NEW AND
COLLECTED
STORIES

ALAN SILLITOE

NEW AND COLLECTED STORIES

CARROLL & GRAF PUBLISHERS
NEW YORK

To H. M. Daleski,
who knows the heart of the storyteller

NEW AND COLLECTED STORIES

Carroll & Graf Publishers
An Imprint of Avalon Publishing Group Inc.
245 West 17th Street
11th Floor
New York, NY 10011

AVALON
publishing group incorporated

Library of Congress Cataloging-in-Publication Data is available.

ISBN: 0-7867-1476-X

Printed in the United States of America
Distributed by Publishers Group West

CONTENTS

The Loneliness of the
Long Distance Runner

As soon as I got to Borstal they made me a long-distance cross-country runner. I suppose they thought I was just the build for it because I was long and skinny for my age (and still am) and in any case I didn't mind it much, to tell you the truth, because running had always been made much of in our family, especially running away from the police. I've always been a good runner, quick and with a big stride as well, the only trouble being that no matter how fast I run, and I did a very fair lick even though I do say so myself, it didn't stop me getting caught by the cops after that bakery job.

You might think it a bit rare, having long-distance cross-country runners in Borstal, thinking that the first thing a long-distance cross-country runner would do when they set him loose at them fields and woods would be to run as far away from the place as he could get on a bellyfull of Borstal slum-gullion – but you're wrong, and I'll tell you why. The first thing is that them bastards over us aren't as daft as they most of the time look, and for another thing I'm not so daft as I would look if I tried to make a break for it in my long-distance running, because to abscond and then get caught is nothing but a mug's game, and I'm not falling for it. Cunning is what counts in this life, and even that you've got to use in the slyest way you can; I'm telling you straight: they're cunning, and I'm cunning. If only 'them' and 'us' had the same ideas we'd get on like a house on fire, but they don't see eye to eye with us and we don't see eye to eye with them, so that's how it stands and how it will always stand. The one fact is that all of us are cunning, and because of this there's no love lost between us. So the thing is that they know I won't try to get away from them: they sit there like spiders in that crumbly manor house, perched like jumped-up jackdaws on the roof, watching out over the drives and fields like German generals from the tops of tanks. And even when I jog-trot

1

on behind a wood and they can't see me anymore they know my sweeping-brush head will bob along that hedge-top in an hour's time and that I'll report to the bloke on the gate. Because when on a raw and frosty morning I get up at five o'clock and stand shivering my belly off on the stone floor and all the rest still have another hour to snooze before the bells go, I slink downstairs through all the corridors to the big outside door with a permit running-card in my fist, I feel like the first and last man on the world, both at once, if you can believe what I'm trying to say. I feel like the first man because I've hardly got a stitch on and am sent against the frozen fields in a shimmy and shorts – even the first poor bastard dropped on to the earth in midwinter knew how to make a suit of leaves, or how to skin a pterodactyl for a topcoat. But there I am, frozen stiff, with nothing to get me warm except a couple of hours' long-distance running before breakfast, not even a slice of bread-and-sheepdip. They're training me up fine for the big sports day when all the pig-faced snotty-nosed dukes and ladies – who can't add two and two together and would mess themselves like loonies if they didn't have slavies to beck-and-call – come and make speeches to us about sports being just the thing to get us leading an honest life and keep our itching finger-ends off them shop locks and safe handles and hairgrips to open gas meters. They give us a bit of blue ribbon and a cup for a prize after we've shagged ourselves out running or jumping, like race horses, only we don't get so well looked-after as race horses, that's the only thing.

So there I am, standing in the doorway in shimmy and shorts, not even a dry crust in my guts, looking out at frosty flowers on the ground. I suppose you think this is enough to make me cry? Not likely. Just because I feel like the first bloke in the world wouldn't make me bawl. It makes me feel fifty times better than when I'm cooped up in that dormitory with three hundred others. No, it's sometimes when I stand there feeling like the *last* man in the world that I don't feel so good. I feel like the last man in the world because I think that all those three hundred sleepers behind me are dead. They sleep so well I think that every scruffy head's kicked the bucket in the night and I'm the only one left, and when I look out into the bushes and frozen ponds I have the feeling that it's going to get colder and colder until everything I can see, meaning my red arms as well, is going to be covered with a thousand miles of ice, all the earth, right up to the sky and over every bit of land and sea. So I try to kick this feeling out and act like

2

I'm the first man on earth. And that makes me feel good, so as soon as I'm steamed up enough to get this feeling in me, I take a flying leap out of the doorway, and off I trot.

I'm in Essex. It's supposed to be a good Borstal, at least that's what the governor said to me when I got here from Nottingham. 'We want to trust you while you are in this establishment,' he said, smoothing out his newspaper with lily-white workless hands, while I read the big words upside down: *Daily Telegraph*. 'If you play ball with us, we'll play ball with you.' (Honest to God, you'd have thought it was going to be one long tennis match.) 'We want hard honest work and we want good athletics,' he said as well. 'And if you give us both these things you can be sure we'll do right by you and send you back into the world an honest man.' Well, I could have died laughing, especially when straight after this I hear the barking sergeant-major's voice calling me and two others to attention and marching us off like we was Grenadier Guards. And when the governor kept saying how 'we' wanted you to do this, and 'we' wanted you to do that, I kept looking round for the other blokes, wondering how many of them there was. Of course, I knew there were thousands of them, but as far as I knew only one was in the room. And there *are* thousands of them, all over the poxeaten country, in shops, offices, railway stations, cars, houses, pubs – In-law blokes like you and them, all on the watch for Out-law blokes like me and us – and waiting to 'phone for the coppers as soon as we make a false move. And it'll always be there, I'll tell you that now, because I haven't finished making all my false moves yet, and I dare say I won't until I kick the bucket. If the In-laws are hoping to stop me making false moves they're wasting their time. They might as well stand me up against a wall and let fly with a dozen rifles. That's the only way they'll stop me, and a few million others. Because I've been doing a lot of thinking since coming here. They can spy on us all day to see if we're pulling our puddings and if we're working good or doing our 'athletics' but they can't make an X-ray of our guts to find out what we're telling ourselves. I've been asking myself all sorts of questions, and thinking about my life up to now. And I like doing all this. It's a treat. It passes the time away and don't make Borstal seem half so bad as the boys in our street used to say it was. And this long-distance running lark is the best of all, because it makes me think so good that I learn things even better than when I'm on my bed at night. And apart from that, what with thinking so much while I'm running I'm getting to be

3

one of the best runners in the Borstal. I can go my five miles round better than anybody else I know.

So as soon as I tell myself I am the first man ever to be dropped into the world, and as soon as I take that first flying leap out into the frosty grass of an early morning when even birds haven't the heart to whistle, I get to thinking, and that's what I like. I go my rounds in a dream, turning at lane or footpath corners without knowing I'm turning, leaping brooks without knowing they're there, and shouting good morning to the early cow-milker without seeing him. It's a treat being a long-distance runner, out in the world by yourself with not a soul to make you bad-tempered or tell you what to do or that there's a shop to break and enter a bit back from the next street. Sometimes I think that I've never been so free as during that couple of hours when I'm trotting up the path out of the gates and turning by that bare-faced, big-bellied oak tree at the lane end. Everything's dead, but good, because it's dead before coming alive, not dead after being alive. That's how I look at it. Mind you, I often feel frozen stiff at first. I can't feel my hands or feet or flesh at all, like I'm a ghost who wouldn't know the earth was under him if he didn't see it now and again through the mist. But even though some people would call this frost-pain suffering if they wrote about it to their mams in a letter, I don't, because I know that in half an hour I'm going to be warm, that by the time I get to the main road and am turning on to the wheatfield footpath by the bus stop I'm going to feel as hot as a potbellied stove and as happy as a dog with a tin tail.

It's a good life, I'm saying to myself, if you don't give in to coppers and Borstal-bosses and the rest of them bastard-faced In-laws. Trot-trot-trot. Puff-puff-puff. Slap-slap-slap go my feet on the hard soil. Swish-swish-swish as my arms and side catch the bare branches of a bush. For I'm seventeen now, and when they let me out of this – if I don't make a break and see that things turn out otherwise – they'll try to get me in the army, and what's the difference between the army and this place I'm in now? They can't kid me, the bastards. I've seen the barracks near where I live, and if there weren't swaddies on guard outside with rifles you wouldn't know the difference between their high walls and the place I'm in now. Even though the swaddies come out at odd times a week for a pint of ale, so what? Don't I come out three mornings a week on my long-distance running, which is fifty times better than boozing. When they first said that I was to do my

4

long-distance running without a guard pedalling beside me on a bike I couldn't believe it; but they called it a progressive and modern place, though they can't kid me because I know it's just like any other Borstal, going by the stories I've heard, except that they let me trot about like this. Borstal's Borstal no matter what they do; but anyway I moaned about it being a bit thick sending me out so early to run five miles on an empty stomach, until they talked me round to thinking it wasn't so bad – which I knew all the time – until they called me a good sport and patted me on the back when I said I'd do it and that I'd try to win them the Borstal Blue Ribbon Prize Cup for Long Distance Cross Country Running (All England). And now the governor talks to me when he comes on his rounds, almost as he'd talk to his prize race horse, if he had one.

'All right, Smith?' he asks.

'Yes, sir,' I answer.

He flicks his grey moustache: 'How's the running coming along?'

'I've set myself to trot round the grounds after dinner just to keep my hand in, sir,' I tell him.

The pot-bellied pop-eyed bastard gets pleased at this: 'Good show. I know you'll get us that cup,' he says.

And I swear under my breath: 'Like boggery, I will.' No, I won't get them that cup, even though the stupid tash-twitching-bastard has all his hopes in me. Because what does his barmy hope mean? I ask myself. Trot-trot-trot, slap-slap-slap, over the stream and into the wood where it's almost dark and frosty-dew twigs sting my legs. It don't mean a bloody thing to me, only to him, and it means as much to him as it would mean to me if I picked up the racing paper and put my bet on a hoss I didn't know, had never seen, and didn't care a sod if I ever did see. That's what it means to him. And I'll lose that race, because I'm not a race horse at all, and I'll let him know it when I'm about to get out – if I don't sling my hook even before the race. By Christ I will. I'm a human being and I've got thoughts and secrets and bloody life inside me that he doesn't know is there, and he'll never know what's there because he's stupid. I suppose you'll laugh at this, me saying the governor's a stupid bastard when I know hardly how to write and he can read and write and add-up like a professor. But what I say is true right enough. He's stupid, and I'm not, because I can see further into the likes of him than he can see into the likes of me. Admitted, we're both cunning, but I'm more cunning and I'll win in the end even if I die in gaol at eighty-two, because I'll have more fun and fire out of my life than he'll ever get out of his. He's read a thousand books I suppose, and for all I know he might even have written a few, but I know for a dead cert, as sure as I'm sitting here, that what I'm scribbling down is worth a million to what he could ever scribble down. I don't care what anybody says, but that's the truth and can't be denied. I know when he talks to me and I look into his army mug that I'm alive and he's dead. He's as dead as a doornail. If he ran ten yards he'd drop dead. If he got ten yards into what goes on in my guts he'd drop dead as well – with surprise. At the moment it's dead blokes like him as have the whip-hand over blokes like me, and I'm almost dead sure it'll always be like that, but even so, by Christ, I'd rather be like I am – always on the run and breaking into shops for a packet of fags and a jar of jam – than have the whip-hand over somebody else and be dead from the toe-nails up. Maybe as soon as you get the whip-hand over somebody you do go dead. By God, to say that last sentence has needed a few hundred miles of long-distance running. I could no more have said that at first than I could have took a million-pound note from my back pocket. But it's true, you know, now I think of it again, and has always been true, and always will be true, and I'm surer of it every time I see the governor open that door and say Good morning lads.

As I run and see my smoky breath going out into the air as if I had ten cigars stuck in different parts of my body I think more on the little speech the governor made when I first came. Honesty. Be honest. I laughed so much one morning I went ten minutes down in my timing because I had to stop and get rid of the stitch in my side. The governor was so worried when I got back late that he sent me to the doctor's for an X-ray and heart check. Be honest. It's like saying: Be dead, like me, and then you'll have no more pain of leaving your nice slummy house for Borstal or prison. Be honest and settle down in a cosy six pounds a week job. Well, even with all this long-distance running I haven't yet been able to decide what he means by this, although I'm just about beginning to – and I don't like what it means. Because after all my thinking I found that it adds up to something that can't be true about me, being born and brought up as I was. Because another thing people like the governor will never understand is that I *am* honest, that I've never been anything else but honest, and that I'll always be honest. Sounds funny. But it's true because I know what honest means according to me and he only knows what it means according to him. I think my honesty is the only sort in the world, and he thinks his is the only sort in the world as well. That's why this dirty great walled-up and fenced-up manor house in the middle of nowhere has been used to coop-up blokes like me. And if I had the whip-hand I wouldn't even bother to build a place like this to put all the cops, governors, posh whores, penpushers, army officers, Members of Parliament in; no, I'd stick them up against a wall and let them have it, like they'd have done with blokes like us years ago, that is, if they'd ever known what it means to be honest, which they don't and never will so help me God Almighty.

I was nearly eighteen months in Borstal before I thought about getting out. I can't tell you much about what it was like there, because I haven't got the hang of describing buildings or saying how many crumby chairs and slatted windows make a room. Neither can I do much complaining, because to tell you the truth I didn't suffer in Borstal at all. I gave the same answer a pal of mine gave when someone asked him how much he hated it in the army. 'I didn't hate it,' he said. 'They fed me, gave me a suit, and pocket-money, which was a bloody sight more than I ever got before, unless I worked myself to death for it, and most of the time they wouldn't let me work but sent me to the dole office twice a week.' Well, that's more or less what I say. Borstal didn't hurt me in that respect, so since I've got no complaints I don't have to describe what they gave us to eat, what the dorms were like, or how they treated us. But in another way Borstal does something to me. No, it doesn't get my back up, because it's always been up, right from when I was born. What it does do is show me what they've been trying to frighten me with. They've got other things as well, like prison and, in the end, the rope. It's like me rushing up to thump a man and snatch the coat off his back when, suddenly, I pull up because he whips out a knife and lifts it to stick me like a pig if I come too close. That knife is Borstal, clink, the rope. But once you've seen the knife you learn a bit of unarmed combat. You have to, because you'll never get that sort of knife in your own hands, and this unarmed combat doesn't amount to much. Still, there it is, and you keep on rushing up to this man, knife or not, hoping to get one of your hands on his wrist and the other on his elbow both at the same time, and press back until he drops the knife.

You see, by sending me to Borstal they've shown me the knife, and from now on I know something I didn't know before: that it's war between me and them. I always knew this, naturally, because I was in

Remand Homes as well and the boys there told me a lot about their brothers in Borstal, but it was only touch and go then, like kittens, like boxing-gloves, like dobbie. But now that they've shown me the knife, whether I ever pinch another thing in my life again or not, I know who my enemies are and what war is. They can drop all the atom bombs they like for all I care: I'll never call it war and wear a soldier's uniform, because I'm in a different sort of war, that they think is child's play. The war they think is war is suicide, and those that go and get killed in war should be put in clink for attempted suicide because that's the feeling in blokes' minds when they rush to join up or let themselves be called up. I know, because I've thought how good it would be sometimes to do myself in and the easiest way to do it, it occurred to me, was to hope for a big war so's I could join up and get killed. But I got past that when I knew I already was in a war of my own, that I was born into one, that I grew up hearing the sound of 'old soldiers' who'd been over the top at Dartmoor, half-killed at Lincoln, trapped in no-man's-land at Borstal, that sounded louder than any Jerry bombs. Government wars aren't my wars; they've got nowt to do with me, because my own war's all that I'll ever be bothered about. I remember when I was fourteen and I went out into the country with three of my cousins, all about the same age, who later went to different Borstals, and then to different regiments, from which they soon deserted, and then to different gaols where they still are as far as I know. But anyway, we were all kids then, and wanted to go out to the woods for a change, to get away from the roads of stinking hot tar one summer. We climbed over fences and went through fields, scrumping a few sour apples on our way, until we saw the wood about a mile off. Up Colliers' Pad we heard another lot of kids talking in high-school voices behind a hedge. We crept up on them and peeped through the brambles, and saw they were eating a picnic, a real posh spread out of baskets and flasks and towels. There must have been about seven of them, lads and girls sent out by their mams and dads for the afternoon. So we went on our bellies through the hedge like crocodiles and surrounded them, and then dashed into the middle, scattering the fire and batting their tabs and snatching up all there was to eat, then running off over Cherry Orchard fields into the wood, with a man chasing us who'd come up while we were ransacking their picnic. We got away all right, and had a good feed into the bargain, because we'd been clambed to death and couldn't wait long enough to get our chops ripping into them thin lettuce and ham sandwiches and creamy cakes.

Well, I'll always feel during every bit of my life like those daft kids should have felt before we broke them up. But they never dreamed that what happened was going to happen, just like the governor of this Borstal who spouts to us about honesty and all that wappy stuff don't know a bloody thing, while I know every minute of my life that a big boot is always likely to smash any nice picnic I might be barmy and dishonest enough to make for myself. I admit that there've been times when I've thought of telling the governor all this so as to put him on guard, but when I've got as close as seeing him I've changed my mind, thinking to let him either find out for himself or go through the same mill as I've gone through. I'm not hard-hearted (in fact I've helped a few blokes in my time with the odd quid, lie, fag, or shelter from the rain when they've been on the run) but I'm boggered if I'm going to risk being put in cells just for trying to give the governor a bit of advice he don't deserve. If my heart's soft I know the sort of people I'm going to save it for. And any advice I'd give the governor wouldn't do him the least bit of good; it'd only trip him up sooner than if he wasn't told at all, which I suppose is what I want to happen. But for the time being I'll let things go on as they are, which is something else I've learned in the last year or two. (It's a good job I can only think of these things as fast as I can write with this stub of pencil that's clutched in my paw, otherwise I'd have dropped the whole thing weeks ago.)

By the time I'm half-way through my morning course, when after a frost-bitten dawn I can see a phlegmy bit of sunlight hanging from the bare twigs of beech and sycamore, and when I've measured my half-way mark by the short-cut scrimmage down the steep bush-covered bank and into the sunken lane, when there's not a soul in sight and not a sound except the neighing of a piebald foal in a cottage stable that I can't see, I get to thinking the deepest and daftest of all. The governor would have a fit if he could see me sliding down the bank because I could break my neck or ankle, but I can't not do it because it's the only risk I take and the only excitement I ever get, flying flat-out like one of them pterodactyls from the 'Lost World' I once heard on the wireless, crazy like a cut-balled cockerel, scratching myself to bits and almost letting myself go but not quite. It's the most wonderful minute because there's not one thought or word or picture of anything in my head while I'm going down. I am empty, as empty as I was before I was born, and I don't let myself go, I suppose because whatever it is

9

that's farthest down inside me don't want me to die or hurt myself bad. And it's daft to think deep, you know, because it gets you nowhere, though deep is what I am when I've passed this half-way mark because the long-distance run of an early morning makes me think that every run like this is a life – a little life, I know – but a life as full of misery and happiness and things happening as you can ever get really around yourself – and I remember that after a lot of these runs I thought that it didn't need much know-how to tell how a life was going to end once it had got well started. But as usual I was wrong, caught first by the cops and then by my own bad brain. I could never trust myself to fly scot-free over these traps, was always tripped up sooner or later no matter how many I got over to the good without even knowing it. Looking back I suppose them big trees put their branches to their snouts and gave each other the wink, and there I was whizzing down the bank and not seeing a bloody thing.

II

I don't say to myself: 'You shouldn't have done the job and then you'd have stayed away from Borstal'; no, what I ram into my runner-brain is that my luck had no right to scram just when I was on my way to making the coppers think I hadn't done the job after all. The time was autumn and the night foggy enough to get me and my mate Mike roaming the streets when we should have been rooted in front of the telly or stuck into a plush posh seat at the pictures, but I was restless after six weeks away from any sort of work, and well you might ask me why I'd been bone-idle for so long because normally I sweated my thin guts out on a milling-machine with the rest of them, but you see, my dad died from cancer of the throat, and mam collected a cool five hundred in insurance and benefits from the factory where he'd worked, 'for your bereavement', they said, or words like that.

Now I believe, and my mam must have thought the same, that a wad of crisp blue-back fivers ain't a sight of good to a living soul unless they're flying out of your hand into some shopkeeper's till, and the shopkeeper is passing you tip-top things in exchange over the counter, so as soon as she got the money, mam took me and my five brothers and sisters out to town and got us dolled-up in new clothes. Then she ordered a twenty-one-inch telly, a new carpet because the old one was covered with blood from dad's dying and wouldn't wash out, and took a taxi home with bags of grub and a new fur coat. And do you know – you wain't believe me when I tell you – she'd still near three hundred left in her bulging handbag the next day, so how could any of us go to work after that? Poor old dad, he didn't get a look in, and he was the one who'd done the suffering and dying for such a lot of lolly.

Night after night we sat in front of the telly with a ham sandwich in one hand, a bar of chocolate in the other, and a bottle of lemonade between our boots, while mam was with some fancy-man upstairs on the new bed she'd ordered, and I'd never known a family as happy as ours was in that couple of months when we'd got all the money we needed. And when the dough ran out I didn't think about anything much, but just roamed the streets – looking for another job, I told mam – hoping to get my hands on another five hundred nicker so's the nice life we'd got used to could go on and on for ever. Because it's surprising how quick you can get used to a different life. To begin with, the adverts on the telly had shown us how much more there was in the world to buy than we'd ever dreamed of when we'd looked into shop windows but hadn't seen all there was to see because we didn't have the money to buy it with anyway. And the telly made all these things seem twenty times better than we'd ever thought they were. Even adverts at the cinema were cool and tame, because now we were seeing them in private at home. We used to cock our noses up at things in shops that didn't move, but suddenly we saw their real value because they jumped and glittered around the screen and had some pasty-faced tart going head over heels to get her nail-polished grabbers on to them or her lipstick lips over them, not like the crumby adverts you saw on posters or in newspapers as dead as doornails; these were flickering around loose, half-open packets and tins, making you think that all you had to do was finish opening them before they were yours, like seeing an unlocked safe through a shop window with the man gone away for a cup of tea without thinking to guard his lolly. The films they showed were good as well, in that way, because we couldn't get our eyes unglued from the cops chasing the robbers who had satchel-bags crammed with cash and looked like getting away to spend it – until the last moment. I always hoped they would end up free to blow the lot, and could never stop wanting to put my hand out, smash into the screen (it only looked a bit of rag-screen like at the pictures)

11

and get the copper in a half-nelson so's he'd stop following the bloke with the money-bags. Even when he'd knocked off a couple of bank clerks I hoped he wouldn't get nabbed. In fact then I wished more than ever he wouldn't because it meant the hot-chair if he did, and I wouldn't wish that on anybody no matter what they'd done, because I'd read in a book where the hot-chair worn't a quick death at all, but that you just sat there scorching to death until you were dead. And it was when these cops were chasing the crooks that we played some good tricks with the telly, because when one of them opened his big gob to spout about getting their man I'd turn the sound down and see his mouth move like a goldfish or mackerel or a minnow mimicking what they were supposed to be acting – it was so funny the whole family nearly went into fits on the brand-new carpet that hadn't yet found its way to the bedroom. It was the best of all though when we did it to some Tory telling us about how good his government was going to be if we kept on voting for them – their slack chops rolling, opening and bumbling, hands lifting to twitch moustaches and touching their buttonholes to make sure the flower hadn't wilted, so that you could see they didn't mean a word they said, especially with not a murmur coming out because we'd cut off the sound. When the governor of the Borstal first talked to me I was reminded of those times so much that I nearly killed myself trying not to laugh. Yes, we played so many good stunts on the box of tricks that mam used to call us the Telly Boys, we got so clever at it.

My pal Mike got let off with probation because it was his first job – anyway the first they ever knew about – and because they said he would never have done it if it hadn't been for me talking him into it. They said I was a menace to honest lads like Mike – hands in his pockets so that they looked stone empty, head bent forward as if looking for half-crowns to fill 'em with, a ripped jersey on and his hair falling into his eyes so that he could go up to women and ask them for a shilling because he was hungry – and that I was the brains behind the job, the guiding light when it came to making up anybody's mind, but I swear to God I worn't owt like that because really I ain't got no more brains than a gnat after hiding the money in the place I did. And I – being cranky like I am – got sent to Borstal because to tell you the honest truth I'd been to Remand Homes before – though that's another story and I suppose if I ever tell it it'll be just as boring as this one is. I was glad though that Mike got away with it, and I only hope he always will, not like silly bastard me.

So on this foggy night we tore ourselves away from the telly and slammed the front door behind us, setting off up our wide street like slow tugs on a river that'd broken their hooters, for we didn't know where the housefronts began what with the perishing cold mist all around. I was snatched to death without an overcoat: mam had forgotten to buy me one in the scrummage of shopping, and by the time I thought to remind her of it the dough was all gone. So we whistled 'The Teddy Boys' Picnic' to keep us warm, and I told myself that I'd get a coat soon if it was the last thing I did. Mike said he thought the same about himself, adding that he'd also get some brand-new glasses with gold rims, to wear instead of the wire frames they'd given him at the school clinic years ago. He didn't twig it was foggy at first and cleaned his glasses every time I pulled him back from a lamp-post or car, but when he saw the lights on Alfreton Road looking like octopus eyes he put them in his pocket and didn't wear them again until we did the job. We hadn't got two ha'pennies between us, and though we weren't hungry we wished we'd got a bob or two when we passed the fish and chip shops because the delicious sniffs of salt and vinegar and frying fat made our mouths water. I don't mind telling you we walked the town from one end to the other and if our eyes worn't glued to the ground looking for lost wallets and watches they was swivelling around house windows and shop doors in case we saw something easy and worth nipping into.

Neither of us said as much as this to each other, but I know for a fact that that was what we was thinking. What I don't know – and as sure as I sit here I know I'll never know – is which of us was the first bastard to latch his peepers on to that baker's backyard. Oh yes, it's all right me telling myself it was me, but the truth is that I've never known whether it was Mike or not, because I do know that I didn't see the open window until he stabbed me in the ribs and pointed it out. 'See it?' he said.

'Yes,' I told him, 'so let's get cracking.'

'But what about the wall though?' he whispered, looking a bit closer.

'On your shoulders,' I chipped in.

His eyes were already up there: 'Will you be able to reach?' It was the only time he ever showed any life.

'Leave it to me,' I said, ever-ready. 'I can reach anywhere from your ham-hock shoulders.'

Mike was a nipper compared to me, but underneath the scruffy draught-board jersey he wore were muscles as hard as iron, and you wouldn't think to see him walking down the street with glasses on and hands in pockets that he'd harm a fly, but I never liked to get on the wrong side of him in a fight because he's the sort that don't say a word for weeks on end – sits plugged in front of the telly, or reads a cowboy book, or just sleeps – when suddenly BIFF – half kills somebody for almost nothing at all, such as beating him in a race for the last Football Post on a Saturday night, pushing in before him at a bus stop, or bumping into him when he was day-dreaming about Dolly-on-the-Tub next door. I saw him set on a bloke once for no more than fixing him in a funny way with his eyes, and it turned out that the bloke was cock-eyed but nobody knew it because he'd just that day come to live in our street. At other times none of these things would matter a bit, and I suppose the only reason why I was pals with him was because I didn't say much from one month's end to another either.

He puts his hands up in the air like he was being covered with a Gatling-Gun, and moved to the wall like he was going to be mowed down, and I climbed up him like he was a stile or step-ladder, and there he stood, the palms of his upshot maulers flat and turned out so's I could step on 'em like they was the adjustable jack-spanner under a car, not a sound of a breath nor the shiver of a flinch coming from him. I lost no time in any case, took my coat from between my teeth, chucked it up to the glass-topped wall (where the glass worn't too sharp because the jags had been worn down by years of accidental stones) and was sitting astraddle before I knew where I was. Then down the other side, with my legs rammed up into my throat when I hit the ground, the crack coming about as hard as when you fall after a high parachute drop, that one of my mates told me was like jumping off a twelve-foot wall, which this must have been. Then I picked up my bits and pieces and opened the gate for Mike, who was still grinning and full of life because the hardest part of the job was already done. 'I came, I broke, I entered,' like that cleverdick Borstal song.

I didn't think about anything at all, as usual, because I never do when I'm busy, when I'm draining pipes, looting sacks, yaling locks, lifting latches, forcing my bony hands and lanky legs into making something move, hardly feeling my lungs going in-whiff and out-whaff, not realizing whether my mouth is clamped tight or gaping, whether I'm hungry, itching from scabies, or whether my flies are open and flashing dirty words like muck and spit into the late-night final fog. And when I don't know anything about all this then how can I honest-to-God say I think of anything at such times? When I'm wondering what's the best way to get a window open or how to force a door, how can I be thinking or have anything on my mind? That's what the four-eyed white-smocked bloke with the notebook couldn't understand when he asked me questions for days and days after I got to Borstal; and I couldn't explain it to him then like I'm writing it down now; and even if I'd been able to maybe he still wouldn't have caught on because I don't know whether I can understand it myself even at this moment, though I'm doing my best you can bet.

So before I knew where I was I was inside the baker's office watching Mike picking up that cash box after he'd struck a match to see where it was, wearing a tailor-made fifty-shilling grin on his square crew-cut nut as his paws closed over the box like he'd squash it to nothing. 'Out,' he suddenly said, shaking it so's it rattled. 'Let's scram.'

'Maybe there's some more,' I said, pulling half a dozen drawers out of a rollertop desk.

'No,' he said, like he'd already been twenty years in the game, 'this is the lot,' patting his tin box, 'this is it.'

I pulled out another few drawers, full of bills, books and letters. 'How do you know, you loony sod?'

He barged past me like a bull at a gate. 'Because I do.'

Right or wrong, we'd both got to stick together and do the same thing. I looked at an ever-loving babe of a brand-new typewriter, but knew it was too traceable, so blew it a kiss, and went out after him. 'Hang on,' I said, pulling the door to, 'we're in no hurry.'

'Not much we aren't,' he says over his shoulder.

'We've got months to splash the lolly,' I whispered as we crossed the yard, 'only don't let that gate creak too much or you'll have the narks tuning-in.'

'You think I'm barmy?' he said, creaking the gate so that the whole street heard.

I don't know about Mike, but now I started to think, of how we'd get back safe through the streets with that money-box up my jumper. Because he'd clapped it into my hand as soon as we'd got to the main road, which might have meant that he'd started thinking as well, which only goes to show how you don't know what's in anybody else's mind unless you think about things yourself. But as far as my thinking went at that moment it wasn't up to much, only a bit of fright that wouldn't budge not even with a hot blow-lamp, about what we'd say if a copper asked us where we were off to with that hump in my guts.

'What is it?' he'd ask, and I'd say: 'A growth.' 'What do you mean, a growth, my lad?' he'd say back, narky like. I'd cough and clutch myself like I was in the most tripe-twisting pain in the world, and screw my eyes up like I was on my way to the hospital, and Mike would take my arm like he was the best pal I'd got. 'Cancer,' I'd manage to say to Narker, which would make his slow punch-drunk brain suspect a thing or two. 'A lad of your age?' So I'd groan again, and hope to make him feel a real bully of a bastard, which would be impossible, but anyway: 'It's in the family, Dad died of it last month, and I'll die of it next month by the feel of it.' 'What, did he have it in the guts?' 'No, in the throat. But it's got me in the stomach.' Groan and cough. 'Well, you shouldn't be out like this if you've got cancer, you should be in the hospital.' I'd get ratty now: 'That's where I'm trying to go if only you'd let me and stop asking so many questions. Aren't I, Mike?' Grunt from Mike as he unslung his cosh. Then just in time the copper would tell us to get on our way, kind and considerate all of a sudden, saying that the outpatient department of the hospital closes at twelve, so hadn't he better call a taxi? He would if we liked, he says, and he'd pay for it as well. But we tell him not to bother, that he's a good bloke even if he is a copper, that we know a short cut anyway. Then just as we're turning a corner he gets it into his big batchy head that we're going the opposite way to the hospital, and calls us back. So we'd start to run . . . if you can call all that thinking.

Up in my room Mike rips open the money-box with a hammer and chisel, and before we know where we are we've got seventy-eight pounds fifteen and fourpence ha'penny each lying all over my bed like tea spread out on Christmas Day: cake and trifle, salad and sandwiches, jam tarts and bars of chocolate: all shared alike between Mike and me because we believed in equal work and equal pay, just like the comrades my dad was in until he couldn't do a stroke anymore and had no breath left to argue with. I thought how good it was that blokes like that poor baker didn't stash all his cash in one of the big marble-fronted banks that take up every corner of the town, how lucky for us that he didn't trust them no matter how many millions of tons of concrete or how many iron bars and boxes they were made of, or how many coppers kept their blue pop-eyed peepers glued on to them, how smashing it was that he believed in money-boxes when so many shopkeepers thought it old-fashioned and tried to be modern by using a bank, which wouldn't give a couple of sincere, honest, hardworking, conscientious blokes like Mike and me a chance.

Now you'd think, and I'd think, and anybody with a bit of imagination would think, that we'd done as clean a job as could ever be done, that, with the baker's shop being at least a mile from where we lived, and with not a soul having seen us, and what with the fog and the fact that we weren't more than five minutes in the place, that the coppers should never have been able to trace us. But then, you'd be wrong. I'd be wrong, and everybody else would be wrong, no matter how much imagination was diced out between us.

Even so, Mike and I didn't splash the money about, because that would have made people think straightaway that we'd latched on to something that didn't belong to us. Which wouldn't do at all, because even in a street like ours there are people who love to do a good turn for the coppers, though I never know why they do. Some people are so mean-gutted that even if they've only got tuppence more than you and they think you're the sort that would take it if you have half the chance, they'd get you put inside if they saw you ripping lead out of a lavatory, even if it weren't their lavatory – just to keep their tuppence out of your reach. And so we didn't do anything to let on about how rich we were, nothing like going down town and coming back dressed in brand-new Teddy boy suits and carrying a set of skiffle-drums like another pal of ours who'd done a factory office about six months before. No, we took the odd bobs and pennies out and folded the notes into bundles and stuffed them up the drainpipe outside the door in the backyard. 'Nobody'll ever think of looking for it there,' I said to Mike. 'We'll keep it doggo for a week or two, then take a few quid a week out till it's all gone. We might be thieving bastards, but we're not green.'

Some days later a plain-clothes dick knocked at the door. And asked for me. I was still in bed, at eleven o'clock, and had to unroll myself from the comfortable black sheets when I heard mam calling me. 'A man to see you,' she said. 'Hurry up, or he'll be gone.'

I could hear her keeping him at the back door, nattering about how fine it had been and how it looked like rain since early this morning – and he didn't answer her except to snap out a snotty yes or no. I scrambled into my trousers and wondered why he'd come – knowing it was a copper because 'a man to see you' always meant just that in our house – and if I'd had any idea that one had gone to Mike's house as well at the same time I'd have twigged it to be because of that seventy quids' worth of paper stuffed up the drainpipe outside the back door about ten inches away from the plain-clothed copper's boot, where mam still talked to him thinking she was doing me a favour, and I wishing to God she'd ask him in, though on second thoughts realizing that that would seem more suspicious than keeping him outside, because they know we hate their guts and smell a rat if they think we're trying to be nice to them. Mam wasn't born yesterday, I thought, thumping my way down the creaking stairs.

I'd seen him before: Borstal Bernard in nicky-hat, Remand Home Ronald in rowing-boat boots, Probation Pete in a pitprop mackintosh, three months clink in collar and tie (all this out of a Borstal skiffle-ballad that my new mate made up, and I'd tell you it in full but it doesn't belong in this story), a 'tec who'd never had as much in his pockets as that drainpipe had up its jackses. He was like Hitler in the face, right down to the paint-brush tash, except that being six-foot tall made him seem worse. But I straightened my shoulders to look into his illiterate blue eyes – like I always do with any copper.

Then he started asking me questions, and my mother from behind said: 'He's never left that television set for the last three months, so you've nowt on him, mate. You might as well look for somebody else, because you're wasting the rates you get out of my rent and the income-tax that comes out of my pay-packet standing there like that' – which was a laugh because she'd never paid either to my knowledge, and never would, I hoped.

'Well, you know where Papplewick Street is, don't you?' the copper asked me, taking no notice of mam.

'Ain't it off Alfreton Road?' I asked him back, helpful and bright.

'You know there's a baker's half-way down on the left-hand side, don't you?'

'Ain't it next door to a pub, then?' I wanted to know.

He answered me sharp: 'No, it bloody well ain't.' Coppers always lose their tempers as quick as this, and more often than not they gain nothing by it. 'Then I don't know it,' I told him, saved by the bell.

He slid his big boot round and round the doorstep. 'Where were you last Friday night?' Back in the ring, but this was worse than a boxing match.

I didn't like him trying to accuse me of something he wasn't sure I'd done. 'Was I at the baker's you mentioned? Or in the pub next door?'

'You'll get five years in Borstal if you don't give me a straight answer,' he said, unbuttoning his mac even though it was cold where he was standing.

'I was glued to the telly, like mam says,' I swore blind. But he went on and on with his looney questions: 'Have you got a television?'

The things he asked wouldn't have taken in a kid of two, and what else could I say to the last one except: 'Has the aerial fell down? Or would you like to come in and see it?'

He was liking me even less for saying that. 'We know you weren't listening to the television set last Friday, and so do you, don't you?'

'P'raps not, but I was *looking* at it, because sometimes we turn the sound down for a bit of fun.' I could hear mam laughing from the kitchen, and I hoped Mike's mam was doing the same if the cops had gone to him as well.

'We know you weren't in the house,' he said, starting up again, cranking himself with the handle. They always say 'We' 'We' never 'I' 'I' — as if they feel braver and righter knowing there's a lot of them against only one.

'I've got witnesses,' I said to him. 'Mam for one. Her fancy-man, for two. Ain't that enough? I can get you a dozen more, or thirteen altogether, if it was a baker's that got robbed.'

'I don't want no lies,' he said, not catching on about the baker's dozen. Where do they scrape cops up from anyway? 'All I want is to get from you where you put that money.'

Don't get mad, I kept saying to myself, don't get mad — hearing mam setting out cups and saucers and putting the pan on the stove for bacon. I stood back and waved him inside like I was the butler. 'Come and search the house. If you've got a warrant.'

'Listen, my lad,' he said, like the dirty bullying jumped-up bastard he was, 'I don't want too much of your lip, because if we get you down to the Guildhall you'll get a few bruises and black-eyes for your trouble.' And I knew he wasn't kidding either, because I'd heard about all them sort of tricks. I hoped one day though that him and all his pals would be the ones to get the black-eyes and kicks, you never knew. It might come sooner than anybody thinks, like in Hungary. 'Tell me where the money is, and I'll get you off with probation.'

'What money?' I asked him, because I'd heard that one before as well.

'You know what money.'

19

'Do I look as though I'd know owt about money?' I said pushing my fist through a hole in my shirt.

'The money that was pinched, that you know all about,' he said. 'You can't trick me, so it's no use trying.'

'Was it three-and-eightpence ha'penny?' I asked.

'You thieving young bastard. We'll teach you to steal money that doesn't belong to you.'

I turned my head around: 'Mam,' I called out, 'get my lawyer on the blower, will you?'

'Clever, aren't you?' he said in an unfriendly way, 'but we won't rest until we clear all this up.'

'Look,' I pleaded, as if about to sob my socks off because he'd got me wrong, 'it's all very well us talking like this, it's like a game almost, but I wish you'd tell me what it's all about, because honest-to-God I've just got out of bed and here you are at the door talking about me having pinched a lot of money, money that I don't know anything about.'

He swung around now as if he'd trapped me, though I couldn't see why he might think so. 'Who said anything about money? I didn't. What made you bring money into this little talk we're having?'

'It's you,' I answered, thinking he was going barmy, and about to start foaming at the chops, 'you've got money on the brain, like all policemen. Baker's shops as well.'

He screwed his face up. 'I want an answer from you: where's the money?'

But I was getting fed-up with all this. 'I'll do a deal.'

Judging by his flash-bulb face he thought he was suddenly onto a good thing. 'What sort of a deal?'

So I told him: 'I'll give you all the money I've got, one and fourpence ha'penny, if you stop this third-degree and let me go in and get my breakfast. Honest, I'm clambed to death. I ain't had a bite since yesterday. Can't you hear my guts rollin'?'

His jaw dropped, but on he went, pumping me for another half hour. A routine check-up they say on the pictures. But I knew I was winning on points.

Then he left, but came back in the afternoon to search the house. He didn't find a thing, not a French farthing. He asked me questions again and I didn't tell him anything except lies, lies, lies, because I can go on doing that forever without batting an eyelid. He'd got nothing on me

20

and we both of us knew it, otherwise I'd have been down the Guildhall in no time, but he kept on keeping on because I'd been in a Remand Home for a high-wall job before; and Mike was put through the same mill because all the local cops knew he was my best pal.

When it got dark me and Mike were in our parlour with a low light on and the telly off, Mike taking it easy in the rocking chair and me slouched out on the settee, both of us puffing a packet of Woods. With the door bolted and curtains drawn we talked about the dough we'd crammed up the drainpipe. Mike thought we should take it out and both of us do a bunk to Skegness or Cleethorpes for a good time in the arcades, living like lords in a boarding house near the pier, then at least we'd both have had a big beano before getting sent down.

'Listen, you daft bleeder,' I said, 'we aren't going to get caught at all, *and* we'll have a good time, later.' We were so clever we didn't even go out to the pictures, though we wanted to.

In the morning old Hitler-face questioned me again, with one of his pals this time, and the next day they came, trying as hard as they could to get something out of me, but I didn't budge an inch. I know I'm showing off when I say this, but in me he'd met his match, and I'd never give in to questions no matter how long it was kept up. They searched the house a couple of times as well, which made me think they thought they really had something to go by, but I know now that they hadn't, and that it was all buckshee speculation. They turned the house upside down and inside out like an old sock, went from top to bottom and front to back but naturally didn't find a thing. The copper even poked his face up the front-room chimney (that hadn't been used or swept for years) and came down looking like Al Jolson so that he had to swill himself clean at the scullery sink. They kept tapping and pottering around the big aspidistra plant that grandma had left to mam, lifting it up from the table to look under the cloth, putting it aside so's they could move the table and get at the boards under the rug – but the big-headed stupid ignorant bastards never once thought of emptying the soil out of the plant pot, where they'd have found the crumpled-up money-box that we'd buried the night we did the job. I suppose it's still there now I think about it, and I suppose mam wonders now and again why the plant don't prosper like it used to – as if it could with a fistful of thick black tin lapped around its guts.

The last time he knocked at our door was one wet morning at five minutes to nine and I was sleep-logged in my crumby bed as usual. Mam had gone to work for the day so I shouted for him to hold on a bit, and then went down to see who it was. There he stood, six-feet tall and sopping wet, and for the first time in my life I did a spiteful thing I'll never forgive myself for: I didn't ask him to come in out of the rain, because I wanted him to get double pneumonia and die. I suppose he could have pushed by me and come in if he'd wanted, but maybe he'd got used to asking questions on the doorstep and didn't want to be put off by changing his ground even though it was raining. Not that I don't like being spiteful because of any barmy principle I've got, but this bit of spite, as it turned out, did me no good at all. I should have treated him as a brother I hadn't seen for twenty years and dragged him in for a cup of tea and a fag, told him about the picture I hadn't seen the night before, asking him how his wife was after her operation and whether they'd shaved her moustache off to make it, and then sent him happy and satisfied out by the front door. But no, I thought, let's see what he's got to say for himself now.

He stood a little to the side of the door, either because it was less wet there, or because he wanted to see me from a different angle, perhaps having found it monotonous to watch a bloke's face always telling lies from the same side. 'You've been identified,' he said, twitching raindrops from his tash. 'A woman saw you and your mate yesterday and she swears blind you are the same chaps she saw going into that bakery.'

I was dead sure he was still bluffing, because Mike and I hadn't even seen each other the day before, but I looked worried. 'She's a menace then to innocent people, whoever she is, because the only bakery I've been in lately is the one up our street to get some cut-bread on tick for mam.'

He didn't bite on this. 'So now I want to know where the money is' — as if I hadn't answered him at all.

'I think mam took it to work this morning to get herself some tea in the canteen.' Rain was splashing down so hard I thought he'd get washed away if he didn't come inside. But I wasn't much bothered, and went on: 'I remember I put it in the telly-vase last night – it was my only one-and-three and I was saving it for a packet of tips this morning – and I nearly had a jibbering black fit just now when I saw it had gone. I was reckoning on it for getting me through today because I don't think life's worth living without a fag, do you?'

22

I was getting into my stride and began to feel good, twigging that this would be my last pack of lies, and that if I kept it up for long enough this time I'd have the bastards beat: Mike and me would be off to the coast in a few weeks' time having the fun of our lives, playing at penny football and latching on to a couple of tarts that would give us all they were good for. 'And this weather's no good for picking-up fag-ends in the street,' I said, 'because they'd be sopping wet. Course, I know you could dry 'em out near the fire, but it don't taste the same you know, all said and done. Rainwater does summat to 'em that don't bear thinkin' about: it turns 'em back into hoss-tods without the taste though.'

I began to wonder, at the back of my brainless eyes, why old copper-lugs didn't pull me up sharp and say he hadn't got time to listen to all this, but he wasn't looking at me anymore, and all my thoughts about Skegness went bursting to smithereens in my sludgy loaf. I could have dropped into the earth when I saw what he'd fixed his eyes on.

He was looking at *it*, an ever-loving fiver, and I could only jabber: 'The one thing is to have some real fags because new hoss-tods is always better than stuff that's been rained on and dried, and I know how you feel about not being able to find money because one-and-three's one-and-three in anybody's pocket, and naturally if I see it knocking around I'll get you on the blower tomorrow straightaway and tell you where you can find it.'

I thought I'd go down in a fit: three green-backs as well had been washed down by the water, and more were following, lying flat at first after their fall, then getting tilted at the corners by wind and rainspots as if they were alive and wanted to get back into the dry snug drainpipe out of the terrible weather, and you can't imagine how I wished they'd be able to. Old Hitler-face didn't know what to make of it but just kept staring down and down, and I thought I'd better keep on talking, though I knew it wasn't much good now.

'It's a fact, I know, that money's hard to come by and half-crowns don't get found on bus seats or in dustbins, and I didn't see any in bed last night because I'd 'ave known about it, wouldn't I? You can't sleep with things like that in the bed because they're too hard, and anyway at first they're . . .' It took Hitler-boy a long time to catch on; they were beginning to spread over the yard a bit, reinforced by the third colour of a ten-bob note, before his hand clamped itself on to my shoulder.

23

III

The pop-eyed potbellied governor said to a pop-eyed potbellied Member of Parliament who sat next to his pop-eyed potbellied whore of a wife that I was his only hope for getting the Borstal Blue Ribbon Prize Cup for Long Distance Cross Country Running (All England), which I was, and it set me laughing to myself inside, and I didn't say a word to any potbellied pop-eyed bastard that might give them real hope, though I knew the governor anyway took my quietness to mean he'd got that cup already stuck on the bookshelf in his office among the few other mildewed trophies.

'He might take up running in a sort of professional way when he gets out,' and it wasn't until he'd said this and I'd heard it with my own flap-tabs that I realized it might be possible to do such a thing, run for money, trot for wages on piece work at a bob a puff rising bit by bit to a guinea a gasp and retiring through old age at thirty-two because of lace-curtain lungs, a football heart, and legs like varicose beanstalks. But I'd have a wife and car and get my grinning long-distance clock in the papers and have a smashing secretary to answer piles of letters sent by tarts who'd mob me when they saw who I was as I pushed my way into Woolworth's for a packet of razor blades and a cup of tea. It was something to think about all right, and sure enough the governor knew he'd got me when he said, turning to me as if I would at any rate have to be consulted about it all: 'How does this matter strike you, then, Smith, my lad?'

A line of potbellied pop-eyes gleamed at me and a row of goldfish mouths opened and wiggled gold teeth at me, so I gave them the answer they wanted because I'd hold my trump card until later. 'It'd suit me fine, sir,' I said.

'Good lad. Good show. Right spirit. Splendid.'

'Well,' the governor said, 'get that cup for us today and I'll do all I can for you. I'll get you trained so that you whack every man in the Free World.' And I had a picture in my brain of me running and beating everybody in the world, leaving them all behind until only I was trot-trotting across a big wide moor alone, doing a marvellous speed as I ripped between boulders and reed-clumps, when suddenly: CRACK! CRACK! – bullets that can go faster than any man running, coming from a copper's rifle planted in a tree, winged me and split my gizzard in spite of my perfect running, and down I fell.

The potbellies expected me to say something else. 'Thank you, sir,' I said.

Told to go, I trotted down the pavilion steps, out on to the field because the big cross-country was about to begin and the two entries from Gunthorpe had fixed themselves early at the starting line and were ready to move off like white kangaroos. The sports ground looked a treat: with big tea-tents all round and flags flying and seats for families – empty because no mam or dad had known what opening day meant – and boys still running heats for the hundred yards, and lords and ladies walking from stall to stall, and the Borstal Boys Brass Band in blue uniforms; and up on the stands the brown jackets of Hucknall as well as our own grey blazers, and then the Gunthorpe lot with shirt sleeves rolled. The blue sky was full of sunshine and it couldn't have been a better day, and all of the big show was like something out of Ivanhoe that we'd seen on the pictures a few days before.

'Come on, Smith,' Roach the sports master called to me, 'we don't want you to be late for the big race, eh? Although I dare say you'd catch them up if you were.' The others catcalled and grunted at this, but I took no notice and placed myself between Gunthorpe and one of the Aylesham trusties, dropped on my knees and plucked a few grass blades to suck on the way round. So the big race it was, for them, watching from the grandstand under a fluttering Union Jack, a race for the governor, that he had been waiting for, and I hoped he and all the rest of his pop-eyed gang were busy placing big bets on me, hundred to one to win, all the money they had in their pockets, all the wages they were going to get for the next five years, and the more they placed the happier I'd be. Because here was a dead cert going to die on the big name they'd built for him, going to go down dying with laughter whether it choked him or not. My knees felt the cool soil pressing into them, and out of my eye's corner I saw Roach lift his hand. The Gunthorpe boy twitched before the signal was given; somebody cheered too soon; Medway bent forward; then the gun went, and I was away.

We went once around the field and then along a half-mile drive of elms, being cheered all the way, and I seemed to feel I was in the lead as we went out by the gate and into the lane, though I wasn't interested enough to find out. The five-mile course was marked by splashes of whitewash gleaming on gateposts and trunks and stiles and stones, and a boy with a waterbottle and bandage-box stood every half-mile waiting for those that dropped out or fainted. Over the first stile, without trying, I was still nearly in the lead but one; and if any of you want tips about running, never be in a hurry, and never let any of the other runners know you are in a hurry even if you are. You can always overtake on long-distance running without letting the others smell the hurry in you; and when you've used your craft like this to reach the two or three up front then you can do a big dash later that puts everybody else's hurry in the shade because you've not had to make haste up till then. I ran to a steady jog-trot rhythm, and soon it was so smooth that I forgot I was running, and I was hardly able to know that my legs were lifting and falling and my arms going in and out, and my lungs didn't seem to be working at all, and my heart stopped that wicked thumping I always get at the beginning of a run. Because you see I never race at all; I just run, and somehow I know that if I forget I'm racing and only jog-trot along until I don't know I'm running I always win the race. For when my eyes recognize that I'm getting near the end of the course – by seeing a stile or cottage corner – I put on a spurt, and such a fast big spurt it is because I feel that up till then I haven't been running and that I've used up no energy at all. And I've been able to do this because I've been thinking; and I wonder if I'm the only one in the running business with this system of forgetting that I'm running because I'm too busy thinking; and I wonder if any of the other lads are on to the same lark, though I know for a fact that they aren't. Off like the wind along the cobbled footpath and rutted lane, smoother than the flat grass track on the field and better for thinking because it's not too smooth, and I was in my element that afternoon knowing that nobody could beat me at running but intending to beat myself before the day was over. For when the governor talked to me of being honest when I first came in he didn't know what the word meant or he wouldn't have had me here in this race, trotting along in shimmy and shorts and sunshine. He'd have had me where I'd have had him if I'd been in his place: in a quarry breaking rocks until he broke his back. At least old Hitler-face the plain-clothes dick was honester than the governor, because he at any rate had had it in for me and I for him, and when my case was coming up in court a copper knocked at our front door at four o'clock in the morning and got my mother out of bed when she was paralytic tired, reminding her she had to be in court at dead on half past nine. It was the finest bit of spite I've ever heard of, but I would call it honest, the same as my mam's words were honest when she really told that copper what she thought of him and called him all the dirty names she'd ever heard of, which took her half an hour and woke the terrace up.

I trotted on along the edge of a field bordered by the sunken lane, smelling green grass and honeysuckle, and I felt as though I came from a long line of whippets trained to run on two legs, only I couldn't see a toy rabbit in front and there wasn't a collier's cosh behind to make me keep up the pace. I passed the Gunthorpe runner whose shimmy was already black with sweat and I could just see the corner of the fenced-up copse in front where the only man I had to pass to win the race was going all out to gain the half-way mark. Then he turned into a tongue of trees and bushes where I couldn't see him anymore, and I couldn't see anybody, and I knew what the loneliness of the long-distance runner running across country felt like, realizing that as far as I was concerned this feeling was the only honesty and realness there was in the world and I knowing it would be no different ever, no matter what I felt at odd times, and no matter what anybody else tried to tell me. The runner behind me must have been a long way off because it was so quiet, and there was even less noise and movement than there had been at five o'clock of a frosty winter morning. It was hard to understand, and all I knew was that you had to run, run, run, without knowing why you were running, but on you went through fields you didn't understand and into woods that made you afraid, over hills without knowing you'd been up and down, and shooting across streams that would have cut the heart out of you had you fallen into them. And the winning post was no end to it, even though crowds might be cheering you in, because on you had to go before you got your breath back, and the only time you stopped running was when you tripped over a tree trunk and broke your neck or fell into a disused well and stayed dead in the darkness forever. So I thought: they aren't going to get me on this racing lark, this running and trying to win, this jog-trotting for a bit of blue ribbon, because it's not the way to go on at all, though they swear blind that it is. You should think about nobody and go your own way, not on a course marked out for you by people holding mugs of water and bottles of iodine in case you fall and cut yourself so that they can pick you up – even if you want to stay where you are – and get you moving again.

On I went, out of the wood, passing the man leading without knowing I was going to do so. Flip-flap, flip-flap, jog-trot, jog-trot, crunchslap-crunchslap, across the middle of a broad field again, rhythmically running in my greyhound effortless fashion, knowing I had won the race though it wasn't half over, won it if I wanted it, could go on for ten or fifteen or twenty miles if I had to and drop dead at the finish of it, which would be the same, in the end, as living an honest life like the governor wanted me to. It amounted to: win the race and be honest, and on trot-trotting I went, having the time of my life, loving my progress because it did me good and set me thinking which by now I liked to do, but not caring at all when I remembered that I had to win this race as well as run it. One of the two, I had to win the race or run it, and I knew I could do both because my legs had carried me well in front – now coming to the short cut down the bramble bank and over the sunken road – and would carry me further because they seemed made of electric cable and easily alive to keep on slapping at those ruts and roots, but I'm not going to win because the only way I'd see I came in first would be if winning meant that I was going to escape the coppers after doing the biggest bank job of my life, but winning means the exact opposite, no matter how they try to kill or kid me, means running right into their white-gloved wall-barred hands and grinning mugs and staying there for the rest of my natural long life of stone-breaking anyway, but stone-breaking in the way I want to do it and not in the way they tell me.

Another honest thought that comes is that I could swing left at the next hedge of the field, and under its cover beat my slow retreat away from the sports ground winning post. I could do three or six or a dozen miles across the turf like this and cut a few main roads behind me so's they'd never know which one I'd taken; and maybe on the last one when it got dark I could thumb a lorry-lift and get a free ride north with somebody who might not give me away. But no, I said I wasn't daft didn't I? I won't pull out with only six months left, and besides there's nothing I want to dodge and run away from; I only want a bit of my own back on the In-laws and Potbellies by letting them sit up there on their big posh seats and watch me lose this race, though as sure as God made me I know that when I do lose I'll get the dirtiest crap and kitchen jobs in the months to go before my time is up. I won't be worth a threepenny bit to anybody here, which will be all the thanks I get for being honest in the only way I know. For when the governor told me to be honest it was meant to be in his way not mine, and if I kept on being honest in the way he wanted and won my race for him he'd see I got the cushiest six months still left to run; but in my own way, well, it's not allowed, and if I find a way of doing it such as I've got now then I'll get what-for in every mean trick he can set his mind to. And if you look at it in my own way, who can blame him? For this is war – and ain't I said so? – and when I hit him in the only place he knows he'll be sure to get his own back on me for not collaring that cup when his heart's been set for ages on seeing himself standing up at the end of the afternoon to clap me on the back as I take the cup from Lord Earwig or some such chinless wonder with a name like that. And so I'll hit him where it hurts a lot, and he'll do all he can to get his own back, tit for tat, though I'll enjoy it most because I'm hitting first, and because I planned it longer. I don't know why I think these thoughts are better than any I've ever had, but I do, and I don't care why. I suppose it took me a long time to get going on all this because I've had no time and peace in all my bandit life, and now my thoughts are coming pat and the only trouble is I often can't stop, even when my brain feels as if it's got cramp, frostbite and creeping paralysis all rolled into one and I have to give it a rest by slap-dashing down through the brambles of the sunken lane. And all this is another uppercut I'm getting in first at people like the governor, to show how – if I can – his races are never won even though some bloke always comes unknowingly in first, how in the end the governor is going to be doomed while blokes like me will take the pickings of his roasted bones and dance like maniacs around his Borstal's ruins. And so this story's like the race and once again I won't bring off a winner to suit the governor; no, I'm being honest like he told me to, without him knowing what he means, though I don't suppose he'll ever come in with a story of his own, even if he reads this one of mine and knows who I'm talking about.

I've just come up out of the sunken lane, kneed and elbowed, thumped and bramble-scratched, and the race is two thirds over, and a voice is going like a wireless in my mind saying that you've had enough of feeling good like the first man on earth on a frosty morning, and you've known how it is to be taken bad like that last man on earth on a summer's afternoon, then you get at last to being like the only man on earth and don't give a bogger about either good or bad, but just trot on with your slippers slapping the good dry soil that at least would never do you a bad turn. Now the words are like coming from a crystal-set that's broken down, and something's happening inside the shell-case of my guts that bothers me and I don't know why or what to blame it on, a grinding near my ticker as though a bag of rusty screws is loose inside me and I shake them up every time I trot forward. Now and again I break my rhythm to feel my left shoulder-blade by swinging a right hand across my chest as if to rub the knife away that has somehow got stuck there. But I know it's nothing to bother about, that more likely it's caused by too much thinking that now and again I take for worry. For sometimes I'm the greatest worrier in the world I think (as you twigged I'll bet from me having got this story out) which is funny anyway because my mam don't know the meaning of the word so I don't take after her; though dad had a hard time of worry all his life up to when he filled his bedroom with hot blood and kicked the bucket that morning when nobody was in the house. I'll never forget it, straight I won't, because I was the one that found him and I often wished I hadn't. Back from a session on the fruit-machines at the fish-and-chip shop, jingling my three-lemon loot to a nail-dead house, as soon as I got in I knew something was wrong, stood leaning my head against the cold mirror above the mantelpiece trying not to open my eyes and see my stone-cold clock – because I knew I'd gone as white as a piece of chalk since coming in as if I'd been got at by a Dracula-vampire and even my penny-pocket winnings kept quiet on purpose.

Gunthorpe nearly caught me up. Birds were singing from the briar hedge, and a couple of thrushes flew like lightning into some thorny bushes. Corn had grown high in the next field and would be cut down soon with scythes and mowers; but I never wanted to notice much while running in case it put me off my stroke, so by the haystack I decided to leave it all behind and put on such a spurt, in spite of nails in my guts, that before long I'd left both Gunthorpe and the birds a good way off; I wasn't far now from going into that last mile and a half like a knife through margarine, but the quietness I suddenly trotted into between two pickets was like opening my eyes underwater and looking at the pebbles on a stream bottom, reminding me again of going back that morning to the house in which my old man had croaked, which is funny because I hadn't thought about it at all since it happened and even then I didn't brood much on it. I wonder why? I suppose that since I started to think on these long-distance runs I'm liable to have anything crop up and pester at my tripes and innards, and now that I see my bloody dad behind each grassblade in my barmy runner-brain I'm not so sure I like to think and that it's such a good thing after all. I choke my phlegm and keep on running anyway and curse the Borstal-builders and their athletics – flappity-flap, slop-slop, crunch-slap, crunchslap-crunchslap – who've maybe got their own back on me from the bright beginning by sliding magic-lantern slides into my head that never stood a chance before. Only if I take whatever comes like this in my runner's stride can I keep on keeping on like my old self and beat them back; and now I've thought on this far I know I'll win, in the crunchslap end. So anyway after a bit I went upstairs one step at a time not thinking anything about how I should find dad and what I'd do when I did. But now I'm making up for it by going over the rotten life mam led him ever since I can remember, knocking-on with different men even when he was alive and fit and she not caring whether he knew it or not, and most of the time he wasn't so blind as she thought and cursed and roared and threatened to punch her tab, and I had to stand up to stop him even though I knew she deserved it. What a life for all of us. Well, I'm not grumbling, because if I did I might just as well win this bleeding race, which I'm not going to do, though if I don't lose speed I'll win it before I know where I am, and then where would I be?

Now I can hear the sportsground noise and music as I head back for the flags and the lead-in drive, the fresh new feel of underfoot gravel going against the iron muscles of my legs. I'm nowhere near puffed despite that bag of nails that rattles as much as ever, and I can still give a big last leap like galeforce wind if I want to, but everything is under control and I know now that there ain't another long-distance cross-country running runner in England to touch my speed and style. Our doddering bastard of a governor, our half-dead gangrened gaffer is hollow like an empty petrol drum, and he wants me and my running life to give him glory, to put in him blood and throbbing veins he never had, wants his potbellied pals to be his witnesses as I gasp and stagger up to his winning post so's he can say: 'My Borstal gets that cup, you see I win my bet because it pays to be honest and try to gain the prizes I offer to my lads, and they know it, have known it all along. They'll always be honest now, because I made them so.' And his pals will think: 'He trains his lads to live right, after all; he deserves a medal but we'll get him made a Sir' – and at this very moment as the birds come back to whistling I can tell myself I'll never care a sod what any of the chinless spineless In-laws think or say. They've seen me and they're cheering now and loudspeakers set around the field like elephant's ears are spreading out the big news that I'm well in the lead, and can't do anything else but stay there. But I'm still thinking of the

Outlaw death my dad died, telling the doctors to scat from the house when they wanted him to finish up in hospital (like a bleeding guinea-pig, he raved at them). He got up in bed to throw them out and even followed them down the stairs in his shirt though he was no more than skin and stick. They tried to tell him he'd want some drugs but he didn't fall for it, and only took the pain-killer that mam and I got from a herb-seller in the next street. It's not till now that I know what guts he had, and when I went into the room that morning he was lying on his stomach with the clothes thrown back, looking like a skinned rabbit, his grey head resting just on the edge of the bed, and on the floor must have been all the blood he'd had in his body, right from his toe-nails up, for nearly all of the lino and carpet was covered in it, thin and pink.

And down the drive I went, carrying a heart blocked up like Boulder Dam across my arteries, the nail-bag clamped down tighter and tighter as though in a woodwork vice, yet with my feet like birdwings and arms like talons ready to fly across the field except that I didn't want to give anybody that much of a show, or win the race by accident. I smell the hot dry day now as I run towards the end, passing a mountain-heap of grass emptied from cans hooked on to the fronts of lawnmowers pushed by my pals; I rip a piece of tree-bark with my fingers and stuff it in my mouth, chewing wood and dust and maybe maggots as I run until I'm nearly sick, yet swallowing what I can of it just the same because a little birdie whistled to me that I've got to go on living for at least a bloody sight longer yet but that for six months I'm not going to smell that grass or taste that dusty bark or trot this lovely path. I hate to have to say this but something bloody-well made my cry, and crying is a thing I haven't bloody-well done since I was a kid of two or three. Because I'm slowing down now for Gunthorpe to catch me up, and I'm doing it in a place just where the drive turns in to the sportsfield – where they can see what I'm doing, especially the governor and his gang from the grandstand, and I'm going so slow I'm almost marking time. Those on the nearest seats haven't caught on yet to what's happening and are still cheering like mad ready for when I make that mark, and I keep on wondering when the bleeding hell Gunthorpe behind me is going to nip by on to the field because I can't hold this up all day, and I think Oh Christ it's just my rotten luck that Gunthorpe's dropped out and that I'll be here for half an hour before the next bloke comes up, but even so, I say, I won't budge, I won't go for that last hundred yards if I have to sit down cross-legged on the grass and have the governor and his chinless wonders pick me up and carry me there, which is against their rules so you can bet they'd never do it because they're not clever enough to break the rules – like I would be in their place – even though they are their own. No, I'll show him what honesty means if it's the last thing I do, though I'm sure he'll never understand because if he and all them like him did it'd mean they'd be on my side which is impossible. By God I'll stick this out like my dad stuck out his pain and kicked them doctors down the stairs; if he had guts for that then I've got guts for this and here I stay waiting for Gunthorpe or Aylesham to bash that turf and go right slap-up against that bit of clothes-line stretched across the winning post. As for me, the only time I'll hit that clothes-line will be when I'm dead and a comfortable coffin's been got ready on the other side. Until then I'm a long-distance runner, crossing country all on my own no matter how bad it feels.

The Essex boys were shouting themselves blue in the face telling me to get a move on, waving their arms, standing up and making as if to run at that rope themselves because they were only a few yards to the side of it. You cranky lot, I thought, stuck at that winning post, and yet I knew they didn't mean what they were shouting, were really on my side and always would be, not able to keep their maulers to themselves, in and out of cop-shops and clink. And there they were now having the time of their lives letting themselves go in cheering me which made the governor think they were heart and soul on his side when he wouldn't have thought any such thing if he'd had a grain of sense. And I could hear the lords and ladies now from the grandstand, and could see them standing up to wave me in: 'Run!' they were shouting in their posh voices. 'Run!' But I was deaf, daft and blind, and stood where I was, still tasting the bark in my mouth and still blubbing like a baby, blubbing now out of gladness that I'd got them beat at last.

Because I heard a roar and saw the Gunthorpe gang throwing their coats up in the air and I felt the pat-pat of feet on the drive behind me getting closer and closer and suddenly a smell of sweat and a pair of lungs on their last gasp passed me by and went swinging on towards that rope, all shagged out and rocking from side to side, grunting like a Zulu that didn't know any better, like the ghost of me at ninety when I'm heading for that fat upholstered coffin. I could have cheered him myself: 'Go on, go on, get cracking. Knot yourself up on that piece of tape.' But he was already there, and so I went on, trot-trotting after him until I got to the rope, and collapsed, with a murderous sounding roar going up through my ears while I was still on the wrong side of it.

It's about time to stop; though don't think I'm not still running, because I am, one way or another. The governor at Borstal proved me right; he didn't respect my honesty at all; not that I expected him to, or tried to explain it to him, but if he's supposed to be educated then he should have more or less twigged it. He got his own back right enough, or thought he did, because he had me carting dustbins about every morning from the big full-working kitchen to the garden-bottoms where I had to empty them; and in the afternoon I spread out slops on spuds and carrots growing in the allotments. In the evenings I scrubbed floors, miles and miles of them. But it wasn't a bad life for six months, which was another thing he could never understand and would have made it grimmer if he could, and it was worth it when I look back on it, considering all the thinking I did, and the fact that the boys caught on to me losing the race on purpose and never had enough good words to say about me, or curses to throw out (to themselves) at the governor.

The work didn't break me; if anything it made me stronger in many ways, and the governor knew, when I left, that his spite had got him nowhere. For since leaving Borstal they tried to get me in the army, but I didn't pass the medical and I'll tell you why. No sooner was I out, after that final run and six-months hard, than I went down with pleurisy, which means as far as I'm concerned that I lost the governor's race all right, and won my own twice over, because I know for certain that if I hadn't raced my race I wouldn't have got this pleurisy, which keeps me out of khaki but doesn't stop me doing the sort of work my itchy fingers want to do.

I'm out now and the heat's switched on again, but the rats haven't got me for the last big thing I pulled. I counted six hundred and twenty-eight pounds and am still living off it because I did the job all on my own, and after it I had the peace to write all this, and it'll be money enough to keep me going until I finish my plans for doing an even bigger snatch, something up my sleeve I wouldn't tell to a living soul. I worked out my systems and hiding-places while pushing scrubbing-brushes around them Borstal floors, planned my outward life of innocence and honest work, yet at the same time grew perfect in the razor-edges of my craft for what I knew I had to do once free; and what I'll do again if netted by the poaching coppers.

In the meantime (as they say in one or two books I've read since, useless though because all of them ended on a winning post and didn't teach me a thing) I'm going to give this story to a pal of mine and tell him that if I do get captured again by the coppers he can try and get it put into a book or something, because I'd like to see the governor's face when he reads it, if he does, which I don't suppose he will; even if he did read it though I don't think he'd know what it was all about. And if I don't get caught the bloke I give this story to will never give me away; he's lived in our terrace for as long as I can remember, and he's my pal. That I do know.

Uncle Ernest

A middle-aged man wearing a dirty raincoat, who badly needed a shave and looked as though he hadn't washed for a month, came out of a public lavatory with a cloth bag of tools folded beneath his arm. Standing for a moment on the edge of the pavement to adjust his cap – the cleanest thing about him – he looked casually to left and right and, when the flow of traffic had eased off, crossed the road. His name and trade were always spoken in one breath, even when the nature of his trade was not in question: Ernest Brown the upholsterer. Every night before returning to his lodgings he left the bag of tools for safety with a man who looked after the public lavatory near the town centre, for he felt there was a risk of them being lost or stolen should he take them back to his room, and if such a thing were to happen his living would be gone.

Chimes to the value of half past ten boomed from the Council-house clock. Over the theatre patches of blue sky held hard-won positions against autumnal clouds, and a treacherous wind lashed out its gusts, sending paper and cigarette packets cartwheeling along unswept gutters. Empty-bellied Ernest was ready for his breakfast, so walked through a café doorway, instinctively lowering his head as he did so, though the beams were a foot above his height.

The long spacious eating-place was almost full. Ernest usually arrived for his breakfast at nine o'clock, but having been paid ten pounds for re-covering a three-piece in a public house the day before, he had stationed himself in the Saloon Bar for the rest of the evening to drink jar after jar of beer, in a slow prolonged and concentrated way that lonely men have. As a result it had been difficult to drag himself from drugged and blissful sleep this morning. His face was pale and his eyes an unhealthy yellow: when he spoke only a few solitary teeth showed behind his lips.

Having passed through the half-dozen noisy people standing about he found himself at the counter, a scarred and chipped haven for

37

hands, like a littered invasion beach extending between two headlands of tea-urns. The big fleshy brunette was busy, so he hastily scanned the list written out in large white letters on the wall behind. He made a timid gesture with his hand. 'A cup of tea, please.'

The brunette turned on him. Tea swilled from a huge brown spout – into a cup that had a crack emerging like a hair above the layer of milk – and a spoon clinked after it into the steam. 'Anything else?'

He spoke up hesitantly. 'Tomatoes on toast as well.' Picking up the plate pushed over to him he moved slowly backwards out of the crowd, then turned and walked towards a vacant corner table.

A steamy appetizing smell rose from the plate: he took up the knife and fork and, with the sharp clean action of a craftsman, cut off a corner of the toast and tomato and raised it slowly to his mouth, eating with relish and hardly noticing people sitting roundabout. Each wielding of his knife and fork, each geometrical cut of the slice of toast, each curve and twist of his lips joined in a complex and regular motion that gave him great satisfaction. He ate slowly, quietly and contentedly, aware only of himself and his body being warmed and made tolerable once more by food. The leisurely movement of a spoon and cup and saucer made up the familiar noise of late breakfast in a crowded café, sounded like music flowing here and there in variations of rhythm.

For years he had eaten alone, but was not yet accustomed to loneliness. He could not get used to it, had only adapted himself to it temporarily in the hope that one day its spell would break. Ernest remembered little of his past, and life moved under him so that he hardly noticed its progress. There was no strong memory to entice him to what had gone by, except that of dead and dying men straggling barbed-wire between the trenches in the First World War. Two sentences had dominated his lips during the years that followed: 'I should not be here in England. I should be dead with the rest of them in France.' Time bereft him of these sentences, till only a dull wordless image remained.

People, he found, treated him as if he were a ghost, as if he were not made of flesh and blood – or so it seemed – and from then on he had lived alone. His wife left him – due to his too vile temper, it was said – and his brothers went to other towns. Later he had thought to look them up, but decided against it: for even in this isolation only the will to go forward and accept more of it seemed worth while. He felt in a dim indefinite way that to go back and search out the slums and

38

landmarks of his youth, old friends, the smells and sounds that beckoned him tangibly from better days, was a sort of death. He argued that it was best to leave them alone, because it seemed somehow probable that after death – whenever it came – he would meet all these things once again.

No pink scar marked his flesh from shell-shock and a jolted brain, and so what had happened in the war warranted no pension book, and even to him the word 'injury' never came into his mind. It was just that he did not care anymore: the wheel of the years had broken him, and so had made life more tolerable. When the next war came his back was not burdened at first, and even the fines and days in prison that he was made to pay for being without Identity Card or Ration Book – or for giving them away with a glad heart to deserters – did not lift him from his tolerable brokenness. The nightmare hours of gunfire and exploding bombs revived a dull image long suppressed as he stared blankly at the cellar wall of his boarding house, and even threw into his mind the scattered words of two insane sentences. But, considering the time-scale his life was lived on, the war ended quickly, and again nothing mattered. He lived from hand to mouth, working cleverly at settees and sofas and chairs, caring about no one. When work was difficult to find and life was hard, he did not notice it very much, and now that he was prosperous and had enough money, he also detected little difference, spending what he earned on beer, and never once thinking that he needed a new coat or a solid pair of boots.

He lifted the last piece of toast and tomato from his plate, then felt dregs of tea moving against his teeth. When he had finished chewing he lit a cigarette and was once more aware of people sitting around him. It was eleven o'clock and the low-roofed café was slowly emptying, leaving only a dozen people inside. He knew that at one table they were talking about horse-racing and at another about war, but words only flowed in his ears and entered his mind at a low pitch of comprehension, leaving it calm and content as he vaguely contemplated the positions and patterns of tables about the room. There would be no work until two o'clock so he intended sitting where he was until then. Yet a sudden embarrassment at having no food on the table to justify a prolonged occupation of it sent him to the counter for tea and cakes.

As he was being served two small girls came in. One sat at a table, but the second and elder stood at the counter. When he returned to his place he found the younger girl sitting there. He was confused and shy, but nevertheless sat down to drink tea and cut a cake into four pieces. The girl looked at him and continued to do so until the elder one came from the counter carrying two cups of steaming tea.

They sat talking and drinking, utterly oblivious of Ernest, who slowly felt their secretive, childish animation enter into himself. He glanced at them from time to time, feeling as if he should not be there, though when he looked at them he did so in a gentle way, with kind, full-smiling eyes. The elder girl, about twelve years old, was dressed in a brown coat that was too big for her, and though she was talking and laughing most of the time he noticed the paleness of her face and her large round eyes that he would have thought beautiful had he not detected the familiar type of vivacity that expressed neglect and want.

The smaller girl was less lively and merely smiled as she answered her sister with brief curt words. She drank her tea and warmed her hands at the same time without putting the cup down once until she had emptied it. Her thin red fingers curled around the cup as she stared into the leaves, and gradually the talk between them died down and they went silent, leaving the field free for traffic that could be heard moving along the street outside, and for inside noises made by the brunette who washed cups and dishes ready for the rush that was expected at midday dinner-time.

Ernest was calculating how many yards of rexine would be needed to cover the job he was to do that afternoon, but when the younger girl began speaking he listened to her, hardly aware that he was doing so.

'If you've got any money I'd like a cake, our Alma.'

'I haven't got any more money,' the elder one replied impatiently.

'Yes you have, and I'd like a cake.'

She was adamant, almost aggressive. 'Then you'll have to want on, because I've only got tuppence.'

'You can buy a cake with that,' the young girl persisted, twining her fingers around the empty cup. 'We don't need bus fares home because it ain't far to walk.'

'We can't walk home: it might rain.'

'No it won't.'

'Well I want a cake as well, but I'm not walking all that way,' the elder girl said conclusively, blocking any last gap that might remain in her defences. The younger girl gave up and said nothing, looked emptily in front of her.

Ernest had finished eating and took out a cigarette, struck a match across the iron fastening of a table leg and, having inhaled deeply, allowed smoke to wander from his mouth. Like a gentle tide washing in under the moon, a line of water flowing inwards and covering the sand, a feeling of acute loneliness took hold of him, an agony that would not let him weep. The two girls sat before him wholly engrossed in themselves, still debating whether they should buy a cake, or whether they should ride home on a bus.

'But it'll be cold,' reasoned the elder, 'walking home.'

'No it won't,' the other said, but with no conviction in her words. The sound of their voices told him how lonely he was, each word feeding him with so much more loneliness that he felt utterly unhappy and empty.

Time went slowly: the minute-hand of the clock seemed as if it were nailed immovably at one angle. The two girls looked at each other and did not notice him: he withdrew into himself and felt the emptiness of the world and wondered how he would spend all the days that seemed to stretch vacantly, like goods on a broken-down conveyor belt, before him. He tried to remember things that had happened and felt panic when he discovered a thirty-year vacuum. All he could see behind was a grey mist and all he could see before him was the same unpredictable fog that would hide nothing. He wanted to walk out of the café and find some activity so that he would henceforth be able to mark off the passage of his empty days, but he had no will to move. He heard someone crying so shook himself free of such thoughts and saw the younger girl with hands to her eyes, weeping. 'What's the matter?' he asked tenderly, leaning across the table.

The elder girl replied for her, saying sternly:

'Nothing. She's acting daft.'

'But she must be crying for some reason. What is it?' Ernest persisted, quietly and soothingly, bending closer still towards her. 'Tell me what's wrong.' Then he remembered something. He drew it like a live thread from a mixture of reality and dream, hanging on to vague words that floated back into his mind. The girls' conversation came to him through an intricate process of recollection. 'I'll get you something to eat,' he ventured. 'Can I?'

She unscrewed clenched fingers from her eyes and looked up, while the elder girl glared at him resentfully and said: 'We don't want anything. We're going now.'

41

'No, don't go,' he cried. 'You just sit down and see what I'm going to get for you.' He stood up and walked to the counter, leaving them whispering to each other.

He came back with a plate of pastries and two cups of tea, which he set before the girls, who looked on in silence. The younger was smiling now. Her round eager eyes were fascinated, yet followed each movement of his hands with some apprehension. Though still hostile the elder girl was gradually subdued by the confidently working actions of his hands, by caressing words and the kindness that showed in his face. He was wholly absorbed in doing good and, at the same time, fighting the feeling of loneliness that he still remembered, but only as a nightmare is remembered.

The two children fell under his spell, began to eat cakes and sip the tea. They glanced at each other, and then at Ernest as he sat before them smoking a cigarette. The café was still almost empty, and the few people eating were so absorbed in themselves, or were in so much of a hurry to eat their food and get out that they took little notice of the small company in the corner. Now that the atmosphere between himself and the two girls had grown more friendly Ernest began to talk to them. 'Do you go to school?' he asked.

The elder girl automatically assumed control and answered his questions. 'Yes, but today we had to come down town on an errand for our mam.'

'Does your mother go out to work, then?'

'Yes,' she informed him. 'All day.'

Ernest was encouraged. 'And does she cook your dinners?'

She obliged him with another answer. 'Not until night.'

'What about your father?' he went on.

'He's dead,' said the smaller girl, her mouth filled with food, daring to speak outright for the first time. Her sister looked at her with disapproval, making it plain that she had said the wrong thing and that she should only speak under guidance.

'Are you going to school then this afternoon?' Ernest resumed.

'Yes,' the spokesman said.

He smiled at her continued hard control. 'And what's your name then?'

'Alma,' she told him, 'and hers is Joan.' She indicated the smaller girl with a slight nod of the head.

'Are you often hungry?'

She stopped eating and glanced at him, uncertain how to answer. 'No, not much,' she told him non-committally, busily eating a second pastry.

'But you were today?'

'Yes,' she said, casting away diplomacy like the crumpled cake-paper she let fall to the floor.

He said nothing for a few moments, sitting with knuckles pressed to his lips. 'Well look' – he began suddenly talking again – 'I come in here every day for my dinner, just about half past twelve, and if ever you're feeling hungry, come down and see me.'

They agreed to this, accepted sixpence for their bus fares home, thanked him very much, and said good-bye.

During the following weeks they came to see him almost every day. Sometimes, when he had little money, he filled his empty stomach with a cup of tea while Alma and Joan satisfied themselves on five shillings'-worth of more solid food. But he was happy and gained immense satisfaction from seeing them bending hungrily over eggs, bacon and pastries, and he was so smoothed at last into a fine feeling of having something to live for that he hardly remembered the lonely days when his only hope of being able to talk to someone was by going into a public house to get drunk. He was happy now because he had his 'little girls' to look after, as he came to call them.

He began spending all his money to buy them presents, so that he was often in debt at his lodgings. He still did not buy any clothes, for whereas in the past his money had been swilled away on beer, now it was spent on presents and food for the girls, and he went on wearing the same old dirty mackintosh and was still without a collar to his shirt; even his cap was no longer clean.

Every day, straight out of school, Alma and Joan ran to catch a bus for the town centre and, a few minutes later, smiling and out of breath, walked into the café where Ernest was waiting. As days and weeks passed, and as Alma noticed how much Ernest depended on them for company, how happy he was to see them, and how obviously miserable when they did not come for a day – which was rare now – she began to demand more and more presents, more food, more money, but only in a particularly naïve and childish way, so that Ernest, in his oblivious contentment, did not notice it.

But certain customers of the café who came in every day could not help but see how the girls asked him to buy them this and that, and how he always gave in with a nature too good to be decently true, and without the least sign of realizing what was really happening. He would never dream to question their demands, for to him, these two girls whom he looked upon almost as his own daughters, were the only people he had to love.

Ernest, about to begin eating, noticed two smartly dressed men sitting at a table a few yards away. They had sat in the same place the previous day, and also the day before that, but he thought no more about it because Joan and Alma came in and walked quickly across to his table.

'Hello, Uncle Ernest!' they said brightly. 'What can we have for dinner?' Alma looked across at the chalk-written list on the wall to read what dishes were available.

His face changed from the blank preoccupation of eating, and a smile of happiness infused his cheeks, eyes, and the curve of his lips. 'Whatever you like,' he answered.

'But what have they got?' Alma demanded crossly. 'I can't read their scrawl.'

'Go up to the counter and ask for a dinner,' he advised with a laugh.

'Will you give me some money then?' she asked, her hand out. Joan stood by without speaking, lacking Alma's confidence, her face timid, and nervous because she did not yet understand this regular transaction of money between Ernest and themselves, being afraid that one day they would stand there waiting for money and Ernest would quite naturally look surprised and say there was nothing for them.

He had just finished repairing an antique three-piece and had been paid that morning, so Alma took five shillings and they went to the counter for a meal. While they were waiting to be served, the two well-dressed men who had been watching Ernest for the last few days stood up and walked over to him.

Only one of them spoke; the other held his silence and looked on. 'Are those two girls your daughters, or any relation to you?' the first asked, nodding towards the counter.

Ernest looked up and smiled. 'No,' he explained in a mild voice, 'they're just friends of mine, why?'

The man's eyes were hard, and he spoke clearly. 'What kind of friends?'

'Just friends. Why? Who are you?' He shuddered, feeling a kind of half-guilt growing inside him for a half-imagined reason he hoped wasn't true.

'Never mind who we are. I just want you to answer my question.'

Ernest raised his voice slightly, yet did not dare to look into the man's arrogant eyes. 'Why?' he cried. 'What's it got to do with you? Why are you asking questions like this?'

'We're from the police station,' the man remarked dryly, 'and we've had complaints that you're giving these little girls money and leading them the wrong way!'

Ernest wanted to laugh, but only from misery. Yet he did not want to laugh in case he should annoy the two detectives. He started to talk: 'But . . . but . . .' – then found himself unable to go on. There was much that he wanted to say, yet he could enunciate nothing, and a bewildered animal stare moved slowly into his eyes.

'Look,' the man said emphatically, 'we don't want any of your "buts". We know all about you. We know who you are. We've known you for years in fact, and we're asking you to leave those girls alone and have nothing more to do with them. Men like you shouldn't give money to little girls. You should know what you're doing, and have more sense.'

Ernest protested loudly at last. 'I tell you they're friends of mine. I mean no harm. I look after them and give them presents just as I would daughters of my own. They're the only company I've got. In any case why shouldn't I look after them? Why should you take them away from me? Who do you think you are? Leave me alone . . . leave me alone.' His voice had risen to a weak scream of defiance, and the other people in the crowded café were looking around and staring at him, wondering what was the cause of the disturbance.

The two detectives acted quickly and competently, yet without apparent haste. One stood on each side of him, lifted him up, and walked him by the counter, out on to the street, squeezing his wrists tightly as they did so. As Ernest passed the counter he saw the girls holding their plates, looking in fear and wonder at him being walked out.

They took him to the end of the street, and stood there for a few seconds talking to him, still keeping hold of his wrists and pressing their fingers hard into them.

'Now look here, we don't want any more trouble from *you*, but if ever we see you near those girls again, you'll find yourself up before a magistrate.' The tone of finality in his voice possessed a physical force that pushed Ernest to the brink of sanity.

He stood speechless. He wanted to say so many things but the words would not come to his lips. They quivered helplessly with shame and hatred, and so were incapable of making words. 'We're asking you in a peaceful manner,' the detective went on, 'to leave them alone. Understand?'

'Yes,' Ernest was forced to answer.

'Right. Go on then. And we don't want to see you with those girls again.'

He was only aware of the earth sliding away from under his feet, and a wave of panic crashing into his mind, and he felt the unbearable and familiar emptiness that flowed outwards from a tiny and unknowable point inside him. Then he was filled with hatred for everything, then intense pity for all the movement that was going on around him, and finally even more intense pity for himself. He wanted to cry but could not: he could only walk away from his shame.

Then he began to shed agony at each step. His bitterness eddied away and a feeling the depth of which he had never known before took its place. There was now more purpose in the motion of his footsteps as he went along the pavement through midday crowds. And it seemed to him that he did not care about anything any more as he pushed through the swing doors and walked into the crowded and noisy bar of a public house, his stare fixed by the beautiful heavily baited trap of beer pots that would take him into the one and only best kind of oblivion.

Mr Raynor the School-teacher

Now that the boys were relatively quiet Mr Raynor looked out of the classroom window, across the cobbled road and into the window of Harrison's the draper's shop. With sight made keener by horn-rimmed spectacles he observed the new girl lift her arms above her head to reach some small drawers of cotton, an action which elongated the breasts inside her dark blue dress until she looked almost flat-chested. Mr Raynor rasped his shoes slightly on the bar of his tall stool, a stool once the subject of a common-room joke, which said that he had paid the caretaker well to put on longer legs so that he could see better out of the window and observe with more ease the girls in Harrison's shop across the road. Most of the boys before him had grown so used to his long periods of distraction – freedom for them – that they no longer found inclination or time to sneer at the well-known reason for it.

When the flat-chested girl went upstairs into the Men's Suits, another girl, small, heavy, and with a satisfyingly larger bosom, came into the centre span of the counter and spread out a box of coloured ties like wheel-spokes before a man who had just come in. But her appeal to his taste was still at an unpalatable extreme, and he again regretted the departure of a girl who had been, to him, perfect in every way. Against a background of road and shop, and movements between the two that his fixed stare kept easily in a state of insignificance, he recalled her image, a difficult thing because faces did not linger clearly for a long time in his memory even though she had only been dead for ten days.

Eighteen, he remembered her, and not too tall, with almost masculine features below short chestnut hair: brown eyes, full cheeks and proportionate lips, like Aphrodite his inward eye had commented time and time again, only a little sweeter. She wore brown sweater and brown cardigan, a union that gave only tormenting glimpses of her upper figure, until one summer's day when the cardigan was set aside, revealing breasts on the same classical style, hips a trifle broad,

complementing nevertheless her somewhat stocky legs and fleshy re-
deeming calves. She had only to move from the counter to the foot of
the stairs that led to the upper part of the shop, and Mr Raynor's
maxims of common arithmetic became stale phrases of instruction to
be given out quickly, leaving his delighted class with an almost free
session.

What memory could not accomplish, imagination did, and he re-
created a tangible image, moved by long-cultivated pre-occupations of
sensuality in which his wife and family took no part. He adjusted his
spectacles, rolled his tongue around the dry back of his teeth, and
grated his feet once more on the bar of the stool. As she walked she had
carried her whole body in a sublime movement conducive to the
attraction of every part of it, so that he was even aware of heels inside
her shoes and finger-tips buried perhaps beneath a bolt of opulent
cloth. A big trolley-bus bundled its green-fronted track along the road,
and carried his vision away on the coloured advertisements decorating
the band between top and bottom decks.

Deprived so suddenly he felt for a cigarette, but there was half an
hour yet for the playtime break. And he still had to deal with the
present class before they went to geography at ten o'clock. The noise
broke into him, sunk him down to reality like cold water entering a
ship. They were the eldest rag-mob of the school, and the most
illiterate, a C stream of fourteen-year-old louts raring to leave and
start work at the factories round about. Bullivant the rowdiest subsided only after his head was well turned from the window; but the
noise went on. The one feasible plan was to keep them as quiet as
possible for the remaining months, then open the gates and let them
free, allow them to spill out into the big wide world like the young
animals they were, eager for fags and football, beer and women and a
forest of streets to roam in. The responsibility would be no longer his,
once they were packed away with the turned pages of his register into
another, more incorrigible annexe than the enclave of jungle he ruled
for his living. He would have done whatever could be done with such
basically unsuitable and unwilling scholars.

'All right,' he called out in a loud clear voice, 'let's have a little
quietness in the room.' Though the noise persisted, an air of obedience
reigned. Mr Raynor was not a strict disciplinarian, but he had taught
for twenty-five years, and so acquired a voice of authority that was
listened to. Even if he didn't hit them very often, it was realized that he

48

was not a young man and could easily do so. And it was consciously felt that there was more force behind a middle-aged fist than a young and inexperienced one. Consequently when he told them to keep quiet, they usually did.

'Take out your Bibles,' he said, 'and open them at Exodus, chapter six.'

He watched forty-five hands, few of them clean, unaccountably opening the Bible, as they did all books, from the back and working to the front. Now and again he caught the flicker of brightly coloured illustrations at different points in the class, on their way through a welter of pages. He leaned forward on the high desk, one elbow supporting his forehead, seeing Bullivant whisper to the boy next to him, and hearing the boy giggle.

'Handley,' Mr Raynor demanded with a show of sternness, 'who was Aaron?'

A small boy from the middle of the class stood up: 'Aaron from the Bible, sir?'

'Yes. Who else, you ass?'

'Don't know, sir,' the boy answered, either because he really didn't, Mr Raynor told himself, or by way of revenge for being called an ass.

'Didn't you read the chapter yesterday I told you to read?'

Here was a question he could answer. 'Yes, sir,' came the bright response.

'Well then, who was Aaron?'

His face was no longer bright. It became clouded as he admitted: 'I've forgot, sir.'

Mr Raynor ran a hand slowly over his forehead. He changed tack. 'NO!' he yelled, so loudly that the boy jumped. 'Don't sit down yet, Handley.' He stood up again. 'We've been reading this part of the Bible for a month, so you should be able to answer my questions. Now: Who was the brother of Moses?'

Bullivant chanted from behind:

> 'Then the Lord said unto Moses
> All the Jews shall have long noses
> Exceptin' Aaron
> He shall 'ave a square'un
> And poor old Peter
> He shall 'ave a gas-meter!'

The low rumble reached Mr Raynor, and he saw several half-tortured faces around Bullivant trying not to laugh. 'Tell me, Handley,' he said again, 'who was the brother of Moses?'

Handley's face became happy, almost recognizable under the unfamiliar light of inspiration, for the significance of the chanted verse had eaten its way through to his understanding. 'Aaron, sir,' he said.

'And so' – Mr Raynor assumed he was getting somewhere at last – 'who was Aaron?'

Handley, who had considered his ordeal to be over on hearing a subdued cheer of irony from Bullivant, lifted a face blank in defeat. 'Don't know, sir.'

A sigh of frustration, not allowed to reach the boys, escaped Mr Raynor. 'Sit down,' he said to Handley, who did so with such alacrity that the desk lid rattled. Duty had been done as far as Handley was concerned, and now it was Robinson's turn, who stood up from his desk a few feet away. 'Tell us who Aaron was,' Mr Raynor ordered.

Robinson was a brighter boy, who had thought to keep a second Bible open beneath his desk lid for reference. 'A priest, sir,' he answered sharply, 'the brother of Moses.'

'Sit down, then,' Mr Raynor said. 'Now, remember that, Handley. What House are you in, Robinson?'

He stood up again, grinning respectfully. 'Buckingham, sir.'

'Then take a credit star.'

After the green star had been fixed to the chart he set one of the boys to read, and when the monotonous drone of his voice was well under way he turned again to span the distance between his high stool and the draper's window. By uniting the figures and faces of the present assistants, and then by dissolving them, he tried to recapture the carnal vision of the girl who had recently died, a practice of reconstruction that had been the mainstay of his sojourn at this school, a line of sight across the cobbled road into Harrison's shop, beamed on to the girls who went to work there when they were fifteen and left at twenty to get married. He had become a connoisseur of young suburban womanhood, and thus the fluctuating labour and marriage market made Mr Raynor a fickle lover, causing him too often to forget each great passion as another one walked in to take its place. Each 'good' one was credit-starred upon his mind, left behind a trail of memories when it went, until a new 'good' one came like a solid fiscal stamp of spiritual currency that drove the other one out. Each memory was thus renewed, so that none of them died.

But the last one was the best one of all, an unexpected beauty back-dropped against the traffic artery of squalid streets. He watched her work and talk or on wet afternoons stand at the counter as if in a trance. The boy on the front row was reading like a prophet, and an agitated muttering sea began to grow about him, and the curtain of Mr Raynor's memory drew back upon the runners of a line recalled from Baudelaire: *'Timide et libertine, et fragile et robuste'* – revealing the secret of her classic beauty and nubility, which vanished when the blood-filled phrase was dragged away by the top deck of a trolley-bus laden with rigid staring faces. A tea-boy carrying a white jug slipped out of the estate agents' offices, dodged deftly through a line of cars and lorries that had stopped for the traffic-lights, and walked whistling a tune into a café further down the road.

The sea of noise surrounding the prophet-like monotonous voice of the reading boy increased to a higher magnitude than discipline would permit, until a wave carried his sonorous words away and another sound dominated the scene. He looked, and saw Bullivant on his feet thumping the boy at the desk in front with all his might. The boy raised his fists to hit back.

Mr Raynor roared with such fury that there was instant silence, his ageing pink face thrust over his desk towards them. 'Come out, Bullivant,' he cried. *Libertine et robuste*: the phrase fought and died, was given a white cross and packed away.

Bullivant slouched out between rows of apprehensive boys. ''e 'it me first,' he said, nearing the blackboard.

'And now I'm going to hit you,' Mr Raynor retorted, lifting the lid of his desk and taking out a stick. His antagonist eyed him truculently, displaying his contempt of the desperate plight he was supposed to be in by turning round and winking at his friends. He was a big boy of fourteen, wearing long drainpipe trousers and a grey jersey.

'Y'aren't gooin' ter 'it me,' he said. 'I ain't dun owt ter get 'it, yer know.'

'Hold out your hand,' Mr Raynor said, his face turning a deep crimson. *Timide*. No, he thought, not likely. This is the least I can do. I'll get these Teddy-boy ideas out of his head for a few seconds.

No hand was extended towards him as it should have been. Bullivant stood still and Mr Raynor repeated his order. The class looked on, and moving traffic in the road hid none of the smaller mutterings that passed for silence. Bullivant still wouldn't lift his hand, and time enough had gone by that could be justified by Mr Raynor as patience.

'Y'aren't gooin' ter 'it me wi' that,' Bullivant said again, a gleam just showing from his blue half-closed eyes.

Robust. An eye for an eye. The body of the girl, the bottom line of the sweater spreading over her hips, was destroyed in silence. His urge for revenge was checked, but was followed by a rage that nevertheless bit hard and forced him to action. In the passing of a bus he stepped to Bullivant's side and struck him several times across the shoulders with the stick, crashing each blow down with all his force. 'Take that,' he cried out, 'you stupid defiant oaf.'

Bullivant shied away. And before any more blows could fall, and before Mr Raynor realized that such a thing was possible, Bullivant lashed back with his fists, and they were locked in a battle of strength, both trying to push the other away, to get clear and strike. Mr Raynor took up a stance with legs apart, trying to push Bullivant back against the desks, but Bullivant foresaw such a move from his stronger adversary and moved his own body so that they went scuffling between the desks. 'Yo' ain't 'ittin' me like that,' Bullivant gasped between his teeth. 'Oo do yo' think yo' are?' He unscrewed his head that was suddenly beneath Mr Raynor's arm, threw out his fists that went wide of the mark, and leapt like a giraffe over a row of desks. Mr Raynor moved quickly and blocked his retreat, grabbed his arm firmly and glowered at him with blood-red face, twisted the captive limb viciously, all in a second, then pushed him free, though he stood with the stick ready in case Bullivant should come for him again.

But Bullivant recognized the dispensation of a truce, and merely said: 'I'll bring our big kid up to settle yo',' and sat down. Experience was Mr Raynor's friend; he saw no point in spinning out trouble to its logical conclusion, which meant only more trouble. He was content to warn Bullivant to behave himself, seeing that no face had been lost by either side in the equal contest. He sat again on the high stool behind his desk. What did it matter, really? Bullivant and most of the others would be leaving in two months, and he could keep them in check for that short time. And after the holidays more Bullivants would move up into his classroom from the scholastic escalator.

It was five minutes to ten, and to ensure that the remaining time was peaceful he took out his Bible and began reading in a clear steady voice: 'Then the Lord said unto Moses (titters here), now shalt thou see what I will do to Pharaoh: for with a strong hand shall he let them go, and with a strong hand shall he drive them out of his land.'

The class that came in at half past ten was for arithmetic, and they were told to open their books and do exercises on page fifty-four. He observed the leaves of many books covered with ink-scrawls, and obscene words written across the illustrations and decorating the 'answer' margins like tattooing on the arms of veteran sailors, pages that would be unrecognizable in a month, but would have to last for another twelve. This was a younger class whose rebellion had so far reached only the pages of their books.

But that, too, was only something to accept and, inclining his head to the right, he forgot the noises of his class and looked across the road at the girls working in the draper's shop. Oh yes, the last one had been the best he could remember, and the time had come when he decided to cure his madness by speaking to her one evening as she left the shop. It was a good idea. But it was too late, for a young man had begun meeting her and seeing her safely, it seemed, to the bus stop. Most of the girls who gave up their jobs at the shop did so because they met some common fate or other. ('*Timide et libertine, et fragile et robuste*' – he could not forget the phrase.) Some were married, others, he had noticed, became pregnant and disappeared; a few quarrelled with the manager and appeared to have been sacked. But the last one, he had discovered, on opening the newspaper one evening by the traffic-lights at the corner, had been murdered by the young man who came to meet her.

Three double-decker trolley-buses trundled by in a line, but he still saw her vision by the counter.

'Quiet!' he roared, to the forty faces before him. 'The next one to talk gets the stick.'

And there was quiet.

The Fishing-boat Picture

I've been a postman for twenty-eight years. Take that first sentence: because it's written in a simple way may make the fact of my having been a postman for so long seem important, but I realize that such a fact has no significance whatever. After all, it's not my fault that it may seem as if it has to some people just because I wrote it down plain; I wouldn't know how to do it any other way. If I started using long and complicated words that I'd searched for in the dictionary I'd use them too many times, the same ones over and over again, with only a few sentences – if that – between each one; so I'd rather not make what I'm going to write look foolish by using dictionary words.

It's also twenty-eight years since I got married. That statement is very important no matter how you write it or in what way you look at it. It so happened that I married my wife as soon as I got a permanent job, and the first good one I landed was with the Post Office (before that I'd been errand-boy and mash-lad). I had to marry her as soon as I got a job because I'd promised her I would, and she wasn't the sort of person to let me forget it.

When my first pay night came I called for her and asked: 'What about a walk up Snakey Wood?' I was cheeky-daft and on top of the world, and because I'd forgotten about our arrangement I didn't think it strange when she said: 'Yes, all right.' It was late autumn I remember and the leaves were as high as snow, crisp on top but soggy underneath. In the full moon and light wind we walked over the Cherry Orchard, happy and arm-in-arm. Suddenly she stopped and turned to me, a big-boned girl yet with a good figure and nice enough face: 'Do you want to go into the wood?'

What a thing to ask! I laughed: 'You know I do. Don't you?'

We walked on, and a minute later she said: 'Yes, I do; but you know what we're to do now you've got a steady job, don't you?'

I wondered what it was all about. Yet I knew right enough. 'Get married,' I admitted, adding on second thoughts: 'I don't have much of a wage to be wed on, you know.'

'It's enough, as far as I'm concerned,' she answered.

And that was that. She gave me the best kiss I'd ever had, and then we went into the wood.

She was never happy about our life together, right from the start. And neither was I, because it didn't take her long to begin telling me that all her friends – her family most of all – said time and time again that our marriage wouldn't last five minutes. I could never say much back to this, knowing after the first few months how right everybody would be. Not that it bothered me though, because I was always the sort of bloke that doesn't get ruffled at anything. If you want to know the truth – the sort of thing I don't suppose many blokes would be ready to admit – the bare fact of my getting married meant only that I changed one house and one mother for another house and a different mother. It was as simple as that. Even my wage-packet didn't alter its course: I handed it over every Friday night and got five shillings back for tobacco and a visit to the pictures. It was the sort of wedding where the cost of the ceremony and reception go as a down payment, and you then continue dishing-out your wages every week for life. Which is where I suppose they got this hire purchase idea from.

But our marriage lasted for more than the five minutes everybody prophesied: it went on for six years; she left me when I was thirty, and when she was thirty-four. The trouble was when we had a row – and they were rows, swearing, hurling pots: the lot – it was too much like suffering, and in the middle of them it seemed to me as if we'd done nothing but row and suffer like this from the moment we set eyes on each other, with not a moment's break, and that it would go on like this for as long as we stayed together. The truth was, as I see it now – and even saw it sometimes then – that a lot of our time was bloody enjoyable.

I'd had an idea before she went that our time as man and wife was about up, because one day we had the worst fight of them all. We were sitting at home one evening after tea, one at each end of the table, plates empty and bellies full so that there was no excuse for what followed. My head was in a book, and Kathy just sat there.

Suddenly she said: 'I do love you, Harry.' I didn't hear the words for some time, as is often the case when you're reading a book. Then: 'Harry, look at me.'

My face came up, smiled, and went down again to my reading. Maybe I was in the wrong, and should have said something, but the book was too good.

'I'm sure all that reading's bad for your eyes,' she commented, prising me again from the hot possessive world of India.

'It ain't,' I denied, not looking up. She was young and still fair-faced, a passionate loose-limbed thirty-odd that wouldn't let me side-step either her obstinacy or anger. 'My dad used to say that on'y fools read books, because they'd such a lot to learn.'

The words hit me and sank in, so that I couldn't resist coming back with, still not looking up: 'He on'y said that because he didn't know how to read. He was jealous, if you ask me.'

'No need to be jealous of the rammel you stuff your big head with,' she said, slowly to make sure I knew she meant every word. The print wouldn't stick any more; the storm was too close.

'Look, why don't *you* get a book, duck?' But she never would, hated them like poison.

She sneered: 'I've got more sense; and too much to do.'

Then I blew up, in a mild way because I still hoped she wouldn't take on, that I'd be able to finish my chapter. 'Well let me read, anyway, won't you? It's an interesting book and I'm tired.'

But such a plea only gave her another opening. 'Tired? You're allus tired.' She laughed out loud: 'Tired Tim! You ought to do some real work for a change instead of walking the streets with that daft post bag.'

I won't go on, spinning it out word for word. In any case not many more passed before she snatched the book out of my hands. 'You booky bastard,' she screamed, 'nowt but books, books, books, you bleddy dead-'ead' – and threw the book on the heaped-up coals, working it further and further into their blazing middle with the poker.

This annoyed me, so I clocked her one, not very hard, but I did. It was a good reading book, and what's more it belonged to the library. I'd have to pay for a new one. She slammed out of the house, and I didn't see her until the next day.

I didn't think to break my heart very much when she skipped off. I'd had enough. All I can say is that it was a stroke of God's luck we never had any kids. She was confined once or twice, but it never came to anything; each time it dragged more bitterness out of her than we could absorb in the few peaceful months that came between. It might have been better if she'd had kids though; you never know.

A month after burning the book she ran off with a housepainter. It was all done very nicely. There was no shouting or knocking each other about or breaking up the happy home. I just came back from work one day and found a note waiting for me. 'I am going away and not coming back' – propped on the mantelpiece in front of the clock. No tear stains on the paper, just eight words in pencil on a page of the insurance book – I've still got it in the back of my wallet, though God knows why.

The housepainter she went with had lived in a house on his own, across the terrace. He'd been on the dole for a few months and suddenly got a job at a place twenty miles away I was later told. The neighbours seemed almost eager to let me know – after they'd gone, naturally – that they'd been knocking-on together for about a year. No one knew where they'd skipped off to exactly, probably imagining that I wanted to chase after them. But the idea never occurred to me. In any case what was I to do? Knock him flat and drag Kathy back by the hair? Not likely.

Even now it's no use trying to tell myself that I wasn't disturbed by this change in my life. You miss a woman when she's been living with you in the same house for six years, no matter what sort of cat-and-dog life you led together – though we had our moments, that I will say. After her sudden departure there was something different about the house, about the walls, ceiling and every object in it. And something altered inside me as well – though I tried to tell myself that all was just the same and that Kathy's leaving me wouldn't make a blind bit of difference. Nevertheless time crawled at first, and I felt like a man just learning to pull himself along with a club-foot; but then the endless evenings of summer came and I was happy almost against my will, too happy anyway to hang on to such torments as sadness and loneliness. The world was moving and, I felt, so was I.

In other words I succeeded in making the best of things, which as much as anything else meant eating a good meal at the canteen every midday. I boiled an egg for breakfast (fried with bacon on Sundays) and had something cold but solid for my tea every night. As things went, it wasn't a bad life. It might have been a bit lonely, but at least it was peaceful, and it got as I didn't mind it, one way or the other. I even lost the feeling of loneliness that had set me thinking a bit too much just after she'd gone. And then I didn't dwell on it any more. I saw enough people on my rounds during the day to last me through the evenings and at week-ends. Sometimes I played draughts at the club, or went out for a slow half pint to the pub up the street.

Things went on like this for ten years. From what I gathered later Kathy had been living in Leicester with her housepainter. Then she came back to Nottingham. She came to see me one Friday evening, payday. From her point of view, as it turned out, she couldn't have come at a better time.

I was leaning on my gate in the backyard smoking a pipe of tobacco. I'd had a busy day on my rounds, an irritating time of it – being handed back letters all along the line, hearing that people had left and that no one had any idea where they'd moved to; and other people taking as much as ten minutes to get out of bed and sign for a registered letter – and now I felt twice as peaceful because I was at home, smoking my pipe in the backyard at the fag-end of an autumn day. The sky was a clear yellow, going green above the housetops and wireless aerials. Chimneys were just beginning to send out evening smoke, and most of the factory motors had been switched off. The noise of kids scooting around lamp-posts and the barking of dogs came from what sounded a long way off. I was about to knock my pipe out, to go back into the house and carry on reading a book about Brazil I'd left off the night before.

As soon as she came around the corner and started walking up the yard I knew her. It gave me a funny feeling, though: ten years ain't enough to change anybody so's you don't recognize them, but it's long enough to make you have to look twice before you're sure. And that split second in between is like a kick in the stomach. She didn't walk with her usual gait, as though she owned the terrace and everybody in it. She was a bit slower than when I'd seen her last, as if she'd bumped into a wall during the last ten years through walking in the cock o'the walk way she'd always had. She didn't seem so sure of herself and was fatter now, wearing a frock left over from the summer and an open winter coat, and her hair had been dyed fair whereas it used to be a nice shade of brown.

I was neither glad nor unhappy to see her, but maybe that's what shock does, because I was surprised, that I will say. Not that I never expected to see her again, but you know how it is, I'd just forgotten her somehow. The longer she was away our married life shrunk to a year, a month, a day, a split second of sparkling light I'd met in the black darkness before getting-up time. The memory had drawn itself too far back, even in ten years, to remain as anything much more than a dream. For as soon as I got used to living alone I forgot her.

Even though her walk had altered I still expected her to say something sarky like: 'Didn't expect to see me back at the scene of the crime so soon, did you, Harry?' Or: 'You thought it wasn't true that a bad penny always turns up again, didn't you?'

But she just stood. 'Hello, Harry' – waited for me to lean up off the gate so's she could get in. 'It's been a long time since we saw each other, hasn't it?'

I opened the gate, slipping my empty pipe away. 'Hello, Kathy,' I said, and walked down the yard so that she could come behind me. She buttoned her coat as we went into the kitchen, as though she were leaving the house instead of just going in. 'How are you getting on then?' I asked, standing near the fireplace.

Her back was to the wireless, and it didn't seem as if she wanted to look at me. Maybe I was a bit upset after all at her sudden visit, and it's possible I showed it without knowing it at the time, because I filled my pipe up straightaway, a thing I never normally do. I always let one pipe cool down before lighting the next.

'I'm fine,' was all she'd say.

'Why don't you sit down then, Kath? I'll get you a bit of a fire soon.'

She kept her eyes to herself still, as if not daring to look at the old things around her, which were much as they'd been when she left. However she'd seen enough to remark: 'You look after yourself all right.'

'What did you expect?' I said, though not in a sarcastic way. She wore lipstick, I noticed, which I'd never seen on her before, and rouge, maybe powder as well, making her look old in a different way, I supposed, than if she'd had nothing on her face at all. It was a thin disguise, yet sufficient to mask from me – and maybe her – the person she'd been ten years ago.

'I hear there's a war coming on,' she said, for the sake of talking.

I pulled a chair away from the table. 'Come on, sit down, Kathy. Get that weight off your legs' – an old phrase we'd used though I don't know why I brought it out at that moment. 'No, I wouldn't be a bit surprised. That bloke Hitler wants a bullet in his brain – like a good many Germans.' I looked up and caught her staring at the picture of a fishing boat on the wall: brown and rusty with sails half spread in a bleak sunrise, not far from the beach along which a woman walked bearing a basket of fish on her shoulder. It was one of a set that Kathy's brother had given us as a wedding present, the other two having been smashed up in another argument we'd had. She liked it a lot, this remaining fishing-boat picture. The last of the fleet, we used to call it in our brighter moments. 'How are you getting on?' I wanted to know. 'Living all right?'

'All right,' she answered. I still couldn't get over the fact that she wasn't as talkative as she had been, that her voice was softer and flatter, with no more bite in it. But perhaps she felt strange at seeing me in the old house again after all this time, with everything just as she'd left it. I had a wireless now, that was the only difference.

'Got a job?' I asked. She seemed afraid to take the chair I'd offered her.

'At Hoskins,' she told me, 'on Ambergate. The lace factory. It pays forty-two bob a week, which isn't bad.' She sat down and did up the remaining button of her coat. I saw she was looking at the fishing-boat picture again. The last of the fleet.

'It ain't good either. They never paid owt but starvation wages and never will I suppose. Where are you living, Kathy?'

Straightening her hair – a trace of grey near the roots – she said: 'I've got a house at Sneinton. Little, but it's only seven and six a week. It's noisy as well, but I like it that way. I was always one for a bit of life, you know that. "A pint of beer and a quart of noise" was what you used to say, didn't you?'

I smiled. 'Fancy you remembering that.' But she didn't look as though she had much of a life. Her eyes lacked that spark of humour that often soared up into the bonfire of a laugh. The lines around them now served only as an indication of age and passing time. 'I'm glad to hear you're taking care of yourself.'

She met my eyes for the first time. 'You was never very excitable, was you, Harry?'

'No,' I replied truthfully, 'not all that much.'

'You should have been,' she said, though in an empty sort of way, 'then we might have hit it off a bit better.'

'Too late now,' I put in, getting the full blow-through of my words. 'I was never one for rows and trouble, you know that. Peace is more my line.'

She made a joke at which we both laughed. 'Like that bloke Chamberlain!' – then moved a plate to the middle of the table and laid her elbows on the cloth. 'I've been looking after myself for the last three years.'

It may be one of my faults, but I get a bit curious sometimes. 'What's happened to that housepainter of yours then?' I asked this question quite naturally though, because I didn't feel I had anything to reproach her with. She'd gone away, and that was that. She hadn't left me in the lurch with a mountain of debts or any such thing. I'd always let her do what she liked.

'I see you've got a lot of books,' she remarked, noticing one propped against the sauce bottle, and two more on the sideboard.

'They pass the time on,' I replied, striking a match because my pipe had gone out. 'I like reading.'

She didn't say anything for a while. Three minutes I remember, because I was looking across at the clock on the dresser. The news would have been on the wireless, and I'd missed the best part of it. It was getting interesting because of the coming war. I didn't have anything else to do but think this while I was waiting for her to speak. 'He died of lead-poisoning,' she told me. 'He did suffer a lot, and he was only forty-two. They took him away to the hospital a week before he died.'

I couldn't say I was sorry, though it was impossible to hold much against him. I just didn't know the chap. 'I don't think I've got a fag in the place to offer you,' I said, looking on the mantelpiece in case I might find one, though knowing I wouldn't. She moved when I passed her on my search, scraping her chair along the floor. 'No, don't bother to shift. I can get by.'

'It's all right,' she said. 'I've got some here' – feeling in her pocket and bringing out a crumpled five-packet. 'Have one, Harry?'

'No thanks. I haven't smoked a fag in twenty years. You know that. Don't you remember how I started smoking a pipe? When we were courting. You gave me one for my birthday and told me to start smoking it because it would make me look more distinguished! So I've smoked one ever since. I got used to it quick enough, and I like it now. I'd never be without it in fact.'

As if it were yesterday! But maybe I was talking too much, for she seemed a bit nervous while lighting her fag. I don't know why it was, because she didn't need to be in my house. 'You know, Harry,' she

62

began, looking at the fishing-boat picture, nodding her head towards it, 'I'd like to have that' – as though she'd never wanted anything so much in her life.

'Not a bad picture, is it?' I remember saying. 'It's nice to have pictures on the wall, not to look at especially, but they're company. Even when you're not looking at them you know they're there. But you can take it if you like.'

'Do you mean that?' she asked, in such a tone that I felt sorry for her for the first time.

'Of course. Take it. I've got no use for it. In any case I can get another picture if I want one, or put a war map up.' It was the only picture on that wall, except for the wedding photo on the sideboard below. But I didn't want to remind her of the wedding picture for fear it would bring back memories she didn't like. I hadn't kept it there for sentimental reasons, so perhaps I should have dished it. 'Did you have any kids?'

'No,' she said, as if not interested. 'But I don't like taking your picture, and I'd rather not if you think all that much of it.' We sat looking over each other's shoulder for a long time. I wondered what had happened during these ten years to make her talk so sadly about the picture. It was getting dark outside. Why didn't she shut up about it, just take the bloody thing? So I offered it to her again, and to settle the issue unhooked it, dusted the back with a cloth, wrapped it up in brown paper, and tied the parcel with the best post-office string. 'There you are,' I said, brushing the pots aside, laying it on the table at her elbows.

'You're very good to me, Harry.'

'Good! I like that. What does a picture more or less in the house matter? And what does it mean to me, anyway?' I can see now that we were giving each other hard knocks in a way we'd never learned to do when living together. I switched on the electric light. As she seemed uneasy when it showed everything up clearly in the room, I offered to switch it off again.

'No, don't bother' – standing to pick up her parcel. 'I think I'll be going now. Happen I'll see you some other time.'

'Drop in whenever you feel like it.' Why not? We weren't enemies. She undid two buttons of her coat, as though having them loose would make her look more at ease and happy in her clothes, then waved to me. 'So long.'

'Good night, Kathy.' It struck me that she hadn't smiled or laughed once the whole time she'd been there, so I smiled to her as she turned for the door, and what came back wasn't the bare-faced cheeky grin I once knew, but a wry parting of the lips moving more for exercise than humour. She must have been through it, I thought, and she's above forty now.

So she went. But it didn't take me long to get back to my book.

A few mornings later I was walking up St Ann's Well Road delivering letters. My round was taking me a long time, for I had to stop at almost every shop. It was raining, a fair drizzle, and water rolled off my cape, soaking my trousers below the knees so that I was looking forward to a mug of tea back in the canteen and hoping they'd kept the stove going. If I hadn't been so late on my round I'd have dropped into a café for a cup.

I'd just taken a pack of letters into a grocer's and, coming out, saw the fishing-boat picture in the next-door pawnshop window, the one I'd given Kathy a few days ago. There was no mistaking it, leaning back against ancient spirit-levels, bladeless planes, rusty hammers, trowels, and a violin case with the strap broken. I recognized a chip in the gold-painted woodwork near the bottom left corner of its frame.

For half a minute I couldn't believe it, was unable to make out how it had got there, then saw the first day of my married life and a sideboard loaded with presents, prominent among them this surviving triplet of a picture looking at me from the wreckage of other lives. And here it is, I thought, come down to a bloody nothing. She must have sold it that night before going home, pawnshops always keeping open late on a Friday so that women could get their husbands' suits out of pop for the week-end. Or maybe she'd sold it this morning, and I was only half an hour behind her on my round. Must have been really hard up. Poor Kathy, I thought. Why hadn't she asked me to let her have a bob or two?

I didn't think much about what I was going to do next. I never do, but went inside and stood at the shop counter waiting for a grey-haired doddering skinflint to sort out the popped bundles of two thin-faced women hovering to make sure he knew they were pawning the best stuff. I was impatient. The place stank of old clothes and mildewed junk after coming out of the fresh rain, and besides I was later than ever now on my round. The canteen would be closed before I got back, and I'd miss my morning tea.

The old man shuffled over at last, his hand out. 'Got any letters?'

'Nowt like that, feyther. I'd just like to have a look at that picture you've got in your window, the one with a ship on it.' The women went out counting what few shillings he'd given them, stuffing pawn-tickets in their purses, and the old man came back carrying the picture as if it was worth five quid.

Shock told me she'd sold it right enough, but belief lagged a long way behind, so I looked at it well to make sure it really was the one. A price marked on the back wasn't plain enough to read. 'How much do you want for it?'

'You can have it for four bob.'

Generosity itself. But I'm not one for bargaining. I could have got it for less, but I'd rather pay an extra bob than go through five minutes of chinning. So I handed the money over, and said I'd call back for the picture later.

Four measly bob, I said to myself as I sloshed on through the rain. The robbing bastard. He must have given poor Kathy about one and six for it. Three pints of beer for the fishing-boat picture.

I don't know why, but I was expecting her to call again the following week. She came on Thursday, at the same time, and was dressed in the usual way: summer frock showing through her brown winter coat whose buttons she couldn't leave alone, telling me how nervous she was. She'd had a drink or two on her way, and before coming into the house stopped off at the lavatory outside. I'd been late for work, and hadn't quite finished my tea, asked her if she could do with a cup. 'I don't feel like it,' came the answer. 'I had one not long ago.'

I emptied the coal scuttle on the fire. 'Sit down nearer the warmth. It's a bit nippy tonight.'

She agreed that it was, then looked up at the fishing-boat picture on the wall. I'd been waiting for this, wondered what she'd say when she did, but there was no surprise at seeing it back in the old place, which made me feel a bit disappointed. 'I won't be staying long tonight,' was all she said. 'I've got to see somebody at eight.'

Not a word about the picture. 'That's all right. How's your work going?'

'Putrid,' she answered nonchalantly, as though my question had been out of place. 'I got the sack, for telling the forewoman where to get off.'

'Oh,' I said, getting always to say 'Oh' when I wanted to hide my feelings, though it was a safe bet that whenever I did say 'Oh' there wasn't much else to come out with.

I had an idea she might want to live in my house again seeing she'd lost her job. If she wanted to she could. And she wouldn't be afraid to ask, even now. But I wasn't going to mention it first. Maybe that was my mistake, though I'll never know. 'A pity you got the sack,' I put in.

Her eyes were on the picture again, until she asked: 'Can you lend me half-a-crown?'

'Of course I can' – emptied my trouser pocket, sorted out half-a-crown, and passed it across to her. Five pints. She couldn't think of anything to say, shuffled her feet to some soundless tune in her mind. 'Thanks very much.'

'Don't mention it,' I said with a smile. I remembered buying a packet of fags in case she'd want one, which shows how much I'd expected her back. 'Have a smoke?' – and she took one, struck a match on the sole of her shoe before I could get her a light myself.

'I'll give you the half-crown next week, when I get paid.' That's funny, I thought. 'I got a job as soon as I lost the other one,' she added, reading my mind before I had time to speak. 'It didn't take long. There's plenty of war work now. Better money as well.'

'I suppose all the firms'll be changing over soon.' It occurred to me that she could claim some sort of allowance from me – for we were still legally married – instead of coming to borrow half-a-crown. It was her right, and I didn't need to remind her; I wouldn't be all that much put out if she took me up on it. I'd been single – as you might say – for so many years that I hadn't been able to stop myself from putting a few quid by. 'I'll be going now,' she said, standing up to fasten her coat.

'Sure you won't have a cup of tea?'

'No thanks. Want to catch the trolley back to Sneinton.' I said I'd show her to the door. 'Don't bother. I'll be all right.' She stood waiting for me, looking at the picture on the wall above the sideboard. 'It's a nice picture you've got up there. I always liked it a lot.'

I made the old joke: 'Yes, but it's the last of the fleet.'

'That's why I like it.' Not a word about having sold it for eighteen pence.

I showed her out, mystified.

* * *

She came to see me every week, all through the war, always on Thursday night at about the same time. We talked a bit, about the weather, the war, her job and my job, never anything important. Often we'd sit for a long time looking into the fire from our different stations in the room, me by the hearth and Kathy a bit further away at the table as if she'd just finished a meal, both of us silent yet not uneasy in it. Sometimes I made a cup of tea, sometimes not. I suppose now that I think of it I could have got a pint of beer in for when she came, but it never occurred to me. Not that I think she felt the lack of it, for it wasn't the sort of thing she expected to see in my house anyway.

She never missed coming once, even though she often had a cold in the winter and would have been better off in bed. The blackout and shrapnel didn't stop her either. In a quiet off-handed sort of way we got to enjoy ourselves and looked forward to seeing each other again, and maybe they were the best times we ever had together in our lives. They certainly helped us through the long monotonous dead evenings of the war.

She was always dressed in the same brown coat, growing shabbier and shabbier. And she wouldn't leave without borrowing a few shillings. Stood up: 'Er . . . lend's half-a-dollar, Harry.' Given, sometimes with a joke: 'Don't get too drunk on it, will you?' – never responded to, as if it were bad manners to joke about a thing like that. I didn't get anything back of course, but then, I didn't miss such a dole either. So I wouldn't say no when she asked me, and as the price of beer went up she increased the amount to three bob then to three-and-six and, finally, just before she died, to four bob. It was a pleasure to be able to help her. Besides, I told myself, she has no one else. I never asked questions as to where she was living, though she did mention a time or two that it was still up Sneinton way. Neither did I at any time see her outside at a pub or picture house; Nottingham is a big town in many ways.

On every visit she would glance from time to time at the fishing-boat picture, the last of the fleet, hanging on the wall above the sideboard. She often mentioned how beautiful she thought it was, and how I should never part with it, how the sunrise and the ship and the woman and the sea were just right. Then a few minutes later she'd hint to me how nice it would be if she had it, but knowing it would end up in the pawnshop I didn't take her hints. I'd rather have lent her five bob instead of half-a-crown so that she wouldn't take the picture, but she never seemed to want more than half-a-crown in those first years. I once mentioned to her she could have more if she liked, but she didn't answer me. I don't think she wanted the picture especially to sell and get money, or to hang in her own house; only to have the pleasure of pawning it, to have someone else buy it so that it wouldn't belong to either of us any more.

But she finally did ask me directly, and I saw no reason to refuse when she put it like that. Just as I had done six years before, when she first came to see me, I dusted it, wrapped it up carefully in several layers of brown paper, tied it with post-office string, and gave it to her. She seemed happy with it under her arm, couldn't get out of the house quick enough, it seemed.

It was the same old story though, for a few days later I saw it again in the pawnshop window, among all the old junk that had been there for years. This time I didn't go in and try to get it back. In a way I wish I had, because then Kathy might not have had the accident that came a few days later. Though you never know. If it hadn't been that, it would have been something else.

I didn't get to her before she died. She'd been run down by a lorry at six o'clock in the evening, and by the time the police had taken me to the General Hospital she was dead. She'd been knocked all to bits, and had practically bled to death even before they'd got her to the hospital. The doctor told me she'd not been quite sober when she was knocked down. Among the things of hers they showed me was the fishing-boat picture, but it was all so broken up and smeared with blood that I hardly recognized it. I burned it in the roaring flames of the firegrate late that night.

When her two brothers, their wives and children had left and taken with them the air of blame they attached to me for Kathy's accident I stood at the graveside thinking I was alone, hoping I would end up crying my eyes out. No such luck. Holding my head up suddenly I noticed a man I hadn't seen before. It was a sunny afternoon of winter, but bitter cold, and the only thing at first able to take my mind off Kathy was the thought of some poor bloke having to break the bone-hard soil to dig this hole she was now lying in. Now there was this stranger. Tears were running down his cheeks, a man in his middle fifties wearing a good suit, grey though but with a black band around his arm, who moved only when the fed-up sexton touched his shoulder – and then mine – to say it was all over.

I felt no need to ask who he was. And I was right. When I got to Kathy's house (it had also been his) he was packing his things, and left a while later in a taxi without saying a word. But the neighbours, who always know everything, told me he and Kathy had been living together for the last six years. Would you believe it? I only wished he'd made her happier than she'd been.

Time has passed now and I haven't bothered to get another picture for the wall. Maybe a war map would do it; the wall gets too blank, for I'm sure some government will oblige soon. But it doesn't really need anything at the moment, to tell you the truth. That part of the room is filled up by the sideboard, on which is still the wedding picture, that she never thought to ask for.

And looking at these few old pictures stacked in the back of my mind I began to realize that I should never have let them go, and that I shouldn't have let Kathy go either. Something told me I'd been daft and dead to do it, and as my rotten luck would have it it was the word dead more than daft that stuck in my mind, and still sticks there like the spinebone of a cod or conger eel, driving me potty sometimes when I lay of a night in bed thinking.

I began to believe there was no point in my life – became even too far gone to turn religious or go on the booze. Why had I lived? I wondered. I can't see anything for it. What was the point of it all? And yet at the worst minutes of my midnight emptiness I'd think less of myself and more of Kathy, see her as suffering in a far rottener way than ever I'd done, and it would come to me – though working only as long as an aspirin pitted against an incurable headache – that the object of my having been alive was that in some small way I'd helped Kathy through her life.

I was born dead. I keep telling myself. Everybody's dead, I answer. So they are, I maintain, but then most of them never know it like I'm beginning to do, and it's a bloody shame that this has come to me at last when I could least do with it, and when it's too bloody late to get anything but bad from it.

Then optimism rides out of the darkness like a knight in armour. If you loved her . . . (of course I bloody-well did) . . . then you both did the only thing possible if it was to be remembered as love. Now didn't you? Knight in armour goes back into blackness. Yes, I cry, but neither of us *did anything about it*, and that's the trouble.

Noah's Ark

While Jones the teacher unravelled the final meanderings of *Masterman Ready*, Colin from the classroom heard another trundle of wagons and caravans rolling slowly towards the open spaces of the Forest. His brain was a bottleneck, like the wide boulevard along which each vehicle passed, and he saw, remembering last year, fresh-packed ranks of colourful Dodgem Cars, traction engines and mobile zoos, Ghost Trains, and Noah's Ark figures securely crated on to drays and lorries.

So *Masterman Ready* was beaten by the prospect of more tangible distraction, though it was rare for a book of dream-adventures to be banished so easily from Colin's mind. The sum total of such free-lance wandering took him through bad days of scarcity, became a mechanical gaudily dressed pied-piper always ahead, which he would follow and one day scrag to see what made it tick. How this would come about he didn't know, didn't even try to find out – while the teacher droned on with the last few pages of his story.

Though his cousin Bert was eleven – a year older – Colin was already in a higher class at school, and felt that this counted for something anyway, even though he had found himself effortlessly there. With imagination fed by books to bursting point, he gave little thought to the rags he wore (except when it was cold) and face paradoxically overfleshed through lack of food. His hair was too short, even for a three-penny basin-crop at the barber's – which was the only thing that bothered him at school in that he was sometimes jocularly referred to as 'Owd Bald-'ead'.

When the Goose Fair came a few pennies had survived his weekly outlay on comics, but Bert had ways and means of spinning them far beyond their paltry value. 'We'll get enough money for lots of rides,' he said, meeting Colin at the street corner of a final Saturday. 'I'll show you' – putting his arm around him as they walked up the street.

'How?' Colin wanted to know, protesting: 'I'm not going to rob any shops. I'll tell you that now.'

Bert, who had done such things, detected disapproval of his past, though sensing at the same time and with a certain pride that Colin would never have the nerve to crack open a shop at midnight and plug his black hands into huge jars of virgin sweets. 'That's not the only way to get money,' he scoffed. 'You only do that when you want summat good. I'll show you what we'll do when we get there.'

Along each misty street they went, aware at every turning of a low exciting noise from the northern sky. Bellies of cloud were lighted orange by the fair's reflection, plain for all to see, an intimidating bully slacking the will and drawing them towards its heart. 'If it's only a penny a ride then we've got two goes each,' Colin calculated with bent head, pondering along the blank flagstoned spaces of the pavement, hands in pockets pinning down his hard-begotten wealth. He was glad of its power to take him on to roundabouts, but the thought of what fourpence would do to the table at home filled him – when neither spoke – with spasms of deep misery. Fourpence would buy a loaf of bread or a bottle of milk or some stewing meat or a pot of jam or a pound of sugar. It would perhaps stop the agony his mother might be in from seeing his father black and brooding by the hearth if he – Colin – had handed the fourpence in for ten Woodbines from the corner shop. His father would take them with a smile, get up and kiss his mother in the fussy way he had and mash some tea, a happy man once more whose re-acquired asset would soon spread to everyone in the house.

It was marvellous what fourpence would do, if you were good enough to place it where it rightly belonged – which I'm not, he thought, because fourpence would also buy a fistful of comics, or two bars of chocolate or take you twice to the flea-pit picture-house or give you four rides on Goose Fair, and the division, the wide dark soil-smelling trench that parted good from bad was filled with wounds of unhappiness. And such unhappiness was suspect, because Colin knew that whistling stone-throwing Bert at his side wouldn't put up with it for the mere sake of fourpence – no, he'd spend it and enjoy it, which he was now out to do with half the pennies Colin had. If Bert robbed a shop or cart he'd take the food straight home – that much Colin knew – and if he laid his hands on five bob or a pound he'd give his mother one and six and say that that was all he'd been able to get doing some sort of work. But fourpence wouldn't worry him a bit. He'd enjoy it. And so would Colin, except in the space of stillness between roundabouts.

They were close to the fair, walking down the slope of Bentinck Road, able to distinguish between smells of fish-and-chips, mussels and brandysnap. 'Look on the floor,' Bert called out, ever-sharp and hollow-cheeked with the fire of keeping himself going, lit by an instinct never to starve yet always looking as if he were starving. The top and back of his head was padded by overgrown hair, and he slopped along in broken slippers, hands in pockets, whistling, then swearing black-and-blue at being swept off the pavement by a tide of youths and girls.

Colin needed little telling: snapped down to the gutter, walked a hundred yards doubled-up like a premature rheumatic, and later shot straight holding a packet with two whole cigarettes protruding. 'No whacks!' he cried, meaning: No sharing.

'Come on,' Bert said, cajoling, threatening, 'don't be bleedin'-well mingy, our Colin. Let's 'ave one.'

Colin stood firm. Finding was keeping. 'I'm savin' 'em for our dad. I don't suppose 'e's got a fag to 'is name.'

'Well, my old man ain't never got no fags either, but I wun't bother to save 'em for 'im if I found any. I mean it as well.'

'P'raps we'll have a drag later on then,' Colin conceded, keeping them in his pocket. They were on the asphalt path of the Forest, ascending a steep slope. Bert feverishly ripped open every cast-down packet now, chucking silver paper to the wind, slipping picture-cards in his pocket for younger brothers, crushing what remained into a ball and hurling it towards the darkness where bodies lay huddled together in some passion that neither of them could understand or even remotely see the point of.

From the war memorial they viewed the whole fair, a sea of lights and tent tops flanked on two sides by dimly shaped houses whose occupants would be happy when the vast encampment scattered the following week to other towns. A soughing groan of pleasure was being squeezed out of the earth, and an occasional crescendo of squeals reached them from the Swingboats and Big Wheel as though an army were below, offering human sacrifices before beginning its march. 'Let's get down there,' Colin said, impatiently turning over his pennies. 'I want to see things. I want to get on that Noah's Ark.'

Sucking penny sticks of brandysnap they pushed by the Ghost Train, hearing girls screaming from its skeleton-filled bowels. 'We'll roll pennies on to numbers and win summat,' Bert said. 'It's easy, you see. All you've got to do is put the pennies on a number when the woman ain't looking.' He spoke eagerly, to get Colin's backing in a project that would seem more of an adventure if they were in it together. Not that he was afraid to cheat alone, but suspicion rarely fell so speedily on a pair as it did on a lone boy obviously out for what his hands could pick up. 'It's dangerous,' Colin argued, though all but convinced, elbowing his way behind. 'You'll get copped.'

A tall gipsy-looking woman with black hair done up in a ponytail stood in the penny-a-roll stall, queen of its inner circle. She stared emptily before her, though Colin, edging close, sensed how little she missed of movement round about. A stack of coppers crashed regularly from one hand to the other, making a noise which, though not loud, drew attention to the stall – and the woman broke its rhythm now and again to issue with an expression of absolute impartiality a few coins to a nicky-hatted man who by controlling two of the wooden slots managed to roll down four pennies at a time. 'He ain't winnin', though,' Bert whispered in Colin's ear, who saw the truth of it: that he rolled out more than he picked up.

His remark stung through to the man's competing brain. 'Who ain't?' he demanded, letting another half-dozen pennies go before swinging round on him.

'Yo' ain't,' Bert chelped.

'Ain't I?' – swung-open mac showing egg and beer stains around his buttons.

Bert stood his ground, blue eyes staring. 'No, y'ain't.'

'That's what yo' think,' the man retorted, in spite of everything, even when the woman scooped up more of his pennies.

Bert pointed truculently. 'Do you call that winning then? Look at it. I don't.' All eyes met on three sad coins lying between squares, and Bert slipped his hand on to the counter where the man had set down a supply-dump of money. Colin watched, couldn't breathe, from fear but also from surprise even though there was nothing about Bert he did not know. A shilling and a sixpence seemed to run into Bert's palm, were straightaway hidden by black fingers curling over them. He reached a couple of pennies with the other hand, but his wrist became solidly clamped against the board. He cried out: 'Oo, yer rotten sod. Yer'r'urtin' me.'

The man's eyes, formerly nebulous with beer, now became deep

74

and self-centred with righteous anger. 'You should keep your thievin' fingers to yoursen. Come on, you little bogger, drop them pennies.'

Colin felt ashamed and hoped he would, wanted to get it over with and lose himself among spinning roundabouts. The black rose of Bert's hand unfolded under pressure, petal by petal, until the coins slid off. 'Them's my pennies,' he complained. 'It's yo' as is the thief, not me. You're a bully as well. I had 'em there ready to roll down as soon as I could get one of them slot things.'

'I was looking the other way,' said the woman, avoiding trouble; which made the man indignant at getting no help: 'Do you think I'm daft then? And blind as well?' he cried.

'You must be,' Bert said quietly, 'if you're trying to say I nicked your money.' Colin felt obliged to back him up: 'He didn't pinch owt,' he said, earnestly, exploiting a look of honesty he could put at will into his face. 'I'm not his pal, mate, but I'll tell you the truth. I was just passin' an' stopped to look, and he put tuppence down on there, took it from 'is own pocket.'

'You thievin' Radford lot,' the man responded angrily, though freed now from the dead-end of continual losing. 'Get cracking from here, or I'll call a copper.'

Bert wouldn't move. 'Not till you've gen me my tuppence back. I worked 'ard for that, at our dad's garden diggin' taters up and weeding.' The woman looked vacantly – sending a column of pennies from one palm to another – beyond them into packed masses swirling and pushing around her flimsy island. With face dead-set in dreadful purpose, hat tilted forward and arms all-embracing what money was his, the man gave in to his fate of being a loser and scooped up all his coins, though he was struck enough in conscience to leave Bert two surviving pennies before making off to better luck at another stall. 'That got shut on 'im,' Bert said, his wink at Colin meaning they were one and eightpence to the good.

The riches lasted for an hour, and Colin couldn't remember having been partner to so much capital, wanted to guard some from the avid tentacles of the thousand-lighted fair. But it fled from their itchy fingers – surrendered or captured, it was hard to say which – spent on shrimps and candyfloss, cakewalk and helter-skelter. They pushed by sideshow fronts. 'You should have saved some of that dough,' Colin said, unable to get used to being poor again.

'It's no use savin' owt,' Bert said. 'If you spend it you can allus get some more' – and became paralysed at the sight of a half-dressed woman in African costume standing by a pay-box with a python curled around her buxom top.

Colin argued: 'If you save you get money and you can go away to Australia or China. I want to go to foreign countries. Eh,' he said with a nudge, 'it's a wonder that snake don't bite her, ain't it?'

Bert laughed. 'It's the sort that squeezes yer ter death, but they gi' 'em pills to mek 'em dozy. I want to see foreign countries as well, but I'll join the army.'

'That's no good,' Colin said, leading the way to more round-abouts, 'there'll be a war soon, and you might get killed.' Around the base of Noah's Ark Bert discovered a tiny door that let them into a space underneath. Colin looked in, to a deadly midnight noise of grinding machinery. 'Where yer going?'

But Bert was already by the middle, doubled up to avoid the flying circular up-and-down world rolling round at full speed above. It seemed to Colin the height of danger – one blow, or get up without thinking, and you'd be dead, brains smashed into grey sand, which would put paid to any thoughts of Australia. Bert though had a cool and accurate sense of proportion, which drew Colin in despite his fear. He crawled on hands and knees, until he came level with Bert and roared into his ear: 'What yer looking for?'

'Pennies,' Bert screamed back above the din.

They found nothing, retired to a more simple life among the crowd. Both were hungry, and Colin told himself it must have been five hours since his four o'clock tea. 'I could scoff a hoss between two mattresses.'

'So could I,' Bert agreed. 'But look what I'm going to do.' A white-scarfed youth wearing a cap, with a girl on his arm working her way through an outsize candyfloss, emerged from a gap in the crowd. Colin saw Bert go up to them and say a few words to the youth, who put his hand in his pocket, made a joke that drew a laugh from the girl, and gave something to Bert.

'What yer got?' Colin demanded when he came back.

Ingenious Bert showed him. 'A penny. I just went up and said I was hungry and asked 'im for summat.'

'I'll try,' Colin said, wanting to contribute his share. Bert pulled him back, for the only people available were a middle-aged man and his wife, well-dressed and married. 'They wain't gi' yer owt. You want to ask courting couples, or people on their own.'

But the man on his own whom Colin asked was argumentative. A penny was a penny. Two and a half cigarettes. 'What do you want it for?'

'I'm hungry,' was all Colin could say.

A dry laugh. 'So am I.'

'Well, I'm hungrier. I ain't 'ad a bite t'eat since this morning, honest.' The man hesitated, but fetched a handful of coins from his pocket. 'You'd better not let a copper see you begging or you'll get sent to Borstal.'

Some time later they counted out a dozen pennies. 'You don't get nowt unless you ask, as mam allus tells me,' Bert grinned. They stood at a tea stall with full cups and a plate of buns, filling themselves to the brim. The near-by Big Wheel spun its passengers towards the clouds, only to spin them down again after a tantalizing glimpse of the whole fair, each descending girl cutting the air with animal screams that made Colin shudder until he realized that they were in no harm, were in fact probably enjoying it. 'I feel better now,' he said, putting his cup back on the counter.

They walked around caravans backed on to railings at the Forest edge, looked up steps and into doorways, at bunks and potbellied stoves, at beautiful closed doors painted in many colours and carved with weird designs that mystified Colin and made him think of a visit once made to the Empire. Gipsies, Goose Fair, Theatre – it was all one to him, a heaven-on-earth because together they made up the one slender bridgehead of another world that breached the tall thickets surrounding his own. A connecting link between them was in the wild-eyed children now and again seated on wooden steps; but when Colin went too near for a closer look a child called out in alarm, and a burly adult burst from the caravan and chased them away.

Colin took Bert's arm as they wedged themselves into the solid mass of people, under smoke of food-stalls and traction engines, between lit-up umbrellas and lights on poles. 'We've spent all our dough,' he said, 'and don't have owt left to go on Noah's Ark wi'.'

'You don't ev ter worry about that. All yer got ter do is get on and keep moving from one thing to another, follering the man collecting the cash so's he never sees yer or catches up wi' yer. Got me?'

Colin didn't like the sound of it, but went up the Noah's Ark steps, barging through lines of onlookers. 'I'll do it first,' Bert said. 'So keep yer eyes on me and see how it's done. Then yo' can go on.'

He first of all straddled a lion. Colin stood by the rail and watched closely. When the Ark began spinning Bert moved discreetly to a cock just behind the attendant who emerged from a hut-like structure in the middle. The roundabout soon took on its fullest speed, until Colin could hardly distinguish one animal from another, and often lost sight of Bert in the quick roaring spin.

Then the world stopped circling, and his turn came: 'Are you staying on for a second go?' Bert said no, that it wasn't wise to do it two times on the trot. Colin well knew that it was wrong, and dangerous, which was more to the point, yet when a Noah's Ark stood in your path spinning with the battle honours of its more than human speed-power written on the face of each brief-glimpsed wooden animal, you had by any means to get yourself on to that platform, money or no money, fear or no fear, and stay there through its violent bucking until it stopped. Watching from the outside it seemed that one ride on the glorious Noah's Ark would fill you with similar inexhaustible energy for another year, that at the end of the ride you wouldn't want to come off, would need to stay on for ever until you were either sick or dead with hunger.

He was riding alone, clinging to a tiger on the outer ring of vehicles, slightly sick with apprehension and at the sudden up-and-down motion of starting. He waved to Bert on the first slow time round. Then the roundabout's speed increased and it was necessary to stop hugging the tiger and follow the attendant who had just emerged to begin collecting the fares. But he was afraid, for it seemed that should only one of his fingers relax its hold he would be shot off what was supposed to be a delicious ride and smashed to pieces on hitting the outside rail – or smash anyone else to pieces who happened to be leaning against it.

However with great effort and a sinking heart he leapt: panic jettisoned only in the space between two animals. In this state he almost derailed a near-by couple, and when the man's hand shot out for revenge he felt the wind of a near miss blowing by the side of his face. The vindictive fist continued to ply even when he was securely seated on a zebra so that, faced with more solid danger than empty space, he put his tongue out at the man and let go once more.

He went further forward, still in sight of the attendant's stooping enquiring back. In his confused zig-zag progress – for few animals were now vacant – he worked inward to the centre where it was safer, under a roof of banging drums and cymbals, thinking at one point to wave victoriously to Bert. But the idea slipped over a cliff as he threw himself forward and held onto a horse's tail.

The roundabout could go no faster, judging by shouts and squeals from the girls. Colin's movements were clumsy, and he envied the attendant's dexterity a few yards in front, and admired Bert who had made this same circular Odyssey with so much aplomb. Aware of peril every second he was more fretful now of being shot like a cannonball against wood and iron than being caught by the money-collector. 'Bogger this,' he cursed. 'I don't like it a bit' – laughing grimly and lunging out on a downgrade, pegged by even more speed to a double seated dragon.

A vacant crocodile gave a few seconds enjoyment before he leapt on to an ant-eater to keep his distance equal from the attendant. He thought his round should have finished by now, but suddenly the man turned and began coming back, looking at each rider to be sure they had paid. This was unprecedented. They weren't lax, but once round in one direction was all they ever did – so Bert had assured him – and now here was this sly rotten bastard who'd got the cheek to come round again. That worn't fair.

The soporific, agreeble summer afternoons of *Masterman Ready*, having laid a trap at the back of his mind, caught him for a moment, yet flew away unreal before this real jungle in which he had somehow stumbled. He had to move back now in full view of the attendant, to face a further apprenticeship at taking the roundabout clockwise. It seemed impossible, and in one rash moment he considered making a flying leap into the solid stationary gangway and getting right out of it – for he was certain the man had marked him down, was about to wring his neck before pitching the dead chicken that remained over the heads of the crowd. He glimpsed him, an overalled greasy bastard whose lips clung to a doused-out nub-end, cashbag heavy but feet sure.

How long's this bleeding ride going to go on? he asked himself. It's been an hour already and Bert swore blind it only lasted three minutes. I thought so as well, but I suppose they're making it longer just because that bloke's after me for having cadged a free ride. This jungle was little different from home and street life, yet alarming, more frightening because the speed was exaggerated. His one thought was to abandon the present jungle, hurl himself into the slower with which he was familiar – though in that also he felt a dragging pain that would fling him forth one day.

He went back the same way, almost feeling an affection now on coming against a nuzzle, ear or tail he'd already held on to going from the sanctuary of ant-eater to dragon to crocodile slowly, then gathering speed and surety in leaping from horse to zebra to tiger and back to lion and cock. No rest for the wicked, his mother always said. But I'm not wicked, he told himself. You'll still get no rest though. I don't want any rest. Not much you don't. Clear-headed now, he was almost running with the roundabout, glancing back when he could – to see the attendant gaining on him – dodging irate fists that lashed out when he missed his grip and smiling at enraged astonished faces as if nothing were the matter, holding on to coat-tail and animal that didn't belong to him.

Things never turn out right, he swore, never never. Rank-a-tank-a-tank-tank went the music. Clash-ter-clash-ter-clash-clash flew the cymbals, up and down to squeals and shouts, and bump-bump-bump-bumpity-bump went his heart, still audible above everything else, lashing out at the insides of his ears with enormous boxing-gloves, throttling his windpipe with a cloven hoof, stamping on his stomach as though he were a tent from which ten buck-navvies were trying to escape, wanting a pint after a week of thirst.

A hand slid over his shoulder, but with a violent twist he broke free and continued his mad career around the swirling Ark. 'He'll get me, he'll get me. He's a man and can run faster than I can. He's had more practice than me.' But he lurched and righted himself, spurted forward as if in a race making such progress that he saw the man's back before him, instead of fleeing from his reaching hand behind. He slowed down too late, for the man, evidently controlled by a wink from the centre, switched back. Colin swivelled also, on the run again.

Compared to what it had been the speed now appeared a snail's pace. The three-minute ride was almost up, but Colin, thinking he would escape, was caught, more securely this time, by neck-scruff and waist. He turned within the grasp, smelling oil and sweat and tobacco, pulling and striking at first then, on an inspired impulse kicking wildly at his ankle, unaware of the pain he was causing because of stabbing aches that spread over his own stubbed toes. The man swore as proficiently as Colin's father when he hit his thumb once putting up shelves in the kitchen. But he was free, and considered that the roundabout up-and-down-about was going slow enough to make a getaway. No need to wait until it really stops, was his last thought.

It was like Buck Rogers landing from a space ship without due care, though a few minutes passed before he was able to think this. Upon leaving the still-swirling platform his body fell into a roll and went out with some force, crashing like a sensitive flesh-and-bone cannonball between a courting couple and piling up against the wooden barrier. The ball his body made without him knowing much about it slewed out when he hit the posts, arms and legs flying against the carved and painted woodwork of the balustrade. Clump-clump – in quick succession – but he wasn't aware of any standstill either beyond or behind his soon-opened eyes. The rank-a-tank-tank-tank played him out, a blurring of red-white-and-blue lights and coloured animals, and a feeling of relief once he was away from his pursuer, no matter what peril the reaching of solid earth might surround him with.

Bert had watched the whole three minutes, had tried pushing a way through the crowd to catch Colin as he came off – a small ragged figure elbowing a passage between lounging semi-relaxed legs that nevertheless were not always easy to move, so that he reached him too late. 'Come on,' he said in a worried voice, 'gerrup. I'll give yer a hand. Did yer enjoy your ride?' – trying to make him stand up. Turning to an enquirer: 'No, he's my cousin, and he's all right. I can tek care on 'im. Come on, Colin. He's still after you, so let's blow.'

Colin's legs were rubber, wanted to stay against the sympathetic hardness of wood. 'He slung me off after speeding it up, the rotten sod. It was a dirty trick.'

'Come on,' Bert urged. 'Let's blow town.'

'Leave me. I'll crawl. I'll kill him if he comes near me.' No spinning now: he felt floorboards, saw legs and the occasional flash of a passing wooden animal. They'd started up again. 'It's your turn now, ain't it?' he said angrily to Bert.

No time was lost. Bert bent down and came up with him on his shoulders like an expert gymnast, going white in the face and tottering down the wooden steps, towards warm soil and dust. On the last step he lost his strength, swerved helplessly to the right, and both donkey and burden crashed out of sight by the bottom roundabout boards where no one went.

They lay where they had fallen. 'I'm sorry,' Bert said. 'I didn't know he was looking out for us. And then you go and cop it. A real bastard.' His hand was under Colin's armpit to stop him sliding sideways. 'Are you all right, though? I wun't a minded if it 'ad bin me, and I mean it. Do you feel sick? Are you going to spew?' – hand clapped over Colin's mouth, that was closed tight anyway. 'The snakey bastard, chasing you off like that. He ought to get summonsed, he did an' all.'

Colin suddenly stood up, leaned against the boards and, with more confidence in his legs, staggered into the crowd, followed by Bert. Abject and beaten, they walked around until midnight by which time, both dead-tired, the idea occurred to them of going home. 'I'll get pasted,' Colin said, 'because I'm supposed to be in by ten.' Bert complained that he was knackered, that he wanted to get back anyway.

Streets around the fair were shrivelling into darkness, took on the hue of cold damp ash. They walked arm-in-arm, inspired enough by the empty space to sing loudly a song that Bert's father had taught him:

> 'We don't want to charge with the fusiliers
> Bomb with the bombardiers
> Fight for the racketeers
> We want to stay at home!
> We want to stay at home!
> We want to stay at home!'

words ringing loud and clear out of two gruff voices slopping along on sandalled feet, mouths wide open and arms on each other's shoulders, turning corners and negotiating twitchells, singing twice as loud by dead cinema and damp graveyard:

> 'We don't want to fight in a Tory war
> Die like the lads before
> Drown in the mud and gore
> We want to go to work . . .'

swinging along from one verse to another, whose parrot-fashioned words were less important than the bellows of steamy breath fogging up cold air always in front of them, frightening cats and skirting midnight prowlers, and hearing people tell them to shurrup and let them sleep from angrily rattled bedroom windows. They stood in the middle of a bigger road when a car was coming, rock still to test their nerves by making it stop, then charging off when they had been successful, to avoid the driver's rage, to reach another corner and resume locked arms, swinging along to the tune of Rule Britannia:

'Rule two tanners
Two tanners make a bob,
King George nevernevernever
SHAVES HIS NOB!'

each note wavering on the air, and dying as they turned a corner; at least it would have sounded like that, if anyone had been listening to it from the deserted corner before. But to Colin, the noise stayed, all around their heads and faces, grinding away the sight and sound of the Noah's Ark jungle he had ridden on free, and so been pitched from.

On Saturday Afternoon

I once saw a bloke try to kill himself. I'll never forget the day because I was sitting in the house one Saturday afternoon, feeling black and fed-up because everybody in the family had gone to the pictures, except me who'd for some reason been left out of it. 'Course, I didn't know then that I would soon see something you can never see in the same way on the pictures, a real bloke stringing himself up. I was only a kid at the time, so you can imagine how much I enjoyed it.

I've never known a family to look as black as our family when they're fed-up. I've seen the old man with his face so dark and full of murder because he ain't got no fags or was having to use saccharine to sweeten his tea, or even for nothing at all, that I've backed out of the house in case he got up from his fireside chair and came for me. He just sits, almost on top of the fire, his oil-stained Sunday-joint maulers opened out in front of him and facing inwards to each other, his thick shoulders scrunched forward, and his dark brown eyes staring into the fire. Now and again he'd say a dirty word, for no reason at all, the worst word you can think of, and when he starts saying this you know it's time to clear out. If mam's in it gets worse than ever, because she says sharp to him: 'What are yo' looking so bleddy black for?' as if it might be because of something she's done, and before you know what's happening he's tipped up a tableful of pots and mam's gone out of the house crying. Dad hunches back over the fire and goes on swearing. All because of a packet of fags.

I once saw him broodier than I'd ever seen him, so that I thought he'd gone crackers in a quiet sort of way – until a fly flew to within a yard of him. Then his hand shot out, got it, and slung it crippled into the roaring fire. After that he cheered up a bit and mashed some tea.

Well, that's where the rest of us get our black looks from. It stands to reason we'd have them with a dad who carries on like that, don't it? Black looks run in the family. Some families have them and some don't. Our family has them right enough, and that's certain, so when we're fed-up we're really fed-up. Nobody knows why we get as fed-up as we do or why it gives us these black looks when we are. Some people get fed-up and don't look bad at all: they seem happy in a funny sort of way, as if they've just been set free from clink after being in there for something they didn't do, or come out of the pictures after sitting plugged for eight hours at a bad film, or just missed a bus they ran half a mile for and seen it was the wrong one just after they'd stopped running – but in our family it's murder for the others if one of us is fed-up. I've asked myself lots of times what it is, but I can never get any sort of answer even if I sit and think for hours, which I must admit I don't do, though it looks good when I say I do. But I sit and think for long enough, until mam says to me, at seeing me scrunched up over the fire like dad: 'What are yo' looking so black for?' So I've just got to stop thinking about it in case I get really black and fed-up and go the same way as dad, tipping up a tableful of pots and all.

Mostly I suppose there's nothing to look so black for: though it's nobody's fault and you can't blame anyone for looking black because I'm sure it's summat in the blood. But on this Saturday afternoon I was looking so black that when dad came in from the bookie's he said to me: 'What's up wi' yo'?'

'I feel badly,' I fibbed. He'd have had a fit if I'd said I was only black because I hadn't gone to the pictures.

'Well have a wash,' he told me.

'I don't want a wash,' I said, and that was a fact.

'Well, get outside and get some fresh air then,' he shouted. I did as I was told, double-quick, because if ever dad goes as far as to tell me to get some fresh air I know it's time to get away from him. But outside the air wasn't so fresh, what with that bloody great bike factory bashing away at the yard-end. I didn't know where to go, so I walked up the yard a bit and sat down near somebody's back gate.

Then I saw this bloke who hadn't lived long in our yard. He was tall and thin and had a face like a parson except that he wore a flat cap and had a moustache that drooped, and looked as though he hadn't had a square meal for a year. I didn't think much o' this at the time: but I remember that as he turned in by the yard-end one of the nosy gossiping women who stood there every minute of the day except when she trudged to the pawnshop with her husband's bike or best suit, shouted to him: 'What's that rope for, mate?'

86

He called back: 'It's to 'ang messen wi', missis,' and she cackled at his bloody good joke so loud and long you'd think she never heard such a good 'un, though the next day she cackled on the other side of her fat face.

He walked by me puffing a fag and carrying his coil of brand new rope, and he had to step over me to get past. His boot nearly took my shoulder off, and when I told him to watch where he was going I don't think he heard me because he didn't even look round. Hardly anybody was about. All the kids were still at the pictures, and most of their mams and dads were downtown doing the shopping.

The bloke walked down the yard to his back door, and having nothing better to do because I hadn't gone to the pictures I followed him. You see, he left his back door open a bit so I gave it a push and went in. I stood there, just watching him, sucking my thumb, the other hand in my pocket. I suppose he knew I was there, because his eyes were moving more natural now, but he didn't seem to mind. 'What are yer going to do wi' that rope, mate?' I asked him.

'I'm going ter 'ang messen, lad,' he told me, as though he'd done it a time or two already, and people usually asked him questions like this beforehand.

'What for, mate?' He must have thought I was a nosy young bogger.

''Cause I want to, that's what for,' he said, clearing all the pots off the table and pulling it to the middle of the room. Then he stood on it to fasten the rope to the light-fitting. The table creaked and didn't look very safe, but it did him for what he wanted.

'It wain't hold up, mate,' I said to him, thinking how much better it was being here than sitting in the pictures and seeing the Jungle Jim serial.

But he got nettled now and turned on me. 'Mind yer own business.'

I thought he was going to tell me to scram, but he didn't. He made ever such a fancy knot with that rope, as though he'd been a sailor or summat, and as he tied it he was whistling a fancy tune to himself. Then he got down from the table and pushed it back to the wall, and put a chair in its place. He wasn't looking black at all, nowhere near as black as anybody in our family when they're feeling fed up. If ever he'd looked only half as black as our dad looked twice a week he'd have hanged himself years ago, I couldn't help thinking. But he was making a good job of that rope all right, as though he'd thought about it a lot anyway, and as though it was going to be the last thing he'd ever do. But I knew something he didn't know, because he wasn't standing where I was. I knew the rope wouldn't hold up, and I told him so, again.

'Shut yer gob,' he said, but quiet like, 'or I'll kick yer out.'

I didn't want to miss it, so I said nothing. He took his cap off and put it on the dresser, then took his coat off, and his scarf, and spread them out on the sofa. I wasn't a bit frightened, like I might be now at sixteen, because it was interesting. And being only ten I'd never had a chance to see a bloke hang himself before. We got pally, the two of us, before he slipped the rope around his neck.

'Shut the door,' he asked me, and I did as I was told. 'Ye're a good lad for your age,' he said to me while I sucked my thumb, and he felt in his pockets and pulled out all that was inside, throwing the handful of bits and bobs on the table: fag-packet and peppermints, a pawn-ticket, an old comb, and a few coppers. He picked out a penny and gave it to me, saying: 'Now listen ter me, young 'un. I'm going to 'ang messen, and when I'm swinging I want you to gi' this chair a bloody good kick and push it away. All right?'

I nodded.

He put the rope around his neck, and then took it off like it was a tie that didn't fit. 'What are yer going to do it for, mate?' I asked again.

'Because I'm fed-up,' he said, looking very unhappy. 'And because I want to. My missus left me, and I'm out o' work.'

I didn't want to argue, because the way he said it, I knew he couldn't do anything else except hang himself. Also there was a funny look on his face: even when he talked to me I swear he couldn't see me. It was different to the black looks my old man puts on, and I suppose that's why my old man would never hang himself, worse luck, because he never gets a look into his clock like this bloke had. My old man's look stares *at* you, so that you have to back down and fly out of the house: this bloke's look looked *through* you, so that you could face it and know it wouldn't do you any harm. So I saw now that dad would never hang himself because he could never get the right sort of look into his face, in spite of the fact that he'd been out of work often enough. Maybe mam would have to leave him first, and then he might do it; but no – I shook my head – there wasn't much chance of that even though he did lead her a dog's life.

'Yer wain't forget to kick that chair away?' he reminded me, and I swung my head to say I wouldn't. So my eyes were popping and I watched every move he made. He stood on the chair and put the rope around his neck so that it fitted this time, still whistling his fancy tune. I wanted to get a better goz at the knot, because my pal was in the scouts, and would ask to know how it was done, and if I told him later he'd let me know what happened at the pictures in the Jungle Jim serial, so's I could have my cake and eat it as well, as mam says, tit for tat. But I thought I'd better not ask the bloke to tell me, and I stayed back in my corner. The last thing he did was take the wet dirty butt-end from his lips and sling it into the empty firegrate, following it with his eyes to the black fireback where it landed – as if he was then going to mend a fault in the lighting like any electrician.

Suddenly his long legs wriggled and his feet tried to kick the chair, so I helped him as I'd promised I would and took a runner at it as if I was playing centre-forward for Notts Forest, and the chair went scooting back against the sofa, dragging his muffler to the floor as it tipped over. He swung for a bit, his arms chafing like he was a scarecrow flapping birds away, and he made a noise in his throat as if he'd just took a dose of salts and was trying to make them stay down.

Then there was another sound, and I looked up and saw a big crack come in the ceiling, like you see on the pictures when an earthquakes's happening, and the bulb began circling round and round as though it was a spaceship. I was just beginning to get dizzy when, thank Christ, he fell down with such a horrible thump on the floor that I thought he'd broke every bone he'd got. He kicked around for a bit, like a dog that's got colic bad. Then he lay still.

I didn't stay to look at him. 'I told him the rope wouldn't hold up,' I kept saying to myself as I went out of the house, tut-tutting because he hadn't done the job right, hands stuffed deep into my pockets and nearly crying at the balls-up he'd made of everything. I slammed his gate so hard with disappointment that it nearly dropped off its hinges.

Just as I was going back up the yard to get my tea at home, hoping the others had come back from the pictures so's I wouldn't have anything to keep being black about, a copper passed me and headed for the bloke's door. He was striding quickly with his head bent forward, and I knew that somebody had narked. They must have seen him buy the rope and then tipped-off the cop. Or happen the old hen at the yard-end had finally caught on. Or perhaps he'd even told somebody himself, because I supposed that the bloke who'd strung himself up hadn't much known what he was doing, especially with the look I'd seen in his eyes. But that's how it is, I said to myself, as I followed the copper back to the bloke's house, a poor bloke can't even hang himself these days.

When I got back the copper was slitting the rope from his neck with a pen-knife, then he gave him a drink of water, and the bloke opened his peepers. I didn't like the copper, because he'd got a couple of my mates sent to approved school for pinching lead piping from lavatories.

'What did you want to hang yourself for?' he asked the bloke, trying to make him sit up. He could hardly talk, and one of his hands was bleeding from where the light-bulb had smashed. I knew that rope wouldn't hold up, but he hadn't listened to me. I'll never hang myself anyway, but if I want to I'll make sure I do it from a tree or something like that, not a light-fitting. 'Well, what did you do it for?'

'Because I wanted to,' the bloke croaked.

'You'll get five years for this,' the copper told him. I'd crept back into the house and was sucking my thumb in the same corner.

'That's what yo' think,' the bloke said, a normal frightened look in his eyes now. 'I only wanted to hang myself.'

'Well,' the copper said, taking out his book, 'it's against the law, you know.'

'Nay,' the bloke said, 'it can't be. It's my life, ain't it?'

'You might think so,' the copper said, 'but it ain't.'

He began to suck the blood from his hand. It was such a little scratch that you couldn't see it. 'That's the first thing I knew,' he said.

'Well I'm telling you,' the copper told him.

'Course, I didn't let on to the copper that I'd helped the bloke to hang himself. I wasn't born yesterday, nor the day before yesterday either.

'It's a fine thing if a bloke can't tek his own life,' the bloke said, seeing he was in for it.

'Well he can't,' the copper said, as if reading out of his book and enjoying it. 'It ain't your life. And it's a crime to take your own life. It's killing yourself. It's suicide.'

The bloke looked hard, as if every one of the copper's words meant six-months cold. I felt sorry for him, and that's a fact, but if only he'd listened to what I'd said and not depended on that light-fitting. He should have done it from a tree or something like that.

90

He went up the yard with the copper like a peaceful lamb, and we all thought that that was the end of that.

But a couple of days later the news was flashed through to us – even before it got to the *Post* because a woman in our yard worked at the hospital of an evening dishing grub out and tidying up. I heard her spilling it to somebody at the yard-end. 'I'd never 'ave thought it. I thought he'd got that daft idea out of his head when they took him away. But no. Wonders'll never cease. Chucked 'issen from the hospital window when the copper who sat near his bed went off for a pee. Would you believe it? Dead? Not much 'e ain't.'

He'd heaved himself at the glass, and fallen like a stone on to the road. In one way I was sorry he'd done it, but in another I was glad, because he'd proved to the coppers and everybody whether it was his life or not all right. It was marvellous though, the way the brainless bastards had put him in a ward six floors up, which finished him off, proper, even better than a tree.

All of which will make me think twice about how black I sometimes feel. The black coal-bag locked inside you, and the black look it puts on your face, doesn't mean you're going to string yourself up or sling yourself under a double-decker or chuck yourself out of a window or cut your throat with a sardine-tin or put your head in the gas-oven or drop your rotten sack-bag of a body on to a railway line, because when you're feeling that black you can't even move from your chair. Anyhow, I know I'll never get so black as to hang myself, because hanging don't look very nice to me, and never will, the more I remember old what's-his-name swinging from the light-fitting.

More than anything else, I'm glad now I didn't go to the pictures that Saturday afternoon when I was feeling black and ready to do myself in. Because you know, I shan't ever kill myself. Trust me. I'll stay alive half-barmy till I'm a hundred and five, and then go out screaming blue murder because I want to stay where I am.

The Match

Bristol City had played Notts County and won. Right from the kick-off Lennox had somehow known that Notts was going to lose, not through any prophetic knowledge of each home-player's performance, but because he himself, a spectator, hadn't been feeling in top form. One-track pessimism had made him godly enough to inform his mechanic friend Fred Iremonger who stood by his side: 'I knew they'd bleddy-well lose, all the time.'

Towards the end of the match, when Bristol scored their winning goal, the players could only just be seen, and the ball was a roll of mist being kicked about the field. Advertising boards above the stands, telling of pork-pies, ales, whisky, cigarettes and other delights of Saturday night, faded with the afternoon visibility.

They stood in the one-and-threes, Lennox trying to fix his eyes on the ball, to follow each one of its erratic well-kicked movements, but after ten minutes going from blurred player to player he gave it up and turned to look at the spectators massed in the rising stands that reached out in a wide arc on either side and joined dimly way out over the pitch. This proving equally futile he rubbed a clenched hand into his weak eyes and squeezed them tight, as if pain would give them more strength. Useless. All it produced was a mass of grey squares dancing before his open lids, so that when they cleared his sight was no better than before. Such an affliction made him appear more phlegmatic at a football match than Fred and most of the others round about, who spun rattles, waved hats and scarves, opened their throats wide to each fresh vacillation in the game.

During his temporary blindness the Notts forwards were pecking and weaving around the Bristol goal and a bright slam from one of them gave rise to a false alarm, an indecisive rolling of cheers roofed in by a grey heavy sky. 'What's up?' Lennox asked Fred. 'Who scored? Anybody?'

Fred was a younger man, recently married, done up in his Saturday afternoon best of sports coat, gaberdine trousers and rain-mac, dark hair sleeked back with oil. 'Not in a month of Sundays,' he laughed, 'but they had a bleddy good try, I'll tell you that.'

By the time Lennox had focused his eyes once more on the players the battle had moved to Notts' goal and Bristol were about to score. He saw a player running down the field, hearing in his imagination the thud of boots on damp introdden turf. A knot of adversaries dribbled out in a line and straggled behind him at a trot. Suddenly the man with the ball spurted forward, was seen to be clear of everyone as if, in a second of time that hadn't existed to any spectator or other player, he'd been catapulted into a hallowed untouchable area before the goal posts. Lennox's heart stopped beating. He peered between two oaken unmovable shoulders that, he thought with anger, had swayed in front purposely to stop him seeing. The renegade centre-forward from the opposing side was seen, like a puppet worked by someone above the low clouds, to bring his leg back, lunge out heavily with his booted foot. 'No,' Lennox had time to say. 'Get on to him you dozy sods. Don't let him get it in.'

From being an animal pacing within the prescribed area of his defended posts, the goalkeeper turned into a leaping ape, arms and legs outstretched, then became a mere stick that swung into a curve – and missed the ball as it sped to one side and lost itself in folds of net behind him.

The lull in the general noise seemed like silence for the mass of people packed about the field. Everyone had settled it in his mind that the match, as bad as it was, would be a draw, but now it was clear that Notts, the home team, had lost. A great roar of disappointment and joy, from the thirty-thousand spectators who hadn't realized that the star of Bristol City was so close, or who had expected a miracle from their own stars at the last moment, ran up the packed embankments, overflowing into streets outside where groups of people, startled at the sudden noise of an erupting mob, speculated as to which team had scored.

Fred was laughing wildly, jumping up and down, bellowing something between a cheer and a shout of hilarious anger, as if out to get his money's worth on the principle that an adverse goal was better than no goal at all. 'Would you believe it?' he called at Lennox. 'Would you believe it? Ninety-five thousand quid gone up like Scotch mist!'

Hardly knowing what he was doing Lennox pulled out a cigarette, lit it. 'It's no good,' he cursed, 'they've lost. They should have walked away with the game' – adding under his breath that he must get some glasses in order to see things better. His sight was now so bad that the line of each eye crossed and converged some distance in front of him. At the cinema he was forced down to the front row, and he was never the first to recognize a pal on the street. And it spelt ruination for any football match. He could remember being able to pinpoint each player's face, and distinguish every spectator around the field, yet he still persuaded himself that he had no need of glasses and that somehow his sight would begin to improve. A more barbed occurrence connected with such eyes was that people were beginning to call him Cock-eye. At the garage where he worked the men sat down to tea-break the other day, and because he wasn't in the room one of them said: 'Where's owd Cock-eye? 'Is tea'll get cold.'

'What hard lines,' Fred shouted, as if no one yet knew about the goal. 'Would you believe it?' The cheering and booing were beginning to die down.

'That goalie's a bloody fool,' Lennox swore, cap pulled low over his forehead. 'He couldn't even catch a bleeding cold.'

'It was dead lucky,' Fred put in reluctantly, 'they deserved it, I suppose' – simmering down now, the full force of the tragedy seeping through even to his newly wedded body and soul. 'Christ, I should have stayed at home with my missus. I'd a bin warm there, I know that much. I might even have cut myself a chunk of hearthrug pie if I'd have asked her right!'

The laugh and wink were intended for Lennox, who was still in the backwater of his personal defeat. 'I suppose that's all you think on these days,' he said wryly.

''Appen I do, but I don't get all that much of it, I can tell you.' It was obvious though that he got enough to keep him in good spirits at a cold and disappointing football match.

'Well,' Lennox pronounced, 'all that'll alter in a bit. You can bet on that.'

'Not if I know it,' Fred said with a broad smile. 'And I reckon it's better after a bad match than if I didn't come to one.'

'You never said a truer word about bad,' Lennox said. He bit his lip with anger. 'Bloody team. They'd even lose at blow football.' A woman behind, swathed in a thick woollen scarf coloured white and black like the Notts players, who had been screaming herself hoarse in support of the home team all the afternoon was almost in tears at the adverse goal. 'Foul! foul! Get the dirty lot off the field. Send 'em back to Bristol where they came from. Foul! Foul! I tell yer.'

People all round were stamping feet dead from the cold, having for more than an hour staved off its encroachment into their limbs by the hope of at least one home-team win before Christmas. Lennox could hardly feel his, hadn't the will to help them back to life, especially in face of an added force to the bitter wind, and a goal that had been given away so easily. Movement on the pitch was now desultory, for there were only ten minutes of play left to go. The two teams knotted up towards one goal, then spread out around an invisible ball, and moved down the field again, back to the other with no decisive result. It seemed that both teams had accepted the present score to be the final state of the game, as though all effort had deserted their limbs and lungs.

'They're done for,' Lennox observed to Fred. People began leaving the ground, making a way between those who were determined to see the game out to its bitter end. Right up to the dull warbling blast of the final whistle the hard core of optimists hoped for a miraculous revival in the worn-out players.

'I'm ready when yo' are,' Fred said.

'Suits me.' He threw his cigarette-end to the floor and, with a grimace of disappointment and disgust, made his way up the steps. At the highest point he turned a last glance over the field, saw two players running and the rest standing around in deepening mist – nothing doing – so went on down towards the barriers. When they were on the road a great cheer rose behind, as a whistle blew the signal for a mass rush to follow.

Lamps were already lit along the road, and bus queues grew quickly in semi-darkness. Fastening up his mac Lennox hurried across the road. Fred lagged behind, dodged a trolley-bus that sloped up to the pavement edge like a man-eating monster and carried off a crowd of people to the city-centre with blue lights flickering from overhead wires. 'Well,' Lennox said when they came close, 'after that little lot I only hope the wife's got summat nice for my tea.'

'I can think of more than that to hope for,' Fred said. 'I'm not one to grumble about my grub.'

''Course,' Lennox sneered, 'you're living on love. If you had Kit-E-Kat shoved in front of you you'd say it was a good dinner.' They turned off by the recruiting centre into the heart of the Meadows, an ageing suburb of black houses and small factories. 'That's what yo' think,' Fred retorted, slightly offended yet too full of hope to really mind. 'I'm just not one to grumble a lot about my snap, that's all.'

'It wouldn't be any good if you was,' Lennox rejoined, 'but the grub's rotten these days, that's the trouble. Either frozen, or in tins. Nowt natural. The bread's enough to choke yer.' And so was the fog: weighed down by frost it lingered and thickened, causing Fred to pull up his rain-mac collar. A man who came level with them on the same side called out derisively: 'Did you ever see such a game?'

'Never in all my born days,' Fred replied.

'It's always the same though,' Lennox was glad to comment, 'the best players are never on the field. I don't know what they pay 'em for.'

The man laughed at this sound logic. 'They'll 'appen get 'em on nex' wik. That'll show 'em.'

'Let's hope so,' Lennox called out as the man was lost in the fog. 'It ain't a bad team,' he added to Fred. But that wasn't what he was thinking. He remembered how he had been up before the gaffer yesterday at the garage for clouting the mash-lad who had called him Cock-eye in front of the office-girl, and the manager had said that if it happened again he would get his cards. And now he wasn't sure that he wouldn't ask for them anyway. He'd never lack a job, he told himself, knowing his own worth and the sureness of his instinct when dissecting piston from cylinder, camshaft and connecting-rod and searching among a thousand-and-one possible faults before setting an engine bursting once more with life. A small boy called from the doorway of a house: 'What's the score, mate?'

'They lost, two-one,' he said curtly, and heard a loud clear-sounding doorslam as the boy ran in with the news. He walked with hands in pockets, and a cigarette at the corner of his mouth so that ash occasionally fell on to his mac. The smell of fish-and-chips came from a well-lit shop, making him feel hungry.

'No pictures for me tonight,' Fred was saying. 'I know the best place in weather like this.' The Meadows were hollow with the clatter of boots behind them, the muttering of voices hot in discussion about the lost match. Groups gathered at each corner, arguing and teasing any girl that passed, lighted gas-lamps a weakening ally in the fog. Lennox turned into an entry, where the cold damp smell of backyards mingled with that of dustbins. They pushed open gates to their separate houses.

'So long. See you tomorrow at the pub maybe.'

97

'Not tomorrow,' Fred answered, already at his back door. 'I'll have a job on mending my bike. I'm going to gi' it a coat of enamel and fix in some new brake blocks. I nearly got flattened by a bus the other day when they didn't work.'

The gate-latch clattered. 'All right then,' Lennox said, 'see you soon' – opening the back door and going into his house.

He walked through the small living-room without speaking, took off his mac in the parlour. 'You should mek a fire in there,' he said, coming out. 'It smells musty. No wonder the clo'es go to pieces inside six months.' His wife sat by the fire knitting from two balls of electric-blue wool in her lap. She was forty, the same age as Lennox, but gone to a plainness and discontented fat, while he stayed thin and wiry from the same reason. Three children, the eldest a girl of fourteen, were at the table finishing tea.

Mrs Lennox went on knitting. 'I was going to make one today but I didn't have time.'

'Iris can mek one,' Lennox said, sitting down at the table.

The girl looked up. 'I haven't finished my tea yet, our dad.' The wheedling tone of her voice made him angry. 'Finish it later,' he said with a threatening look. 'The fire needs making now, so come on, look sharp and get some coal from the cellar.'

She didn't move, sat there with the obstinacy of the young spoiled by a mother. Lennox stood up. 'Don't let me have to tell you again.' Tears came into her eyes. 'Go on,' he shouted. 'Do as you are told.' He ignored his wife's plea to stop picking on her and lifted his hand to settle her with a blow.

'All right, I'm going. Look' – she got up and went to the cellar door. So he sat down again, his eyes roaming over the well-set table before him, holding his hands tightly clenched beneath the cloth. 'What's for tea, then?'

His wife looked up again from her knitting. 'There's two kippers in the oven.'

He did not move, sat morosely fingering a knife and fork. 'Well?' he demanded. 'Do I have to wait all night for a bit o' summat t'eat?'

Quietly she took a plate from the oven and put it before him. Two brown kippers lay steaming across it. 'One of these days,' he said, pulling a long strip of white flesh from the bone, 'we'll have a change.'

'That's the best I can do,' she said, her deliberate patience no way to stop his grumbling – though she didn't know what else would. And the fact that he detected it made things worse.

'I'm sure it is,' he retorted. The coal bucket clattered from the parlour where the girl was making a fire. Slowly, he picked his kippers to pieces without eating any. The other two children sat on the sofa watching him, not daring to talk. On one side of the plate he laid bones; on the other, flesh. When the cat rubbed against his leg he dropped pieces of fish for it on to the lino, and when he considered that it had eaten enough he kicked it away with such force that its head knocked against the sideboard. It leapt on to a chair and began to lick itself, looking at him with green surprised eyes.

He gave one of the boys sixpence to fetch a *Football Guardian*. 'And be quick about it,' he called after him. He pushed his plate away, and nodded towards the mauled kippers. 'I don't want this. You'd better send somebody out for some pastries. And mash some fresh tea,' he added as an afterthought, 'that pot's stewed.'

He had gone too far. Why did he make Saturday afternoons such hell on earth? Anger throbbed violently in her temples. Through the furious beating of her heart she cried out: 'If you want some pastries you'll fetch 'em yourself. And you'll mash your own tea as well.'

'When a man goes to wok all week he wants some tea,' he said, glaring at her. Nodding at the boy: 'Send him out for some cakes.'

The boy already stood up. 'Don't go. Sit down,' she said to him. 'Get 'em yourself,' she retorted to her husband. 'The tea I've already put on the table's good enough for anybody. There's nowt wrong wi' it at all, and then you carry on like this. I suppose they lost at the match, because I can't think of any other reason why you should have such a long face.'

He was shocked by such a sustained tirade, stood up to subdue her. 'You what?' he shouted. 'What do you think you're on wi'?'

Her face turned a deep pink. 'You heard,' she called back. 'A few home truths might do you a bit of good.'

He picked up the plate of fish and, with exaggerated deliberation, threw it to the floor. 'There,' he roared. 'That's what you can do with your bleeding tea.'

'You're a lunatic,' she screamed. 'You're mental.'

He hit her once, twice, three times across the head, and knocked her to the ground. The little boy wailed, and his sister came running in from the parlour . . .

Fred and his young wife in the house next door heard a commotion through the thin walls. They caught the cadence of voices and shifting chairs, but didn't really think anything amiss until the shriller climax was reached. 'Would you believe it?' Ruby said, slipping off Fred's knee and straightening her skirt. 'Just because Notts have lost again. I'm glad yo' aren't like that.'

Ruby was nineteen, plump like a pear not round like a pudding, already pregnant though they'd only been married a month. Fred held her back by the waist. 'I'm not so daft as to let owt like that bother me.'

She wrenched herself free. 'It's a good job you're not; because if you was I'd bosh you one.'

Fred sat by the fire with a bemused, Cheshire-cat grin on his face while Ruby was in the scullery getting them something to eat. The noise in the next house had died down. After a slamming of doors and much walking to and fro outside Lennox's wife had taken the children, and left him for the last time.

The Disgrace of Jim Scarfedale

I'm easily led and swung, my mind like a weather-vane when somebody wants to change it for me, but there's one sure rule I'll stick to for good, and I don't mind driving a nail head-first into a bloody long rigmarole of a story to tell you what I mean.

Jim Scarfedale.

I'll never let anybody try and tell me that you don't have to sling your hook as soon as you get to the age of fifteen. You ought to be able to do it earlier, only it's against the law, like everything else in this poxetten land of hope and glory.

You see, you can't hang on to your mam's apron strings for ever, though it's a dead cert there's many a bloke as would like to. Jim Scarfedale was one of these. He hung on so long that in the end he couldn't get used to anything else, and when he tried to change I swear blind he didn't know the difference between an apron string and a pair of garters, though I'm sure his brand-new almost-beautiful wife must have tried to drum it into his skull before she sent him whining back to his mother.

Well, I'm not going to be one of that sort. As soon as I see a way of making-off – even if I have to rob meters to feed myself – I'll take it. Instead of doing arithmetic lessons at school I glue my eyes to the atlas under my desk, planning the way I'm going to take when the time comes (with the ripped-out map folded-up in my back pocket): bike to Derby, bus to Manchester, train to Glasgow, nicked car to Edinburgh, and hitch-hiking down to London. I can never stop looking at these maps, with their red roads and brown hills and marvellous other cities – so it's no wonder I can't add up for toffee. (Yes, I know every city's the same when you come to weigh it up: the same hostels full of thieves all out to snatch your last bob if you give them half the chance; the same factories full of work, if you're lucky; the same mildewed backyards and houses full of silverfish and black-clocks when you suddenly switch on the light at night; but nevertheless, even though they're all the same they're different as well in dozens of ways, and nobody can deny it.)

Jim Scarfedale lived in our terrace, with his mam, in a house like our own, only it was a lot nearer the bike factory, smack next to it in fact, so that it was a marvel to me how they stuck it with all the noise you could hear. They might just as well have been inside the factory, because the racket it kicked up was killing. I went in the house once to tell Mrs Scarfedale that Mr Taylor at the shop wanted to see her about her week's grub order, and while I was telling her this I could hear the engines and pulleys next door in the factory thumping away, and iron-presses slamming as if they were trying to burst through the wall and set up another department at the Scarfedales'. It wouldn't surprise me a bit if it was this noise, as much as Jim's mam, that made him go the way he did.

Jim's mam was a big woman, a Tartar, a real six-footer who kept her house as clean as a new pin, and who fed Jim up to his eyeballs on steam pudding and Irish stew. She was the sort of woman as 'had a way with her' – which meant that she usually got what she wanted and knew that what she wanted was right. Her husband had coughed himself to death with consumption not long after Jim was born, and Mrs Scarfedale had set to working at the tobacco factory to earn enough for herself and Jim. She stayed hard at it for donkey's years, and she had a struggle to make ends meet through the dole days, I will say that for her, and Jim always had some sort of suit on his back every Sunday morning – which was a bloody sight more than anybody else in the terrace had. But even though he was fed more snap than the rest of us he was a small lad, and I was as big at thirteen as he was at twenty-seven (by which time it struck me that he must have stopped growing) even though I'd been half clambed to death. The war was on then – when we in our family thought we were living in the lap of luxury because we were able to stuff ourselves on date-jam and oxo – and they didn't take Jim in the army because of his bad eyes, and his mam was glad at this because his dad had got a gob full of gas in the Great War. So Jim stayed with his mam, which I think was worse in the end than if he'd gone for a soldier and been blown to bits by the Jerries.

It worn't long after the war started that Jim surprised us all by getting married.

102

When he told his mam what he was going to do there was such ructions that we could hear them all the way up the yard. His mam hadn't even seen the girl, and that was what made it worse, she shouted. Courting on the sly like that and suddenly upping and saying he was getting married, without having mentioned a word of it before. Ungrateful, after all she'd done for him, bringing him up so well, even though he'd had no dad. Think of all the times she'd slaved for him! Think of it! Just think of it! (Jesus, you should have heard her.) Day in and day out she'd worked her fingers to the bone at that fag-packing machine, coming home at night dead to the wide yet cooking his dinners and mending his britches and cleaning his room out – it didn't bear thinking about. And now what had he gone and done, by way of thanks? (Robbed her purse? I asked myself quickly in the breathless interval; pawned the sheets and got drunk on the dough, drowned the cat, cut her window plants down with a pair of scissors?) No, he'd come home and told her he was getting married, just like that. It wasn't the getting married she minded – oh no, not that at all, of course it wasn't, because every young chap had to get married one day – so much as him not having brought the girl home before now for her to see and talk to. Why hadn't he done this? Was he ashamed of his mother? Didn't he think she was respectable enough to be seen by his young woman? Didn't he like to bring her back to his own home – you should have heard the way she said 'home': it made my blood run cold – even though it was cleaned every day from top to bottom? Was he ashamed of his house as well? Or was it the young woman he was ashamed of? Was she *that* sort? Well, it was a mystery, it was and all. And what's more it wasn't fair, it wasn't. Do you think it's fair, Jim? Do you? Ay, maybe you do, but I don't, and I can't think of anybody else as would either.

She stopped shouting and thumping the table for a minute, and then the waterworks began. Fair would you say it was – she sobbed her socks off – after all I've struggled and sweated getting you up for school every morning when you was little and sitting you down to porridge and bacon before you went out into the snow with your topcoat on, which was more than any of the other little rag-bags in the yard wore because their dads and mams boozed the dole money – (she said this, she really did, because I was listening from a place where I couldn't help but hear it – and I'll swear blind our dad never boozed a penny of his dole money and we were still clambed half to death on

103

it . . .) And I think of all the times when you was badly and I fetched the doctor, she went on screaming. Think of it. But I suppose you're too self-pinnyated to think, which is what my spoiling's done for you, aren't you? Eh?

The tears stopped. I think you might have had the common decency to tell me you wanted to get married and had started courting. She didn't know how he'd managed it, that she didn't, especially when she'd kept her eyes on him so well. I shouldn't have let you go twice a week to that Co-op youth club of yourn, she shouted, suddenly realizing where he'd seen his chance. That was it. By God it was, that was it. And you telling me you was playing draughts and listening to blokes talk politics! Politics! That's what they called it, was it? First thing I knew. They called it summat else in my day, and it worn't such a pretty name, either. Ay, by God. And now you've got the cheek to stand there, still with your coat on, not even offering to drop all this married business. (She hadn't given him the chance to.) Why, Jim, how could you think about getting married (tap on again) when I've been so good to you? My poor lad, hasn't even realized what it's cost me and how I've worked to keep us together all these years, ever since your poor dad died. But I'll tell you one thing, my lad (tap off, sharp, and the big finger wagging), you'd better bring her to me and let me see her, and if she ain't up to much, yer can let her go and look for somebody else, if she still feels inclined.

By God, I was all of a tremble myself when I climbed down from my perch, though I wouldn't have took it like Jim did, but would have bashed her between the eyes and slung my hook there and then. Jim was earning good money and could have gone anywhere in the country, the bloody fool.

I suppose you'll be wondering how everybody in the yard knew all about what went on in Jim's house that night, and how it is that I'm able to tell word for word what Jim's mam said to him. Well, this is how it was: with Jim's house being so near the factory there's a ledge between the factory roof and his scullery window, the thickness of a double-brick wall, and I was thin-rapped enough to squeeze myself along this and listen-in. The scullery window was open, and so was the scullery door that led to the kitchen, so I heard all as went on. And nobody in the house twigged it either. I found this place out when I was eight, when I used to go monkey-climbing all over the buildings in our yard. It'd 'ave been dead easy to burgle the Scarfedales' house, except that there worn't anything much worth pinching, and except that the coppers would have jumped on me for it right away.

Well, we all knew then what went off right enough, but what surprised everybody was that Jim Scarfedale meant what he said and wasn't going to let his mam play the bully and stop him from getting married. I was on my perch the second night when sucky Jim brought his young woman to face his tub-thumping mother. She'd made him promise that much, at least.

I don't know why, but everybody in the yard expected to see some poor crumby-faced boss-eyed tart from Basford, a scruffy, half-baked, daft sort of piece that wouldn't say boo to a goose. But they got a shock. And so did I when I spied her through the scullery window. (Mrs Scarfedale was crackers about fresh air, I will say that for her.) I'd never heard anybody talk so posh, as if she'd come straight out of an office, and it made me think that Jim hadn't lied after all when he said they'd talked about politics at the club.

'Good evening, Mrs Scarfedale,' she said as she came in. There was a glint in her eye, and a way she had, that made me think she'd been born talking as posh as she did. I wondered what she saw in Jim, whether she'd found out, unbeknown to any of us, that he'd been left some money, or was going to win the Irish Sweepstake. But no, Jim wasn't lucky enough for either, and I suppose his mam was thinking this at the same time as I was. Nobody shook hands.

'Sit down,' Jim's mam said. She turned to the girl, and looked at her properly for the first time, hard. 'I hear as you're wanting to marry my lad?'

'That's right, Mrs Scarfedale,' she said, taking the best chair, though sitting in it stiff and not at her ease. 'We're going to be married quite soon.' Then she tried to be more friendly, because Jim had given her the eye, like a little dog. 'My name's Phyllis Blunt. Call me Phyllis.' She looked at Jim, and Jim smiled at her because she was so nice to his mam after all. He went on smiling, as if he'd been practising all the afternoon in the lavatory mirror at the place where he worked. Phyllis smiled back, as though she'd been used to smiling like that all her life. Smiles all over the place, but it didn't mean a thing.

'What we have to do first,' Jim said, putting his foot in it, though in a nice sociable way, 'is get a ring.'

I could see the way things were going right enough. His mam suddenly went blue in the face. 'It ain't like *that*?' she brought out. 'Is it?'

She couldn't touch Phyllis with a barge-pole. 'I'm not pregnant, if that's what you mean.'

Mrs Scarfedale didn't know I was chiking, but I'll bet we both thought together: Where's the catch in it, then? Though it soon dawned on me that there wasn't any catch, at least not of the sort we must have thought of. And if this had dawned on Mrs Scarfedale at the same time as it did on me there wouldn't have been the bigger argument that night – all of them going at it worse than tigers – and perhaps poor Jim wouldn't have got married as quick as he did.

'Well,' his mother complained to our mam one day at the end of the yard about a month after they'd got spliced, 'he's made his bed, and he can lie on it, even though it turns out to be a bed of nettles, which I for one told him it was bound to be.'

Yet everybody hoped Jim would be able to keep on lying on it, because they'd always had something against such domineering strugglers as Mrs Scarfedale. Not that everybody in our yard hadn't been a struggler – and still was – one way or another. You had to be, or just lay down and die. But Jim's mam sort of carried a placard about saying: I'm a struggler but a cut above everybody else because I'm so good at it. You could tell a mile off that she was a struggler and that was what nobody liked.

She was right about her lad though. Sod it, some people said. Jim didn't lie on his bed for long, though his wife wasn't a bad-looking piece and I can see now that he should have stayed between those sheets for longer than he did. Inside six months he was back, and we all wondered what could have gone wrong – as we saw him walking down the yard carrying a suit-case and two paper bundles, looking as miserable as sin and wearing the good suit he'd got married in to save it getting creased in the case. Well, I said to myself, I'll be back on my perch soon to find out what happened between Jim and his posh missis. Yes, we'd all been expecting him to come back to his mam if you want to know the dead honest truth, even though we *hoped* he wouldn't, poor lad, because in the first three months of being married he'd hardly come to see her at all, and most people thought from this that he'd settled down a treat and that married life must be suiting him.

But I knew different, for when a bloke's just got married he comes home often to see his mam and dad – if he's happy. That's only natural. But Jim stayed away, or tried to, and that showed me that his wife was helping all she could to stop him seeing his mam. After them first three months though he came home more and more often – instead of the other way round – sometimes sleeping a night, which meant that his fights with Phyllis was getting worse and worse. That last time he came he had a bandage round his napper, a trilby hat stuck on top like a lop-sided crown.

I got to my perch before Jim opened his back door, and I was able to see him come in and make out what sort of a welcome his mam gave him. She was clever, I will say that for her. If she had thought about it she could have stopped his marriage a dozen times by using a bit of craft I'll bet. There was no: 'I told you so. You should have listened to me and then everything wouldn't have happened.' No, she kissed him and mashed him a cup of tea, because she knew that if she played her cards right she could have him at home for good. You could see how glad she was – could hardly stop herself smiling – as she picked up his case and parcels and carried them upstairs to his room, meaning to make his bed while the kettle boiled, leaving him a blank ten-minute sit-down in peace which she knew was just what he wanted.

But you should have seen poor old Jim, his face wicked-badly, forty-five if he looked a day, as if he'd just been let out of a Jap prisoner-of-war camp and staring – like he was crackers – at the same patch of carpet he'd stared at when he was only a kid on his pot. He'd always had a bit of a pain screwed into his mug – born that way I should think – but now it seemed as though he'd got an invisible sledgehammer hanging all the time in front of his miserable clock ready to fall against his snout. It would have made my heart bleed if I hadn't guessed he'd been such a sodding fool, getting wed with a nice tart and then making a mess of it all.

He sat like that for a quarter of an hour, and I'll swear blind he didn't hear a single one of the homely sounds coming from upstairs, of his mam making his bed and fixing up his room, like I did. And I kept wishing she'd made haste and get done with it, but she knew what she was doing all right, dusting the mirror and polishing the pictures for her sucky lad.

Well, she came down all of a smile (trying to hide it as best she could though) and set his bread and cheese out on the table, but he didn't touch a bite, only swigged three mugs of tea straight off while she sat in her chair and looked at him as if she, anyway, would make a good supper for him.

'I'll tell you, mam,' he began as soon as she came and set herself staring at him from the other end of the table to get him blabbing just like this. 'I've been through hell in the last six months, and I never want to go through it again.'

It was like a dam breaking down. In fact the crack in a dam wall that you see on the pictures came into his forehead just like that, exactly. And once he got started there was no holding him back. 'Tell me about it then, my lad' – though there was no need for her to have said this: he was trembling like a jelly, so that I was sometimes hard put to it to know what was going on. Honest, I can't tell it all in Jim's own words because it'd break my heart; and I really did feel sorry for him as he went on and on.

'Mam,' he moaned, dipping bread and butter in his tea, a thing I'm sure he'd never been able to do with his posh missis at the table, 'she led me a dog's life. In fact a dog would have been better off in his kennel with an old bone to chew now and again than I was with her. It was all right at first, because you see, mam, she had some idea that a working bloke like myself was good and honest and all that sort of thing. I never knew whether she'd read this in a book or whether she'd known working blokes before that were different from me, but she might have read it because she had a few books in the house that I never looked at, and she never mentioned any other blokes in her life. She used to say that it was a treat to be able to marry and live with a bloke like me who used his bare hands for a living, because there weren't many blokes in the world, when you considered it, who did good hard labouring work. She said she'd die if ever she married a bloke as worked in an office and who crawled around his boss because he wanted to get on. So I thought it would go off all right, mam, honest I did, when she said nice things like this to me. It made the netting factory look better to me, and I didn't so much mind carrying bobbins from one machine to another. I was happy with her and I thought that she was happy with me. At first she made a bigger fuss of me than before we were married even, and when I came home at night she used to talk about politics and books and things, saying how the world was made for blokes like me and that we should run the world and not leave it to a lot of money-grubbing capitalist bastards who didn't know any more about it than to talk like babies week after week and get nothing done that was any good to anybody.

'But to tell you the truth, mam, I was too tired to talk politics after I'd done a hard day's graft, and then she started to ask questions, and would get ratty after a while when she began to see that I couldn't answer what she wanted to know. She asked me all sorts of things, about my bringing up, about my dad, about all the neighbours in the terrace, but I could never tell her much, anyway, not what she wanted to know, and that started a bit of trouble. At first she packed my lunches and dinners and there was always a nice hot tea and some clothes to change into waiting for me when I came home, but later on she wanted me to have a bath every night, and that caused a bit of trouble because I was too tired to have a bath and often I was too fagged out even to change my clothes. I wanted to sit in my overalls listening to the wireless and reading the paper in peace. Once when I was reading the paper and she was getting mad because I couldn't get my eyes off the football results she put a match to the bottom of the paper and I didn't know about it till the flames almost came into my face. I got a fright, I can tell you, because I thought we were still happy then. And she made a joke about it, and even went out to buy me another newspaper, so I thought it was all right and that it was only a rum joke she'd played. But not long after that when I'd got the racing on the wireless she said she couldn't stand the noise and that I should listen to something better, so she pulled the plug out and wouldn't put it back.

'Yes, she did very well by me at first, that I will say, just like you, mam, but then she grew tired of it all, and started to read books all day, and there'd be nowt on the table at tea time when I came home dead to the wide except a packet of fags and a bag of toffees. She was all loving to me at first, but then she got sarcastic and said she couldn't stand the sight of me. "Here comes the noble savage," she called out when I came home, and used longer words I didn't know the meaning of when I asked her where my tea was. "Get it yourself," she said, and one day when I picked up one of her toffees from the table she threw the poker at me. I said I was hungry, but she just told me: "Well, if you are, then crawl under the table to me and I'll give you something." Honest, mam, I can't tell you one half of what went on, because you wouldn't want to hear it.'

(Not much, I thought. I could see her as large as life licking her chops.)

'Tell me it all, my lad,' she said. 'Get it off your chest. I can see you've had a lot to put up with.'

'I did and all,' he said. 'The names she called me, mam. It made my hair stand on end. I never thought she was that sort, but I soon found out. She used to sit in front of the fire with nothing on, and when I said that she should get dressed in case a neighbour knocked at the door, she said she was only warming her meal-ticket that the noble savage had given her, and then she'd laugh, mam, in a way that made me so's I couldn't move. I had to get out when she carried on like that because I knew that if I stayed in she'd throw something and do damage.

'I don't know where she is now. She packed up and took her things, saying she never wanted to see me again, that I could chuck myself in the canal for all she cared. She used to shout a lot about going down to London and seeing some real life, so I suppose that's where she's gone. There was four pounds ten and threepence in a jam-jar on the kitchen shelf and when she'd gone that was gone as well.

'So I don't know, our mam, about anything, or what I'm going to do. I'd like to live here again with you if you'll have me. I'll pay you two quid a week regular for my board, and see you right. I can't put up with any of that any more because I can't stand it, and I don't suppose I'll ever leave home again after all that little lot of trouble. So if you'll have me back, mam, I'll be ever so glad. I'll work hard for you, that I will, and you'll never have to worry again. I'll do right by you and pay you back a bit for all the struggle you had in bringing me up. I heard at work the other day as I'm to have a ten bob rise next week, so if you let me stay I'll get a new wireless and pay the deposit on it. So let me stay, our mam, because, I tell you, I've suffered a lot.'

And the way she kissed him made me sick, so I got down from my monkey-perch.

Jim Scarfedale stayed, right enough, the great big baby. He was never happier in his life after getting the OK from his old woman. All his worries were over, he'd swear blind they were, even if you tried to tell him what a daft sod he was for not packing his shaving tackle and getting out, which I did try to tell him, only he thought I was cracked even more than he was himself, I suppose. His mother thought she'd got him back for good, though, and so did we all, but we were off the mark by a mile. If you weren't stone-blind you could see he was never

110

the same old Jim after he'd been married: he got broody and never spoke to a soul, and nobody, not even his mam, could ever get out of him where he went to every night. His face went pudgy-white and his sandy mouse-hair fell out so much that he was nearly bald in six months. Even the few freckles he had went pale. He used to slink back from wherever he'd been at twelve o'clock, whether the night was winter or summer, and never a bloke would know what he got up to. And if you asked him right out loud, like as if you were cracking a bit of a joke: 'Where you been, Jim?' he'd make as if he hadn't heard a sound.

It must have been a couple of years later when the copper came up our yard one moonlight night: I saw him from my bedroom window. He turned the corner, and I dodged back before he could spot me. You're in for it now, I said to myself, ripping lead from that empty house on Buckingham Street. You should have had more sense, you daft bogger (frightened to death I was, though I don't know why now), especially when you only got three and a tanner for it from Cooky. I always said you'd end up in Borstal, and here comes the copper to get you.

Even when he went on past our house I thought it was only because he'd got mixed up in the numbers and that he'd swing back at any minute. But no, it was the Scarfedales' door he wanted, and I'd never known a happier feeling than when I heard that rap-rap-rapping and knew that this time they hadn't come for me. Never again, I sang to myself, never again – so happy that I got the stitch – they can keep their bleeding lead.

Jim's mam screamed as soon as the copper mentioned her name. Even where I was I heard her say: 'He's never gone and got run over, has he?'

Then I could hear no more, but a minute later she walked up the yard with the copper, and I saw her phizzog by the lamplight, looking set hard like granite, as if she would fall down and kick the bucket if you as much as whispered a word to her. The copper had to hold her arm.

It all came out next morning – the queerest case the yard had ever known. Blokes had been put inside for burglary, deserting, setting fire to buildings, bad language, being blind drunk, grabbing hold of grown women and trying to give them what-for, not paying maintenance money, running up big debts for wireless and washing machines and then selling them, poaching, trespassing, driving off in cars that didn't belong to them, trying to commit suicide, attempted murder, assault and battery, snatching handbags, shoplifting, fraud, forgery, pilfering from work, bashing each other about, and all sorts of larks that didn't mean much. But Jim did something I hadn't heard about before, at least not in our yard.

He'd been at it for months as well, taking a bus for miles across town to places where nobody knew him and waiting in old dark streets near some lit-up beer-off for little girls of ten and eleven to come walking along carrying jugs to get their dads a pint. And sucky Jim would jump out of his hiding place near pieces of waste-ground and frighten the life out of them and get up to his dirty tricks. I can't understand why he did it, I can't, I really can't, but did it he did, and got copped for it as well. He did it so often that somebody must have sprung a trap, because one hard-luck night they collared him and he was put inside for eighteen months. You should have heard the telling-off he got from the judge. I'll bet the poor sod didn't know where to put his face, though I'm sure there's many a judge that's done the same, if not worse, than Jim. 'We've got to put you in clink,' the judge said, 'not only for the good of little girls but for your own good as well. People have to be protected from the likes of you, you dirty sod.'

After that we never saw him again in our yard, because by the time he came out his mother had got a house and a new job in Derby, so's they could settle down where nobody knew them I suppose. Jim was the only bloke in our yard that ever got a big spread in *all* the newspapers, as far as I can remember, and nobody would have thought he had it in him, though I think it was a bit like cheating, getting in on them with a thing like that.

Which is why I think nobody should hang on to his mother's apron strings for such a long time like Jim did, or they might go the same way. And that's why I look at that atlas under my desk at school instead of doing sums (up through Derbyshire and into Manchester, then up to Glasgow, across to Edinburgh, and down again to London, saying hello to mam and dad on the way) because I hate doing sums, especially when I think I can already reckon up all the money I'm ever likely to scoop from any small-time gas-meter.

The Decline and Fall of
Frankie Buller

Sitting in what has come to be called my study, a room in the first-floor flat of a ramshackle Majorcan house, my eyes move over racks of books around me. Row after row of coloured backs and dusty tops, they give an air of distinction not only to the room but to the whole flat, and one can sense the thoughts of occasional visitors who stoop down discreetly during drinks to read their titles:

'A Greek lexicon, Homer in the original. He knows Greek! (Wrong, those books belong to my brother-in-law.) Shakespeare, The Golden Bough, a Holy Bible bookmarked with tapes and paper. He even reads it! Euripides and the rest, and a dozen mouldering Baedekers. What a funny idea to collect them! Proust, all twelve volumes! I never could wade through that lot. (Neither did I.) Dostoevsky. My God, is *he* still going strong?'

And so on and so on, items that have become part of me, foliage that has grown to conceal the bare stem of my real personality, what I was like before I ever saw these books, or any book at all, come to that. Often I would like to rip them away from me one by one, extract their shadows out of my mouth and heart, cut them neatly with a scalpel from my jungle-brain. Impossible. You can't wind back the clock that sits grinning on the marble shelf. You can't even smash its face in and forget it.

Yesterday we visited the house of a friend who lives further along the valley, away from the town noises so that sitting on the terrace with eyes half-closed and my head leaning back in a deck-chair, beneath a tree of half-ripe medlars and with the smell of plundered oranges still on my hands, I heard the sound of a cuckoo coming from the pine woods on the mountain slopes.

The cuckoo accomplished what a surgeon's knife could not. I was plunged back deep through the years into my natural state, without books and without the knowledge that I am supposed to have gained from them. I was suddenly landed beyond all immediate horizons of the past by the soft, sharp, fluting whistle of the cuckoo, and set down once more within the kingdom of Frankie Buller.

We were marching to war, and I was part of his army, with an elderberry stick at the slope and my pockets heavy with smooth, flat, well-chosen stones that would skim softly and swiftly through the air, and strike the foreheads of enemies. My plimsoll shoes were sprouting bunions, and there must have been a patch at the back of my trousers and holes in my socks, because I can never remember a time when there weren't, up to the age of fourteen.

The roll-call revealed eleven of us, yet Frankie was a full-blown centurion with his six-foot spear-headed railing at the slope, and his rusty dustbin lid for a shield. To make our numbers look huge to an enemy he marched us down from the bridge and across the field in twos, for Frankie was a good tactician, having led the local armies since he was fifteen years old.

At that time his age must have stood between twenty and twenty-five. Nobody seemed to know for sure, Frankie least of all, and it was supposed that his parents found it politic to keep the secret closely. When we asked Frankie how old he was he answered with the highly improbable number of: ''Undred an' fifty-eight.' This reply was logically followed by another question: 'When did you leave school, then?' Sometimes he would retort scornfully to this: 'I never went to school.' Or he might answer with a proud grin: 'I didn't leave, I ran away.'

I wore short trousers, and he wore long trousers, so it was impossible for me to say how tall he was in feet and inches. In appearance he seemed like a giant. He had grey eyes and dark hair, and regular features that would have made him passably handsome had not a subtle air of pre-pubescent unreliability lurked in his eyes and around the lines of his low brow. In body and strength he lacked nothing for a full-grown man.

We in the ranks automatically gave him the title of General, but he insisted on being addressed as Sergeant-Major, because his father had been a sergeant-major in the First World War. 'My dad was wounded in the war,' he told us every time we saw him. 'He got a medal and shell-shock, and because he got shell-shock, that's why I'm like I am.'

He was glad and proud of being 'like he was' because it meant he did not have to work in a factory all day and earn his living like other men of his age. He preferred to lead the gang of twelve-year-olds in our street to war against the same age group of another district. Our street was a straggling line of ancient back-to-backs on the city's edge, while the enemy district was a new housing estate of three long streets which had outflanked us and left us a mere pocket of country in which to run wild – a few fields and allotment gardens, which was reason enough for holding an eternal grudge against them. People from the slums in the city-centre lived in the housing estate, so that our enemies were no less ferocious than we, except that they didn't have a twenty-year-old backward youth like Frankie to lead them into battle. The inhabitants of the housing estate had not discarded their slum habits, so that the area became known to our streets as 'Sodom'.

'We're gooin' ter raid Sodom today,' Frankie said, when we were lined-up on parade. He did not know the Biblical association of the word, thinking it a name officially given by the city council.

So we walked down the street in twos and threes, and formed up on the bridge over the River Leen. Frankie would order us to surround any stray children we met with on the way, and if they wouldn't willingly fall in with us as recruits he would follow one of three courses. First: he might have them bound with a piece of clothes-line and brought with us by force; second: threaten to torture them until they agreed to come with us of their own free will; third: beat them across the head with his formidable hand and send them home weeping, or snarling back curses at him from a safe distance. I had come to join his gang through clause number two, and had stayed with it for profitable reasons of fun and adventure. My father often said: 'If I see yo' gooin' about wi' that daft Frankie Buller I'll clink yer tab-'ole.'

Although Frankie was often in trouble with the police he could never, even disregarding his age, be accurately described as a 'juvenile delinquent'. He was threatened regularly by the law with being sent to Borstal, but his antics did not claim for him a higher categorical glory than that of 'general nuisance' and so kept him out of the clutches of such institutions. His father drew a pension due to wounds from the war, and his mother worked at the tobacco factory, and on this combined income the three of them seemed to live at a higher standard than the rest of us, whose fathers were permanent appendages at the dole office. The fact that Frankie was an only child in a district where some families numbered up to half a dozen was accounted for by the rumour that the father, having seen Frankie at birth, had decided to run no more risks. Another whispered reason concerned the nature of Mr Buller's pensionable wound.

We used to ask Frankie, when we made camp in the woods and squatted around a fire roasting plundered potatoes after victory, what he was going to do when the Second War started.

'Join up,' he would say, non-committally.

'What in, Frankie?' someone would ask respectfully, for Frankie's age and strength counted for much more than the fact that the rest of us knew roughly how to read and write.

Frankie responded by hurling a piece of wood at his interrogator. He was a crackshot at any kind of throw, and rarely missed hitting the shoulder or chest. 'Yer've got to call me "SIR"!' he roared, his arms trembling with rightful anger. 'Yer can get out to the edge of the wood and keep guard for that.' The bruised culprit slunk off through the bushes, clutching his pole and stones.

'What would you join, sir?' a more knowing ranker said.

Such respect made him amiable:

'The Sherwood Foresters. That's the regiment my dad was in. He got a medal in France for killin' sixty-three Jerries in one day. He was in a dug-out, see' – Frankie could act this with powerful realism since seeing *All Quiet on the Western Front* and *The Lives of a Bengal Lancer* – 'behind his machine gun, and the Jerries come over at dawn, and my dad seed 'em and started shootin'. They kept comin' over, but the Old Man just kept on firin' away – der-der-der-der-der-der-der – even when all his pals was dead. My Old Man was 'it with a bullet as well, but 'e din't let go of 'is gun, and the Jerries was fallin' dead like flies, dropping all round 'im, and when the rest o' the Sherwoods come back to 'elp 'im and stop the Jerries coming over, 'e counted sixty-three dead bodies in front of 'is gun. So they gen 'im a medal and sent 'im back ter England.'

He looked around at the semicircle of us. 'What do yer think o' that, then?' he demanded savagely, as if he himself were the hero and we were disputing it. 'All right,' he ordered, when we had given the required appreciation to his father's exploits, 'I want yer all ter scout round for wood so's the fire wain't goo out.'

Frankie was passionately interested in war. He would often slip a penny into my hand and tell me to fetch the *Evening Post* so that I could read to him the latest war news from China, Abyssinia, or Spain, and he would lean against the wall of his house, his grey eyes gazing at the roofs across the street, saying whenever I stopped for breath: 'Go on, Alan, read me a bit more. Read me that bit about Madrid again . . .'

Frankie was a colossus, yet a brave man who formed us up and laid us in the hollows of a field facing the railway embankment that defended the approaches to the streets of Sodom. We would wait for an hour, a dozen of us with faces pressed to the earth, feeling our sticks and trying to stop the stones in our pockets from rattling. If anyone stirred Frankie would whisper out a threat: 'The next man to move, I'll smash 'im with my knobkerrie.'

We were three hundred yards from the embankment. The grass beneath us was smooth and sweet, and Frankie chewed it by the mouthful, stipulating that no one else must do so because it was worse than Deadly Nightshade. It would kill us in five seconds flat if we were to eat it, he went on, but it would do him no harm because he was proof against poison of all kinds. There was magic inside him that would not let it kill him; he was a witch doctor, and, for anyone who wasn't, the grass would scorch his guts away.

An express train came out of the station, gathered speed on the bend, and blocked the pink eavings of Sodom from view while we lifted our heads from the grass and counted the carriages. Then we saw our enemies, several figures standing on the railway tracks, brandishing sticks and throwing stones with playful viciousness into a pool of water down the slope.

'It's the Sodom gang,' we whispered.

'Keep quiet,' Frankie hissed. 'How many do you see?'

'Can't tell.'

'Eight.'

'There's more comin' up.'

'Pretend they're Germans,' Frankie said.

They came down the slope and, one by one, lifted themselves over to our side of the railings. On the embankment they shouted and called out to each other, but once in the field they walked close together without making much noise. I saw nine of them, with several more still boldly trespassing on the railway line. I remembered that we were eleven, and while waiting for the signal to rush forward I kept saying to myself: 'It won't be long now. It can't be long now.'

Frankie mumbled his final orders. 'You lot go left. You other lot go right. We'll go in front. I want 'em surrounded.' The only military triumph he recognized was to surround and capture.

He was on his feet, brandishing an iron spear and waving a shield. We stood up with him and, stretched out in a line, advanced slowly, throwing stones as fast as our arms would move in to the concentric ring of the enemy gang.

It was a typical skirmish. Having no David to bring against our Goliath they slung a few ineffectual stones and ran back helter-skelter over the railings, mounting the slope to the railway line. Several of them were hit.

'Prisoners!' Frankie bellowed, but they bolted at the last moment and escaped. For some minutes stones flew between field and embankment, and our flanks were unable to push forward and surround. The enemy exulted then from the railway line because they had a harvest of specially laid stones between the tracks, while we had grass underfoot, with no prospect of finding more ammunition when our pockets were emptied. If they rallied and came back at us, we would have to retreat half a mile before finding stones at the bridge.

Frankie realized all this in a second. The same tactical situation had occurred before. Now some of us were hit. A few fell back. Someone's eye was cut. My head was streaming with blood, but I disregarded this for the moment because I was more afraid of the good hiding I would catch from my father's meaty fist at home for getting into a fight, than blood and a little pain. ('Yer've bin wi' that Frankie Buller agen, ain't yer?' Bump. 'What did I tell yer? Not ter ger wi' 'im, didn't I?' Bump. 'And yer don't do what I tell yer, do you?' Bump. 'Yer'll keep on gooin' wi' that Frankie Buller tell yer as daft as 'e is, wain't yer?' Bump-bump.)

We were wavering. My pockets were light and almost empty of stones. My arms ached with flinging them.

'All right if we charge, lads?' Frankie called out.

There was only one answer to his words. We were with him, right into the ovens of a furnace had he asked it. Perhaps he led us into these bad situations, in which no retreat was possible, just for the fine feeling of a glorious win or lose.

'Yes!' we all shouted together.

'Come on, then,' he bawled out at the top of his voice:

'CHARGE!'

His great strides carried him the hundred yards in a few seconds, and he was already climbing the railing. Stones from the Sodom lot were clanging and rattling against his shield. Lacking the emblematic spear and dustbin lid of a leader we went forward more slowly, aiming our last stones at the gang on the embankment above.

As we mounted the railings on his left and right Frankie was half-way up the slope, within a few yards of the enemy. He exhorted his wings all the time to make more speed and surround them, waving his dangerous spear-headed length of iron now before their faces. From lagging slightly we suddenly swept in on both flanks, reaching the railway line in one rush to replenish our stocks of ammunition, while Frankie went on belabouring them from the front.

They broke, and ran down the other slope, down into the streets of Sodom, scattering into the refuge of their rows of pink houses whose doors were already scratched and scarred, and where, it was rumoured, they kept coal in their bathrooms (though this was secretly envied by us as a commodious coal-scuttle so conveniently near to the kitchen) and strung poaching nets out in their back gardens.

When the women of our street could think of no more bad names to call Frankie Buller for leading their children into fights that resulted in black eyes, torn clothes, and split heads, they called him a Zulu, a label that Frankie nevertheless came to accept as a tribute, regarding it as being synonymous with bravery and recklessness. 'Why do you run around with that bleddy Zulu?' a mother demanded from her child as she tore up one of father's old shirts for a bandage or patch. And immediately there was conjured up before you Frankie, a wild figure wielding spear and dustbin lid, jumping up and down before leading his gang into battle. When prisoners were taken he would have them tied to a tree or fence-post, then order his gang to do a war dance around them. After the performance, in which he in his fierce panoply sometimes took part, he would have a fire built near by and shout out that he was going to have the prisoners tortured to death now. He once came so near to carrying out this threat that one of us ran back and persuaded Frankie's father to come and deal with his son and set the prisoners free. And so Mr Buller and two other men, one of them my father, came striding down the steps of the bridge. They walked quickly across the field, short, stocky, black-browed Chris, and bald Buller with his walrus moustache. But the same person who had given the alarm crept back into Frankie's camp and gave warning there, so that when the three men arrived, ready to buckle Frankie down and drive him home, they found nothing except a kicked-out fire and a frightened but unharmed pair of captives still tied to a tree.

It was a fact that Frankie's acts of terrorism multiplied as the war drew nearer, though many of them passed unnoticed because of the pre-occupied and brooding atmosphere of that summer. He would lead his gang into allotments and break into the huts, scattering tools and flower seeds with a maniacal energy around the garden, driving a lawn-mower over lettuce-heads and parsley, leaving a litter of decapitated chrysanthemums in his track. His favourite sport was to stand outside one of the huts and throw his spear at it with such force that its iron barb ran right through the thin wood.

We had long since said farewell to the novelty of possessing gasmasks. Frankie led us on a foray over the fields one day, out on a raid with masks on our faces – having sworn that the white cloud above the wood was filled with mustard gas let loose from the Jerry trenches on the other side – and they became so broken up in the scuffle that we threw each one ceremoniously into a fire before going home, preferring to say we had lost them rather than show the tattered relics that remained.

So many windows were broken, dustbins upturned, air let out of bicycle tyres, and heads split as a result of pyrrhic victories in gang raids – for he seemed suddenly to be losing his military genius – that it became dangerous for Frankie to walk down our street. Stuffing a few shreds of tobacco into one of his father's old pipes – tobacco that we collected for him as cigarette-ends – he would walk along the middle of the street, and suddenly an irate woman would rush out of an entry wielding a clothes-prop and start frantically hitting him.

'I saw you empty my dustbin last night, you bleddy Zulu, you grett daft baby. Take that, and that, and that!'

'It worn't me, missis. I swear to God it worn't,' he would shout in protest, arms folded over his head and galloping away to avoid her blows.

'Yo' come near my house agen,' she shouted after him, 'and I'll cool yer down wi' a bucket o' water, yo' see'f I don't.'

Out of range, he looked back at her, bewildered, angry, his blood boiling with resentment. He shouted out the worst swear-words he knew, and disappeared into his house, slamming the door behind him.

It was not only the outbreak of the war that caused Frankie's downfall. Partly it came about because there was a romantic side to his nature that evinced itself in other means than mock warfare. At the end of many afternoons in the summer he stood at the top of our street and waited for the girls to come out of the tobacco factory. Two thousand worked there, and about a quarter of them passed by every evening on their way home to tea.

He mostly stood there alone in his black corduroy trousers, patched jacket, and a collarless shirt belonging to his father, but if an older member of the gang stayed for company it by no means inhibited his particular brand of courtship. He had the loudest mouth-whistle in the street, and this was put to good and musical use as the girls went by with arms linked in twos and threes.

'Hey up, duck!' he would call out. 'How are yer?'

A shrug of the shoulders, a toss of the head, laughter, or a sharp retort came back.

'Can I tek yer out tonight?' he cried with a loud laugh. 'Do you want me to treat you to t'pictures?'

Occasionally a girl would cross to the other side of the road to avoid him, and she would be singled out for his most special witticism:

'Hey up, good-lookin', can I cum up and see yer some time?'

Responses flew back like this, laced around with much laughter:

'It'll cost yer five quid!'

'Yer'r daft, me duck, yer foller balloons!'

'I'll meet you at the Grand at eight. Don't forget to be there, because I shall!'

It was his greatest hour of mature diversion. He was merely acting his age, following, though in a much exaggerated manner, what the other twenty-year-olds did in the district. The consummation of these unique courtships took place among the bulrushes, in the marsh between the River Leen and the railway line where Frankie rarely led his gang. He stalked alone (a whistled-at girl accompanying him only as a dim picture in his mind) along concealed paths to catch tadpoles, and then to lie by himself in a secret place where no one could see him, self-styled boss of osiers, elderberry and bordering oak. From which journey he returned pale and shifty-eyed with guilt and a pleasurable memory.

He stood at the street corner every evening as the summer wore on, at first with many of the gang, but later alone because his remarks to the passing factory girls were no longer innocent, so that one evening a policeman came and drove him away from the street corner for ever.

121

During those same months hundreds of loaded lorries went day after day to the edge of the marsh and dumped rubble there, until Frankie's secret hiding place was obliterated, and above it lay the firm foundation for another branch of the tobacco factory.

On the Sunday morning that my mother and father shook their heads over Chamberlain's melancholy voice issuing from the webbed heart-shaped speaker of our wireless set, I met Frankie in the street.

I asked what he would do now there was a war on, for I assumed that in view of his conscriptable age he would be called-up with the rest of the world. He seemed inert and sad, and I took this to be because of the war, a mask of proper seriousness that should be on everybody's face, even though I didn't feel it to be on my own. I also noticed that when he spoke he did so with a stammer. He sat on the pavement with his back leaning against the wall of some house, instinctively knowing that no one would think of pummelling him with a clothes-prop today.

'I'll just wait for my calling-up papers,' he answered. 'Then I'll get in the Sherwood Foresters.'

'If I get called up I'll go in the navy,' I put in, when he did not offer an anecdote about his father's exploits in the last war.

'The army's the only thing to join, Alan,' he said with deep conviction, standing up and taking out his pipe.

He suddenly smiled, his dejection gone. 'I'll tell you what, after dinner we'll get the gang together and go over New Bridge for manoeuvres. I've got to get you all into shape now there's a war on. We'll do a bit o' training. P'raps we'll meet some o' the Sodom lot.'

As we marched along that afternoon Frankie outlined his plan for our future. When we were about sixteen, he said, if the war was still on – it was bound to be because the Germans were tough, his old man told him so, though they wouldn't win in the end because their officers always sent the men over the top first – he'd take us down to the recruiting depot in town and enlist us together, all at the same time. In that way he – Frankie – would be our platoon commander.

It was a wonderful idea. All hands were thrust into the air.

The field was clear over New Bridge. We stood in a line along the parapet and saw without comment the newest proof of the city's advance. The grazing lands and allotments were now cut off from the main spread of the countryside by a boulevard sprouting from Sodom's new houses, with cars and Corporation double-deckers already running along it.

There was no sign of the Sodom lot, so Frankie ordered three of us to disappear into the gullies and hollows for the rest of the gang to track down. The next item on the training programme was target practice, a tin can set on a tree trunk until it was knocked over with stones from fifty yards. After fencing lessons and wrestling matches six of the Sodom gang appeared on the railway line, and at the end of a quick brutal skirmish they were held fast as prisoners. Frankie wished neither to keep them nor harm them, and let them go after making them swear an oath of allegiance to the Sherwood Foresters.

At seven o'clock we were formed up in double file to be marched back. Someone grumbled that it was a late hour to get home to tea, and for once Frankie succumbed to what I clearly remembered seeing as insubordination. He listened to the complaint and decided to cut our journey short by leading us across the branch-line that ran into the colliery. The factories and squalid streets on the hill had turned a sombre ochred colour, as if a storm would burst during the night, and the clouds above the city were pink, giving an unreal impression of profound silence so that we felt exposed, as if the railwayman in the distant signal box could see us and hear every word we spoke.

One by one we climbed the wire fence, Frankie crouching in the bushes and telling us when he thought the path was clear. He sent us over one at a time, and we leapt the six tracks yet kept our backs bent, as if we were passing a machine-gun post. Between the last line and the fence stood an obstacle in the form of a grounded railway carriage that served as a repair and tool-storage shed. Frankie had assured us that no one was in it, but when we were all across, the others already rushing through the field and up on to the lane, I turned around and saw a railwayman come out of the door and stop Frankie just as he was making for the fence.

I didn't hear any distinct words, only the muffled sound of arguing. I kept down between the osiers and watched the railwayman poking his finger at Frankie's chest as if he were giving him some really strong advice. Then Frankie began to wave his hands in the air, as though he could not tolerate being stopped in this way, with his whole gang looking on from the field, as he thought.

Then, in one vivid second, I saw Frankie snatch a pint bottle from his jacket pocket and hit the railwayman over the head with it. In the exaggerated silence I heard the crash, and a cry of shock, rage, and pain from the man. Frankie then turned and ran in my direction, leaping

123

like a zebra over the fence. When he drew level and saw me he cried wildly:

'Run, Alan, run. He asked for it. He asked for it.'

And we ran.

The next day my brothers, sisters and myself were loaded into Corporation buses and transported to Worksop. We were evacuated, our few belongings thrust into paper carrier-bags, away from the expected bombs, along with most other children of the city. In one fatal blow Frankie's gang was taken away from him, and Frankie himself was carried off to the police station for hitting the railwayman on the head with a bottle. He was also charged with trespassing.

It may have been that the beginning of the war coincided with the end of Frankie's so-called adolescence, though ever after traces of it frequently appeared in his behaviour. For instance he would still tramp from one end of the city to the other, even through smokescreen and blackout, in the hope of finding some cinema that showed a good cowboy film.

I didn't meet Frankie again for two years. One day I saw a man pushing a handcart up the old street in which we did not live anymore. The man was Frankie, and the handcart was loaded with bundles of wood, the sort of kindling that housewives spread over a crumpled-up *Evening Post* before making a morning fire. We couldn't find much to talk about, and Frankie seemed condescending in his attitude to me, as though ashamed to be seen talking to one so much younger than himself. This was not obvious in any plain way, yet I felt it and, being thirteen, resented it. Times had definitely altered. We just weren't pals any more. I tried to break once again into the atmosphere of old times by saying:

'Did you try to get into the army then, Frankie?'

I realize now that it was an indiscreet thing to say, and might have hurt him. I did not notice it then, yet I remembered his sensitivity as he answered:

'What do you mean? I *am* in the army. I joined up a year ago. The Old Man's back in the army as well – sergeant-major – and I'm in 'is cumpny.'

The conversation quickly ended. Frankie pushed his barrow to the next entry, and began unloading his bundles of wood.

I didn't meet him for more than ten years. In that time I too had done my 'sodjerin', in Malaya, and I had forgotten the childish games we used to play with Frankie Buller, and the pitched battles with the Sodom lot over New Bridge.

I didn't live in the same city any more. I suppose it could be said that I had risen from the ranks. I had become a writer of sorts, having for some indescribable reason, after the evacuation and during the later bombs, taken to reading books.

I went back home to visit my family, and on my way through the streets about six o'clock one winter's evening, I heard someone call out:

'Alan!'

I recognized the voice instantly. I turned and saw Frankie standing before a cinema billboard, trying to read it. He was about thirty-five now, no longer the javelin-wielding colossus he once appeared, but nearer my own height, thinner, an unmistakable air of meekness in his face, almost respectable in his cap and black topcoat with white muffler tucked neatly inside. I noticed the green medal-ribbon on the lapel of his coat, and that confirmed what I had heard about him from time to time during the last ten years. From being the sergeant-major of our gang he had become a private soldier in the Home Guard, a runner indeed in his father's company. With tin-hat on his sweating low-browed head Frankie had stalked with messages through country whose every blade of grass he knew.

He was not my leader any more, and we both instantly recognized the fact as we shook hands. Frankie's one-man wood business had prospered, and he now went around the streets with a pony and cart. He wasn't well-off, but he was his own employer. The outspoken ambition of our class was to become one's own boss. He knew he wasn't the leader of kindred spirits any more, while he probably wondered as we spoke whether or not I might be, which could have accounted for his shyness.

Not only had we both grown up in our different ways since the days when with dustbin lid and railing-spear he led his battalion into pitiless stone-throwing forays, but something of which I did not know had happened to him. Coming from the same class and, one might say, from the same childhood, there should have been some tree-root of recognition between us, despite the fact that our outer foliage of leaves would have wilted somewhat before each other's differing shade of colour. But there was no contact and I, being possessed of what the world I had moved into often termed

125

'heightened consciousness', knew that it was due as much to some-thing in Frankie as in me.

''Ow are yer goin' on these days, Frankie?' I asked, revelling in the old accent, though knowing that I no longer had the right to use it.

His stammer was just short of what we would once have derisively called a stutter. 'All right now, I feel a lot better, after that year I had in hospital.'

I looked him quickly and discreetly up and down for evidence of a lame foot, a broken limb, a scar; for why else did people go to hospital? 'What were you in for?' I asked.

In replying, his stammer increased. I felt he hesitated because for one moment he did not know which tone to take, though the final voice he used was almost proud, and certainly serious. 'Shock treatment. That's why I went.'

'What did they give you shock treatment for, Frankie?' I asked this question calmly, genuinely unable to comprehend what he told me, until the full horrible details of what Frankie must have undergone flashed into my mind. And then I wanted power in me to tear down those white-smocked mad interferers with Frankie's coal-forest world, wanted to wipe out their hate and presumption.

He pulled his coat collar up because, in the dusk, it was beginning to rain. 'Well, you see, Alan,' he began, with what I recognized now as a responsible and conforming face, 'I had a fight with the Old Man, and after it I blacked out. I hurt my dad, and he sent for the police. They fetched a doctor, and the doctor said I'd have to go to the hospital.' They had even taught him to call it 'hospital'. In the old days he would have roared with laughter and said:

''Sylum!'

'I'm glad you're better now, then,' I said, and during the long pause that followed I realized that Frankie's world was after all untouchable, that the conscientious-scientific-methodical probers could no doubt reach it, could drive it into hiding, could kill the physical body that housed it, but had no power in the long run really to harm such minds. There is a part of the jungle that the scalpel can never reach.

He wanted to go. The rain was worrying him. Then, remembering why he had called me over, he turned to face the broad black lettering on a yellow background. 'Is that for the Savoy?' he asked, nodding at the poster.

'Yes,' I said.

126

He explained apologetically: 'I forgot me glasses, Alan. Can you read it for me, and tell me what's on tonight.'

'Sure, Frankie,' I read it out: 'Gary Cooper, in *Saratoga Trunk*.'

'I wonder if it's any good?' he asked. 'Do you think it's a cowboy picture, or a love picture?'

I was able to help him on this point. I wondered, after the shock treatment, which of these subjects he would prefer. Into what circle of his dark, devil-populated world had the jolts of electricity penetrated? 'I've seen that picture before,' I told him. 'It's a sort of cowboy picture. There's a terrific train smash at the end.'

Then I saw. I think he was surprised that I shook his hand so firmly when we parted. My explanation of the picture's main points acted on him like a charm. Into his eyes came the same glint I had seen years ago when he stood up with spear and shield and roared out: 'CHARGE!' and flung himself against showers of sticks and flying stones.

'It sounds good,' he said. 'That's the picture for me. I'll see that.'

He pulled his cap lower down, made sure that his coat collar covered his throat and neck and walked with stirred imagination off into the driving rain.

'Cheerio, Frank,' I called out as he turned the corner. I wondered what would be left of him by the time they had finished. Would they succeed in tapping and draining dry the immense subterranean reservoir of his dark inspired mind?

I watched him. He ignored the traffic-lights, walked diagonally across the wide wet road, then ran after a bus and leapt safely on to its empty platform.

And I with my books have not seen him since. It was like saying goodbye to a part of me, for ever.

The Ragman's Daughter

I was walking home with an empty suitcase one night, an up-to-date pigskin zip job I was fetching back from a pal who thought he'd borrowed it for good, and two plainclothed coppers stopped me. They questioned me for twenty minutes, then gave up and let me go. While they had been talking to me, a smash-and-grab had taken place around the corner, and ten thousand nicker had vanished into the wide open spaces of somebody who needed it.

That's life. I was lucky my suitcase had nothing but air in it. Sometimes I walk out with a box of butter and cheese from the warehouse I work at, but for once that no-good God was on my side – trying to make up for the times he's stabbed me in the back maybe. But if the coppers had had a word with me a few nights later they'd have found me loaded with high-class provision snap.

My job is unloading cheeses as big as beer barrels off lorries that come in twice a week from the country. They draw in at the side door of the warehouse, and me and a couple of mates roll our sleeves up and shoulder them slowly down the gang-plank into the special part set aside for cheeses. We once saw, after checking the lists, that there was one cheese extra, so decided to share it out between a dozen of us and take it home to our wives and families. The question came up as to which cheese we should get rid of, and the chargehand said: 'Now, all look around for the cheese that the rats have started to go for, and that's the one we'll carve between us, because you can bet your bottom dollar that that's the best.'

It was a load of choice Dalbeattie, and I'd never tasted any cheese so delicious. For a long time my wife would say: 'When are you going to get us some more of that marvellous cheese, Tony?' And whatever I did take after that never seemed to satisfy them, though every time I went out with a chunk of cheese or a fist of butter I was risking my job, such as it is. Once for a treat I actually bought a piece of Dalbeattie from another shop, but they knew it wasn't stolen so it didn't taste as good as the other that the rats had pointed out to us. It happens now and again at the warehouse that a bloke takes some butter and the police nab him. They bring him back and he gets the push. Fancy getting the push for half a pound of butter. I'd be ashamed to look my mates in the eye again, and would be glad I'd got the sack so's I wouldn't have to.

The first thing I stole was at infants' school when I was five. They gave us cardboard coins to play with, pennies, shillings, half-crowns, stiff and almost hard to bend, that we were supposed to exchange for bricks and pieces of chalk. This lesson was called Buying and Selling. Even at the time I remember feeling that there was something not right about the game, yet only pouting and playing it badly because I wasn't old enough to realize what it was. But when I played well I ended up the loser, until I learned quickly that one can go beyond skill: at the end of the next afternoon I kept about a dozen of the coins (silver I noticed later) in my pocket when the teacher came round to collect them back.

'Some is missing,' she said, in that plummy voice that sent shivers down my spine and made me want to give them up. But I resisted my natural inclinations and held out. 'Someone hasn't given their money back,' she said. 'Come along, children, own up, or I'll keep you in after all the other classes have gone home.'

I was hoping she'd search me, but she kept us in for ten minutes, and I went home with my pockets full. That night I was caught by a shopkeeper trying to force the coins into his fag and chewing-gum machines. He dragged me home and the old man lammed into me. So, sobbing up to bed, I learned at an early age that money meant trouble as well.

Next time at school I helped myself to bricks, but teacher saw my bulging pockets and took them back, then threw me into the play-ground, saying I wasn't fit to be at achool. This showed me that it was always safest to go for money.

Once, an uncle asked what I wanted to be when I grew up, and I answered: 'A thief'. He bumped me, so I decided, whenever anybody else asked that trick question to say: 'An honest man' or 'An engine driver'. I stole money from my mother's purse, or odd coppers left lying around the house for gas or electricity, and so I got batted for that as well as for saying I wanted to be a thief when I grew up. I began to see that really I was getting clobbered for the same thing, which made me keep my trap shut on the one hand, and not get caught on the other.

In spite of the fact that I nicked whatever I could lay my hands on without too much chance of getting caught, I didn't like possessing things. Suits, a car, watches – as soon as I nicked something and got clear away, I lost interest in it. I broke into an office and came out with two typewriters, and after having them at home for a day I borrowed a car and dropped them over Trent Bridge one dark night. If the cops cared to dredge the river about there they'd get a few surprises. What I like most is the splash stuff makes when I drop it in: that plunge into water of something heavy – such as a T V set, a cash register and once, best of all, a motorbike – which makes a dull exploding noise and has the same effect on me as booze (which I hate) because it makes my head spin. Even a week later, riding on a bus, I'll suddenly twitch and burst out laughing at the thought of it, and some posh trot will tut-tut, saying: 'These young men! Drunk at eleven in the morning! What they want is to be in the army.'

If I lost all I have in the world I wouldn't worry much. If I was to go across the road for a packet of fags one morning and come back to see the house clapping its hands in flames with everything I owned burning inside I'd turn my back without any thought or regret and walk away, even if my jacket and last ten-bob note were in the flames as well.

What I'd like, believe it or not, is to live in a country where I didn't like thieving and where I didn't want to thieve, a place where everybody felt the same way because they all had only the same as everyone else – even if it wasn't much. Jail is a place like this, though it's not the one I'd find agreeable because you aren't free there. The place that fills my mind would be the same as in jail because everybody would have the same, but being free as well they wouldn't want to nick what bit each had got. I don't know what sort of system that would be called.

While as a youth I went out with girls, I used to like thieving more. The best of all was when I got a young girl to come thieving with me. The right sort was better than any mate I could team up with, more exciting and safe.

I met Doris outside the fish-and-chip shop on Ilkeston Road. Going in to get a supply for supper she dropped her purse, and a few obstinate shekels rolled into the road. 'Don't worry,' I said, 'I'll find them, duck.'

A couple of other youths wanted to help, but I got one by the elbow. 'Bale out. She's my girl-friend. You'll get crippled for life.'

131

'All right, Tony,' he laughed. 'I didn't know it was you.'

I picked her money up: 'This is the lot' – followed her into the light of the fish-and-chip shop where I could see what she was made of. 'I'm going for some chips as well,' I said, so as not to put her off.

'Thanks for getting my money. I have butterfingers sometimes.' Her hair was the colour of butter, yellow and reaching for her shoulders, where my hands wanted to be. We stood in the queue. I'd just eaten a bundle of fish-and-chips downtown, so even the smell in this joint turned my guts. 'Haven't I seen you somewhere before?' I asked.

'You might, for all I know. I've been around nearly as long as you have.'

'Where do you live, then?'

'Up Churchfield Lane.'

'I'll see you home.'

'You won't.' She was so fair and goodlooking that I almost lost heart, though not enough to stop me answering: 'You might drop your purse again.' I didn't know whether I'd passed her on the street some time, dreamed about her, or seen her drifting across the television screen in a shampoo advertisement between 'Blood Gun' and 'The Kremlin Strikes Again'. Her skin was smooth, cheeks a bit meaty, eyes blue, small nose and lips also fleshy but wearing a camouflage of orange-coloured lipstick that made me want to kiss them even more than if it had been flag-red. She stood at the counter with a vacant, faraway look in her eyes, the sort that meant she had a bit more thought in her rather than the other way round. She gave a little sniff at the billowing clouds of chip steam doubled in size because of mirrors behind the sizzling bins. It was impossible to tell whether or not she liked the smell.

'You're a long way from Churchfield Lane,' I said. 'Ain't you got chip shops up that part?'

'Dad says they do good fish here,' she told me. 'So I come to get him some, as a favour.'

'It's better at Rawson's though, downtown. You ought to let me take you there some time – for a supper. You'd enjoy it.'

It was her turn at the counter. 'I'm busy these days. Two shillings' worth of chips and six fish, please.'

'Where do you work, then?'

'I don't.'

I laughed: 'Neither do I.'

She took her bundle: 'Thank you very much' – turned to me: 'You won't be able to take me out then, will you?'

I edged a way back to the door, and we stood on the pavement. 'You're a torment, as well as being goodlooking. I've still got money, even if I don't go to work right now.' We walked across the road, and all the time I was waiting for her to tell me to skid, hoping she would yet not wanting her to. 'Does it fall from heaven, then?'

'No, I nick it.'

She half believed me. 'I'll bet you do. Where from?'

'It all depends. Anywhere.' I could already see myself taking her the whole way home – if I kept my trap flapping.

'I've never stolen anything in my life,' she said, 'but I've often wanted to.'

'If you stick around I'll show you a few things.'

She laughed: 'I might be scared.'

'Not with me. We'll go out one night and see what we can do.'

'Fast worker. We could do it for kicks, though.'

'It's better to do it for money,' I said, dead strict on this.

'What's the difference? It's stealing.'

I'd never thought about it this way before. 'Maybe it is. But it's still not the same.'

'If you do it for kicks,' she went on, 'you don't get caught so easily.'

'There's no point in doing something just for kicks,' I argued. 'It's a waste of time.'

'Well,' she said, 'I'll tell you what. You do it for money, and I'll do it for kicks. Then we'll both be satisfied.'

'Fine,' I said, taking her arm, 'that sounds reasonable.'

She lived in a big old house just off Churchfield Lane, and I even got a kiss out of her before she went into the garden and called me a soft goodnight. Doris, she had said, my name's Doris.

I thought she was joking about stealing stuff for kicks, but I met her a few days later outside a cinema, and when the show was over and we stood by a pavement where five roads met, she said: 'I suppose you just prowl around until you see something that's easy and quiet.'

'More or less' – not showing my surprise. 'It might be a bit harder than that though.' I held up a jack knife, that looked like a hedgehog with every blade splayed out: 'That one ain't for opening pop bottles; and this one ain't for getting stones out of horses' hoofs either. A useful little machine, this is.'

'I thought you used hairgrips?' She was treating it like a joke, but I said, deadpan: 'Sometimes. Depends on the lock.' A copper walked across the road towards us, and with every flat footstep I closed a blade of the knife, slipping it into my pocket before he was half-way over. 'Come on,' I said, lighting a fag, and heading towards Berridge Road.

The overhead lights made us look TB, as if some big government scab had made a mistake on the telephone and had too much milk tipped into the sea. We even stopped talking at the sight of each other's fag-ash faces, but after a while the darker side streets brought us back to life, and every ten yards I got what she'd not been ready to give on the back seat of the pictures: a fully-fledged passionate kiss. Into each went all my wondering at why a girl like this should want to come out on nightwork with a lout called me.

'You live in a big house,' I said when we walked on. 'What does your old man do?'

'He's a scrapdealer.'

'Scrapdealer?' It seemed funny, somehow. 'No kidding?'

'You know – rag and metal merchant. Randall's on Orston Road.'

I laughed, because during my life as a kid that was the place I'd taken scrap-iron and jamjars, lead and woollens to, and her old man was the bloke who'd traded with me – a deadbeat skinflint with a pound note sign between his eyes and breathing LSD all over the place. Dead at the brain and crotch the fat gett drove a maroon Jaguar in an old lounge suit. I'd seen him one day scatter a load of kids in the street, pumping that screaming button-hooter before he got too close, and as they bulleted out of his way throw a fistful of change after them. He nearly smashed into a lamp-post because such sudden and treacherous generosity put him off his steering.

'What's funny about it?' she wanted to know.

'I'm surprised, that's all.'

'I told a girl at school once that my dad was a scrapdealer, and she laughed, just like you did. I don't see what's funny about it at all.' You stupid bastard, I called myself, laughing for nothing when before you'd been getting marvellous kisses from her. A black cat shot through the light of a lamp-post, taking my good luck with it.

'He's better off than most people, so maybe you laugh because you're jealous.'

'Not me,' I said, trying to make amends. 'Another reason I laughed, if you want to know the truth, is that I've always wanted to be a scrapdealer, but so far I've never known how to get started. It was just the coincidence.' While she was wondering whether to believe me I tried changing the subject: 'What sort of school did you go to where they'd laugh at a thing like that?'

'I still go,' she said, 'a grammar school. I leave at the end of the year, though.' A school kid, I thought. Still, she's a posh one, so she can be nearly seventeen, though she looks at least as old as me, which is eighteen and a half. 'I'll be glad to leave school, anyway. I want to be independent. I'm always in top class though, so in a sense I like it as well. Funny.'

'You want to get a job, you mean?'

'Sure. Of course. I'll go to a secretarial college. Dad says he'd let me.'

'Sounds all right. You'll be set for life, the way you're going.' We were walking miles, pacing innumerable streets out of our systems, a slow arm-in-arm zig-zag through the darkening neighbourhood. It was a night full of star holes after a day of rain, a windy sky stretching into a huge flow over the rising ground of Forest Fields and Hyson Green and Basford, through Mapperley to Redhill and carried away by some red doubledecker loaded with colliers vanishing into the black night of Sherwood. We made a solitary boat in this flood of small houses, packed together like the frozen teeth of sharp black waves and, going from one lighthouse lamp-post to another, the district seemed an even bigger stretch than the area I was born and brought up in.

An old woman stood on a doorstep saying: 'Have you got a fag, my duck? I'd be ever so grateful if you could manage it.' She looked about ninety, and when I handed her one she lit up as if ready to have a nervous breakdown. 'Thanks, my love. I hope you'll be happy, the pair of you.'

'Same to you, missis,' I said as we went off.

'Aren't old women funny?' Doris said.

We kissed at every corner, and whenever it seemed I might not she reminded me by a tug at my linked arm. She wore slacks and a head scarf, a three-quarter leather coat and flat-heeled lace-ups, as if this was her idea of a break-and-entry rig. She looked good in it, stayed serious and quiet for most of the walking, so that all we did now and again was move into a clinch for a good bout of tormenting kisses. She moaned softly sometimes, and I wanted to go further than lipwork, but how could we in a solid wide open street where someone walking through would disturb us? With the air so sweet and long lasting, I knew it would be a stretch past her bed time before she finally landed home that night. Yet I didn't care, felt awake and marvellous, full of love for all the world – meaning her first and then myself, and it showed in our kisses as we went at a slow rate through the streets, arms fast around each other like Siamese twins.

Across the main road stretched a wall covering the yard of a small car-body workshop. As soon as I saw it my left leg began trembling and the kneecap of my right to twitch, so I knew this was the first place we'd go into together. I always got scared as soon as the decision was made, though it never took long for fright to get chased off as I tried to fathom a way into the joint.

I told Doris: 'You go to the end of the street and keep conk. I'll try to force this gate, and whistle if I do. If you see anybody coming walk back here, and we'll cuddle up as if we're courting.' She did as she was told, while I got to work on the gate lock, using first the bottle-opener and then the nail-file, then the spike. With a bit more play it snapped back, and I whistled. We were in the yard.

There was no word said from beginning to end. If I'd been doing it with a mate you'd have heard scufflings and mutterings, door-rattlings and shoulder-knocks and the next thing we'd be in a cop car on our way to Guildhall. But now, our limbs and eyes acted together, as if controlled by one person that was neither of us, a sensation I'd never known before. A side door opened and we went between a line of machines into a partitioned office to begin a quiet and orderly search. I'd been once in a similar place with a pal, and the noise as we pulled out drawers and slung typewriters about, and took pot shots with elastic and paperclips at light bulbs was so insane that it made me stop and silence him as well after five minutes. But now there wasn't a scratch or click anywhere.

Still with no word I walked to the door, and Doris came after me. In two seconds we were back on the street, leaning against the workshop wall to fill each of our mouths with such kisses that I knew I loved her, and that from then on I was in the fire, floating, burning, feeling the two of us ready to explode if we didn't get out of this to where we could lie down. Nothing would stop us, because we already matched and fused together, not even if we fell into a river or snow-bank.

There was no gunning of feet from the factory so that a lawful passing pedestrian could suspect we were up to no good and squeal for the coppers. After five minutes snogging we walked off, as if we'd just noticed how late it was and remembered we had to be at work in the morning. At the main road I said: 'What did you get?'

She took a bundle of pound notes from her pocket: 'This, what about you?'

I emptied a large envelope of postage stamps and cheques: 'Useless. You got the kitty, then.'

'I guess so,' she said, not sounding too full of joy.

'Not bad for a beginner. A school kid, as well!' I gave her half the stamps and she handed me half the money – which came to twenty quid apiece. We homed our way the couple of miles back, sticking one or two stamps (upside down) on each of the corners turned. 'I don't write letters,' I laughed. It was a loony action, but I have to do something insane on every job, otherwise there's no chance of getting caught, and if there's no chance of getting caught, there's no chance of getting away. I explained this to Doris, who said she'd never heard such a screwy idea, but that she was nearly convinced about it because I was more experienced than she was. Luckily the stamps ran out, otherwise the trail would have gone right through our back door, up the stairs and into my bedroom, the last one on my pillow hidden by my stupid big head. I felt feather-brained and obstinate, knowing that even if the world rolled over me I wouldn't squash.

By the banks of the Leen at Bobber's Mill we got under the fence and went down where nobody could see us. It was after midnight, and quiet but for the sound of softly rolling cold water a few feet off, as black as heaven for the loving we had to do.

Doris called for me at home, turned the corner, and came down our cobbled street on a horse. My brother Paul ran in and said: 'Come and look at this woman (he was only nine) on a horse, our Tony' – and having nothing better to do while waiting for Doris but flip through the *Mirror* I strode to the yard-end. It was a warm day, dust in the wind making a lazy atmosphere around the eyes, smoke sneaking off at right angles to chimneys and telly masts. By the pavement I looked down the street and saw nothing but a man going across to the shop in shirt-sleeves and braces, then swivelling my eyes the other way I saw this girl coming down the street on a walking horse.

It was a rare sight, because she was beautiful, had blonde hair like Lady Godiva except that she was dressed in riding slacks and a white shirt that set a couple of my Ted mates whistling at her, though most stayed quiet with surprise – and envy – when the horse pulled up at our yard-end and Doris on it said hello to me. It was hard to believe that last night we'd broken into a factory, seemed even more far gone than a dream; though what we'd done later by the river was real enough, especially when I caught that smell of scent and freshness as she bent down from the horse's neck. 'Why don't you come in for a cup of tea? Bring your horse in for a crust as well.'

It was a good filly, the colour of best bitter, with eyes like priceless damsons that were alive because of the reflector-light in them. The only horses seen on our street – pulling coal carts or bread vans – had gone to the knackers' yards years ago. I took the bridle and led it up the yard, Doris talking softly from high up and calling it Marian, guiding it over the smooth stones. A man came out of a lavatory and had a fit in his eyes when he nearly bumped into it. 'It wain't bite you, George,' I laughed.

'I'll have it for Sunday dinner if it does,' he said, stalking off.

'It wain't be the first time,' I called. My mother was washing clothes at the scullery sink, and it pushed its head to the window for a good look – until she glanced up: 'Tony! What have you got there!'

'Only a horse, mam,' I shouted back. 'It's all right: I ain't nicked it' – as she came out drying her hands.

'A friend of mine come to see me,' I told her, introducing Doris, who dropped to her proper size on the asphalt. My mother patted the horse as if it were a stray dog, then went in for a piece of bread. She'd been brought up in the country, and liked animals.

'We had a good time last night,' I said to Doris, thinking about it.

'Not bad. What shall we do with the money?'

'Spend it.'

Our fence was rickety, looked as if it would fall down when she tethered the horse to it. 'Funny,' she said. 'But what on?'

'How much does a horse cost?' I asked, tapping its nose.

'I'm not sure. Dad got me Marian. More than twenty pounds, though.' I was disappointed, had pictured us riding in the country, overland to Langley Mill and Matlock Bath without using a road once, the pair of us making a fine silhouette on some lonely skyline. Then as on the films we'd wind our way far down into the valley and get lodgings at a pub or farmhouse. Bit by bit we'd edge to Scotland and maybe at the end of all our long wanderings by horse we'd get a job as man and wife working a lighthouse. Set on a rock far out at sea, the waves would bash at it like mountains of snow, and we'd keep the lights going, still loving each other and happy even though we hadn't had a letter or lettuce in six months.

The sun shone over our backyards, and I was happy anyway: 'I'll just get rid of my dough, enjoy myself. I'm out of work, so it'll keep me for a month.'

'I hope we don't have to wait that long before doing it again,' she said, brushing her hair back.

'We'll go tonight, if you like. I'll bet the coppers don't know we went into that factory yet.' My mother came out with a bag of crusts for the horse: 'I've just made a pot of tea,' she said. 'Go and pour it, Tony.'

When we got behind the door I pulled Doris to me and kissed her. She kissed me, as well. Not having to chase and fight for it made it seem like real love.

We went on many 'expeditions', as Doris called them. I even got a makeshift job at a factory in case anybody should wonder how I was living. Doris asked if it would be O K to bring a school pal with us one night, and this caused our first argument. I said she was loony to think of such a thing, and did she imagine I was running a school for cowing crime, or summat? I hoped she hadn't mentioned our prowling nights to anybody else – though she hadn't, as it turned out, and all she'd wanted was to see if this particular girl at her school would be able to do this sort of job as cool as she could. 'Well, drop it,' I said, sharp. 'We do all right our oursens, so let's keep it to oursens.'

Having been brought up as the ragman's daughter and never wanting for dough, she had hardly played with the kids in the street. She hadn't much to do with those at school either, for they lived mostly in new houses and bungalows up Wollaton and would never come to Radford to call on her. So she'd been lonely in a way I never had been.

Her parents lived in a house off Churchfield Lane, a big ancient one backing its yards (where the old man still kept some of his scrap mountains) on to the Leen. Her dad had worked like a navvy all day and every day of his life, watching each farthing even after he was rich enough to retire like a lord. I don't know what else he could have done. Sucked icecream at the seaside? Gardened his feet off? Fished himself to death? He preferred to stick by sun, moon or electric light sorting metal or picking a bone with his own strength because, being a big and satisfied man, that was all he felt like doing – and who could blame him? Doris told me he was mean with most things, though not with her. She could have what she liked.

'Get a hundred, then,' I said.

But she just smiled and thought that wouldn't be right, that she'd only have from him what he gave her because she liked it better that way.

Every week-end she came to our house, on her horse except when the weather was bad. If nobody else was in she fastened her steed to the fence and we went up to my bedroom, got undressed and had the time of our lives. She had a marvellous figure, small breasts for her age, yet wide hips as if they'd finished growing before anything else of her. I always had the idea she felt better out of her clothes, realizing maybe that no clothes, even if expensive like gold, could ever match her birthday suit for a perfect fit that was always the height of fashion. We'd put a few Acker Bilks low on my record player and listen for a while with nothing on, getting drowsy and warmed up under the usual talk and kisses. Then after having it we'd sit and talk more, maybe have it again before mam or dad shouted up that tea was ready. When on a quiet day the horse shuffled and whinnied, it was like being in a cottage bedroom, alone with her and in the country. If it was sunny and warm as well and a sudden breeze pushed air into the room and flipped a photo of some pop singer off the shelf and felt softly at our bare skins I'd feel like a stallion, as fit and strong as a buck African and we'd have it over and over so that my legs wobbled as I walked back down the stairs.

People got used to seeing her ride down the street, and they'd say: 'Hellow, duck' – adding: 'He's in' – meaning me – 'I just saw him come back from the shop with a loaf.' George Clark asked when I was going to get married, and when I shouted that I didn't know he laughed: 'I expect you've got to find a place big enough for the horse as well, first.' At which I told him to mind his own effing business.

Yet people were glad that Doris rode down our street on a horse, and I sensed that because of it they even looked up to me more – or maybe they only noticed me in a different way to being carted off by the coppers. Doris was pleased when a man coming out of the bookie's called after her: 'Hey up, Lady Luck!' – waving a five-pound note in the air.

Often we'd go down town together, ending up at the pictures, or in a pub over a bitter or babycham. But nobody dreamed what we got up to before finally parting for our different houses. If we pinched fags or food or clothes we'd push what was possible through the letterbox of the first house we came to, or if it was too big we'd leave good things in litter-bins for some poor tramp or tatter to find. We were hardly ever seen, and never caught, on these expeditions, as if love made us invisible, ghosts without sound walking hand in hand between dark streets until we came to some factory, office, lock-up shop or house that we knew was empty of people – and every time this happened I remember the few seconds of surprise, not quite fear, at both of us knowing exactly what to do. I would stand a moment at this surprise – thankful, though waiting for it to go – until she squeezed my hand, and I was moving again, to finish getting in.

I was able to buy a motorbike, a secondhand powerful speedster, and when Doris called she'd leave her horse in our backyard, and we'd nip off for a machine-spin towards Stanton Ironworks, sliding into a full ton once we topped Balloon House Hill and had a few miles of straight and flat laid out for us like an airport runway. Slag heaps looked pale blue in summer, full triangles set like pyramid-targets way ahead and I'd swing towards them between leaf hedges of the country road, hoping they'd keep that far-off vacant colour, as if they weren't real. They never did though, and I lost them at a dip and bend, and when next in sight they were grey and useless and scabby, too real to look good any more.

On my own I rode with L plates, and took a test so as to get rid of them on the law's side of the law, but I didn't pass because I never was good at examinations. Roaring along with Doris straight as goldenrod behind, and hearing noises in the wind tunnel I made whisper sweet nothings into our four ear-holes, was an experience we loved, and I'd shout: 'You can't ride as fast as this on a horse' – and listen to the laugh she gave, which meant she liked to do both.

She once said: 'Why don't we go on an expedition on your bike?' and I answered: 'Why don't we do one on your hoss?' adding: 'Because it'd spoil everything, wouldn't it?'

She laughed: 'You're cleverer than I think.'

'No kidding,' I said, sarky. 'If only you could see yoursen as I can see you, and if only I could see mysen as you can see me, things would be plainer for us, wouldn't they?'

I couldn't help talking. We'd stopped the bike and were leaning on a bridge wall, with nothing but trees and a narrow lane round about, and the green-glass water of a canal below. Her arm was over my shoulder, and my arm was around her waist: 'I wonder if they would?' she said.

'I don't know. Let's go down into them trees.'

'What for?'

'Because I love you.'

She laughed again: 'Is that all?' – then took my arm: 'Come on, then.'

We played a game for a long time in our street, where a gang of us boys held fag lighters in a fair wind, flicking them on and off and seeing which light stayed on longest. It was a stupid game because everything was left to chance, and though this can be thrilling you can't help but lose by it in the end. This game was all the rage for weeks, before we got fed up, or our lighters did, I forget which. Sooner or later every lighter goes out or gives in; or a wind in jackboots jumps from around the corner and kicks it flat – and you get caught under the avalanche of the falling world.

One summer's week-end we waited in a juke-box coffee bar for enough darkness to settle over the streets before setting out. Doris wore jeans and sweatshirt, and I was without a jacket because of the warm night. Also due to the warmth we didn't walk the miles we normally did before nipping into something, which was a pity because a lot of hoof-work put our brains and bodies into tune for such quiet jobs, relaxed and warmed us so that we became like cats, alert and ready at any warning sound to duck or scram. Now and again the noise of the weather hid us – thunder, snow, drizzle, wind, or even the fact that clouds were above made enough noise for us to operate more safely than on this night of open sky with a million ears and eyes of copper stars cocked and staring. Every footstep deafened me, and occasionally on our casual stroll we'd stop to look at each other, stand a few seconds under the wall of a side-lit empty street, then walk on hand in hand. I wanted to whistle (softly) or sing a low tune to myself, for, though I felt uneasy at the open dumb night, it was also the kind of night that left me confident and full of energy, and when these things joined I was apt to get a bit reckless. But I held back, slowed my heart and took in every detail of each same street – so as to miss no opportunity, as they drummed into us at school. 'I feel as if I've had a few,' I said, in spite of my resolution.

'So do I.'

'Or as if we'd just been up in my room and had it together.'

'I don't feel like going far, though,' she said.

'Tired, duck?'

'No, but let's go home. I don't feel like it tonight.'

I wondered what was wrong with her, saying: 'I'll walk you back and we'll call it a day.'

In the next street I saw a gate leading to the rear yard of a shop, and I was too spun up to go home without doing anything at all: 'Let's just nip in here. You needn't come, duck. I wain't be five minutes.'

'O K.' She smiled, though my face was already set at that loot-barrier. It wasn't very high, and when I was on top she called: 'Give me a hand up.'

'Are you sure?'

'Of course I am.' It was the middle of a short street, and lamp-posts at either end didn't shed radiance this far up. I got to the back door and, in our usual quiet way, the lock was forced and we stood in a smell of leather, polish and cardboard boxes.

'It's a shoe shop,' Doris said. I felt my path across the storehouse behind the selling part of the shop, by racks and racks of shoe boxes, touching paper and balls of string on a corner table.

We went round it like blind people in the dark a couple of times just to be sure we didn't miss a silent cashbox cringing and holding its breath as our fingers went by. People on such jobs often miss thousands through hurrying or thinking the coppers are snorting down their necks. My old man insists I get the sack from one firm after another because I'm not thorough enough in my work, but if he could have seen me on this sort of task he'd have to think again.

There was nothing in the back room. I went into the shop part and in ten seconds flat was at the till, running my fingers over them little plastic buttons as if I was going to write a letter to my old man explaining just how thorough I could be at times. To make up for the coming small clatter of noise I held my breath – hoping both would average out to make it not heard. A couple of night owls walked by outside, then I turned the handle and felt the till drawer thump itself towards my guts. It's the best punch in the world, like a tabby cat boxing you with its paw, soft and loaded as it slides out on ballbearing rollers.

My hand made the lucky dip, lifted a wad of notes from under a spring-weight, and the other scooped up silver, slid it into my pocket as if it were that cardboard money they used to lend us at infants' school to teach us how to be good shoppers and happy savers – not rattling good coin ready for grown-ups to get rid of. I went to the back room and stood by the exit to make sure all was clear.

The light went on, a brilliant blue striplight flooding every corner of the room. I froze like a frog that's landed in grass instead of water. When I could speak I said to Doris: 'What did you do that for?' – too scared to be raving mad.

'Because I wanted to.' She must have sensed how much I felt like bashing her, because: 'Nobody can see it from the street' – which could have been true, but even so.

'Kicks are kicks,' I said, 'but this is a death trap.'

'Scared?' she smiled.

'Just cool' – feeling anything but. 'I've got about fifty quid in my pocket.'

She stood against a wall of shoe boxes, and even a telly ad couldn't have gone deeper into my guts than the sight of Doris now. Yellow arms of light turned full on her left me in the shade – which was fine, for I expected to see the dead mug of a copper burst in at any moment. Yet even at that I wouldn't be able to care. I felt as if music was in my head wanting to get out, as if it had come to me because I was one of those who could spin it out from me, though knowing I'd never had any say in a thing like that.

She didn't speak, stood to her full fair height and stared. I knew we were safe, that no copper would make any capture that night because the light she had switched on protected us both. We were cast-iron solid in this strongbox of shoes, and Doris knew it as well because when I couldn't help but smile she broke the spell by saying:

'I want to try some shoes on.'

'What?'

'Maybe they've got some of the latest.'

The idea was barmy, not so that I wanted to run like a shot stag out of the place, but so that I could have done a handstand against the wall of boxes. I lifted out an armful and set them on the floor like a game of dominoes. She chose one and opened it gently. I took up a box and split it down the middle: 'Try these.'

They were too small, a pair of black shiners with heels like toothpicks. 'I wish the shopkeeper was here,' she said, 'then he could tell me where the best are. This is a waste of time.'

I scoffed. 'You don't want much, do you? You'd have to pay for them, then. No, we'll go through the lot and find a few pairs of Paris fashions.'

'Not in this shop' – contemptuously slinging a pair of plain lace-ups to the other side of the room, enough noise to wake every rat under the skirting board. From the ladder I passed down a few choice boxes, selecting every other on the off chance of picking winners. 'I should have come in skirt and stockings,' she said, 'then I could have told which ones suit me.'

'Well, next time we go into a shoe shop I'll let you know; I'll wear an evening suit and we'll bring a transistor to do a hop with. Try these square toes. They'll go well with slacks.'

They fitted but, being the wrong colour, were hurled out with the other misfits. The room was scattered with shoes, looked as if one of them Yank cyclones – Mabel or Edna or whatever you call them – had been hatched there, or as if a meeting of cripples and one-legs had been suddenly broken up by news of the four-minute warning. She still hadn't found the right pair, so went on looking as if she lived there, ordering shop-assistant me about, though I didn't mind because it seemed like a game we were playing. 'Why don't you find a pair for yourself?' she said.

'No, we'll get you fixed. I'm always well shod.'

I knew that we were no longer safe in that shop and sprang to switch off the lights. 'You silly fool,' she cried.

Darkness put us into another world, the real one we were used to, or that I was anyway because it was hard to tell which sort of world Doris felt at home in. All she wanted, I sometimes thought, was a world with kicks, but I didn't fancy being for long at the mercy of a world in pitboots. Maybe it wore carpet slippers when dealing with her – though I shouldn't get like that now that it's been over for so long.

'Why did you switch off the light?' she yelled.

'Come on, let's get outside.'

We were in the yard, Doris without any pair of shoes except those she'd come out in that evening. The skyline for me ended at the top of the gate, for a copper was coming over it, a blue-black tree trunk bending towards us about twenty yards away. Doris was frozen like a rabbit. I pushed her towards some back sheds so that she was hidden between two of them before the copper, now in the yard, spotted the commotion.

He saw me, though. I dodged to another space, then ricochetted to the safe end of the yard, and when he ran at me, stinking of fags and beer, I made a nip out of his long arms and was on the gate saddle before he could reach me.

'Stop, you little bogger,' he called, 'I've got you.'

But all he had was one of my feet, and after a bit of tugging I left my shoe in the copper's hand. As I was racing clippitty-clop, hop-skip-and-a-jump up the street, I heard his boots rattling the boards of the gate as he got over – not, thank God, having twigged that Doris was in there and could now skip free.

I was a machine, legs fastened to my body like nuts and bolts, arms pulling me along as I ran down that empty street. I turned each corner like a flashing tadpole, heart in my head as I rattled the pavement so fast that I went from the eye of lamp-post in what seemed like no seconds at all. There was no worry in my head except the need to put a mile of zig-zags between that copper and me. I'd stopped hearing him only a few yards from the shoe shop gate, but it seemed that half an hour passed before I had to give up running in case I blew to pieces from the heavy bombs now getting harder all over me.

Making noises like a crazy elephant, I walked, only realizing now that one of my shoes was missing. The night had fallen apart, split me and Doris from each other, and I hoped she'd made a getaway before the copper gave me up and went back to check on what I'd nicked.

I threw my other shoe over the wall of an old chapel and went home barefoot, meaning to buy myself some more next day with the fifty quid still stuck in my pocket. The shoe landed on a heap of cinders and rusting cans, and the softness of my feet on the pavement was more than made up for by the solid ringing curses my brain and heart played ping-pong with. I kept telling myself this was the end, and though I knew it was, another voice kept urging me to hope for the best and look on the bright side – like some mad deceiving parson on the telly.

I was so sure of the end that before turning into our street I dropped the fifty pound bundle through somebody's letter box and hoped that when they found it they'd not say a word to anybody about such good luck. This in fact was what happened, and by the time I was safe for a three-year lap in Borstal the old woman who lived there had had an unexpected good time on the money that was, so she said, sent to her by a grateful and everloving nephew in Sheffield.

Next morning two cops came to our door, and I knew it was no good lying because they looked at me hard, as if they'd seen me on last night's television reading the news. One of them held my shoes in his hand: 'Do these fit you?'

A short while before my capture Doris said, when we were kissing good night outside her front door: 'I've learnt a lot since meeting you. I'm not the same person any more.' Before I had time to find out what she'd learnt I was down at the cop shop and more than half-way to Borstal. It was a joke, and I laughed on my way there. They never knew about Doris, so she went scot-free, riding her horse whenever she felt like it. I had that to be glad about at least. As a picture it made a stove in my guts those first black months, and as a joke I laughed over and over again, because it would never go stale on me. I'd learned a lot as well since meeting Doris, though to be honest I even now can't explain what it is. But what I learned is still in me, feeding my quieter life with energy almost without my noticing it.

I wrote to Doris from Borstal but never received an answer, and even my mother couldn't tell me anything about her, or maybe wouldn't, because plenty happened to Doris that all the district knew of. Myself though, I was kept three years in the dark, suffering and going off my head at something that without this love and worry I'd have sailed through laughing. Twenty of the lads would jump on me when I raved at night, and gradually I became low and brainless and without breath like a beetle and almost stopped thinking of her, hoping that maybe she'd be waiting for me when I came out and that we'd be able to get married.

That was the hope of story books, of television and B B C; didn't belong at all to me and life and somebody like Doris. For three solid years my brain wouldn't leave me alone, came at me each night and rolled over me like a wheel of fire, so that I still sweat blood at the thought of that torture, waiting, without news, like a dwarf locked in the dark. No Borstal could take the credit for such punishment as this.

On coming out I pieced everything together. Doris had been pregnant when I was sent down, and three months later married a garage mechanic who had a reputation for flying around on motorbikes like a

147

dangerous loon. Maybe that was how she prolonged the bout of kicks that had started with me, but this time it didn't turn out so well. The baby was a boy, and she named it after me. When it was two months old she went out at Christmas Eve with her husband. They were going to a dance at Derby on the motorbike and, tonning around a frosty bend, met a petrol bowser side on. Frost, darkness, and large red letters spelling PETROL were the last things she saw, and I wondered what was in her mind at that moment. Not much, because she was dead when the bowser man found her, and so was her husband. She couldn't have been much over eighteen.

'It just about killed her dad as well,' my mother said, 'broke his heart. I talked to him once on the street, and he said he'd allus wanted to send her to the university, she was so clever. Still, the baby went back to him.'

And I went back to jail, for six months, because I opened a car door and took out a transistor radio. I don't know why I did it. The wireless was no good to me and I didn't need it. I wasn't even short of money. I just opened the car door and took the radio and, here's what still mystifies me, I switched it on straightaway and listened to some music as I walked down the street, so that the bloke who owned the car heard it and chased after me.

But that was the last time I was in the nick – touch wood – and maybe I had to go in, because when I came out I was able to face things again, walk the streets without falling under a bus or smashing a jeweller's window for the relief of getting caught.

I got work at a sawmill, keeping the machines free of dust and wood splinters. The screaming engine noise ripping through trunks and planks was even fiercer than the battle-shindig in myself, which was a good thing during the first months I was free. I rode there each morning on a new-bought bike, to work hard before eating my dinner sandwiches under a spreading chestnut tree. The smell of fresh leaves on the one hand, and newly flying sawdust on the other, cleared my head and made me feel part of the world again. I liked it so much I thought it was the best job I'd ever had – even though the hours were long and the wages rotten.

One day I saw an elderly man walking through the wood, followed by a little boy who ran in and out of the bushes whacking flowers with his stick. The kid was about four, dressed in cowboy suit and hat, the other hand firing off his six-shooter that made midget sharp cracks splitting like invisible twigs between the trees. He was pink-faced with grey eyes, the terror of cats and birds, a pest for the ice-cream man, the sort of kid half stunned by an avalanche of toys at Christmas, spoiled beyond recall by people with money. You could see it in his face.

I got a goz at the man, had to stare a bit before I saw it was Doris's father, the scrap merchant who'd not so long back been the menace of the street in his overdriven car. He was grey and wax in the face, well wrapped in topcoat and hat and scarf and treading carefully along the woodpath. 'Come on,' he said to the kid. 'Come on, Tony, or you'll get lost.'

I watched him run towards the old man, take his hand and say: 'Are we going home now, grandad?' I had an impulse, which makes me blush to remember it, and that was to go up to Doris's ragman father and say – what I've already said in most of this story, to say that in a way he was my father as well, to say: 'Hey up, dad. You don't know much, do you?' But I didn't, because I couldn't, leaned against a tree, feeling as if I'd done a week's work without stop, feeling a hundred years older than that old man who was walking off with my kid.

My last real sight of Doris was of her inside the shoe shop trying on shoes, and after that, when I switched off the light because I sensed danger, we both went into the dark, and never came out. But there's another and final picture of her that haunts me like a vision in my waking dreams. I see her coming down the street, all clean and golden-haired on that shining horse, riding it slowly towards our house to call on me, as she did for a long time. And she was known to men standing by the bookie's as Lady Luck.

That's a long while ago, and I even see Doris's kid, a big lad now, running home from school. I can watch him without wanting to put my head in the gas oven, watch him and laugh to myself because I was happy to see him at all. He's in good hands and prospering. I'm going straight as well, working in the warehouse where they store butter and cheese. I eat like a fighting cock, and take home so much that my wife and two kids don't do bad on it either.

The Other John Peel

When the world was asleep one Sunday morning Bob slid away from the warm aura of his wife and padded downstairs – boots in hand – to fix up a flask and some bacon sandwiches.

Electric light gave the living-room an ageless air, only different from last night in that it was empty – of people. He looked around at the house full of furniture: television set, washing machine glinting white from the scullery, even a car on the street – the lot, and it belonged to him. Eric and Freda also slept, and he'd promised to take them up the Trent and hire a rowing-boat this afternoon if they were good. Wearing his second-best suit, knapsack all set, he remembered Freda's plea a few days ago: 'Will you bring me one o' them tails, our dad?' He had to laugh, the fawce little bogger, as he combed his dark wavy hair at the mirror and put on his glasses. I must tell her not to blab it to her pals though.

He opened the cellar door for his guns and pouches, put them under his arm to keep them low – having a licence for the twelve-bore, but not the .303 service rifle – and went out into the backyard. The world was a cemetery on short lease to the night, dead quiet except for the whine of factory generators: a row of upstairs windows were closed tight to hold in the breath of sleep. A pale grey saloon stood by the kerb, the best of several left out on the cobbles, and Bob stowed his guns well down behind the back seat before lighting a cigarette.

The streets were yours at six on a Sunday morning, flying through the cradle of a deadbeat world with nothing to stop you getting what fun and excitement you wanted. The one drawback to the .303 was that out of fifty bullets from the army he'd but twenty left, though if he rationed himself to a shot every Sunday there'd still be six months' sport for the taking. And you never knew: maybe he could tap his cousin in the Terriers for a belt of souvenirs.

He bounded through the traffic lights, between church and pub, climbing the smooth tarmac up Mansfield Road, then pouring his

151

headlights into the dip and heading north under a sky of stars. Houses fell endlessly back on either side, a gauntlet trying to cup him but getting nowhere. The wireless had forecast a fine day and looked like being right for a change, which was the least they could do for you. It was good to get out after a week cooped-up, to be a long-range hunter in a car that blended with the lanes. He was doing well for himself: wife and kids, a good toolsetting job, and a four-roomed house at fifteen bob a week. Fine. And most Sunday mornings he ranged from Yorkshire to Lincolnshire, and Staffordshire to Leicestershire, every map-point a sitting duck for his coolly sighted guns.

On the dot of six-thirty he saw Ernie by the Valley Road picture house. 'Hey up,' Ernie said as he pulled in. 'That was well timed.' Almost a foot taller than Bob, he loomed over the car dressed in an old mac.

'It's going to be fine,' Bob said, 'according to the radio.'

Ernie let himself in. 'The wireless's allus wrong. Spouts nowt but lies. I got welloes on in case it rains.'

They scooted up the dual carriageway. 'Is this the best you can do?' Ernie asked. 'You can fetch ninety out of this, I'm sure. 'Ark at that engine: purring like a she-cat on the batter.'

'Take your sweat,' Bob said. 'This is a mystery trip.'

Ernie agreed. 'I'm glad there's no racing on a Sunday. It's good to get out a bit like this.'

'It is, an' all. Missis well?'

'Not too bad. Says she feels like a battleship with such a big belly' – and went silent. Bob knew him well enough: he'd never talk just to be friendly; they could drive for an hour and he'd stay shut, often in an icy far-off mood that didn't give him anything to say or think of. They worked a dozen feet from each other all week, Bob on his precision jobs, Ernie watching a row of crankshaft millers. 'What guns you got then?' he asked.

Bob peered ahead, a calm and measured glance along the lit-up wastes of the road to Ollerton. 'A twelve-bore and a .303.'

'I wish you had,' Ernie laughed. 'You never know when you're going to need a .303 these days. Best gun out.'

'Keep your trap shut about it though,' Bob said. 'I got it in the army. I wouldn't tell you except that I know I can trust you by now.'

Maybe he wasn't joking, Ernie thought. Bob was clever with hands and brain, the stop-gap of the shop with micrometer and centre-lathe, a toolmaker who could turn off a candlestick or fag-lighter as soon as look at you. 'Do you mean it about a .303?'

Bob pulled into a lay-by and got out. 'Keep clear of the headlights,' he said, 'but catch this.' Ernie caught it, pushed forward the safety catch, the magazine resting in the net of his fingers. 'God Almighty! Anything up the spout?'

'I've a clip in my pocket. Strictly for rabbits' – Bob smiled, taking it back.

'A waste,' Ernie said. 'The twelve-bore would do. Mixermatosis has killed 'em all off, anyway.'

They drove on. 'Had it since I left the army,' Bob told him. 'The stores was in a chronic state in Germany at the end of the war. Found myself with two, so kept one. I have a pot-shot with it now and again. I enjoy hunting – for a bit o' recreation.'

Ernie laughed, wildly and uncontrolled, jerking excited shouts into the air as if trying to throw something out of his mouth, holding his stomach to stop himself doubling up, wearing down the shock of what a free-lance .303 meant. He put his arm around Bob's shoulder by way of congratulation: 'You'd better not let many people know about it, or the coppers'll get on to you.'

'Don't worry. If ever they search, it's a souvenir. I'd get rid of the bolt, and turn another off on the lathe when I needed it.'

'Marvellous,' Ernie said. 'A .303! Just the thing to have in case of a revolution. I hope I can get my hands on one when the trouble starts.'

Bob was sardonic: 'You and your revolution! There wain't be one in our lifetimes, I can tell you that.' Ernie had talked revolution to him for months, had argued with fiery puritanical force, guiding Bob's opinion from voting Labour to a head-nodding acceptance of rough and ready Communism. 'I can't see why you think there'll be a revolution though.'

'I've told you though,' Ernie said loudly. 'There's got to be some-thing. I feel it. We wok in a factory, don't we? Well, we're the backbone of the country, but you see, Bob, there's too many people on our backs. And it's about time they was slung off. The last strike we had a bloke in a pub said to me: "Why are you fellows allus on strike?" And I said to 'im: "What sort o' wok do you do?" And he said: "I'm a travelling salesman." So I said, ready to smash 'im: "Well, the reason I come out on strike is because I want to get bastards like yo' off my back." That shut 'im up. He just crawled back into his sherry.'

153

At dawn they stopped the car in a ladle of land between Tuxford and the Dukeries, pulling on to a grass verge by a gate. A tall hawthorn hedge covered in green shoots bordered the lane, and the bosom of the meadow within rose steeply to a dark skyline, heavy rolls of cloud across it. Ernie stood by the gate: 'The clouds smell fresh' – pulling his mac collar up. 'Think we'll get owt 'ere?'

'It's good hunting country,' Bob told him. 'I know for a fact.'

They opened flasks and tore hungrily into sandwiches. 'Here, have a swig of this,' Ernie said, pouring some into his own cup. 'It'll do you good.'

Bob held it to the light. 'What is it?'

'Turps and dash. Here's the skin off your lips.'

'Don't talk so loud. You'll chase all the wild life away. Not a bad drop, is it?'

'A rabbit wouldn't get far with a .303 at its arse.' A sort of loving excitement paralysed his fingers when he picked up the rifle: 'Can you get me one?'

'They don't grow on trees, Ernie.'

'I'd like one, though. For the next war. I'd just wait for somebody to try and call me up!' They leaned on the gate, smoking. 'Christ, when the Russians come I'll be liberated.'

'It's a good job everybody ain't like you,' Bob said with a smile. 'You're a rare 'un, yo' are.'

Ernie saw a movement across the field, beginning from the right and parting a diagonal line of grass, ascending towards the crest on their left. The light from behind showed it up clear and neat. 'See it?' he hissed, ramming a shell in the twelve-bore. Bob said nothing, noiselessly lifted the .303. No need to use that, Ernie thought. It'd bring a man down a mile off; a twelve-bore's good enough for a skinful of mixermatosis.

A sudden wind blew against the dawn, ruffling the line of their prey. Bob's eye was still on it: a single round went into the breech. 'I'll take it,' he said softly. It was already out of buck-shot from Ernie's twelve-bore. Both lost it, but said nothing. A lull in the wind didn't show it up. 'I expect it's a hare.'

Bob lowered his .303, but Ernie signalled him to be quiet: it seemed as if a match were lit in the middle of the field, a slow-burning brown flame moving cautiously through shallow grass, more erratic now, but still edging towards the crest. The cold, star-flecked sky needed only a slow half turn to bring full daylight. What the bloody hell is it? Ernie wondered. Fields and lane were dead quiet: they were kings of the countryside: no houses, no one in sight. He strained his eyes hoping to discover what it was. A squirrel? Some gingernut, anyway.

A smile came on to Bob's face, as when occasionally at work his patience paid off over some exacting job, a flange going into place with not half a thou' to spare. Now it was more heightened than that: a triumph of hunting. Two sharp ears were seen on the skyline, a hang-dog tail, a vulpine mouth breakfasting on wind – with Ernie's heart a bongo drum playing rhythms on his chest wall: a fox.

The air split open, and from all directions came a tidal wave of noise, rushing in on every ear but that to which the bullet had been aimed. Together they were over the gate, and speeding up the slope as if in a dawn attack. Gasping, Bob knelt and turned the dead fox over: as precise a job as he had ever done. 'I always get 'em in the head if I can. I promised one of the tails to a neighbour.'

'Ain't this the first fox you've shot, then?' Ernie couldn't fathom his quiet talk: a fox stone dead from a .303 happened once in a lifetime. They walked down the hill. 'I've had about half a dozen,' he said by the car door, dragging a large polythene bag from under the seat and stuffing the dead fox into it. 'From round here most on 'em. I'll knock off a bit and go to Lincolnshire next time.' The fox lay as if under a glass case, head bashed and tail without colour. 'It never stood a chance with a .303,' Ernie grinned.

He took the wheel going back, flying down lanes to the main road, setting its nose at Mansfield as if intent on cutting Nottinghamshire in two. Bob lounged behind using a pull-through on the .303. 'I've allus liked hunting,' he shouted to Ernie. 'My old man used to go poaching before the war, so we could have summat to eat. He once did a month in quod, the poor bastard. Never got a chance to enjoy real hunting, like me.'

'I want the next tail, for the kid that's coming,' Ernie said, laughing.

Bob was pleased with himself: 'You talk about revolution: the nobs around here would go daft if they knew I was knocking their sport off.'

It was broad daylight: 'Have another turps and dash,' Ernie said, 'you clever bleeder. You'll find the bottle in my haversack.'

The road opened along a high flat ridge through a colliery village, whose grey houses still had no smoke at their chimneys. Silent head-stocks to the left cowered above the fenced-off coppices of Sherwood Forest.

The Firebug

I smile as much as feel ashamed at the memory of some of the things I did when I was a lad, even though I caused my mother a lot of trouble. I used to pinch her matches and set fire to heaps of paper and anything I could get my eyes on.

I was no bigger than sixpennorth o' coppers, so's you'd think I wasn't capable of harming a fly. People came straight out with it: 'Poor little bogger. Butter wouldn't melt in his mouth.' But my auntie used to say: 'He might not be so daft as he looks when he grows up' – and she was right, I can see that now. Her husband had a few brains as well: 'He's quiet, nobody can deny it, but still waters run deep. I wouldn't trust him an inch.' At this the rest of the family got on to him and called him bully with neither sense nor feeling, said I was delicate and might not have long for this world – while I went on eating my way through a fistful of bread-and-jam as if I hadn't heard a dickybird and would last forever.

This match craze must have started when, still in leggings, I was traipsed downtown by my mother one day midweek. The streets weren't all that crowded and I held on to her carrier-bag, dragging a bit I should think, slurring my other hand along the cold glass of shop windows full of tricycles and forts for Christmas that I would never get – unless they were given to me as a reward for being good enough not to pinch 'em. As usual my mother was harassed to death (on her way to ask for a bit more time to pay off the arrears of 24 Slum Yard I shouldn't wonder) and I was grizzling because I couldn't share as much as I'd have liked in the razzle-dazzle of the downtown street.

Suddenly I left off moaning, felt the air go quiet and blue, as if a streak of sly lightning had stiffened everybody dead in their tracks. Even motor cars stopped. 'What's up, mam?' I said – or whined I expect, because I could only whine up to fourteen: then I went to work and started talking clear and proper, from shock.

Before she could tell me, a bloody great bell began clanging – louder

157

than any school or church call – bowling its ding-dong from every place at once, so that I looked quickly at the up-windows to wonder where it was coming from. I felt myself going white, knees quaking. Not that I was terrified. I was right in the middle of another world, as if the one and only door to it had a bell on saying PRESS, and somebody was leaning his elbow spot-on and drilling right into my startled brain.

The bells got louder, so's I couldn't any longer hope it was only the cops or an ambulance. It was something I'd never seen before nor dreamt of either: a flying red-faced monster batting along the narrow street at a flat-out sixty, as if it had been thrown there like a toy. Only this weighed a ton or two and made the ground shake under me, like a procession for the Coronation or something – but coming at top speed, as if a couple of Russian tanks were after its guts and shooting fire behind. 'What is it, mam? What is it?' I whined when it got quiet enough to speak.

'Only a fire,' she told me. 'A house is on fire, and they're fire-engines going to put it out.' Then another couple of engines came belting through the deadened street, both together it seemed, turning all the air into terrifying klaxons. I started screaming, and didn't stop until I'd gone down in a fit.

Mam and a man carried me into the nearest shop and when I woke up there was nothing but toys all around, so's I thought I was in heaven. To keep me calm the shopkeeper gave me a lead soldier which I was glad to grab, though I'd rather have had the toy fire-engine that caught at my sight as soon as I stood up. It was as if my eyes had opened for the first time since I was born: red with yellow ladders and blue men in helmets – but he turned me away to ask if I was all right, and when I nodded walked me back into the street out of temptation. I was a bit of a bogger in them days.

The long school holidays of summer seemed to go on for years. When I could scrounge fourpence I'd nip to the continuous downtown pictures after dinner and drop myself in one of the front seats, to see the same film over and over till driven out by hunger or God save the king. But I didn't often get money to go, and now and again mam would bundle me into the street so's her nerves could have a rest from my 'give-me-this-and-I-want-that' sort of grizzling. I'd be quite happy – after the shock of being slung out had worn off – to sit on the pavement making wrinkles in the hot tar with a spoon I'd managed to grab on my way through the kitchen, or drawing patterns with a piece of slate or matchstick. Other kids would be rolling marbles or running at rounders, or a string of them would scream out of an entry after playing hide and seek in somebody's backyard. A few would be away at seaside camp, or out in the fields and woods on Sunday treats, so it worn't as noisy as it might have been. I remember once I sat dead quiet all afternoon doing nothing but talking to myself for minutes at a time on what had happened to me in the last day or two and about things I hoped to do as soon as I got either money or matches in my fist – chuntering ten to the dozen as if somebody unknown to me had put a penny in the gramophone of my brain as they walked by. Other people passing looked at me gone-out, but I didn't give a bogger and just went on talking until the noise of a fire-engine in the distance came through to my locked-in world.

It sounded like a gale just starting up, an aeroplane of bells going along at ground level with folded wings, about ten streets off but far enough away to seem as if it was in another town behind the big white clouds of summer, circling round a dream I'd had about a fire a few nights ago. It didn't sound real, though I knew what it meant now, after my downtown fit a long time back in the winter. Hot sun and empty sky stopped it being loud I suppose, but my heart nearly fell over itself at the brass-band rattle, it went so fast – sitting in my mouth like a cough-drop or dollymixture getting bigger as the bells went on. Most of the other kids ran hollering to where the noise came from, even when I thought they were too far off for anybody else to hear, went clobbering up the street and round a corner until everywhere was quiet and empty except the bells now reaching louder all the time.

I wanted to join in the chase, fly towards fire and smoke as fast as my oversize wellingtons would take me, to see all them helmeted men with hatchets and ladders and hosepipes trying to stop the red flames but not managing so that the only thing left was a couple of cinders one on top of the other. And then I'd try to sneak up and blow the top one off. But I'd never be able to catch them, that much I knew as sure as God made little apples, so I waited till my face changed back from white to mucky and my blood stopped bumping, and went on playing tar games in the sun.

But sometimes I'd sit and hear the bells of a fire engine that none of the other kids would hear, would leave off playing and listen hard for it to come closer, hoping to see one swivel around the bend at the top of our street and pour down with its big nose getting closer – and if it did I wouldn't know whether to stick by and see what happened or run screaming in to mam and get her to hide me under the stairs. I was always hoping for a sweltering fire close by so that I could watch them trying to put it out – hope for one at the bike factory or pub or in some shop or other. But I just heard them now and again in my mind, sat (before I cottoned on to this) waiting for the others to hear it and run yelling to where it came from, but they didn't and then I knew it was just in me the bells had played. This was only on summer days though, as if the sun melted wax in my tabs and let me hear better than anybody else – even things that didn't happen at all.

But fire-engine fires were rare as five-pound notes, and up to then the nearest a big blaze ever came to our street was on Bonfire Night. They told us about Bonfire Night at school, about how this poor bloke Guy Fawkes got chucked on a fire because he wanted to blow up parliament, and I learned as well about the Great Fire of London where all the town got lit because everything was built of wood. What a sight that must have been! Thousands and thousands of houses going up like matchboxes. Still, I didn't like to think of people getting burnt to death, I do know that. I was terrified on it, and so was dad, and though he used to poke the fire cold out every night, and pull the rugs a long way back from the grate and set the chairs under the window, I was still worried in bed later in case a hot coal lit up again and walked to right across the room where the rugs were; or that somebody next door would go to sleep with his pipe lit and the first thing I'd know was a rubber hose slooshing water through the window and onto us four kids. I wouldn't even have heard the ding-dong-belling of the fire-engine I slept so deep – and that would have broken my heart.

On Bonfire Night fires were lit like cherry trees, two or three to a long street like ours, and the only thing I ever prayed for was that it wouldn't rain after the bigger lads got busy and set their matches under piles of mattresses, boxes and old sofas. The flames climbed so high by ten that house walls glowed and shone as if somebody had scrubbed them clean, and I used to go from one fire-hill to another eating my bread and jam and jumping out of the way when firecrackers got close. I was so excited the bread almost wouldn't go down, and my breath gulped as the warmth tried to ram itself through my throat when I went too near the fire.

If only flames like this blazed all winter, was my one big wish. But they didn't, my brain told me: they flared for one night, hands of fire waving hello and good-bye while we shouted and danced, then died to a glowing hump of grey ash for corporation carts to clear away like the bodies of big runover dogs next morning. Christmas was a letdown after these mountainous fires.

This Bonfire Night I stayed out till twelve hoping, now that everybody else had gone, for a last-minute flame to shoot up for one second and show its face only to me; but all that remained was the smell of fire-ash and gunpowder. Then in the dead quietness I heard the bell of a far-off fire-engine, flying down some empty street with bells full on, passing houses that were so quiet you might think God had gone before and like some fat publican shouted TIME in each. I looked at the fire again in the hope that it would flare and bring the distant engine to where I was, frightened a bit at the same time because I was on my own and would have nobody to stand with if it did. All I got for my waiting though was a spot of icecold rain on my arm, and the sound of another big drop burying itself with a hiss chock in the middle of the ash. And the fire-engine went tingling on till I couldn't hear it no more, off to some street where, I thought, they had a bigger fire than could ever be built in ours.

My first fires were nothing to speak of: baby ones built in the backyard with a single sheet of paper that burned out in half a second like celluloid, scattering like black butterflies at the draught of another kid. Mam clouted my tabhole and took the matches off me – to begin with – but realizing after a while how it kept me occupied at a time when she was hard-up for peace and quiet she let me play: a couple of old newspapers and half a dozen matches stopped me whining for an hour, which was cheap at the price. For mam was badly right enough, holding her heart all the time and blue in the face when anything harassed her, so that even if I'd wanted to make a row dad would have thumped me one.

So nobody bothered me and my midget fires, because they could see I wasn't doing no harm. One or two of the nosey parkers went as far as to tut-tut loud when they looked over the fence in passing and saw wisps of smoke floating in front of my eyes, but they soon got used to the sight of it and stopped pulling meagrims. They must have known mam knew I'd got the matches, and didn't want a row with her because she was still a wild fighter badly or not. I soon stopped making fires outside our back door, though, because one day I collected a whole tin of matchsticks off the street and they burnt so long in a bad wind that when mam smelled them up in the bedroom dad kicked the fire out with his boots and locked the gate on me. I'd only got a couple matches left, and had forgotten to snatch up the newspaper when dad's fist lifted me, so I was feeling hard done by as I sulked near the yard lavatories.

At the first nip of a cold rainspot I went into the nearest because if there was one thing I didn't like it was getting wet. It made me feel so miserable I could have put my head in the gas-oven or gone to the railway line and played with an express till I was bumped into, rolled over, and blacked-out for good. Whenever a spot of rain fell I sheltered in a shop doorway or entry until it stopped even if I was there for hours, because when rain landed on me it was like a shock of pins and needles sending me off my nut, as if every bit of me was a funny bone. And big rain was worse than ever, for it seemed to stick into me like falling penknives.

If I hadn't opened the door and gone in to get out of the rain I'd never have noticed the wad of newspapers stuffed behind the lavatory pipe. Two or three thick Sunday ones, the sort I liked because they'd got bigger letters on the front page than any. Once at Aunt Ethel's one of my grown-up cousins was reading the Sunday paper and his brother put a light to the bottom for a lark, and the other didn't know what was going off till flames reached the terrible headlines and started licking his nose. Or maybe he did, for he stayed as calm as if it had happened before: he was near the range and when the whole paper was in flames just leaned over and let it fall in the firegrate to burn itself out – as if he'd read all he wanted to anyway – and calmly asked his mam if there was any more tea in the pot. I laughed at the thought of it for days and days.

As soon as the heap of papers caught I ran out of the yard and rattled to the bottom of the street, went up to a gang of pals and played marbles so's nobody'd twig anything. I was so excited at what I'd done, and at listening all the time for a fire-engine (that I hoped somebody had called to come rumbling full tilt down the cobbled street with bells ringing), that I lost all my five marbles because I hardly knew what I was doing.

I didn't hear the bells of a fire-engine though: the only ringing that went on was all night in my ears after the old man had given me a good pasting when I went home a long time later. The whole yard talked about my fire-making for days: 'The little varmint wants taming. He's got too much on it.'

'You'd better lock your door when you go over the road shopping, or he might sneak in and send your home up in flames.'

'If I was his mother I'd take him to have his brains tested, though she can't do a sight at the moment, poor woman. So he gets neglected. I don't know, I don't.'

'He'd be better off at Cumberland Hall,' another woman said – which made me shiver when I heard it because Cumberland Hall's a stark cold place they send kids to as ain't got no mam and dad, where they hit you with sticks, feed you on bread and porridge, and get you up at six in the morning – or so mam once told me when I asked her about it. And it was a long way in the woods, she said, so's I knew if I got sent there I wouldn't be able to hear a fire-engine for years and years. Unless I made a fire on the sly and one had to come and put it out, then I might, but you couldn't depend on it because I knew by now that fire-engines didn't fly ding-donging to every bit of fire in the open air: they had to be big ones, which meant I was beginning to learn. Also I didn't want to get caught again and have my head batted, for as well as it hurting a long time afterwards it might send me daft or dead which would be terrible because then I wouldn't be able to make the fires or hear the engines.

So I knew I'd got to be careful next time and thought about how secret you could be if you did it in a wood and how big a fire it'd grow to if once it got going and the wind blew on it. I dreamed about it for weeks, saw yellow matchlight jump to paper, spread to dry leaves and twigs, climb to dead wood and branches and bushes and little trees and big trees, changing colour from red to blue and green and back to red as the big bell ding-donged through everything, racing from the main road. And all the firemen would just stand there, helmets off and scratching their heads because they wouldn't have a dog's chance of putting it out. I was sweating myself at the thought of it. Once on the pictures I saw where a big oil well caught fire, and they had to have dynamite to put it out. Dynamite! Think of that! Many's the pasting I got from the teacher at school for being half asleep in these daydreams. Once I was called out to the front for it, and as he was holding the strap up to let me have it, the thundery quiet of the classroom was filled with the roar of a fire-engine out on the boulevard. A few seconds went by as everybody wondered where it was going, and I thought the teacher would let me off at such a fire-awful noise, (though I don't know why he should), but the next thing I knew the strap had hit the outstretched palm of my hand as if a large stone had fallen on it from a thousand feet up. The bastard. I should have been listening to him telling us about how the army of some batchy king or other chopped up the senseless blokes of another army; then the two kings shook hands and signed a bit of paper to say things should be the same, but peaceful, and all the soldiers just sat in gangs around their little fires boiling soup and laughing, when all I thought of was how all these little fires could be joined together into a big blaze, as big as a mountain, with the two kings on top instead of that poor bloke called Guy Fawkes – just because he had a funny name.

I went off early one morning, a sunny day one Sunday, all by myself after a breakfast of tomatoes and bacon. Dad was glad to get rid of me because mam was still badly and the doctor was up with her. She hadn't spoken to me for a week because she'd been sleeping most of the time – and all I had to do, dad said, was keep out of her way and then she'd get better quicker.

Well, I was glad to because I'd got other things to brood on, walking down the street well into the wall with a box of matches and some folded paper in my pockets, my hand clutching the matches because I didn't want them to jump out – or fall through the hole that might get wider as I walked along. I'd be hard put to it to get any more if they did, because I hadn't got a penny to my name. Admitted, I could always stop and ask people to give me a match, but it was risky, because I'd often tried it, though sometimes I managed to beg one or two from a bloke who didn't care what I was up to and perhaps wanted me to smoke myself to death, or set Nottingham on fire. But mostly the people I asked either pushed me away and said clear off, or told me they were sorry but their matches were safeties and no good without a box. Now and again a bloke with safeties would give me a few anyway – wanting to help me and hoping I'd find some way to strike them, though I never did, unless I lit them with proper matches I latched on to later. The people I never asked were women, after the first one or two had threatened to fetch a copper, being clever enough to twig what I was up to.

Wind blew my hair about as I crossed the railway bridge by the station. Trolley buses trundled both ways and mostly empty, though even if I'd had a penny I'd still have walked, for walking my legs off made me feel I was going somewhere, strolling along though not too slow and enjoying the faces of fresh air that met me by the time I got out to the open spaces of Western Boulevard. I was feeling free and easy, and hoped a copper wouldn't stop me and ask what I was doing with paper and matches sticking out of my pockets. But nobody bothered me and I turned down from the bridge and onto the canal bank, looking in deep locks now and again, at the endless bottoms of water, as if the steep sides of the smooth wall still went on underneath – to the middle of the earth as far as I knew. A funny thought came to me: how long would it take for this canyon with water at the bottom to be filled to the brim with the fine and flimsy ash from cigarettes, only that? I sat on a lock gate and wondered: how many people need to smoke how many fags for how many years? Donkey's years, I supposed. I'd be an old man on two sticks by then. Even teachers at school wouldn't be able to work that sum out. I stood up and had a long pee down into the smooth surface, my pasty face in the mirror of it shivered to bits when the first piss struck.

After a good while of more walking I cut off along a lane at the next bridge leading towards the wood I'd set my heart on: a toy for Christmas. I was excited, already heard fire-engines crossing the sky, bells going off miles away, a sound that thrilled me even though I did know I was hearing things. The wheat was tall, yellow and dusty-looking over hedges and gates, bushes so high along the lane that sometimes I couldn't see the sky. Faded fag packets and scorched newspaper had been thrown among nettles and scrub by lads and courting couples out from Nottingham, for the fields weren't all that far off from the black and smothercating streets. My teeth still felt funny at the screams of tree-trunks from Sunday overtime at the sawmill not far off, though after a while I couldn't hear anything at all, except the odd thrush or blackbird nipping about like bats trying to get their own shadows in their beaks. I'd been out here a time or two with pals looking for eggs in birds' nests but I wasn't interested in that any more because my uncle once caught me with some and told me it was wicked and wrong to rob birds of their young 'uns.

So I walked by the hedge, keeping well down till I got to a gap. It was dim and cool in the wood, and so lonely that I'd have been frightened if I hadn't a pocketful of paper and matches to keep me company. Bushes were covered in blackberries, and I stopped now and again to take my pick, careful not to scratch myself or eat too many in case I got the gut ache when I went to bed at night.

It was long and narrow, not the sort of wood you could go deep into, so I jumped over a stream and found the middle quick enough, a clearing, more or less, with a dry and dying bush on one side that looked just ready for a fire. I worked like a galley slave, piling up dead twigs and leaves over my bit of paper that soon you could hardly see. I wondered about the noise but what could I do? and anyway soon forgot my worry and went on working. I knew it must be past dinner-time when I stood back to look at my bonfire heap. Sweating like a bull (though nothing to how them trees would be sweating in a bit, I grinned) I measured the chances of a fire-engine fire: the bush was sure to light and so would the two small trees on either side, but unless there was a good wind the main trees would be hard put to it.

The first match was slammed out by the wind that blew strong over my shoulder as if it had been lurking there specially; the head of the second fell off before I could get under the paper; the third-time lucky one caught a treat, was like a red, red robin breaking out of its shell, and I soon had to stand back to keep the burning blazes off my hand. I wanted to put it out at first: the words nearly choked me; 'Stread on it. Kick it to bits.' I twisted my hands up in front of me, but couldn't move, just stood there like the no good tripehound dad often called me (and which I dare say I was) until the smoke made me step further back – and back I went until my head scraped into a big-barked tree. The noise of the fire must have been what frightened me: it was as hungry as if it had got teeth, went chewing its way up into the air like a shark in Technicolor. A stone of blood settled over my heart, but smoke and flame hypnotized me, stood me there frozen and happy, rubbing my hands yet wanting to put it out, but not being able to any more than I could kill myself.

I didn't know fires could grow like that. My little ones had always gone out, shrunk up to black bits and flew into the air when I set half a breath against it. But then, that was only true with a scrap of news-paper on an asphalt yard. This was in a wood, and fire took to it like a kid to hot dinners: it was a sheet of red flame and grey smoke, a choking wall and curtain that scared me a bit, because I was back to life, as if big hands would reach out and grab me in for good and all. Like my uncle had said hell was – though I never believed him till now.

166

It was time to run. I sped off like a rabbit, scratched and cindered as my ankles caught on thorns and sharp grass. The hammer-and-tongs of a fire-engine were a long way from me now, and I was a ragged-arsed thunderbolt suddenly tangled in a high bush, stuck like a press-stud that fought a path out, and went on again lit-up and cursing. At the edge of the wood I slowed down, and halfway to the lane looked back, expecting to see a sheet of fire and smoke bending out over the trees with flags flying and claws sharp.

But nothing. I could have burst into a gallon of tears. Nothing: not a butterfly of smoke, not an ant of flame. Maybe I'm too close to see, I thought. Or should I run back and stoke up again, blow it and coax, pat and kick it into life? But I went on. If the wood caught fire, as I still hoped, who'd get the fire-engines? And if nobody did would I hear and see them? Being as how I'd caused the fire I had to get miles away quick without being spotted, so how could I poke my nose in at the nearest copperbox and bawl out there was a fire in Snakey Wood and not risk getting sent to an Approved School for my good deed? I wished I'd thought of this already, but all I could hope for now was that some bloke at the local sawmill or a field-digger from the farm would twig things while I wasn't too far off and get the fire-engine on its way so's I could run and see it.

By the lane I turned, and there it was: no fire yet but a thin trail of smoke coming up like a wavy blue pole above the crowded trees. I'd expected it all to be like it was on the pictures, boiling away and me having to run for my life, with a yellow-orange carpet of flame snap-dragging at my heels, but it just showed how different things were to what you expected. Not that I didn't know they always were, but it still came as a shock I don't mind admitting. The wood was burning, which was a start, and though I couldn't see any flame yet I didn't wait for it either, but dodged under the hedgebottom and crossed the open field to the big outstanding arm-beam of a canal lock. I puffed and grunted to get it shut, then crept across on all fours – using it as a bridge – to the towing path on the other side. Nobody saw me: a man was humped over the bank fishing a bit further down, but he never even turned to see who was passing. Maybe he ain't got a licence to fish, I thought, and no more wants to be seen than I do – which I can easy understand.

The wind blew stronger and the sun still shone but I daren't look back towards my pet wood which I hoped by now was crackling away to boggery. Walking along I looked like a fed-up kid out for an airing who was too daft and useless to have been in mischief – but because it seemed as if butter wouldn't melt in my mouth didn't mean I hadn't set a fire off in which butter wouldn't stand an earthly. I didn't want anybody to twig anything though, as I walked up to the main road and into a world of people and traffic where I wasn't so noticeable any more.

Back along the canal, far-off thick smoke was going up to the bubble-blue sky, black low down as if from an oil-well, but thinning a bit on top. It was burning all right, though people walking by didn't seem to think much was amiss. I sat on the bridge wall, unable to take my eyes off it, rattled a bit that people didn't turn to open their mouths and wonder what I was looking at. I wanted to shout out: 'Hey missis, hey mester, see that smoke? It's Snakey Wood on fire, and I done it' – but somehow the words wouldn't come, though God knows I remember wanting them to.

I started off towards home, one minute happy that I'd brought off my own big fire, and the next crippled by a rotten sadness I couldn't explain, hands in pockets as I walked further and further away from the column of my fire and smoke that, if you think about it, should have made me the happiest kid in Radford.

From this changeable mood I was neither one thing nor the other as I went downhill towards the White Horse – almost home, having nothing else in my head but a shrill-whistled Al Jolson tune. Then into my ears and brain – through the last barbed-wire of my whistling – came the magic sound I'd longed all day to hear. The air went blue and electric, as it sometimes does before a terrible sheet-ripping thunderstorm, and cars at the crossroads stopped and waited, drivers winding their windows down to look out. My mouth opened and I stared and stared, the only picture in my mind for the next few seconds being that of the last Bonfire Night but one, in which I'd wandered off on my own up Mitchell Street and come across the best fire I'd ever seen. It was already twice as high as any man, and impossible to stoke anything else on top. A pile of mattresses still had got to be burned and a couple of big lads dragged them one at a time up on top of a chapel roof by whose side-walls the fire had been lit. When all of the two dozen bug-eaten mattresses were stacked high on the slates, the lads swung each one out, perched up there like demons in the blaze of the rattling flames, and let them crash down one by one into the very middle of the red bed. Everybody said the church would go, but it didn't, and when I saw that it wouldn't I walked away.

My eyes were open again on broad daylight, and from the top of the opposite hill sounded the bells I remembered hearing that very first time as a kid when downtown with mam. But this time there were more bells than I'd ever heard; a big red engine, fresh out of the vast sheds of town and coming between the shops and pubs, shot the crossroads as if out of a flashgun, all bells at full throttle so that two blokes talking outside the pub couldn't make themselves heard and stopped till it had gone by. But they still couldn't start talking again, because another engine was almost right behind.

My legs trembled and I thought my ears would fall away from my head. One of the two men looked so hard at me that his face swam, and I thought: What's he making himself go all blurred like that for? – but when my ankles became heavy as lead and my legs above them turned into feathers I knew it was my eyes swimming, that I was about to cave in again like I'd done that long time ago with mam. I took a step forward, screwing my eyes and opening them, then held on the window ledge for a second, until I knew I'd be all right, and was able to stand another engine bursting in and out of my brain; then another.

Four! No sooner could I have shouted with joy, than I found it hard to stop myself letting the tears roll like wagons out of my eyes. I'd never seen four fire-engines before. The whole wood must be in flame from top to bottom, I thought, and was sorry now I hadn't stayed close by to watch, wondering if I should go back, because I knew that even four engines wouldn't get a fire like that down before tonight or even later. All that work and walking gone for nothing, I cursed, as another engine broke the record of the last one down the hill. I waved as it shot by, yet felt as if I'd had my fill of fire-engines for a long while.

Six passed altogether. By this time I was sobbing, almost stone-dead and useless. 'What's up, kid?' one of the two men said to me.

'I'm frightened,' I managed to blurt out. He patted me on the shoulder. 'There's no need o' that. The fire's miles away, up Wollaton somewhere, by the look on it. It wain't come down 'ere, so you needn't worry.' But I couldn't stop. It was as hard to dry up as it had been for me to start, and I went on heaving as if the end of the world was just around the corner.

'Do you live far?' he asked.

'I'm frightened,' was all I said, and he didn't know what to do, wished by this time he'd left me alone: 'Well, you shouldn't be frightened. You're a big lad now.'

I walked towards home along Eddison Road, my eyes drying up with every step, the great stone in my chest not jumping about so much. Six fire-engines made it a bigger day than Christmas, each red engine being better than a Santa Claus, so that even after my fire-bugging I never got over red being my favourite colour. When I went in through the scullery dad looked happy, and such a thing was hard for me to understand.

'Come on my old lad,' he said. I'd never seen him so good-tempered. 'Where've you bin all this time, you young bogger? It's nearly tea time.' He pulled a chair to the table for me: 'Here you are, get this down you. You must be clambed to death' – took a plate of dinner out of the oven. 'I thought you'd got lost, or summat. Your mam's bin asking for you.'

'Is she all right then, dad?'

'She's a bit better today,' he smiled. 'I expect we'll pull her through yet' – which I was so glad to hear that it made me twice as hungry, as if the fire had burned a hole in me as well as Snakey Wood, because a whole load of food was needed to fill it. Dad brought in the teapot, and I drank two mugs of that as well. 'My Christ,' he said, sitting opposite me with a fag on and enjoying the sight of me eating, 'I heard a lot of fire-engines going by just now. Some poor bogger's getting burned out of house and home by the sound of it.'

Nobody knew who started that big fire all them years ago, and I know now that nobody will ever care, because Snakey Wood has gone forever, even better flattened than by any fire. Its trees have been ripped up and soil pressed down by a housing estate that spread over it. As it turned out I only burned down half, according to the *Post*, and though everybody in our yard knew I was a bit of a firebug nobody thought for a minute it might have been me who set fire to Snakey Wood. Or if they did, nowt was said.

In the next load of weeks and months I lost all interest in lighting fires. Even the sound of a fire-engine rattling by didn't bother me as much as it had. Maybe it was strange, me giving it up all of a sudden like that, but I just hadn't got the heart to put match to paper, couldn't be bothered in fact, after mam got better – which happened about the same time. I expect that big fire satisfied me, because whatever I did again would need to be bloody huge to get more than six engines called out to it. In any case there was something bigger than me to start fires, for after a couple of years came an air raid from the Germans and I remember getting out of the shelter at six one morning when the all-clear had gone and standing in the middle of our street, seeing the whole sky red and orange over the other side of Nottingham – where, I heard later, two whole factories were up in flames. They burned for days, and I wanted to go off and see them but dad wouldn't let me. People said that fifty fire-engines had to come before that was put out – spinning into Nottingham from Mansfield and Derby and all over everywhere.

And not long afterwards I was fourteen, went to work and started courting, so what was the use of fires after that?

The Magic Box

I

Fred made his way towards the arboretum bench.

Though it was well gone eleven he hadn't yet clocked in, and wouldn't, either. There were some things a man would be glad to work for, but that morning his head was full of thoughts that would have got him hung – if anything could have been gained by swinging.

He sat down, drew two porkpies from their cellophane wrappers and exposed them to daylight. Half closing his eyes (as if his palate were up there and not in his mouth) he bit into the first pie: the meat wasn't bad, but the pastry was chronic. When the crumpled bag settled in the prison of the half-filled litter basket he chewed through a prolonged stare towards the ornamental pond and park wall, hearing the breathtaking gear-change of traffic chewing its way up the hill outside.

Morning was the worst time. He hated going to bed, and he hated getting up even more, but since these two actions were necessary for life and work he preferred getting up – by himself. God alone knew why Nan had risen with him this morning, but she had, and that, as much as anything else, had been the cause of the row that had burst over them – from her. In six years of marriage he'd learned that to argue at breakfast always led to a blow-up. It was better to argue in the evening (if you had any choice) because sooner or later you went to bed.

Though in many ways pleasant, half a day off work wasn't the sort of thing he could keep from Nan, since she saw his wage-packet on Friday night. Not that she nosed into everything, but her skill at housekeeping demanded that each bob and tanner be accounted for. He would be laughed at by his workmates if they knew, though many of them lived by the same arrangement, and that was a fact. In any case how could they find out? Nan wouldn't drive by in a speaker van and let

173

them know, for she often claimed: 'My place is to go shopping and clean the house, not to wait for you outside that stinking factory. When we go to the pictures on Friday you can get me a place in the queue, and I'll meet you there.'

He only hoped that one day Nan would see him as the good man from the many bad, a bloke who didn't deserve to be bossed and tormented so much. But she hated the factory, as if to punish him not only for having married her but also for stipulating soon after that she should stop going out to work. He'd only insisted on it because he loved her, thinking she wanted him to press her on this and prove even greater love than he was capable of. Not many would have loved a woman enough to see it that way. But since the gilt had worn off she became bitter about having left work at all, hinting that staying on would have made her a forewoman by now. In fact she had only offered to give in to his manly insistence because she wanted him to see that she loved him more than was considered normal, and he had been blind and selfish enough to take her up on it.

'Well' – now wanting some peace in the house – 'why don't you go and ask them to set you on again if that's the way you feel? I'm not a bleddy mind reader.'

This took the row to a higher pitch, as he'd known it would, but he hadn't the sense to sit down and say nothing, or walk out of the house whistling. 'How can I?' she called. 'I'd have to start again on a machine. I'd never get back to the old position I had when I was loony enough to take note o' you and pack my good job in.'

He didn't know how it had begun that morning. He didn't suppose she did, either. He would like to think of her as still brooding on it, but not likely. No sooner had the door closed than she'd smashed the cup he'd drunk from, though he'd bet his last dollar she was out shopping now, and laughing with other women as if there'd been no quarrel at all.

It was fine enough weather to make everyone forget their troubles. Autumn sun warmed the green banks of the park, ants and insects proliferating among juicy-looking blades of grass. Small birds fed at a piece of his cast-off porkpie beyond the diamond wirespaces of the litter basket, like a dozen thumbnail sketches that had come to life. Two pigeons joined the feast, enormous in comparison to the thrushes, but there was no bullying. Both pigeons and thrushes seemed unaware of any difference in size, and the fact that both wanted to get at the same piece of pie was, after all, a similarity.

He smoked a cigarette. A young man walked by with a back-combed suicide-blonde in a black mac, who looked as if she hadn't had a square meal for a month, and she was saying angrily: 'I'll bleddy-well nail him when I see him, I bleddy-well will, an' all' – with such threat and vengeance that Fred felt sorry for whoever this was meant for. The world thrives on it, he thought, but I don't, and in any case life's not always like that. Bad luck and good luck: it's like a swing on a kids' playground, always one thing or the other. We've had more than our share of the bad though, by bloody Christ we have, too much to think about, and the last bit of good luck was almost more trouble than it was worth. He thought back on it, how a year ago, at the start of the football season, a cheque had come one morning for two hundred and fifty quid, and a few hours later his mug (and Nan's) was grinning all over the front of the newspaper. She enjoyed it so much that it certainly didn't occur to him to remind her of all the times she had threatened to burn the daft football coupons on which he had wasted so much time and money. No, they got in a dozen quarts of beer and a platter of black puddings, and handed manna around to anyone with the grace or avarice to drop in. The man from the *Post* had asked: 'What are you going to do with the money?' Fred was surprised at so much bother when all he felt was disappointment at not hitting the treble chance and raking in a hundred thousand. Two hundred and fifty nicker seemed so little that before Nan could spin some tale of intent to the reporter Fred butted in: 'Oh, I expect we'll just split it and use it as pocket-money.' Which was duly noted in heavy type for the day's editions (POOLS WIN: POCKET-MONEY FOR NOTTINGHAM COUPLE) so prominently displayed that though Nan had the spirit left to tell Fred he should have kept his trap shut she hadn't the nerve to make him do anything else with the money but what he'd said he would for fear of being known to defy the bold public print of a newspaper that, as far as Nan knew, everyone had read.

To spend a hundred quid in one fell bout of shopping demanded bravery, and Fred was the sort in which, if bravery existed, it was anything but spontaneous. Still, he had seen things worth buying which, so far, was more than could be said for Nan. Walking around town Fred had come across an all-wave ex-army wireless receiver staring him out from behind plate glass, the exact communications set he'd worked during his war stint with the signals in Egypt. It stayed in the same window for months, being, he surmised, too expensive for anyone to step in and say: 'I want it.' So he took his time in sparking up courage to walk by that array of valves and morse tappers, to make a purchase by pointing between heart beats towards the window.

Many afternoons he'd stood at the window fixed by the magic black box of the communications receiver, and at so many long and regular absences Nan began to wonder whether he had set himself up with a piece of fancy work met in the factory – and she said as much when he once came home looking piqued and sheepish. He still hadn't been able to walk in and buy the radio, and so felt poor enough in spirit to go straight over and kiss her: 'Hello, my angel, how are we today?'

She turned her face away. Half a dozen books were stacked on the sideboard after a visit to the library. 'What's the idea? What do you want?'

'I don't want anything.'

'You'd better not, either, until you tell me where you go and what you get up to every Saturday afternoon.'

So that was what he'd seen boiling up, something so far from his mind that he could only say: 'I've bin down town looking around the shops.'

She pulled the curtains across and set the table, while Fred dug himself in the fireside chair, watching her as she worked. Her face had altered, become sterner in the last year or two, as if it had done enough battle with the world since Ivor had been drowned. But at thirty she was still good-looking, pretty almost, with her small even features and smooth skin. Her face was round and pleasantly fleshed, her eyes cool and outgiving when she was not anguished or perturbed. He smiled as she reached into the crockery cupboard: the best might be yet to come. How can she think I'd ever look at another woman? We've been through a lot together, the worst of it being the terrible way that Ivor went. If there's anything worse than her blaming me for him having fallen into that canal while reaching for a batch of tadpoles, it's her blaming herself, which I know she does even though it was three years ago and an accident. To think we paid that batchy girl half a crown every time she took him out, and she let this happen. My first thought on hearing he'd been killed like that was: 'The daft little bogger. Wait till I get my hands on him. I'll give him what for.' I couldn't believe it then, but I can now, just about.

'Have you been looking at the shops thinking how to spend your football money?' she asked in a more amiable voice, passing a cup of tea. They'd married on his demob leave in forty-six, after a mere week of kisses five years before, and four hundred letters in which by an inexhaustible permutation every aspect of common romantic love had been exchanged between them. Distance had made both hearts grow fonder, and out of sight out of mind had been disproved, apart from the long letters, by a frequent transmission of photographic images on which were stamped the thousand proofs of far-off love that kept Fred and Nan alive for each other. It was as if they were married after the first three months apart, as if they had already spent a honeymoon at Matlock and been wrenched from it by the first year, and had been long settled into an unthinking matrimonial rut by the fourth. They wrote of houses and work and children, and by the time they stood outside the church posing for their first photo together Fred anyway felt that the marriage about to begin was a plain print of black and white on positive paper, as opposed to the flimsy and transient negative of the preceding years.

Nan didn't see it like this, found it necessary to distinguish between the correspondence course and her new full status as a housewife, became more competent than Fred at tackling problems after returning from a week at Matlock. To go shopping – pale, young and full of thought – in the raw fog of a December morning and come home to see that the fire had died, brought reality closer than Fred's daily dash to his factory incarceration in which machines warmly hummed and men baited him still on his recent honeymoon. Through the war Nan had stayed in a cold and exacting climate, while Fred had picked dreamily at radio sets in his monastic army life. Fascinated by the Nile Valley, he had ventured with his pals on a trip to the Great Pyramid, and his lean young unsure face looked down from the high back of a camel in a Box Brownie snapshot sent to Nan who, though stuck with the hardships of air-raids and rationing, saw him as adventuring around wild desert with an independence boding good for when they were married.

Not that she'd had much to complain about; in fact during her pregnancy Fred was as good as gold – she told her mother. And when Ivor came along he was even better, so she was now in the position of knowing that something was wrong yet not being able to complain, a state for which she couldn't but blame him, and which led to frenzied unreasonable quarrels which he could only define as 'temper' and blame on her.

'You're always curious about how I'm going to spend my share of the football money,' he said, 'but you haven't got rid of your whack yet. What are you going to do with it?' Answers to this question lacked venom, for money was now the only discussable topic which did not disturb the unstable bed of their emotions. She looked up from the newspaper: 'I haven't thought about it much, though I daresay I shall one of these days.'

A waterhen went out from the nearest bank, going as smoothly over the water as if drawn by a piece of cotton pulled by an invisible boy on the other side. Its head with button-eye and yellow beak was perfectly proud and still, and the green and blue back-feathers were comparable to colours made by flames appearing on the surface of a fire that had acted dead and out. The sun was good, and he didn't intend going to work until after dinner-hour, even if it meant another big row with Nan. The sound of machinery would cripple all reflection, and its manufacturing teeth pulling him back like a bulldog to earning a living for himself, Nan, and a possible future kid, seemed appalling in this unexpected sunshine – just as did the idea of going home to Nan again after their awful purposeless scrap of the morning.

It was the first time such a thing had happened, and it gnawed at his peace of mind because he'd had no intention of pushing her back so hard against the sofa. His hand had left the hot side of the cup and collided with her before he could do anything about it. It frightened him. If only I'd done it deliberately, known what was in me. The gone-out stare in her face drove him from the house, and he doubted whether he'd get back into it. Then again maybe she'd have forgotten it by evening, which would only go to show how much effect these rows had on her. He wasn't even sure he wanted to get back into the house anyway. Out of it the pain was less, and sitting in the park having eaten two porkpies and a thimble of sunshine sent it right away except for occasional stabs of the memory knife.

He walked through the main gate, towards the radio shop in the middle thoroughfare of the driving city. His football winnings took on value at last, a lump sum of over a hundred pounds to be handed in for a high-class radio set that would put him in touch with the short-wave world, give him something to do and maybe stop him being such a bastard to Nan. If he ordered it now the shop van would deliver it to-morrow. And after the dinner-hour he'd go back to work, otherwise, with it being Friday, he would get no wages.

II

Earphones on, he sat alone in Ivor's room, tuned-in to the Third Programme like a resistance radio operator receiving from abroad instructions that were the life blood of his cause. A fastidious voice was speaking unintelligibly on books and, as if not getting his money's worth, Fred clicked on to short wave and sent the needle rippling over hundreds of morse stations. Sounds chipped and whistled like clouds of tormented birds trying to get free, but he fixed one station and, as if from the fluttering of wings pinned firm at the middle by the hair-thin tuning needle, he deciphered its rhythm as: MEET ME TILBURY DOCK THURSDAY 24TH STOP AM DYING TO BE WITH YOU AGAIN ALL MY LOVE DARLING – MARY.

Alistair Crossbanks, 3 Hearthrug Villas, Branley was the lucky man, yet not the only one, since Fred took several more such messages. They came from sea-liners and went to waiting lovers who burned with the anguish of tormented separation – though he doubted whether any had spanned the same long time as Nan and himself before they were married. But the thought of ships steaming through a broadly striped sea at its sudden tropical darkening caused him to ignore further telegrams. He pictured a sleek liner in a thousand miles of ocean, a great circle bordering its allotted speed as, day after day, it crawled on an invisible track towards Aden or Capetown. He felt its radio pulse beating softly in his ear, as if by listening he had some control of it, and the remoteness of this oceanic lit-up beetle set off his own feeling of isolation in this sea-like suburb spreading in terraces and streets around his room.

The room had belonged to Ivor before he had been killed. Wallpaper of rabbits and trees, trains and aeroplanes, suggested it, as well as the single bed and the cupboard of toys that, even so long afterwards, neither had the heart to empty. Ivor had dark hair and brown eyes, and up to the age of four had been sharp and intelligent, thin, voracious and bright, all running and fighting, wanting and destroying. Yet for several months before slipping into the cold pocket of the canal he had turned back from this unnatural liveliness as if, not having such life responded to, the world had failed to get through to him, to make touch with his spirit in a way he could understand. Fred couldn't even regret having ill-treated him – that anyway would have made him easier remembered. All he saw was his wild boy breaking up an alarm clock and screaming off into a corner when the bell jangled his unready ears. But the lasting image of Ivor's face was one of deprivation, and this was what Fred could not explain, for it wasn't lack of food, clothes, toys, even money that gave this peculiar look, but an expression – now he saw it clearly – bound into Ivor's soul, one that would never let him respond to him.

He threw the master switch, and sat in evening silence, overpowered by this bleak force of negative feedback. Trust me to blame an innocent dead kid for what could only have been my fault and maybe Nan's. Ships were moving over untroubled oceans, set in such emptiness and warmth that for the people on them the tree of ecstasy was still a real thing. He switched on and, by the hairsplitting mechanism of the magic box, such poems were extractable out of the atmosphere. Another telegram from ELIZABETH said HOPE YOU BOOKED US A ROOM STOP CAN'T WAIT, and to break such torment he turned to news agency Tass explaining some revolutionary method of oil drilling in the Caucasus – a liquid cold chute of morse that cleared all passion from his mind.

He stayed undisturbed in Ivor's room, knowing that Nan would sit feasting at the television until calling him down for supper at half-past nine. He felt strange tonight; a bad tormenting cold depressed him: at such times his senses were connected to similar bad colds in the past, and certain unwrapped scenes from them hit him with stunning vividness.

Egypt was a land of colds, brought on by a yearly inundation of the Nile widening its valley into a sea of water and mud. Triangular points of the dark brown pyramids that reared beyond appeared sordid, like old jettisoned cartons fallen somehow in such queer shapes, and looking from this distance as if, should a prolonged breeze dry them of rain and flood-water, a more violent wind might uproot and lose them in the open desert like so much rubbish. In Cairo he had been a champion at morse, writing it at thirty-two words a minute and reading it at thirty-six. His brain, perfect for reception, drew in streams of morse for hour after hour and jerked his fingers to rapid script with no thought barrier between, work from which other less dedicated operators were led glassy-eyed and muttering to some recuperation camp by the blistering bonny banks of the Suez Canal. Fred enjoyed his fame as speed king, which, though pre-supposing a certain yoga-like emptiness of mind, demanded at the same time a smart brain and a dab hand. Yet in nothing did he look speedy: his sallow face made him seem always deep in slow thoughts beyond the understanding of his noisier pals – who were less efficient as radio men. Their respect for him was for his seriousness as much as for an uncommon rate of morse, which must have been so because even those in the cookhouse, to whom signalling prowess meant nothing, didn't bawl so sharply when a gap lay between Fred and the plate-filling man ahead. He was a priest of silence among blades of bed-tipping and boozing, singing and bawling and brothel-going. Some who didn't muck in were subjected at least to apple-pie beds, but Fred was on good terms even without trying. He was somehow found congenial, and would often have tea brought back for him from the mess by someone who came off watch at a late hour. When Fred returned this favour it was even more appreciated for being unexpected.

Mostly he would sit by himself in the library writing long letters to Nan, but the one friend he made was flown up one day from Kenya in the belly of a Mosquito fighter-bomber – which dropped its extra fuel tanks like turds somewhere over the desert. The shortage of good operators was so desperate (at a time of big offensive or retreat – nobody could ever tell which, since all differences were drowned in a similar confusion) that Fred was working a hundred hours a week. Not that he felt shagged by it, but the Big Battle had started and another man was needed, so in stepped Peter Nkagwe, a tall cheek-scarred black African from Nairobi – freshly changed into clean pressed khaki drill and smiling a good afternoon boys as he entered the signals office. The sergeant assigned him a set, and Fred amazed, then envious, saw his long-fingered hands trembling the key like a concert pianist at an evenness and speed never before seen.

Peter Nkagwe was no ascetic sender and receiver like Fred, but smiled and looked around as he played the key with an accurate, easy, show-off proficiency. He not only read Reuter's cricket scores from Australia but, which was where Fred failed, his fingers were nimble enough to write them down, so that his sheets of neat script went from hand to hand around the base until falling apart.

One day Fred called over, words unrehearsed, ignited from such depth that he didn't even regret them after he'd spoken: 'You beat out them messages, mate, like you was at a tom-tom.'

Peter, unflinching, finished the message at his usual speed. He then took off his earphones and stood over Fred in silence.

Fred was uncomfortable at the length of it: 'Lost owt?'

'There's a look in your eyes, MATE,' Peter said, 'as if your head's full of shit.' He went back to his radio, and from then on Fred's signalling championship was divided. They became friends.

Night after night at his communications receiver, Fred hoped to hear messages from his old HQ unit that, though long closed down, would magically send the same signals rippling between familiar stations. He might even pick up the fast melodious rhythms of Peter Nkagwe, that vanished ghost of a friend who, somewhere, still sat keying out indispensable messages whose text and meaning, put into code and cypher by someone else, were never made known to him. He turned the dial slowly, hoping to recognize both callsign and sending prowess of his old friend. It was impossible, though much time at the set was spent shamefaced in this way as if, should he try hard and stay at it long enough, those lost voices would send out tentacles and pull him back to the brilliant sun-dazzle of the Mokattam Hills.

His lean face, and expert hands moving over the writing-pad, were set before his multi-dialled altar, the whole outlined by a tassel-shaded table lamp. If I'd had this radio in Ivor's day, he laughed, the little bogger would have been at it till the light didn't shine and the valves packed in. Talk about destruction! 'Destruction, thy name is Ivor!' He remembered him, as if he were downstairs drinking tea, or being bathed in front of the fire, or gone away to his grandma's and due back next week. Anything mechanical he'd smash. He took a day on a systematic wipe-out of the gramophone, then brought the pieces to Fred, who suggested he put them together again. Ivor tried (I will say that for him) but failed, and when Fred mended it he was so overjoyed at the record spinning loud and true once more that he treated it as one thing to stay henceforth free of his hammer.

Ivor with a round, empty-eyed happiness, took huge bites of bread, and wiped jamstains down his shirt. Fred couldn't keep the sarcasm from his voice when telling him to stop, so that the bites had changed to tiny, until Fred laughed and they returned to big again, relaxing the empty desperation of his tough face. Such memories were buried deep, going down like the different seams and galleries of a coalmine. In the few months before his birth Ivor had moved inside Nan, kicking with life that had been distinct enough to wake Fred at night – and send him back to sleep smiling.

The small lamp gave one-tenth light, leaving most of the room in darkness. Fixed at the muttering radio and reaping an occasional message out of the air with his fast-moving hook of a pencil, Fred felt his mind locked in the same ratio, with that one-tenth glimmer unable to burst like a bomb and explode the rest of himself into light. He composed silent questions about Ivor, like sending out telegrams that would get no answer. Why was I born? Why didn't I love him so that he stayed alive? Could I love anybody enough to make them stay alive and kicking? Would it have made any difference if I'd loved him even more than I did? He couldn't lift the dominating blackness from his brain, but struggled to free himself, ineffectually spinning the knobs and dials of his radio, fighting to keep even the one-tenth light in his consciousness.

He opened the radio lid and peered in at the valves, coloured lights of blue flame deep in bulbs as if he had cultivated in his one-tenth light a new shape of exotic onion. Thoughts passed through his mind, singly and in good order, though the one just gone was never remembered – only the sensation remained that it had been. He tried to recall the thought or picture slipping from his mind in order to lynchpin it to the one now pushing in – which might, he hoped, be seen to have some connection to the one following. It turned out to have nothing in common at all.

'Never mind, sweetheart,' I said, when Ivor was drowned. 'Never mind' – rocking her back to sense. But she turned on him, words burning now as if he had taken them down in morse: 'Always "My sweetheart",' she cried. 'You never say "My wife".' He was hurt and bitter, unable to understand, but saw now that not saying 'My wife' and never getting through to Ivor with his love, were the same thing.

The earphones blocked all sounds of children, traffic, next-door telly, and he wrote another message from the spot-middle of some ocean or other, a man-made arrowhead of peace steering from land to land: ARRIVING HOME 27TH CAN'T WAIT TO SEE MY MUMMY AND DADDY – LOVE JANET. The big ship sailed on: aerials sensitive, funnels powerful, people happy – sleeping, eating, kissing or, if crew, heavy with work. He saw himself in a smaller craft, marooned in a darkening unmapped ocean where no one sent messages because he was the only passenger, and no person would think to flash him a telegram anyway. Neither could anyone wish him a good journey because he had never announced his port of destination, and in any case no one knew he was afloat, and there was no one to whom he could send a marconigram stating his imminent arrival because even if he were going somewhere he wouldn't even know where nor when he would get there, and there was even less chance of anyone being at that end than from where he'd started. All he could do was fight this vision, and instead keep the big jewel-lit liner in his mind, read what messages flashed to and from it.

Earphones swung from the jacks-socket, and in the full overhead light he snapped open Ivor's cupboard. Horses and trainsets, teddy bear and games and forts and tricycle were piled where the boy had last thrown them. Morse sounds no longer hit him like snowflakes from his lit-up fabulous ship. He stared blindly as each toy was slung across the room, towards window, door, fireplace or ceiling, until every limbless piece had found a new resting place. He went back to his wireless as the stairfoot door snapped open and heavy sounds thumped their way up at his commotion.

The ship remained. Its messages of love and arrival for some, godspeed for others, birthday wishes and the balming oil of common news, still sped out from it; but such words from the black box made a picture that he couldn't break like the limbless toys all around him. His breath scraped out of his lungs at the real and coloured vision mercilessly forming. The ship was off centre, but he was able to watch it slowly sinking, the calm grey water of tropical dusk lapping around it with cat-like hunger, as if finely controlled by a brain not apparent or visible to anyone. The ship subsided to its decks, and the endless oil-smooth sea became more easy-going and polite, though kept the hidden strength to force it under. As the ship flooded, people overflowed the lifeboats, until nothing remained but an undisturbed grey sheet of water – as smooth and shiny as tin that can be used for a mirror – and a voice in the earphones saying something Fred could not at first decipher. It was a gruff, homely, almost familiar tone, though one that he knew he would never be able to recognize no matter how long he concentrated.

The lock on the bedroom door burst, and several people were trying to pull him away from the radio, Nan's voice imploring above the others. Fingers of both hands – white and strong as flayed twigs – held on to the radio, which was so heavy that those pulling at him thought it was nailed to the bench and that the bench was riveted to the floor. Fred held on with great strength, without speaking, cunning enough at the crucial moment to withdraw his hands from the radio (before superior odds could pull him clear) and clamp them with an equally steel-grip on to the bench, strange grunts sounding like trapped animals trying to jump from his mouth.

Eventually they dragged him free. Sweat glistened on him, as he waved his arms in the middle of the room: 'I heard God!' he shouted. 'Leave me be,' he roared. 'I heard God!' – then dropped.

III

Nan said not to bother with a doctor and, when they argued, stood to her full height, thanked everyone very much, and bundled them out of the house. Neighbours were a godsend, but there was an end to what goodness you could let them show. When Fred was undressed and into bed she stood by the window of Ivor's room, wondering why exactly he'd had such a fit. Hadn't he been happy? As far as she knew he lacked nothing, had all that most men had. She thought a lot of him, in spite of everything, and was quite sure he thought a lot of her, in spite of the fact that he was incapable of showing it. Neither had any reproaches to make, and apart from poor Ivor being drowned their life hadn't been so bad. Of course, she could never understand how he'd survived Ivor's death so well, though maybe it was bravery and self control that hadn't let him show what this barbaric piece of luck had done to him – which was all very well, but such dumb silence had made it ten times worse for her. She'd paid for it, by God, and it had just about done her in. It was hard to believe he'd felt it as hard as she had, in any case, when the first action of his fit had been to pulverize poor Ivor's toys. That wasn't something she could forgive and forget in a hurry, even though he may not have realized what he was doing. If he'd been full of drink it would have been a different matter, maybe, but Fred only drank much at Christmas or birthdays. Still, it wasn't like him to have such a black paralytic fit.

Next morning she phoned a doctor. He was violent and screaming all night, had ripped off great strips of wallpaper in his unreachable agony. During these long hours she was reminded of a new-born baby gripped for no reason by a blind unending temper, and there is nothing to do except draw on all the patience you have and try to soothe. Thinking of this kept her calm and able to manage. In a few bleak minutes of early morning she persuaded him to enter a mental hospital. 'I don't want you to go, love. But everybody thinks it'll be for the best. And I think so as well. They know what to do about such things there. You'll be as right as rain then in a couple of months.'

'All right,' he said, unable to care. Afloat in the ocean like his favourite unanchorable ship, he was carried away by a restful warm current beyond anyone's control.

She packed a case as if he were going again on a five-year jag to the army. She looked anxious and sorry, unable to stop her tears falling, her hand trembling as she turned out drawers for handkerchiefs and pyjamas. Fred sat in the armchair, his dressing-gown collar pulled up to his white immobile face, shaking with cold though the room was warmed by a huge, expert fire.

She travelled in the ambulance and saw him into the hospital, registered, examined, sedated, finally laid full-length in a narrow immaculate bed. Everything happened so quickly that she began to doubt that they could do any good. 'It's very nice,' she remarked, while his eyes stayed open, looking at the cream-painted blank ceiling of the ward. 'You couldn't be in a better place. I know they'll look after you, and I'll come twice a week to see you.'

'Aye,' he acknowledged, though out of it all.

'I've got to go now, love, or I'll miss the bus.'

At first there was nothing to do except keep the house clean. Polishing glass on the pictures, shining knives and forks, putting fresh paper on the kitchen shelves, she hoped his nervous breakdown wouldn't take too long to cure, though tears fell at the huge cannonball blow that had landed its weight against her: such mental things could last years. First Ivor gone, and now Fred; it was a bit bloody much. She cried to the empty house between sobs. She came in for sympathy from the neighbours: 'He was as good as gold,' a woman met shopping said, as if he'd already been buried and prayed over, 'but them's the sort that suffers first. It's a shame. Still, Mrs Hargreaves, if there's anything I can do for you, duck, just let me know.'

The novelty of living alone wore off. She began to feel young again, but it was a different sort of youth to when, every Thursday during the war, she walked across the road with her allowance book to collect Fred's fourteen shillings from the post office. It was a lonely, thrilling sort of freedom that began to dawn. She begrudged the frequent visits of both families who thought she wanted to stay in a continual state of being cheered-up, and when she told all of them in a loud voice that this wasn't so, her own parents retired hoping that she, after all, wasn't going the same way as 'that poor Fred', while Fred's mother and father went away thinking they could see at last who had made their poor son the way he was.

Dates changed on each evening paper, and months passed. Men began noticing her in the street (or she noticed them noticing her again) giving looks which meant that they would like to get in bed with her. She found this far from agreeable, but it did hold back the full misery of Fred's incarceration from turning her into an old woman. Anyway, why shouldn't she feel pleased when men smiled or winked at her in passing? she thought, seeing that it had taken misfortune to make her realize how firm her figure was at the bust and hips, how smooth-skinned and pale her face under dark hair. These sentiments descended on her with as little warning as Fred's illness had on him. To everyone else she stuck it out like a widow waiting for her husband to come back from the grave.

Twice a week she took a bus through curving lanes to the sudden tower that dominated the camplike spread of lesser buildings. Getting off the bus with her bundles and magazines, flowers and grapes, and clean handkerchiefs with the odour of ironing still on them, she felt desolate at being one of so many, as if such numbers visiting sick-minded men and women made it a shameless and guilty job that fate had hooked them into, and that they should try and hide their own stupidity and bad luck from each other.

She hurried head down to be first in the ward, going along corridors whose low ceilings sported so many reptilian pipes that it seemed as if she was deep in one of those submarine ships seen on the pictures. She then entered a light-enough ward, to find a waxen spiritual embalming of her husband that even pins would not wake up.

'Fred,' she said, still on her feet and spreading gifts over the bed, 'I've brought you these.'

'Aye,' he answered, an affirmation used by their parents, which he had taken to since his illness.

'Fred, they tell me you'll be getting better soon.'

'Aye' – again.

'Did they give you them new drugs yet?'

'Aye.'

'As long as you don't get that shock treatment. Everything's OK at home. I'm managing all right.' She had to sit and look at him for an hour, because to leave before then, even though there was nothing left to say, was unthinkable. His mind might be a thousand miles away under his skin, but he'd remember it. She wondered what weird force had turned his life into a half sleep that she could no longer penetrate. He wasn't suffering, and that was a good job. Sometimes they saw snakes and dragons and screamed for hours, but Fred looked quiet enough, though there was no saying what he was like on days she didn't come. His brown calm eyes watched her, and she wondered if he still heard those morse codes he'd been so cranky on when they came from his expensive black radio. Of course, she nodded to her thoughts, that's what sent him, hearing those terrible squeaking messages night in and night out. Once, she had switched off the television and listened by Ivor's door, and to her the swift high-pitched dots and dashes had sounded like a monkey laughing – or trying to, which was worse. God knows what he made of such noise, and there was no way of finding out because he set fire to his papers every night, saying in his maddening know-all voice how wireless operators had to keep secret all messages they took down, otherwise it was prison for them. If she'd been the jealous sort she would have told him off about spending so much time at his wireless because, back from work, he could hardly wait to get his tea and a wash before he was up those stairs and glued to it. Still, most blokes would have been throwing their money away in a pub, and getting ulcers into the bargain. You can't have everything, and that was a fact, she supposed.

'I'll bring you a custard next week, love,' she said, wondering how else she could cheer him up.

'Aye.'

'If you want anything, drop me a postcard.' She didn't see him as helpless, treated him almost as if he had chosen to lie in that fashion and could come out of it at will – though from the way he smiled it was obvious he couldn't. In his locker were half a dozen paperback books she'd brought him, but she knew he hadn't read them. Still, they looked good in a place like this, and maybe he'd need them soon. You never knew when the steel band at the back of his eyes would snap and set him free again. She held his hand, shyly because many other visitors were in the ward, though they were too busy holding other hands to notice.

Always first into the hospital, she came out last, and so had to find a seat on the top deck of the bus, where pipe and cigarette smoke spread thickly. Surging, twisting movement was a relief – the bus eating its headlit way through winter's approaching darkness, speeding when the black canyon of trees straightened. She arched her back after the busy day, stared along the bus where other people talked out the highlights of their visit. Up to now her grief had been too new to allow for making friends, or do more than nod to a greeting, but when the man next to her asked:

'How was he today?' she replied:

'About the same,' and blushed as red as the sun which, hovering on the fields, resembled a beetroot going into the reverse of its existence, slipping back to the comfortable gloom of winter soil from which it had come. I'm a fool she thought, not daring to look. Why did I answer the cheeky devil like that? But she glanced at him, while his own eyes took in the bleak fall of night outside which, from his smile, made the bus interior feel like snug home to him. He was a young man who seemed born for nothing but work, awkward when his best clothes claimed their right to dominate him one day of the week. He was about thirty, she guessed, unmarried perhaps, since his approach was anything but furtive.

'It's a long job,' he said, 'once they get in a place like that. Longer than TB I reckon.'

'Well,' she said, thinking his face too red and healthy-looking for him to be a collier, 'they wouldn't keep 'em in longer than they had to either, would they? Cost too much.'

He took out a cigarette and, in spite of her retort, the smoke didn't increase her annoyance, for his lighting-up was debonair, matched to the feel of his dressed-up best. A cigarette suited him more than a collar and tie, and she didn't doubt that a pint of ale would suit him even more. Maybe he's nervous, she smiled, underneath it all. 'I don't suppose they would,' he said, having taken his time over it.

'It ain't the sort of thing they die from, either,' she added.

'There's that to be thankful for. I'm sorry' – out came his twenty-packet again – 'Smoke, duck?'

'No, thanks.' Who did he think he was? Who does he think I am, as well? 'Yes, I will have one.'

'I like a fag,' he said. 'Keeps me company.'

The opening was plain a mile off, but she refused it: 'Who do you see at the hospital, then?'

'A pal o' mine. He's in surgical though. Fell off some scaffolding last winter. He only broke an arm – that's what we thought, anyway – but he ain't been the same in the head since. He's an Irish bloke, a paddy, you know, and none of his family get to see him, so me and the lads tek turns at having half a day off to see he's all right. Shovel in a few fags and things. Be out in a couple of months, according to the doctor.'

She hardly listened. 'You're a brickie, then?'

'Brickie's labourer. Who do *you* go and see? I mek good money though.'

'My husband.' At Redhill the lights of Nottingham blistered the sky in front, drew them down to its welcoming horseshoe. His naïve glance seemed too good, and she wondered if such an expression weren't the ultimate extension of his guile. 'I shan't be sorry to get home,' she told him. 'It's a long day, coming all this way.'

The frown left his face as soon as he thought she might see it: 'You can spend too much time at home. I like staying out, having a good time.'

She saw where his glance went, and began to fasten her coat. 'There is something to be said for it, I suppose.'

'There is, an' all,' he grinned.

'It's a long time since I had a drink,' she claimed, self-righteousness seeming the only defence left.

'Come and have one with me then, before you go home. You'll enjoy it.'

She flushed: he thinks I'm trying to knock on with him, and the idea made her so angry that she said, though not too loud in case she was heard and shown-up more for the flirt she might seem to be: 'What you need is a smack across the face.'

'I suppose so.' His voice verged on sadness. 'I'm sorry if I offended you, duck. But come and have a drink with me, then we can make it up.'

He was the limit. 'What do you tek me for?' – a question that puzzled him since it was too early to say. 'In any case,' she told him, 'I'm married, respectably married.'

'So am I,' he answered, 'but I'm not narrow-minded' – then kept his trap shut while the bus went slowly through bright lights and traffic, stopping and starting like possible future answers formulating in Nan's mind in case he had the nerve to speak again.

190

At the terminus they filed out onto the asphalt, and when he repeated his proposition in the darker shadows of the station yard both were shocked at the unequivocal 'yes' that for a few seconds kept them apart, then pulled them passionately together.

IV

Fred's brainstorm thinned-out at a predictable speed, leaving an un-clouded blue-sea vision of a mind from which the large ship had slid away. He walked out of the ward with a suitcase in one hand and morning paper tucked under the other arm. His fervent kiss irritated Nan, but all she could say was: 'You'll be better off at home.'

'I know I shall. And I'll never want to leave it again love.' He stared with pleasure at the lush green of middle spring, the febrile smell of grass and catkins beating petrol smells through the open bus-window. Water charged under the lane, into an enormous pipe, a swollen silver arm speckling a field that cows drank from. He rubbed sun from his eyes as if after a fair spell in prison, was too absorbed in his journey to say much, enjoying his way out and back, Nan thought, as she herself had revelled in his absence once the shock of breakdown had worn off.

The first bungalows lay like tarted-up kennels over suburban fields, and he turned from them: 'I feel good, love. I feel marvellous.'

She smiled. 'I thought you did. You look as though you've had a long holiday.'

'I suppose it was, in a way.' He took her hand and squeezed it: 'Let's go down town this afternoon. Go for a stroll round, then spend a couple of hours at the pictures. We can have a real holiday between now and Monday.'

'All right' – doubting that they would.

As he walked down the yard, the neighbours thought him another of Nan's fancy men who had gone into the house via the back door late at night in the last months, and slid out of the front door early next morning. She had been sly about it, but not sly enough, they grinned. Not that Fred was in danger of being informed, for it was hard to imagine him pasting her: she was beyond that by now, and in any case he would never be man enough for it. And when he did find out – as he must in time – then there'd be no point in knocking her about for what had become history.

They had to look twice before recognizing the Fred they'd known for years. His sallow face had filled out, and he had lost the lively movements of his brown eyes that, through not being sure of themselves, had given and received sufficient warmth and sympathy to make him popular. His best suit would have shown as too tight if Nan hadn't thought to take his mac which, having always been slightly too big, hid the worst of his weight increase from curious eyes. Most obvious was his face, which had broadened. The expression of it was firmly tainted by middle age, though the neighbours were to swear how much better he looked, and what a lot of good the country air had done. 'It's fattened him,' they said, 'and it'll turn out to have fattened her as well – though it wasn't fresh air and good food as did that.' Fred caught their laughter by the back door.

The smells of the yard were familiar, tea-leaves and coal dust, car fuel and midday stew. He revelled in it, couldn't wait to get back to work next Monday and walk among those hot, oilburning machines, which would make his homecoming complete. Nan hung up his mac, while he turned to the living-room. He thought they'd walked into the wrong house. 'What's this, then?'

'What's what?' She smiled at his frown, though it seemed like insult to her: 'What's what, Fred?'

'All this' – waving his arm, as if it indicated something that wasn't worth a light. He shifted his stance, uncomfortable at the change that had taken place while he was away.

'Don't you like it?'

'It's all right,' he conceded after a pause. 'It's a surprise though.'

'Aye.' He looked carefully, again. The old furniture, the old wallpaper, the old curtains and pictures – all gone, swept away by a magic wand of six dead months. The room was brighter, stippled green-contemporary and (though this didn't occur to them) resembled more the hospital he had just left than the previous homely decoration of their married life. 'You don't like it, then?'

He saw a thundercloud-quarrel looming up, and only ten minutes back from the hospital. 'It's lighter. Yes, I reckon it's OK. It's marvellous, in fact.'

'Thanks,' she said. 'I thought you'd jump for joy. I'll make you a cup of tea now.'

'It must have cost a good bit,' he called into the scullery, losing some of his strangeness at being home.

'I spent my football money on it,' she said. 'All but a few quid.'

'I suppose that's how you was able to look after me so well, bring me things every time.'

'It was,' she said.

'And I thought it was because you was such a good manager.'

'Don't be sarcastic. I often wondered what I'd do with it, you know that, and now you can see. I suppose you think I'm a dope, blowing it on the house when you spent your share on yourself, on a . . . wireless set. Well, I expect I am, but I like to keep the home nice. As long as you've got a pleasant place to live in there ain't much as can happen to you.'

'That's true.'

'Takes work and money though to keep it going, but it's worth it. Not that there's owt wrong with work.'

He stood by the fire, drinking his first cup of tea: 'You can say that again. I'll be glad to clock-in on Monday.'

'It's what makes people live,' she went on, almost happily, he thought, 'and you as well, if I know you. You've always been a lad for work. Course, after a while there gets as if there's not enough for a woman to do when she's got no kids. That's why most women in my position should be in a factory. No good moping around all day, or gossiping, or just sitting by the fire pulling a meagrim because you've read all the books at the library. You need a proper job. You can fit your housework in easy enough, and let them as say you can't come to your house and prove it.'

'What are you going on like this for, then?' he cried.

'Because I'm going to start work as well on Monday, at my old firm.'

Knowing what her game was, he became calmer. 'Maybe they don't need anybody.' They sat for a meal: cold ham, fresh salad and bread, sardines, a porkpie each in a cellophane wrapper. 'I went the other day to see 'em. They'd love to have me back, as an overlooker as well. The processing hasn't altered a bit since I was last there.'

He smiled: 'It wouldn't, not in a hundred years, no more than it would where I work.'

'I'll be like a fish back in water after an hour or two,' she exulted. 'I didn't tell 'em I'd only be there about three months, though while I am I'll put a bit of money by.'

193

'We don't need money,' he said, his appetite failing, 'because we'll be all right when I've pulled in a few wage-packets.'

'Not as I see it. We'll want all we can get, because I'm pregnant.' He smiled, then the smile ran from his face before the claws of her meaning savaged it. 'Pregnant?'

'Yes,' she said. 'Can't you see it? My belly's up. We'll have a kid in the house in six months. You won't know the place.' She glared, as if hoping he'd try denying it. But the healthy bloom of fresh air had already left his cheeks.

'You've got things fixed up, then, haven't you?'

'Things often fix themselves up, whatever you do.' Her heartbeats were visible, breasts lifting and falling, making it seem to him as if her blouse were alive.

'Whose kid is it?'

'Nobody's as matters.'

He trembled the teacup back into its saucer. 'It matters to me, it bloody-well does.'

'We can have another kid between us after this, so you needn't carry on.'

He stood from his half-finished meal. 'That's what you think. You're a lunatic' – and his slow intimidating tread of disappointment on the stairs filled her more with sorrow for him than for herself.

She hadn't expected him to cave-in so deeply at the first telling, hoped he would argue, settle what had to be settled before going off to soothe his injuries in solitude. 'Maybe I am a lunatic' – and though she never imagined he lacked guts for such a vital set-to, it could be that she'd accepted too blindly the advice that things have a way of working themselves out better than you expect – given by Danny on telling him she was pregnant, and before he lit off for a new construction job at Rotherham. She remembered him saying, after their first night together, that whenever he met a woman the first thing that crossed his mind was 'If I have a kid by her, which of us will it look like?' 'And is that what you thought about me when you started talking to me on the bus?' 'What do you think?' he'd laughed. 'Of course it was, you juicy little piece.' But now he'd gone, and only she would be able to see how the kid turned out. Maybe that was why he wondered – because he knew he'd never be there to see. The bloody rotter – though there wasn't much else he could have done but hopped-it. Still, (her sigh was a sad one), the last few months had been heaven, a wild spree on what was left from her football money. She'd boozed and sang with Danny, in a pub tucked somewhere in the opposite end of town. It was a long while since she'd laughed so much, played darts and argued with the young men (some no older than teddy boys) all earning fair money at Gedling pit and out for a good time while they could get it. She'd never imagined her pool winnings would come in so handy, had even taken to filling coupons in again, which she and Fred had sworn never to do once they cleared a packet. Getting home at night she had felt Danny's hands and lips loving her: warm and ready for him, she came alive once more as the sweet shock of orgasm twisted her body. She hadn't bargained on getting pregnant, but couldn't feel sorry either, in spite of Fred clattering about upstairs. She'd hoped that the bliss of his absence would turn into the heaven of his coming back, but that had been too much to hope for, like most things. Tears forced a way out. Thoughts of Fred and their past life were too vivid and accurate now. 'I couldn't help it,' she said. 'I didn't want to have anything to do with Danny, but I wasn't myself.' She'd often forgot Fred's existence, her mind withdrawing to a time even before meeting him, a sense of paradise so far distant that she'd sometimes write on a postcard: VISIT HOSPITAL TOMORROW and lean it against the clock, so as not to lose him altogether.

There seemed no doubt to Fred upstairs than an end was reached but, seeing his half-filled suit-case on a chair, the end was like a sheer smooth wall blocking a tunnel in which there wasn't room enough to turn round and grope for a new beginning, though that seemed the only hope.

The fag-end nipped his fingers, fell and he let his foot slide over it. In the darkness of the cupboard he saw pictures of his London journey that afternoon, a long packed train rattling him to some strange impersonal bedroom smelling of trainsmoke and damp, and a new job, struggle, solitude, and even less reason for living than he had now. Still, there's not much for it but to get out. The moves of his departure were slow, but he smiled and told himself there was no hurry.

Ivor's toys had gone, cleared away by Nan after he'd been carted-off that morning. The jig-saw made sense, showed her returning alone from the hospital and not knowing what to do because he, Fred, was no longer part of the house. He saw himself smashing Ivor's toys by boot and hand, a lunatic flailing after a brainstorm harvest too abundant of life and energy.

Something half-concealed by a piece of clean sacking flashed into the back door of his eye before turning away from the cupboard. Pulling it clear he saw the radio set, black, deathly, and switched off, lying like some solid reproachful monster in place of the dustbinned toys. He grinned: Nan had intended hiding it where she imagined he was unlikely to see it, and he wondered why she hadn't scrapped it with the toys. He knelt towards the eyes and dials, touching and spinning in the hope that agreeable noises would lift from it.

Its size and dignity were intimidating, made him stand back and view it from a point where it disturbed him less. The vision began as half a memory striving to enter his brain. It edged a way sharply in. He laughed at it, tapped a pleasant hollow-sounding noise on the lid with his fingers, not like an army drum but something more satisfying, primitive and jungle-like. It reminded him of Peter Nkagwe, whose illuminated face was locked like stone as he battered out messages hour after hour in the signals office years ago.

The black box weighed a hundred pounds. Two hands flexed and stretched over it, pressing the sharp rim into his groin as he moved, breathless and foot by foot. His dark hair fell forward, joined beads of sweat in pricking his skin. Hospital had made him soft, but he resisted shifting the radio in two stages, found enough strength to do it the hard way, drawing on the rock-middle of himself to reach the table at one agonizing go, and set it so delicately down it would have been impossible either to see or hear the soundless contact of wood and metal.

It was a minute's work to screw on aerial and power, click in earphones and switch a current-flow through valves and superhet. Energy went like an invisible stoat into each purple and glowing filament. The panels lit up and background static began as if, when a child, he had pressed a sea-shell to his ear and heard the far-off poise and fall of breakers at Skegness; then such subtlety went, and noise rose to the loud electric punching of a full-grown sea in continual motion. He turned the volume down and sent the fly-wheel onto morse code.

The sea calmed for its mundane messages of arrival and departure, of love and happy birthday and grandma died and I bought presents in Bombay, and from this festive liner – white, sleek and grandiose – once more seen between clear sky and otherwise desolate flat sea – signals were emitted saying that a son had been (or was it would be?) born with love from Nancy in a place where both were doing well.

He slung the pencil down and stared at the accidental words, grew a smile at the irony of the message. He frowned, as if a best friend taunted him. The calm boat flowed on and a voice spoke over his shoulder: 'What have you got there, Fred?'

'A message,' he answered, not looking round, sliding his hand over so that she wouldn't see it. 'I take them down from ships at sea.'

'I know you do.'

'All sorts of things,' he added, sociable without knowing why. The earphones fell to his neck and he needle-spun the wavelength, a noise that reminded Nancy of running by the huge arboretum birdcages as a kid: 'What though?'

'Telegrams and things. Ordinary stuff. Listen to what this funny one says' – sliding his hand away – "FRED HARGREAVES LEFT HOME AT ONE O'CLOCK THURSDAY AFTERNOON."

She turned: 'You're not going, Fred, are you? I don't believe it.'

'That's what the telegram said. Everyone I take down says the same thing. I can't get over it.'

'Talk proper,' she cried. 'It's not right to go off like this.'

He laughed, a grinding of heart and soul. 'In't it?'

'What about your job?'

'There's plenty more where that came from.'

'What about me?'

He laid his earphones down, and spoke with exaggerated awful quietness. 'You should a thought of that before you trolloped off and got a bastard in you.'

'It's all finished now. Didn't I tell you? It's about time you believed me.'

'You told me a lot of things.' It was more of a grouse than a reproach. 'All on 'em lies.'

'I thought it was better that way.'

'And going with that bloke? Was that better as well?' His shout startled her, brown eyes, glittering under darkening shadows, as if his exhaustion had never been lifted by a sojourn at the hospital. Neighbours from next door and out in the yard could hear them shouting. Don't tell me he's found out already. Well, well!

She was still in the new dress worn to fetch him home, and it showed already a slight thickness at the waist. 'I couldn't help it,' she cried, able to add, in spite of tears on her face: 'Anyway, what did you expect? We'd had no life between us since Ivor died. I was fed up on it. I had to let myself go.'

'It was too bad though, worn't it?'

'I'm not saying it wasn't. But I'm not going to go on bended knees and ask you to stay. I'm not an' all.' She stiffened, looked at him with hatred: 'It's as much your fault as mine.'

'I'm leaving,' he said, 'I'm off.'

'Go on, then.' Her face turned, the tone mechanical and meant, the quiet resignation of it a hot poker burning through his eyes. It was a final torment he could not take. Dazed by the grief of her decision she didn't see his hand coming. A huge blow, like a boulder flying at top speed in a gale, hit the side of her face, threw her back, feet collapsing. Another fist caught her, and another. She crashed on to the bed, a cry of shock beating her to it there. As she was to tell her mother: 'He hadn't hit me before then, and he wain't hit me again, either. Maybe I deserved it, though.'

He tore the message off and screwed it tight, flung it to the far corner of the room. Then he went to Nan and tried to comfort her, the iron hooves of desperate love trampling them back into the proportions of matrimonial strife.

The Bike

The Easter I was fifteen I sat at the table for supper and Mam said to me: 'I'm glad you've left school. Now you can go to work.'

'I don't want to go to wok,' I said in a big voice.

'Well, you've got to,' she said. 'I can't afford to keep a pit-prop like yo' on nowt.'

I sulked, pushed my toasted cheese away as if it was the worst kind of slop. 'I thought I could have a break before starting.'

'Well you thought wrong. You'll be out of harm's way at work.' She took my plate and emptied it on John's, my younger brother's, knowing the right way to get me mad. That's the trouble with me: I'm not clever. I could have bashed our John's face in and snatched it back, except the little bastard had gobbled it up, and Dad was sitting by the fire, behind his paper with one tab lifted. 'You can't get me out to wok quick enough, can you?' was all I could say at Mam.

Dad chipped in, put down his paper. 'Listen: no wok, no grub. So get out and look for a job tomorrow, and don't come back till you've got one.'

Going to the bike factory to ask for a job meant getting up early, just as if I was back at school; there didn't seem any point in getting older. My old man was a good worker though, and I knew in my bones and brain that I took after him. At the school garden the teacher used to say: 'Colin, you're the best worker I've got, and you'll get on when you leave' – after I'd spent a couple of hours digging spuds while all the others had been larking about trying to run each other over with the lawn-rollers. Then the teacher would sell the spuds off at threepence a pound and what did I get out of it? Bogger-all. Yet I liked the work because it wore me out; and I always feel pretty good when I'm worn out.

I knew you had to go to work though, and that rough work was best. I saw a picture once about a revolution in Russia, about the workers taking over and everything (like Dad wants to) and they lined

199

everybody up and made them hold their hands out and the working blokes went up and down looking at them. Anybody whose hands was lily-white was taken away and shot. The others was OK. Well, if ever that happened in this country, I'd be OK, and that made me feel better when a few days later I was walking down the street in overalls at half-past seven in the morning with the rest of them. One side of my face felt lively and interested in what I was in for, but the other side was crooked and sorry for itself, so that a neighbour got a front view of my whole clock and called with a wide laugh, a gap I'd like to have seen a few inches lower down – in her neck: 'Never mind, Colin, it ain't all that bad.'

The man on the gate took me to the turnery. The noise hit me like a boxing-glove as I went in, but I kept on walking straight into it without flinching, feeling it reach right into my guts as if to wrench them out and use them as garters. I was handed over to the foreman; then the foreman passed me on to the toolsetter; and the toolsetter took me to another youth – so that I began to feel like a hot wallet.

The youth led me to a cupboard, opened it, and gave me a sweeping brush. 'Yo' do that gangway,' he said, 'and I'll do this one.' My gangway was wider, but I didn't bother to mention it. 'Bernard,' he said, holding out his hand, 'that's me. I go on a machine next week, a drill.'

'How long you been on this sweeping?' I wanted to know, bored with it already.

'Three months. Every lad gets put on sweeping first, just to get 'em used to the place.' Bernard was small and thin, older than me. We took to each other. He had round bright eyes and dark wavy hair, and spoke in a quick way as if he'd stayed at school longer than he had. He was idle, and I thought him sharp and clever, maybe because his mam and dad died when he was three. He'd been brought up by an asthmatic auntie who'd not only spoiled him but let him run wild as well, he told me later when we sat supping from our tea mugs. He'd quietened down now though, and butter wouldn't melt in his mouth, he said with a wink. I couldn't think why this was, after all his stories about him being a mad-head – which put me off him at first, though after a bit he was my mate, and that was that.

We was talking one day, and Bernard said the thing he wanted to buy most in the world was a gram and lots of jazz records – New Orleans style. He was saving up and had already got ten quid.

200

'Me,' I said, 'I want a bike, to get out at week-ends up Trent. A shop on Arkwright Street sells good 'uns second hand.'

I went back to my sweeping. It was a fact I've always wanted a bike. Speed gave me a thrill. Malcolm Campbell was my bigshot – but I'd settle for a two-wheeled pushbike. I'd once borrowed my cousin's and gone down Balloon House Hill so quick I passed a bus. I'd often thought how easy it would be to pinch a bike: look in a shop window until a bloke leaves his bike to go into the same shop, then nip in just before him and ask for something you knew they hadn't got; then walk out whistling to the bike at the kerb and ride off as if it's yours while the bloke's still in the shop. I'd brood for hours: fly home on it, enamel it, file off the numbers, turn the handlebars round, change the pedals, take lamps off or put them on . . . only, no, I thought, I'll be honest and save up for one when I get forced out to work, worse luck.

But work turned out to be a better life than school. I kept as hard at it as I could, and got on well with the blokes because I used to spout about how rotten the wages was and how hard the bosses slaved us – which made me popular you can bet. Like my old man always says, I told them: 'At home when you've got a headache, mash a pot of tea. At work, when you've got a headache, strike.' Which brought a few laughs.

Bernard was put on his drill, and one Friday while he was cleaning it down I stood waiting to cart his rammel off. 'Are you still saving up for that bike, then?' he asked, pushing steel dust away with a handbrush.

'Course I am. But I'm a way off getting one yet. They rush you a fiver at that shop. Guaranteed, though.'

He worked on for a minute or two then, as if he'd got a birthday present or was trying to spring a good surprise on me, said without turning round: 'I've made up my mind to sell my bike.'

'I didn't know you'd got one.'

'Well' – a look on his face as if there was a few things I didn't know –'I bus it to work: it's easier.' Then in a pallier voice: 'I got it last Christmas, from my auntie. But I want a record player now.'

My heart was thumping. I knew I hadn't got enough, but: 'How much do you want for it?'

He smiled. 'It ain't how much I want for the bike, it's how much more dough I need to get the gram and a couple of discs.'

I saw Trent Valley spread out below me from the top of Carlton Hill – fields and villages, and the river like a white scarf dropped from a giant's neck. 'How much do you need, then?'

201

He took his time about it, as if still having to reckon it up. 'Fifty bob.' I'd only got two quid – so the giant snatched his scarf away and vanished. Then Bernard seemed in a hurry to finish the deal: 'Look, I don't want to mess about, I'll let it go for two pounds five. You can borrow the other five bob.'

'I'll do it then,' I said, and Bernard shook my hand like he was going away in the army. 'It's a deal. Bring the dough in the morning, and I'll bike it to wok.'

Dad was already in when I got home, filling the kettle at the scullery tap. I don't think he felt safe without there was a kettle on the gas. 'What would you do if the world suddenly ended, Dad?' I once asked when he was in a good mood. 'Mash some tea and watch it,' he said. He poured me a cup.

'Lend's five bob, Dad, till Friday.'

He slipped the cosy on. 'What do you want to borrow money for?' I told him. 'Who from?' he asked.

'My mate at wok.'

He passed me the money. 'Is it a good 'un?'

'I ain't seen it yet. He's bringing it in the morning.'

'Make sure the brakes is safe.'

Bernard came in half an hour late, so I wasn't able to see the bike till dinner-time. I kept thinking he'd took bad and wouldn't come at all, but suddenly he was stooping at the door to take his clips off – so's I'd know he'd got his – my – bike. He looked paler than usual, as if he'd been up the canal-bank all night with a piece of skirt and caught a bilious-bout. I paid him at dinner-time. 'Do you want a receipt for it?' he laughed. It was no time to lark about. I gave it a short test around the factory, then rode it home.

The next three evenings, for it was well in to summer, I rode a dozen miles out into the country, where fresh air smelt like cowshit and the land was coloured different, was wide open and windier than in streets. Marvellous. It was like a new life starting up, as if till then I'd been tied by a mile-long rope around the ankle to home. Whistling along lanes I planned trips to Skegness, wondering how many miles I could make in a whole day. If I pedalled like mad, bursting my lungs for fifteen hours I'd reach London where I'd never been. It was like sawing through the bars in clink. It was a good bike as well, a few years old, but a smart racer with lamps and saddlebag and a pump that went. I thought Bernard was a bit loony parting with it at that price, but I supposed that that's how blokes are when they get dead set on a gram and discs. They'd sell their own mother, I thought, enjoying a mad dash down from Canning Circus, weaving between the cars for kicks.

'What's it like, having a bike?' Bernard asked, stopping to slap me on the back – as jolly as I'd ever seen him, yet in a kind of way that don't happen between pals.

'You should know,' I said. 'Why? It's all right, ain't it? The wheels are good, aren't they?'

An insulted look came into his eyes. 'You can give it back if you like. I'll give you your money.'

'I don't want it,' I said. I could no more part with it than my right arm, and he knew it. 'Got the gram yet?' And he told me about it for the next half-hour. It had got so many dials for this and that he made it sound like a space ship. We was both satisfied, which was the main thing.

That same Saturday I went to the barber's for my monthly D A and when I came out I saw a bloke getting on my bike to ride it away. I tagged him on the shoulder, my fist flashing red for danger.

'Off,' I said sharp, ready to smash the thieving bastard. He turned to me. A funny sort of thief, I couldn't help thinking, a respectable-looking bloke of about forty wearing glasses and shiny shoes, smaller than me, with a moustache. Still, the swivel-eyed sinner was taking my bike.

'I'm boggered if I will,' he said, in a quiet way so that I thought he was a bit touched. 'It's my bike, anyway.'

'It bloody-well ain't,' I swore, 'and if you don't get off I'll crack you one.'

A few people gawked at us. The bloke didn't mess about and I can understand it now. 'Missis,' he called, 'just go down the road to that copperbox and ask a policeman to come up 'ere, will you? This is my bike, and this young bogger nicked it.'

I was strong for my age. 'You sodding fibber,' I cried, pulling him clean off the bike so's it clattered to the pavement. I picked it up to ride away, but the bloke got me round the waist, and it was more than I could do to take him off up the road as well, even if I wanted to. Which I didn't.

'Fancing robbing a working-man of his bike,' somebody called out from the crowd of idle bastards now collected. I could have mowed them down.

But I didn't get a chance. A copper came, and the man was soon flicking out his wallet, showing a bill with the number of the bike on it: proof right enough. But I still thought he'd made a mistake. 'You can tell us all about that at the Guildhall,' the copper said to me.

I don't know why – I suppose I want my brains testing – but I stuck to a story that I found the bike dumped at the end of the yard that morning and was on my way to give it in at a copshop, and had called for a haircut first. I think the magistrate half believed me, because the bloke knew to the minute when it was pinched, and at that time I had a perfect alibi – I was in work, proved by my clocking-in card. I knew some rat who hadn't been in work though when he should have been.

All the same, being found with a pinched bike, I got put on probation, and am still doing it. I hate old Bernard's guts for playing a trick like that on me, his mate. But it was lucky for him I hated the coppers more and wouldn't nark on anybody, not even a dog. Dad would have killed me if ever I had, though he didn't need to tell me. I could only thank God a story came to me as quick as it did, though in one way I still sometimes reckon I was barmy not to have told them how I got the bike.

There's one thing I do know. I'm waiting for Bernard to come out of Borstal. He got picked up, the day after I was copped with the bike, for robbing his auntie's gas meter to buy more discs. She'd had about all she could stand from him, and thought a spell inside would do him good, if not cure him altogether. I've got a big bone to pick with him, because he owes me forty-five bob. I don't care where he gets it – even if he goes out and robs another meter – but I'll get it out of him, I swear blind I will. I'll pulverize him.

Another thing about him though that makes me laugh is that, if ever there's a revolution and everybody's lined-up with their hands out, Bernard's will still be lily-white, because he's a bone-idle thieving bastard – and then we'll see how he goes on; because mine won't be lily-white, I can tell you that now. And you never know, I might even be one of the blokes picking 'em out.

To Be Collected

Donnie came out of the snackshack in Heanor marketplace, paused to wipe crumbs from his mouth with a damp sleeve of raincoat. 'Belt-up, you rag-bags,' he shouted, to his two brothers beckoning from their government surplus lorry.

He ploughed into waterpuddles, socks and flesh soaked. 'Can't you see I'm coming? Now look at what they've made me do!' Curses ate into him like a corkscrew – 'I'm wet through now. I'll catch me death o' cold. You poxed-up bastards,' he raved, a fist pushed further into his groin pocket when he'd like it to be out and slamming them. He broke his tirade to grin at a couple of wide-eyed shopping women who thought he might have less dirty talk. 'Can't you wait a bit? You must have drainpipes, not guts, swallowing scorched tea like that.'

Tall Dave leaned out of the cab. His rawboned face, and grizzled-grey hair topped by a faded cap, jutted over a little boy pushing a tricycle. 'There ain't all day. We want to get cracking to Eastwood, see what we can get' – his voice raised but reasonable. Back inside he lit a cigarette, shifted to the middle: 'Hudge up, Flaptabs wants to park hissen.'

Bert, foot on the clutch and revving up loud, pressed himself against the door. He was the driver so, though the youngest of the three brothers, held the balance of which-way-turn and what-snackbar-stop decisions. He'd worked some time at the pitface, but too many changes of temperature, dampness and water, had marked him with pleurisy, menaced him with TB. Illness was shameful and unmanly, neither to be tolerated nor surrendered to, so he opted while sound for an outdoor life. This situation made him even more violent and morbid, see-sawed between pessimism, and hilarious pipedreams which came to nothing because he was so busy earning a living, though at the same time they enabled him to face making one.

'It's pissing down,' Donnie observed, installing himself in the warm, smoke-filled cab.

205

'Do you good,' Bert said, changing gear, 'get you a wash.'

'You can't beat a drop o' rain,' Donnie said, 'keeps 'em home for when the ragman calls.' He'd been involved in the last few days, in sporadic argument with Bert, though he'd given signs of wanting to pack it in without losing pride: 'I 'ad a wash this morning before I came out, which is more than yo' did, our Bert, you blackfaced bastard' – he grinned from his perished, intense face.

Dave hated argument: 'Why don't you two stop fucking-well needling each other? I'm not kidding, but you're driving me off my bleddy nut, day in and day out.' Neither took him up on this so, map reading, systematic and sharp for detail, he said: 'Left at the market then, out o' these crowds. Watch you don't hit that post office van – or you might accidentally knock-off a few thousand postal orders.'

'If I did it'd be enough to keep us for a year at the wage we mek.' Bert took Dave's directions smoothly, as if thinking them out for himself.

As the eldest Dave felt it his right to give orders, though he was careful to modify his voice and phrases when doing so. 'Get round this corner and we'll head for Eastwood. We've got to call at them houses we left hand-bills at this morning.' An old man, macless and without umbrella, shuffled off the pavement. 'I'll run that old bastard down,' Bert said. 'Can't see a foot before 'im.' He cupped a hand to his mouth: 'Get off home and DIE!'

'Less to feed,' Donnie laughed, no longer the butt-end of their fun: 'Don't hit him, though.'

'Listen at old soft-heart,' Bert jeered.

Dave agreed: 'Wappy bleeder' – scornful because they obviously wouldn't run the man over, and because Donnie's sympathy reminded them that they daren't. Able to cross between studs, the old man held his pace and shambled towards safe pavement. 'Join the army,' Bert shouted. 'They're crying out for blokes like yo', dad!' The man turned. A worn white death-mask of a starvo face opened into a smile. He shook his fist and stood on the pavement laughing.

They waved back. They all laughed, and the lorry shot forward. Shop awnings were pelted by violent rain: 'Whose idea was it to come out today?' he moaned, a side-glance at Donnie. 'Shaking it down in buckets and nowt between us and getting into debt but the price o' five fags and a gallon o' petrol. What a life. Out on the road in all this weltering piss.' He grumbled with a deadpan face, drew back his gears

206

to the pitchdown of a steep hill, going fast between houses and towards a railway on the valley bottom, scarves of mist and black smoke boiling from pit-chimneys and train funnels. 'I wouldn't live out 'ere for a pension.'

'Go on,' Donnie cried, the optimist who, even in the most terrible glasshouse of the British Army, averred that things might have been worse in a German deathcamp, and that pigswill was better than no swill at all. 'We might strike lucky at Eastwood, with an old copper or a mangle. Or an old firegrate. A few stone o' woollens. You never know.'

'All we'll get,' Bert prophesied, 'is a couple of bugged-up bedticks that a consumptive man and wife have just pegged out on. We'll be lucky to get eighteen pence the two: a cup of tea and a bun each.'

'That wain't keep my gang o' kids,' Donnie put in. 'But we'll get more than that though, yo' see.'

'I don't know why you have so many kids, Donnie. I don't, honest. You know you can't afford to keep 'em.'

'They don't tek any bread out o' your mouth.' Donnie's family was a great consolation to him, and though he could understand why it was made a joke of by his brothers, he had never been able to see the justice of it. His face steeled hard: 'And I do keep 'em though, don't I, eh?'

'Well,' Dave killed the joke before it went too far, 'even me and Alice don't get enough to live on.'

'You might just as well put your head in the gas-oven and be done wi' it,' Bert said.

'That wouldn't do, either,' Donnie smiled. 'You've got no right to talk like that. No use dying, is it?' Bert's eyes half closed at Donnie spinning things out to such a dead-end conclusion and, turning a corner, he roared into his ear:

'Wrap up. Brainless bastard' – so loud that even above the engine noise a policeman heard its subhuman command and glared into the cab to see what was the matter. Dave's eyes flashed out a picture of what possessions sprawled on the open back: a coil of rope, heaps of sacks, and a folded tarpaulin that covered nothing because it had been fine when they set out. Everything soaked. But nothing for the copper to get big ideas at either. The eyes of the law swivelled out of sight. 'You want to be careful what you say,' Donnie called. 'I'm a few years older than yo', you know.'

207

Bert became solemn, then melancholy, and gave himself up to grandiose dreams as he held the lorry fast to an uphill shove into Eastwood. 'I'd like to build eight machine-guns into this vehicle – into the bonnet – and blast my way through owt as stood in our way,' he said with a laugh, slowing at MAJOR ROAD AHEAD. 'To blast coppers, that's what I'd use it for.'

'What about the Blackshirts?' Donnie said. 'They're coppers, aren't they?'

'Who's talking about Blackshirts? Shurrup.'

'Course they are,' Dave told him.

'One 'ud put his hand out to get my licence' – Bert went on, grinning, 'six on 'em at a roadblock, and I'd slow down a bit, as if I was all for the law and going to stop.'

'To give 'em a Woodbine out of the ten thousand we'd got in the back?'

He pulled a face at Donnie. 'So I'd press this specially built-in button, and hear them bullet-belts starting to move under our feet, and the road in front would get churned up and go all grey and black, and the lorry would go bump-bump over the rubble we'd made of everything, and we'd all laugh together at six coppers snuffing it behind.'

'Well,' Dave said, winking towards Donnie, 'you'd get summonsed then if you killed 'em, I know you would.'

'That's what used to 'appen in Chicago though,' Bert put in. 'Like in them old pictures, with James Cagney and George Raft.'

'Well' – from Donnie – 'it don't 'appen anywhere now.'

'Not even in Russia,' Bert laughed. 'Like it did in that revolution.'

Donnie turned serious: 'If you did such a thing there now you'd end up filling saltbags, in the geranium mines.' And their laughter exploded, louder than any bomb or gunfire.

Eastwood was wetter than Heanor. They ascended the hill, patrolled rows of drenched uniform houses, desolate and scruffy at the backs, scruffier when TV aerials lifted Martian claws above slate-roofs and chimney stacks. Children were in school, and no one else seemed out on such a day. 'Pull up,' Dave rapped out. 'Let's get cracking on a couple o' these streets.'

'Maybe somebody's left a crust o' bread for us, or a claprag,' Bert scoffed, drawing into the kerb. 'I'll bet we don't see the sweat off a gnat's knackers – nor even as much as an old gas-stove.' Donnie caught on to this further wave of descending gloom, kept his monkey-face glum and silent. The lorry stayed by the kerb before any of them had the stomach to get out: the smell of their cigarettes and bodies made an atmosphere of homely warmth that they were loth to leave for wet unwelcoming backyards. 'It ain't all that bad,' Dave retorted to Bert's bitter weighing-up of their prospects, reaching under the steering-wheel for a pack of newly printed handbills. 'Before the war it was, but not since. Course, everything still looks the same.'

'And smells the same.'

'But all the colliers is on full time.'

'For a bit, anyway.'

Bert laughed. 'Everybody's got dough but us, I know that much.' For a moment their thoughts and voices had met in harmony, but drew away again when Donnie demanded: 'We got the lorry, ain't we?'

'Well' – Bert turned as if to rub the nub-end into his face – 'we wokked for it, din't we?' It was impossible to deny this triumphant assertion, and all three brooded for a minute on the months of monstrous overtime in the summer as brickies' labourers on the new estates – heaving high-loaded hods on bony shoulders, unstacking fresh-baked bricks from lorry-backs and hosing them down, lugging cement bags in the sun, lips cracking under hot tea and the blinding heat of shaving fires – a nightmare that nevertheless made a good memory in this wet daylight of a Monday morning – and which ended each with a hundred pounds to club-in for their rag-and-bone lorry. Dave glared savagely at the top handbill:

EX-SERVICEMAN'S COLLECTION
We give good CASH for
GAS-STOVES MANGLES LEAD
METALS OF ANY DESCRIPTION
RAGS AND BEDSTEADS
EVERYTHING
gratefully received
WE
call back in half an hour
THANK YOU.

'A lot o' bleeding good that does us,' Bert said, digging at Dave, whose idea the handbills had been. 'If we don't start making some money I'm going back to labouring.'

Dave groaned. They had discussed chucking it in before, but he prevailed on optimist Donnie to wield the casting vote that kept them at it. 'What's up with you? We made ten quid a-piece last week. You can't expect to get a millionaire's whack the first few months can you? Or p'raps you like working for a bleeding gaffer? I don't. I've 'ad enough o' that. You've only got to pull out a fag and you get your cards. Or see whether or not you backed a winner at dinner-time. You can bogger that for a lark. I'm not going to chuck it yet. I'd give it a longer try and see what we can do.' He reached for the map: 'We'll try Bolsover next week. The trouble with these places near Nottingham is they've allus bin done by some graballing bastard half an hour before; but up there, nobody ever bothers.'

'Like that place last week,' Bert thought, cheerful at having egged Dave to go on justifying and encouraging for so long – which was one of the few ways he knew of getting him to talk.

'If we make a living wage,' Donnie put in, 'what does it matter?'

Dave steered them back to work: ''Ark at 'im – bin listening to the Conservatives. Thinks he's got a right to a living wage. Come on, let's stop boggering around, and get cracking.' At which they alighted onto the pavement, took up their particular sacks, and spread in three directions into rainshot streets.

Such free-lance fending had sharpened Donnie's powers of reconnaissance. Each backyard – from dustbin to lavatory, clothes-line to wooden palings – was assessed for articles of value: a thrown-out bicycle, a zinc bathtub on the wall, a sack-covered mangle waiting for washday. He noticed blinds down for a funeral, milk bottles on doorsteps and, on entering a street or terrace, immediately looked for what chimney-stacks sent out no smoke in this land of mineral plenty. Not, of course, that he would walk off with anything that didn't belong to him – his thieving days had ended during the war, when to go on living demanded a definite long spate of thieving – but to remove some backyard eyesore of mildewed pram or stack of scrap copper or ripped up firegrate would be a favour he couldn't be bad tempered enough to deny anyone. Hadn't a woman pleaded with them only the other week to shift stuff they knew they wouldn't get five bob for?

His roped-together mackintosh was darkened by rain. The wind rose, couldn't make up its mind which way to scatter the floods. He'd collected nothing. Locusts and desert, he thought. Every crumb scratched and scraped – and saw himself in the same mind maybe as those poor enormous animals in prehistoric times come to the end of their tether because the sun had dried up the earth– which was better than this wet.

He knocked at a back door and, after a prolonged rattling of bolts and latches it was pulled violently inwards, irritation sounding even in the squeak of its hinges. A tall, thin, middle-aged collier stood there, still in his shirt-sleeves from the night shift. His deep grey eyes flashed:

'What do yo' want?'

Donnie usually spoke first, making his request against a blank stare. But this time he was stopped dead by abrupt rage in the collier's face as if, should it turn out he had been dragged from his breakfast for nothing, he would swing the hand from behind and wield a pick over Donnie's head, ready to bring down a well-aimed prostrating blow.

'Any old rags, mate?'

The collier's scarred features took time off to consider. Then: 'Ar,' he bawled, 'tek me' – and slammed the door at his face.

He wondered whether his brothers were having better luck. A whippet, entombed in some distant kennel, howled dismally at the general condition of the rheumatic world. Rain belted down, yet the sun shone in Donnie's brain of day-dream and optimism, illuminating the sudden find of lead-rolls outside some half-built church he would never pray in, laughing like mad with his brothers as they set upon the gold-find with axe and crowbar, stuffing sack after sack which would weigh on their shoulderbones till they felt sick with lugging it to the lorry. A raindrop running down to his ear caused him to scrub away the itch of it. He missed half a dozen houses due to his daydream. The collier's rebuff seemed so comic that he thought to tell it later to his brothers for a laugh.

He knocked at another door, and a woman opened it, a cherubic tow-headed kid making an aeroplane out of the collection leaflet. She held an old brass kettle: 'If you've come for scrap, you can tek this, my lad.'

'How much do you want for it?' he said, thinking it better than nothing.

'Nay, lad, I'll tek nowt from thee, seeing as tha's had such a lot to put up with in the war, while many a one was staying at home.'

He looked modestly into the kitchen beyond. 'That's the way it is.'

211

'It's a bleddy shame they don't look after you better when you've been all them miles away fighting for 'em, it is and all.'

'Well,' Donnie said, 'as long as they fill their own pockets. I was in a Jap prison camp seven years. I've still got scars all over me, and one of my lungs is gone. I don't like to think about it. There's many a night I wake up all of a groan and sweat. And what did we get when we come back? Twenty-six bob a week. No good to a living soul. But I've got eleven kids now, so I suppose I'm good for something.' He stuffed the kettle into his sack, left his thanks as the door closed. He heard her going through the parlour muttering loudly to the uncomprehending kid: 'Seven years! Poor bogger. Seven – that's funny, though.'

At the end of the street stood a red-bricked chapel, a body-snatcher guarded by railings and fronted by wide steps leading to the principal door. It was a chapel no longer, but a get-together of shabby drill-hall and dead-beat billiard saloon. Donnie found a nub-end pinned under the crossband of his cigarette case. Maybe they're clearing the place out, he thought, for it looked as if it were about to fall flat on its face. He pushed open a side gate and walked up the entry. The backyard hadn't seen sunshine since its walls were built. Windows were wooden-barred and barbed-wired. Broken bottles spiking the top bricks turned it into a well-defended backyard of the house of God. Donnie noticed a row of dustbins, each caved-in or holed, which several experienced kicks showed to be empty. He grunted at the dampness, a dispiriting waterlogged atmosphere more tied to an out-law's heart than any other smell and feeling.

He glanced back for a last check-up. Under an awning of corrugated tin stood a canvas kitbag tied at the neck. He went over and, giving it an immediate kick, expected the unresistant cave-in of cardboard and paper, but was not surprised (already suspecting that it looked too good for any old rubbish) when his boot hit against some kind of metal. He thumped it for being so puzzling, closed his fingers over corners of whatever was inside. Undo the string, you silly bogger, and have a look – an irritating and unrewarding job, for his fingernails broke at the first try. He stood back a moment: the cord was knotted and double-knotted, and shrunk and solidified in the damp air.

He was bemused, at what a kitbag meant to many but had never meant to him. Gunner Donnie Hodson – you didn't keep your kitbag long: came on leave one day and never went back – stayed by the fireside in a long paralysis of fear and rage, smoking what fags you could cadge until your mother chucked you out and told you to get some money or clamb. Them was funny times. One day he was at the kitchen table when knocks – back and front – sounded from the wide-awake street. He was hungry for his tea, holding a sharp knife and not knowing whether to cut his throat or a slice of bread. His mother did what was needed of her. Donnie ran up to the attic, coolly setting the skylight down when once on the roof. And there he was, hanging out on the slates like Monday washing, under the summer sky and counting German planes that slid over low and let rip with machine-guns. Shellbursts like dirty wool seemed to be exploding not many feet from his head. The sirens were moaning like a runover cat, and it was hard to imagine anyone in his right mind out on the roof – so the coppers must have thought. But Donnie wasn't in anybody's mind except his own, which turned out to be right enough, and his instinct told him one sure thing, that it was better to risk a bullet from German planes than go back through that skylight and get parcelled off to the army again. 'What did mam do with them two full cups of tea she'd just poured? Did she sling 'em in the sink before the coppers could see 'em?' – were his sole speculations as shrapnel (from AA shells he would have been firing had he not been where he was) zipped viciously by like petrified dead sparrows onto the slates, breaking some, others ricochetting, one piercing the skylight window that finally stopped the coppers' courage from thinking he was out there.

Looking back on this one uncomfortable glory of his life, he couldn't help but laugh. Nothing from the past was sad, no matter how awful it might have been at the time. Only the present was classifiable into good or putrid, but every incident that he could remember was laughable for the simple reason that it was past, and that he had survived it without mortal damage. While Donnie was sitting on the rooftop with shrapnel and bullets pissing all around, his mother was being questioned by coppers and redcaps, unable to speak out where he was, yet wanting to in order to get him off that dangerous roof.

They got him in the end, cornered as a rat by bigger rats in a cul-de-sac one dark night, a suitcase of plundered whisky at his feet. Dave had got away, rattled his longer legs among streets at different angles to Donnie's, until dark distance drew him into a maw of safety. Donnie was pounced on by a couple of stalwart Specials and manhandled to the police station: 'We're helping our country' – bump – 'and trying to do our bit,' – bump – 'but you blokes are worse than the bloody Germans' – bump-thud. 'You want bleeding-well exterminating, then maybe we could get this war finished' – crash. No bail (the black eyes and cuts had disappeared by quarter-sessions time). Twenty-two cases to be taken into consideration, sir. Three years, then. And let that be a lesson to you. Yes, sir. Thank you, sir.

That was the only way to get the war over. Go and fight, they had said. What for? Show me what I've got to fight for, and then I'll go. You can't though, can you? There's nobody in this bloody country can show me that. 'You're a pacifist,' Dave dinned into him. 'Like me. See?' It was still the middle of the war when they let him out of jail and turned him over to the redcaps, so he hopped it a second time, and uniform number two burst into paraffin-flame from the bedroom grate.

In 1945 the redcaps collared him for the final bout, made him pay for having kept out of the war as successfully as they had by declaring on him a private and spiteful war of their own. Even that terrible time was laughable. He had wakened up one fine day to find himself between the clean sheets of heaven. 'A mental home,' the man in the next bed grinned. Marvellous. No more bread-and-water, cells, packdrill, kicks and punches and buckets of freezing pond-scum splashing against thin denims. You had to laugh, at what men who should have been your own mates in factory or on building site did to you. You just couldn't help laughing, though you could bet that some bastards had put them up to it as well. Such a grin gave you toothache on the lips. It was funny, too funny even to tell anyone about, and so Donnie had a reputation for being soft, almost daft and, unlike his brothers, slow in ways of self-preservation. He was also reluctant with his speech, dense it was said, often unable to make his opinions fit the subject under discussion, or make them influence it when they did. His family and friends began to think that such attitudes had been there from birth, to be pointed out and taken advantage of.

The rain was a mere drizzle, easier to accept and fight, and he shook himself to regard the actual physical bulk of the kitbag. This one stored rubbish – a useful purpose to what most carried. He searched for another cigarette, but found none. 'I'll ask Dave to lend me one when I get back. I'd better start moving, or they'll wonder where I've got to.'

He pulled the bag forward, held it from the ground by unyielding strings. It weighed heavy and, replacing it, a piece of cardboard finished its journey and slid onto the stones behind. Torn from a shoebox and crayoned on the white surface, the words he held up were: TO BE COLLECTED.

His heart bumped. By who else but him? A find, it looked like. Who'd have thought it in all this drenching rain? It was meant for the scrapman to pick up and relieve whoever had left it of an unwanted rubbish-burden. It felt like old metal against his boot, a mixture of bits and bobs no doubt, that would need sorting but hadn't been considered valuable enough to sell. It was no use sorting it now: he pictured his brothers doing that like vultures later, cursing him, he shouldn't wonder, because the stuff – after his dreams of a unique find – wasn't worth much after all. Still, it was marvellous to get something. He spat on both palms and honed them well, lifted the bag onto his broad shoulders and lugged it out into the street, a miracle that such a light heart supported it.

Most of their time back at the lorry had been spent cursing Donnie – 'the dilat'ry bastard' – for dawdling, when from their vantage point of the high cab they saw him staggering along the street with what looked like a treasure of a load. Old rags didn't weigh that much, for Donnie was a carthorse, a man of iron never known to flinch or tire under the most back-breaking weights. So what could it be and where had he clicked to be shouldering such heavy responsibility?

'Trust old mental to get all the luck,' Bert said. A grateful feeling lurked somewhere behind his scowl, though he could only show it by feeling envious. 'We didn't even get a bleddy claprag between us. Where did you find it?' he bawled.

'From a church.'

The metal was all sharp elbows, dug corner after merciless corner into the muscle of Donnie's shoulders. The pressure had now passed aching point, become pain – fiery and unbearable. At Bert's abrupt question, though only a few yards from the lorry, he let the sack roll over his head and crash logwise on the wet pavement. It pulled his new cap off: 'Can't you bleddy-well wait till I get to the lorry?' he shouted angrily at Bert. Dave was helping him to carry it there.

Bert hung back, opening and closing the blade of his jack-knife. The crash sounded tinny, like kids' toys hammered together to take up less room – but Donnie wouldn't know the difference. Old wool-nut thought all metal a miracle of gold and silver, and only leapt into life at the noise it made. Which perhaps was a good thing for a bloke on this job, for look how he'd toted that sack from God knew where. Bert slid

215

to the pavement when all work was done, snapping strings with his razorsharp knifeblade.

'Steady-on,' Donnie cried. 'Give me a chance to get the bleddy thing down. You'll slice my finger off if you aren't careful.' He stood back, sullen while they ravaged his prize. Bert started to unthread the cord through each eye-hole, but was beaten to it by nimble, systematic Dave. All three fixed their eyes on it at the same time.

Dave held it as he must at some time have been taught to during his various brief stays with the army: left hand under the barrel a little behind the spout, arm out at a sufficient angle to give rest to the magazine – which he instinctively slotted on; right hand at the trigger; and skeleton-butt under his arm. Then it swivelled downwards, mouth pouting to the pavement.

'Christ!' he said, all breath shocked from him. Bert balanced a slender tin casing of magazine on his palm. It was full of bullets. 'What sort of a chapel did you say you got it from?' He was amused, as much at Dave's tight-set face seeing prison and death and all the discomforts that oscillated between for possessing such a thing, as at the sight of the Sten machine-gun he unwillingly toted. Donnie was the least surprised or perturbed, still thought of it as scrap, guns and magazines to be sledge-hammered into solid unrecognizable slabs and flogged at the junkyard. Nobody would know. It had been done before; and they might be as much as a quid each to the good.

Dave turned on him: 'You *barmy* bleeder. You crazy bastard. Bringing things like this!'

Maybe he was putting on a rare joke, though the pained face made Donnie suspect him in earnest. 'What do you mean? What are you calling me like that for?'

A woman, carrierbags hooked to each hand, came around the corner from the main road. Dave rammed the gun under cover and they talked about last night's film. 'I suppose you're going to tell me you found 'em in a dustbin next?' he demanded when she had passed.

'They was near a dustbin,' Donnie explained, hurt at such ingratitude. 'A card was on top of the bag saying: TO BE COLLECTED. Somebody meant it for us, I'm dead sure o' that. It's government surplus maybe, that's all.'

Dave's anguished face showed he was nowhere convinced. He set the bag down a yard from himself: 'Carry 'em up the street again.'

'Not me. Yo' can do it if you like.'

'We'll get ten years each in bleeding jail if you don't.'

Donnie climbed into the cab and slammed the door on himself. 'That's the bleddy thanks I get for struggling all that way with it.'

'He might get nicked taking 'em back,' Bert said. 'We'd better dump 'em on the lorry and get shot on 'em when we come to a lonely place.'

The whole day boggered, Dave plainly saw. Would you believe it? That was the worst o' working with batchy bleeders like Donnie. His narrowed eyes, grizzled hair and creased forehead gave an impression of forcefulness that would never break. 'It's looney,' he said, yet saw reason in Bert's advice. He slung the sack on the lorry-back. 'All right, Bert' – giving unrepentant Donnie a black look – 'let's get cracking out of here. We'll drop 'em in a reservoir somewhere.'

Bert drove to the main road as if to go quietly from the pitch of their crime, filtered through the traffic of Hilltop and descended into the valley, eager to put distance between them and Eastwood. 'I expect it's only scrap though, you know.'

'Course it is' – a desperate note in Donnie's voice – 'They wouldn't 'ave put it there if it worn't. I don't know. All this bother over a few bits o' junk.'

'You mental bastard,' Dave cried. 'You think it's scrap – with ammunition? It might have been army surplus but we worn't supposed to tek it. Anybody with a bit o' sense would have known it. I expect you thought they put it there for us, specially? "Perhaps somebody'll want to start a revolution," I suppose you thought they said. "Or maybe somebody'll want to do a bit o' target practice at the rent man, or knock off the odd copper or two?" Christ!' He banged his fist against the lorry door, emphasizing a decision that needed no democratic majority to force it through: 'We'll get rid of it somewhere past Ripley, then beat it back to Nottingham. I only hope nobody gets onto us about it, that's all. If they do, I'll brain you. You might want to get away from your ten kids for a few years, but I don't.'

'It'd be better if we could sell it though,' Bert said. 'I know an IRA bloke who'd give his right arm for stuff like this. Happen we could dump it somewhere, and then let him know where it is, at a price.'

Fields, hedged by mounds of stone, rose from either side of the road. Towns were left far behind. Dave turned to his brother: 'Look, nut, if you think I'm going to get twenty years, you're wrong.' His hand went to the door: 'I'm getting out.'

'I was only joking,' Bert said, though slowing down in case Dave

217

really wanted to get out. But he pulled the door to and they drove on in silence, three factions as much as three brothers.

Beyond Ambergate lay tranquil countryside, low cloud and rainmist on purple inhospitable hills around the Matlocks. The road contoured into another valley, and no one spoke. Such wild land kept words penned in. Donnie's normal face was one of open good-humoured speculation as to whether the day would yield fair loads and a living wage, but his triumphant find at the chapel ('It couldn't have been a chapel,' he told himself now) gave it a self-importance that his brothers would not acknowledge; at which his face gave way to gloom, like some forlorn box-headed terrier that retrieves a succulent rabbit for its poaching master but feels it change into a rat while the smile of achievement awkwardly persists.

Rain hung, a carbide sheet of blue above grey-green rolling hills around. Trees were bowed down by the weight of water, bare twigs shining silver with it, the soaked smell of the green and soily earth more extreme and frightening than the rancid stink of protective streets. Hopeful Donnie assumed that every wayside house was a missed opportunity of a brass bedstead or heap of iron and lead. But Dave sat immersed in the webbed roads of his map, and Bert's eyes showed only a flat concern for his firm motionful steering along the highway.

Dave grunted them into a by-road and Bert silently obeyed, putting the lorry at grinding first gear for a steep incline. The high-roaring life of the engine plunged Donnie's memory back to another faraway lorry that, in the depths of a smoke-screen, increased speed regardless of what might be in its way. He was going on foot through a paraffin midnight, each quiet step betrayed by a choking cough, delayed by a case bulging with silk stockings snaffled from a shop hidden within the bull's-eye of a few dozen shrouded streets.

On the boulevard a woman screamed, and Donnie jumped (the first time afraid that evening) thinking she was under its double wheels. He was close enough to touch her. 'Where are you, duck?' he called, as the unheeding vehicle thundered away. 'Are you all right?'

The voice that answered sounded young and sweet, even behind such swearing laid on at the unthinking driver: 'The bleddy swine might a killed me.'

'Tek my arm,' Donnie said. 'I'll see you 'ome. Did you miss your last bus?'

'Aye,' she answered, quick off the mark, 'I did.'

'What a shame,' Donnie said, leading her along, and thinking that most likely some chap had ditched the poor gel.

Her name was Dora and, talking readily, they made a harmless couple passing the copper propping up the labour-exchange in the artificial fog. They went home to Donnie's, and slept a sinful sweet kip together. From his attache-case Dora thought he was a nice young man, a commercial traveller perhaps (which he was but not in the way she thought) and fairly well-off when he opened the case in the morning and gave her a dozen pairs of fully-fashioned stockings; and Donnie, when they decided that same day to live together ('I've got a house in Cuckney Terrace just down the road,' she told him) deduced her to be living alone because her husband was in the Forces. Both, thinking they were on to a good thing, were disappointed. Dora found soon enough that Donnie was on the run and thieving for a living; and Donnie discovered even sooner that Dora already had four children in the house (floors and faces well-scrubbed though to receive him) and that she was separated from her husband because he was in jail. Such disappointments cancelled out, and they were happy together. Donnie stole hard to keep her and the kids, liked being the master of his house and having something to go steady for. Dora loved him and bred well so that there were three more kids by Victory Day. 'We'll buy the silly bleeder a dartboard, or a game of ludo,' Dave said. 'He thinks there ain't owt else to do in the world but that.'

'You'd do better to whitewash his cellar out and knock a few bunks together,' Bert answered. 'If it worn't already full up.'

One of the children could not have been Donnie's, not well enough synchronized with his spells in prison, but he accepted it just the same. This, he found, lowered him still further in the eyes of his brothers: 'She's done it on him, the poor bogger. If she was my woman I'd paste her from one end of Hyson Road to the other,' he heard Bert say once when he came in from the bookie's because he'd lost his money sooner than intended. 'I shouldn't be a bit surprised if none o' them kids are 'is,' his mother was saying. 'She's an old bag, and nowt else,' Dave said sternly as Donnie came in through the scullery. 'How else could she have lived, though, while he was in clink?' was the final verdict.

Riding along with a load of hot guns, all silent because they'd share a life sentence if caught, Donnie felt they were ripping away his credit for what could be a profitable find. His grievance came from the memory of his desperate yet strangely happy years during the war, and of what he had overheard after his bad luck on the horses which only now did he relate to himself – and so long ago, he thought, beaming his mortally injured sight on the set visages of Dave and Bert.

A sun blade made the road shine like a roll of liquorice. Clouds moved above wooded spurs and crags of the lonely Pennines whither Dave had guided them by constant reference to his magic map. 'They have wicked weather out here,' he said. 'Only a month ago the snow nearly covered the telegraph poles. I'd rather be in streets.' It was a long time since they passed a house, and none were now in sight. The woods seemed dead and February bare, yet when Bert stopped the lorry under a hill bushes showed spring buds like the green tips of novelty matchsticks.

They got down, stamped their feet morosely against wind and the smell of open country beating up their limbs; it felt clean and agreeable to the stale stink of cab and backyards. Dave led them over a five-barred gate and down a bank. Bert carried the kitbag to a large pool of stagnant water, hurled a stone towards the middle that landed with a healthy penetrating sound: gluck! 'It's deep. Be good enough to swim in, if it worn't so cold.'

Dave, slashing the bag with a penknife, looked at Donnie as if he would slash him next: 'All we want now is for a copper to come by. Think of the time and petrol we've lost on this stunt.'

Shirtsleeves rolled up, Bert rubbed the beneficial ointment of wind into his white heavily veined skin. 'It's like a holiday. Leave Donnie be,' he said. 'We know how you feel by now.'

Donnie stood by the rising ground, feeling the injustice of their so-called democracy. His great effort of the rain-soddened morning had come to this! – slung into deep and muddy water, sunk out of sight when they had stood to make a fiver each – which he for one could do with, Dora being pregnant and soon to leave for the hospital. He'd often thought how this ragman job was too low paid, having such a mob of kids to look after, but the family allowance helped, and it was better than working for a gaffer no matter how low the money. He had been the one brother reluctant to part with his hundred pounds, giving in eventually because without it there'd be no business – something they had willingly forgotten. And now they'd got the sort of find often imagined with glowing eyes and pints suspended they were chucking it away, just like that. 'Come on,' Dave cried. 'Give a hand to get rid o' this stuff.'

Donnie couldn't move. 'I'm for keeping it. What about yo', our Bert?'

'I'm snatched,' Bert said, struggling back into his coat. He turned to Donnie: 'I don't know. Honest to God, I don't.'

Dave picked out the top Sten gun. 'I do. It's got to be slung away. If it ain't I'm not getting in that lorry again. I'd rather walk back to Nottingham.' His words burned with righteousness, and of all three he had the clearest ideas of right and wrong (though he didn't always abide by them), which made him a hard man to argue with. At election times Donnie never voted; Bert sometimes dragged himself between one pint and the next; Dave always did, being at heart a simple political man and swearing at others whom he suspected of not having bothered. With him an idea once expressed stuck until a new one took its place, causing the old one to fuse with the hard core of his personality.

Bert turned to Donnie: 'I reckon we'd better sink 'em. They aren't any good to us. Too risky to keep, as well' – an opinion sending Dave into action before Donnie tried once more to swing the vote. The first gun sailed to the middle of the water. It sank. Another followed. Bert joined in, threw a gun and tailed it with a hollow magazine.

Donnie strolled casually over and picked out a gun, as if to help, then sorted through rusting magazines until he reached one that was loaded. He clipped it onto his gun, the sound hidden by resplendent water-spouts caused by the hard work of his brothers. 'This is what they should a done in the war,' Dave said.

'I thought that was what yo' did,' Bert laughed.

'I mean everybody though.'

'Maybe they will in the next one.'

'There wain't be a next one, or time to do this if there is' – Dave spun the last weapon as high as it would go, the two of them drawing their heads back – seeing bordering rocks, treetops and a gulf of cloud – to follow the upward and downward flight. 'A bull's-eye,' Bert shouted, blinking at its impact. 'Chock in the middle.'

Dave gave in to a rare bout of self-praise. 'I can't help it if I'm a crackshot!'

A savage, sharp explosion burst through the air, a needling crack of white fire directly connected with the chip that flew from the moss-covered rock a bare yard from Bert's foot. The shot itinerated every crevice-point of the hills, came back again and again, each time with diminishing vigour.

The sight of Donnie holding the machine-gun, as if he had been a professional guerilla all his life, sent a pain through Dave's feet that seemed to come from the soil he stood on, fastening him to earth and shrubs like a charge of electricity high enough to cause a rheumatic pain but not to sling him a dozen yards away. He was afraid to move, to try and rid himself of it in case it would increase – or for fear a bullet from Donnie's gun would strike him all unbeknowing – smack in the guts. He stared at the apparition of his brother, was startled by Bert calling: 'Drop it, Donnie, you daft sod. Come on, knock it off. You'll do some damage if you aren't careful.'

'That's right,' Dave said, and to Bert: 'You should a kept your bloody eye on him.' The derogatory tone, stabbing through to Donnie's incensed brain, brought forth a further terrifying shot. Dave and Bert scampered towards different boulders beyond the pool. 'Why don't you mind what you're saying?' Bert hissed across to Dave. Then in a commanding yet considerate tone: 'Donnie, put that bleeding gun down. I'll get mad in a minute.'

Donnie's fallen cap lay at the edge of the pool, half in and half out of the water like a turtle emerging for a breath of air. His face was rigid, all lines and muscles clamped into place by the grip of his teeth. His hair blew in the wind. 'You bastards' – a tearful implacable roar – 'you rotten lousy bastards.'

'What's bitin' you?' Bert shouted. 'What 'ave we done to you?'

'I'll kill you both,' he responded loudly, his brain shut hard against the wind, and all their talk. 'You've 'ad it your own way too long. I'll show you whether I'm kidding or not. That's what Dora's allus telling me, that you put on me. Only I ain't believed her up to now.'

'Pack your game up,' Dave said reasonably, 'and let's get cracking. We've lost enough time as it is.'

'Chuck that gun in the water,' Bert ordered. 'Or I'll get mad, our Donnie.' The sun came out and, standing between them, gave Bert confidence to move nearer Donnie. He knelt at the kitbag to fold it: 'We'd better tek this with us and burn it. We don't want anybody to find it.'

'I suppose not,' Dave winked.

'You bastards,' Donnie said. 'You think you're the bosses and can get away with everything.' His eyes were set on them, unmoving, as hard as the spout of the ever-pointing gun. 'You should a kept them Stens and not thrown 'em away. You'll be sorry you wasted 'em like that one day.'

222

'I told you it was dangerous,' Dave said. 'Our Bert said so as well. You don't want to go to clink for ten years, do you? I don't, anyway, I know that much. What would Dora do if you got sent down? Eh?'

Donnie pressed a foot forward. 'I don't give a fuck for owt now. I'll do you both in.'

'Put it away,' Dave shouted. 'You cranky sod.'

Bert eyed him coolly: 'If you do owt daft, you'll swing.'

'I don't care.'

'You will. Wain't he, Dave?' – nonchalantly.

'Not much he wain't. He'll get my fist as well when I catch hold of him.'

Bert was nearer now, pushing the spacious kitbag over his boots in a kneeling-down position and easing his feet forward while he talked: 'I know a bloke in the army had his arm shot off, only by accident, but the bloke who done it got ten years. I reckon he deserved it though: an arm's an arm, and a pension's no good to anybody. I don't like guns being pointed at me our Donnie, so you'd better drop it; it brings my cough back, and I feel bad for days then. I get laid-up and earn no dough, so stop it.'

'You never listen to what I say,' Donnie complained, crashing in on Bert's monologue. 'You think I'm daft. Two on to one. That's how it is all the time. I've only got to say: "Let's do this," and you two rotten bastards allus vote it down. But my share in this lorry's the same as yourn, you know. You forget that, you do an' all.'

'I never say it ain't,' Bert reassured him. 'You know I don't' – forward again, still closer. Dave, watching, wondered how it was going to end – 'I'm allus on your side, but you forget that as soon as I see fit to vote with Dave once in a while. Don't he, Dave?'

'That's what I tell him.'

'You remember that time you wanted to tek Dora and the kids on an outing to Gunthorpe, and Dave said we couldn't afford the time, and that we should collect some stuff from Derby instead? I voted with you then. So you won, and all your tribe had a smashing day by the Trent.'

Dave backed him up: 'Course they did. He's a madhead though, wain't listen to anybody.'

He was deeply hurt, accused of disloyalty. 'Yes I do,' was all he could think of.

'No you don't. If you do, put that gun down and prove it. You've

223

already made enough noise to bring all the coppers of Derby onto us, and I don't want to see yo' nor any on us copped. Come on, I'm clambed to death. Aren't yo', Bert?'

Dave imagined a reasonable tone would now creep into their discussion, then: 'I'm going to count to seven,' Donnie said slowly, 'and when I've counted seven I'm going to empty this magazine into the pair of you. Then we'll see who's got a vote and who ain't. One, two, three' – loud like bullets already flying, a supercharged tone of voice he had often heard ordering him about, but had never been able to use himself.

Bert broke in. 'Donnie, you rat' – and moved closer, covered by his ruse of the kitbag. Dave stood, graven.

'Four, five' – slow and definite, each echo overriding Bert's plea, moving the gunspout now in a circular pointing motion that, though not making for accuracy, gave fate a chance to operate and seemed more menacing. 'Donnie, chuck it,' Dave yelled. 'You can have the bleeding lorry, but drop that gun.' Bert had stopped moving, was fastened by Donnie's eyes.

'Six, Seven!'

Nothing happened. 'Who are you kidding?' Bert said, standing up.

Donnie grinned. 'You thought I meant it, didn't you? Well I do. But if you think I'm going to do it when you expect it though, you're both bleddy-well wrong.' Bert's senses were fixed hard between guile and humour, and he said with a smile: 'Drop that rod, and I'll strip stark naked and swim in to get them guns out, one at a time – then we'll flog 'em to the I R A. Eh? What do you think o' that, then?'

It made no impression against Donnie's maniacal stare. Without warning, his arms lifted for the aim.

Bert fell to the ground, flattened like a spread-out frog. Dave followed, keeling over like a post, low-current electricity of fear moving like a threat through his limbs. Donnie's arms spun like propellers working in competition, and after several illogical movements both gun and magazine somehow parted and leapt free of his swinging arms, falling into the water. On lifting their heads – a broad margin of some seconds after the splash – they saw Donnie widely grinning.

'Oh you should a seen yer! Christ, you should a seen yer! Frightened to death, the pair of you. What a treat! Never in all my born days . . .'

They ran at him, wild for vengeance, and before they reached him Donnie knew it was no use making out it had been a joke. Gaiety withered on his face.

'You swine,' Dave screamed, gripping his waist and dragging him down. He had wanted to smash Donnie's life out, had promised himself the marvellous vicious treat of it while petrified by the Sten in such crazy hands – but a relatively harmless grip was all he could give now that the time had come. Bert found Donnie's head from out of the scuffle, and thumped him between the eyes in a business-like way, hard. 'You cranky bastard, doing a thing like that.'

In spite of smoke-stacks and colliery headstocks the distant landscape was clear: sun out to stay and clouds lingering only to the cold watery north. Bert manoeuvred the lorry like a madman, light hearted now that their incriminating load had been cast off. The lorry, it seemed, was a sort of zip mechanism causing the road to fasten-off the hills behind them as they descended. Dave sang snatches of songs they had beaten out together in last Saturday's pub, the map crushed and stained under his muddy boots. Donnie sat between them, smiling, his face dirty, hand at last taken from the swollen eye sustained in the final settlement at the pool. Dave put an arm around his shoulders, pulled him close, hugged him: 'Old barmy sod. Old madhead' – yet with a certain deference that Donnie was too happy, and Bert too careful at the corner before Tipley, and Dave too close to it, to notice.

Donnie pulled away. 'Less of the barmy,' he threatened, as if still holding the Sten.

'Hark at him,' Dave sang back. 'Scarface. Al Capone. It's a good job we got rid o' them guns, or he'd a bin down at Barclays tomorrow asking for a loan.'

'Bogger off,' Donnie retaliated, though laughing with them at such a Robin Hood picture and grateful that it saved him feeling foolish for having stuck them up. 'I wouldn't do owt as daft as to rob a bank.' Here was a story they could talk and laugh about for ever among themselves, without being able to tell it to another and so mock Donnie with.

'Well, I don't know about that,' Dave said. 'In a way maybe we should a kept one o' them guns. If there's a war and they come to call us up we could take to the hills with it. Mow down a few Civil Defence bastards on the way. All three on us, wi' the lorry. We'd never get caught.'

Donnie was indignant. 'Now hark at who's talking. Christ! That's what I was trying to tell you back there. It's too bleddy late now.'

Dave's imagination drew back, having touched on some too open wound. He was the calm and thoughtful leader once more. 'Forget it. I'm only kidding.'

'Perhaps we should 'ave though,' Bert said, feeling for the crumpled kitbag between his legs, aiming punches that swerved the lorry from one side of the house-lined street to the other. 'We could a kept two or three. Donnie was right.'

'No he worn't,' Dave said, but quietly. 'And I'm telling the pair of you – that you don't know owt about no guns – that you've never seen any. Forget 'em, see?'

'They'll never find 'em,' Bert said.

'What a bloody time we 'ad though,' Dave laughed, nudging Donnie.

'I wonder if Dora's had her kid yet?' Bert asked, spitting out of the window. 'I can see owd Donnie ending up better off than any of us. He'll be sitting back like a sheik while his twenty kids bring their wage packets back from the factory every week.'

'It's not due for a day or two,' was all Donnie said. Drab windswept houses funnelled them up the hill, and dinner could be detected journeying from gas-ovens to tables of waiting children home from school. 'It's only one o'clock,' Bert said, stopping at the marketplace, 'but I feel as if a week's gone by since this morning.'

'Shall we eat here, or in Heanor?' Dave wanted to know. Smells from a snackbar drifted over the cobbles as a bus conductor opened the door and stood fastening his silver-buttoned coat over a just-fed belly.

'Here,' Bert opted, 'I'm clambed.'

'I reckon we should go to Heanor,' Donnie said. 'It ain't far off.' Bert said they could eat just as well where they were, so Donnie turned to Dave: 'What about yo'? At that place in Heanor you can get a big plate o' stuff for a couple o' bob.'

Bert pulled the door shut. 'Let's make our bleddy minds up.' Cigarettes were lit to relieve the strained atmosphere of voting. Fingers drummed hard on the drumsounding door. Dave's long face made up its mind, yet no sign was showed of a decision: 'Heanor.'

Even on the second syllable Bert had given in and pulled out the choke, and they were rolling down the hills again towards Eastwood. Once a majority vote was reached it became a unanimous decision. A hard wind drove tension clear of the cab. 'I forgot to tell you,' Donnie said. 'It was a scream.' He laughed until Dave told him to get on with it then. 'Well, I went to this house at Eastwood, before I found the guns, and a collier comes to the door, a great big bastard still in his helmet and pit-muck, his trousers patched and his vest in tatters. "What do *yo'* want?" he bawls out at me. I thought he was going to smash me with the pick he's got in his hand. So I says: "Got any old rags, mate?" and he looks at me for half a minute, then says, "Ar, TEK ME!" and slams the door in my face.'

It was the best joke in years: three crimson faces choking behind the windscreen of the descending lorry. Bert pulled into the side of the road and switched off, tears flowing from all but Donnie, who knew it was a good story, but wasn't paralysed by it. When the lorry started again he felt happy – in spite of the half-soaked cap (rescued at the last minute from the pool) whose damp side ate through to his hair – singing to himself because Dora might have another boy. He still didn't know why he'd insisted that they eat in Heanor because, all said and done, it didn't matter to him where they ate, as long as he was able to fill his aching guts with something.

Revenge

The service was over, and we signed the book, stood outside the late-English Perpendicular nondescript church, while the buffed-up blackened eye of the camera fixed us forever in the bewildered yet happy world.

Confetti snowed down, coloured snow, tips of spring flowers falling over our bent backs as we got into the car. Life was beginning, and we laughed, never wondering whether or not we would cry at the far end of it all. The preacher's claptrap still fed my humour, though it wasn't long before I began to look back on it as one big farce. My mates didn't even grin when I agreed to a church wedding. They thought I was quite right to give in to her, the spineless lot, and so I was glad to change into another department where the hypocrisy of friendship hadn't had time to jell, so that we could all concur how soft I'd been to slide back on my principles, even though it hurt me to say so.

I was nearing forty, and Caroline who became my wife had just turned thirty, so it was late for both of us. But every old sock finds an old shoe, as those at work laughingly put it. With my parents dead, I lived alone in the house I had just finished buying, and that as an only son I had grown up in. It was a house of the better sort, with three floors instead of two, and set a few yards back from the pavement. My bride now came there for the reception.

She looked so beautiful, among all our friends at the table, that I wondered how she'd come to marry me, which explains why I'd let us be spliced in church perhaps. But looks never counted for much between us. I'm well set up and stocky, with all my hair still and swept back neat. What's more I've never been got at by illness. All that bothered me was a tape-worm in Gibraltar during the war, but it wasn't so rare as to be a real sickness, though such a thing growing inside me, no matter how much they pulled it out, took weeks to get rid of. In fact I became so badly that I was shipped home, and sometimes I wonder if I'm not still harbouring it, I feel so jumpy.

Maybe it's just the memory, and time will tell, though it has enough to live on in the meantime if it really is down there chewing away.

I was looking at the darling I'd married, tall and thin-faced, with fine fair hair that I hoped she'd now grow long (though she never did), and good features when she was pleasantly smiling. Otherwise I'd stick my thumb towards the earth and enjoy feeling a swine – but it's too early to start being hard on myself. I'd only met her six months before, and what all the hurry was I couldn't now say. Certainly, I didn't know then that she'd gone through a bout of mental trouble at twenty. Even if I had known there'd have been no backing out, but rather I would have worn the fact in my buttonhole to show everyone what a noble sort I was.

So many presents piled on the sideboard gave me a funny feeling, a disturbance I couldn't remark on because it hardly existed, and in any case it wouldn't have been polite to do so at such a time. Around the glory of the cake was a spread-out zone of toasters, dinner-services and tea-sets, electric blankets, transistor radios, horseshoes and telegrams, records and ashtrays, plastic fruit and paper flowers, kettles and bedside lights, that everyone looked avidly over, stuff which almost brought tears into Caroline's eyes when she passed them by to take off her dress upstairs.

Two rooms had been opened into one, and the space was full, tables put together down the middle and bordered by every chair in the house, plus a few brought by her brother in his brand-new estate car. Trimmings were up, lights on, and drink was flowing. What could go wrong with such a spread of cake and salad, ham and wine? I said so in my speech after we'd all set to. A friend from work mumbled something about going at it like a bull at a gate, but I stopped him in mid-flight. I didn't like a thing like that, because I considered it the vilest kind of talk. Times were changing, and there was no call for smutty humour any more. It brought silence for a few moments, but I noticed how Caroline smiled her thanks, and that was good enough for me. As for Bernie, I'd plaster him when I got back to work, unless it slipped my mind, which it most likely would. I was glad again. The lights were back on in the attics of my brain – except when they glimpsed that sideboard-pile of presents.

'Ladies and gentlemen!' I shouted, and they fell quiet. 'Friends, boys and girls, I've come here today' – they were already rocking with laughter because it was good clean fun, and I was known as a bit of a jokester – 'to let you know that I am now . . . oh my God! I've forgotten the word. Now, what was the word I wanted? Eh? Tell me somebody, please.'

'Married!' Bernie shouted, my old friend.

'Married. Thank you. That was it. To tell you that I am now *married*! You can't know how much it means to me when I tell you that, but I thought I'd explain the presence of all this food and drink, and those gifts you can see behind me, all that fantastic stack of gifts . . . otherwise you might wonder!'

'Good old Richard.'

'Get on with it then!' That was from Bernie again. He never could leave well alone.

'So here's a toast to my presence here, and to Caroline, and to all of you who've come to honour us. We left it rather late, but better that, I feel, than the other way. I'm not much of a hand at weddings, this being my first. I didn't go to my parents', like some people I've met who might have done, so excuse any lack of formality, dear friends.' I was sweating now, and more and more toasts didn't help. Neither did the food, which I wasn't able to touch. The arrangement was that we'd stay in the house that night, and leave for Hastings at ten the next morning, and train times kept going round in my head.

The only thing now was to render a couple of songs for them, which I did. My voice was good, and I'd often entertained at friends' houses and on bus-outings from work. I gave them, but mainly for Caroline's sake, because I knew she loved both: 'I'll Walk Beside You' and 'Abide With Me'. But that was the last time I did any such thing, which was a pity, because I was always proud of my voice.

One by one they left, wishing me luck and happiness. I felt like going with them, shaking hands with the bride and invisible bride-groom, bestowing on them the best of health, then vanishing into the autumn dusk of chip smells, fog and freedom. Yet it was my wedding, proved by those glittering and intimidating presents on the sideboard, above all by that pagoda of pots, the kingpin dinner-service in dazzling flowers and cottages. I couldn't believe I'd have to use them for the rest of my life, drink out of them, eat off them, warm myself by them. One or two people didn't want to leave, or were too drunk to do so, and the trouble is I wasn't too drunk to envy them. But I remembered my position as man and husband of the house, and helped them out into the street.

Everything had gone like clockwork and by the book. The last women to depart had washed the pots and straightened up. Neatness made the house so barren, yet I'd been looking forward to this moment for weeks and, I believe, so had Caroline. The fire was burning well, and now we could sit by it and relax, laugh over the day's routine.

I kicked off with a harmless enough remark: 'It went easier than I expected.'

'Perfect,' she smiled, 'thanks to you, Richard. The service was beautiful. "Whom God hath joined together let no man put asunder".'

'Ay,' I assented. 'They know how to say it.'

'That was it, wasn't it?'

'It was.' I was conscious and absolutely clear in my brain of the effect every word was going to have before I said it, though it had no brake whatsoever on my self-control. 'They ought to get out an EP record of the marriage service.'

'What a marvellous idea.'

'Add on the first night and make it an LP.'

'What, Richard?'

'The morning after would make it an album, I expect. Sell like hot cakes.'

'Are you a bit jangled?' she asked, having just caught the reek that all wasn't well.

'If you like.'

'Can I get you some aspirin?' My head was burning, but I said no, that I was all right. She smiled, forgiving when there was no need to be. If there had been, the balloon would have gone up already. 'You don't have any regrets, do you love?'

It was too early to say. Did she think that nothing more was to come? 'None,' I said, putting my arms around her. I loved her even more than I loved myself, and no man could say fairer than that. I was taken out of myself, as happy as if I were flying over a desert that was just sprouting flowers again. My arms tightened, and her head leaned comfortably on my shoulder. I'd drunk enough that day and perhaps it helped, yet it was something more that set my blood melting. Certainly I didn't have to tell myself that I was four hours married in order to feel all the breeding and manners ever instilled into me drifting away.

She stood up quickly. 'I can't, Richard. It must be in the right way. Not yet.'

'Why not?' I shouldn't have said that, but it came before I could help myself, throwing me back on to a filthy pavement at the butt-end of summer – which is about the only sort of earth I've ever known in my deeper moments.

'It was the same before we were married,' she cried. 'Always in too much of a hurry. It's almost uncouth.'

The 'almost' clawed right through me, a mincing qualification that would have made a plain 'uncouth' laughable by comparison. It bit deep, sounded like the worst of insults, because a real insult is when somebody tells something about yourself you've half-known all along. That's the cut. If you are told something you couldn't possibly have known, you just laugh, because it's not true, what you could not know.

I was unable to answer, and she thought I was sulking in order to get my own back. 'Why spoil it?' she said. 'Would you like a glass of sherry?'

I screwed out a smile. Maybe Bernie had been right after all about a bull at a gate. 'Please, love.'

'A slice of ham?' she called from the kitchen.

Blood in my mouth: I'd bitten my tongue. 'No thanks.' I looked around and the spread of presents shrivelled my brain. It was a carnival that lacked a death's head, skull and crossbones and the King Snap-dragon of the lot. I closed my eyes, then opened them with the thought that if I didn't they might stay shut forever. I spied a heavy poker standing by the fire, one of the gifts already unpacked, squared-off at one end and falling to a point, a beautiful instrument made by a couple of friends at work, the firm's metal but their skill and sweat – and regard for me.

I picked it up, weighed and balanced it, lifted it high and stood over the whole patchwork regalia. I've always taken pride in my arm strength, felt it gathering now in my shoulders for a job to be bloody well done.

There was a shout from the doorway: 'Richard!'

Her face was white, thinner than I'd ever seen it, and I saw then how much this so-called marriage ceremony had worn her out. I was filled with pity, which I knew to be good and honest because I lowered the poker.

'What are you doing?' she righteously demanded.

'Feeling the weight of it. It's a lovely piece of work. Last forever, if you ask me.'

She put the tray down. 'You were going to do something you'd never forgive yourself for. And I wouldn't want you to do that, because I've got to live with you.' She was always lucid during trouble, and I admired her for it. We looked at each other. She couldn't stand the silence like I could, after such a day, and I can't blame her. 'Oh dear,' she said in sudden exultation as if that organ music was starting all over again. 'I was right.'

I had a blinding vision of our four wounded parents squatting among that trash like a collection of grinning gnome-faced jugs, prophesying and winking at each other over the idiotic unknown step I'd taken with the darling of my life, their hats askew and atremble in delight at what we were about to do to ourselves, which was all that they had done, right to the point of out-living regret and bitterness by the time old age came upon them, which lasted a few years and enabled them to fix a grin forever that advised us to live through the rottenness like them, because we'd come to enjoy it in the end and join them in helping to pass it down to oncoming innocents forever.

The force of my arm drove a canyon down that dinner-service and split it asunder, quartered and shattered it by wave after wave of strength and agony. It was rocking, knocking every transistor out of its pocket, buckling ashtrays, irons, pot-dogs, bowls, bows, a shop-window of all the catalogue-goods of servitude spending under my poker quicker than they'd ever reach the dustbin by normal wear and tear. When I thought there was nothing left, I noticed a walnut polished biscuit-barrel untouched at one corner on the edge of the bomb damage. Coaxing it into the middle – no cooper would ever own it from henceforth – I splayed it flat like a star.

I must have taken my time over it, because Caroline had her coat on, a suitcase by her side that she'd gone to Butlin's with the year before. 'Right,' I said, sitting exhausted on one of the stools, 'going home, are you?'

'Yes,' she answered coolly, while my own breath could hardly move.

'But this is your home, so let's have your coat off. Put that case away and be sensible.'

'You really want me to?'

'Yes.'

She waited a while, the silence on her side now. 'All right, Richard, I will stay.'

I didn't like the way she looked at me while taking off her coat, but then, had I any right to?

Every time Caroline came up in the morning and placed a cup of tea at my bedside she said: 'How do you know it's not poisoned?' and walked downstairs again, leaving me to wonder.

I knew it wasn't, but how could a man be sure? Not me, certainly, because even in the face of anyone as good as gold I'd never have the nerve to be sure of them. Blind love and adoration would only make me suspicious, while the pure hatred I was now getting couldn't make it much worse. But the world had to go on, and I never knew whether or not my tea was poisoned till I'd stepped on the bus for work, for if the gripes hadn't struck by then I could begin to hope again. Usually the bus was so cold I even stopped sweating. It was a bad winter.

According to a newspaper read at lunchbreak one day, marital difficulties are the greatest cause of divorce. As if I didn't know, being a realistic man. I've known some people though, and I won't mention any names, who seem to regard marriage as a pact wherein each party promises to drive the other mad or kill in the attempt. But it appears to me that most divorces come about because people grow bored with each other – though Caroline and I never got bored, and consequently we had to find another way to split up.

For Christmas she gave me a box of Cuban cigars, plastered with labels looking like birth-certificates and hundred-pound notes. She sat with a loving smile, anticipating thanks, while I spent five minutes with a pen-knife trying to find the slit of the lid, getting more impatient till I broke the box from end to end along the wrong side, cracked it to splinters so that wood and cigars and bits of label tumbled on to the rug. 'I'm just not good at opening boxes of cigars,' I said.

She stood up and walked out of the room, vowing never to speak to me again, but later that night when I was taking off my shirt she said: 'Hasn't anyone ever told you that patience and understanding are needed in this world?' She spoke with lips close together, as if to stop her false teeth falling out should she grow too emotional – but she had no false teeth.

'Not yet, they haven't,' I answered with a smile.

'What you want,' she said sharply, 'is for some barbarian to come along and civilize you.'

I fell in love with her again, kept falling in love at forty as much as I had done at twenty. When I admitted this she called me a case of arrested development, not to have altered in all those years. The fact that I'd married someone like her, she said, proved it.

The trouble was, I'd married late, for while living was pleasant I took my time and held it off. When the world was good I felt no reason to be good back to it. I worked too hard for that. I know now that I'd been selfish, but if I saw in those days all that I know now I don't see how I could have gone on living, so it's a good job I didn't. You're too busy making what's in store for you to think about the future when it comes – or when it doesn't, I told myself. The world's got to go round, after all.

She called me a monster of selfishness when I told her all this, and maybe I did become one, yet I wasn't too selfish not to fall in with her wish and have a church wedding. I've never believed in religious claptrap, but I loved her, and she was fervent in wishing for it, to say the least, and love makes a man honourable in that he'll do anything for his beloved. He might undo it all again later, though I wasn't to know that at the time.

Love is like childhood – golden to recall. Galling moments are forgotten, and all those wasted words and waves of anguish vanish before the mystic flights of going to bed, fall like lees of sand to the sea-bottom. I know it, especially if I keep telling myself, over and over again. But I can place the end of what might be called our love with the exactitude of a carpenter's rule.

We were lying on the bed one summer's evening after making love, naked and calm, and full of affection, even though our modesty had gone. Her face looked at mine, and she smiled, beautiful and tender, as if we had never known anyone else but each other and had been continually in a state of sublime love from the very first moment. Our kisses were pure, the prime height of emotional life. Caroline smiled again, and as I looked at her an unexpected voice, out of place but unmistakable, came into my mind and said to her: 'Goodbye, goodbye, goodbye.' She was not allowed to hear it, and I smiled back, alarmed yet thrilled at the intruding voice, which I knew to be as true as the dead wood in my heart.

But it wasn't over yet – not by a long way. We had our distractions, being a serious couple. She read magazines and romantic fiction, while I went in for a better class of book because I was hard to satisfy in that spiritual way. Otherwise I might have gone to church on Sunday morning like she kept on doing. But I'd only twiddle my thumbs there, want to take a book out and read till it was all over. So I didn't shame her by going, preferred to brood and read, and hug my mood in the hope of becoming familiar with what was happening inside myself. I'd never allow any preacher to tell me anything, or stop me knowing myself. I sometimes thought I might like to, but the fact was that I couldn't. I never talked much to other men, being a foreman at work, which gave me some advantage in that at least I could talk to myself with some possibility of not being misunderstood.

In spite of our ups and downs, and the times when we knew in our hearts that it was finished for sure, we were in love for a long time – two years to be precise and show you the exact nature of our optimism. We'd occasionally talk about what we'd do if we had all the money in the world, the charities she'd help, the places I'd visit, the common joy of having no set work. What I omitted in my cowardly way to remind her was that if I hadn't been going to work forty hours a week we wouldn't have lasted together three months, because our bitterest quarrels usually took place when she got back from evensong on Sunday night. She walked in in her lilac-blue hat and high-heeled shoes, pale suit, umbrella if it was raining, and at that night's supper when I'd been longest away from my workshop of friends and machines our fatal, final, common incompatibilities would break in on us like vixens.

One Saturday morning, when we were clearing away breakfast things, she looked straight and tenderly into my eyes. 'Richard, I love you. You know that, don't you?'

We stood by the kitchen door: 'Yes, I know you do' – and kissed her.

'I'd never do anything to hurt you, you know that. You're the only man I've ever loved, in spite of everything.'

'Sweetheart,' I said, wondering a little bit what was up, but thinking she was just being affectionate.

The vicar came to see her that afternoon. I'd normally have been at a football match, but the pitch was deep in snow, so I sat in the living room playing one of my classical records – I forget which. I had to turn the stereo off when he came in – though two frustrations in one day didn't seem overmuch for me at the time.

I hadn't seen him since that day in his cold and draughty church. Not that I had any real dislike for him, for no doubt it would have been somebody else who married us, even if only in a registry office. He was a good man as far as I knew, with a harassed wife and four kids, who lived in a crumbling vicarage opposite his place of work. An ex-RAF man (like myself, who'd been an airframe fitter through the war), he was about fifty, bald, well built, and might have been a stoker in another age.

Caroline gave an embarrassed hello, then went away busily to get tea ready. The parson sat opposite me by the fire, a sweat on his face in spite of the snow, which I suppose he'd hurried through in order to get out of.

'Some people like snow,' he grinned, 'because they find it picturesque, but I think it's a damned nuisance, really.'

'I have inside work myself,' I said, wanting to be agreeable. 'As long as it doesn't hold up the buses, and I'm able to get there. "Whom God hath joined let no man put asunder" – especially concerning his work.' I suddenly had an idea as to why he'd come to see us, and in a detached sort of way could feel my heart choking on its own blood because of it. It was no good. I didn't love Caroline any more. If one can ever believe in God one can only do so when one is in love. To believe at such a time is the most sublime state of all, I am sure, but I had lost even love, and therefore everything. He had come a bit too late for me to credit his help, though at the same time he could never have been early enough, either.

'To a certain extent you're right,' he argued, 'but man was created before work.'

'I always thought God put in a good six days,' I answered, 'before he clocked off for the weekend and sat down to rest.'

'All right, Mr Butler, but you know, Caroline is very unhappy about the way your marriage is going, and as she is a good member of our parish church, and as I had the great pleasure of marrying you both, I simply think that it must then be my duty as a friend and a Christian to ask if I can help you in your trouble. You must excuse this unannounced visit to your home but I imagine, rightly,' – here he gave a fair laugh – 'that you might not have stayed in if I'd given you notice. And I couldn't talk to you at church because you don't come, I'm sorry to say.'

'Was this Caroline's idea?'

'Well, yes. In a way it was. But I can't say exactly.'

I stood up. 'Mind your own business, and clear out.'

Caroline was at the door, our best wedding-present tea-tray loaded: 'Richard, what are you saying? Please!' She put the tray down to unload it, as if such activity would diminish the saltpetre air of the room.

'I'll solve my own problems,' I cried at them both.

'We were made to help our fellow-men,' the parson said in a quiet and dignified way. He stood and took me by the elbow, surprised at my violence, though confident he could handle it. But his self-assurance, sparking from insolent generations of bossiness, drew blood from my eyeballs. I was surprised at still being able to talk.

'But not to preach to them,' I shouted. 'What gives you a right to understand me?' I snapped his hand away. 'You've been to college? You've got faith? That'll never be enough, mate. If I need help – and I'm not so sure it's me that needs it – then it'll come from inside me in its own good time. You'll just mix it up and push it back. So get out and find some slobbering grateful arthritic terrified godfearing parishioner who's ready to peg out and needs your ministrations. Then get the Good Lord on the blower and tell Him how good you've been. Reverse the charges if you can't afford it. Go on, get out of my house.'

He didn't even say goodbye, and picked up his coat to get it on in the snow. I stood on my own two feet, though aching to hug the earth in my black piercing rage. Pride had got me like a rat, and wouldn't let go. I was left with Caroline, whose big eyes shone mistily from a pale face. Where had I seen it before? Greens and yellows and long hair, large eyes like candleflames, pupils reaching up to the flaring tip, face derelict and phosphorous, all of it looking at bestial barbaric me through a heavy glass window. But the glass broke, and I staggered across the room at a savage blow from the tray.

I didn't go to work for three days. Nor did I eat during that time, and I think it was this more than me actually hitting her back which finally made her turn the way she did. If I'd just hit her and carried on as if nothing had happened, things might in some strange way have got better between us, in spite of my inability at the moment to see how they ever could. But in breaking the normal routine of life I had cracked, and this disconcerted her so much that she could never forgive me.

I went in the spare room and lay on the single bed without a mattress, would not open the door in spite of her sobbing and knocking. In my darkness I railed at her having called in a parson to try and sort out our troubles (which after all were only a way of life and could have been stuck to the end of our days) so that the more I brooded on it the smaller my heart became. I'd grown up proud and hardworking and independent, lived by all those dead-true clichés that only mean so much when somebody spits on them.

239

If I belched on my way to work I'd know I hadn't been poisoned. The sun promised and sweet April threatened, a fusing scene of unease and well-being which made the streets feel friendlier and more protective than on other days. Mist was blue and fresh in early morning, the first breath of skinless springtime over the city, and if I didn't inhale too deeply on the doorstep it smelled pleasantly nostalgic and reminded me of the happiness I'd once had. Fortunately it didn't pierce deeply enough to get through to the irrevocable layer of smoke and swamp underneath, which would make me wish I hadn't lit that cigarette after putting on my hat, and that I had never got married in the first place. The trees were less brittle and blue on this particular day, faintly streaked with the emerald of spreading buds. It was a more colourful morning than I could ever remember, and it didn't occur to me to wonder why until I reached for the rail of the bus and slid back into the gutter.

Since my encounter with the parson she'd been out to get me. 'How do you know it isn't poisoned?' she'd smile on bringing my tea up in the morning, said it so often that after a couple of months I didn't believe it was any more. If I'd had any sense I should have booted her out the first time she said it, but it had always been my biggest fault, to think quick and act slow.

I might have known something was wrong when she said goodbye in an almost affectionate tone. The tea tasted strange, but she said the milk had gone off, and I thought no more about it till my legs weakened and my heart raced, and it burst as I reached out for the bus. She'd been grinding up sleeping pills, and because of overtime I hadn't got in till ten the night before. I fell into bed and slept like an ox, and welcomed the bedside tea next morning with a smile.

I woke up in hospital, and for the first time in my life I both thought and acted quick at the same time. What made me spout the right words I don't know, but it wasn't reason, and it wasn't emotion either. Nor was it a sense of love and protection I owed to my wife, because from then on Caroline would never be a wife to me again. We'd mean nothing to each other. She had brought on us the law of the jungle by trying to kill me, and I'd never let myself live in a jungle. And yet, who knows really what the jungle is like, and what goes on in the mind of animals who live in it? Do animals kill more of one another than men do? Maybe this was spinning in my mind when I woke up and blurted out: 'I didn't mean to kill myself. I took the tablets by mistake.' I smiled when I saw how easy it was to make them believe me no matter what Caroline might say.

But she knew how to handle her side of life too; came to see me during my few days in hospital, walked up to the bed with a bunch of flowers and a widow's smile, as if just back from my burial service at church. We'd finished each other off with such utter completeness that it almost made me sad. I wanted to shout to the nurse: 'Take her out! Go on, or I'll really kill myself!' – except that it would have showed up my lie on coming out of the dark.

She sat by the bed, so triumphant I could almost have fallen in love with her for the last time.

'What did you tell them?' she asked.

'That I didn't mean to kill myself. What nice flowers.'

'They're for you.'

'They'd have looked more fitting on my grave. Take them away.'

'I'll ask one of the nurses to put them in water as I go out. Why did you tell them that?' She straightened my pillow, all wifelike.

'Will you do it again?'

Her smile was wide, right at the deep end. 'Do what?'

'Try to murder me.'

A blush of anger went over her. 'I don't know what you're talking about.'

I laughed, really happy for the first time that she hadn't succeeded. 'That's the stuff. Better to have it on your conscience than me on mine.' The nurse, smiling a young beautiful unencumbered smile, came up with my tea-tray.

'You always were good at self-sacrifice,' Caroline said.

'Better than sacrifice,' I quipped. 'Don't go. Let them see how you love me, or they'll suspect you tried to kill me. Stay and pour my tea.'

Tears were in her eyes, and she stood up. 'How can you joke about it?'

'Look,' I pleaded, 'let's go hand-in-hand into the loony-bin: they'll separate us at the gate, but what an end for us! What a gesture! You can show me the way there since you've been in already.'

'I hope it's not true,' she said, 'that men and women aren't made to live together.'

'I know two that aren't, anyway.'

'You are mad,' she said. 'Now I do know.'

'Get away,' I cried. 'Don't come here to torment me. I forgive you, so what more do you want?' And I did forgive her, because that was the only thing left for me to free myself from her completely.

It was the end, and should have been the beginning, but I stamped it right out of us. Some people split up after ten years in a state of emotional squalor, a decade of under-development, but at least we'd done better than that, in about half the time. Our marriage had been a terrifying mistake which had been allowed to go on only through inanition and neurosis. I for one couldn't go back. I didn't want to. And there were certain things I wouldn't go forward to, either. What have I got to lose? I wondered. Everything, I told myself, but lose it, nevertheless, because underneath the love you have for someone else, the battle for your own survival goes on even more remorselessly.

It was the end, also, of what went into the psychiatrists' tape-recorder. They wanted to hear about my childhood and the earliest memories of family life, but I was only willing to tell them what had been bothering me. I've reconstructed the tape out of my head, because I naturally never got a copy of it. I spent a long time in that office, sitting in an ordinary leather armchair, and talking while those infernal wheels of the tape-machine slowly revolved.

When I first went in the two psychiatrists were chatting normally about what was on at the pictures and what books they'd been reading, altogether ignoring me for a few minutes, as if this was part of their policy. Then I was offered a cigarette, which I was glad of, though they never really put me at ease. Doctor Brown, the one in charge, was short, slim, and had ginger hair, and reminded me of a man who works at the factory – under me. Yet I was half-afraid of them, tardy at going in and diffident when I got there, taking the lift to their big room of an office in a building behind the council house.

Since I'd admitted trying to kill myself the idea of my going there was rather insisted on, though at least I was able to choose a good private man recommended by my own GP. I didn't want my brain chopping about just because I'd reacted with the finer instinct of an animal in trying not to get the same thing done or worse to Caroline. It was bad enough having the neighbours point at me when I walked up the street, bad for any man to stand, while she was talked to with deference and understanding because she had a husband who was sick in the head. Once your pride starts to go, the wind takes it a long way. Still, she needed people to talk to her more than I needed them to talk to me. I never spoke another word to her, because, when I'd said it was the end between us, that was the way I made it turn out. I've always been a moral man who realizes his value to society, but there's a limit to what one can be expected to take – or should be. Social laws are to be kept up to a point because they make life easier among the pain and squalor, but when you stray by mistake into a swamp you are obliged to fight for your life and get out of it. If you can't keep your dignity, then all laws have to be thrown overboard.

During that long talk to the psychiatrists I held on to mine, though it wasn't easy, doing something no part of my soul wanted to, yet having to whether I liked it or not. I simply told my story, and almost felt pleased that they and the tape were listening to me, sensed the good that might come if I gave myself into it, the comfort at being able to spout hour after hour about myself and my so-called troubles and having no one to chelp me back, only to help me when and if they could. I suppose that was the nearest I got to real madness, because there was nothing wrong with me, seeing how they should have had someone else under the arc-lights.

'Doctor Ridgeway and I will go through this tape,' Brown said, 'and we'll have another session at the same time next week. All we need do in your case is continue these little talks for a while.'

He seemed lighthearted about it, and I can't blame him, since he was dealing with a sane man. Maybe other people he treats are sane also. Still, I was thankful it wasn't as unpleasant as I'd imagined, and that I didn't have reason to wish that Caroline hadn't under-estimated the dose necessary to kill me.

The drizzle and mist of the city felt good outside, mid-morning traffic quietened by it. A comforting sense of freedom fell on me as I stood in the doorway and lit a cigarette before stepping into it. I'd go for a cup of coffee before taking the bus home. Yet the gulf seemed to be actually and physically under my feet, and I tried to step lightly in my walk. It was now, having talked it out, that I felt as if there was nothing left between me and Caroline, and in another way between me and the world. We were finished, pulling ourselves apart and to pieces, and I thought for a minute that every man and woman married or living together were really also in this state, the whole of their way of life about to fly apart. And you might ask, what would we have then? Well, you tell me.

But I was fed up with the past, after all that tape-work. To think so much about the past is like a desperate and unhappy person running back to his mother for comfort. Life would be so much easier if what you thought and what you did bore some relationship to each other. And yet when I felt for the macintosh on my arm, and realized that I'd left it in the psychiatrists' office, I had a clean and uncomfortable feeling that they did in too many vital ways.

I went up on the lift, and back in again. There was no receptionist to announce me, but I didn't think it mattered, since they were such pleasant informal people. Those inside didn't notice my entrance, being so involved in what they were listening to. An inane tune was jigging through my head, and this may have helped me to remain self-absorbed and unnoticed for so long.

Hearing them replay the tape, it was now that I properly enumerated the furnishings of the office. Desk, pictures, books, three chairs – how bare and empty it was, how hollow now that I stood in as one of them, but for a minute unbeknown to them, no longer part of the furniture, listening to my own voice going towards every corner of the room. I'd heard myself on tape before, so recognized its low-keyed, precise, cocksure, rambling vibration touching off their laughter.

Doctor Brown, who was controlling the machine, switched it to another section of my talk that he was anxious for them to hear. All three were in on it, one a tall broad man, as well as those I already knew. 'He tried to kill himself, and now he says it was his wife who tried to murder him.'

'Delusions of paranoia,' said the new man knowingly.

'Listen to this then,' laughed Doctor Brown, and clicked the reel forward with as much zeal as if the forthcoming funny bit had actually been made up by him, and he wanted the credit for it, so that they could gag about it all through lunch.

So on my voice went, telling of my fight with the parson. At first I couldn't believe they were amused by me, and my mind was flitting around inside itself searching for some parallel motive which might be entertaining them. It was as if, while listening seriously to my talk, they remembered a joke spent between them an hour before and were merely laughing at that. But they were too engrossed in the tape for such to be true, which was also lucky, in that I stayed by the door some time before anyone noticed me. The pain was compounded when part of me also, on hearing their continual laughter, thought that my long confession was funny, and I felt grateful to them for laughing at it, and almost wanted to join in and relax about it with them. But this was only a passing slim impulse – which was the forerunner of the most total black rage I've ever felt. It was beyond shame, spoiled vanity, insult, not even a matter of them being wrong in what they were doing. Everything in my mind was quick and clear, and I've never known black anger to do that, because it left my judgement free when it seemed more necessary than ever in my life before or since.

They flicked the reel, and it hummed along till it settled on the final meeting with my wife by the hospital bedside. They even found this hilarious, but to me it was interesting, my carefully rehearsed story that had been going through my head for weeks at last pinned down. I didn't think it funny though, and wanted them to stop joking about it so that I could follow what was being said, as if it weren't me on the tape at all.

'You always were good at self-sacrifice,' Caroline said.

'Better than sacrifice,' I quipped. *'Don't go. Let them see how you love me, or they'll suspect you tried to kill me. Stay and pour my tea.'*

Tears were in her eyes, and she stood up. 'How can you joke about it?'

'Look,' I pleaded, *'let's go hand-in-hand into the loony-bin: they'll separate us at the gate, but what an end for us! What a gesture! You can show me the way there since you've been in already.'*

'I hope it's not true,' she said, *'that men and women aren't made to live together.'*

'I know two that aren't, anyway.'

'You are mad,' she said. *'Now I do know.'*

'Get away,' I cried. *'Don't come here to torment me. I forgive you, so what more do you want?'* And I did forgive her, because that was the only thing left for me to free myself from her completely.

They laughed. 'Priceless,' said Doctor Brown.

'Turn it to the wedding, then,' said his colleague.

'Let's have lunch first. We'll go right through it this afternoon.' Nevertheless he flicked back the tape to the marriage part, as if it were going to play them out like a signature tune. 'The thing is,' he said, 'these damn schizos give me the horrors. Which is why I listen to them, I suppose.'

'Must be,' said the other, with a dry laugh.

Then Doctor Brown saw me.

I'd been listening to the tape, true, but also I spied a heavy walking-stick standing in a corner. My rage was back in full, and so was

245

my clarity, and they gave me wolfish strength. The swing of it made a magic circle around me. I wasn't the one at bay, because I heard their voices asking me to put it down, almost pleading. 'It wasn't nice, ethical, or clever,' I said, 'to laugh at me.'

Down came a blow that shot the tape out and up into the air, sent it spiralling towards the ceiling as if the flies up there were holding a victory parade. What was left in the other half also ticker-taped up, coils of brown ribbon shooting and snapping over the room, and all three afraid to touch me or move in case I turned on them, which in my finely conscious state I had no intention of doing, though they were too cowardly to realize it.

'I trusted you,' I shouted, with another burst at the disintegrating tape jerking and squirting away from me as I finally threw down the walking-stick and went out of the room.

I worked on a building-site in London as a labourer, a very high building, and all the men wondered why I had so much nerve, how it was possible that after so short a time on the job I wasn't in the least afraid of such terrifying heights. The foreman had a good word for me, told me I knew what to do without much explanation and carried out my work calmly. He talked about giving me my own gang on a big job coming up the following year.

As I worked, so high up, there was the sound of aeroplanes passing all day towards the airport, gracefully sloping down between me and the sky, beautiful pieces of machinery that are so much more perfect than men, and more useful. The sight of them inspired me one minute and depressed me the next. If it weren't for the fact that men had made them, I would no longer have wanted to go on living. I was often sad at night when I could no longer see those beautiful machines. Yet I could still hear them as I lay trying to sleep, thinking that aeroplanes had replaced the old romantic noise of trains and train-whistles, and that one could fly a much longer way in them.

Back on earth my escape had been made, out of the swamp I'd landed in but couldn't swim in because there were too many monsters out for my arms and legs. I thought at first I might be brought back for what I did in the psychiatrists' office and for not carrying on my treatment with them. But I heard nothing, touch wood. Perhaps they realized what damage they'd done, and so made it all right for me. If so, it's the least (and most) they could do, and those particular ones are the sort of people a human being can deal with, if he ceases at a lucky and crucial moment to be a human being who is dependent on them – which is the least I can say for such wayward immoral bastards.

I work hard on my job, because at the moment not much else is left, though it will be. Often on my fetching and carrying high above the river I look up into the sky. Clouds are shrouds to wrap the sun in, hustle it away to doom and ruin. But I can look down as well. In my house there are many mansions – with different coloured wallpaper, maybe, and it's a hard house to get out of, especially if you are walking on the roof, and you can look between your feet into every room at once.

I was looking down at the crowds beckoning me back to earth, but, damn them, I would not go till I was ready, not without the safe wings of flying which I felt growing in place of my arms. I would not live among them any more, not in such impersonal chaos. When I go down I might finally end up in the place I'd tried to avoid all my life, though it was true that Caroline has already been there before me without ever actually having said what it was like. I thought that if I went there she would sooner or later join me, and I didn't want that. I imagined it to be a pretty ordered sort of existence, too much so, as I mildly walked towards the edge of the girder and began to climb down for dinner-break.

Life is long, long enough always to start again. The black pitch of energy is inexhaustible in the barrel, the spirit-fire burning underneath to keep it always at the boil and bubble. Nothing can stop it, not in me. And if we ever meet again, maybe we'll meet as equals.

Chicken

One Sunday Dave went to visit a workmate from his foundry who lived in the country near Keyworth. On the way back he pulled up by the laneside to light a fag, wanting some warmth under the leaden and freezing sky. A hen strutted from a gap in the hedge, as proud and unconcerned as if it owned the land for miles around. Dave picked it up without getting off his bike and stuffed it in a sack-like shopping-bag already weighted by a stone of potatoes. He rode off, wobbling slightly, not even time to kill it, preferring in fact the boasting smiles of getting it home alive, in spite of its thumps and noise.

It was nearly teatime. He left his bike by the back door, and walked through the scullery into the kitchen with his struggling sack held high in sudden light. His mother laughed: 'What have you done, picked up somebody's best cat?'

He took off his clips. 'It's a live chicken.'

'Where the hell did you get that?' She was already suspicious.

'Bought it in Keyworth. A couple of quid. All meat, after you slit its gizzard and peel off the feathers. Make you a nice pillow, mam.'

'It's probably got fleas,' Bert said.

He took it from the sack, held it by both legs with one hand while he swallowed a cup of tea with the other. It was a fine plump bird, a White Leghorn hen feathered from tail to topnotch. Its eyes were hooded, covered, and it clucked as if about to lay eggs.

'Well,' she said, 'we'll have it for dinner sometime next week' – and told him to kill it in the backyard so that there'd be no mess in her clean scullery, but really because she couldn't bear to see it slaughtered. Bert and Colin followed him out to see what sort of job he'd make of it.

He set his cap on the window-sill. 'Get me a sharp knife, will you, somebody?'

'Can you manage?' Colin asked.

'Who are you talking to? Listen, I did it every day when I was in

Germany – me and the lads, anyway – whenever we went through a farm. I was good at it. I once killed a pig with a sledge hammer, crept up behind it through all the muck with my boots around my neck, then let smash. It didn't even know what happened. Brained it, first go.' He was so lit up by his own story that the chicken flapped out of his grasp, heading for the gate. Bert, knife in hand, dived from the step and gripped it firm: 'Here you are, Dave. Get it out of its misery.'

Dave forced the neck on to a half-brick, and cut through neatly, ending a crescendo of noise. Blood swelled over the back of his hand, his nose twitching at the smell of it. Then he looked up, grinning at his pair of brothers: 'You thought I'd need some help, did you?' He laughed, head back, grizzled wire hair softening in the atmosphere of slowly descending mist: 'You can come out now, mam. It's all done.' But she stayed wisely by the fire.

Blood seeped between his fingers, making the whole palm sticky, the back of his hand wet and freezing in bitter air. They wanted to get back inside, to the big fruit pie and tea, and the pale blinding fire that gave you spots before the eyes if you gazed at it too long. Dave looked at the twitching rump, his mouth narrow, grey eyes considering, unable to believe it was over so quickly. A feather, minute and beautiful so that he followed it up as far as possible with his eyes, spun and settled on his nose. He didn't fancy knocking it off with the knife-hand. 'Bert, flick it away, for Christ's sake!'

The chicken humped under his sticky palm and hopped its way to a corner of the yard. 'Catch it,' Dave called, 'or it'll fly back home. It's tomorrow's dinner.'

'I can't,' Bert screamed. He'd done so a minute ago, but it was a different matter now, to catch a hen on the rampage with no head.

It tried to batter a way through the wooden door of the lavatory. Dave's well-studded boots slid along the asphalt, and his bones thumped down hard, laying him flat on his back. Full of strength, spirit and decision, it trotted up his chest and on to his face, scattering geranium petals of blood all over his best white shirt. Bert's quick hands descended, but it launched itself from Dave's forehead and off towards the footscraper near the back door. Colin fell on it, unable to avoid its wings spreading sharply into his eyes before doubling away.

Dave swayed on his feet. 'Let's get it quick.' But three did not make a circle, and it soared over its own head and the half-brick of its execution, and was off along the pock-marked yard. You never knew which way it would dive or zigzag. It avoided all hands with uncanny skill, fighting harder now for its life than when it still had a head left to fight for and think with: it was as if the head a few feet away was transmitting accurate messages of warning and direction that it never failed to pick up, an unbreakable line of communication while blood still went through its veins and heart. When it ran over a crust of bread Colin almost expected it to bend its neck and peck at it.

'It'll run down in a bit, like an alarm clock,' Dave said, blood over his trousers, coat torn at the elbow, 'then we'll get the bleeder.' As it ran along the yard the grey December day was stricken by an almost soundless clucking, only half-hearted, as if from miles away, yet tangible nevertheless, maybe a diminution of its earlier protests.

The door of the next house but one was open, and when Bert saw the hen go inside he was on his feet and after it. Dave ran too, the sudden thought striking him that maybe it would shoot out of the front door as well and get run over by a trolley-bus on Wilford Road. It seemed still to have a brain and mind of its own, determined to elude them after its uncalled-for treatment at their hands. They all entered the house without thinking to knock, hunters in a state of ecstasy at having cornered their prey at last, hardly separated from the tail of the hen.

Kitchen lights were full on, a fire in the contemporary-style grate, with Mr Grady at that moment panning more coal on to it. He was an upright hard-working man who lived out his life in overtime on the building sites, except for the treat of his Sunday tea. His wife was serving food to their three grown kids and a couple of relations. She dropped the plate of salmon and screamed as the headless chicken flew up on to the table, clearly on a last bound of energy, and began to spin crazily over plates and dishes. She stared at the three brothers in the doorway.

'What is it? Oh dear God, what are you doing? What is it?'

Mr Grady stood, a heavy poker in his hand, couldn't speak while the animal reigned over his table, continually hopping and taking-off, dropping blood and feathers, its webbed feet scratching silently over butter and trifle, the soundless echo of clucking seeming to come from its gaping and discontinued neck.

Dave, Bert and Colin were unable to move, stared as it stamped circle-wise over bread and jelly, custard and cress. Colin was somehow expecting Mr Grady to bring down the poker and end this painful and ludicrous situation – in which the hen looked like beating them at last.

251

It fell dead in the salad, greenery dwarfed by snowing feathers and flecks of blood. The table was wrecked, and the reality of his ruined, hard-earned tea-party reached Mr Grady's sensitive spot. His big face turned red, after the whiteness of shock and superstitious horror. He fixed his wild eyes on Dave, who drew back, treading into his brothers' ankles:

'You bastards,' Grady roared, poker still in his hand and watched by all. 'You bastards, you!'

'I'd like my chicken back,' Dave said, as calmly as the sight of Grady's face and shattered table allowed.

Bert and Colin said nothing. Dave's impetuous thieving had never brought them anything but trouble, as far as they could remember – now that things had gone wrong. All this trouble out of one chicken.

Grady girded himself for the just answer: 'It's *my* chicken now,' he said, trying to smile over it.

'It ain't,' Dave said, obstinate.

'You sent it in on purpose,' Grady cried, half tearful again, his great chest heaving. 'I know you lot, by God I do. Anything for devilment.'

'I'd like it back.'

Grady's eyes narrowed, the poker higher. 'Get away from my house.'

'I'm not going till I've got my chicken.'

'Get out.' He saw Dave's mouth about to open in further argument, but Grady was set on the ultimate word – or at least the last one that mattered, under the circumstances. He brought the poker down on the dead chicken, cracking the salad bowl, a gasp from everyone in the room, including the three brothers. 'You should keep your animals under control,' he raved. 'I'm having this. Now put yourselves on the right side of my door-step or I'll split every single head of you.'

That final thump of the poker set the full stop on all of them, as if the deathblow had been Grady's and gave him the last and absolute right over it. They retreated. What else could you do in face of such barbarity? Grady had always had that sort of reputation. It would henceforth stick with him, and he deserved it more than ever. They would treat him accordingly.

Dave couldn't get over his defeat and humiliation – and his loss that was all the more bitter since the hen had come to him so easily. On their way to the back door he was crying: 'I'll get that fat bleeding navvy. What a trick to play on somebody who lives in the same yard!

I'll get the bastard. He'll pay for that chicken. By God he will. He's robbed a man of his dinner. He won't get away with a thing like that.'

But they were really thinking about what they were going to say to their mother, who had stayed in the house, and who would no doubt remind them for the next few weeks that there was some justice left in the world, and that for the time being it was quite rightly on the side of Mr Grady.

Canals

When Dick received the letter saying his father hadn't long to live he put a black tie in his pocket, got leave from the school where he taught, and took the first train up.

In a tunnel his face was reflected clearly, brown eyes shadowed underneath from the pressure of a cold that had been trying to break out but that his will-power still held back. He considered that there had never been a good photograph taken of him, certainly none reflecting the fine image he saw when looking in the mirror of the thin-faced, hard, sensitive man whose ancestors must all have had similar bones and features. But photographs showed him weak, a face that couldn't retain its strength at more than one angle, and that people might look at and not know whether this uncertainty was mere charm or a subtle and conscious form of deception. He had a wide mouth and the middling forehead of a practical man whose highest ambition was, once upon a time, to be a good tool-setter, until he joined the army and discovered that he was intelligent in a more worldly sense. And when he left he knew that he would never go into a factory again.

In his briefcase were a shirt and two handkerchiefs his wife had forced on him at the last moment, as well as a razor, and some magazines scooped up in case he had nothing to think about on the journey.

Sitting in the dining-car for lunch, alone yet surrounded by many people, he remembered his mother saying, when he was leaving home ten years before: 'Well, you'll always be able to come back. If you can't come home again, where can you go?' But on a visit after four years he walked into the house and, apart from a brief hello, nobody turned from the television set to greet him, though they'd been a close-blooded family, and on and off the best of friends all their lives.

So he never really went back, didn't see himself as the sort of person who ever would. Whether he ever went forward or not was another question, but he certainly knew there was no profit in looking back. He preferred a new block of flats to a cathedral any day, a good bus-service to a Rembrandt or historic ruin, though he realized it was better to have *all* these things and not be in a position of having to choose.

He remembered his father saying: 'A good soldier never looks back. He don't even polish the backs of his boots. You can see your face in the toecaps, though.' His father had never been a soldier, yet this was his favourite saying – because he'd never been forward anywhere, either.

So the only time he did go back was when his father was dying. It wasn't a question of having to, or even thinking about it: he just went, stayed for a week while his father died and got buried, then came back, leaving his mother in charge of brothers and sisters, even though he was the eldest son.

He stayed with his father day and night for three days, except when he queued for pills at the all-night chemist's downtown. He felt there was no need to make a song-and-dance about anyone dying, even your own father, because you should have done that while they were alive. He hoped he'd get better, yet knew he wouldn't. At fifty-four a lavish and royal grip of rottenness that refused to let go had got him in the head, a giant invisible cancerous rat with the dullest yet most tenacious teeth in the world, pressing its way through that parchment skull. He sweated to death, died at a quarter to five in the afternoon, and no one had ever told him he was going to die.

His mother didn't shed a tear. She was afraid of death and of her husband, hated him with reason because he had always without intending it turned her on to the monstrous path of having no one to hate but herself. She had hardly been in to see him during the last three days, and neither had his two daughters. Dick and his brother held each other in an embrace, two grown men unable to stop themselves sobbing like children.

A young thin woman of the neighbourhood laid the father out, and Dick went to get the doctor, who filled in a death-certificate without bothering to come and see that his patient had actually died.

The undertakers took him away. The mattress was rolled up and put outside for the dustbin men. Then the bed he'd lain on was folded back into a settee, making the small room look empty – all within an hour of him dying. An aunt who'd also lost her husband hadn't shed a tear either. Maybe it runs in the family, he thought. At the funeral, walking from the house to the waiting car, his mother wept for the first and last time – in front of all the neighbours. Of his father's five brothers none came to see him off, though all knew of it. It was almost as if he'd died in the middle of a battlefield, there were so few witnesses. But at least he didn't know about it, and might not have worried much if he had. And who am I to talk? Dick wondered, much later. I never went back to his grave, and I doubt if anyone else did, either. His mother's lack of tears didn't strike him as strange at the time considering the life she and their father had led.

Between the death and burial he was nut-loose and roaming free. At first, the brothers, sisters and mother went out together in the evenings, sticking close in a single corner of a bar-room snug, not talking except to stand up and ask who wanted what. Once they went to the pictures, but afterwards drifted into their separate ways.

It was early May, and all he wanted to do was walk. The low small sky of the bedroom ceiling had turned to blue, white angels and angles of cloud shifting across between factory and house skyline. It was vast above, and made the streets look even smaller. He hated them, wished a fire-tailed rocket would spin from the sky and wash them clean with all-enduring phosphorus. He was thirty-three, and old enough to know better than wish for that, or to think it would come when he wanted it to, or that it would make any difference if ever it did.

The greatest instinct is to go home again, the unacknowledged urge of the deracinated, the exiles – even when it isn't admitted. The only true soul is the gipsy's, and he takes home and family with him wherever he drifts. The nomad pushes his roots about like the beetle his ball of dung, lives on what he scavenges from the rock and sand of the desert. It's a good man or woman who evades it and is not poisoned precisely because he has avoided it while knowing all about it. You take on the soul of the Slav, and if you can eventually find that sort of soul it falls around you like a robe and makes you feel like a king. The wandering Jew carried the secret of creation in the pocket of his long overcoat, and now he has ploughed it into the fields of Israel. The Siberian nomad has formed his collective or joined a work-gang on some giant dam that will illuminate the wilderness his ancestors were free to wander in. Is the desert then all that is left? If the houses and factories stretching for miles around are a desert for one's soul, then maybe the desert itself is the Garden of Eden, even if one dries up and dies in it.

But he knew at the same time that life had two sides, and a base-line set firmly on the earth. The good air was blowing through the fresh-leafed trees of the cemetery he was passing. There was moss between the sandstone lumps of the wall, well bedded and livid where most damp had got at it. Between spring and summer there was a conscious feeling to the year, a mellow blight of reminiscence and nostalgia blending with the softening sweet air of late afternoon. The atmosphere made buildings and people stand out clearly, as if the meadow-and-water clouds of the Trent had not dispersed and still held that magical quality of light while passing high over the hills and roof-tops of the city. It was a delight to be alive and walking, and for some reason he wanted the day to go on for ever. There was a terrible beauty in the city he belonged to that he had never found anywhere else.

He walked over Bobber's Mill bridge, far enough out to smell soil of allotment gardens, loam of fields, water of the mill-racing Leen that had streamed down from beyond Newstead. In spite of petrol, the reek of upholstery, and fag-smoke coming from a bus-door when it stopped near him, he held on to this purity of vision that made him believe life was good and worth living.

He walked by the railway bank and through the allotment gardens – still exactly there from fifteen years ago. Feeling himself too old to be indulging in such fleshly reminiscence, he enjoyed it all the more, not as a vice but as if it were food to a starving man. Every elm tree, oak tree, apple tree, lime tree represented a leaning-post for kisses, a pausing place to talk and rest at, light cigarettes, wait while Marian fastened her coat or put on more lipstick. Every wooden gateway in the tall hedges that were as blind as walls brought to mind the self-indulgent embraces and love-making of his various courting mates. Different generations of thrushes were still loud in the same tree-tops, hawthorn, and privet, except that their notes and noise were more exactly the same.

The brook was as usual stagnant, yet water came from somewhere, green button-eyed weed making patterns on the surface to blot out cloud reflections and blue sky. Tadpoles had passed away, and young frogs were jumping under the unreachable part of the hedge. To observe all this, connect it to his past life and give it no part in his future, made him feel an old man, certainly far older than he was. Maybe he was merely mature, when what you saw and thought about no longer drove you on to the next action of your life no matter how small that action turned out to be.

The uterine flight of reminiscence, the warm piss of nostalgia as he stood by a hedge and relieved himself where the shaded pathway stretched emptily in both directions, was a way of filling in the void that a recent death created, especially the death of a person whose life had been utterly unfulfilled – of which there are so many, and which makes you feel it deeply because on the watershed of such sorrow you sense that your life too could turn out at the end to have been equally unfulfilled. The vital breezes of clean air shaking the hedgetops don't let such thoughts stay long. The lack of your own persistence in real life is often bad, while the lack of it in self-destroying thoughts at such times as this is occasionally good.

The canal had dried up, been dammed and drained and in places built over. In the mouldering soft colour of dusk he walked from one bank to another. The old stone bridge had been allowed to drop into the canal below and fill it in, hump and all, and a white-lined and tarmacked road had been laid straight across it.

He followed what was left, walked along its old tow-path towards the country. A large open pond lay down to the right with indistinct banks except for a scrap of wood on the western side now touched by a barleycorn dip of the sun. A smell of raw smoke and water was wafted in his direction. The headstocks of the colliery where his grandfather had worked blocked off an opposite view, and it was so close that the noise of turbines and generators made a fitting counterpoint to re-awakening senses.

It was dark by the time he stepped into the Ramrod and Musket and ordered a pint of beer. A fire burned in one of the side rooms, and he sat by it, loosening his raincoat. Everyone he saw he felt pity for. The wells of it had not stopped pumping, and the light of it was too blinding for him to turn it round on himself, a beam he alone could explore the world with, prise it from the darkness it lived in. He had come here thinking he might meet someone known from years ago, though he would never acknowledge such a lapse in case its nerve-racking mixture of pride and weakness might poison all hope in him.

Going outside to the back, there was no bulb in the socket to light his way. Indigo had faded completely from the sky, and he stepped slowly across the yard with eyes shut tight, under the illusion that he could see better than if he walked with them open and arms held out for fear of colliding with something.

The liquid in his pint went down, a spiritual nilometer latched by the river of his momentarily stilled life. He felt comfortable, hearing the homely accents of the few other men dealing out chitchat that in London he wouldn't give tuppence for. Nostalgia was sweet, and he allowed it to seep into him with a further jar of beer. The others sat back from the fire, glasses set on labelled mats, sliding them around to make a point.

He hated beer after the third pint, a senseless water-logging of the body that adiposed it to the earth one tried to get away from. He thought of going on to another place when no one came in that he knew, but considered a pub-crawl futile – except that the ground covered between them is different and shakes the stuff to a lower level to make room for more. Otherwise stay at the first one you stumble into.

The more he drank the more his cold bothered him. Death and the funeral had held it off, but now it spread the poison and colour of infection, a slight shifting of every feature from its spot-on proportion in order to recoup the truth and clarity of things past. One's feelings were important during a cold, in showing what you are really like and what stirs your mind from one decade to the next. It was almost as if the real you was a reactionary because it rooted you so firmly to the past without calling on detail as a support, giving it the slightly sick air which all reactionaries must have as a permanent condition. In so many cases the only key to the past is sentimentality – unless one has that cold or sickness which puts it in its place. He had reviled the past, but to loathe something was the first step to understanding it, just as to love something was the first step towards abandoning it. The past is a cellar, twisting catacombs or filled-in canals, but a cellar in which you have to walk in order to put a bullet into the back of the head of whatever monarch may be ruling too autocratically there. Only you have to tread slowly, warily, to make sure you get the right one, because if by any chance you get the wrong one you might end up putting a bullet into the back of your own head.

He was married, and had three children, one of them a few weeks old, so that his wife had not been able to come up from London with him. It was years since he had been so alone, and it was like a new experience, which he did not quite know how to handle, or realize what might come of it. People so alone rarely had chance meetings, yet the day after his father had died, walking across the city centre on his way to register the death, he heard someone from the roof-tops calling his name.

He didn't think he was hearing things, or going mad, because it was not in his nature to do so. His physical build seemed absolutely to preclude it. But he stopped, looked, then felt foolish at having been mistaken. It was a fine, blustery Nottingham day, with green double-decker buses almost surrounding the market square, and a few people actually crossing the road.

'Dick!' The voice came again, but he walked away since it was obviously some workman shouting to his mate. 'Dick! Dick!' The voice was closer, so he stopped to light a cigarette in case it really wasn't meant for him.

His cousin came scurrying down a series of ladders and dropped on the pavement a few yards away. He was, as the saying goes, 'all over him' – they hadn't met for so long, and had been such close friends, born on the same fish day of March, a wild blizzarding day in which no fish had a chance of swimming.

Bernard was thin and wiry, even through the old jacket and trousers of a builder's labourer. His grey eyes were eager with friendship, and they embraced on the street: 'I didn't know you was in Nottingham,' he said fussily. 'Why didn't you write and tell me? Fancy meeting like this.' He laughed about it, seeing himself as having climbed down from the sky like a monkey.

'I came up all of a sudden. How did you recognize me from right up there?'

'Your face. And that walk. I'd know it anywhere.'

'Dad was ill. He died last night.'

'Uncle Joe?' he took off his cap, pushed back fair and matted hair in the wind, bewildered at the enormity of the event and, Dick thought, at not being able to say anything about it.

'He had cancer.'

There was a pub near by: 'Let's go for a drink,' Bernard said.

'Won't the foreman mind?'

'I expect so. Come on. They've had enough sweat out of me. I'm sorry Joe died.'

They sat in the otherwise empty bar. 'Come up and see us all before you go back,' he said. 'We'd be glad if you would. I don't know what you live in London for, honest I don't. There's plenty of schools you could teach at in Nottingham. They're crying out for teachers, I'll bet. I suppose it's a bit of a dump, but you can't beat it. At least I don't reckon so.'

'It's all right,' Dick said, 'but London's where I belong – if I belong anywhere.' They talked as if it were on the other side of the world, which it was against the background of their common memories – even further.

261

'Well, you can't beat the town you were brought up in – dragged up, I mean!' Bernard said. Dick remembered, and talked about it before he could stop himself, of when they were children, and he and Bernard used to go around houses asking for old rags and scrap, which they would then sell for picture-money and food. The houses whose gardens backed on to the recreation ground were somewhat better off than the ones they lived in, and therefore good for pickings. At one a youngish woman gave them bread and jam and cups of tea, which they gladly accepted. They didn't call often, and not many others went around to spoil their pitch. And yet, good as she was, sweet as the tea and jam tasted, they couldn't keep going there. There was some slight feeling of shame about it, probably quite unjustified, yet picked up by both of them all the same. Without even saying anything to each other they stopped calling. Dick wondered what the woman had thought, and whether she had missed them.

Though he remembered this common incident clearly, it soon became obvious that Bernard did not, and that his mind was a blank regarding it, though at first he had looked as if he did vaguely recollect it, and then as if he wanted to but couldn't quite pull it back. 'Still,' Dick said, laughing it away, 'you can't go home again, I know that.'

'You can't?' Bernard asked, full of surprise. 'Why can't you?'

'I can't, anyway.'

'You can do what you like, can't you?'

'Some people can.'

They drank to it.

'Bring your wife and kids here to live. Get a house up Sherwood Rise. It's healthy there. They'll love it.'

'I can't, because I don't want to.'

He laughed. 'Maybe you are better off down there, at that. I can't trap yo' into owt. I'm sorry about Uncle Joe though; Mam'll be upset when I tell her.'

'It'll be in the paper today.'

'She'll see it, then. Let me get you one now.'

'Next time. I must be off.'

Dick watched him ascend the ladders, up from the pavement to the first storey, then to the second. From the roof he straddled a parapet, turned and looked down, a gargoyle for one moment, then he took off his cap and waved, a wide frantic smile on his far-off face. Dick had time to wave back before he leapt up and was hidden by a chimney-stack.

The past is like a fire – don't put your hand in it. And yet, what is to stop you walking through it upright, all of you, body and soul? It was a weekday, and the pub hadn't filled up. Near to ten o'clock he couldn't bear the thought of going home. His impulse was to flee towards London, but he'd promised to stay on a few days. It was expected of him, and for once in his life he had to obey.

He'd called here often for a drink with Marian, though she'd always insisted on having her shandy outside because she wasn't yet eighteen, as if it would have made much difference. After a summer's night on Bramcote Hills the thirst was killing, and he drank more beer in those days than he could ever stomach now. The good food of London living had peppered his gut with ulcers – or so it felt, without having been to any doctor – and the heartburn was sure to grip him next day if he put back too much.

The last bus was at half past ten, and he thought he might as well walk home. Outside, fastening his coat in the lighted doorway, the insane idea came to call on Marian, to go down to the estate and knock on her door. Why think about it, if you intended doing it? The one advantage of dwelling on the past was to act without thought if you were to get the utmost from it. In that way, of course, it would end up getting the utmost out of you, but that was nothing to be afraid of.

Fifteen years was a long time, judging by the excitement the hope of meeting her again let loose in him. It was similar to that when they had been 'going out' with each other for what seemed a decade, but which had not felt much like being in love at the time.

Having started factory work at fourteen, he was a seasoned man by the age of eighteen, and those four years had slowed down to become the longest in his life, possibly because there was an end to them which he hadn't foreseen at the time. In them, he grew up and died. His courtships had seemed eternal, even when they only lasted several months – looking back on them. The time with Marian went on longest of all, and being the last it was also the most important in that micro-cosmic life.

A fine drizzle powdered across the orange sodium lights of the housing estate. The roads were just as wide as he'd remembered them. If so little alters in a man's life, who but the most bigoted can believe in progress? Such a question came, he knew, of having too little faith, and of too complete immersion in a past so far away and severed that it couldn't be anything else but irrelevant fiction. Yet it didn't feel like it, and it did not disturb him that it didn't. The familiar dank smell of coal-smoke hovered even along the wide avenues and crescents, and the closeness of his cigarette tasted the same in his mouth and nostrils as it had all those years ago. Privet hedges shone with water under the street-lamps, and a well-caped railwayman rode by on a bicycle that seemed to have no light until only a yard away. He pulled up by the kerb, and the latch clattered as he went up the path and round to his own back door.

It was a good distance, yet he wished it were longer, both because he was apprehensive at meeting Marian and because it would spin out further the pleasant anticipation of her being at home. She'd been going with his friend Barry when he first met her, a carnal and passionate love similar to the one he at the time was pursuing with someone else. But Barry went into the army, driven from home by a black-haired bossy mother and a house full of sisters, lit off at seventeen into the Engineers just as the war ended. Letters and the occasional leave were no way to keep love's fires stoked between him and Marian, and one night Dick met her by chance and, on seeing her home, fell into honeyed and violent kisses by her gate. She agreed to see him again, and he didn't realize to what extent he had run his mate off until Barry clocked on with the army for twelve years and went straight off to Greece to serve two of them. They even stayed friends over it, yet the blow to Barry had been hard, as he admitted when they met, years later.

He made up his mind to turn at the next corner and go home, to leave the past in its matchwood compartment and not smash over it with the bulldozer of his useless and idiotic obsession. She would be out, or a husband would meet him at the door and tell him he'd got the wrong house. He smiled to remember how, during the war, an American soldier had called one night on the woman next door, as had been his habit for some months. But this time his opening of the door was answered by the husband, who had unexpectedly finished his stint on nights. The American stared unbelievingly at the pudgy and belligerent face. After a few seconds he backed out with the lame remark, 'Sorry, I thought it was a public house.' The husband had accepted it as a genuine mistake, but there were some snide comments going around the street for a long time on how lucky Mrs So-and-so was to have such a numb-skull for a husband. So if Marian's husband was at home, or some man she might be living with, he'd merely say: 'Is Mrs Smith in?' and make some excuse about getting the number of the house wrong.

Having decided to go home and not be such a fool, he kept on his track towards Marian's as if locked in some deep and serpentine canal, unable to scale its side and get back to sane air. He even went more quickly, without feeling or thought or sense of direction. From the public house he had forgotten the exact streets to follow, but it didn't matter, for he simply walked looking mostly towards the ground, recognizing the shadows of a bus-shelter, the precise spot reached by the spreading rays of a particular street-lamp, the height of a kerb, or twitchel posts at the end of a cul-de-sac.

He found the road and the number, opened the gate, and walked down the path with even more self-assurance than he ever had after courting her for a year. There was a light on in the living room. The fifteen years had not been a complete blank. He'd heard that her mother had died and that she had married a man who had been sent to prison and whom she had refused to see again. Barry also told him that there had been one child, a son. The first five years after they split up must have been agony to her, blow after blow, and it was as if he were going back now to see how she had borne the suffering that followed in his wake. But no, he could never admit to so much power. He stood at the back door, in darkness for some minutes, torn at last by the indecision that should have gripped him on his way there, and splintered by the remorse he might feel after he had left. The noise of a television set came from inside, music and crass speech that made it impossible to tell whether one or a dozen people were at home.

He too had gone into the army, and when her letters grew less frequent he was almost glad at the sense of freedom he felt. But her thoughts and feelings were not of the sort she could put easily in writing and transmit that way, as he found when they met on his first leave. Passion, because it was incommunicable, was her form of love. It was fully flowered and would go on forever with regard to him, incapable of development yet utterly complete. He expected letters, subtlety, variation, words, words, words, and couldn't stand the emptiness of such fulfilment. She could foresee no greater happiness than that they get married, and would have demanded little more than the most basic necessities of life. If he had been a man he would have accepted this, because he also loved her; and if he were a man now he would not have come back looking for her, unable to say what he wanted, whether it was love or chaos he hoped to resurrect.

It was no use standing in the dark with such thoughts, so he knocked

265

at the door. She opened it, set up the two steps in an oblong of pale orange light. 'What do you want?' she said, seeing only a stranger and at this time of night. The protective voice of a boy called from inside:

'Who is it, Mam?'

Regret, indecision, dread had gone, for he had acted, had the deepest instincts of his heart carried out for him, which really meant that he had been acted upon. He smiled, telling her who it was.

She repeated his name, and looked closer, eyes narrowing almost to a squint, 'You! Fancy you!'

'Well,' he said, 'I was passing and thought I'd see if you still lived here.'

She asked him in, and they stood in the small kitchen. He saw it was painted white instead of cream, had an electric stove in place of the old gas one, but with the same sink now patched and stained.

'Who is it, Mam?'

'I'm surprised you still knew where I lived.'

'I don't suppose I could ever forget it. In any case it's not that long ago.'

'No? It is, though.'

'It doesn't feel like it to me.'

But, to look at her, it was. And she was thinking the same. She seemed taller, was more full-bodied, no longer the pale, slim, wildlife girl of eighteen. The set lines running from her mouth, which he remembered as being formed by that curious smile of wanting to know something more definite and significant about what had caused her to smile in the first place, had hardened and deepened because her curiosity hadn't been responded to, and because the questions could never be formed clearly enough in her to ask them. The smile had moved to the grey eyes, and was more forthright in its limitations, less expressive but no longer painful.

'Come in,' she said. 'I'll make you a cup of tea, if you'd like one.'

'All right. I will for a minute.' Once inside he forgot his absence and hesitancy and took off his coat. Her twelve-year-old son lay as far back as he could get in an armchair, watching television from too close by, a livid perpetual lightning flicker to Dick, who wasn't facing it. His mother made him turn it down. 'This is Peter,' she said. 'Peter, this is an old friend of your Mam's.'

Peter said nothing, an intelligent face blighted by sudden resentment at another man in the house. He looked harder into the telly in case his mother should ask him to turn it right off. Marian's hands shook as she poured the tea, put in sugar and milk. 'I can't get over it,' she said, 'you coming to see me. Of all people! Do you know anybody else around here?'

'Nobody. Only you.'

She was happy at the thought that he had come especially to see her. 'You haven't altered much in all these years.'

'Neither have you.'

Her ironic grin was the same: 'Not much I haven't! You can't lie to me any more. You did once though, didn't you, duck?'

He might have done, and the fact that he'd forgotten was made to seem unforgivable by the slight shock still on her face at his sudden reappearance. Still, she managed to laugh about the thought of him having lied to her once, though he knew better than to take such laughs at their face value. 'Did you come up by car?' she asked. 'What sort is it?'

'I don't have a car.'

'I thought you would have. Then you could have taken me and Peter for a ride in it some time. Couldn't he, Peter?'

A 'yes' broke from the back of Peter's mind. 'You know,' she said, 'when I heard you'd become a schoolteacher I had to see the funny side of it. Fancy me going out for so long with a man who was going to become a schoolteacher! No wonder you chucked somebody like me up. I don't blame you, though.'

'That wasn't why I chucked you up. If I did.'

'You might have done – anyway,' she reflected.

'I don't remember who chucked who up.'

'You loved me though, didn't you?' She said this so that Peter wouldn't hear, from within the clatter and shouting of his private gunfight.

'I did,' he answered.

'You said you wanted to stay in the army for good, and so getting married wouldn't be fair to either of us. I remember all of it clearly. But I could see that that wasn't it at all, though. You'd just lost interest. There was nowt else you could get to know about me, after all the times we had. We didn't even fall out with each other. I didn't know what to tell the girls at work when they asked about you.'

Every word and nuance of her recollected past was accurate. It was no use saying he was only eighteen at the time, because he (as well as she) held himself totally responsible for his actions. Four years at work made him man enough already, and it wasn't so much shame he felt now as a failure of masculine responsibility. Yet some innate and ruthless sense had steered him from a life he was unfitted for. She spoke as if it were last year, whereas to him it was a whole lifetime ago, and could be considered in one way as the immature skirt-chasing of a callow youth, and in another as the throwback past of a man who, being incapable of forgetting it, had been unable to grow up. And if, beyond all this, he had stepped from one world and settled himself securely in another with a wife, three children, and an all-absorbing job, why had he made this painful and paranoid expedition to the world he had launched out from? His age didn't justify it. Maybe in his deracinated life he was forgetting where he had come from, yet wasn't a visit home enough to remind him? One had to make journeys in all directions, was the only answer that came while listening to Marian. Happy are those who don't make journeys and never need to, he thought, yet luckier are those who do.

Peter had gone to bed, more willingly than he expected. He opened a half-bottle of whisky bought in the pub, and Marian set out two glasses: 'To you and your life,' he said.

'To yourn,' she answered. 'I hardly ever drink, but this tastes good for a change. It might buck me up.' She sat on the sofa they had made love on countless times, and he stayed on a straight-backed chair at the table on which plates, cups, and sauce-bottle still rested. A clothes-horse barricaded the fire from them.

'I work at the same place still,' she said, 'at the stocking factory. I've got a better job now, though: I fault them, prick them under a glass so that they won't last more than three months. It's a good job, faulting. I can make twelve pounds a week on piecework. It's hard though in wintertime, because I go to work on my bike, riding up the hill with a January wind hitting me head-on. I went on a bus once, but halfway there the driver had a dizzy spell. He turned round, shouting for everybody to jump off, before he was able to stop it. The only time I ever went on the bus, as well! Everything happens to me!'

'What was this I heard about your husband?' he asked, noticing the regularity of her teeth. All were false, and none of his had come out yet.

'Him?' she said. 'Oh, when you left me I got married a year later. I met him at a dance, and never realized he was no good. Not long after we were married, while Mam was still alive – though on that morning she'd gone out shopping, thank God, or she'd have died at the shock I'm sure – I was in here washing up when two policemen knocked at the back door and asked if Arthur Baldwin lived here. I felt my heart going like mad, pitter-patter, and thought he'd been run over or killed in a machine at work, ready for the tears to burst out of me. But it wasn't that at all. They'd picked him up on the street because they'd found out he'd been breaking into houses, and I don't know what else he'd done. I didn't go to court, and never even read the papers about it. In fact he hadn't been at work for a long time, and I thought he had. I was such a baby I never realized what was going on. He'd been in trouble with the police before we met, but I didn't know anything about it, and nobody thought to tell me. He'd even got another woman he was keeping, in the Meadows. His mother asked me to go down to the court and plead for him, because I was pregnant already, but I didn't. I wouldn't have anything to do with it. "He's got hisself into it," I told her, "so he can get hisself out of it." She threatened me, but I still wouldn't do it, and then my mother nearly threw her out of the house. It wouldn't have helped much, anyway, I know that, because the police had really got it in for him, just as I had as well for the way he'd done it on me.

'He was sent to prison for two years, and I haven't seen him since. As I say, I was pregnant, and Peter was born while he was in prison. He don't know anything about it yet, though he'll have a right to some day. I just tell him that his father left me when he was a baby. Mam and me got a bed down from upstairs when I had Peter, and fixed it up in this corner, and I had him on it. Then a year later Mam went, and I've lived alone ever since, the last ten years. I wouldn't get married again now, though, not for a fortune. All I've got is Peter, and it's enough for me, bringing him up. He's a bit of a handful at times, being without a dad, but when he is he gets my fist. Mind you, we have some good times together as well. We go fishing now and again, and he loves it, sitting by the canal with all his tackle and bait, net and floats. He feels a proper man, and I don't mind buying him the best stuff to do it with. He's very clever though at mechanical things. All he does is build things up. He's got all sorts of radio kits and construction sets. I never have to touch a fuse: he mends them all. He fixed a transistor radio last week for Mrs Barnes next door, and she was ever so pleased. She gave him ten bob.

'I work hard, so we live well. Last year we rented a caravan at Cleethorpes with the couple next door, and stayed a fortnight. I look a sight in a bathing costume, but we went swimming every day, and had a marvellous time. Mr Barnes got a car and we went all over Lincolnshire picnicking. It won't be all that long now before Peter starts work, and then he'll be bring in some money as well. He doesn't want to stay on at school, at least he says he don't, though I don't think he'll be able to change his mind if he decides to.

'I suppose it was hardest for me though when Mam went. It was cancer, but she wasn't badly for very long. She never went to bed, stopped going when she knew she was going to die, though nobody told her, just lay on this sofa at night and sat in that armchair during the day. I don't know how we managed with just each other. I knew she was going to die, and that when she went there'd be no one left. Then I'd hear Peter crying, and knew that there would be, but it didn't make much difference for a long time. Still, we've all got to go, though it don't do to think about it.'

'We're young yet,' Dick said. 'We're just over thirty.' He sat by her on the sofa and took her hand. Was it true then that in all the troubles people had, no one could help anyone else, be of much use to soothe and comfort? Was everyone alone in their own black caverns and never communicating by tunnel or canal?

'I had help,' she said. 'The neighbours did what they could. At a time like that only God can help you, and it's only then you realize He can't. We aren't taking a holiday this year. I can't afford it because I got Peter a pickup and tape-recorder. But the year after, if we're still here, we're hoping to go to Norfolk for ten days. Give us summat to look forward to.'

'I expect you'll get married again one day,' he said.

'Married?' she jeered. 'Not me, mate. I've had my life. No more kids, either. The woman next door had a baby last week, and when she came in to see me with it I laughed at her for being so quick in her visiting and said: "Hey, don't come in here spreading your feathers!" And she laughed as well, as if it might not be a bad idea, but I knew it worn't. All I want to do is bring Peter up, give him a good start in life. I don't mind working for that, and living for it. I'll work till I drop, but as for getting married, you don't know what I've had to go through. And don't think I'm squealing about it. I might have done at one time, but not any more, because it's all over. I'm not going to get married and have them all come back.'

'You can fall in love, you know.' He detected a weakness in her that she had obviously long brooded on.

'No, I won't.'

'That's what you say now. There's no telling when it'll come.'

270

'I loved you,' she said, 'and you can only be in love once in your life, the first time. There ain't any other.' Her conviction was quiet, all jeering gone. She pressed his hand, and he leaned over to kiss her on the cheek. 'It's like a dream,' she said, smiling, her eyes shining as if the tears would break. 'You coming back. I can't believe it. I can't, duck, honest I can't.'

She wasn't in love with him, no more than he was with her, but he had lured her into the spider-trap of the past, and she was sweetening within it. 'No,' she said, 'I'll never fall in love.'

'You don't have to be in love to get married,' he said.

'That's what I thought before,' she answered, 'and look what happened.'

'Love is a destroyer if you wait for it too long. If you like somebody, love can come out of it. It's no use wrecking your life for want of being in love. Sometimes I think that as soon as you start talking about love it's on its way out, that really it's nothing more than the bloody relic of a bygone age that civilization no longer needs. There's something wicked and destructive about it.'

'I don't properly understand you,' she said gently, 'but you're wrong, anyway. You're only saying it to soothe me. You don't need to, you know, I'm all right. I'm not as sour as I sound.'

The door opened without warning and Peter appeared in his dressing-gown, eyes blinded by the light as if he'd already been half asleep, though Dick thought he may have been listening to their talk for a while. 'What do you want?' Marian asked.

'I'm looking for my comic.' He found it, under a cushion of the sofa they were sitting on. 'Don't stay up late, duck,' she said. 'You've got to go to school in the morning.'

He stood by the door, looking at them. 'Are you coming to bed then, Mam?'

'Soon. We're just having a talk about old times. I shan't be long.'

He went up the stairs, slowly, drawing the sleeve of his dressing-gown against the wall.

She made more tea, took out a box of photographs and went through them one by one, then got him to empty his wallet and show pictures of his wife and children. The past was impotent, finally, with no cleansing quality in its slow-burning fires. Yet they could never be put out because the canals that led to them were baked dry at the bottom with the rusting and tattered debris of the life you lead.

271

'I didn't think you'd ever go to live in London, though,' she said. 'It's a long way off.'

'Two hours by train. There and back in half a day. Nothing.'

'Not if you live there, and was born here. Shall you come and see me again?'

He stood up and put on his coat. 'I'd like to, if you won't kick me out.'

'Well, maybe I won't.'

'I don't come up too often, though.'

'It don't matter. We could go to a pub or summat, couldn't we?'

He held her close. 'We could.'

'It don't matter though, if you don't want to. But come in and see me.'

'All right, love.'

They held each other close, and kissed for a few seconds, standing near the kitchen door. 'I can't believe it,' she said. 'I still can't. Why did you come back? Why?' He couldn't say. He didn't know. The fifteen years fizzled down to nothing. It wasn't that he'd been a man at eighteen. He was a youth, and the raging sweet waves of it crushed into him, two flat heads of vice-steel closing with nothing in between.

'What did you say?' he asked.

'Nothing. I didn't say owt.' He kissed the tears out of her eyes.

After midnight he walked through fire, tattered and burned, going the same track home as on the hundreds of occasions when he had stayed late and missed his bus, blinded and blindfolded across the wide roads and by the black hedge-bound footpath of Collier's Pad. Only the train might take him out of it.

Lights crouched in the distance all around, every tree-root holy, the foliage damned. The narrow path was hedged in by uncertainty and chaos, life's way spun out of suffering and towards death. Artificially lighted air blighted your lungs, and you now and again stopped on your walk by some half-concealed bran-tub to dip your hands into the entrails of the past when destruction wasn't coming on you fast enough; the past is only good when what you pull up can be seen as part of the future.

But his heart was full of Marian's fate, up to her death and his death, and he felt better in knowing that at least they had this much in common whether they saw each other again or not.

The Road

When Ivan was five his parents took him on a day-trip to Skegness. They wanted to spend a few hours out of the city and see the coast where they had languished for ten days of a misty frustrating honeymoon of long ago, but Stanley said: 'Let's take Ivan to the seaside. It'll do him good.'

'Yes,' his mother said. 'He'll love it.'

And Ivan, sucking a lollipop as they walked up Arkwright Street, was oblivious to the responsibility they had put on to his shoulders. Yesterday the car had broken down, so they were going by train. To Stanley everything always happened at the crucial moment, otherwise why did it happen at all?

Ivan wore a new navy blazer, and long trousers specially creased for Whitsun. His shoes were polished and tight around his checked socks. Dark thin hair was well parted, and shy blue eyes looked out of a pale face that tapered from a broad forehead down to his narrow chin and royal blue tie. He held his father with one hand, and gripped his lollipop with the other.

'It'll be marvellous to get to the sea,' Stanley said. 'It's a hard life being a waiter, and good to have a whole day off for a change.'

Amy agreed on all counts, though didn't say so aloud. Ivan wondered if there'd be boats, and she answered that she dare say there would be. Stanley picked Ivan up and put him high on his shoulders: 'We'd better hurry.'

'You'll have a heart attack if you're not careful,' she laughed. 'Like in them adverts!'

'We've got to get going, though.'

'There's still half an hour,' she said, 'and we're nearly there.' Such bleak and common rush seemed to expose her more to the rigours of the world than was necessary, so she would never run, not even for a bus that might make her late for work if she missed it. But then, she never was late for work, and it was part of Stanley's job to get a move on.

He fought his way into the carriage to get seats, and even then Amy had to sit a few rows down. Ivan stayed with his father, now and again standing on his grey flannel trousers for a better view. The carriage was full, and he adjusted quickly to his new home, for all the unfamiliar people in the compartment became part of his family. Strange faces that he would be half afraid of on the street or in dreams seemed now so close and large and smiling, loud in their gaze or talk, that they could not but be uncles and aunts and cousins. In which case he could look with absolute safety at everything outside.

His blue eyes pierced with telescopic clarity the scene of a cow chewing by green indistinct waterbanks of a flooded field that the sky, having been fatally stabbed, had fallen into. A hedge unfurled behind the cow that stood forlorn as if it would be trapped should the water rise further – which it could not do under such moist sunshine.

Gone.

Railway trucks at station sidings fell back along the line like dominoes.

Gone.

An ochred farmhouse came, and stood for a second to show a grey slate roof, damp as if one big patch had settled all over it, the yard around flooded with mud and a man standing in it looking at the train. He waved. Ivan lifted his hand.

Gone.

A junction line vanished into the curve of a cutting.

Gone. All going or gone. They were still, who were gazing out of the windows, and everything was passing them.

The train found its way along, seemed to be making tracks as it went and leaving them brand-new behind, shining brightly when they turned a wide bend and Ivan stretched his neck to look back. An older boy smiled: 'Have you seen my new toy?'

He was sullen at being taken from such never-ending pictures that seemed to belong to him. 'No.'

'Do you want to?' He put an object on the table, ovoid, rubber, with four short legs as hands and arms. A length of fine tubing ran from its back to a hollow reservoir of air – which the boy held in his hand. Ivan stared at the rubber, in spite of not wanting to, then at the object on the table that sprang open and up, a horrific miniature skeleton, ready to grow enormously in size and grab everyone in sight, throttle them one and all and send them crushed and raw out of the window – starting with Ivan.

He drew back, and Stanley laughed at his shout of panic, hoping the boy would go on working it so that he too could enjoy the novelty. 'Stare at it like a man, then you won't be frightened! It's only a skeleton.'

When the boy held it to Ivan's face, it became the arms and legs of a threatening silver spider brushing his cheeks. Fields rattled by but gave no comfort, so closing his eyes he buried his head against his father. 'You are a silly lad. It's only a toy.'

'Make him stop it. I don't like it.' But he looked again at the glaring death-head, phosphorus on black, shaking and smiling, arms and legs going in and out as if in the grip of some cosmic agony. Amy came along the gangway at his cry and knocked the boy away, daring his near-by mother to object. She took Ivan on her knee: 'He was frightening him, you damned fool,' she said to Stanley. 'Couldn't you see?'

The train stopped at a small station. A gravel depot was heaped between two wooden walls, and beyond the lines a rusting plough grew into an elderberry bush. No one got on or off the train, which made the stop boring and inexplicable. People rustled among baskets and haversacks for sandwiches and flasks of drink.

'I want some water,' Ivan said, staring at the open door of the waiting room.

'You'll have to wait,' Amy said.

'There's an hour yet,' Stanley reminded her. 'He can't.'

The train jolted, as if about to start. 'I'm thirsty. I want a drink of water.'

'O my God,' his mother said. 'I told you we should have bought some lemonade at the station.'

'We had to get straight on. We were late.'

'A couple of minutes wouldn't have mattered.'

'I wanted to get seats.'

'We'd have found some somewhere.'

To argue about what was so irrevocably finished infuriated him, but he deliberately calmed himself and rooted in the basket for a blue plastic cup. His whole body was set happily for action: 'I'll just nip across to the tap.'

'The train's going to start,' she said. 'Sit down.'

'No, it won't.' But he didn't get up, paralysed by her objection.

'Are you going?' she said, 'or aren't you?' A vein jumped at the side of his forehead as he pushed along the crowded gangway, thinking that if he didn't reach the door and get free of her in a split second he would either go mad or fix his hands at her throat. Their carriage was beyond the platform, and he was out of sight for a moment. Then she saw him running between two trolleys into the men's lavatory as another playful whistle sounded from the engine.

'Where's Dad gone, Mam?'

'To get some water.'

Everyone was looking out of the window, interested in his race: 'He won't make it.'

'I'll lay a quid each way.'

'Don't be bleddy silly, he'll never get back in time. You can hear the wheels squeaking already. Feel that shuddering?'

'You're bleddy hopeful. We'll be here an hour yet.' The face disappeared behind a bottle: 'I'll live to see us move.'

Money was changing hands in fervid betting.

'He will.'

'He won't.'

At the second whistle he bobbed up, pale and smiling, a cup held high, water splashing over the brim.

'What's Dad out there for?' Ivan asked, lifting his face from a mug of lemonade someone had given him. The wheels moved more quickly, and Stanley was halfway along the platform. Odds were lengthening as he dropped from view, and pound notes were flying into the bookie's cap. A woman who wanted to place two bob each way was struggling purple-faced to get from the other end of the carriage. Her coins were passed over.

Amy sat tight-lipped, unwilling to join in common words of encouragement even if it meant never seeing him again. Their return tickets were in his wallet, as well as money and everything else that mattered, but she wouldn't speak. He can wander over the earth till he drops, she thought, though the vision of him sitting outside some charming rustic pub with twelve empty pint jars (and the plastic cup still full of water) in front of him, while she explained at the other end about their lost tickets and destitution, didn't make his disappearance too easy to keep calm about.

The carriage slid away, a definite move of steel rolling over steel beneath them all. He was trying not to spill his hard-won water. A roar of voices blasted along the windows as the train gathered speed. 'He's missed it!'

The door banged open, and a man who had slept through the betting spree jumped in his seat. He had come off nights at six that morning, and his false teeth jerked so that only a reflex action with both hands held them in the general neighbourhood of his mouth. Red in the face, he slotted them properly in with everyone looking on.

'What's the hurry, you noisy bogger?' he asked, at Stanley standing upright and triumphant beside him.

They clamoured at the bookie to pay up, and when his baffled face promised to be slow in doing so they stopped laughing and threatened to throw him off the bleeding train. He'd seen and grabbed his chance of making a few quid on the excursion, but having mixed up his odds he now looked like being sorted out by the crowd.

'Leave him alone,' the winners shouted. But they clapped and cheered, and avoided a fight as the train swayed with speed between fields and spinnies. Stanley stood with the plastic cup two-thirds full, then made his way to Ivan and Amy, unable to understand what all the daft excitement was about.

'What did you have to make a laughing-stock of yourself like that for?' she wanted to know.

'He needed some water, didn't he?'

'You mean you had to put on a show for everybody.' Their argument went unnoticed in the general share-out. 'You can see how much he wanted water,' she said, pointing to his closed eyes and hung-down lower lip fixed in sleep.

The sea was nowhere to be seen. They stood on the front and looked for it. Shining sand stretched left and right, and all the way to the horizon, pools and small salt rivers flickered under the sun now breaking through. The immense sky intimidated them, made Skegness seem small at their spines. It looked as if the ocean went on forever round the world and came right back to their heels.

'This is a rum bloody do,' he said, setting Ivan down. 'I thought we'd take a boat out on it. What a place to build a seaside resort.'

She smiled. 'You know how it is. The tide'll be in this afternoon. Then I suppose you'll be complaining that all the sand's under water. It's better this way because he can dig and not fall in.'

A few people had been on the beach but now, on either side,

hundreds advanced on to the sand, hair and dresses and white shirts moving against the wind, a shimmering film of blue and grey, red and yellow spreading from the funnel of the station avenue. Campstools and crates of beer staked each claim, and children started an immediate feverish digging as if to find buried toys before the tide came back.

'Can I have a big boat?' Ivan asked as they went closer to the pier and coastguard station. 'With a motor in it, and a lot of seats?'

'Where do you want to go?' Stanley asked.

Ivan wondered. 'A long way. That's where I want to go. A place like that. Up some road.'

'We'll get you a bus, then,' his father laughed.

'You want to stay at home with your mam,' she said. They walked further down the sand, between people who had already set out their camps. Neither spoke, or thought of stopping. Gulls came swooping low, their shadows sharp as if to slice open pools of water. 'How much more are we going to walk?'

'I didn't know you wanted to stop,' he said, stopping.

'I didn't know you wanted to come this far, or I wouldn't have come. You just walk on and on.'

'Why didn't you speak up then?'

'I did. Why didn't you stop?'

'I'm not a mind-reader.'

'You don't have to be. You don't even think. Not about other people, anyway.'

'I wanted to get beyond all this crowd.'

'I suppose you wanted to dump us in the sea.'

'I didn't want to sit all day in a café like you did, and that's a fact.'

'You're like a kid, always wanting to be on your own.'

'You're too bossy, always wanting your own way.'

'It usually turns out to be better than yours. But you never know what you do want, anyway.'

He was struck dumb by this irrational leap-frogging argument from someone he blindly loved. He stood and looked at the great space of sand and sky, birds, and a slight moving white beard of foam appearing on the far edge of the sand where the sea lay fallow and sleepy.

'Well?' she demanded. 'Are we traipsing much further, or aren't we? I wish you'd make up your mind.'

He threw the basket down. 'Here's where we stay, you hasty-tempered bitch.'

'You can be on your own, then,' she said, 'because I'm going.'

He opened a newspaper, without even bothering to watch her go – which was what she'd throw at him when she came back. 'You didn't even watch me go!' He should have been standing up and keeping her retreating figure in sight – that was fast merging with the crowd – his face frowning and unhappy in wondering whether or not he had lost her for ever.

But, after so long, his reactions would not mesh into gear. They'd become a deadeningly smooth surface that struck no sparks any more. When she needed him to put an arm around her and tell her not to get excited – to calm down because he loved her very much – that was when his mouth became ashen and his eyes glazed into the general paralysis of his whole body. She needed him most at the precise moment when he needed her most, and so they retreated into their own damaged worlds to wait for the time when they again felt no need of each other, and they could then give freely all that was no longer wanted, but which was appreciated nevertheless.

'Where's Mam gone?' Ivan asked, half-hidden in his well-dug hole.

'To fetch us something.'

'What, though?'

'We'll see.'

'Will she get me a tractor?'

'You never know.'

'I want a red one.'

'Let's dig a moat,' Stanley said, taking the spade. 'We'll rig a castle in the middle.'

He looked up from time to time, at other people coming to sit near by. An old man opened a campstool and took off his jacket. He wore a striped shirt over his long straight back, braces taut at the shoulders. Adjusting his trilby hat, he looked firmly and unblinking out to sea, so that Stanley paused in his work to see what he was fixing with such determination.

Nothing.

'Shall we make a tunnel, Dad?'

'All right, then, but it'll crumble.'

The thin white ray was coming towards them, feather-tips lifting from it, a few hundred yards away and suddenly no longer straight, pushed forward a little in the centre, scarred by the out-jutting pier. It broke on the sand and went right back.

'She'll be in in a bit, don't worry. We're in the front line, so we'll have to move,' the old man said. 'Half an hour at the most. You can't stop it, and that's a fact. Comes in shoulder-high, faster than a racehorse sometimes, and then you've got to watch out, even from this distance, my guy you have. Might look a fair way and flat one minute, then it's marching in quick like the Guards. Saw a man dragged in once, big six-footer he was. His wife and kids just watched. Found 'im in the Wash a week later. Pulls you underfoot. Even I can find my legs and run at times like that, whether I'm eighty or not.'

If it weren't for the trace of white he'd hardly have known where sky ended and sand began, for the wetness of it under the line was light purple, a mellower shade of the midday lower horizon. The mark of white surf stopped them blending, a firm and quite definite dividing of earth and water and air.

'Come here every year, then?' Stanley asked.

'Most days,' the man said. 'Used to be a lifeboatman. I live here.' His hand ran around the inside of a straw basket like a weasel and pulled out a bottle of beer. He untwisted the tight cork, up-ended it, and swigged it into his bony throat. 'You from Notts, I suppose?'

Stanley nodded. 'I'm a waiter. Wangled some time off for a change. It don't make so much difference at a big hotel. There used to be a shortage, but we've got some of them Spanish chaps now.' His jacket and tie lay on the sand, one sleeve hidden by a fallen rampart of Ivan's intricate castle.

Looking up he saw Amy making her way between patchwork blankets of people, a tall and robust figure wearing a flowered dress. A tied ribbon set hair spreading towards her shoulders. She never tried to look fabricated and smart, even on her job as a cashier at the local dance hall. He was almost annoyed at being so happy to see her, yet finally gave in to his pleasure and watched her getting closer, while hoping she had now recovered from her fits of the morning. Perhaps the job she had was too much for her, but she liked to work, because it gave a feeling of independence, helped to keep that vitality and anger that held Stanley so firmly to her. It was no easy life, and because of the money she earned little time could be given to Ivan, though such continual work kept the family more stable than if as a triangle the three of them were too much with each other – which they wanted to be against their own and everyone's good.

She had sandwiches, fried fish, cakes, dandelion-and-burdock, beer. 'This is what we need to stop us feeling so rattled.'

He wondered why she had to say the wrong thing so soon after coming back. 'Who's rattled?'

'You were. I was as well, if you like. Let's eat this though. I'm starving.'

She opened the packets, and kept them in equal radius around her, passing food to them both. 'I didn't know how hungry I was,' Stanley said.

'If anything's wrong,' she said, 'it's usually that – or something else.' She reached out, and they pressed each other's hand.

'You look lovely today,' he said.

'I'm glad we came.'

'So am I. Maybe I'll get a job here.'

'It'd be seasonal,' she said. 'Wouldn't do for us.'

'That's true.'

While Ivan had his mouth full of food, some in his hand, and a reserve waiting in his lap, she asked if he wanted any more. Even at home, when only halfway through a plate, the same thing happened, and Stanley wondered whether she wanted to stuff, choke or stifle him – or just kill his appetite. He'd told her about it, but it made no difference.

After the meal Ivan took his bread and banana and played at the water's edge, where spume spread like silver shekels in the sun and ran around his plimsolls, then fell back or faded into the sand. He stood up, and when it tried to catch him he ran, laughing so loudly that his face turned as red as the salmon paste spread on the open rolls that his mother and father were still eating. The sea missed him by inches. The castle-tumulus of sand was mined and sapped by salt water until its crude formations became lopsided, a boat rotted by time and neglect. A sudden upsurge melted it like wax, and on the follow-up there was no trace. He watched it, wondering why it gave in so totally to such gentle pressure.

They had to move, and Amy picked up their belongings, unable to stop water running over the sleeve of Stanley's jacket. 'You see,' she chided, 'if you hadn't insisted on coming all this way down we wouldn't have needed to shift so early.'

He was sleepy and good-natured, for the food hadn't yet started to eat his liver. 'Everybody'll have to move. It goes right up to the road when it's full in.'

'Not for another twenty minutes. Look how far down we are. Trust us to be in the front line. That's the way you like it, though. If only we could do something right for a change, have a peaceful excursion without much going wrong.'

He thought so, too, and tried to smile as he stood up to help.

'If everything went perfectly right one day,' she said, 'you'd still have to do something and deliberately muck it up, I know you would.'

As he said afterwards – or would have said if the same course hadn't by then been followed yet again – one thing led to another, and before I could help myself . . .

The fact was that the whole acreage of the remaining sand, peopled by much of Nottingham on its day's outing, was there for an audience, or would have been if any eyes had been trained on them, which they weren't particularly. But many of them couldn't help but be, after the first smack. In spite of the sea and the uprising wind, it could be heard, and the second was indeed listened for after her raging cry at the impact.

'You tried me,' he said, hopelessly baffled and above all immediately sorry. 'You try me all the time.' And the jerked-out words, and the overwhelming feeling of regret, made him hit her a third time, till he stood, arms hanging thinly at his side like the maimed branches of some blighted and thirsty tree that he wanted to disown but couldn't. They felt helpless, and too weak to be kept under sufficient control. He tried to get them safely into his pockets, but they wouldn't fit.

A red leaf-mark above her eye was slowly swelling. 'Keep away,' she cried, lifting her heavy handbag but unable to crash it against him. She sobbed. It was the first time he had hit her in public, and the voices calling that he should have less on it, and others wondering what funny stuff she had been up to to deserve it, already sounded above the steady railing of the nerve-racking sea. An over-forward wave sent a line of spray that saturated one of her feet. She ignored it, and turned to look for Ivan among the speckled colours of the crowd. Pinks and greys, blues and whites shifted across her eyes and showed nothing.

She turned to him: 'Where is he, then?'

He felt sullen and empty, as if he were the one who'd been hit. 'I don't know. I thought he was over there.'

'Where?'

'Just there. He was digging.'

'O my God, what if he's drowned?'

'Don't be so bloody silly,' he said, his face white, and thinner than she'd ever seen it. Bucket and spade lay by the basket between them. They looked into the sea, and then towards land, unable to find him from their mutual loathing and distress. They were closer than anyone else to the sea, and the old lifeboatman had gone. Everyone had moved during their argument, and the water now boiled and threw itself so threateningly that they had to pick up everything and run.

'What effect do you think all this arguing and fightin's going to have on him?' she demanded. He'd never thought about such outside problems, and considered she had only mentioned them now so as to get at him with the final weapon of mother-and-child, certainly not for Ivan's own and especial good. Yet he was not so sure. The horror of doubt came over him, opened raw wounds not only to himself but to the whole world for the first time as they walked towards the road and set out on a silent bitter search through the town.

For a long while Ivan sat on the steps of a church, the seventh step down from the doors, beating time with a broken stick as blocks of traffic sped by. He sang a song, dazed, enclosed, at peace. A seagull sat at his feet, and when he sneezed it flew away. He stayed at peace even after they found him, and went gladly on the train with them as if into the shambles. They seemed happily united in getting him back at last. The effort of the search had taken away all their guilt at having succumbed to such a pointless quarrel in front of him. He watched the fields, and heavy streams like long wavy mirrors that cows chewed at and clouds flowed over and ignored.

He sat on his father's knee, who held him as if he were a rather unusual but valuable tip a customer in the restaurant had left. Ivan felt nothing. The frozen soul, set in ancestry and childhood, fixed his eyes to look and see beyond them and the windows. The train wasn't moving after a while. He was sleeping a great distance away from it, detached, its jolting a permanent feature of life and the earth. He wanted to go on travelling forever, as if should he ever stop the sky would fall in. He dreamed that it had, and was about to black him out, so he woke up and clung to his father, asking when they would be back in Nottingham.

The Rope Trick

While making an efficient fire on which to roast sausages, on a rock bed built between carob and olive trees in Greece, one of the happy-go-lucky girls called June, who was nothing if not stoned and with it (and with me) said: 'I can see you've done your time in Sherwood Forest.'

'Listen,' I snapped, feeding brittle wood into the smoke. 'There are two ways you can do time in Sherwood Forest. One is in the army, and the other's in the sanatorium. I did mine in the sanatorium, but as a stoker not an invalid, which was after I came out of prison and met the girl of my life — if I remember.'

They laughed. Yes, it was very funny. We were all recovering from a strong dose of the pot, and lay in deadbeat poses eating at bread, and sausages burnt in pine and juniper branches. A hot wind came from up the grey wall of mountain as if someone were wafting it down through the asphodel for our especial benefit. We got to talking about love, and to my surprise none of them thought much of it — though we all had our birds, the birds were there, and they didn't wear feathers, either. Neither did I believe in love — though I had an idea I was lying as usual.

'The sooner you lose all trace of love, the better,' I said. 'I can see that now, having never got her, yet realized that she was the love of my life and was bound to have some influence on it.'

June moved over to let me sit on the tree-trunk after such a selfless stint by the fire. 'Love is the end,' said Michael, 'the end; so go to greet love as a friend!'

'And turn queer,' someone shouted, I forget who.

The blue sea puffed its spume tops along all the caves of the coast, fisherboats smacking down into it, and swooping along. 'I can never turn anything,' I said. 'But I'll try and tell you about her, if you'll pass me some more of that resinated fishwater that in these parts goes for wine.'

I didn't even know her name — no name, no photo and hardly a face, yet the memory bites at me so often that I think it must end up a good one. Either that, or it will rot my soul.

They looked at me, my travelling companions, friends of the fraternity that one bumped into on the Long Grand Tour. They listened as always, which was pleasant for me, because if you don't have anything to say how can anybody know you're alive? And if people aren't sure whether or not you're alive how can you be expected to know yourself?

I was lucky to have a few good pennies left in my pocket on that raw October morning, for it meant I still had one at least without a hole in it, which may have accounted for the fine and heady feeling as I walked down Mansfield Road. Stepping off the kerb I almost became good for nothing but a few black puddings as a petrol lorry flowed an inch from my foot, but even that shock didn't shake my tripes, and the flood-roar of swearing stopped in half a minute. Buns in a baker's window looked as if pelted with coal-specks and baked in canary-shit, so I thought I'd rather throw my remaining coppers on a cup of cold tea in a dirty cracked cup with lipstick round the edges, for the half-hour buckshee sitdown would be a break from the never-ending traipse over concrete and cobblestones looking for a job, a hard thing to find after a long stretch of the penthouse.

But at least I'd paid society for my crimes, which as you can imagine made me feel a lot better. You think it did? When you've stopped laughing, I'll go on. No matter how much quod you get you don't pay back anything. Some who thieve were born to make good, can't wait between snatching the loot and getting pulled in, but I'm not like that, didn't hand back a shilling of all I took in spite of my spell in the nick, for it was spent before they got me.

When the powdery rain eased off, a blade of sun leapt a row of pram and toy shops, as sharp and sudden as if God had whipped out a gold-plated flick-knife to prise open a door and break in. But the sun went back. He'd changed his mind because the shops weren't rich enough, being the sort that could go bankrupt any day. I pulled up my collar for the umpteenth time, the changeable weather lifting clouds high only to let them fall low again. If this sly and treacherous rain kept on peeing itself I'd sit in the library for a dose of reading, I said to myself.

Being still so close to clink I told the other half of me things it might have thought healthier to forget. I remembered a tall man inside, with black hair and a Roman conk whose brown eyes stared too much for his own good. Up to then I'd thought only blue eyes could stare so much, but his brown ones gazed as if a fire blazed between him and the world. Maybe he glimpsed something that could never be reached, even beyond the blue skies of outside. He was down for a seven-year stretch after manslaughtering a pal who'd knocked on with his wife, and he had a habit of pushing a scrap of paper into anyone's hand he passed close to. One day I happened to be going by on exercise and felt something pressed into my own. Despite the friendliness I wondered how much of a good thing it was, for if it had been a cigarette you had to be careful it wasn't a choir-boy getting round you, for it was a common move of theirs.

Back in my cell I opened the postage-stamp of lavatory paper and read LENIN written in wavy capital letters. He's a brittle worm-eaten nut, I said, throwing it away. Yet I changed my mind, spent time looking till my fingers groped over it, then swallowed hard into my stomach and went back to reading Byron – which was all I was fit for in those not so far-off days.

One morning he threw a terrible fit in the grub hall, and smashed everything his hands could reach. He looked consumptive, thin, almost without muscle, yet I saw a match of strength I'd never seen before. But the screws battened the roaring bleeder down and humped him off to the loony bin.

So he was buried alive, and I was stomping the cobbles in my freedom, rooting for work to stop me starving. Not that you're at liberty the minute you set your snout beyond that iron gate. Being let loose after a thousand days was both fine and dangerous, a well-concealed trap in front of eyes and feet to trip me up and send me a header into some well-stocked shop or house, and so once more into the bullock-box. It's like recovering from a broken leg or pneumonia, when you need a few weeks' convalescence for fear of dropping back. So I trod softly for my own raw good, looking normal but stepping along that piece of taut rope, which is all right when it's on the ground and your head is solid, but after jail it's as though the line is six foot above the pavement and needs but one flick of an eyelid to send you arse over backwards. You may be lucky and pick yourself up from the right side of the rope-walk, but then again you might wake with a black eye in a cell at the copshop before you know where you are, supping a cup of scalding tea that one of the bastards had brought so's you'll look good in front of the magistrate next morning

– all because an unexpected windfall made you slip on to the bad side.

Air and bridgestones shook by the station as a black muscle-bound express boned its way out towards Sheffield. Coiling rubbernecks of smoke and steam shot above the parapet to spar with the sky, and I wanted to be in one of those carriages with a ticket and ten quid padding my pocket, fixed on a seat with a bottle of ale by one paw and a filled fag-case in the other, looking out at fields and collieries and feeling good wearing a new suit got from somewhere, my eyes lit up with the vision of a sure-fire job.

The steamy tea bar was full of drivers and conductors, hawkers, tarts, and angels of the dole, but nobody I knew, thank God, for I wasn't in any mood to moan about the weather and shake my head over the next war. They couldn't drop the Bomb soon enough for me, right there and then. I had no property to lose, caught sight of myself in the mirror, not looking good for much, because prison and long walks searching for work had kept me thin, my suit elbow-and-arse-patched, and prime King Edward spuds at the back of my socks, and a gap in one of my boot-toes big enough to compete with Larry Adler on the mouth organ. I never was a handsome brute, with a low forehead, thin face, and starvo eyes, and a change of fashion hadn't yet made me as prepossessing as I am now – with hair nearly on my shoulders.

I'd shaved that morning with a razor-blade sharpened on the inside of a jam-jar, but still looked as if I'd spent three years in jungle not jail, hunted by tigers, and enormous apes, swinging like an underdone Tarzan over streams and canyons with never a second's rest from chasing and being chased by devils inside and out. You can see what a man is by looking into his eyes, I thought, though I hope not everything he ever will be. I'd stared myself out while shaving, because the mirror in our kitchen was no bigger than a postage stamp ripped in half, which was why the safety razor cut me to ribbons. That's how you see anybody though, through smashed bits of mirror, and nobody can say which way and in how many pieces the mirror was going to break when it dropped and gave that seven years' bad luck. But through the pattern of such glittering scraps it's easy to tell whether a person is used to being knocked about by the world and has no option but to let it, or whether he's got something in his brain and stomach that makes him spin into action like an ant with bladder trouble against all the Bible-backed pot-loathing bastards of the universe.

The café had once been smart, done up for old ladies and Tory widows to sup tea in while waiting for buses to take them home to matchbox bungalows and yapping mole-dogs, but now the chairs were slashed and battered, a late-night hideaway for beats and riff-raff, and the wet floor was scraped from hob-nailed boots and specked with nub-ends.

A swish bint behind the counter with a soft white face and long hair asked what I wanted, and I would like to have told her the truth, though even so her heart seemed pleased when I answered: 'A cup of tea, duck.'

I must have been dug right into myself, because I'd sat next to a girl without knowing it. Not that I'd have shuffled off to a quiet corner and brooded alone if I had seen her, but I might have sparked an opening shot before sitting down. Giving the sly once-over with one eye, I watched my drink slooshing from a hundred-watt brass tea-tub with the other.

The maroon coat had padded shoulders and thick cuffs, and she must have been walking in the rain, because I could whiff the fresh wetness of autumn on stale cloth drifting through tea-fumes and fag-smoke, and saw where raindrops had dried on the nearest cheek to me. Her face was dark, going to sallow because of thinness, and would have had a better complexion with more meat on it.

I liked the dark hair she had, for it fell on her neck in ringlets, as if the wind had blown it around before she'd had time to think of drawing a comb through it. I couldn't see her full face, but enough at this cockeyed angle to sense that something was wrong.

I made up a story saying that maybe she'd lost either husband, parents or perhaps a baby, was in a bad way and didn't know what to do now she'd finished her cup of tea.

A hand reached up to her face, a movement that startled me as if before then I'd been looking at a person not quite alive. She stared at the sheer mirror that rose like an empty sea above a rocky shore of Woodbines and matches, and the only two faces looking back from it were hers and mine, me at her and she at nothing.

I pushed my hot and untouched cup of tea across to her. 'Are you all right, duck?'

'What are you staring at me for?' she demanded – in such a tone that I knew she wouldn't feel too good if I answered the same way.

'I like looking at people.'

'Pick somebody else, then.'

'I'm sorry. I've been seeing the same dead mugs year in and year out behind bars, and that's enough to drive even a sane man crazy. The government's had me worried and bullied blind, and I'm just about getting back into my heart.'

After such a reason she became more sociable. 'I see what you mean. I've never been in one of those places, but I suppose it is strange to be loose again.' She spoke softly, yet jerked her words out in a breathless way.

'You catch on quick.' I pushed a fag over, one of a couple lifted from the old man's packet that morning before he pushed me into the yard and told me never to come back because the sight of me made mother ill. I took him at his word, and never did see either of them again.

She hesitated. 'I shouldn't smoke.'

I scraped a match along the brass rail. 'Don't take down, then it wain't hurt.'

'I haven't the price of a cigarette,' she said, 'to tell you the truth.' Hair and eyes made her sallow skin look darker than it was, and she could almost have been the sister of the bloke in clink who'd plagued me with his Lenin message month after month. Smoking gave her more colour, coupled to the tea she sipped. 'I've neither digs nor a job at the moment. I was kicked out of both as from this morning.'

I lowered my fag, to get a clearer view of her face: 'What happened, then?'

'I worked as a wardmaid at the hospital.'

'I shouldn't think that'd be up to much.'

'It wasn't. I was scrubbing floors and serving meals from morning till night, and looking after dying men. It was a cancer ward. Did you ever see anyone die of that? Nothing kills the pain with some. They spin like crazy animals, right under the bed, and I had to help the nurses get them back and give them a jab.'

'It's the sort of work somebody's got to do.'

'I tried. But it wasn't possible.'

'Sure you did.'

'I went on all right for quite some time, though I didn't enjoy it, but then I got ill and had to be looked after myself. Now I'm better, but I can't do that sort of work any more.' She wasn't the kind of girl I'd normally meet in the district I lived in, and maybe this as much as anything drew me to her. She wasn't so rare and extraordinary, but her nervous face hinted at more intelligence than usual, and I imagined that on happier days her slightly curved nose and thin lips would mark her as being witty and fond of a good time. She spoke in a clearer way than I did then, the headlights of that Nottingham accent dipped almost as if she came from some other town. I wondered how old she was, and thought she could easily have been thirty from the lines around her face. 'What part of the world do you come from?' I wanted to know.

She didn't like my question, but answered: 'Nottingham.'

I guessed she wanted me to mind my own business, yet went on: 'Why do you stay here, then, if you don't like it?'

'My husband.'

'He don't seem to look after you very well.'

'I've no idea where he is, and I don't much care.'

In spite of everything she seemed easier when I went on pumping her. 'Why did you split up?'

'He'd never work, expected me to go out and keep him. He's a wireless mechanic, quite clever, but I couldn't stand him any longer and left. Or he left me, rather. We had a room, and I had to leave that this morning because I couldn't pay the rent.'

The waitress was talking to a couple of postmen, so left us in the clear. I gave all the sympathy I'd got, for there wasn't much else I could part with, and feeling sorry for her made it seem less like trying to pick her up, for I wasn't sure whether I wanted to.

'That's the worst of working for these great institutions,' I said. 'They slave you to death then throw you out. They've got no heart. I know, because I was in one myself, with a big wall around it. They said my time was up, contract finished. I was a model worker and earned my remission, so I argued about the contract and rates of pay, said remission didn't worry me, yet told them that wages and conditions were rotten. But the boss swore at me, said he'd not take me on again when times were bad, that he'd let me starve if I didn't have less of my lip. I threatened him with a strike even, but before I knew where I was I was outside the gate, a hole in the arse of the suit I'd been taken in in.'

I looked at her through the mirror, and knew that nothing could dislodge the boulder of apathy across her brain and eyes. When people talk about apathy at election times they don't know what it means, I thought, hearing a speaker-van passing by outside asking us to vote for something or other.

Beyond her shoulders I saw rain falling, followed by hailstones in an

October madness, a revolution of proletarian ice-heads rushing downwards to be softened by the still warm earth. A red bus came out of a rank, left gravel for tarmac and took a turning for Newark when the eyelids of the traffic lights lifted to a prolonged stare of green.

'I'd even like to be on that drowned rat of a bus going north along an up-and-down road,' I said, 'or rocketing down the motorway towards London.'

'Are you another who's always running away?'

People listened to the hail and rain as if the dim voice of God would start to come through it, so that her question couldn't be heard by anyone except me among the semi-darkness and clink of cups. 'I'm either running away from something,' I answered, 'or running into something, I don't know which. But I'm not a shirker, if that's what you mean.'

'Amen,' she said. 'Try running on nothing to eat, and no money.'

'You're right. I've never done much on an empty stomach. That's why I've always landed in trouble.'

Tea and fags were finished, and she asked if I'd ever tried working. 'Many a time,' I said, feeling grim and rotten whenever I told the truth.

'I'm sorry. I'm sure you did. You seem wide awake enough.'

'Too pepped-up to find it easy. There's a shortage of work now: the bosses are frightened of losing their profits.'

She laughed – which in my stupidity I took as a good sign.

'My husband used to say that. I don't think it means much. Not that you're anything like him, though!' – remembering her previous opinion – 'Nobody could be as bad as he was, regarding work. He wouldn't go to bed at night and wouldn't get up in the morning. So we never had money, except what dole he wheedled, or National Assistance, or what I brought in. He didn't mind half starving, as long as he could sleep, and I think he'd really have been happy enough to see me on the streets.' This insistence upon work was grinding my nerves down, especially when I'd been wearing my legs off for the last fortnight trying to corner some.

She had no make-up on, not even lipstick, nothing to disguise the fact that she'd just fought clear of an illness. I wanted to get outside, but to leave her seemed too much of a risk. I glanced at her, not through the mirror but into flesh and blood, and, seeing her eyes closed felt afraid she'd faint, so put my arm behind her in case. Her mouth trembled, and tears came from beneath her eyelids, which gave me real distress, because in a way I liked her and felt sorry there was no useful help in me. I couldn't even offer my handkerchief, it was so black.

The girl behind the bar thought we were having a silent set-to, so stayed away and punched open the till as she served a customer, dropped a coin in with a dull click (which told me how full it was) and scooped out some change. Money. That's all she needed, a good meal, a few drinks and a warm bed, and she'd be a different woman. I pressed her hand till she looked at me. 'Wait half an hour, duck, and I'll have something for you, to help while you get a job.'

She nodded, unbelievingly. 'You wain't go away?' I said. She shook her head. 'Everything'll be all right when I come back.' She couldn't answer, was numb inside and out, and had no faith in what I was trying to say. 'You believe me, don't you? I won't be long. I know where I can get some money.'

I could have smashed my dum-dum head against a wall I felt so useless, but she nodded when I asked her again to wait just half an hour.

The rain had stopped. Nothing and no one – the sky least of all – has a mind of its own.

There were no pictures in the sky, so I looked at the gutters running with brown water, a full spate of production thrusting a straight way between kerb and cobblestones and leaving fresher air in its wake, dragged under further down by sewer grates and carried unwilling to the black and snaky Trent. Whether you fight with all the force in your spring-jack arms to make headway, or roll along like oil and water, you're sucked into the black grates of death just the same.

Thoughts come to me in grey and enclosed places, and in clink I closed my hand over and set them in the warm nest of my brain to stop me going into screaming madness. I remember the pals I had at school and see their lives, how they were mostly married by twenty-one, and an aeroplane flies out of heaven, sky-writing THE END across their world. Or they finish with the army and see the same message. But I was in the nick till twenty-four, and the army would never have me, so I'm still on the advance towards new fields and marshes. The two-word telegram can't frighten me, and when I came from the cell and under an archway the plane quickly wrote THE BEGINNING and flew away from the chaos that surrounds my life. Hemmed in with my shattered brain I sometimes saw myself as the man who, after hydrogen bombs have splattered the earth, will roar around the emptiness crying out word by word the first chapter of the Bible, because nothing else will be in my head except that, and whoever I meet won't have anything in their heads at all. Sometimes you go mad to stop yourself going mad.

Slab Square's dominating timepiece handed out twelve o'clock like charity. How could I get money for what's-her-name sitting in the tea bar? Print it, mould it, stamp it out like a bloody blacksmith? I zigzagged through the bus station and stood by the market watching people go in and out. She's expecting me back with something borrowed from a barrow-boy pal who happened to be conveniently near, and I thought: if only the world was made like that.

I walked between the stalls with weasel eye and hungry hand set for any chance at all. Above the bustle of women buying supplies for their family fortresses, and old men looking at stuff they were too slow to pinch and too broke to buy I listened to cash-tills ringing in and out like the bells of Hell. Ping! Ping! Here, they were saying, here! Pinging like shots against a barricaded bank, while I stood spellbound in midstream of a strong crowd current, petrified with pleasure at the irregular rhythm and chorus of it, coupled with the call of voices, the clash of pots from crock stalls, breezes of fish and fruit and meat and the low thundering pass of traffic from outside. Money was pouring into pockets and tills, filling baskets and banks, hearts with greed and eyes with incurable blindness. Ping! Ping! And here was I with a poor bit of a rundown woman who was short of a few bob to stand on her feet, while a poster outside told me in dazzling colours I'd never had it so good and would soon have it better.

A sweet old Dolly-on-the-tub swayed by, a head-scarfed hot-slot from Notts with a homely mangel-wurzel face, a dyed army overcoat on her back. A purse lay in the basket between a packet of soapflakes and a wrapped loaf, so I followed the trail of her steamy breath. The place was jammed, and if my life had depended on a clear way through, all trouble would have been finished for good. Near the wide entrance my hand snaked and struck towards the basket, and in my imagination had already opened the purse, cursing my luck as I flung away bus tickets and pawn tags, pension book and worn-out photos, wading through all that to find only eighteen pence, because she'd never had it so good either. She swung towards the fish section, leaving my hand in mid-air and my bent back locked in a terrible lumbago cramp.

The fishmonger lapped paper around her bundle, slapped it on top of the purse. A pal of Dolly's pulled her by the elbow, nearly crushing my toes. 'Can't abide this weather,' she said, after greetings. 'I just can't abide it, Mary, my duck.'

Mary couldn't, either, because it brought on her railway-husband's bronchitis. Such talk gave my hand the twitches, for it hovered like a semi-black meaty rare tropical butterfly near the back of my neck and was trying to get down between a butcher's assistant and a bus conductress, then through to the basket and purse that I couldn't even see any more. I had to look as if I were moving without really doing so, appearing cheerful and treadmilly mobile as if on my way to the tea-stall whose cups steamed not far beyond.

'Aye, it does take some beating, don't it? I wouldn't mind it so much, except that I can never get my washing done, and it stokes my rheumatics up summat wicked.'

A deep sigh came from Mary, and I was close enough to blow in her ear, though still couldn't steer my mauler through. A couple of other women were jammed near. 'Well,' Mary grumbled, 'you mustn't grumble. You'll allus find somebody worse off than yourself.' You're looking right at him, I thought, unless I can get my hand on your pal's change-bag.

The way cleared, and I could see through to the basket, and when my hand was getting scratched on the straw I noticed the glassy eyes of the mackerel that had rolled from their paper specially to glare at me: 'You bring your thieving fingers any closer,' they seemed to say, 'and we'll scream.' Someone pushed, not heavy enough to be on purpose, but I was a few inches back again. He had difficulty getting through, and the roll of his fat neck came dead-level with me.

My heart crashed in and out like an oxygen bag, and my feet moved from the cloth I was staring at, because I'd seen the colour of that uniform a good few times before: blue-black and ready for that stainless Sheffield flick-blade I'm glad I didn't have or, being so close to falling from the post-penthouse tight-rope I might have buried it between his shoulder-bones and run for my spent life. I made for the exit, the purse out of my mind, and hearing only the quick dying trail of someone swear as I put my foot on theirs without stopping to apologize.

I leaned against the wall outside, my heart and blood signalling far and wide the news of my miraculous escape. Then I remembered the girl in the café who was down on her luck and waiting for me to lope in, my sound pocket stuffed by the wherewithal to do her a lot of good. And in the same crashing breath I hated myself like arsenic because I'd thought of robbing a poor old trot of her short-changed purse, a woman worth ten of me because she'd suffered more and was older, while I hadn't and was still young. I could have smashed my head on a railing spike and ended it all, because if I robbed anyone at all it shouldn't be anybody like her.

A bus drew in at the stop and people got off, stuffing used tickets like good citizens into the slot provided, being as afraid of dirtying the street as they were of shitting their own pants, wanting to keep the roads clean even though their hearts might be black. One four-eyed bowler-hat even put some coins into a little red box for uncollected fares. Luck puts the wind up some people. You've got to pay for everything in this life, old-fashioned church voices whisper from the insides of their hollow skulls, and so they believe it, young and old, clutching a conscience like an extra arm they can't do without, but which is really a rudder steering them through a life they've got used to and never want to change, since they're dead scared of anything new. And you can only change such a system by chopping that arm right off and burying it six feet under like any corpse. I was hungry and bitter, and knew it was wrong to be either, so told myself to stop it, stop it, or I wouldn't be free much longer.

I considered getting on a bus and opening one of those little red boxes, but threw the idea out because even though I might be a robbing bastard I was no fool. Walking towards Hockley I felt sure the girl would wait till I got back, for her present mood was familiar to me, had often nailed my body and soul into the ground and kept it there for countless hours so that I hardly knew time was passing and didn't care whether I died or not.

But now I was a man of action and wondered whether I should go to a bookshop and nick an expensive manual on engineering and sell it secondhand for ten bob or a quid. Useless. I turned from the clothes shops whose fronts were decorated with overalls, cheap suits, and rows of boots. I passed their prices labelled in big creosote figures, then walked between deserted lace factories and tall warehouses, booting a black rat-killing tomcat that ran from under a wooden gate. A few office tarts were strolling around, but I went through them like a ghost, and sat on a stone bench by a churchyard thinking that maybe I ought to go into Woolworth's and sneak my hand up like a cobra to drag down a few fountain pens.

Pacing the green old gravestones I came face to face with a church door, pushed it open and went in. There were rows of empty seats and a deserted altar, as if it were never used even by the rats. I read notices about this and that meeting, or service, or charity, and on a table lay booklets telling of church and parish history. But my eyes moved to a lightly padlocked box on which was painted in white letters: RESTORATION FUND.

I was outside in a second, but stopped for some reason on the steps. Feeling rain I had good reason to go back inside, but seeing granite scrolls and marble slabs, caskets with hangdog flowers, railings with heads like barbarian spears, emptiness crossing the narrow streets like an unhurrying copper, an exhausted sky only stopped from falling flat on its guts because of sharp chimneypots and pointed eaves, I had better reasons for staying where I was. Yet something put its hooks in me, and necessity like boiling oil burned away conscience and hesitation. I can't say I stood there reflecting like an honest man on good and evil, because it would be a lie if I did, but it was something to my credit that I stood there at all.

A few minutes later I pushed that oak-stained door once more and stood inside the church before it had time to slide to behind me. A piece of matting lay in front of the padlocked box, as if to encourage people with cold feet to step on it for long enough to part with their lolly, and I hoped it had been successful as I too stood and took a last glance around the church to make sure it was empty.

I looked at that lovely phrase saying RESTORATION FUND, which was the right one anyway, for I could think of two people at least who wanted restoring. Gripping the padlock as if about to do a clever judo move and sling the box skyhigh over my shoulder, I gave it a maniacal twist, my other hand pressed down hard on top. The wrench was strengthened by desperate need choking the girl I'd left in the café and it was plain, as the screws gave and the lock buckled, that a tenth of such force would have been sufficient.

I threw the lock on to the matting, and lifted the lid to see at least a pound in coin. It was strange how most of the money had dropped in and rolled to the left side of the box. I couldn't get a grip on the last few with my fingers, took some time getting fingernails under each before flicking them up into my hands where they rattled with a willing heart at freedom, glad like a bunch of prisoners at being in circulation again. An idea of gratitude struck me, of which I was always full, and because I rarely had the opportunity to give it I felt in my pocket for a pencil and wrote plainly under RESTORATION FUND: 'Thank you, dear friends.' I then dropped the cash pell-mell into my pocket and walked out.

People might think I've been in to light a candle for my grandmother's soul, and that I'm pleased she's being warmed at last in stone-cold heaven – I laughed as I went between gravestones into the street, then back towards the bus station café, where the girl no doubt sat looking into an empty teacup, unable to read her fortune because a leafless tea-urn had taken even that kick away.

Calmness left me. The older I was the more scared I got afterwards, not like the old days when I stashed open a post office in a light-hearted devil-may-care way and came out with a cashbox under my coat – and ran straight into the arms of a copper. The old lags had weighed me up right in saying I'd lose my nerve sooner or later. I used to think they were wrong and couldn't tell a cut lip from a black eye no matter how long they looked, but truth was somewhere at the back of it, because my legs would hardly hold as I turned by the market. With my rattling pocket I felt as if fifty sharp-cornered cashboxes hung around me like a Christmas tree at the wrong season. But losing your nerve doesn't matter so much, as long as you keep a tight control over yourself.

I was some way down from the bus station café where I'd left my dark and beautiful stranger, and being so close I dared at last to plunge my hand in and feel those cool shapes of money. A strong and wilful hand fell on my shoulder.

I'd have dropped stone dead on the spot if the life force hadn't thought I was worth saving at the last moment. Bleak terror sent me totally cold – before the voice broke. I was in court, given up as a bad job and put away this time for good, plunged into the cattlepen of no-man's-land for what days were left to me, finished at the turn of a frost-filled iron key. My mouth was full of iodine and sawdust, coal gas and common bird-lime, and it stayed just as strong as ever when I heard the big bluff voice that followed the blow on my shoulder: 'You thought I was a copper, didn't you, you rogue! Still the same Jack

Parker who can't keep his hands to hisself! I'd a known you a mile off, walking along like a hungry jack-rabbit.'

I turned, and who should it be but my old pal Terry Jackson, whom I hadn't seen for three years and wouldn't have known but for his face, for he was dressed like a millionaire in a charcoal-grey suit and striped shirt, a small knotted tie and spick-and-span shoes. He was smoking a long cigarette and looked so well turned out that labels should have been stuck on him saying 'Fragile' and 'This Side Up' and 'Don't Bend', which made him altogether different to the cross-eyed scruff in a shattered coat who'd gone with me into that warehouse. He was well fed, built on meat and solid salad, not so tall as I was, but his fair combed hair smelled of scent and his shaved chops of eau-de-cologne. He hadn't exactly a film star's features, but money had lifted his chin higher and given an extra sparkle to his eyes, seemed to have made sure that wherever he stepped in his tailor-made shoes everything would shift out of his way. Even the pimples had gone without trace, packed up their pus in a hurry and left.

'I'll bet you thought your number was up. I can just see both your pockets stuffed with fivers,' he laughed.

'I wish they was,' I said, glad to see him. 'How did you drop into all this wealth? And don't tell me you earned it as an errand boy.'

He grinned, spent another bash on my shoulder. I bashed him back. 'I ain't seen you for years,' he said. 'My old pal! I thought you'd signed on for twenty-one with the army, or killed yourself in some other way. And driving along in my new sports bus I see you. As if that could be anybody else but Jack Parker, I thought to myself! Where you bin, then?'

'All over. After a month sunning myself in the Isles of Greece I went to live in France. Worked there a couple of years. Had a marvellous time. Better than this dump.'

'Why did you come back then?'

'Got fed up. You know how it is. Which is your car?'

He pointed down the kerb, at an open sports with a girl in it. It was red and thin like a lobster, the sort you'd buy at the fish shop rather than a garage, looking as if it would crack in two if you sat on the middle of it.

'It can do a hundred in the shade,' Terry said. 'The other day on the road to Newark, you should have seen it, skimming along like a speed boat. I daren't look at the clock. It was smashing.' The girl waved to him, to hurry back and stop talking to that scruff. From a distance she looked a stunner, fair-haired and well dressed, little pink fingers drumming the side of the car, but not too hard in case she dented it or disturbed her C & A hat.

'Nice piece,' I said.

This made him happy. 'She ain't a piece. She's my wife. Married her a year ago. Her old man owns roundabouts and sideshows at the fair. Loaded with dough, and lets me help myself. Loves me like a son – which he never had. Come on the fairground next week and look us up. She's got an aunt who tells fortunes. It's a scream. Allus says I'll come to a bad end, but it's only because I can't stop laughing. She'll tell your fortune if you come.'

I took one of the fags he offered. 'If I've got time.'

Gold cigarette-lighter. 'Mek time. What are you doing these days?'

I'd nothing to hide. 'Looking for a job.'

'You ought to find a wife. Settle down. If you want a job I know a factory office you could do. Dough comes in from the bank on Thursday night for payday time. Need a drop of gelly though, that's all.'

I pulled him up: 'I've just been inside for three years and want to stay out for good now. Anyway I think my luck's changed as from an hour ago.' I said this to save him offering me a job on his roundabouts, because he'd be scared of me walking off with the week's takings of some coconut stall, and I'd be afraid of ending up on a spinning roundabout that got me nowhere. 'Still live in Denman Terrace?' he asked. 'We had some good times there, didn't we? A terrible crumb-dump. Has it been bombed yet, do you know?'

'Don't think so.'

'Let me know when it has. I'll have a double whisky on it.'

'I'm going back to London next week,' I said. 'Get a job on a building site. Or work as a railway porter. You have better times down there.'

He was impressed. 'No kidding? I'd go with you, but' – nodding towards his piece of skirt – 'I'm hooked.' He couldn't take his eyes off her.

'What's she like then?' I asked.

'In bed?' Before I could stop him his grey eyes lit as if to burn through any she-cat: 'Boy, she's marvellous. I never get tired. When I come it's like Siberia. It goes on and on, and there's no end to it. I'm flying, man! Flying!'

'Introduce me. You've set me on.'

300

'Come to Goose Fair next week, then I will. Don't forget.'

'All right. Meanwhile lend's a quid or two. I'll pay it back when I see you there.' I said this in spite of myself, because up to that moment I'd preferred to steal rather than borrow.

Like a good friend, he pushed a couple of five-notes into my hand, and even laughed over it. 'Plenty more where that came from!'

We cracked each other a few more times on the shoulder, then I watched him drive off, his ringed fingers waving farewell like a king as he clipped the traffic lights.

My pocket bursting its seams with money I went back to find Floradora, who'd at least have a good few quid till she found work enough to stay on her feet. The time I'd seen her had set my mad brain going about her marvellous hair, and unhappy face that was good-looking if she'd ever escape from the uppers of her luck. I hoped I'd be able to know her better and though it might not come off, I thought, pushing open the door, it could be worth a bit more than my dead life to get in there and try. What with that, and bumping into Terry Jackson, I didn't give a sod for any job or body, saw the nick as a fading bad dream, and the rain now behind me washing out the past and what blame was latched to it, making the way clear for some future I was ever too blind to see.

The same wet smoke and tea smells, and the stink of beans-on-toast greeted me, but I'd never felt less hungry in my life, eyed the line of backs stuck on each seat over supped cups and nibbled plates, so many people in caps and coats, I couldn't immediately find the girl for whom my pocket jingled and rustled. Terry's long cigarette was still young, and flipping off the ash I walked between the tables but knew she couldn't be at any one of them. The search was casual, went to the more likely bar, and from head to head again looking for dark ringlets on one bent slightly forward.

I put off the truth as long as possible, unwilling to tell myself she wasn't there, had vanished, flipped-out with worries that a few quid and what care I could give might have fixed, gone also with her red lips and dark skin and agile thinness and all the madness and gaiety that lurks in a girl who can become buried by such lunatic unhappy weather. Still unable to believe it, I said to the waitress: 'Remember me, duck?'

She leaned all her softness forward: 'Who wouldn't?'

'What happened to the woman I was sitting with half an hour ago?'

301

There was a quick dark scuffle in her memory. 'Wore a maroon coat?'

I nodded.

'She went just after you left. I thought she'd gone to look for you.' Perhaps she saw my disappointment, but there was no use hiding it. What they can't see they sense, and think you less of a man for keeping it quiet under your coat. She asked me who she was, and I lied for the third time that day: 'My wife.'

I walked out of the café and back into the streaming rain to look for her, my good pocket full like my heart to bursting, weeping and cursing that she hadn't even waited the promised half-hour.

I'd find a job, but I'd never see her again. To look for both in the next few days was possible, but the search turned out to be hopeless. That's the way things are arranged, in this super and abundant world, which must go on turning, like a dead pig over the slow fire of my body and soul.

After three months in the sanatorium working as a stoker and doing my penance for the sick and healing, I looked again, but all I found was Terry Jackson. I took him up on the job he'd offered, and one day after a ragbag year of saving, during which time I was often tempted to rinse my fingers in the till but didn't, a year of all work and no expensive pleasures, I set out on a gang-hitch to ancient Greece, to the happy isles, the lotus hash-land where I'll stay forever, meaning for as long as I'm able to think back on what I am and have been. The sun is good and healing, the sausages here are real meat, the sky blue and the wind some-times bitter, but my love has gone and will never come back.

We walked slowly up the stony track, zigzagging like donkeys after a hard day in the blinkers, between cork and carob and pine and olive, flashes of sea to keep us happy in the sweat and heat of the climb, taking an hour to reach the village where somebody's friend had promised us another night's doss on the stone floor of a wash-house.

'You're a long way from Nottingham and all that now,' Michael said. Not as far as you might think, I told him. I thought distances were small to all of us, and time had less meaning still. I'm right, they say. Life has no meaning after all, so long live life! That way we'll live forever, I say. It goes on like this ever upward path, my bright bird chips out from two loops below. I love you for that, I say, blowing a kiss that she doesn't see. My feet are free and my eyes are hot.

Down here in the olive grove I'm a great one for my stories, because what else is there except the gift of the gab, the talk, talk, talk, to stop the black sea rushing in? But all I've got left is enough LSD for half a trip, and hash for half a blow. My foot-fare home I've got, and as for June I think she'll make out, staying or leaving, unless I throw her off the Acropolis the day after tomorrow on our way through.

All the cash is spent, until I can peddle another selection of Turkish Delight, or Indian Rope that you can vanish up easily enough, or Persian chopped rug you can actually fly on. So in the meantime I'll bum around or starve, in the hands of pot, pot God, hash heaven, the acid bath of hell and all delight, on the straight but corrugated path that widens when it gets closer and closer and over the deep dip on the edge of the world. But I'll go over it thinking of my dark-haired beauty, thin-faced and maybe at death's door, the one I never got, so lost. And a man like me can't ask for more than that. If he does he suffers too much, and that sort of thing went out with the angels, didn't it?

Guzman, Go Home

Bouncing and engine-noise kept the baby soothed, as if he were snug in the belly of a purring cat. But at the minute of feeding-time he screamed out his eight-week honeyguts in a high-powered lament, which nothing but the nipple could stop. Somewhere had to be found where he could feed in peace and privacy, otherwise his cries in the narrow car threatened the straight arrow on Chris's driving.

He often had fifty miles of road to himself, except when a sudden horn signalled an overtaking fast-driven Volkswagen loaded to the gills. 'Look how marvellously they go,' Jane said. 'I told you you should have bought one. No wonder they overtake you so easily, with that left-hand drive.'

Open scrub fanned out north and west, boulders and olive trees, mountains combing the late May sky of Spain. It was sombre and handsome country, in contrast to the flat-chested fields of England. He backed into an orange grove, red earth newly watered, cool wind coming down from the fortress of Sagunto. While Jane fed the baby, he fed Jane and himself, broke off pieces of ham and cheese for a simultaneous intake to save time.

The car was so loaded that they looked like refugees leaving a city that the liberating army is coming back to. Apart from a small space for the baby the inside was jammed with cases, typewriter, baskets, flasks, coats, umbrellas, and plastic bowls. On the luggage-rack lay a trunk and two cases with, topping all, a folded pram-frame, and collapsible bath.

It was a new car, but dust, luggage, and erratic driving gave it a veteran appearance. They had crossed Paris in a hail and thunderstorm, got lost in the traffic maze of Barcelona, and skirted Valencia by a ring road so rotten that it seemed as if an earthquake had hit it half an hour before. Both wanted the dead useless tree of London lifted off their nerves, so they locked up the flat, loaded the car, and sailed to Boulogne, where the compass of their heart's desire shook its needle towards Morocco.

They wanted to get away from the political atmosphere that saturated English artistic life. Chris, being a painter, had decided that politics ought not to concern him. He would 'keep his hands clean' and get on with his work. 'I like to remember what happened in 1848 to Wagner,' he said, 'who fell in with the revolution up to his neck, helping the workers to storm the arsenal in Dresden, and organizing stores for the defence. Then when the revolution collapsed he hightailed it to Italy to be "entirely an artist" again.' He laughed loud, until a particularly deep pothole cut it short in his belly.

Flying along the straight empty road before Valencia they realized the meaning of freedom from claustrophobic and dirty London, from television and Sunday newspapers, and their middle-aged mediocre friends who talked more glibly nowadays of good restaurants than they had formerly about socialism. The gallery owner advised Chris to go to Majorca, if he must get away, but Chris wanted to be near the mosques and museums of Fez, smoke *kif* at the tribal gatherings of Taroudant and Tafilalt, witness the rose-hip snake-green sunsets of Rabat and Mogador. The art dealer couldn't see why he wanted to travel at all. Wasn't England good enough for other painters and writers? 'They like it here, so why don't you? Travel broadens the mind, but it shouldn't go to the head. It's a thing of the past – old-fashioned. You're socially conscious, so you can't be away from the centre of things for long. What about the marches and sit-downs, petitions, and talks?'

For ten hours he'd driven along the hairpin coast and across the plains of Murcia and Lorca, wanting to beat the previous day's run. They hadn't stopped for the usual rich skins of sausage-protein and cheese, but ate biscuits and bitter chocolate as they went along. He hardly spoke, as if needing all his concentration to wring so many extra miles an hour from the empty and now tolerable road.

His impulse was to get out of Spain, to put that wide arid land behind them. He found it dull, its people too beaten down to be interesting or worth knowing. The country seemed a thousand years older than it had on his last visit. Then, he'd expected insurrection at any time, but now the thought of it was a big horse-laugh. The country smelt even more hopeless than England – which was saying a lot. He wanted to reach Morocco which, no matter how feudal and corrupt, was a new country that might be on the up and up.

So when the engine roared too much for good health at Benidorm, he chose to keep going in order to reach Almeria by nightfall. That extra roar seemed caused by a surcharge of rich fuel at leaving the choke out too long, that would right itself after twenty miles. But it didn't, and on hairpin bends he had difficulty controlling the car. He was careful not to mention this in case his wife persuaded him to get it repaired – which would delay them God knew how many days.

When the plains of Murcia laid a straight road in front of them, it wasn't much after midday. What did hunger matter with progress so good? The roaring of the engine sometimes created a dangerous speed, but maybe it would get them to Tangier. Nothing could be really wrong with a three-month old car – so he drove it into the remotest part of Spain, sublime indifference and sublime confidence blinding him.

He shot through Villa Oveja at five o'clock. The town stood on a hill, so gear had to be changed, causing such a bellowing of the engine that people stared as if expecting the luggage-racked car to go up any second like the Bomb, that Chris had fought so hard to get banned. The speed increased so much that he daren't take his foot from the brake even when going uphill.

The houses looked miserable and dull, a few doorways opening into cobblestoned *entradas*. By one an old woman sat cutting up vegetables; a group of children were playing by another; and a woman with folded arms looked as if waiting for some fast car full of purpose and direction to take her away. Pools of muddy water lay around, though no rain had fallen for weeks. A petrol pump stood like a one-armed veteran of the Civil War outside an open motor workshop – several men busy within at the bonnet of a Leyland lorry. 'These Spanish towns give me the creeps,' he said, hooting a child out of the way.

He waved a farewell at the last house. Between there and Almeria the earth, under its reafforestation skin of cactus and weed, was yellow with sand, desert to be traversed at high speed with eyes half-closed. The road looped the hills, to the left sheer wall and to the right precipices that fell into approaching dusk. Earth and rocks generated a silence that reminded him of mountains anywhere. He almost expected to see snow around the next bend.

In spite of the faulty engine he felt snug and safe in his sturdy car, all set to reach the coast in a couple of hours. The road ahead looked like a black lace fallen from Satan's boot in heaven. No healthy tune was played by the sandy wind, and the unguarded drop on the right was enough to scare any driver, yet kilometres were a shorter measure than

307

miles, would soon roll him into the comfort of a big meal and a night's hotel.

On a steep deserted curve the car failed to change gear. Chris thought it a temporary flash of overheated temper from the clutch mechanism, but, trying again – before the loaded car rolled off the precipice – drew a screech of igniting steel from within the gearbox.

He was stopped from trying the gears once more by a warning yell from Jane, pulled the handbrake firmly up. The car still rolled, its two back wheels at the cliff edge, so he pressed with all his force on the footbrake as well, and held it there, sweat piling out on to the skin of his face. They sat, the engine switched off.

Wind was the only noise, a weird hooting brazen hill-wind from which the sun had already extricated itself. 'All we can do,' he said, 'is hope somebody will pass, so that we can get help.'

'Don't you know *anything* about this bloody car? We can't sit here all night.' Her face was wound up like a spring, life only in her righteous words. It was as if all day the toil of the road had been preparing them for just this.

'Only that it shouldn't have gone wrong, being two months old.'

'Well,' she said, 'British is best. You know I told you to buy a Volkswagen. What do you *think* is wrong with it?'

'I don't know. I absolutely don't bloody well know.'

'I believe you. My God! You've got the stupidity to bring me and a baby right across Europe in a car without knowing the first thing about it. I think you're mad to risk all our lives like this. You haven't even got a proper driving licence.' The wind, too, moaned its just rebuke. But the honeyed sound of another motor on the mountain road filtered into the horsepower of their bickering. Its healthy and forceful noise drew closer, a machine that knew where it was going, its four-stroke cycle fearlessly cutting through the silence. While he searched for a telling response to her tirade, Jane put her arm out, waving the car to stop.

It was a Volkswagen (of course, he thought, it bloody well had to be), a field-grey low-axled turtle with windows, so fresh-washed and polished that it might just have rolled off the conveyor line. Its driver leaned out while the engine still turned: '*Que ha pasado?*'

Chris told him: the car had stopped, and it wasn't possible to change gear, or get it going at all. The Volkswagen had a Spanish number plate, and the driver's Spanish, though grammatical, was undermined

308

by another accent. He got out, motioned Chris to do the same. He was a tall, well-built man dressed in khaki slacks and a light-blue open-necked jersey-shirt a size too small: his chest tended to bulge through it and gave the impression of more muscle than he really had. His bare arms were tanned, and on one was a small white mark where a wristwatch had been. There was a more subtle tan to his face, as if it had done a slow change from lobster red to a parchment colour, oil-soaked and wind-worn after a lot of travel.

To Chris he seemed like a rescuing angel, yet there was a cast of sadness, of disappointment underlying his face that, with a man of his middle-age, was no passing expression. It was a mark that life had grown on him over the years, and for good reason, since there was also something of great strength in his features. As if to deny all this – yet in a weird way confirming it more – he had a broad forehead, and the eyes and mouth of an alert benign cat, and like so many short-sighted Germans who wore rimless spectacles he had that dazed and distant look that managed to combine stupidity and ruthlessness.

He sat in the driver's seat, released the brake, and signalled Chris to push. *'Harémos la vuelta.'*

Jane stayed inside, rigid from the danger they had been in, weary in every vein after days travelling with a baby that was feeding from herself. She turned now and again to tuck the sheet under the baby. The man beside her deftly manoeuvred the car to the safe side of the road, and faced it towards the bend leading back to Villa Oveja.

He started the engine. The turnover was healthy, and the wheels moved. Chris saw the car sliding away, wife, luggage, and baby fifty yards down the road. He was too tired to be afraid they would vanish for ever and leave him utterly alone in the middle of these darkening peaks. He lit a cigarette, in a vagrant slap-happy wind that, he had time to think, would never have allowed him to do so in a more normal situation.

The car stopped, then started again, and the man tried to change gear, which brought a further roaring screech from the steel discs within. He stopped the car, leaned from the window and looked with bland objective sadness at Chris. Hand on the wheel, he spoke English for the first time, but in an unmistakable German accent. He grinned and said, a high-pitched rhythmical rise and fall, a telegraphic render-ing of disaster that was to haunt Chris a long time:

'England, your car has snapped!'

'Lucky for you, England, I am the owner of the garage in Villa Oveja. A towing-rope in my car will drag you there in five minutes.

'My name is Guzman – allowing me to introduce myself. If I hadn't come along and seen your break-up you would perhaps have waited all night, because this is the loneliest Iberian road. I only come this way once a week, so you are double lucky. I go to the next town to see my other garage branch, confirm that the Spaniard I have set to run it doesn't trick me too much. He is my friend, as far as I can have a friend in this country where, due to unsought-for happenings, I have spent nearly the same years as my native Germany. But I find my second garage is not doing too wrong. The Spaniards are good mechanics, a very adjustable people. Even without spare parts they have the genius to get an engine living – though under such a system it can't last long before being carried back again. Still, they are clever. I taught my mechanics all I know: I myself was once able to pick tank engines into morsels, under even more trying conditions than here. I trained mechanics well, and one answered by taking his knowledge to Madrid, where I don't doubt he got an excellent job – the crooked, ungrateful. He was the most brainful, so what could he do except trick me? I would have done the same in his place. The others, they are fools for not escaping with my knowledge, and so they will never get on to the summit. Likewise they aren't much use for me. But we will fix your car good once we get right back to the town, have no fear of it.

'You say it is only three months old? Ah, England, no German car would be such a bad boy after three months. This Volkswagen I have had two years, and not a nut and bolt has slipped out of place. I never boast about myself, but the Volkswagen is a good car, that any rational human being can trust. It is made with intelligence. It is fast and hard, has a marvellous honest engine, that sounds to last a thousand years pulling through these mountains. Even on scorched days I like to drive with all my windows shut-closed, listening to the engine nuzzling swift along like a happy cat-bitch. I sweat like rivers, but the sound is beautiful. A good car, and anything goes wrong, so you take the lid off, and all its insides are there for the eye to see and the hand-spanner to work at. Whereas your English cars are difficult to treat with. A nut and bolt loose, a pipe snapped, and if you don't burn the fingers you surely sprain the wrist trying to get at the injured fix. It's as if your designers hide them on purpose. Why? It isn't rational why, in a people's car that is so common. A car should be natural to expose and easy to understand. On the other hand you can't say that because a car is new nothing should happen to it. Even an English car. That is unrealistic. You should say: This car is new, therefore I must not let anything happen to it. A car is a rational human being like yourself.

'Thank you. I've always had a wanton for English cigarettes, as I have for the language. The tobacco is more subtle than the brutal odours of the Spanish. Language is our best lanes of communication, England, and whenever I meet travellers like yourself I take advantage from it.

'You don't like the shape of the Volkswagen? Ah, England! That is the prime mistake in choosing a car. You English are so aesthetic, so biased. When I was walking through north Spain just after the war – before the ink was dry on the armistice signatures, ha, ha! – I was very poor and had no financial money – and in spite of the beautiful landscapes and marvellous towns with walls and churches, I sold my golden spectacles to a bruto farmer so that I can buy sufficing bread and sausage to feed me to Madrid. I didn't see the pleasant things so clearly, and being minus them the print in my Baedeker handbook blurred my eyes, but here I am today. So what does the shape of a car mean? That you like it? That you don't wear spectacles yet, so you'll never have to sell them, you say? Oh, I am laughing. Oh, oh, oh! But England, excuse me wagging the big finger at you, but one day you may not be so fortunate.

'Ah! So! Marvellous, as you say: clever Guzman has flipped into second gear, and maybe I do not need my towing rope to get you back to town. I don't think you were so glad in all your life to meet a German, were you, England? Stray Germans like me are not so current in Spain nowadays.'

Shadows took the place of wind. A calm dusk slunk like an idling panther from the hips and peaks of the mountains. A few yellow lamps shone from the outlying white houses of Villa Oveja. Both cars descended the looping road, then crept up to the lights like prodigal moths.

As he stopped outside Guzman's garage, Chris remembered his ironic goodbye of an hour ago. A small crowd gathered, who'd perhaps witnessed other motorists give that final contemptuous hand-wave, only to draggle back in this forlorn manner. God's judgement, I suppose they think, the religious bastards. Guzman finished his inspection, sunlight seeming to shine on his glasses even in semi-darkness – which also hid what might be a smile: 'England, I will take you to a hotel where you can stay all night – with your wife and child.'

'All night!' Chris had expected this, so his exclamation wasn't so sharp.

'Maybe two whole nights, England.'

Jane's words were clipped with hysteria: 'I won't spend two nights in this awful dump.' The crowd recognized the livelier inflections of a quarrel, grew livelier themselves. Guzman's smile was less hidden: 'Rationally speaking, it must be difficult travelling with a family-wife. However, you will find the Hotel Universal modest but comfortable, I'm sure.'

'Listen,' Chris said, 'can't you fix this clutch tonight?' He turned to Jane: 'We could still be in Almeria by twelve.'

'Forget it,' she said. 'This is what . . .'

'. . . comes of leaving England with a car you know nothing about? Oh for God's sake!'

Guzman's heavy accent sometimes rose to an almost feminine pitch, and now came remorselessly in: 'England, if I might suggest . . .'

The hotel room smelled of carbolic and Flit; it was scrupulously clean. Every piece of luggage was unloaded and stacked on the spacious landing of the second floor – a ramshackle heap surrounded by thriving able-bodied aspidistras. The room dosed so heavily with Flit gave Jane a headache. Rooms with bath were non-existent, but a handbasin was available, and became sufficient during their three days there.

Off the squalor of the main road were narrow, cobblestoned streets. White-faced houses with over-hanging balconies were neat and well cared for. The streets channelled you into a spacious square, where the obligatory church, the necessary town hall, and the useful *telegrafos*, emphasized the importance of the locality. While Guzman's tame mechanics worked on the car Chris and Jane sat in the cool dining room and listened to Guzman himself. On either side of the door leading to the kitchen were two bird cages, as large as prisons, with an austere primitive beauty about the handiwork of them. In each was a hook-beaked tropical bird, and while he talked Guzman now and again rolled up a ball of bread that was left over from dinner and threw it with

312

such swift accuracy at the cage that it was caught by the scissor-beak that seemed eternally poked without.

'I come here always for an hour after lunch or dinner,' he said, lighting a small cigar, 'to partake coffee and perhaps meet interesting people, by which I signify any foreigner who happens to be moving through. As you imagine, not many stay in our little God-forgotten town – as your charming and rational wife surmised on your precipitant arrival here. My English is coming back the more I talk to you, which makes me happy. I read much, to maintain my vocabulary, but speech is rare. I haven't spoken it with anyone for fourteen months. You express motions of disbelief? It's true. Few motorists happen to break up at this particular spot in Spain. Many English who come prefer the coasts. Not that the mosquitoes are any lesser there than here. Still, I killed that one: a last midnight black-out for the little blighter. Ah, there's another. There, on your hand. Get it, England. Bravo. You are also quick. They are not usually so bad, because we Flit them to death.

'I suppose the English like Spain in this modern epoch because of its politics, which are on the right side – a little primitive, but safe and solid. Excuse me, I did not know you were speeding through to Africa, and did not care for political Spain. Not many visit the artistic qualities of Iberia, which I have always preferred. You are fed up with politics, you say, and want to leave them all behind? I don't blame you. You are wisdom himself, because politics can make peril for a man's life, especially if he is an artist. It is good to do nothing but paint, and good that you should not linger among this country. Why does an artist sit at politics? He is not used to it, tries his hand, and then all is explosioned in him. Shelley? Yes, of course, but that was a long time ago, my dear England. Excuse me again, yes, I will have a *coñac*. When I was in London, in 1932, somebody taught me a smart toast: health, wealth, and stealth! *Gesundheit!*

'Forgive my discretion, England, but I see from your luggage that you are an artist, and I must talk of it. I have a great opinion of artists, and can see why it is that your car broke down. Artists know little of mechanical things, and those that do can't ever be great artists. I myself began as a middling artist. It is a long story, which starts when I was eighteen, and I shall tell you soon.

'Your car is in good hands. Don't worry. And you, madam, I forbid you. We can relax after such a dinner. My mechanics have taken out the engine, and are already shaping off the spare necessary on the lathe.

There are no spare parts for your particular name of car in this section of Spain, therefore we have to use our intelligent handicraft – to make them from nothing, from scrape, as you say. That doesn't daunt me, England, because in Russia I had to make spare parts for captured tanks. Ah! I learned a lot in Russia. But I wish I hadn't ever been there. My fighting was tragical, my bullets shooting so that I bleed to death every night for my perpetrations. But bygones are bypassed, and are a long time ago. At least I learned the language. *Chto dyelaets?*

'Well, it is a pity you don't have a Volkswagen, which I have all the spare pieces for. Yet if you'd had a Volkswagen we wouldn't have been talking here. You would have been in Marrakech. Like my own countrymen: they overtake every traveller on the road in their fast Volkswagens, as if they departed Hamburg that morning and have to get the ferry ship for Tangier this evening, so as to be in Marrakech tomorrow. Then after a swift weekend in the Atlas Mountains they speed back to the office work for another economic miracle, little perceiving that I am one of those that made that miracle possible. What do I mean? How?

'Ah, ah, ah! You are sympathetic. When I laugh loud, so, you don't get up and walk away. You don't stare at me or flinch. Often the English do that, especially those who come to Spain. Red-faced and lonely, they stare and stare, then walk off. But you understand my laugh, England. You smile even. Maybe it is because you are an artist. You say it is because I am an artist? Oh, you are so kind, so kind. I have been an artist and a soldier both, also a mechanic. Unhappily I have done too many things, fallen between cleft stools.

'But, believe it or not, I earned a living for longer years by my drawing than I have done as a garage man. The first money I earned in my life was during my student days in Königsberg – by drawing my uncle who was a ship-captain. My father wanted me to be a lawyer but I desired to be an artist. It was difficult to shake words with my father at that time, because he had just made a return from the war and he was very dispirited about Germany and himself. Therefore he wanted me to obey him as if I had lost the war for him, and he wouldn't let me choose. I had to give up all drawing and become a lawyer, nothing less. I said no. He said yes. So I departed home. I walked twenty miles to the railway station with all the money I'd saved for years, and when I got there, the next day, it transpires that the young fortune I thought I had wouldn't even take me on a mile of my long journey. All my banknotes were useless, yet I asked myself how could that be, because houses and factories still stood up, and there were fields and gardens all around me. I was flabbergasted. But I set off for Berlin with no money, and it took me a month to get there, drawing people's faces for slices of bread and sausage. I began to see what my father meant, but by now it was too late. I had taken the jump, and went hungry for it, like all rebellious youths.

'In my native home-house I had been sheltered from the gales of economy, because I saw now how the country was. Destituted. In Frankfurt a man landed at my foot because he had dropped from a lot of floors up. England, it was terrible: the man had worked for forty years to save his money, and he had none remaining. Someone else ran down the street screaming: "I'm ruined! Ruined utterly!" But all those other shop-keepers who would be ruined tomorrow turned back to their coffee and brandy. No one was solid, England. No solidarity anywhere. Can your mind imagine it? In such a confusion I decided more than ever that the only term one could be was an artist. Coming from Königsberg to Berlin had shown me a thrill for travel. But Berlin was dirty and dangerous. It was full of people singing about socialism – not national socialism, you understand, but communist socialism. So I soon left and went to Vienna – walking. You must comprehend that all this takes months, but I am young, and I like it. I do not eat well, but I did eat, and I have many adventures, with women especially. I think that it was the best time of my life. You want to go, madam? Ah, goodnight. I kiss your hand, even if you do not like my prattle. Goodnight, madam, goodnight. A charming wife, England.

'I didn't like Vienna, because its past glories are too past, and it was full of unemployed. One of the few sorts of people I can't like are the people without work. They make my stomach ill. I am not rational when I see them, so I try not to see them as soon as I can. I went to Budapest, walking along the banks of the Danube with nothing except a knapsack and a stick, free, healthy, and young. I was not the old-fashioned artist who sits gloomily starving in his studio-garret, or talks all day in cafés, but I wanted to get out among the world of people. But in every city there was much conflict, where maybe people were finishing off what they had started in the trenches. I watched the steamers travelling by, always catching me up, then leaving me a long way back, until all I could listen was their little toots of progress from the next switch of the river. The money crashed, but the steamers went on. What else could Germany do? It was a good time though, England, because I never thought of the future, or wondered where I would be in the years to reach. I certainly didn't see that I should throw so much of my good years in this little Spanish town – in a country even more destituted than the one in Germany after I set off so easily from my birth-home. Excuse me, if I talk so much. It is the brandy, and it is also making me affectionate and sentimental. People are least intelligent when most affectionate, so forgive me if I do not always keep up the high standard of talk that two artists should kindle among them.

'No, I insist that it is my turn this time. Your wife has gone, no, to look after the baby? In fact I shall order a bottle of brandy. This Spanish liquid is hot, but not too intoxicating. Ah! I shall now pour. It's not that I have the courage to talk to you only when I am up to my neck in bottle-drink, as that I have the courage to talk to you while you are drunk. You can drink me under the table, England? Ah! We shall see, dear comrade. Say when. I have travelled a long way, to many places: Capri, Turkey, Stalingrad, Majorca, Lisbon, but I never foresaw that I should end up in the awkward state I am now in. It is unjust, my dear England, unjust. My heart becomes like a flitterbat when I think that the end is so close.

'Why? Ah! Where was I? Yes, in Budapest there was even more killing, so I went to Klausenburg (I don't know which country that town is in any more) and passed many of these beautiful clean Saxon towns. The peasants wore their ancient pictorial costume, and on the lonely dusty road were full of friendships and dignity. We spoke to each other, and then went on. I walked through the mountains and woods of Transylvania, over the high Carpathians. The horizons changed every day; blue, purple, white, shining like the sun; and on days when there were no horizons because of rain or mist I stayed in some cowshed, or the salon of a farmhouse if I had pleased the family with my sketching likenesses. I went on, walking, walking (I walked every mile, England, a German pilgrim), across the great plain, through Bucharest and over the Danube again, and into Bulgaria. I had left Germany far behind, and my soul was liberal. Politics didn't interest me, and I was amazed, in freedom at my father being sad at the war.

'How the brandy goes! But I don't get drunk. If only I could get drunk. But the more brandy I drink the colder I get, cool and icy on the heart. Even good brandy is the same. Health, wealth, and stealth! I got to Constantinople, and stayed for six months. Strangely, in the poorest city of all, I made a good living. In an oriental city unemployment didn't bother me: it seemed natural. I went around the terraces of hotels along the Bosphorus making portraits of the clientèles, and of all the money I made I gave the proprietors ten per cent. If they were modern I drew them or their wives also against the background of the Straits, and sometimes I would take a commission to portray a palace or historic house.

'One day I met a man who questioned if I would draw a building for him a few kilometres along the coast. He would give me five English pounds now, and five more when we came back to the hotel. Of course I accepted, and we drove in his car. He was a middle-aged Englishman, tall and formal, but he'd offered me a good price for the hour's drawing necessary. By now I had developed the quickness of draughtsmanship, and sat on the headland easily sketching the building on the next cape. While I worked your Englishman, England, walked up and down smoking swiftly on a cigar, and looked nervous about something. I had ended, and was packing my sketches in, when two Turkish soldiers stood from behind a rock and came to us with rifles sticking out. "Walk to the car," the Englishman said to me, hissing, "as if you haven't done anything."

'"But," I said, "we've made nothing wrong, truly."

'"I should say not, my boy," he told me. "That was a Turkish fort you just sketched."

'We run, but two more soldiers stand in front of us, and the Englishman joked with them all four, patted them on the savage head, but he had to give out twenty pounds before they let us go, and then he cursed all the way back.

'It might have been worse, I realize at the hotel, and the Englishman is pleased, but said we'll have to move on for our next venture, and he asked me if I'd ever thought of hiking to the frontier of Turkey and Russia. "Beautiful, wild country," he told me. "You'll never forget it. *You* go there on your own, and make a few sketches for me, and it'll prove lucrative – while I sit back over my sherbet here. Ha, ha, ha!"

'So I questioned him: "Do you want me to sketch Turkish forts, or Soviet ones?"

'"Well," he said, "both."

'That, England, was my first piece of stealthy work, but it never made me wealthy, and I already was healthy. Ah, ah, ah, ho, ho! You are strong, England. I cannot make you flinch when I hit you on the back like a friend. So! Before then I had been too naïve to feel dishonest. Once on the Turkish border I was captured, with my sketches, and nearly hanged, but my Englishman pays money, and I go free. Charming days. I wasn't even interested in politics.

'I hear a baby crying. What a sweet sound it is! England, I think your wife calls for you.'

III

'It is fine night tonight, England, a beautiful star-dark around this town. I have travelled most of my life. Even without trouble I would have travelled, never possessing one jot of wealth, only needing food at the sunset and hot water for breakfast. During the war my voyaging was also simple.

'In my youth, after I was exported from Turkey by the soldiers (They took all my money before letting me go. If only we had conquered them during the war, then I would have met them again and made them repay it with every drop of their blood!) I travelled in innumerable countries of the Balkans and Central East, until I was so confused by the multiple currencies that I began to lose count of the exchange. I would recite my travellers' cataclysm as I crossed country limits: "Ten Slibs equals one Flap; a hundred Clackies makes one Golden Crud; four Stuks comes out at one Drek" – but usually I went to the next nation with not Slib Flap Clackie or Golden Crud to my name, nothing except what I wear and a pair of worn sandals. I joke about the currencies, because there is no fact I cannot remember. Some borders I have crossed a dozen times, but even so far back I can memory the dates of them, and stand aside to watch myself at that particular time walking along, carefreed, towards the custom post.

'One of my adventures is that I get married, and my wife is a strong and healthy girl from Hamburg who also likes the walking life. Once we trampled from Alexandria, stepping all along the coast of Africa to Tangier, but it was hard because the Mussulmans do not like to have their faces drawn. However, there were many white people we met, and I also sketch a lot of buildings and interesting features – which were later found to be of much use to certain circles in Berlin. You understand, eh?

318

'We went back to Germany, and walked in that country also. We joined groups of young people on excursions to the Alps, and had many jolly times on the *hohewege* of the Schwarzwald. My wife had two children, both boys, but life was still carefreed. There were more young people like ourselves to enjoy it with. My art was attaining something, and I did hundreds of drawings, all of which made me very proud, though some were better than others, naturally. Most were burned to cinders by your aeroplanes, I am sad to say. I also lost many of my old walking friends in that war, good men . . . but that is all in the past, and to be soonest forgotten. Nowadays I have only a few comrades, in Ibiza. Life can be very sad, England.

'In that time before the war my drawings were highly prized in Germany. They hung in many galleries, because they showed the spirit of the age – of young people striving in all their purity to build the great state together, the magnificent corporation of one country. We were patriotic, England, and radical as well. Ah! It is good when all the people go forward together. I know many artists who thought that anarchism was not enough to cure the griefs of the globe as they swung into black shirts. Children do not like the dark when they go to bed, and what can blame them? Someone has to build a fire and put on lights. But you shouldn't think I liked the bad things though, about inferior races and so on. Because if you consider, how could I be living in Spain if I did? It was a proud and noble time when loneliness was forgotten. It contained sensations I often spend my nights thinking about, because I felt that after all the travels of my young days I was getting at last some look-on at my work, as well as finding the contentment of knowing a leader who pointed to me the fact that I was different from those people I had been through on my travels. He drew me together. Ah! England, at that you get more angry than if I had banged you on the shoulder like a jolly German! You think I am so rotten that when I cut myself, maggots run out. But don't, please don't, because I can't stand that from any man. I don't believe anything now, so let me tell you. Nothing, nothing . . . nothing. Everyone was joining something in those days, and I couldn't stop myself, even though I was an artist. And because I was an artist I went the whole way, to the extremes, right beyond the nether boundaries. I was carried along like this *coñac* cork, floating down a big river. I couldn't swim out of it, and in any case the river was so strong that I liked it, I liked being in it, a strong river, because I was as light as a cork, and it would never carry me under. He . . . he made us as light as a cork, England. But politics are gone from my life's vision. I make no distinction any more between races or systems. One of my favourite own jokes is that of Stalin, Lenin and Trotsky playing your money game Monopoly together in the smallest back room of the Kremlin in 1922. Ha, ha, ha! You also think it is funny, England, no?

'No, you don't think it is funny, I can see that. I am sorry you don't. Your face is stern and you are gazing far away. But listen to me though, you are lucky. So far you don't know what it is to belong to a nation that has taken the extreme lanes, but you will, you will. So I can see it coming because I read your newspapers. Up till now your country has been lucky, ours has been unlucky. We have no luck, none at all. We are rational, intelligent, strong, but unlucky. You cut off the head of your King Karl; we didn't of our Karl. Ah, now you smile at my wit. You laugh. You have the laugh of the superior, England, the mild smile of those who do not know, but once on a time, if any foreigner laughed at me like that I could kill them. And I did! I did!

'Stop me if I shout. Forgive me. No, don't go, England. Your baby is not crying. Your wife does not call. Listen to me more. I don't believe anything except that I am able to repair your car and do it good. And that is something. How many men can set you on the road again? It is a long way from my exhibitions of drawings, one of which, at Magdeburg, was opened and appreciated by You-know-who, a person who also knew about art. Yes, actually him. He shook my own hand, this hand! I was reconciled to my father by then: I who hated my father more than any hatred that was ever possible since the beginnings of the civilized world was brought back to respect him, to view his point with proper sympathy. To be able to again give respect to one's father in middle-age! Can you imagine it ever, England? And who did it? He is truly a great man who can make the different generations understand each other, a dictator maybe, but great, still a genius. I tell you that my father was the proudest man in all Germany because he who had done it had shaken this – this hand!

'Well, I will not ennui you any more about my adventures in those days. Let us skip a few years and talk about romantic Spain. Not that it was romantic. It can be a very dirty place, and annoying, unlike the cleaner countries, such as ours, my dear England. Just after crossing

320

the mountains on foot in 1945, I stayed in a shepherd's hut for two weeks of hiding. Someone paid the shepherd a terrible high rent for this stenching sty, and all the while I was attacked by ants, so that I go nearly mad. I looked mad – with my long beard and poor clothes, dreamed I was the King of Steiermark with my loptilted crown. Ants came in the door, and I start to kill them with hammer and sceptre – then I spare some lives in the hope that they would scuttle back and tell their friends that they had better not come near that hut because a crazy bone-German is conducting a proficient massacre. But it made no difference, and they kept coming on into the kill-feast. I worked for days to stop them, but they came continuously I suppose to see why it was that those before them were not coming back. There were thousands, and my romantic nature won because I got tired first. Strength and intelligence finally let me down. Ants are inhuman. Nowadays, if I see ants in my house or garage I use a Flit gun – bacteriological warfare, if you like, and that is quicker. I can let science take over and so don't need to beg stupid questions. It stops them. I think of all those poor ants who get killed, and maybe the ants themselves have no option but to start this war on me. If only they were all individuals, England, like you – or me – then maybe only one or two would have been killed before the others turned and ran. But no, they have their statues to the war, the tomb of the Unknown Ant, who dies so that every ant could have his pebble of sugar, but who died in vain, of course. I have a sense of humour? Yes, I have. But it didn't protect me from doing great wrong.

'How did I get to Spain? My life is full of long stories, but this time I came to Spain from necessity, from dire necessity. It was a matter of life and death. To get here I set out from Russia on a journeying much longer than the one I told you about already in my youth. Name a country, and I have been in it. Say a town and I can call the main street, because I have slept on it. I can tell you about the colour of the policeman's uniform, and where you can get the cheapest food; which is the best corner to stand and ask for money. I have done many things since the end of the war that I would not naturally do, that I should be ashamed of, except that it is man's duty to survive. And man's duty to let him? you said. Of course, quite right, quite so. Humanitarian people are right next door to my heart, my dear friend. But during the war I thought men couldn't survive, and when the war started to end I taught myself that they could. How did I come to obtain my garage business? you ask. It takes much money to buy a garage, and I tell you something now that I wouldn't tell a walking soul, not even my wife, so that instead of forgiving me, you will try to understand.

'I got to Algeria. To say how would damage a few people, so I mustn't. Part of my time I was a teacher of English in Setif, and passed myself as an Englishman. I imitated in every manner that man who was a spy back on the Turkish Bosphorus until nobody in this new place spied the difference. I taught English to Moslems as well, but earned a bad living at it. To augment my inmoney I made intricate maps of farmers' land in the area. I am a good reconnaissance man, and if a farmer had only a very poor and tiny square of land the map I drew made it look like a kingdom, and he was glad to have it square-framed, seeing something to fight for as he gazed at it hanging on the wall of his tinroofed domicile, at night when the mosquitoes bit him mad, and he was double mad worrying about crops, money, and drought – not to mention rebellion. Then I began selling plots of land in the *bled* that weren't accurately possessed by me – to Frenchmen who came straight out of the army from the mix-in of Indo-China – by telling people it was rich with oil. Nowadays I hear that it really is, but no matter. I sold the land only cheap, but I soon had enough real finance to buy many passports and escape to Majorca. I got fine work as a travel-agent clerk in Palma, and worked good for a year, trying to save my money like an honest man. Spain was a stone country to make a living in then – things are much easier these days since the peseta is devalued. I couldn't save, because all the time I had before me the remembering of the man in Frankfurt who dropped at my feet completely dead because his life savings wouldn't buy a postal stamp. But then an Italian asks me to look after his yacht one winter, which for him was a huge mistake, because when I had sold it to a rich Englishman I took an aeroplane to Paris.

'There I thought I had done such a deal of travelling in my scattered life that I should turn such knowing into my own business. To commence, I announced in a good newspaper that ten people were desired for a trip around the world, that it would be a co-operative venture, and that only little money would be needed, comparatively. When I saw the ten people I told that two thousand dollars each would be enough, but they had to be fed-up sufficiently with modern world-living to qualify for my expedition. I explained that out of our collective money we would comprise a lorry, and a moving-camera to take documentary films of strange places, that we would sell. Everybody said it was a shining brainwave, and I soon got the lorry and camera cheap. For two weeks we had map meetings while I planned each specific of the trip. I spent as much money on maps as on the lorry, almost, and pinned them to the wall at these gatherings. I gave them labour of cartography and collecting stores. They were all good people, so trusted me, even when I said that a supplementary cost would be laid because of the high price of film. No one would be leader of the expedition, I stipulated: it would be run by committee, with myself as the chairman. But somehow, and against my will, I achieved control. Because I was more interested in getting reactions from other people than from myself I became the real leader of them. In this aspect my good heart triumphed, because they needed me to be their overboss.

'Much of the money I put in the bank, but the peril was I began to like the idea of this world-round journey so much that I couldn't make myself disappear with it. I kept on, obsessed at the plan. I wrote to many shops and factories and (even in France) they gave me equipment. I charged it all to my clients – as I called them in my secret self. Unfortunately the newspaper wrote stories about my scheme, and put my photo in the print.

'So our big lorry set out of Paris, and snapped on the road to Marseilles. I repaired it, and from Marseilles our happy gathering steamed to Casablanca on a packet-boat. I had moved battalions of men and tanks (and many prisoners) in every complication over the eye-dust and soul-mud and numb snow of Russia, but this was a happy situation with these twenty people (by this time others had been entered to our committee). It was like being young again. Everyone loved me. I was *popular*, England, by total consent of all those dear, good friends. Tears fall into my eyes when I think of it – real tears that I can't bear the taste of. The further I gave in to my sentimental journeying and went on with my dear international companions, the less was the money that I intended to go off and begin my garage with in Spain. I had never had such a skirmish in my conscience. What could I do? Tell me, England, what could I do? Would you have done any better than such? No, you wouldn't, I know. My God! I am shouting again. Why don't you stop me?

'The lorry snapped awfully, at Colomb-Bechar, just before we intend to cross the real desert. But my talents triumph again, and I repaired it, and say I am going to try it out. They are still in the tents, eating some lunch, and I drive off, round and round in big circles. Suddenly I make a straight line and they never see me again. I don't know what became of them. They were nearly penniless. I took petrol and the cameras, everything expensive, as well as funds. It is too painful for me to speculate, so ask me nothing else, even if I tell you. From Casablanca I come to here, and when I have collected all from my banks I see there is enough to get my garage, and much to spare.

'And now I am in Spain, you think I have as much as a man could want? I have a Spanish wife, two children and an interesting work. I have had several wives, and now a Spanish woman. She is dark, beautiful, and plump (yes, you have seen her) but in bed she doesn't act with me. My children go to the convent school, and kiss crosses, tremble at nuns and priests. These I cannot like at all, but what can I do? It has been a dull life, because there's not much here. Sometimes we go to a bullfight. But I don't like it. It is a good ritual, but not attractive to a rational human being like myself. All winter we see no travellers, and hug the fireplace like damp washing. Now and again I still do some drawings. Yes, that is one of them over there, that I presented to this hotel. You don't like it? You do? Ah, you make me very happy, England. Often I go down the coast road to Algeciras, a short trip in my dependable Volkswagen. It is a very pleasant port, and I make many sketches. I know some Russians who have a hotel and let me stay at cost rate. Gibraltar is a fascinating shape to make on paper, which I see from the terrace. I also go across to your famous English fort-rock to shopping, and maybe purchase one of those intellectual English Sunday newspapers there. One of them lasts me a month at least. I find them very good, exceptionally lively and interesting to a mind like mine.

'Ah, England, let us take a walk and I will tell you why my life is finished. That's better. The air smells fresh and good. Why, we have talked the whole night through. I tell lies to everyone – with no exception. But to myself – and I talk free to you and myself now – I tell the precise ice-cold truth as far as it is possible. Telling lies to everyone else makes it more possible to tell a more accurate truth to myself. Does that make me happy? For most people happiness is letting them follow the habits their fathers developed. But *he* changed all that, that's why we loved him, drilled truths into us so that we didn't need to live by habit. That would be worse than death – because death is at least something positive.

'That green speck in the sky over there is the first dawn, a little light, a glow-worm that the sun sends in front to make sure that all is dark for it. Your wife will never forgive you. But women are not rational human beings. Oh, oh, oh – England, you think they are? I can prove to you that they are not so, quicker than you can prove to me that they are. You say that the sun is a red sun? I can see that it will be. But I have been in Spain many times. In 1934 I came here, walking all through, sketching farmhouses and touristic monuments – later published as an album in Berlin. I surveyed the land. Spain I know exceedingly well. This beautiful land we saved from Bolshevism – though I sometimes wonder why. I am afraid of a communist government here, because if it comes, I am ended. The whole world gets dark for me. Maybe Franco will make a pact with communist Germany, and send me back to it. It has happened before. I feel my bed is not so safe to lie on.

'My life has been tragic, but I am not one of those who self-pities. It will be hot today. I sweat already. I must sell my garage and leave, go to another country. I am forced to abandon my wife and children, which is not a good fate. It gives me suffering in the heart that you cannot imagine. I am slowly taking secret luggage to my other garage, and one day I shall tell her I'm going to inspect things over there, and she will never see me again. I travel lightly, England, but I am nearly sixty years. You will notice that I have not talked about the war, because it is too hurtful to me. My home was in East Prussia: but the Soviets took the family land. They enslaved and murdered my fellow countrymen. England, don't laugh. You say they should keep the Berlin Wall there for ever? Ah, you don't know what you are saying. I can see that my misfortune makes you glad. I was not there, of course, but I know what the Soviets did. My wife was killed in one of their bombardments.

'England, please, do not ask me that question. I do not know who started such wicked bombings of the mass. A war begins, and many things happen. Much water flows under the bridge-road. Let me march on with my story. Please, patience. My two sons are in the communist party. As if that was why I fought, used in my body and soul the most terrible energies for one large Germany. I want to go there and beat them both, beat them without mercy, hit at them until they are dead.

'Once I had a letter from them, and they ask me to come back to my homeland – not fatherland, but homeland. How the letter gets me I don't know, but a person in Toledo sends it. They beg me to come back and work for democratic Germany. Why do you think they ask me this? That they are innocent, and only love their father as sons should? Ah! It's because they know I shall be hanged when I get there. That is why they ask. They are devils, devils.

'I am leaving Villa Oveja, quitting Spain, because someone came to this town a few weeks ago and saw me. I think from my photo in the Paris paper and other photos issued by my enemies, he recognized me. They have fastened me down, hunted me like an animal, and know where I am now. I know they are leaving me for the time being, because perhaps there is a bigger job – someone more important before they concentrate on the small fish. This Jew wasn't like the others. He was tall, young and blond. He was browned by the sun, he was handsome, as if he'd been in Spain as much as I had, and one day he came to the door of my garage and looked in at me. He looked, to make sure. I could not compete his stare, and they could have used my face for the chalk of Dover. How did I know he was a Jew, you ask? Don't mock me, England, because I am no longer against them. I hardly look at his face, but I *knew* because his eyes were like sulphur, a nice young man who could have been a pleasant tourist, but I knew, I knew without knowing why I knew, that he was one of their people. They have their own country now: if only they had their own country before the war, England. His eyes burned my heart away. I could not move. The next day he went off, but at any time they will come for me. I am still young, even while sixty, yet think that perhaps I don't care, that I will let them carry me, or that I will kill myself before they come.

'It is not possible I stay here, because the people have turned. Maybe the Jew told something before he went away, but a man stopped me in one of the alley-streets and said: "Guzman, get out, go home." The man had been one of my friends, so you can imagine how it bit deep at me. And then, to hammer it harder, I have been seeing it written on walls in big letters: "Guzman, go home," – which makes my brains burst, because this *is* my home. No one understands, that I am wanting to be solitary, to have peace, to labour all right. When I make tears like this I feel I am an old man.

'I should not have killed those people. I sat down to eat. They were hungry in the snow, and I could not stop myself. I could not tolerate the way they stood and looked, people who couldn't work because they had no food to take into them. They kept looking, England, they kept looking. I thought: their life is agony. I will end it. If I feed them Christmas food for three months they will never be strong again. I wanted to help them out of their life and suffering, to get them peace, so that they would be no more cold and hungry. I fired my gun. My way went terrible after that, out of control. I was rational. My soul was black. I killed and killed, to stop the spread of the suffering that came on to me. While I killed I was warm, and not aware of the suffering, the rheumatism of my soul. How could I have done it? I wasn't like the others. I was an artist.

'Look, don't go yet. Don't stand and leave me by. The sun is making that mountain drink fire. I shall always see mountains on fire, whenever I go and wherever else my feet tread, red mountains shaking flames out of their hat top. Even before the Jew came a dream was in me one night. I was a young scholar at the high-school, and circles were painted in the concrete groundspaces, for gymnasium games and drill. I stood in one, with a book in my hand to read. Everything changed, and the perfect circle was of white steel. A thin rod it was, a hot circle that glowed metal. I wanted to get out of it but I couldn't, because the heat from it was scorching my ankles. All the force of me was pressing against it, and though I was a highgrown man I couldn't jump out. I had a gun in my hand instead of a book, and I was going to shoot myself, because I knew the idea that if I did I should get out and be able to walk off a freed man. I shot someone passing by, a silent bullet. But then I woke, and nothing had worked for me.

'In military life they say there is a marshal's rank in every soldier's kitbag. In peace-life I think there is a pair of worn sandals in every cupboard, because you don't ever know when the longest life-trudge is going to start – whether you are criminal or not. I dig blame into my heart like donkey-dung into good soil. If I was an aristocrat I could claim that all my uncles had been hung up on meat-hooks because they tried to revolt. If I was from a factory I could say I didn't know any better. Everybody who dies dies in vain, England, so I can't do that. What shall I do? Your questions are pertinent, but I am practical. I am rational. I won't give in, because I am always rational. Maybe it is the best thing of quality obtained from my father. I look at my maps, and have the big hope of a hunted man. Do you have any dollars in currency that I could exchange? You haven't? Can you pay the repair bill on your car in dollars, then? Ah, so. I have another Volkswagen I could sell you, only a year old and going like a spark, guaranteed for years on rough roads. The man I bought it from had taken it to Nyasaland – overearth, the whole return. Pay me in pound-sterling then, in Gibraltar if you like. I can get the ferry there and back in a day, make my purchasing of necessaries for a long trek . . . no, you can't?

'It is going to be a cloudy day, good for driving because it will not be too hot. Your car is now in excellent order, and will run well for long hours. It is a reasonable car, with a stout motor and strong frame. It is not too logical for repairing, and will not have such long life as you thought when you bought it. Next time, if you want some of my best caution, you will purchase a Volkswagen. You won't regret it, and will always remember me for giving you such solid advice.

'I am tired after being up all night. Mind how you drive, on those mountain curves. Don't you see what it speaks in the sky over there? You don't? Your eyes are not good. Or perhaps you are deceiving me to save my feelings. It says: GUZMAN, GO HOME. Where can I go? I own two houses and my garage here. I own property, England, property. All my life I wanted to own property, and shall have to sell it to them in Villa Oveja for next door to nothing. Go home, they say to me, go home.

'Rational and intelligent! Everybody is being rational and intelligent. What beautiful words – but they have to be kept in a case and admired, like those two parrots that the hotel keeper brought back from a trip to South America. You look at them, and their beauty gives you heart. An unfortunate American client once wanted to touch them, put his finger too close to the bars, and then the blood flowed after the razor-beak snapped over it. Their colour gives you soul also, but when you are at last hunted down, and only the corner wall is behind you, then what use are being rational and intelligent? Use them, and slowly rolls the big destruction. Hitler made them kill each other in every man jackboot of us.

'I am light-headed when I don't sleep the dark, but I must go to work, think some more while I am working. My name is not Guzman. That is a name the Spaniards gave me, proud, sly, and envious, because of my clever business ways. It has always surprised me that I could make my commerical career so well, when I started off life only as a poor hiker drawing faces. Now I am a wanderer, when I don't want to be.'

* * *

328

Chris, his face the grey-green colour of a living tree branch that had had the bark stripped from it, turned away and walked quickly through the quiet town to the hotel. His wife was feeding the baby. The day after tomorrow, they would be in Africa. Six months after that, back in London.

The car broke down again in Tangier. 'That crazy Nazi,' he thought, 'can't even mend a bloody car.'

Mimic

I

I learned to mimic at an early age, probably at two or three when I sat in front of the fire and stared at the cat. A mimic has a long memory, fine hands, and a face he can't bear to look at in the mirror, unless he puts on somebody else's with such intensity that he cannot recognize himself there. His soul is his own, but he buries it deeply with many others because under such a mound it is finally safe. Eventually of course it is so far lost and gone that he is unable to get down to it when he wants to, but that is another matter, and finally unimportant when one knows that age and death will settle everything.

In the early days of infancy I did not know I was becoming a mimic. By all accounts I was such a handsome baby that when my mother pushed me through town in a pram men would stop to admire me and give her five shillings to buy me a new rattle. At least that was her story, though my memory is better than any story, for another line was that because she was so pretty they gave money to me as an excuse for getting off with her.

A still further version could be I was so rotten-faced and ugly they gave her money to show sympathy at her being loaded with such a terrible burden. Anyway, that's how she met her second husband, which only proves that mimics usually have pretty and wayward mothers, while they may be fair-to-ugly themselves. You can't be a mimic with a fine-featured face, but for the first few years must stare at the world and take nothing in so that your face stays flat and putty-coloured, with a button-nose, beehive-mouth, and burdock-chin that deflects what sunlight hopes to make your features more heavenly to the world.

While father was at work and my mother in the scullery I'd romp on the rug for a while, then settle down and look at the cat, a black tabby with a white spot between its ears. I'd stare right into its splinter eyes till it opened its great mouth and yawned. Then, facing it on all fours, I'd open my mouth as well, full of small new teeth, stretching the side skin as far as it would go. The way the cat looked at me I knew I was successful, and because of this it seemed as if I felt alive for the first time in my life. I'll never forget this strong impression. When I mimicked, the light went on, as if somebody had sneaked up behind and slyly lifted off the dark glasses I didn't have. Finally the cat walked away, as if embarrassed.

I practised on animals for years, on the assumption, rightly I think, that if I could mimic animals so that they recognized themselves in me when I was doing it in front of them, then it would be quite easy to do it to human beings when I was ready for the changeover.

I remember at the age of nine that a young woman in our yard had a puppy, a small dark fat one that had been ill, that she wanted to get rid of. So she asked me to take it to the PDSA, gave me a shilling to put into their contribution box, and threepence to myself for the errand of taking it. The place was about a mile away, and going there I called in many sweet shops, buying chocolate at every stop. The puppy was wrapped in a towel in my arms, and after stocking up at a shop I would sit on a wall to eat the loot, and take another goz at the puppy who was going to be 'put to sleep' as the woman had said. I knew of course what that meant, and though the puppy squinted at me and licked my hand when I gave it chocolate it still looked as if it might welcome what was in store for it. I stared hard at those brown eyes, at that fat half-blind face that could never have any say in how the world was run, and between one snap of chocolate and the next I'd borrow its expression, take on that look, and show it to the puppy to let him feel he was not alone.

A mimic does what he is paid to do. By the time I got to the PDSA I had only threepence left for the contribution box. A shilling had gone on chocolate for me and the dog, and for the dog it was the last thing it would ever eat.

On the way home a hump-backed bridge crossed a canal. I went down through a gate on to the towpath. On the opposite side was a factory wall, but on my side was a fence and an elderberry bush. The water was bottle green, and reflected both sides in it. My eyes turned from grey to brown, and I barked as the dog had barked when the woman in the white overall had taken him from me.

This isn't a story about childhood. It is about a mimic, and mimics have no childhood. In fact it would almost be fair to say that they don't even have a life of their own. There is a certain price to pay for taking on another face, another voice, even though mimicry need bring no profit. But what mimicry does give is a continuation of one's life when for some reason that life had been forfeited even before birth. Whether one had done it oneself as a spirit from another age, or whether someone in another age had got hold of your spirit before it was born and squeezed the life out of it, who can ever be able to say? One may be born innocent, but in order to make one's mark on life, one has to get rid of that innocence.

One puts one's devilries as a mimic into other people if one is guilty of what blasted one's life before birth; one takes others' devilries upon oneself if one was innocent before birth.

To borrow a face is to show no mercy to it. In order to call it your own, you leave the owner of it with nothing. Not only do you see something of an advantage in using someone else's face, but you seek to rob them of what strength they also get from wearing it. At the same time you mimic them to hide yourself. A mimic therefore can't lose, except of course that he has lost everything before birth, more than anyone else can lose unless he is a mimic too.

The first *person* I mimicked, or tried to, was my mother, and I did this by falling in love with her. This is not so easy as it sounds, especially since she had been responsible for giving me birth, but being the person with the power of life and death over me there surely wasn't any fitter person to fall in love with. But I didn't let her see it, because my way of doing it was to mimic her one day, and I expected that since she had already given me so much she wouldn't mind this at all, would be flattered by it in fact. But all she saw was that I was taking everything.

She'd just had a blinding row with my father, and he'd stormed off to see his mates in the pub. At the heart-rending smash of the door behind him she sat by the fire waiting for the kettle to boil. When it did, she burst into tears. I thought to myself that if I did the same, her misery would be halved, so I put on the same expression (the half-closed eyes and twisted mouth, hands to my face-side with two fingers over my ear) and drew tears out with almost exactly the same noise. I'd meant to let my heart flow with hers, to be with it as a sort of comfort, but what I didn't know was that I'd only irritated her, mocked her – which is what she called mimicking for many years. This barefaced imitation made it worse, though instead of increasing her tears (it could hardly do that) it stopped them altogether. This was what I had hoped for, but only in such a way as to soften her heart, not to harden her. She smacked my face: 'Don't mock me, you little bleeder. You're almost as bad as he is.' I don't need to say who 'he' was, though in spite of our similarity he never became the mimic that I did.

So I mimicked my father, seeing how my attempt at love for mother had failed. It was quite a while before I stopped tormenting my mother by only mimicking my father in front of her, and began mimicking him to his face. When I did, he laughed, and I'd never seen him in such a good mood. Life is full of surprises for a mimic. He'd loosened his belt one Sunday dinner because he was too full of beer and food. He pulled me on to his knee and kissed me, my mother looking wryly over her shoulder now and again as she washed the pots. He was so pleased at my exact imitation of him, of seeing himself so clearly in me, that he gave me a shilling.

This momentary gain went to my head and, before he could fall into a doze by the fire, I thought I would put on the best show he'd seen by mimicking my mother for him. If he could laugh at himself in me, he'd be more touched than ever to see mother in my face.

I drew myself up on the hearthrug as if I were tall and thin, curved my arms outward from my side, tilted my head, and drew in my cheeks, completely altering the shape of my mouth and putting that fire into my eyes that expected to be swamped out any second by a tidal wave.

'You've been a long time at the pub,' I said in her voice, 'don't you know your dinner's burnt? It's a wonder you couldn't smell it right from the bar.'

His eyes grew small, and the smile capsized like a boat in a gale. Before I knew where I was I was flat on my face. Then a boot got me in the ribs and I was curled up by the stairfoot floor.

Somehow, mimicking my mother in front of my father hadn't upset *her* at all, not like when I'd done it for her alone. In fact she was amused now, so when the old man lashed out at me with the old one-two of fist and boot, she cried and railed in my defence, calling him all the cruel gets under the sun.

'You leave my son alone,' she shouted, 'you drunken bully. I'll get the police in next time you kick him like that. He's never done any harm to a living soul, and you've never treated him right, either.'

Father was baffled. He'd not liked me being disrespectful, he said, as if he'd been at church instead of a pub. I hadn't any right to mock her. As for him, he could stand it because it was only a bit of a joke, but he didn't like me doing it to her, the wife and mother of the house.

By this time I'd uncurled myself from the hedgehog position (I could imitate a hedgehog very well at times) and had seated myself at the table. I wasn't crying. A mimic soon learns to stop that sort of thing, otherwise he'd never do any mimicking at all. To get kicked was one of the risks you ran. And because I wasn't in tears, they soon made up their quarrel which, after all, had only started because of me. He put more coal on the fire, and she made him some fresh tea. When that was finished they talked and laughed, and she sat on his knee. Then they went upstairs together for a Sunday sleep, and I was left downstairs alone on the hearthrug wondering where I'd gone wrong. I didn't even have the energy to mimic a strong man booting the cat out of the way because things hadn't gone too well for him at work.

Some people believe that simplicity can only come out of madness, but who wants to go through madness in order to achieve the dubious advantage of becoming simple? Only a mimic can straddle these two states and so avoid being himself. That is to say, he finds a way of not searching for himself in order to avoid discovering that he has no self, and therefore does not exist. To see finally that there is nothing behind all the faces of one's existence is to find real madness. And what simplicity is there in that?

At school, I was the sort of person of whom the other boys asked: 'Is it going to rain today?' even though I looked nothing like a sage or weatherman. But the clouds or empty sky seemed to be on my side, and I was often right when I told them one thing or the other. It wasn't so much that I could guess the weather as that I'd take a chance on saying what I thought was going to happen. This comes easy to a mimic, because every person or object that he decides to imitate has a vein of risk in it.

In my young days it took a long while for me to realize that whenever I decided to mimic someone, and actually went through the process of doing so, I was filled with a deep interest in life and did no harm to anybody. But in between times I was remote and restless in turn, and liable to delve into all kinds of mischief. If I was not inspired for weeks to mimic, and at the same time found no opportunity otherwise to work off my bilious spirit by getting into trouble, then I took ill with some current letdown of the body such as pneumonia or mumps. My father and mother would have liked to have blasted me for the bother I gave them but after I had mimicked them successfully so early on they went out of my life for ever in any important way, and I took so little notice of their rage against me that many people and other members of my family began to look on me as a saint – until my next rampage.

One Christmas at school there was a fancy-dress party before breaking up for the holidays. I went as a moth, with two great wings and white powder all over me. Some came as musketeers and spacemen, but most appeared as nothing at all, simply wearing a badge, or hat. It was an old school, but there was a stage at one end of a big classroom. I received first prize, somebody else got second, and another boy third. The other two were told to get on the stage and act out what they were supposed to be. They did their best, then I went up.

A teacher put a candle on a low table, and I became a moth, weaving around it so that everybody stopped talking and looked. Maybe the teachers told them to be quiet. It was raining in the street, and perhaps being out of it and in the warmth made it easier for me to mimic a moth, with two wings and dry powder all over me. I went round and round the candle, my eyes half closed, and the flame hardly moving. I took the moth into me, and later heard that they began to laugh. I must have known this, yet didn't know it, at the time. But I went on circling the candle, and nobody thought to stop me, to break my spell and their spell.

If life is one long quest to avoid deciding what you are, I suddenly knew that I was a moth when one whole wing was touched off by the candle.

The flame came up suddenly and without smoke, but it wasn't as swift to others as it was to me, and before more than a slight scorch was done the flame was killed stone dead by two of the teachers.

Everybody thought that my days of mimicking were done for good. So did I, because on that occasion it seemed to have got out of control, and though I thought I might like such a thing to happen at some time in my life, I wasn't ready for it yet.

Before leaving that part of my life for ever (I still can't bring myself to call it childhood) I remember a photograph of me, that showed a big self-absorbed boy of thirteen. It was taken by an uncle, and then enlarged, and my mother had it framed and put on the sideboard in the parlour where nobody went and so hardly anybody, thank God, ever looked at it. I'd been out of her care and bother for a long time, but she'd taken to liking me again. It made no difference, because once a decision is taken through a failure to mimic, nothing can alter it. Maybe I reminded her of my father who had long since gone and given place to another person, and who she still in some way liked. But I'd never mimic him for her, even so, though I could have done it so that the house would have crowed around us.

This photo seemed to have no connection with me, but everybody swore that it had, and that there couldn't be a better one. In my heart I'd come to the age where I wanted to please them, so I decided I must mimic that photo so as to become like the image on it. It wasn't long before I saw that such a thing was not feasible. If you don't know what you are, how is it possible to imitate yourself? This was the issue that burned me. I could not imitate something that had no life, not even myself if I didn't have any. And certainly judging by the photo there was no life there whatever. That was what everyone liked about it, my mother most of all, who stuck it on the sideboard in what was to her the place of honour.

Nevertheless, I looked at that photo for a long time, since other people had given it so much meaning. It was there for the world to see, above all, those who close their hearts and say: Know thyself. But I say: Get me a mirror, and according to the antics performed in it you can then (if you have that sort of desire) know everybody in the world.

But a photograph is not a mirror. You do not even see yourself as others see you. For a moment I almost went into the spirit of that photograph, but pulled myself back in time. That would have been evil. I preferred not to know what I was. There was almost triumph in that decision. If I don't know what I am, nobody can know, not even God. And if God doesn't know, then there is no God.

Rather than mimic the photograph of myself and believe in God I decided that I'd sooner be a moth.

Being such a good mimic I couldn't hold down any job for long. Sooner or later the foreman was bound to turn up when I was doing an imitation of him before all my mates. I worked harder than most though because I was so self-absorbed that nothing was too difficult or arduous for me. It was always with great regret that I was sacked.

On the other hand, all women love a mimic, except the mimic's mother, who ceases to matter by the time he becomes interested in other women. If you want to get off with a woman all you have to do is talk. Let the steamroller roll, and talk, talk, talk. Flatter her if you must, but the main thing is to talk. No woman can resist a constant stream of fulsome talk, no matter how inane and irrelevant, as long as you keep it up and make her laugh. Even if she laughs at you, it doesn't matter. By that time she's softening, you can bet.

And a mimic, even if he's so much speechless putty when left alone with himself, can mimic a funny and talkative man when the need arises. Of course, when the girl falls in love she never gets what she thinks she is getting. But then, who does? There is much wisdom in the world. Certain basic rules were formulated for me by Sam England who worked in the plywood factory where I took my first job. Never, he said, marry a girl who hates her mother, because sooner or later she will start to hate you. He also added that if you want to know what your girl-friend is going to look like in thirty years' time, look at her mother now. And if you want to know what your girl-friend expects you to look like in *ten* years' time, look at her father.

Whenever I met a girl I had to decide, by her face and talk, and the sort of home she came from, what sort of a person she'd like me to be. There weren't many girls who could ever put up with a strong silent type for the first three dates while he weighed up the situation. But after that I fell into the slot, and the talk began, the endless jokes and self-revelations that come from anyone no matter what sort he is.

If I wanted to get rid of a girl, I made an abrupt change of character. None of them could stand this. They thought I had either gone mad, or lost my respect for them. In the soiled territory of the heart the precise configuration of the land only comes with continual and intense familiarity.

One girl I could not get rid of. I changed character no less than five times, but she wouldn't go away, so there was nothing I could do except marry her.

If there's one thing I've always found it hard to mimic it's a happy man. I've often been happy, but that was no help when I was indifferent and wanted to let someone else see that I was full of the joy of life.

I knew that I had to overcome this problem and prayed that on this vital issue my talent for mimicry would not let me down.

In the very act of getting married, in order to appear happy to the girl I was to live with, I had to behave like a fool. When I should have slipped the ring on her finger I put it on mine – then on to hers. When we were declared married I attempted to kiss the best man, a fellow clerk from an office I was then working at. He fought free and pleaded with me not to be bloody silly, so then I kissed the bride, and apologized to everyone later by saying I'd been too happy to know what I was doing. They believed this, and forgave me, and I loved them so much I could have mimicked them all, one after another to the end of time.

When I changed for the sixth time it was only to mimic a man getting married. That was the one character she couldn't stand, and by the time I had come to believe in the act, and had almost grown to like it, it was the one finally by which I got rid of her. When we parted six months later I did a very tolerable job of mimicking an amicable man, who had taken one step wrong in life and wanted to go two steps back. She went home to her parents, and took the television set among all her cases in the second run of the taxi. We had always made love in the most perfect way, because I'd had enough experience to mimic that like a stallion, but it had made no difference to our final feeling for each other. She'd never been able to get through to the real me, no more than I had. And after a year of trying she imagined she never would, and I couldn't help but admire her promptitude in getting out as quickly as she did.

This is not a tale of love, or the wail of a broken marriage, or a moan about impossible human relationships. I won't dwell long on any of that. I can go on for years telling you what all this is *not*. It'll be up to you to tell me what it is.

Ambition has never been strong in my veins. To be ambitious you have first to know what you are. Either that, or you do not have to be concerned with what you are. My talent for mimicry was an end in itself. If I could observe someone, I thought in the early days, and then become exactly the same, why should I go through years of work to accomplish it in the reality of society?

I had never any intention of working, but what society demands of you is in fact what life itself wants. So you must imitate it – instead of allowing your soul to be destroyed by believing in it. As soon as you accept something, and cease to play a role regarding it, you are done for.

339

Your soul is in danger. You have even less chance then of ever getting to know the real nature of yourself.

The same must be with everything you are called upon to do in life, whatever action, whether it lasts a minute or a year. Mimic it, I told myself at times of danger when caught by a suspicious joy of life I was about to acquiesce to. The successful mimic is he who not only takes on a role completely so that everyone is deceived, but actually from a distance sees himself with his own eyes doing it so that he himself is never deceived. I only learned to do this later, probably after I broke up with my first wife.

One might imagine that if the main thing in life was the survival of the fittest, then one as a mimic would be wise to imitate and continue to imitate one of the fittest. But not only would that be boring, it would be inhuman, and above all foolish. We know that it is not the fittest who survive, but the wise. The wise die, but the fittest perish, and they perish early on from having settled on to one role in life. They have determined to keep it to the very end, and also to defend it to the death against those who would try to show them that the world is richer than they have made it.

It is the easiest thing in the world for me to recognize those who believe in the survival of the fittest, which means most people. It is, conversely, difficult for me to meet another person like myself, because there are so few of us.

But I once met a woman who was also a mimic. What I could never understand was why those qualities that I had, made people trust and love me, especially women. If to mimic is to betray (which it certainly is) then you would expect to be generally disliked, but strangely enough it was more often the opposite. She said exactly the same thing, except that it was especially men who loved and trusted her.

A friend of mine from the insurance office where I worked was getting married, and I met her at the reception for it. She was a thin green-eyed girl from the tobacco factory, and I listened to her during the meal mimicking the parson, for she had also been at the church. As a lesser friend of the bride's she was assigned to a more remote table, and I happened to be passing on my way back from the lavatory, where I had mimicked a disgusted man and thrown up what food I'd already eaten.

The people around her didn't know whether to be amused or offended. I was merely interested. Her face lost its pallor and grew weightier with the sombre voice she put on. She had great range of tone, and as she went through the service I took the part of bridegroom. Instead of saying 'I will,' at the correct moment, I said: 'I'm damned if I will,' and the two nearest tables joined in the applause.

The actual bride, as this went on, shook at the mouth and dropped tears on to her cheeks. The best man and the bridegroom demanded that we pack it in, but some devil was in us both, and our duet went on as if we were in the middle of a field with no audience at all. There was silence for a few minutes before the uproar. A pair of fine mimics had met, an accident of two stars clashing in interstellar space, and nothing could stop us getting to the end of the act.

The last word was with the best man. I suppose the bridegroom was saving himself for the first night. He only nodded in despair, knowing that it couldn't end in any other way. When the man hit me I pulled two chairs over and half dragged the tablecloth on to the floor. I sprang up and, mimicking an outraged partygoer whose best piece was being unjustly spat on, punched him right over the table, where his head spliced down through the four-tier cake.

The bride screamed as if her husband had been killed. I'd had enough. Grabbing the slender fingers of my fellow mimic I ran out of that doom-laden party for all I was worth, wondering how long the marriage would last after such an inauspicious beginning.

Our association was interesting, but disastrous from the start. We didn't live together, but shared each other's rooms. For a few months it was champagne and roses. Coming back to one of the rooms from our respective jobs we would eat a supper (imitating each other's mastication all the way through), then we would dare each other to mimic certain characters, such as an airline pilot, a policewoman, an insurance man, girl shop assistant. We played with each other, tested each other, acted God and the Devil with the deepest penetrable parts of our hearts and souls. We mimicked each other mimicking each other. We mimicked each other mimicking people we both knew. We mimicked the same person to see who could do it best. When we emptied each other we made love, and it came marvellously on such occasions. We thought we had come to the end of the road, gone over the cliff hand in hand like a couple of Gadarene swine and found we had landed in paradise.

But to think such things only means that the road is about to enter a swamp. I wanted her to marry me, but it turned out she was already married. So was I. Her husband knocked on my door one Sunday afternoon, and what could I do but ask him in? He was a van driver of thirty, but with his sweater and quiff he looked seventeen. He appeared stupid and sensitive, a not uncommon combination. 'I know you're living with him,' he said, 'but I've come to ask you to come back and live with me. That's why I've come.'

I stood up and made a quiff in my hair, threw off my jacket, and pulled the sweater down. Then I repeated his speech in exactly the same voice. It's dangerous mimicking simple people, but I couldn't resist. He must have gone through all the possible situations that could arise before he knocked at my door, but this wasn't one of them. He looked horror-struck, and leaned against the outside door. At this, Jean, who'd said nothing so far, got up and stretched her spine against the door to the kitchen with exactly the same expression.

'What's going on?' he demanded.

'What's going on?' I mimicked.

He lifted his fist as if about to fly through the room and crash against me. Jean lifted her fist and prepared to spring in exactly the same way. They would have collided and died in an apotheosis of glorious mimicry.

He turned to the door and opened it. Jean pulled at the kitchen door. We heard him running downstairs, and he never came back.

I passed him a few months later as I was walking through town. A girl was with him, and he didn't notice me in my misery. But I saw him all right because I hadn't seen anyone so obviously happy for a long time.

I followed Jean from the factory one night, and she met another man. She'd been seeing me less and less. I'd expected it, but because we couldn't live together, could only exist like two cripples, taking turns to hold each other up, I was struck by jealousy as if a javelin.had shuddered deep between my shoulder blades.

When two vampires meet, they meet for ever, until another comes to set them free. But freedom is painful, for a while. For a mimic who doesn't believe in it, it can be catastrophic.

I rang the bell of his flat one Sunday morning. As he opened the door Jean made a good imitation of the ringing noise. I saw that I was in for a bad time. Think of what situation you want from the bottom of your soul to avoid, and when you have decided what it is, consider what you'll do when it comes about.

He was grinning by the window, and Jean actually offered me a cup of tea. While she was giving it to me I could see her imitating her actions. She had learned a lot, and I wondered where. I never knew his name. To the world he was an ordinary chap in some trade or other, but to me I saw he was trying to mimic something and I didn't know what it was. I was puzzled, but sat and drank my tea.

I asked Jean how she was, but she only smiled, and didn't seem to know. I wondered if she was happy, and could only say that she was. I knew that if I asked direct questions they would combine to defeat me in mimicry, and I had no wish to bring on to myself what Jean and I had poured on to her husband. They knew this. He stayed by the window, grinning, and I withered under the stare that went with it. Nevertheless I looked up at him from time to time. His face seemed a shade paler and thinner. I would fight on my own ground, in other words get up and go – but not before I could see what he was imitating.

But the stare grew ashen and luminous, especially after I had nothing left to say. I stood up and made for the door, but Jean blocked it. Where had she met such a person?

'I'm going,' I said calmly. A mimic cannot give up the ground he stands on, without knowing that another piece of land is waiting for him. Here, I was isolated, and the ocean was wide. It wasn't an honour to be defeated at this moment, but it was essential to me as a man. In defeat one can begin to know what one is, in victory – never. 'Get out of my way.'

Behind my back I heard: 'I'm going. Get out of my way' – in my own voice exactly.

'Guess what he's mimicking?' she said.

Without turning around I saw reflected in her eyes the sky-blue bones of his skull head, and the fixed grin of the victory I'd been forced to give him.

I mimicked her: 'Guess what he's mimicking?' and didn't give her time to answer. 'A corpse,' I said, forcing her gently aside, opening the door, and walking away.

Between bouts of mimicking one person and another, my entity becomes blank. To be able to mimic someone I had to like them. That was the first rule, just as, in the reverse sense, in order to love someone you have to be able to mimic them. When I mimicked people now, they ceased to like me, if they had ever done so. But then, treachery always begins with a kiss. For these reasons I had found it impossible to imitate God, and not only because I'd never seen Him.

Later, in my isolation, I only mimicked people to myself instead of out loud or for the benefit of others. Don't force the pace. This isn't a story. Switch off if you're not with me. I'll go on as long as you can, if not longer. I've had everything: booze, pot, shock, solitary. Yet though I may be sane, and a mimic of the world, can I imitate Mr Sand or Mr Water, Mr Cloud or Mr Sky with sufficient conviction to become all of them rolled into one realistic and convincing ball?

I mimic myself trying to mimic myself when I don't know who I am or what my real self is. I sit on my own in a pub laughing inwardly because I am more king of the world than anyone else. I see faces around me both troubled and serene, and don't know which one to choose for the great grand mimic of the night. I give up trying to mimic myself, and choose a man talking earnestly to his wife. I stand in the middle of the floor. Everything is clear and steady, but no one looks at me. I talk as if the man's wife were standing two inches from my face, grinning at the jokes I'm (he's) obviously making, then looking slow-eyed and glum when she mentions the children. Somebody pushes by with an empty glass as if I don't exist. I pull him back and he knocks me down. I do exist. I live, and smile on the floor before getting up. But only he notices me, and does so no more as his glass is filled and he steps by me back to his table. It is quite a disturbance, but they don't even call the police.

Was Jean's new man mimicking himself, or was it me? I shall never know. But I would not see her again, even though she might want to take up with me. She'd been in contact with evil, and the evil had rubbed off on to her. Some of it in that short time had jumped to me, and I was already trying to fight free of it.

When I was mimicking someone I was walking parallel with the frontiers of madness. When I did it marvellously well, the greater was the drop of madness below me. But I didn't know this. I was driven to mimicry by threat and fear of madness. For some months I totally lost the skill to mimic, and that's why I got a note from my doctor and presented myself at the door of the local head-hospital. They welcomed me with open arms, and I was able to begin making notes from the seven millionth bed.

I did well there, announced to all assembled that I was now going to put on a show of mimicking Doctor So-and-so, and what to me was a brilliant act for them turned out to be perfectly still flesh and a blank stare from a person who was me in the middle of the room.

I had to start again, from the beginning. In order to imitate a sneeze I was thrown on to the floor by the force of it. I turned into a dog down one side of my face, and a moth on the other.

As I came up from the pit I started to write these notes. I have written them out five times already, and on each occasion they have been snatched from me by the attendant and burned. While I write I am quiet; when I stop, I rave. That is why they are taken from me.

II

I didn't stay long: it took me two years to recover. To imitate was like learning to speak again. But my soul was filled with iron, and I went on and on. The whole world was inside of me, and on any stage I chose I performed my masterpiece of mimicry. These were merely rehearsals for when I actually figured as the same person over and over again, a calm, precise, reasonable man who bore no relation to the real me seething like a malt-vat inside. The select audience appreciated my effort. I don't think anything was lost on them, except perhaps the truth.

No one can mimic time and make it go away, as one can sometimes make friends and enemies alike disappear when you mimic them. I had to sit with time, feed it my bones in daylight and darkness.

This great creation of mine, that I dredged up so painfully from the bottom of my soul, was someone I'd sidestepped from birth. I breathed life in him, a task as hard as if he were a stone, yet I had to perfect him and make him live, because in the looney bin I realized the trap I'd walked into.

I made a successful imitation of a sane man, and then they let me out. It felt like the greatest day of my life. I do not think my perform-ance could have been better than it was.

An insane man can vanish like a fish in water, and hide anywhere. I am not insane, and it was never my intention to become so. But one is forced to mimic to perfection a sane man so as to become free, and what greater insanity is there than that? Yet it widens the horizons of the heart, which is no bad thing for someone who was born a mimic.

Years have passed, and in my pursuit and mimicry of sanity I have become the assistant manager of a large office. I am thirty-five years of age, and never married again. I took some winter leave and went to Switzerland. Don't ask me why – that means you, the one I'm imitating, and you, who I am not. I planned the space off work and set off for London with my pocket full of traveller's cheques and a passport. In my rucksack was a hammock, nylon groundsheet, blanket, tobacco, matches, soap, toothpaste, toothbrush, compass, a book, notebook, and pencils. That's all. I don't remember where I got such a list from but I did, and stuck to it religiously. I was determined that every action from now on should have some meaning, just as in the past every time I had ever mimicked anyone had also had some important significance. One cannot live in the world of chance. If fate will not act for you, then take it by the neck.

It was so cold I thought my head would break like an old teapot, but as I walked away from the lake and along the narrow road between banks of trees I got used to it. The walls of the mountains on either side were so steep it seemed that if anybody were foolhardy enough to climb up they would fall off and down – unless they were a fly. Perhaps I could mimic a fly, since already in the cold I had conjured a burning stove into my belly. A car passed and offered me a lift. I waved it on.

It was getting dark by five, and there wasn't much snow to be seen, a large sheet of luminous basilisk blue overhead, and behind me to the south a map-patch of dying fluorescent pink. The air was pure, you could certainly say that for it. The sun must have given the valley an hour each day, then a last wink before it vanished on its way to America.

There was snow underfoot, at certain higher places off the road, good clean snow that you could eat with honey on it. I could not see such snow and fading sun without death coming into my heart, the off-white powder humps in the dusk thrown between rock and tree-boles, flecked among the grey and scattered rooftops of a village I was coming to.

Bells were sounding from the church, a leisurely mellow music coming across the snow, so welcoming that they made me think that maybe I had had a childhood after all. I walked up the steep narrow lanes, slipping on the snow hardened into beds of ice. No one was about, though lights were in the windows of dark wooden houses.

Along one lane was a larger building of plain brick, and I went inside for something to eat. A girl stood by the counter, and said good evening in Italian. I took off my pack and overcoat, and she pointed to tables set in the room behind.

They did not ask me what I wanted but brought soup, then roast meat, bread, and cabbage. I gave in my passport, intending to stay the night. A woman walked in, tall, blonde, rawboned, and blue-eyed. She sat at another table, and fed half her meal to the cat. After my long trek from the railway station (stopping only in the town to buy a map) I was starving, and had eyes for nothing but my food. The first part of the walk was agony. I creaked like an old man, but now, in spite of my exhaustion, I felt I could walk on through the night.

I did not sleep well. In dreams I began to feel myself leaving the world. My hand was small and made of copper, tiny (like hammers that broke toffee when I was a child), and I placed it on my head that was immense and made of concrete, solid, but that suddenly started to get smaller. This was beginning to be an actual physical state, so I opened my eyes to fight it off. If I didn't I saw myself being pressed and squeezed into extinction, out of the world. It didn't seem as if I would go mad (nothing is that simple) but that I would be killed by this attrition of total insecurity. It seemed as if the earth were about to turn into concrete and roll over my body.

I got out of bed and dressed. The air in the room, which had firmly shut double windows and radiators, was stifling. When you think you're going mad it's a sign you're getting over it. The faces of everyone I'd ever mimicked or made love to fell to pieces in turn like a breaking jigsaw puzzle.

My boots bit into the snow as I closed the door behind. It wasn't yet midnight. There was a distinct ring around the full and brilliant moon. There was snow on the mountain sides, and it seemed as if just over the line of their crests a neon light was shining. I walked along the lanes of the village, in the scorching frosty cold.

To question why one is alive means that one is only half a person, but to be a whole person is to be half dead.

Sun was shining over the snow next morning as I sat by the window drinking coffee. I was near the head of the valley, and the mountain slopes opened out. Most of it was sombre forest with occasional outcrops of rock, but to the west, at a place shone on directly by the sun, I could see green space. Then nothing but rock and snow, and blue sky. My eyes were always good. I never needed glasses or binoculars, and just above the meadow before the trees began was a small hut. No smoke came from it.

I paid my bill, collected my pack, and said good-bye. At the road a cow had been hit by a car and lay dying. The car's headlamp was shattered and the animal lay in a pool of blood, moving its hoofs slightly. A group of people stood around, and the driver was showing his papers. Another man rested a notebook on the car-top to write. It was all very orderly. I pushed through and looked into the eyes of the dying animal. It did not understand. As a last gesture it bellowed, but no one was interested in it, because the end was certain. No one even heard it, I was sure. The damson eyes were full of the non-comprehension of understanding.

The mountains were reflected in one, and the village in the other – or so it seemed as I paced back and forth. Another bellow sounded, even after it was dead, and when all the people looked at me at last to make sure that the noise was coming from me and not out of the sky I walked on alone up the road, away from the spoiled territory of the heart, and the soiled landscape of the soul.

I am wild. If I lift up my eyes to the hills a child cries. A child crying makes me sad. A baby crying puts me into a rage against it. I imagine everything. If I go into the hills and sit there, birds sing. They are made of frost, like the flowers. Insanity means freedom, nothing else. Tell me how to live and I'll be dangerous. If I find out for myself I'll die of boredom afterwards. When I look along the valley and then up it seems as if the sky is coming into land. The mountains look as tall as if they are about to walk over me. If they want to, let them. I shall not be afraid.

The wind is fresh except when it blows smoke into my face. I build a fire by the hut, boil water on it for tea. The wind is increasing, and I don't like the look of the weather.

The hut is sheltered, and when I came to it I found as if by instinct a key just under the roof. There's nothing inside, but the floor is clean, and I have my hammock as well as food. When it is dark it seems as if the wind has been moaning and prowling for days, plying its claws into every interstice of the nerves. I wanted to get out and go after it, climb the escarpment above the treeline with a knife between my teeth, and fight on the high plateau in the light of the moon, corner that diabolic wind and stab it to death, tip his carcass over the nearest cliff.

I cannot mimic either Jack Frost or a windkiller. It's too dark, pit-shadows surround me, but there's no fear because outside in the mountains the whole fresh world stretches, waiting for children like me to get up in the morning, to go out into it and be born again.

I have finished with mimicking. I always thought the time would come, but could never imagine when or where. I cannot get into anyone any more and mimic them. I am too far into myself at last, for better or worse, good or bad, till death do me part.

One man will go down into the daylight. In loneliness and darkness I am one man: a spark shot out of the blackest pitch of night and found its way to my centre.

A crowd of phantoms followed me up, and I collected them together in this black-aired hut, tamed them and tied them down, dogs, moths, mothers, and wives. Having arrived at the cliff-face of the present there's little else to say. When my store of food is finished I'll descend the mountainside and go back to the inn, where I'll think some more as I sit drinking coffee by the window, watching the snow or sunshine. I'll meet again the tall, blonde, rawboned, blue-eyed woman who fed half her meal to the cat – before setting off on my travels. Don't ask me where, or who with.

Before Snow Comes

The lights below glowed red like lines of strawberries. Snow had been forecast, and when it fell he thought they would be buried. The smell of frost and smoke had softened, and he could taste snow on his lips even before the first flake drifted down on to his hair.

The only thing was to drink, drink, drink, and try not to forget. With glass after glass her face came back with much greater clarity than when he was sober. In full ordinary everyday light she stayed dim and far away, out of sight and all possibility of mind. But in memory she never stood so close that he could touch her.

He recognized the garden because of the rosebush growing in it. The palings leaned as if they would never get up again. They had not been thumped by a good-natured drunk, for then they could have been willingly straightened, but sagged as if someone had deliberately kicked them in passing because he was fed up with life when he had no need to be. They should be totally uprooted and thrown away for bonfire night. Then I'd get some of those new-smelling planks and laths from the woodyard and put good fences around the rosebush. He would get clean steel nails and set out those laths and offshoot wasted planks from the trunks of great trees that he got cheap because one of his mates worked there, and brush off the sawdust lovingly from each one, feeling it collect like the wooden gold-dust of life in the palm of his hands and sift between the broad flesh of his lower fingers. That half-sunk sagging fence wanted a good dose of the boot, to be followed of course by a bit of loving skill for her sake.

He had it because he was divorced. His spirit was turned upside down, the sand in his brain rifting through as in the old days to body and heart, an eggtimer letting its intoxication into the crevice of every vein and vesicle, bone and sinew. He worked and worked, walked from one step to another between elevation and misery. At work they thought him a happy and reliable mate, but every second night he forgot to wind up his watch and had to call on a neighbour to check

351

the time in order to say hello in the morning, otherwise he'd be late getting up for work (or might never get up at all) and that would never do.

He had four brothers and two sisters, all of them married, and all divorced, except one who was killed in a car crash. It wasn't that his family was unlucky or maladjusted, simply that they were normal and wholesome, just conforming like the rest of the world and following in the family tradition with such pertinacity that at the worst of times it made him laugh, and at the best it sent him out in carpet slippers on Sunday morning to buy a newspaper and read what was happening to other families. What else could you do and think, if the razor-blade of fate isn't to cut you down and spare you even more sufferings? Sometimes he thought he'd buy a Bible and make prayer-wheels to send zipping into outer space, which seemed the only possible alternative to drinking himself to death, which he couldn't afford to do. But the world keeps going round, and it was no use asking what had happened to all the good times. The ocean was too deep and wide to escape from the island on which he found himself.

She kept her roses well, and he remarked on them when passing the backyard where her fence was ready to lie down and never get up again, though it wasn't the worst of them in that terrace by any means. She leaned on the gate smoking a cigarette, a young woman with dark short curly hair, sallow and full in the face below it. Her eyes, a sharp light-blue, gave her expression a state of being lit up and luminous, aware of everything inside her but not of the world. Why she was standing there he didn't know, because there was nothing to look at but a brick wall two yards away. He stopped, nothing else in his mind except: 'I like those roses. I could smell 'em as I went by.'

'They aren't exactly Wheatcroft specials,' she said, not smiling.

'Where'd you get 'em?'

'My brother lives in Hertfordshire, and he gen me a few cuttings from his garden. Only one took, but look how it blossomed!'

'It has, an' all,' he said. Neither of them could think of anything else to say.

'Good-bye, missis.'

'Good-bye, then.'

He didn't see her for a long time, but thought about her. He worked at a cabinet-making factory as a joiner, making doors one week and window frames the next, lines of window frames and rows of doors.

The bandsaws screamed all day from the next department like the greatest banshee thousand-ton atomic bomb rearing for the spot-middle of the earth which seemed to be his brain. Planing machines went like four tank engines that set him looking at the stone wall as if to see it keel towards him for the final flattening, and then the milling machines buzzing around like scout cars searching for the answers to all questions . . . It was like the Normandy battlefield all over again when he was eighteen, but without death flickering about. Not that noise bothered him, but he often complained to himself of minor irritations, and left the disasters to do their worst. It was like pinching himself to make sure he was alive.

He gave her names, but none seemed to fit. Her face was clear, but he couldn't remember what clothes she had been wearing. It was just after midday and he wrenched his memory around like wet plywood to try and remember if the smell of any cooking dinner had been drifting from her kitchen door, whether she'd been leaning there waiting for her husband to come up the street from the factory. He expected that she had, though it didn't seem important.

After heavy spring rain the Trent flowed fast at Gunthorpe, as if somebody was feeding it along the narrows with an invisible elbow and tipping it towards the weir that was almost levelled out. But after rain there was sunshine and he cycled up the hill. At Kneeton hamlet he stood at the top of the hill with his bike, looking down through the gloomy bracken, along the descending hedge-tunnel towards the ferry and over the opposite flat bank. But for a better view he turned and leaned his bike against a wall, and went into Kneeton churchyard. The river was as grey as battleship paint, none of the small white clouds of the sky visible in it. They were reflected rather on the glistening fields beyond, and the dry red-roofed houses of various farms and villages.

He walked over the soddened grass, around the small cemetery. The gravestone of Sarah Ann Gash had split in the middle and fallen. She was born on September 1st but it didn't say what year because the split of the slate had gone right through it. Where was Sarah now? he wondered, Sarah who no longer walked around these high woods and looked now and again across the Trent for signs of storm and sunshine.

He'd left his room early, hoping to get in the full brightness of Sunday before the piss of heaven belted down again. He looked across the valley as he'd done dozens of times and brooded on it as he always did, a valley fair and shallow as himself. He told himself it was different now, without being sharp enough at the moment to know why. Locked in his Nottinghamshire room he thought about the past, but seeing this blue sky and so much open land, he wondered about the future, though in such a way that he would allow no useful answer to come out of his musing. He doubted that an answer could come under any conditions, though however unsatisfied he did not want to return to his room and brood without the benefit of such good and placid scenery.

He was a man of forty who considered that nothing had happened in life so far – apart from the death of his parents, and the loss of his wife and child by a divorce which she had wanted, and been willingly given. Just as he believed that a clerk did not work because you could not see his calloused hands and blackheads dotting his face, so he believed that he hadn't suffered because he wasn't physically scarred, crippled, or blind. It seemed that a sense of realism regarding the world and what it could do to you, and you to it, hadn't yet given him the opportunity of being fully born to its wrath, and whenever he felt something near to peace – gazing for too long over the snaky Trent and slowly rising fields on the far side – his face looked more puzzled than pleased. The wind blew against his jersey shirt, and he felt it to the flesh. Anything he felt, he noticed, and this if nothing else brought a smile to his face.

The lane descending to the river went between high hedges with sharp buds scattered over them like green snow, bent slightly on its route to the narrow band of meadow bordering the river-bank. A smell of wet cloud and fields came from the bushes. He wanted to reach the river, but not to plough in his bike and boots through the mud when a paved lane behind would get him there in a little more time but far less trouble.

Four great engines were detonated against the sky, and over the trees to his right a huge plane slid off an aerodrome runway and carried its grey belly far off across the opposite flat fields, suddenly climbing and merging completely with the sky like a bird. Something in him waited for a blue-white flash along the body, a silent unobtrusive packed explosion that would make it vanish for ever from both world and sky, as if it had no right up there where only birds of flesh and feathers could travel. But when it went on its flight he was happy and relieved that nothing happened to it. There is something greater than love, he thought. Far greater. I feel it, something that makes love seem

354

primitive. I can't say what it is, but I know that it exists, though one can only get to it through love.

He cycled over the long tarmac bridge, considered stopping on the pavement to look at the river's floodspeed over the parapet, but knew it finally could only interest a child, so turned across the line of traffic and down the lane towards field and gravel-stones sloping between the inn and the water's edge. The nearby weir was almost level yet still let out a thunderous roar of water from its depths, and in various side-pools of the river men sat fishing, oblivious to it. He laid his bike down, and set off for a walk.

A woman and two children were picnicking beyond the first clump of bushes, and not having a very good time of it. A khaki groundsheet had been fixed on two sticks as a shield against the irritating windbite gusting across the river to scatter sandwich papers and salt. They crouched under it, and he heard the grit of discontented voices. It was difficult to light a cigarette in such a cunning wind, except by opening his jacket and holding it as a buffer. So as not to intrude upon their private feast he walked behind them, but when he was closest he knew he had seen the woman before, leaning against the backyard gate of a house in Radford. A boy of seven felt under a blanket and pulled out a transistor radio the size of a two-ounce tobacco tin, and switched on a thin screech of music. Ducks flew over from the woods, and when their beaks moved during a low swerve towards the fishermen behind, he heard no sound because of the radio.

The mother switched it off: 'You can play it after you've had something to eat' – and gave him and his sister a hardboiled egg. He heard the soft crack of shell on a stone, and remembered that he had eaten no breakfast. Her thick plum-coloured coat was open to show a pale-green sweater. His stare drew her head around, and he was astounded now that he had a full view of her face, to see how much it had altered, or how much his memory had embellished it with features it had probably never possessed. The sallowness lay on thinner and smaller bones, and she was darker under her eyes. But she drew him with the same force, like a girl he'd been in love with as an adolescent and just by accident met again, suddenly bringing back to him youth and naïvety and the unforgettable depth and freshness of first love that he knew could never come twice in anybody's lifetime. It struck him that whenever he thought of something that happened a few years ago it always felt as if he were recapturing adolescence.

He stood back, but said when she looked hard at him: 'I was passing, and recognized your face. You live down Radford, don't you?'

'Who's that, mam?'

'Shurrup and get your picnic.' She was puzzled, and not pleased at this plain intrusion.

'I remember your rosebush,' he said with a smile. 'How's it getting on?'

'Not very well. I didn't know you knew me.'

'I passed your gate, and yours was the only back garden with roses in it.'

She gave each child a radish, and the girl who got the biggest held it like a doll, then grasped the green sprouts and chewed it while thoughtfully looking at the river. 'What's your name?'

'Jean,' she said, 'if you like.'

He smiled. 'That's a funny way of putting it.'

'Jean then, whether you like it or not.'

'We talked about your roses. Don't you remember?'

She pulled her coat to. 'Wipe your nose, Paul. Don't let it go all over your food. A lot's happened since.' She was not eating, handled all food respectfully and passed it to her children. A gang of boys went by, waving sticks and swinging tadpole jars at the end of string.

'That's lucky,' he said, 'no matter how bad it is.'

'I don't care, one way or the other.' Yet her face had relaxed almost into a smile at the few words bartered since he'd stopped.

'That's no way, either,' he said. 'You know what they say about Don't Care?' The boy and girl looked up at him, with more interest than their mother. The girl smiled, waiting.

'It goes like this, I think:

> 'Don't Care had golden hair
> Don't Care was green at the face
> Don't Care was tall and lame
> Don't Care wore a shirt of lace
> Don't Care took the Devil's name
> Don't Care was hung:
> Don't Care fell down through the air
> Into a pit of dung!'

He felt foolish at such recitation, yet less so when he saw that all three were amused.

'Where did you learn that?'

He winked. 'Read it in a book.'

'What sort of book?' asked the boy.

'Any book. No, I tell a lie. I remember my father saying it to me as a boy.'

'A rum thing to tell a child,' she said. Wet blue clouds were coming eastwards over the summit of the woods, cold grey at the edges, but a line of sun still cut the mother from her children, moving and warming them in turn.

'I hope it doesn't think to rain,' she said.

'So do I. I biked up from Nottingham, and now I'm off for a walk. What happened to you in the last two years, then?' He saw she wouldn't want to talk about it, but asked just the same, because it was up to her to decide, not him.

'It's a long story,' she said, snubbing him by the silence that followed.

It must be a bloody bad one, he thought, from the way she looks: 'I'll tell you one thing, though: no stories have an ending. They never end. So maybe it won't turn out to be as bad as you think. Take me, for instance. I'm only really happy when I'm working.'

His way of speaking had aroused her interest, as if she was un-accustomed to hearing people speak at all. She asked if he lived alone.

'I do,' he said.

'Me too; but I've got two kids. You keep yourself looking well and clean for a man who lives alone!'

He laughed: 'It's not too difficult.'

'Some men find it so.'

'I'll be going for a stroll then.'

'What's your name, anyway?'

'Mark,' he told her. 'Maybe I'll pass your house again for another look at your roses. I've never seen such fine ones in Radford.'

He climbed a gate and made his way through wet nettles that came up to his knees and brushed his trousers above the tops of his leather boots. Across the path striated puddles barred his way, an edge of the yellow round sun reflected in them. The sky was blue and heavy, patched, rimmed, and streaked with thinning grey cloud. Whenever faced with a long walk he began to feel self-indulgent, wished he hadn't set out, and speculated on his point of no return. The fields stretched into the distance, reluctant to slope up through mist into the hills beyond Southwell. He stood by the edge of a copse that barred his way, black trunks and evergreen tops forming an impenetrable heart in his path. There was a paralysis in his legs that would not allow him to find the free flow around it so as to continue his roaming. What was the point in going on if you could not get easily to the heart? Two pigeons flew out of the field and buried themselves in it without difficulty. It looked even more of a job to get into that than one's own soul, a million times harder, in fact.

It started to rain. The soul was a moth fluttering in smoke, down on the concrete floor of his personality, sometimes touching it with the tips of its wings, flying above it, but always conscious that it was there in the smoke and darkness, and that it could never get through to the richer fields below, where connection with the universe and the clue to the real meaning of life lay. He could not burst that concrete as others presumably had, blast a way through to his soul with the dynamite of hardship and suffering. It was a mystery to him how it was done. Where does one begin? What is the secret or quality of disposition towards nature that one must have in one's marrow? Two pigeons, back out of the copse, were flying through the rain towards the river, and without thinking he headed back in that direction himself. Jean and her children had packed up and gone – which didn't surprise him because the thin consistent rain already reached through to his skin. He rubbed the beads of water from his bicycle handlebars and rode with head down along the main road back towards Nottingham.

The rose bushes had indeed withered: some organic malevolence had bitten them at the root and travelled up to every point of life. The blight had crippled them, in spite of all hope and intermittent care between bitter and useless quarrels with her husband. His departure had been the talk of the yard, but everyone had known right from the beginning that their marriage had been broken-backed and would dissolve one day. So did Jean know, now that it was all over. Even the children had stopped asking for him after a few weeks, knowing that to go on doing so would make her unendurably irritable for hours.

She tried to revive them, bought various compost powders from the ironmonger's and dug up the rock-cake soil around each one, but they seemed unwilling to risk flowering in the closed-off urban air. Their thorns stayed rusty in summer, shining under the blue complacent sky.

While cooking the children's breakfast she remembered the man who had talked to them on their last excursion to Gunthorpe. If only it had been as fine a day as this, she thought, glancing out of the window at a clean warm sky, I'd have felt more like chatting him back instead of driving him away with megrims and miseries. She could find excuses for it, but no reason, though the memory by no means depressed her as she stirred porridge and put sausages under the grill. They had a meal at school, and got their own tea till she came in at six. As for men, she did not care if she never had another one near her for the rest of her life. She'd had two bellyfuls from Ken, and got no joy out of either. Any of that, and she could manage it herself, as most self-respecting women had to do.

Janice came down, dressed already, but Paul still had his pyjama-bottoms on and his clothes bundled up like a bomb under his arm. She snapped and tugged him into a dressed creature in two minutes, and Janice was pouring cold milk into his porridge when she went out of the back door to catch the bus for work.

Mark cycled over in his dinner hour, but she wasn't in. He didn't like being seen in his overalls, but was able to look towards her back door while smoking a cigarette, careful not to lean on the sagging fence which looked as if it would stay up for ever it was so rotten. The neighbours assumed he was her boy-friend, and couldn't understand that someone who must have crept into her house now and again when it was dark – though no one had actually seen him – should be so gormless as to come here in the middle of the day merely to stand and look at the scullery window.

I ought to mend that fence, he told himself. A few good posts and a line of deep holes filled with concrete, and I'd ram in the supports to last till the slum clearance brigade comes round. Wouldn't take me a day.

He'd had the disease most of his life of asking questions before the time was ripe – if it ever was – and so destroying what pleasure he might be destined to feel if he did the impossible and kept his mind closed. But at half past eight that evening (while it was still light: the neighbours thought he had a cheek) he knocked at the back door with a definite proposition in mind.

A large white towel was swathed around her sopping head, just up from its final rinse at the scullery tap. The two top buttons of her blouse were open, and he turned red at the face. 'I was passing, so I thought I'd say hello.'

'Oh!' she said, the green-eyed twilight blank and clear at the back of his head. 'It's you! I thought it was going to be Flo Holland. What do you want?' The offputting brutality of this abrupt question was lessened by an assumption in her tone that he had a right to come here and want something, and that for some reason she by no means considered him a total stranger. Her face seemed less pale, a little more healthy with the dark hair invisible, lines slightly hard like a woman's in a bathing cap and devoid of make-up or lipstick. Through the main window he saw the white electric flash of the telly reflection. 'I've just washed my hair,' she said. 'It saves a few bob to do it at the sink. You can come in for a cup of tea in a minute.'

She closed the door, and he was sure she'd forget him, accidentally-on-purpose, as it were. He stood by the fence smoking, only this time on her side of the gate, and it was amazing how strong that gate looked in comparison to the rotten decrepit lines of paling on either side.

When he was about to walk away the door pulled open. The scarf that bundled the drying hair gave her a gipsy look, darkened her eyes and narrowed the face. 'Come on,' she said, 'I've got the kettle on.' Sometimes when cycling he would go for miles deep in thought, and suddenly realize he could not remember passing any of the familiar landmarks on the road behind. So now, filled with happiness instead of thought, he could not recollect details of getting to the table and facing her from his abstracted melancholy stance by the gate.

'What made me call,' he said, 'was the sight of that fence.'

'I thought it was me,' she said.

'Don't get sarky. I'm a chippie and can fix it for you.'

'How much do you want for it?' she asked.

'I'll do it for fun.'

She held a slice of bread at the fire with a long fork. 'I wouldn't bother. It's been like that for so long. Anyway, if we have a bad winter like the last one I'll use it for firewood to save me or the kids queuing at the coke-yard.'

'The toast's burning,' he said. She buttered it, and poured a mug of tea. 'I don't eat till the kids are upstairs. I get indigestion at their antics. When Paul broke a cup tonight I screamed as if somebody had thrown a knife at me. Frightened the poor little bogger out of his wits.'

'No use getting nervous,' he laughed.

'It's no use telling me that. I was born like it.'

'Who wasn't? Sometimes it goes.'

'In middle age,' she said, 'I'm waiting.'

'There's a long time yet,' he said.

She leaned over for a light. 'Ever go to the pubs?'

'Not as a rule. Do you?'

'Not really. It'd get me out a bit if I did, I suppose.'

'Where do you go for your holidays?' he said.

'You met me on them.'

'Up Gunthorpe?'

'I take the kids now and again. Last year it was Matlock for the day, boating on the Derwent and then into the caves. They enjoyed it, I'm glad to say. We have better times since Ken left, though there's a bit less money to throw around.'

'I expect he'll be back,' he said, as if very happy at the idea.

'When the kids asked me where he's gone – they didn't like him all that much, but they missed him at first – I said he was off to work in London for a while. But they know he won't come back. I was down town a few weeks ago with Janice, and we was just crossing the road in Slab Square when a bus stopped at the traffic lights, and out of the window I heard this voice shout: 'How are you, Jean, my duck?' and when I looked it was him sitting there as large as life with another bloody woman! Janice asked me who it was so I said it was nothing to do with us, and pulled her round when she tried to look. No, he'll never come back to me. Not that it would do him much good if he tried. More tea?'

'Please. I'll do that fence on Saturday. I often go to work then, but I can leave off overtime for once.'

Neighbours stopped and looked into the small of his back as they passed along the yard, or from the end of it turned to see what he was on with. Clouds were low, and the heavy oppressive warmth of summer weighed over the kitchens and lines of lavatories. Once started on a job he didn't want to stop till it was over and done with. It was a change from making the eternal doors and windows at the factory. He uprooted the rotten palings and prised out rusty nails so that he could lay each piece of redundant wood under the front window for next winter's kindling. The holes were plotted with a ruler,

361

marked by temporary sticks while he mixed the concrete. He'd pushed the new palings up on two journeys by bike the evening before, and she grumbled but gave in when he insisted on them staying overnight in the kitchen. Out in the garden, someone would be bound to pinch them, as he had done.

Janice and Paul watched, chewing caramels he'd treated them to. 'You're making a good job of it,' Jean said, bringing a mug of tea.

'I might as well, while I'm at it.'

'I'm off shopping. I shan't be long' – as if he should be embarrassed left all alone in a strange yard.

He straightened and took the tea. The first three posts were in, packed upright by bricks. 'If you're going out to do a week's shop you might need some money. Take this' – holding a few pounds.

'No,' she said, with a finality that he could neither change nor broach, 'it's all right.'

He crushed the notes back in his hand, fingers kneading till the knuckles went white, hoping they would disappear and prove he hadn't been so stupid as to offer it.

'I'm not being fussy,' she smiled, 'but I just don't need it. You're doing enough as it is.'

'It's good tea,' he said, 'and I was ready for it. I thought I'd help out, that's all.' He took off his cap and rubbed the sweat back into his hair. 'Do you play draughts?'

Arms were folded under her breasts, drawing in her blouse. 'Not for years, but I can.'

'I'll give you a game tonight.'

'All right then. I'll bring some fags back.'

He couldn't refuse them, as she had rebuffed him over the money; in fact such fine tenderness on her part sent as much pleasure through him as if they had indulged in a secret and unexpected kiss.

When the fence was finally up, and the kids packed off to bed, they sat down to a peaceful supper of sliced meat and farmhouse bread, coffee and pickles, cobs and jam. 'You've worked hard,' she said, 'and I'm glad of what you've done.'

'I've worked hard,' he said, his mouth full. 'Hard or soft, it's all the same. It'll stand up a long while. I'll guarantee that.'

They went through three games of draughts, and he beat her every time, though the last one wasn't so easy. 'I don't think we'll play any more,' he laughed, standing to put on his jacket. He felt in a pocket for his clips. 'Ever thought of taking a lodger?' he said, looking close at her.

She had, but wouldn't say so. It was too soon. He came close to kiss her, but she pushed him gently away and went with him to the door. She liked him, because he seemed to think about everything and took nothing for granted. What's more, he was kind and helpful, and such a man was rare. The sky was clear, but stars weren't often in it. Only telly aerials and chimneys were between you and the sky, and they helped to keep you warm.

'I'll think about it,' she said, touching his arm.

He seemed dejected, being at the end of the best day he'd spent in years, as he walked up the yard and out by his new-made fence.

The gate clicked, so she shut the door and went back to clear the table.

He didn't come for a month, but every day she expected him. She saw her husband several times in various parts of the city, but never once did she bump into Mark. Why doesn't he come? she wondered. He builds a brand-new marvellous fence, and then thinks he can just go off like any cock-a-doodle dandy and say no more about it. I suppose he can, she thought, sitting alone one night. He must have been offended when I wouldn't take money towards my shopping, but that's just like a man, to get haughty when they can't make a kept woman out of you in the first five minutes. They either do nothing, or want to do everything too quickly.

But he was close to her, so near, so close that sometimes she could see him clearly, though if she tried to touch him he vanished. She waited for him, but it seemed he'd gone for ever, either because he was scared of her and two children, or because he'd been discouraged by her coldness. She considered herself more hot-blooded than he knew, and as proof thought of the many times she had not been able to tolerate the knowledge of her husband going to bed with other women, until all vestige of love between them had been destroyed. Even Ken lost his jauntiness, and often his desire for whoever he was running after at the time. Their continual battles were fought with such unplanned unconscious spite that a note of fate and heroism crept into them both, bent as they then became on the complete destruction of each other's emotional base. Neither won, and neither lost – unless Ken could be said to have done so because he was the one who had walked out. She used to think during such fighting that the longer two people lived together the less possible did it become for them to do so. When she didn't speak to him for three days, at least not to say anything civilized, the atmosphere seemed to be damaging her actual brain cells, as if she would never again be able to see anything clearly without the most desperate effort. And when she did nothing else except speak to him for three days it was just as much of a torment, and the damage seemed to be even worse, because neither had a civil word left to say to each other.

But these memories vanished as soon as she thought of Mark, and she felt almost happy again. Then he came back.

He felt the soft warmth of midsummer, and an agreeable wind whose noiselessness was drowned by a gentle continuous brush of incoming water. For the first time in his life he was at peace not only with the world but also with those who lived in it. The clash of the children's spades into the stones sounded somewhere beyond his closed eyes. It was impossible to brood on the misery that had brought such good fortune. The sea excluded all unnecessary reflection. Its rhythms cut him off from any past machinery that may have had control over him. The place he lay on was a bridgehead on the land, and the stones pressing under his body were all that he owned. He reached out and met Jean's thigh, lifted higher until he could take her hand and press it tenderly. You went near the sea so that it could claim you, though it never did, dared it to send up an arm to try and pluck you off the precipitous shelf of life and happiness you had just by a miracle found, and drag you back to the death of its depths where you had come from. It couldn't. Both of them were firm in that. You were dreamy, and in any case had chosen a calm summer's day to lie there when there could be no danger whatsoever.

Jean sat up to spread their lunch, and he heard the children throw down spades and pull themselves over without standing up. 'Mark,' she said, 'I can't get the tops of these flasks off.'

'Knock 'em with a stone. That'll loosen 'em.'

She threw a pebble which struck his shoe. 'If you don't move I'll kiss you, lazy good-for-nothing.'

'Kiss me.'

She bent over, the sea on her lips, hair cutting out light when he opened his eyes. 'You weren't so lazy in bed last night.'

'The mattress was hard.' He jumped up yelling from a sharp nudge in the ribs, then got on his knees to twist the caps off. He couldn't screw his eyes down to the very stones and earth they sat on, but stared vacantly while exerting his strength, towards the far-off grey break-water that divided a pale blue sea and a pale blue sky, its nearer arm coming out from grey shingle and off-white cliffs. They had come for a fortnight on his hundred pounds saved, taken two rooms half an hour inland on the uppers of the town, but with a wide view over the sea.

At night when the kids were sleeping they went to the front, along it and back, the sky still on fire and the sea blood-black and flat, walking out to the waterline without shoes or socks, and standing under the cry of the nightbirds, holding hands.

When they lay naked in bed together, lightbulb shining directly over them, he in her and both locked in restfulness after making love, he thought he saw her eyes screwed up with pain, until he realized it was the light from above shining through the strands and lines of her hair and reflecting them on the skin surrounding her closed eyes. The nights were becoming one night, days one day now that the holiday was ending. The children would remember the days, but they would only remember the nights. She felt the warm thickness of his shoulders and back, the relaxed flesh of his buttocks. It was all comfort, and love, and silence, and she wondered when it would break up into the violent colours of chaos, then smiled at her pessimism and drew deeply on the hope that it never would.

'Happy, love?' he said, sensing it, never daring to ask if he knew she was not.

'Oh yes. You?'

They shifted on to their sides. 'Never more happy,' he told her. 'You know that.'

'I do.'

It was raining when they climbed into the train next day, a soft warm summer letdown from low cloud that made them happier than if they'd left the seaside with sun still shining. 'I'll save up,' he said, 'and we'll come again next year.'

'How many months is that?' Paul asked, digging his spade into the carriage floor.

Mark told him.

'How many weeks, then?'

'Fifty-odd.'

'How many minutes?'

He took out a biro and wrote on the margin of his *Daily Mirror*. 'Twenty-one thousand,' he laughed.

'I'll count them,' Paul said, as the train jerked and he fell against his mother.

The fence stood up, and so did the rosebush, every branch stem lined with concealed thorns among the remnants of decaying blossoms. More than a year had passed, and the sooty frost of winter lay over factories and houses. The factory covered more acreage than the houses. Across Ilkeston Road whole streets were cleared, a ground plan of cobbled laneways revealed. Blocks of flats, thin and high up the hill towards Canning Circus, stood like strands of hair stiffening at some apparition on the horizon that no human being could see because they were not made of concrete and girders, windows and seasoned wood. Such flats had now replaced the bucket-hovels that had held down the daisies for a hundred years, he thought, riding home on his way for dinner.

Home was where Jean and the children had once lived with her husband, and now allowed him to stay, though not in the man and wife sense, for his bed was in the parlour. 'I don't see why we can't share one bedroom,' he said.

'I do,' she retorted. 'I want some privacy in my life.'

Coming back to Nottingham after their sublime fortnight by the sea had the opposite effect to what he'd expected. The bliss of it seemed to have broken the back of their tenuous need for each other. Instead of the fabulous beginning of a full rich life together he now looked on their holiday as the height of affection and intimacy from which, through some unexplained perversity in Jean, they began to descend. Though not afraid to have the neighbours think they were living together, she seemed ashamed that she and Mark should actually do so.

At times she regretted having 'taken a lodger', useful and loving though he was. He was calm and tender, nothing upset him, neither the fact that his tea was late, nor the surge of kids jumping like mad things over him after an evening consumed in the sweat of overtime. He was goodness itself. Silver spoons must have been laid out for him at some time in his life, no matter what state he was born in. His goodness increased her feeling of guilt at having driven her husband away – though knowing in her heart that she was at least no more at fault than he had been.

Mark came home in the evening with a wide smile at the sight of her, and she tried to match him in it, would stand up from the table to greet him, while feeling desperately shy if the children were there. If they were out playing she would not even stand up. Because he was happy all of her moods were a torture to him. When he asked what was wrong, and she could not reply, it only proved that he was superfluous in the house.

'I'll go then,' he said late one night.

She jumped up. 'No, don't Mark, don't.'

'What else can I do?'

'Stay, stay. I'd die if you left me.'

He held her. 'I don't want to go. My god I don't. I couldn't. But why aren't you happy, love?'

'You're too good,' she said, her tears wetting his close face. 'You're too good to me, Mark. I don't deserve this.'

'You do,' he said, fighting back a bleak inner weeping of his own. He questioned what she called his goodness, but it seemed no time to argue about that. 'You deserve any good thing that can happen to you,' he went on, pleading with her to accept whatever he had to give. But she went on crying, as if a moss-grown moon of despair had lodged itself in her heart that she had no hope of ever prising loose. It was hard to give comfort, impossible to reach her, but he stayed close and stroked her hair, saying that he loved her, loved her, thought she was beautiful, wonderful, the only woman of his life. But he felt empty, knew he was saying all this at the wrong time, that none of it was getting through, for she was beyond all aid and sympathy, untouchable. 'Leave me,' she moaned, 'leave me.'

'I can't. I never will.'

'Leave me alone. Go away.' It wasn't the first time she'd been so upset, but now it felt so bad that he thought his heart would burst, suffering so much himself at the manifestation of her grave unhappiness that he could in no way help her. She had so much, everything when you knew there was nothing further that she could attain or reach for.

Sometimes her sister came to look after the children and they went to see a good film, or walked around the streets talking and holding hands, going later into a pub to sit alone and lost in their own common glow. Every weekend they took the children either boating to Beeston Weir or for a picnic over Catstone Hill. He not only did his best for them, but enjoyed it so that he didn't seem to be doing anything at all. She sensed this, hoping that if he did put himself out he would perform miracles and make her life worth living after all. If she could not have everything, then the world was a desert in the depths of the night that could never be walked away from.

He was inadequate before her desolation. 'Don't be so upset, Jean. What is it? What can I do for you?'

The very fact of asking meant that he could do nothing. 'I don't know,' she said, 'I feel frightened all the time. Something's wrong, and I don't know what it is. I don't even know why I'm on this earth.'

'What does it matter? What do you want to know for? It doesn't bother me, not knowing.'

'I know it doesn't. That's why you're so good!' Her cries shook against the house, as if she were being deliberately tormented by some totally unfeeling person. But it was all coming from inside her, he thought, tightening his grip. The torture of helplessness passed on to him, the fact that his selfless love could do nothing to prevent the unexplained agony of her suffering – that he could not bear to be close to. It shook his heart to the core, and his own tears fell, filled with remorse because he could not follow Jean where some anguish he was not privileged to be part of had taken her right away from him.

They held each other tightly, sat on the floor, and wept aloud.

He got up one morning and fried an egg for breakfast. Jean did not go to work any more, and he took up a cup of tea before leaving.

A black dawn drizzle was falling outside, rattling against the loose window frame. It was a shame to sally into it, yet he liked going to work, being absorbed all day among noise and sawdust, fitting together unending rows of doors and windows. As labour it was less monotonous because he was now head man in the department, an unofficial foreman whose position was not yet confirmed by the management because they wanted to delay his increase in wages. But it would come, though he was already paying for it by having less jocular talks with his friends than before. Still, it was a better life, even if he did take a stint on actual chipping to make sure the quota was rushed out at the end of each day.

The stairs creaked under him as he went up with the tray. The children were staying for a week with her sister, and they had slept the last few nights together in her bed. 'I'm off to work,' he said, bending to her ear.

Her white shoulders and the pink straps of her nightdress shone under the bed light, dark long hair spreading back across the pillow. She opened her eyes, and saw his thin-faced smile turned on her, an expression of uncertainty because he was never sure in what sort of mood she was going to wake up. Their faces were like the two covers of a book, and when they pressed together everything was packed between them, and nothing got out. They kissed several times, rare for a morning. 'Did you sleep well?' he asked, pouring her tea.

'Right under,' she smiled.

'You'll feel better today, then.'

She thought how good his face was, how handsome and thin, full of intelligence and feeling and everything a woman might want and be happy living with. She was tranquil and happy. 'Don't go to work.'

'I can't let a drop of rain put me off,' he smiled.

'All right. Give me another kiss before you go.'

When he went home in the evening he saw from the yard-end that the blinds were down. The gate was padlocked and bolted against him. It was dusk, and a sharp fresh wind came between the houses as if to clean out the backyards. A radio played from the lit-up house next door. He stared, as if to penetrate the bricks, fixed in his own desperate musing. In a moment the lights would mushroom and he would hear the hollow voice of the television set, and when the lock dropped away from his cold fingers he would open the back door and see her sitting there in the warmth they had created for themselves.

A man and woman passed him in complete silence, and walked into a house further down the yard. He pushed at the gate as if to split its hinges. It held firm. Then his whole weight went against the fence, wanting to smash down every foot and paling of it. He grunted and moaned, pitting black strength at it till his shoulder felt cracked and shattered. It stood straight, unbendable. Looking into the garden he saw that the rosebush had rotted and withered right to the tips of its branches, but remembered it as beautiful, petals falling, a circle of leaves and pink spots on the soil.

He went to the neighbour's house and knocked at the door. 'Where's Jean, then?' he asked when the scullery light fell over him.

'I'm sorry,' Mrs Harby said. 'Her husband fetched her in a taxi this afternoon. She left your case here. Would you like a cup of tea?'

'Was there anything else?'

'I can soon make you a cup of tea if you'd like one.'

'No thanks.'

She pulled a letter from her apron pocket. 'There was this she asked me to give you. It's a shame, that's all I can say.'

He balanced the heavy case over the crossbar of his bike. Why had she gone, in such a way and without telling him? If he had talked to her she would never have done it. They could have loved each other for ever but, having gone to the threshold of a full and tolerable life, they had shied back from it. But he didn't know. You never did know, and he wondered whether you had to live without knowing all your life, and in wondering this he had some glimmer as to why she had blown up their world and left him.

He leaned his bike against a wall, and stood the case close by. Street lamps glowed up the sloping cobbled street. Nothing had ever seemed so completely finished. The hum of the factory swamped into him, a slight relief on the pain.

He went to another lamp post, and under its light tore the unopened letter into as many pieces as he had strength for, held them above his head, gripped them tight in his fist. When his arm ached, he spread all fingers. The wind snapped the scraps of paper away, up and into the darker air beyond the lamp light, as quickly as a hundred birds vanishing before snow comes. He stood there for some time, then clenched his fist again. After a while he walked on.

Enoch's Two Letters

Enoch's parents parted in a singular way. He was eight years of age at the time.

It happened one morning after he had gone to school, so that he didn't know anything about it till coming home in the evening.

Jack Boden got up as usual at seven o'clock, and his wife, who was Enoch's mother, set a breakfast of bacon and egg before him. They never said much, and spoke even less on this particular morning, because both were solidly locked in their separate thoughts which, unknown to each other, they were at last intending to act on.

Instead of getting a bus to his foundry, Jack boarded one for the city centre. He sought out a public lavatory where, for the price of a penny, he was able to draw off his overalls, and emerge with them under his arm. They were wrapped in the brown paper which he had put into his pocket before leaving the house, a sly and unobtrusive movement as he called from the scullery: 'So long, love. See you this afternoon.'

Now wearing a reasonable suit, he walked to the railway station. There he met René, who had in her two suitcases a few of his possessions that he had fed to her during clandestine meetings over the past fortnight. Having worked in the same factory, they had, as many others who were employed there saw, 'fallen for each other'. René wasn't married, so there seemed nothing to stop her going away with him. And Jack's dull toothache of a conscience had, in the six months since knowing her, cured itself at last.

Yet they got on the train to London feeling somewhat alarmed at the step they had taken, though neither liked to say anything in case the other should think they wanted to back out. Hardly a word was spoken the whole way. René wondered what her parents would say when they saw she'd gone. Jack thought mostly about Enoch, but he knew he'd be safe enough with his mother, and that she'd bring him up right. He would send her a letter from London to explain that he had gone – in case she hadn't noticed it.

*　*　*

371

No sooner had Jack left for his normal daylight stint at the foundry than his wife, Edna, attended to Enoch. She watched him eat, standing by the mantelshelf for a good view of him during her stare. He looked up, half out of his sleep, and didn't smile back at her.

She kissed him, pushed sixpence into his pocket, and sent him up the street to school, then went upstairs to decide what things to take with her. It wasn't a hard choice, for though they had plenty of possessions, little of it was movable. So it turned out that two suitcases and a handbag held all she wanted.

There was ample time, and she went downstairs to more tea and a proper breakfast. They'd been married ten years, and for seven at least she'd had enough. The trouble with Jack was that he'd let nothing worry him. He was so trustworthy and easy-going he got on her nerves. He didn't even seem interested in other women, and the worst thing about such a man was that he hardly ever noticed when you were upset. When he did, he accused you of upsetting him.

There were so many things wrong, that now she was about to leave she couldn't bring them to mind, and this irritated her, and made her think that it had been even worse than it was, rather than the other way round. As a couple they had given up tackling any differences between them by the human method of talking. It was as if the sight of each other struck them dumb. On first meeting, a dozen years ago, they had been unable to say much – which, in their mutual attraction, they had confused with love at first sight. And nowadays they didn't try to talk to each other about the way they felt any more because neither of them thought it would do any good. Having come this far, the only thing left was to act. It wasn't that life was dull exactly, but they had nothing in common. If they had, maybe she could have put up with him, no matter how bad he was.

For a week she'd been trying to write a letter, to be posted from where she was going, but she couldn't get beyond: 'I'm leaving you for good, so stop bothering about me any more. Just look after Enoch, because I've had my bellyful and I'm off.' After re-reading it she put it back and clipped her handbag shut.

Having decided to act after years of thinking about it, she was now uncertain as to what she would do. A sister lived in Hull, so her first plan was to stay there till she found a job and a room. This was something to hang on to, and beyond it she didn't think. She'd just have to act again, and that was that. Once you started there was probably no stopping, she thought, not feeling too good about it now that the time had come.

An hour later she turned the clock to the wall, and walked out of the house for good, safe in knowing that shortly after Enoch came in from school his father would be home to feed him. They had lavished a lot of love on Enoch – she knew that – maybe too much, some of which they should have given to each other but had grown too mean and shy to.

She left the door unlocked so that he could just walk in. He was an intelligent lad, who'd be able to turn on the gas fire if he felt cold. When Mrs Mackley called from her back door to ask if she was going on her holidays, Edna laughed and said she was only off to see Jack's mother at Netherfield, to take some old rags that she needed to cut up and use for rug-clippings.

'Mam,' Enoch cried, going in by the back door. 'Mam, where's my tea?'

He'd come running down the road with a pocketful of marbles. His head in fact looked like one of the more psychedelic ones, with a pale round face, a lick of brilliant ginger hair down over his forehead, and a streak of red toffee-stain across his mouth.

Gossiping again, he thought scornfully, seeing the kitchen empty. He threw his coat, still with the sleeves twisted, over to the settee. The house did have more quiet than usual, he didn't know why. He turned the clock to face the right way, then went into the scullery and put the kettle on.

The tea wasn't like his mother made. It was too weak. But it was hot, so he put a lot of sugar in to make up for it, then sat at the table to read a comic.

It was early spring, and as soon as it began to get dark he switched the light on and went to draw the curtains. One half came over easily, but the other only part of the way, leaving a foot-wide gap of dusk, like a long, open mouth going up instead of across. This bothered him for a while, until it got dark, when he decided to ignore it and switch the television on.

From hoping to see his mother, he began to wonder where his father was. If his mother had gone to Aunt Jenny's and missed the bus home, maybe his father at the foundry had had an accident and fallen into one of the moulds – from which it was impossible to get out alive, except as a skeleton.

Jam pot, butter dish, knife, and crumbs were spread over the kitchen table when he got himself something to eat. Not that it bothered him, that his father might have been killed, because when they had left him for an hour on his own a few months ago he had wondered what he would do if they never came back. Before he'd had time to decide, though, they had opened the door to tell him to get a sandwich and be off to bed sharp, otherwise he'd be too tired to get up for school in the morning. So he knew they'd be back sooner than he expected. When Johnny Bootle's father had been killed in a lorry last year he'd envied him, but Johnny Bootle himself hadn't liked it very much.

Whether they came back or not, it was nice being in the house on his own. He was boss of it, could mash another pot of tea if he felt like it, and keep the gas fire burning as long as he liked. The telly was flickering but he didn't want to switch it off, even though heads kept rolling up and up, so that when he looked at it continually for half a minute it seemed as if they were going round in a circle. He turned to scoop a spoonful of raspberry jam from the pot, and swallow some more cold tea.

He sat in his father's chair by the fire, legs stretched across the rug, but ready to jump at the click of the outdoor latch, and be back at the table before they could get into the room. His father wouldn't like him being in his chair, unless he were sitting on his knee. All he needed was a cigarette, and though he looked on the sideboard and along the shelf there were none in sight. He had to content himself with trying to whistle in a thick manly style. Johnny Bootle had been lucky in his loss, because he'd had a sister.

If they didn't come back tonight he wouldn't go to school in the morning. They'd shout at him when they found out, but that didn't matter if they were dead. It was eight o'clock, and he wondered where they were. They ought to be back by now, and he began to regret that he'd hoped they never would be, as if God's punishment for thinking this might be that He'd never let them.

He yawned, and picked up the clock to wind it. That was what you did when you yawned after eight in the evening. If they didn't come soon he would have to go upstairs to bed, but he thought he would get some coats and sleep on the sofa down here, with the gas fire shining bright, rather than venture to his bedroom alone. They'd really gone for a night out, and that was a fact. Maybe they were late coming back because they'd gone for a divorce. When the same thing had happened to Tom Brunt it was because his mam had gone to fetch a baby, though he was taken into a neighbour's house next door before he'd been alone as long as this.

He looked along the shelf to see if he had missed a cigarette that he could put into his mouth and play at smoking with. He had good eyes and no need of glasses, that was true, because he'd been right first time. In spite of the bread and jam he still felt hungry, and went into the scullery for some cheese.

When the light went, taking the flickering telly with it, he found a torch at the back of the dresser drawer, then looked for a shilling to put in the meter. Fortunately the gas fire gave off enough pink glow for him to see the borders of the room, especially when he shone the torch beam continually around the walls as if it were a searchlight looking for enemy planes.

'It was a long wait to Tipperary' – as he had sometimes heard his father sing while drunk, but his eyes closed, with the piece of cheese still in his hands, and he hoped he would drop off before they came in so that they'd be sorry for staying out so late, and wouldn't be able to be mad at him for not having gone to bed.

He walked across the room to the coat hooks in the recess, but his mother's and father's coats had gone, as he should have known they would be, since neither of them was in. There was nothing to put over himself when he went to sleep, but he still wouldn't go upstairs for a blanket. It would be as bad as going into a wood at night. He had run across the road when a bus was coming, and seen Frankenstein once on the telly, but he wouldn't go into a wood at night, even though lying Jimmy Kemp claimed to have done so.

Pushing one corner at a time, he got the table back against the sideboard. There was an oval mirror above the mantelshelf, and he leaned both elbows on it to get as good a look at himself as he could in the wavering pink light – his round face and small ears, chin in shadow, and eyes popping forward. He distorted his mouth with two fingers, and curled a tongue hideously up to his nose to try and frighten himself away from the bigger fear of the house that was threatening him with tears.

It was hard to remember what they'd done at school today, and when he tried to imagine his father walking into the house and switching on the light it was difficult to make out his face very clearly.

375

He hated him for that, and hoped one day to kill him with an axe. Even his mother's face wasn't easy to bring back, but he didn't want to kill her. He felt his knee caps burning, being too close to the gas bars, so he stood away to let them go cool.

When he was busy rolling up the carpet in front of the fire, and being away from the mirror, his parents suddenly appeared to him properly, their faces side by side with absolute clarity, and he wished they'd come back. If they did, and asked what the bloody hell he thought he was doing rolling up the carpet, he'd say well what else do you expect me to do? I've got to use something for a blanket when I go to sleep on the settee, haven't I?

If there was one skill he was glad of, it was that he could tell the time. He'd only learned it properly six months ago, so it had come just right. You didn't have to put a shilling in the clock, so that was still ticking at least, except that it made him feel tired.

He heaved at the settee, to swivel it round in front of the fire, a feat which convinced him that one day he'd be as strong as his father — wherever he was. There was certainly no hope of the gas keeping on till the morning, so he turned it down to number two. Then he lay on the settee and pulled the carpet over him. It smelled of stone and pumice, and of soap that had gone bad.

He sniffed the cold air, and sensed there was daylight in it, though he couldn't open his eyes. Weaving his hand as far as it would go, he felt that the gas fire had gone out, meaning that the cooking stove wouldn't work. He wondered why his eyelids were stuck together, then thought of chopping up a chair to make a blaze, but the grate was blocked by the gas fire. This disappointed him, because it would have been nice to lean over it, warming himself as the bottom of the kettle got blacker and blacker till it boiled at the top.

When his eyes mysteriously opened, old Tinface the clock said it was half past seven. In any case there were no matches left to light anything. He went into the scullery to wash his face.

He had to be content with a cup of milk, and a spoon of sugar in it, with more bread and cheese. People were walking along the backyards on their way to work. If they've gone for good, he thought, I shall go to my grandma's, and I'll have to change schools because she lives at Netherfield, miles away.

His mother had given him sixpence for sweets the morning before, and he already had twopence, so he knew that this was enough to get him half fare to Netherfield.

That's all I can do, he thought, turning the clock to the wall, and wondering whether he ought to put the furniture right in case his parents came in and got mad that it was all over the place, though he hoped they wouldn't care, since they'd left him all night on his own.

Apart from not wanting to spend the sixpence his mother had given him till she came back, he was sorry at having to go to his grandma's because now he wouldn't be able to go to school and tell his mates that he'd been all night in a house on his own.

He pushed a way to the upper deck of the bus, from which height he could look down on the roofs of cars, and see level into the top seats of other buses passing them through the town. You never know, he thought, I might see 'em – going home to put a shilling each in the light and gas for me. He gave his money to the conductor.

It took a long time to get clear of traffic at Canning Circus, and he wished he'd packed up some bread and cheese before leaving the house. Men were smoking foul fags all around, and a gang of boys going to People's College made a big noise until the conductor told them to stop it or he'd put them off.

He knew the name of his grandmother's street, but not how to get there from the bus stop. A postman pointed the direction for him. Netherfield was on the edge of Nottingham, and huge black cauliflower clouds with the sun locked inside came over on the wind from Colwick Woods.

When his grandmother opened the back door he was turning the handle of the old mangle outside. She told him to stop it, and then asked in a tone of surprise what had brought him there at that time of the morning.

'Dad and mam have gone,' he said.

'Gone?' she cried, pulling him into the scullery. 'What do you mean?' He saw the big coal fire, and smelled the remains of bacon that she must have done for Tom's breakfast – the last of her sons living there. His face was distorted with pain. 'No,' she said, 'nay, you mustn't cry. Whatever's the matter for you to cry like that?'

The tea she poured was hot, strong, and sweet, and he was sorry at having cried in front of her. 'All right, now?' she said, drawing back to watch him and see if it was.

377

He nodded. 'I slept on the couch.'

'The whole night! And where can they be?'

He saw she was worried. 'They had an accident,' he told her, pouring his tea into the saucer to cool it. She fried him an egg, and gave him some bread and butter.

'Our Jack's never had an accident,' she said grimly.

'If they're dead, grandma, can I live with you?'

'Aye, you can. But they're not, so you needn't worry your little eyes.'

'They must be,' he told her, feeling certain about it.

'We'll see,' she said. 'When I've cleaned up a bit, we'll go and find out what got into 'em.' He watched her sweeping the room, then stood in the doorway as she knelt down to scrub the scullery floor, a smell of cold water and pumice when she reached the doorstep. 'I've got to keep the place spotless,' she said with a laugh, standing up, 'or your Uncle Tom would leave home. He's bound to get married one day though, and that's a fact. His three brothers did, one of 'em being your daft father.'

She held his hand back to the bus stop. If Uncle Tom does clear off it looks like she'll have me to look after. It seemed years already since he'd last seen his mother and father, and he was growing to like the adventure of it, provided they didn't stay away too long. It was rare going twice across town in one day.

It started to rain, so they stood in a shop doorway to wait for the bus. There wasn't so many people on it this time, and they sat on the bottom deck because his grandma didn't feel like climbing all them steps. 'Did you lock the door behind you?'

'I forgot.'

'Let's hope nobody goes in.'

'There was no light left,' he said. 'Nor any gas. I was cold when I woke up.'

'I'm sure you was,' she said. 'But you're a big lad now. You should have gone to a neighbour's house. They'd have given you some tea. Mrs Upton would, I'm sure. Or Mrs Mackley.'

'I kept thinking *they'd* be back any minute.'

'You always have to go to the neighbours,' she told him, when they got off the bus and walked across Ilkeston Road. Her hand had warmed up now from the pumice and cold water. 'Don't kick your feet like that.'

If it happened again, he would take her advice. He hoped it wouldn't, though next time he'd sleep in his bed and not be frightened.

378

They walked down the yard, and in by the back door. Nothing was missing, he could have told anybody that, though he didn't speak. The empty house seemed dead, and he didn't like that. He couldn't stay on his own, so followed his grandmother upstairs and into every room, half expecting her to find them in some secret place he'd never known of.

The beds were made, and wardrobe doors closed. One of the windows was open a few inches, so she slammed it shut and locked it. 'Come on down. There's nowt up here.'

She put a shilling in the gas meter, and set a kettle on the stove. 'Might as well have a cup of tea while I think this one out. A bloody big one it is, as well.'

It was the first time he'd heard her swear, but then, he'd never seen her worried, either. It made him feel better. She thought about the front room, and he followed her.

'They kept the house clean, any road up,' she said, touching the curtains and chair covers. 'That's summat to be said for 'em. But it ain't everything.'

'It ain't,' he agreed, and saw two letters lying on the mat just inside the front door. He watched her broad back as she bent to pick them up, thinking now that they were both dead for sure.

A Trip to Southwell

Alec leaned from the window of the empty compartment to fix the time by the platform clock.

Even if she ran down the stone stairs in her click-heelers shouting for him to stop he'd shrug and turn away with a slit-grin that would grip the heart painfully – knowing there was no chance of her coming whatever he felt or hoped.

At the age of seventeen, if you fall in love with a girl younger than yourself, you don't know what you're letting yourself in for. It pulled you to the middle of the earth and was hard to get out of once you were that far down. There was so much honey you got stuck like any black and orange bee. When you weren't gassed with sweetness your feet got burned.

To begin with he hadn't even known he was in love, and she was still fifteen, what's more. Things shifted under you like on the cakewalk at Goose Fair, but it had always been like that with him, and he expected it never to alter. If he hadn't lived in Nottingham he wouldn't have met her, which might have been for the best. When things went wrong what could you do except wish they hadn't happened?

Then his old man got a better-paid job managing a butcher's shop in Leicester instead of cutting up chops and joints under somebody else down Radford. But you couldn't blame him for the break-up no more than you could for getting me in the world in the first place. So they moved, and there he was as well, or would be (and for good) when the train got there in forty minutes – time enough to go back over the whole tormenting issue.

Everybody was het-up after spilling from the late-night pictures, and the distant smell of a fish-and-chip shop came through the thick and icy fog. Alec saw her standing apart from her sister and saying nothing, while noise from the rest of them clattered around the lamp post.

381

The best compliment you could make in those days was that some-body was 'quiet'. He once heard Doris Mackin say a boy named Bernard was smashing because he talked so quiet. Well, when he saw Mavis Hallam, and heard her reply to her sister who called out to come and join the gang, he thought how marvellous that her voice was soft.

Even though it was quiet he heard her say: 'I don't want to, our Helen. We'll have to be going soon, or dad'll shout at us when he sees us coming in late' – as if shouting was the worst punishment anybody could have, and that they should do anything to avoid it.

'Don't be daft,' Helen called, punching Bill Cotgrave who tried to get too much out of her: 'We aren't even courting,' she bawled at him, 'so get your scabby 'ands off of me.'

Mavis turned without answering, and sensed Alec looking at her. While he thought of what to say, in an equally low voice if he could manage it, he remembered that her softened tone was nevertheless a bit sarcastic. Though not lost on him, it didn't matter at a time when he'd give his right arm to know more about her.

Joshing and laughing the whole gang turned from the lamp post and straggled up Berridge Road. The world had divided into moving through the dark mist, and the quiet presence of Mavis who came on not far behind.

Between the two, Alec surmised that even though she lagged out of sight, and in spite of her soft voice and sarky tone, she still wanted to mill in with the rest. There was much of that in him too. Larking about bored him, and he didn't go for the dirty jokes and swinging hands (though he thought he could hold his own with both), yet he was glad to put up with it for the palliness and warmth. Bill Cotgrave and Alf Meggison worked at the same electrical firm, and with them Alec went twice a week to the youth club, completing a triangle of home, work, and leisure.

He waited for her. 'Why don't you catch up?'

'Why don't *you*?' she asked, quiet and unhurried, and close enough for him to see her smile.

'I wanted to drop back a bit and talk.'

'Talk, then.'

He tried to hold her hand, but she pulled it away.

'If that's how it is,' he said.

'I said talk, not grab. I don't know you that well.'

382

She didn't raise her voice through this, or even sound harsh, which made him want all the more to hold her. He saw it was going to be a long job, especially after this rebuff, and what he thought of as his first mistake.

He'd only seen her a couple of times, because Helen, her elder sister, didn't consider her old enough to mix with the rough and tumble she herself kept. A couple of the lads had already 'had it' with Helen, but he couldn't ever see himself getting on the same track with Mavis – though you never know how things might turn out. He felt something more than that towards her, and didn't know what it was, unable to put it down to her soft voice, which would be too easy.

'Anyway,' she said, pushing the silence away, 'I don't know whether I like people with ginger hair.'

She was the first who'd ever objected to it, which he supposed was something else that made her different. 'I've got blue eyes,' he said. 'I expect they put your back up as well. I'll dye 'em if you like. If I'm too tall for you I'll take a correspondence course in shrinking. Maybe I could even do it at night school.'

Her laugh was more an attempt at one, though he liked her for it because it showed he was on the right track. He'd never seen her properly in broad day or electric light, always in the shifting flicker of a street lamp or the dim colours outside a cinema, and he longed now, searching for the wit to make her laugh properly, to see her clearly.

He had a fair idea of what she looked like, but being unsure of himself he wondered, if he met her in the possible sunlight of tomorrow's mid-day walking along the street and wearing a different coat, whether he'd be able to tell her well enough to risk saying hello Mavis and how are you?

Going to the pictures once, on his own, he got talking to a girl inside, and before the end they were kissing as if they'd known each other six weeks. Afterwards, her mother was outside to see her home, but they'd already arranged another meeting. In the following days he forgot what she looked like, not knowing whether she was tall or short or fair or dark – or anything whatever about her appearance. It might even have been a matter of conjecture whether or not she had a wooden leg, for all he noticed.

When the time came he approached the only other girl outside the cinema, and almost got into a fight because her boyfriend who had just dropped off a bus thought he was bothering her. He went up to several girls in the next half hour, none of whom was the dated one, though he would have gone in with any who said they were. He thought he was going off his head, but told himself that life was like that. When the right girl turned up he spotted her straight away.

He would know Mavis, however, not so much from her distinct features as from a feeling of her presence that would bring instant recognition. He felt more than saw her slightly plump figure and long coat, her head held back, and short black curly hair, her small curved mouth and full cheeks, shapely ears and pale skin. She wore no make-up, as if to emphasize the fact of not mixing in. There was no taint or smell to disguise any part of her, which he supposed was due to her being only fifteen (though sixteen in a fortnight, she said) and made him think that if he got off with her he'd hear his pals yelling he was a cradle-snatcher, since he himself was already seventeen.

'I've known you long enough,' he answered, which sounded too much like a jocular complaint that one of his mates might use, and one he'd often put on with other girls. Since her voice was softly controlled he imagined she was repeating this in her mind and laughing at him, so he went on to make it worse – trying to forget what an older man at work once said: that ginger-nuts often thought people were laughing at them when they weren't. 'I'll meet you Sunday afternoon if you like, and we can go to Sunday School together.'

She missed his clumsy joke, and said: 'I've never been to such a place. In any case I wouldn't go with you. People'd know your sort a mile off – two miles, in fact.'

He felt better that she'd already gone to the trouble of putting him into a 'sort', though he realized this couldn't have been very difficult. 'What is my sort, anyway?' He managed to keep his voice as soft as hers, but only when asking questions.

'Always after the girls,' she scorned. 'Johnny Wiley told me about you.'

He wondered how Johnny Wiley had ever got close enough to tell her anything she'd listen to from a bastard like him. 'The world's full of big mouths,' he answered, gritting his teeth at being jealous so early on. 'People have dirty minds, that's all I can say.'

'He knows a thing or two, though, Johnny Wiley.'

'I'm not going out with anybody,' he told her. They walked side by side, and she didn't seem to mind. To make an impression he had to spill an interesting piece of news or gossip, as Johnny Wiley had done.

Then maybe she'd remember it, and repeat that too. It would be one sort of step forward at least. 'I went out with Doreen Buckle, but we got fed up with each other. Her old man came back early from the pub and caught us in the house alone. We was only watching the box. But he put a stop to it. You know how it is.'

'That was her excuse,' Mavis said. 'She made up lies for all I know. But she blabbed out to everybody that *she* got fed up with *you*.'

He knew he should have spun off some lurid and filthy tale about Johnny Wiley, instead of telling her about his own dull self, both to get his revenge and to make her more interested in him. But he hadn't thought to lie, because it didn't seem necessary. Even if it was he wouldn't bother. Some people were too idle to tell lies, and he felt this was true of him.

But he was narked by the accuracy of her news: 'Why do they spill it all to you?'

She didn't respond, and he thought they confided so much in her because they never imagined she'd repeat what they said – with that quiet way of hers. Or she was so young they got kicks out of shocking her. He hadn't noticed that she had that sort of face, but the idea began to intrigue him. On the other hand, maybe her soft voice brought it out of them. 'I ought to keep my trap shut,' he added, putting an arm around her.

'You can if you like,' she said, meaning it would make no difference. 'We'd better get a move on or we won't catch the others up.'

'Not that I want to.'

'I do,' she jibed, 'with you hanging round me.' But she didn't shake his arm off, nor walk more quickly when the gang in front flowed round a corner.

Meeting her towards the end of a rainy winter they went to a snack bar and ate cheese cobs with a cup of coffee.

The place was empty but for them, which made her less shy than if it'd been full. But it was the first time he'd got her so much on her own, and he could see she was uneasy about it. He wondered if that was why he liked her, for if she was nervous there was something worth getting to know, especially when she spoke softly as well. Other such girls, he'd found, were often pan-mouths, shouting and snapping all around the place, and that sort could go and jump over a high wall with glass on top as far as he was concerned.

Mavis ate her cheese cob and said nothing, and that was the trouble because being so quiet it was up to him to talk, and he'd never been very good at that, especially with girls. So trust him to fall for one that needed the lipwork from him. But he hoped she might improve one day, and that the odds would equalize.

'Cob all right, duck?'

She wiped a crumb from her mouth. 'I'm not hungry, but it tastes good. I like not eating at home for a change. They tease me summat rotten, just because I'm the youngest. I'm fed up of it.'

That's why she's quiet and hangs back. Never gets a word in edgeways because she can't stand being chaffed. 'We'll go out and have a proper dinner some-time,' he said. 'I know a nice café up Pelham Street.'

'We could do,' she smiled.

He told her about his father getting ready to move to Leicester, which meant he'd be shifting that way as well.

'When's this?' she asked.

'In a couple of months.'

'There's no castle at Leicester,' she said.

'What difference does that make?'

'Nor a river, either.'

'So what?'

'It ain't got no middle then, has it?'

'Know-all!' he laughed. 'When did you go there? I've never seen you down there.'

'That's what everybody says.'

'You don't believe everybody, do you?' he scorned.

'It's not as good as Nottingham, I'm sure.'

She took his move more seriously than necessary, as if weighing up the points of living there herself. Then he knew he was imagining things. You always did if something was too good to be true. But it frightened him a bit, so he got back to reality: 'Anybody'd think it was my fault Leicester wasn't up to much.'

Maybe it wasn't. His father had snapped up the chance to go there, not only for a better job, but because Alec's sister had got pregnant. A change of place would stop all talk about her, and get her away from the man who was still pestering her but couldn't marry her because he'd already got a wife and kids of his own.

Mavis didn't answer. Nothing was his fault; nothing was her fault.

Getting her into a café and away from the others meant he could sit opposite and take his time seeing her plain. You had to see somebody like that before you could view them in any way at all, and when you did see them clear you could tell whether there was anything there or not. It was hard to do outside because she was mostly in shadow or never still, or the others were jumping around and pulling at them to go here or there. And while kissing, they were too close to see each other.

He'd known his sister was pregnant even before his parents twigged it. A certain warmth came into her, a particular and not unpleasant smell as he passed her, plus a sudden weariness in her eyes at something like terror as she tried to subdue a good feeling she felt might gain the upper hand but ought not to.

He watched Mavis. Her lids were heavy and her eyes looked down, her lips still but always as if about to break into the smallest of sly smiles. Yet at the same time it seemed as if her face were made of stone.

It stopped raining, so they walked down Alfreton Road. He put his arm over her back and around her waist, noticing how small she was. Other girls had latched their arm about him as well at this stage, but Mavis didn't, emphasizing perhaps that with her it was no game, rather some sort of going out together that might have more seriousness in it. He realized with an inner laugh how hope latched on to nothing.

'I suppose you'll be away for good,' she said, 'when you go to Leicester.'

'I expect so. But it's a stone's throw. I went there on my bike a couple of months ago, and it only took two hours.'

She laughed in a way he didn't like, and wasn't meant to. 'You aren't going to come on your bike and see me, are you? All that way!'

'There's a train. A bike 'ud be handy if I missed the last one, though.'

'Don't worry,' she said, 'that wain't happen. It'll be funny – if you do come to see me on a bike.'

There were times when he just couldn't fathom her, when she wasn't friendly and made him wonder why she bothered to meet him in the first place. It seemed the world glittered so much for her that a bike was old-fashioned and out of place, like a horse-and-cart on a motorway.

The only test was when he tried to kiss her a few doors up from where she lived. The first time he'd got nothing out of her, but now the kiss was good and sweet, as if she'd been dreading it but liked it when it came.

She let him have most when on the back row of the Saturday-night pictures, where it was all right because nobody could see them. It was the only time she showed a bit of passion, and didn't always shift his hand when he put it under her coat and over her breasts. But the further they went together in the cinema the cooler she was when they got outside.

Now that he'd broken the ice all the lads of the gang were after her, whereas a month ago she'd been too young and remote and set apart to bother with, protected by her sister and her own quiet scorn. At the club Pete Whatton would come up behind and try to kiss her, or make a grab for her in other places. But the uproar from her sister stopped it, drowning the words that Mavis quietly spat back. If Alec was there he bumped Pete or anybody else away, threatening to blaze a red trail with them across town.

So Mavis, now desired, stood her ground among them, and knowing she was safe from all and sundry gave her face a livelier look, an expression that made the kisses for Alec more than marvellous because they were for him alone, though there wasn't always the warmth behind them that he would have liked.

They got on a bus and went up Trent Valley to Southwell. Why he took her there he didn't know. He'd never been himself, had merely seen it marked on his brother's one-inch walking map and thought it a good place to make arrangements for since it seemed to be out in the country among lots of fields.

The bus called at villages along the river, and though spring was far on by the calendar it was only just coming in fact, water at half-flood lifting the edge of its leaden grey line up towards the narrow road, a cold wind flapping from the opposite direction unable to beat it back. Darkly packed trees on the other side went right up the steep line of hills, and he wished they'd gone that way instead, where the cover seemed better.

They walked from the bus stop back to the Minster, which he felt they must look into because he'd often heard about it. He'd never bothered with churches, yet liked the look of this one, possibly because

Mavis was with him, a reason that made him feel stupid, as if threatening him with something he not only didn't understand but also disliked.

'*That's* an old gravestone,' she said, when they were in the churchyard. She took his hand. 'It's worn already, and he wasn't buried more than sixty years ago.'

'Look at this one then: he was only twenty-four. Gives me another seven years!'

'Cheerful,' she said. 'I want somebody who's going to last.'

'Don't worry about that, duck! I'll live to be a hundred.'

'All right, *duck*,' she mocked. He'd only said it in fun, but noticed how she often used his own jokes, which she pretended not to understand, just to get back at him.

He liked the Minster, pleased it wasn't a city church but one placed on its own, an island among green lawns. You could walk all round it, see every angle of its middle tower and two end pinnacles.

'Are you going in then, or aren't you?' she said with a smile, as if he needed dragging through the door.

'Can I carry you across the threshold?'

'We aren't going to live in it, dope! Anyway, you'd drop me.'

'Yes,' he said, holding the wooden door open for her, 'it's a lovely hard floor!'

They walked around the walls, a few feet apart. He saw how the sun shone through the small panes of plain windows. Other people were about, but far off down the nave. He went quietly behind and tried to kiss her.

'Stop it.' She swung away more quickly than he thought necessary. 'We're in a church.'

'It's all right. I've never been christened.'

'Leave me alone,' she hissed, buttoning her coat against the cold.

He felt stalled and irritated, though this feeling went when they strolled into the Chapter House. He reached it first, and stood by himself. He knew it was a beautiful place, the round room and arched ceiling, built so cleverly he couldn't think how and soon stopped trying to. Looking up and out of the small windows of plain glass he could see the indistinct shapes of the rest of the cathedral, clouds floating by in the light of the sky, like some magic scene which he knew was particular to the spot where he stood.

Mavis walked around the room, looking at each wooden seat specially built for the prelates of the neighbouring parishes. He read them aloud as he walked, feeling flippant now that Mavis had come into the room. He sat on a seat that had no village name: 'They must have kept this one for me!'

She was about to smile at his antic, but her expression changed to one of fury. 'Get up,' she cried.

'What?'

'Why don't you get up?'

He was puzzled at her rage. 'I like it. It fits me.'

'Somebody'll see you.'

'I've got as much right to sit in it as anybody,' he retorted.

'You're the end,' she said. 'Mocking things.'

She walked out quickly, ahead of him.

He caught her up at the door. 'I'm not serious. It was only a bit of fun.'

She smiled when they were in the sunlight. 'It's a nice church.'

Her bad mood had vanished.

'It is,' he agreed, taking her arm, and sweating inwardly because you never knew where you were with her.

They bought two Mars bars and walked into the fields. The grass was dark and rich, but cold looking.

'We went biking last year,' she said, 'and you should have seen the things that went on. It was hot, and Whitsun. We ate our stuff up Gotham Hills, and must have stayed a couple of hours. I was bored but they wouldn't come away. Everybody was in the bushes except me.'

He laughed. 'I wish I'd been there. Then we could have taken a turn. Just for a lie down. You need a bit of rest after biking out from Nottingham.'

'Our Helen had it off Johnny Wiley.'

'How do you know?'

She took the Mars bar from her pocket, peeled off the paper, and bit a third of it away. 'You could tell, that's all.' Then she wrapped up the rest and put it back for later. 'The way they crept out . . . They could hardly bike home.'

'You don't miss much, do you?' The tone of her voice hadn't indicated whether she was telling it as a hint not to do anything like that with her, or whether she was trying to work herself into letting him do as he wanted.

It was hard to say, when you weren't sure what was in the offing, so they walked without talking. He cursed himself for his silence, knowing she thought he'd taken her tale as a warning. Wanting to break it, but unable to, made him feel worse. There were things to say but his mouth was full of concrete. He'd expected this before coming on the trip, and all week he'd been storing tales in his mind to tell her, but now he'd forgotten them.

The sun came out. He took her hand and it was warm, slightly sticky from the sweets she had eaten.

'Maybe we'll go biking at Easter,' he said. 'Just the two of us. I can't stand going in a big crowd with all the others.'

'I've got an aunt at Blidworth,' she told hm. 'We could ride up there. It's not far, but it's hard in a wind. She might give us a piece of cake. She makes ever such good cake.'

'I went to Worksop last year,' he said, to prove it wasn't beyond him. 'Twenty-seven miles, each way. Coming back I got a puncture and there was still twelve miles to get home.'

He stopped talking, to find a way for them through a hedge. A twig stuck up his sleeve, and he pulled it free.

'Anyway, I thought I'd better mend it, and called at a farm to ask for a bowl of water so's I could find the bubble in the inner tube.'

'You aren't back'ards at coming forward.'

'She was a nice woman, and put one outside for me. Had an apron on and wore glasses. Even gave me a cup of tea after I'd fixed it up.'

'I expect there was a lot of sugar in it,' she said, tartly.

'Stacks. Sweet as honey.'

They stopped near the hill top, a straight line of dark wood in front. 'Nearly as sweet as you are.' When he kissed her she held herself stiffly.

'Don't you like it?' He sifted through his past life for another story to tell.

She said: 'Don't be daft' in such a way he was no wiser, but he kissed her again till she slipped aside and said they ought to get on or they'd be seen. You never knew who was chiking around.

The field was empty, and he couldn't see anything except green stubble, and sky with the odd hole of blue in it, blue flame drawing itself out and pulling more behind. It made him dizzy to look too long. It was a queer feeling, because though you felt alone in an empty field you couldn't be sure that the hedges surrounding it weren't filled with people. He disliked her mood leaping over on to him, having noticed how skilled she was at giving it a push.

There was no wind to disturb them, but she trod warily into the wood – as if afraid of snakes or toadstools. 'I don't know why you're bringing me here. There aren't any bluebells yet.'

'Are you frightened of being seen?'

'Course not.'

Her sharp denial told him that she was, yet it annoyed him that he couldn't finally be sure what unease was gripping her. 'Where *else* can we go? It's a change from the field. Would you like to live in the country?'

The path was muddy in places, and he guided her to the drier ridges. 'It's all right for an outing,' she said. 'I like pavements best.' It was green and dark, with a strong smell of soft bark and rotting ferns, soil, and hidden water. 'Let's get out of it.'

Like a good city dweller he'd noted the way in, and soon they were on the lane going downhill. There was a brook at the bottom, and it was hard getting her across. Being sarcastic and quiet of voice, and so cool towards him he thought she was the same with everyone else, she was finally physically timid when it came to distances, and brooks, and going into woods.

When he kissed her on the other side she clung to him. He was surprised and glad, and thought he was getting somewhere at last, but tried not to think of it in this way because it didn't tally with the holier feeling of love that swept in and took him over. Her body was hot through both their coats, and her kisses so firm it was difficult to get breath.

They walked towards a hedge and lay on his mackintosh in the driest part, grappling with such force they could not even kiss, clinging as if falling down through space and terrified at the impact that was coming soon.

They caught the bus from Thurgarton, and the city lights were on by the time it dragged up Carlton Hill. She sat on the inside seat, arm in his and head on his shoulder.

There was no doubt they loved each other, and though she hadn't exactly said so while they were by that hedge, he himself had murmured it a dozen times – which seemed to make up for it. He nevertheless wondered whether she hadn't held him so fiercely because such a grip would stop her getting the words out, though words, he knew, pushing his misgivings away at the expense of his better judgement, could not express everything. You had to take account, when all was said and done, of how people acted and the feelings shown that could never be mistaken.

They had lain by the hedge for a couple of hours, hands roaming at every part of each other, though they hadn't, as the gang phrase went, 'had it'. Because of this the sweet passion still lingering between them was more like real love than when he'd gone all the way with other girls.

During his half-hour walk home from a brief kiss of goodbye at the end of the street where she lived, and a promise to meet in a few days at the club, he felt a strange disheartenment gnawing underneath the incredible ebullient happiness that carried him along.

He saw her little in the next six weeks, and knew from the loud hearsay bandied about that she was going now and again with George Butler, and even that he had 'had it off her'. When more names were mentioned to her fast-maturing credit he was determined not to let grass grow under his feet. The fresh dates he made with other girls carried him further in a week than he'd got in months with her. But it wasn't the same, and he was tormented by her face, her soft voice, and dark hair.

Her smile at him was knowing and friendly, and promised less than when it had been cold and she had wanted him to do all the talking. It was true he was going to Leicester in a few weeks, but he did not see what that had to do with it, for with trains all day he could see her so often she wouldn't know the difference.

She had taken to using lipstick, and her voice had not the same pull-back into her own quiet centre. Her sister didn't come to her aid any more because there was no need to. This made little difference because she had still not become one of the loud and merry talkers, but when she hung back there was more confidence in it, almost as if she did it for a purpose. It seemed now that anybody could take her out, and this included Alec, because when he asked her to come to the café in Pelham Street she agreed.

They sat in a corner of the hushed and modern room, and Mavis said how nice a place it was, and that if ever she got married this was the sort of decoration she wanted for the front room of her house.

Her gaze was drawn by the coloured shade of the lamp whose light fixed itself on her cheeks and the soft coating of make-up she had put there. The faint smell of it drifting across reminded him of the presence of his aunts when they came for a visit as a child. It was disturbing, and he wished she hadn't taken to lipstick and powder because of this faint connection with the dimness of years gone by.

'When do you go?'

'Next week,' he said. 'But I'll come up and see you, you know that.'

'Will you?'

If she had said 'Shall you?' it would have sounded more encouraging. But she didn't, and that was that. He picked up the card: 'Let's have some soup. All right?'

She wore a white blouse with a wide collar, which made her look broader and older. 'If you like.'

'I'll be up to see you, you can bet.' He saw it was a mistake to repeat it, as if he were trying to convince himself, not her.

'When?'

'Next weekend. I've got a job already. The pay's even better than here.'

She folded her paper serviette into triangles, until she couldn't make it any smaller. 'What do they make?'

'Electrical stuff. Same as where I'm at now.'

'I wish I was going away.'

'Where would you go?'

'I don't know,' she said.

He wouldn't come at the weekend, even though she didn't draw her hand away when he reached under the table.

'I might not be in when you come,' she added. 'I might be out. I might not want to see you' – and he wondered why she went on teasing him like this.

'I love you,' he said, blind to everything. 'You know that, don't you?' He meant it, he told himself, and knew it to be more true than anything he'd ever said, which was why it would be so hard to come and see her, in case she wasn't there, as she had threatened.

She took her hand away. 'Are you sure?'

He had a feeling, and hoped he was wrong, and ended up knowing he was wrong, that she had only come out to supper with him because she was making a story from it like that sloppy sort in magazines he'd seen her with. It was something in her eyes that told him this, and the way her lips were about to move but never did when she looked at him. Her head was always slightly turned when she opened her mouth.

After a few days in Leicester he got a note saying she'd like it very much if they never saw each other again.

There wasn't an hour that she was out of his thoughts. He even dreamed about her when he'd hardly ever dreamed in his life before. He talked long hours to her, persuading her to go for a walk, get engaged, marry him, anything to end the torment and start real happiness for the rest of their lives. Happiness began in his dreams when he made love to her.

Going with other girls wasn't the same, and there was less talent to click with because he didn't feel like it. Even when there was they sensed a lack in him, or lost interest because something which griped at his heart would bode no good for them. He seemed too different, wasn't all there, and so nothing lasted. Not that he wanted it to.

A fair-looking blonde girl with a mole on her neck talked to him at work, and they started going out together. She was nice and pleasant, and open in everything she said, letting him go all the way with her providing he took the trouble to stop her getting pregnant.

He was surprised she could find much to stick with in a person like him, but he was struck most of all by what she said when they were walking back one night from the field they'd been making love in: 'I like you because you don't say much in a loud-mouthed way, like some of the chaps at our place. You talk quiet, and I like that.'

The next day was Saturday and he could stand it no longer. He got on a train for Nottingham.

He took a bus from Midland Station, and changed to another in the town centre, already feeling better at being closer to Mavis. From the top deck he looked at places where they'd walked a year ago – and might again if she felt in any small way for him as he did for her.

In the old days he'd never actually gone to her house and knocked at the door to ask if she was in. He didn't know how she'd take such brashness, but it was the only thing he could do. As he got closer he was afraid of having nothing to say when they came face to face, but she might not be at home anyway, at which he thought of several things, mostly daft and unimportant, but at least he wouldn't be rooted there like a dumb gawk.

The familiar air encouraged him, together with his heart pushing at the inside of his best suit. It would be better to go to the back door so as to cause least disturbance, and she'd get more quickly to that than the front, anyway, so that if the worst happened and she slammed it in his face it would be over quickly. It was pointless wasting time on something that harrowed you so much.

He had an impulse to run, as if the boiling surf of hell were waiting to pull him in. But his legs, more determined than they'd ever been, took him along the entry where he opened the wooden gate with its rusty latch.

His knee-joints seized up in hesitation, then got to work and took him by the coalhouse and lavatory till there was nothing he could do but get a tight hand from his pocket and knock at the door. Even then he thought of going away, until wrenched by the alarming noise of his knuckles tapping a second time on the wood. He noticed how paint was blistering on the middle panel.

It would be better if her sister Helen came to the door, and he started to rephrase his greetings just in case. It might even be one of her parents.

The door opened and Mavis stood before him, leaning towards one of the lintels.

At least it appeared to be her, and he stared a bit too hard for anybody to feel pleased at him suddenly turning up. She wore heels that made her seem taller. 'I thought I'd come to say hello,' he said, 'being in Nottingham a few days.'

She was almost fat, he saw while waiting for an answer, or a formal greeting at least. Her lips and cheeks were heavily made up, and he could smell it where he stood. Arms showed plump from the shortened sleeves of her damson-coloured sweater.

She was looking at him in the hope that he would vanish, a petulant expression on her lips as if wondering why he'd got the cheek to come knocking at her door and imagine she would go out with somebody like him.

'Do you want to come for a drink tonight?' he said.

She must have a regular boyfriend, for the look he was given could mean nothing else. Her eyes seemed to get smaller at the flush of sharp resentment on her cheeks, and he wondered in fact whether there wasn't a youth in the house at this moment with whom she had been about to make love.

He knew she still saw herself as the much-wanted dark beauty of good figure and small stature, and he twigged that because of this she thought he had no right to come pestering her. But to him she had changed so much as to be almost a different person, while she still considered herself to be worth more than him and able to do twenty times better. It was clear that she did not know how much she had altered. It made him sorry for himself, but sorrier for her, which did nothing therefore to damp down his love.

He said to himself, after another quick glance directly into her eyes, that even so, even if she was, though he couldn't be finally sure she was pregnant, he'd keep on going out with her if she was only half-way willing but nevertheless wanted to, and even marry her if she thought it might be a good way out of her trouble.

She broke her silence, and he knew she hadn't sensed anything of what was in his mind. Her world was miles away from him and his. 'I don't want to go out with you.'

He made one last try: 'Can't you?'

'No.'

She closed the door even before he reached the gate.

It gave him something to think about on his way back to the station, to brood on for months afterwards till he forgot her or, to be more truthful, remembered her only as he'd recall a dream, the final blow of it leading to the earlier time when he'd thought she was the first and last and only girl he had been in love with.

When the train was ready to leave he was certain there'd be no chance of her hurrying down the stone steps to call him back and say anything it might do him the least bit good to hear.

He opened his sandwich pack when the train began, and sat back to think about where he'd gone wrong. He considered that twenty-five miles was long enough to do it in – not yet knowing he would never lose that feeling of having loved in vain, and would hardly realize through the years that followed where the strength came from that he grew to need.

Yet a presentiment of this led him to wonder whether everything that had happened to Mavis could be blamed on him, and he decided against it when the pit that opened was too deep and black.

The Chiker

'What would you rather have to keep you warm, my little pee-thing, or a new fur coat?' Ken whispered to his girl-friend in the fertile darkness of a double entry.

'Your little pee-thing,' she giggled, which pleased him so much he gave her a fur coat as well.

The trouble was that while he was still paying for the fur coat on hire purchase his little pee-thing gave her a baby, so he had to marry her and be done with it.

If he'd been a few years older she'd have been young enough to be his daughter. He wouldn't have minded, but she wasn't even pretty, and soon looked as old as he was, which served him right for getting carried away in the first place.

He didn't like things to happen so fast. When they did he got angry and wanted to go to sleep. Perhaps that's because he had been twelve years in the army and without a trouble in the world, a time when nothing happened that was his own fault.

Even four years as a prisoner of the Japanese wasn't on his con-science, so it hadn't really happened, except that he knew it had. You could blame the bleeding generals for that. Such people were the same in civvy street or out. The managing director of the firm he worked at had a face similar to the CO of his old battalion.

Ken had fought like a mad bastard. In an attack he'd scream louder than the Japs, and couldn't forget the contemptuous look from his platoon commander as they were moving between the rubber trees. The next thing was, *he'd* snuffed it, and Ken didn't stop to pick him up or turn to see if he was only wounded.

He remembered sitting by a tree eating the last of his rations, and when a Jap stood over him with fixed bayonet what could he do but offer some? He cracked the butt on top of his head though, and took the lot, which Ken supposed he'd have done in his place anyway.

He lost half his weight and nearly died a few times. Scurvy, beri-

beri, and Mongolian footrot chased themselves in and out of his system till his face was so pitted it looked like the front of a Sheffield pikelet.

His teeth went and his hair got thin, but six months back in lovely old Nottingham and he was as right as rain. It's funny how quick you change from good to bad. Other way as well, I dare say. But he never wanted to go through that lot again, knowing there are things in a man's life he can't survive twice. You could tell by his face that he used to be an optimist.

All he had to show for nearly four years was a cigarette lighter taken from a Japanese guard when the war ended. Looting was forbidden by the British officers. It simply wasn't done. You had to leave it for them to do. But he chased the Jap into the bush and beat the living shit out of him to get that lighter. He'd been weak enough at the time, with only a fortnight's good grub in him, but with fists so full of greed and vengeance nothing could stop them.

It was a fine-looking gold-plated titbit, fit to last a lifetime. Even now it was a good igniter, wind or no wind, though he'd had it repaired a few times since.

He was thirty when he came back, and looked fifty. Now he appeared the fifty that he was, a small muscular man with short curly hair that had grown like a miracle as soon as he got home to the land of rain and fog. He worked for a firm that baled waste paper from local factories and sent it off to be repulped. He screwed the press-top as high as it would go, piled in the rammel, and pushed the button that formed it into a compact bale and laced it up with wire. Then he released it from its box, and hauled out as neat a cube as any man could who'd been so long on the job.

So because of his pee-thing twenty years ago he'd had to marry her, and if it hadn't been for his mother dying of the shock of it, or near enough in time for him to think so, they wouldn't have had a house to live in.

He'd craved for his life to settle into a long routine, but the child he married her for had died at birth. Another didn't come for three more years, a girl who was now fifteen, so buxom and sloppy he'd have to keep an eye on her, though she'd already had one boyfriend from what he had seen.

But he was no angel either, and his marriage had been on the run a few times since, when the mutton-dagger dance came at him. Standing by his press at work he thought the only solution was to have it cut off, but then he got to wondering what he'd pee with if it was.

'That's what frightens me,' he said to his mates in the pub, throwing his last dart and missing the double-seven down from three-o-one which would have wiped the floor with them in one deft stroke. 'Otherwise I'd have the bloody thing done tomorrow.'

On a warm evening in June he stood up from the hearth and told his wife not to forget to feed the canary because he was going to the pub for an hour or two.

'Don't get drunk,' she said, 'and try not to be too late. It's work tomorrow. I expect I'll be in bed by the time you get home.'

Such orders satisfied them, because even though everything was dead between them, at least they understood each other. He would be glad of some fresh air, and she to see the back of him till morning.

The collar of his white shirt was spread outside his jacket, and he smoked a cigarette contentedly. Alone and on the loose he felt at peace, as if he'd swallowed a dose of pep-pills young kids talk about.

Girls he passed on the street looked fresh and smart, jolly dollies with lovely joggletits pushing their blouses out, sights that bucked him up so much he felt like singing and not being responsible for his actions. Yet the only thing left for such a runagate as himself if he craved a bit on the side was a juiceless old dawn-plucker for thirty bob who might put the finishing touches on him. It was best to walk the streets and look at it, for all the harm it did.

Fifty if he was a day, he felt fourteen and hoped he looked it to young girls he winked at in passing – but so faintly they might have thought he'd gone a bit rheumy at the eyes and couldn't help himself. Maybe all men of his age felt young enough to be their own sons. What a shame that at fourteen he hadn't realized how they saw themselves as no older than he was then, and didn't know much more about the world.

They only tricked you into thinking they did by putting on a swank about it, wearing their age or grey hairs like the corporal his stripes in the army. Now he was in the same boat and felt as if, on his way up through the orphanage and army, marriage and factory, he'd not been allowed to grow older properly like some people he knew.

It was the best part of the year, a calm summer evening when everybody had stopped work, and time had put its brakes on so that he would live for ever. When you had that feeling what could you do but think of love and let your little pee-thing stir?

One small cloud dented the sky, but on reaching the hilltop at Canning Circus it had gone, as if sucked in by the Trent and blown out to sea. He didn't feel like going into a pub, being held from such human joshing on an evening that seemed too good to waste. Something in his chemical set-up made him already half merry to himself, but it was a faint inebriation caused through a definite lack, and not from having had too much of anything.

People sat around Slab Square, and after a leisurely patrol he went down Wheeler Gate, but not too fast, nor looking into the sky. It was the wrong side of the city to bump into any friends, which seemed a good reason for coming here, then crossing the canal and going on by the station. He thought how good it would be to meet an old flame who would suddenly turn a corner and say: 'Hey up, Kenny, how are you, my duck?' – especially if neither of them had grown a day older.

It wasn't likely. Not widow, wife, or whore with a door to knock on in the whole dead-beat district, nothing to stir the entrails of the heart in this or any other part of town during the last few years.

It was more than that he wanted. It must have been, because he couldn't think what it was. A young chap walked from the bus stop with two suitcases, into the station to take a train somewhere.

He wondered what other town he'd get to, and saw him reaching it in two hours time, a strange place whose streets he didn't know, smelling of bus fumes and dust. He'd get a room at a boarding house and sleep content in a different bed, rising early in the morning to go out and look for a job. Or maybe he had pals where he was going, or his family, or even a girl friend.

He walked faster at such questions since he had no hope of answering them, though he felt happier at speculating on the life of one man who was travelling, for it made the world bigger and more interesting, and he less alone in it. If people could still get on trains there was a chance for him yet, though he knew he would never catch one himself because he didn't need to strongly enough.

He only wanted to go where he was walking, but where that was he didn't know, except that his steps took him to a beer-off with a fading sign painted on a sheet of tin above the door saying: 'CAKES PASTRIES SWEETS AND MINERALS.' During a guarded

402

walk from the orphanage in the olden days such a placard would have made his mouth water, but now it only brought back the memory of his early times.

With a comforting chink of cupro-nickel in his pocket he went in for a packet of cigarettes. The meaty smell of ale and cooked ham reminded him that he hadn't yet supped his nightly pint, but he preferred to wait till it was dark so as to get the full benefit of leaving the shadowy street and entering the lighted guts of a pub.

It was nine o'clock and almost dusk by the time he leaned on the parapet of Trent Bridge. A streak of snake-yellow lay in the western sky, and the river glistened below as if it had a deep black sky of its own.

He'd had a short life so far, even though he'd done so much of it. It had passed him by in big chunks that now seemed no time at all. Every change had been set off by a hidden fuse. When he was three his father left his mother, so she put him into Bulwell Hall orphanage till he was fifteen because she couldn't afford to keep him. Then she brought him out so that he could go to work and earn her some money. A few years later she got into bed with him one morning saying: 'I've loved you ever since you was a baby, Kenny.' The next day he joined the army.

He didn't know why he thought of it now, though it never left him. Other knocks were too recent to be considered. Perhaps they really hadn't mattered all that much, he thought, letting his fag-end drop into the sky below.

He crossed the road and went down a lane along the river bank. A breeze shaking in from the countryside made him feel colder than he'd done all day. His eyes got used to the darkness and he noticed how the twilight was lasting. Away from the river he could make out hedges, and hummocks of grass.

A courting couple lingered by a bush, arms around each other as they moved into one shape. Ken knelt to tie the shoelace that had bothered him since leaving the bridge, his eyes level on the two people, a clump of osiers keeping him hidden. The shadow came apart and he squinted as if to bring it closer.

Satisfied that no one was nearby, the man spread his overcoat. 'What are we up to then?' Ken wondered. 'As if I didn't know!' The girl must have sat down also, for they went out of sight for another kiss.

He wanted to clear his throat, but the trundling river some way behind wasn't loud enough to hide the noise he would make. A pint of beer would ease his gullet, but he was too intent on going forward, knees bent, hands splayed as if about to fall on all fours and push himself through the grass as he had once done so skilfully in the Malayan jungle. You don't forget anything, he thought, and that's a fact, wanting to light a cigarette but having to postpone that too till later.

A rustling from close by sounded as if an animal were stirring itself before making up its mind to lumber out and get him. Over the field was a thin white moon when he lifted his head.

The man was on top of the woman, and one of her white legs showed plainly, the almost luminous flesh moving about like a dismembered part of her. They were murmuring as they made love, and he craved to hear what was being said, as much as see what was done, because he never spoke at such times, leaving it to the woman if she felt that way.

He took the lighter from his pocket, to comfort the palm of his hand with a compact and metal object that worked to perfection and asked no questions. It helped to calm him at something he hadn't done since a child when, escaping for an hour from playtime at the orphanage, he had chiked a courting couple in the woods near by.

He felt guilty at chiking, and thought he should go back before the pubs put their towels on. The only sound was one of mutual appreciation going out to the moon. They must love each other, considering how they moaned while at it. He wondered what he sounded like at home, though not being able to chike himself it was something he'd never know.

The lighter rolled in his palm. He wanted to stop it and press the top, see its flame spurt into a yellow shape and glow on the damp grass that was wetting his trousers at the knee-cap. Though it might warm his windbitten face it would give the game away.

They went on longer than him, and didn't complain at the chill. He made up his mind to pull back and go but was fixed in their act and unable to move. His eyes grew large, outweighed his body and rooted him there.

A light drizzle blew across the fields. They ended suddenly and the man stood up. Half-way to his own feet Ken felt the lighter slide from his hand.

He glanced at the couple to make sure they had finished. The man turned but, thinking he was some low bush that had grown while they were making love, or seeing nothing strange because the details of the landscape had failed to impress him while searching for a place to lie down, he turned back to ask the girl if she was all right.

Ken ran his hand through the grass to pick up his lighter. It was time to make his secret retreat. But he didn't want to go. He was happy enough to stay there for ever.

The girl was smoothing her skirt: 'We'll be late.'

Late for what? he wondered, his hand moving quickly to look for his lighter. They were kissing again, in a subdued and tender mood, and he paused in case he might miss something, then hoped they would get down a few more minutes so that he could search for his lighter without being seen.

Extending the area, he lost the exact spot where he supposed he had dropped it. Swearing, he sent his arms in wider circles, half on his feet as if for a better view of what was too dark to see anyway.

He stood up and kicked at the grass he had been lying on, longing to feel its gentle knock against his toecap.

'There's somebody there,' the girl said, in a voice of shame and alarm. 'He's been there all the time,' she wailed. 'Look!'

'Hey you, you bastard,' a gruff voice called, responding to her clear invitation to get him.

Ken would normally have squared whoever named him such a thing into a similar pulverized shape to that which came out of his press when he had given it the works. But it was raining, and who could be bothered at such a time? Having watched them at their games, he'd rather not show his face – though what could they expect but get looked at if they did it in the open?

There was a rushing of feet through the grass: 'Come 'ere, you dirty bleeding chiker.'

He felt he ought to run, but could not do a thing like that. A grip latched at his elbow, more than any man could bear who was out on a harmless walk before going into a pub for his evening pint. He swung, and caught the man a full hard blow in the stomach.

'Oh Bill!' the girl cried, as if she had felt the pain of it, and now thinking that a chiker might be more dangerous than her boyfriend seemed to.

The fact that Ken's solid fist landed where it did, when he had meant it for a higher place, showed how much taller the man was. He had time to wonder not only why he hadn't run when there was still a chance, but why he had strayed by the river at all.

He brooded afterwards. Being taller, the man had the advantage of a longer reach, apart from being half his age. He took Ken by the lapels and lammed into him, not just out of revenge for the first strike which, Ken felt as the stars spun, must have been feeble by comparison, but also because he had moral right on his side at having been disturbed in his sweet evening fuck on the grass.

Ken fell under the vicious hailstorm, and the man stood with fists poised for when he should get up. 'I'll kill you,' he said.

At the feel of wet blood and flesh on fire Ken stayed kneeling, afraid the man might actually try to. 'I was looking for my lighter,' he explained. 'I lost my lighter.'

'Tell me another, you chiker. *You chiker!*' – and he aimed a screaming kick that knocked him flat.

The girl pulled his arm: 'Leave him, Bill. He's just a rotten animal. They can't help it.'

'I ought to throw him in the river.'

'Oh shut up, and come on.'

They went away, arguing.

Things were never as bad as they seemed, though the pain told him that they almost were. He stood up when the couple were beyond sight and earshot and walked back to where he had lain. He couldn't find his lighter in a month of Sundays, nor ever recognize the man who had bashed him up. Revenge was out of the question, a desolate sensation.

He smoothed his jacket, glancing around in case the man in his poisonous rage was waiting to paste him once more. But he was alone, and dipped his handkerchief in a pool to wipe his face. Got in a fight in a pub, he said on his way to the bridge. Gave the bastard what-for. I know I'm bruised, but you should see his mangled clock. Lighter? Got my pocket picked. I'll have to get a new one. I was fed up with it, anyway.

Talking thus to his wife, or even his mates at work, he walked into the lights to get the last bus home, feeling far away from any convivial pub.

The usual lamp post didn't shine, because somebody had put its bulb out the night before, but going towards home it felt as if the scalding burn of its filament had been transferred to his own flesh. The window was in darkness, so it seemed everybody was in bed.

From the pavement the front door opened straight into the parlour, and pressing the light-switch he saw Janice lying under her boyfriend on the settee. The place stank so much it nearly pushed him back into the street.

They straightened themselves. Janice, expecting him to rant and bawl, was more frightened the longer he kept quiet. Usually so talkative, he held his face at an angle, not wanting to take in what he plainly saw, even though it only heightened the bruises on his cheeks and forehead.

'What's wrong with your face, dad?'

'I saw you,' he cried, his hand brushing her question away as if it were a troublesome fly.

'We was lying down,' said Bernard, a youth who lived a few doors along the street.

'Is that what you call it?'

'What did it look like?'

'Less o' your bloody cheek!' But he hung his jacket on the back of the door with a gesture that took the bite from his words and made Janice think it might yet be all right.

She straightened her skirt: 'I don't see what you've got to shout about.'

'It stinks like a brothel.' He turned to Bernard: 'Get out, you.'

'I was going to make him a cup of tea,' his daughter said.

Ken reached her quickly and the sound of his smack at her face bounced from the four walls right back against him. 'Pick up your pants, you filthy bitch!'

'I'm not a filthy bitch,' she wept, reaching down to the settee.

'Touch her once more, and I'll do you,' Bernard said, though plainly afraid of him.

'Get to bed,' he ordered Janice.

'I'm fifteen,' she cried out at the injustice of life, 'and I go to work. I'm fed up with this.' On seeing his hand move she rushed out of the room and up the stairs.

Bernard was sullen. 'You'd better not do that again.'

'Piss off, you.'

'She'll let me know tomorrow if you do.'

He lit a cigarette from a box of matches on the shelf. The door clicked softly as Bernard left. He'd show 'em. She was too young for it yet, even though she'd had it already. There wasn't much you could do about it if the world was to go on, but at least they could stop using his front room.

Smoke from his cigarette inflated him with a sort of warmth. The good mood he'd started the evening with came back to him, and reminded him of his lost lighter. He sat and brooded on it, and didn't like brooding because it got you nowhere. Anybody knew that, so it was best not to do it, except when you couldn't help it.

The canary woke and made merry, while Ken was black with a grieved sort of worry. It sang as if wound tight by some mysterious force that wouldn't let up no matter how late it was. A piece of his own heart had been ripped away, and he didn't like it: 'For God's sake, stop your noise.'

It might have heard, but took no notice, flitted around its circular cage and went on whistling. Birds had to sing when they were cooped up, though why did it go on without stopping? It was no good putting your hands to your ears because such noise could get through anything. Its beak pointed at him when he stood, opening and closing as if trilling a tune to the four corners of the room in turn.

'Be quiet, you bastard. Knock off.'

He smiled when it stopped, as if obeying him, but suddenly it started again, more full-throated and clogged with life than ever.

A blaze joined his eyes together, packed in with ice at the temples. He set the cage on the rug and, careful to prevent the bird escaping, opened the door and stuffed in crumpled newspaper, one piece after the other till it filled half the cage. The bird sat on top, flitting around in the small space left to continue its endless and piercing song.

He took the firescreen away. The cage fitted the grate as perfectly as his packs of waste paper slotted into the press-jig when he baled them.

Lighting another cigarette, he threw the dead match down. There was no time left. He felt neither young nor old, neither lit up nor black dead, only a cubic area of matter sitting by a cool summer fireplace that had a bird cage in it, from which a concatenating whistle chipped away the last fibres of his organism.

Face set hard with emptiness, he struck a match and held it through the bars of the cage: '*Now* stop it.'

He had a vision of smoke and flame drawn swiftly up the chimney. With a roar and rustle it would put a final stop to the singing. He dropped the match when it burned his finger.

Being alive again, he bent and opened the cage, put his hand in to get the bird again and set it free.

The firescreen fell at his attempts to grasp it, and blood flooded his head from the quick change of position. He sat exhausted in the armchair. The bird stayed where it was, in spite of the door being open, but it didn't sing any more.

A car went by, like a heavy blanket being dragged along the street. Stones weighed at his heart with so much force that it was even more difficult to say what was tormenting him. He exchanged the silence for deep sobs which rent every part of his body.

His wife came downstairs, wondering what it was, softly in case it was nothing. She stood behind the door, breathing slowly so that he shouldn't hear her through his weeping. 'That's twice he's done that in the last year,' she said to herself. 'I'd better leave him alone so's he can get over it.'

She walked slowly up to bed, needing her sleep because she had to get him to work in the morning.

Ken drew the curtains fully back and opened the window on to the street. He looked blankly at the bird and the wide open door of its cage, but it seemed as if it would never make a move.

It sat on its perch and kept quiet, waiting for him to shut it before beginning its song again.

The End of Enoch?

I was asked by the matron of a clinic where I recently had an operation whether I would ever write a sequel to 'Enoch's Two Letters', which she had read in a magazine. She wanted to know, and quite rightly, what finally happened to an eight-year-old boy who had been abandoned by his parents.

At the time I was in no position to consider her request, and now that I am I can only argue in her favour. Perhaps I should have finished the story properly at the time, but I felt then that the important thing was why he was abandoned, and not so much what took place after he was. Yet thinking about it, it seemed quite natural that Miss E——, or indeed anybody else, should want to know more about Enoch. I would also like to know, and so decided to find out for the possible benefit of all concerned.

Of course, this is a story, not a case history, and so it isn't simply a matter of writing a few letters, or going to Nottingham to read the newspaper files, or talking to the neighbours in the street where Enoch stayed with his grandmother. It's not as easy as that.

Nor is it easy to write the end of the story. Even after finishing this one I might be lucky enough to get a letter from some reader, irate or otherwise, asking what happened after that. And then after that. There is rarely an end to any story, only an arbitrary decision by the writer when he's had enough and can't think of anything else to say, or when various demons in the people of the story have temporarily run out of mischief. Or let's say he tries to stop writing when something definite has happened, when the climb down from a big event has landed the main character either in marriage, a mental home, or a state of near-contentment according to the rules and expectations of the society we live in.

The first story about Enoch happened many years ago, and I can bring you up to press (as they say) in a few more pages. Enoch's mother left the house one morning intending never to come back to the husband, and as the demon that held them apart would have it, the father left home on the same day determined not to return to his wife. Each thought that the other (whom they had had enough of, to put it succinctly) would still be there to look after the fruit of their ten-year misalliance – red-haired, round-faced Enoch – when he came home that afternoon from school.

But no one was there, and after staying the long night by himself – poor little bogger, as the neighbours said sympathetically when the story got out – he had the gumption to get on a bus and go to his grandma's house miles away across town.

When his mother reached Hull she wrote to her husband, and when his father arrived in London he dropped a line to his wife – one envelope white and the other blue (as if it made any difference) – and both were picked up by the grandmother when she went back with Enoch the following day. She took Enoch and the letters home with her, and all three items stayed unopened for years, the letters propped behind the walnut-wood biscuit barrel on the sideboard, waiting, like Enoch himself, to be claimed, or sent on when news was heard.

Many a time when Enoch was in bed and she sat by the fire waiting for her forty-year-old son Tom to come back from his surreptitious courting, she picked them up and turned them over. She saw herself opening them, heard the sound of crinkling paper as she unfolded it, to see if any address was inside so that maybe she could put Enoch back in touch with his parents. But a letter was a letter, and neither one was addressed to her. They had stamps on that had been bought with money, and she had no right to touch or read anything that was inside. All she could do was wait until they came back – one or the other of them – so that she could hand them over, together with a piece of her mind, which meant the biggest bloody rollicking they'd ever had in their selfish and unthinking lives.

Whatever they'd done they'd done it for good though, or so it appeared, which was something she helped to make sure of by selling off their furniture and telling the agents that they'd left the house. When she walked past it a few weeks later it was already filled with another family. What bit of money she got for the furniture and belongings bought a secondhand telly and a few clothes for Enoch – at one canny blow providing for his physical and spiritual wellbeing.

She told the Child Welfare when they nosed around that Enoch's parents had farmed him on her 'by prior arrangement'. That was Tom's phrase, and she added, as if only by afterthought, that she hadn't heard from them since they left more than six months ago.

'No,' she repeated firmly, 'I ain't heard a dicky-bird in all that while.' Unwilling to mix things up too much, she did not mention that they had heard from each other, or at least that some attempt had been made at it.

The Child Welfare Officer was no more than a girl, who from her face didn't seem to know much about the world as yet, though no doubt she did on paper. Still, she was given a cup of tea and a chair to sit on. As a result of the visit a few forms drifted through Grandma's life, but seeing that Enoch was obviously well looked after they were happy to let him stay there.

It took Enoch a long time to get used to living at his grandmother's. He'd often been there visiting with his mother, and always liked the trip across town and the fuss his grandmother made, but actually staying for good in the house was strange to him. It was somewhat quieter than if he'd been living with his parents still, and rare enough because nobody ever seemed to quarrel. For this reason time went more slowly and in a dreamier way.

But though the process was a lot softened by his going to a new school, he was all the time looking forward to living at his grandmother's properly, so that it would become like being with his mother. Even after a year such a state seemed a long time coming. He thought that if it hadn't been for Uncle Tom taking him fishing or to the pictures now and again it wouldn't have looked like coming at all.

By the time he'd forgotten about expecting his life to be normal, he stopped thinking about it, so that it more or less became so, except that at certain times of the year it seemed still as if there was something missing.

Tom was like a lighthouse with his guiding principles and care. He had a fad about memory training, and 'cultivating the powers of observation'. He sat by the fire facing Enoch, who was looking hard at him. Tom took several objects out of his pockets – a few coins, a penknife, a watch, a pencil, a cigarette lighter – and put them into a handkerchief without saying a word but making sure that Enoch's big eyes were on every move. Then, at the same time next day, he asked Enoch to write on a piece of paper all that he'd seen go into the handkerchief the evening before. The idea was, he explained, to find out whether he'd observed correctly, and remembered. Enoch passed often and too easily, so Tom gave it up, though he went on inventing other games and wit-tests.

A long time went by until Enoch was ten. One day he wondered sharply to himself when his mother was coming back, and piped up to his grandmother: 'Where do you think my mam is?'

She looked at him hard and a bit long, as if he'd said a dirty word, or farted at Sunday dinner. Then she smiled, and pushed her glasses back up her nose: 'She's gone off with a black man, for all I know. Get over there while I lay the table.'

'What shall I do, then?' he asked.

She opened the knife-and-fork drawer, and put her hands in without looking: 'You're all right here, aren't you? You're as right as rain, with me and Tom.'

'I know I am,' he said, thinking that was that. There were bushes in the back garden, and a lilac tree, more growing green than there'd been in the house down Radford.

In spring he wondered the same questions as he sat at the table for dinner. Outside, it was sun one minute and snow the next, the greenery either black, or dazzling its way back to emerald. It was the worst spring for a long time, the worst this year, any road up. Only the birds were doing well out of it, having gorged the breakfast scraps. One was so fat that when it swallowed a piece of bread it waddled away like a duck. It just got to a bush before it fell over.

She went out for an hour on business of her own and it seemed as if she'd been gone for years, and that it would take years getting to know her again when she came back. Whenever she walked out of the house, especially in summer, he thought she had gone for ever, and wondered who he'd move on to now.

At times of black frost it was a different matter. You knew how things stood, and could sit by the fire eating bread and best butter. But this time he didn't feel so good because he'd got the hot flushes. Even the television made his head ache, and when his grandma thought as much she switched it off and sat dozing opposite. He not only wondered why his mother had gone, but what he'd done with her. He must have done something with her if she'd gone, and she must have gone because he hadn't seen her for such a long time.

The fact that he'd sold her to a circus played on his mind whenever he thought about it. When the big tall man with a top hat and whip had come to fetch her Enoch had taken the four pounds ten that had been pushed into his hand and gone off to spend it on sweets.

His mother must be roaring in a cage somewhere, though he supposed she'd grown to like it by now, since she didn't think to escape and come back. Maybe she'd even married a lion, you never knew. Anything like that could happen. But he was the one who sold her to a circus, so it was all his fault that she wasn't here no more.

When the man gave him the money he'd winked at him, and squeezed his fingers so hard that his ear began to itch. He remembered it plainly, almost as plain as a dream. And when he scratched his ear to stop it itching, he got the hiccups, and he hiccuped while his mother was being taken out to join the circus he'd wickedly sold her to, and the hiccups didn't properly stop till he stuffed the first sweets into his mouth while still standing in the shop. You had to get something for doing a thing like that to your mother. He hoped she'd done well at the circus, otherwise the man might turn up and snarl for his money back, saying she was no good to them. If she came back as well he'd have to sell her to another one, to get more sweets.

'You look as if you're ready for a talk with the chimney-sweep,' his grandmother would say to him, after a supper of cocoa and bread-and-cheese, meaning that he should go to bed and get some sleep.

In summer-time he rarely thought about his mother. His grandma asked him to carry a chair into the garden, on a sunny day when it was warm and humid, so that she could sit there and read the paper. When she got tired of that she went into the house for the scissors, then sat on the chair cutting her toe-nails, while he stayed inside feeling shy about it and doing his homework.

He thought that if she went on cutting her toe-nails like that in the garden, with the hard bits flying all over the grass, maybe a tree would grow in a few years' time. What sort of tree though was beyond him to say. But he knew that any sort of tree would be a miracle.

Three years after his mother left, she came back. The time had been very short to her, so little had happened in it. When Enoch grew up and looked back it seemed a very short time to him as well, until he began to think about it, when it became longer and longer, almost as long as it had been at the time.

He only thought properly about it after his grandmother had died.

His own mother is still alive, because she married another man and Enoch, who didn't care one way or the other because he spent much time at his grandma's till she died, grew up and got to university, and never regretted the burning fact that he had started it all off by selling his mother to a circus. In any case, she must have had a good time in it, though it hadn't stopped her growing old, nor, at last, coming back to search him out and say nothing at all when she looked at him about what he'd done to her.

His father also came back to Nottingham, and lived with his fancy woman. Enoch saw him from time to time with his other new kids, and was occasionally taken for a treat up Colwick, and even sent something at Christmas and birthdays, though Enoch never forgave him, not until he grew up and realized that nothing that anybody did was their fault, since you were always liable to do the same yourself.

The two letters that his grandmother had saved finally got to where they should have gone a long time ago, but didn't make much difference to Enoch. He saw his mother tear up the one to her from his father into little pieces after hardly reading it. And what his father did with hers he never knew, and forgot to even wonder about.

Enoch only knew that when nothing was happening, everything was happening. The action was only mime. He knew as well that by doing nothing we all connive in our own disasters. One letter would have been enough, if it had been addressed to him – who alone knew what had caused the whole thing.

Scenes from
the Life of Margaret

The budgerigar greeted her as she came in and laid her basket down. The kids ate at school but she needed a meal herself, so took off her coat and lit the gas. Rain swept over fences and clattered against the window as if spring would never cease, she thought, hoping one day for sunshine.

A year ago the bird had got out of his cage and flown into the fire, and though Michael was there to dart in a hand and pull him free, the smell of singed feathers and burned skin was everywhere, and the poor bird lay for days doctored on warm milk and coddled in clean handkerchiefs. Bit by bit it came to life, its warm breast throbbing with song after song, and half-speech imitations that she and the kids had taught him before the accident.

His feathers had grown back in places, vivid emerald and blue, with a patch of white over the left eye. She'd never expected it to live, and found it surprising what fire and grief and God knew what else such a creature could survive. It didn't seem much to do with its own will whether it got back to life or not, but something else which neither of them knew about.

Such reminiscing reminded her of her father's death the year before, and she wondered whether it had been any worse to him than the fire the bird flew into. She'd been afraid to walk into the other ground-floor room and see him, though he was beyond all help and wouldn't have known her. She was too proud of him to see him die, and didn't want to witness what he might in after-life (if there was such a thing, but you never knew) feel ashamed that she had seen.

She mashed some tea, then ate bread and cheese. It was strange how lonely you could be with three strong kids, for they went out hand in hand after breakfast, and didn't roar in again till tea-time. The budgerigar woke from its perch of sleep near the window and sent a trill of stone-chipping notes through its wire cage.

She put in a hand and held the warm soft-feathered body, now singing out its second life as if nothing terrible had ever happened to it. Michael, who was eight at the time, willed it to get through the tunnel of that suffering, while she had given it up. Only the children's tears had brought her faith that it might choose to live after all.

When she opened the cage it darted like a blue pebble over the settee and settled near the front window. For a while they hadn't let it out when the fire was lit. Not that it would have gone there anyway, but it had become too precious for such rash chances. Nowadays it was safer because the chimney was closed, and a less harmful mock-electric fire fitted in the grate.

Carefully closing the door she walked down the path to meet the baker's van. The grey house-roofs were drying, and the freshening air reminded her how some neighbours even grumbled because the estate wasn't so black and cosy as the slum they'd not long left.

One of the eight kids who lived across the road came to buy two loaves. The baker held one hand out to get the money, and the other with the bread, but the child didn't have money to give so he put the bread back.

'I suppose his dad sent him out to try it on,' Margaret laughed, collecting her own loaves.

When he was ready to drive off the kid came again, this time with coins, so that he got the bread. Then three other kids ran from the same house to buy cakes with equally ready cash.

'You'd be surprised at some of the antics people get up to,' the roundsman said, 'just to save a couple o' bob.'

Being on National Assistance and her husband's allowance, money was short for her as well, but they still weren't as bad off as in the old days because she had a council house for one thing, and for another the rest of the family helped her along. Her mother worked at a food warehouse and brought a load of purloined groceries up on the bus every weekend. Her sister was in a shoe factory, so they never had wet feet. Her brother served at a clothing shop and rigged them out when he could. Another was a radio mechanic, so she had a reject telly in the living room. A cousin who helped in a butcher's shop did his best not to forget her.

Now and then she could swap shoes and food and clothes with somebody in the next avenue who worked at a toy depot, or she'd barter with the woman next door who packed up pots and pans for a mail order firm. Her aunt was an overlooker at a tobacco factory and Margaret, not smoking herself, was able to give pilfered fags to a man who dug her garden and occasionally whitewashed the kitchen. What was life worth if you couldn't help each other? The bird flew back to the top of its cage and whistled its agreement from there.

A radio voice talked about a leper colony in Africa, so she switched it to light music. A blue stream of soap powder spun into boiling water and she stirred at the bubbles with a huge wooden spoon that Edie across the way had brought her as a present from Majorca: 'You can use it to bash the kids with when they chelp you,' she laughed.

'Not mine, duck,' Margaret said, standing by the hole in the fence that connected the two houses. 'They do as I tell 'em without that. My kids have to be good, not having any dad. Sometimes I tell myself he don't know the joy he's missing.'

Fifty bright round faces shifted among the bubbles, rainbows breaking in the stream. 'They'll see you right,' Edie said, 'when they go to work. You'll have your joy of 'em yet.'

'They'll get married then, duck,' Margaret prophesied soberly. 'I'll find another man, maybe, when I've got 'em off my hands.'

'I shouldn't wait too long if I was you,' Edie said. 'You're still young. Get a bit of it back up you before you're too old to feel it.'

It made Margaret laugh just to look at her sallow and serious face with its glasses and long false teeth to match, every second waiting for her to say something foul and funny. She didn't know how Edie's husband put up with it yet he seemed to like her well enough.

'I can do without that for a while,' Margaret told her. 'I keep myself company in bed at night, I do' – which sent Edie cackling back to her kitchen. It was good to laugh, even if it did show a bad tooth or two. The only chance she got was when they showed old silent comedies on the telly, which she'd look at all night if they were on.

She thought maybe Edie was right, because if somebody was found it wouldn't do to turn him down. Life was too short, but the trouble with men was that they're just like women, she reflected, no better and no worse. And who'd want to take anybody on who's got three kids already? It'd be a rope around his neck right enough, though she'd heard people say there were men who didn't want the bother of a woman having babies, and would rather step into a brood of kids ready-made or half grown up.

419

But if that was the case where did the woman come in? Maybe he treated her as one of the kids, a pat on the head now and again for good measure. It was surprising what you might end up doing for the kids' sake, if you didn't watch yourself, though if mine don't have a father it's no more than a lot of others have to put up with. Still, it does touch my heart when I ask in the tally-man or window-cleaner for a cup of tea and see them jumping all over his legs.

Men aren't the be-all and end-all of my life, she thought, taking the long prop and wedging the line high, all signals hoisted. Pants, vests, stockings, and socks straightened and flapped in the uprising wind. The less you want something the more likely it is to take place, and the more you picture it, the less chance of it becoming real. What you never imagined were the bad things that hit you, and what you always thought of were the good things that never did.

She had got over her husband leaving her. She had been too shattered and upset by it not to survive.

The sallow catkins were full of yellow dust. It was good to go up the Grove for an afternoon walk, smell the spring water of the Trent flooding by down the steep bank. There was nothing else to do but laugh, except cry, she smiled.

With three kids to be fed and looked after there'd been no time to brood herself into the grave or Mapperley Asylum. There was some justice in the world, though you only thought so when it kicked you in the chops, or hoped so when it was about to. In his rough and cunning fashion he'd made certain she'd never be able to take up with anyone else, though maybe in one sense it was generous of him to leave her the kids, otherwise she might not have got over it.

He and his 'fancy woman' had prospered after opening a corner shop to sell new and second-hand bicycles. He bought old ones at scrap prices and tarted them up in his clever way, while *she* looked after the book-keeping and window-dressing. Margaret met his mother one day in Slab Square, and was told all about it.

It didn't even hurt any more to brood on it, though a man who could forget his children so absolutely must be a real blackguard. He might stop living with his wife, but if he went on loving his kids she could at least console herself that some of this contained a bit of hidden regard for her as well. He never saw them or wrote, nor sent Christmas presents, but had rubbed them out of his life. She sat on a broken elm trunk to rest, wondering how she of all people had ever met such a man.

She thought of the man who courted her before him, as if that might give some clue to it. The war had been on for a long time, though everyone knew it was coming towards its end. Margaret was sixteen, and after two years working in a food factory she joined the Women's Land Army so as to get away from home and 'see life'. All she saw were bulls' heads and pigs' arses, glowering woods and wet fields, and a poky room in a mildewed and leaking cottage which she shared with six other girls, a muddy and sweating life which paid thirty bob a week and a rough sort of keep.

She began to feel like a slave-labouring appendage to the animals, till one of the farmer's men taught her to drive a tractor. She learned quickly and got a licence, but because things were now so much better she was able to look back on how bad they had been, and in a fit of anger that she should have been so much put upon, packed her things one Saturday and walked to the village bus stop. Reaching Nottingham in two hours, she left her case at home and went down Slab Square to see which of her girl friends were in any of the pubs.

After the cold black-out night, bruised by huddled gangs of soldiers, the Eight Bells was like a secret cave cut into the hillside of the street-cliff.

She bought a shandy and, every seat being taken, stood near the bar. An American soldier put his hand on the arm of a girl near by, who shrugged it away:

'Get your hands off me, Yank!'

'Sorry, sister.'

'I'm not your sister.'

'All right, baby.'

'I'm not your bloody baby, either. If you don't lay off I'll part your hair with this pint jar.'

Margaret knew the voice, and saw the face. Smoke and beer-smells, breath and pungent boot-dust exhilarated her. The backs and faces set colourfully along each line of mirrors after two years in the rural dullness heightened the flush in her face and made her stretched limbs tingle.

She laughed at the raucous rat-crack of the protesting voice, knowing it to come from one of her cousins. 'That's right,' she called over. 'You tell him, Eileen.'

The snow-white hair of a suicide-blonde flashed around: 'Hey up, Margaret!'

'I could tell you a mile off,' she said.

'What are yo' doin' 'ere? Up to no good, like me?'

She wished she hadn't spoken, for Eileen's reputation, even in her own family, was almost as low as you could get, her back-chat to the American being only another form of come-on, so that she smiled at him before edging over to Margaret: 'I had a nobble on an hour ago,' she said, apologizing for her lack of success so far, 'but the poor bogger went out to be sick and I ain't seen 'im since. When did you get back from the cow sheds?'

'An hour ago.'

'I'd pack it in, if I was yo'.'

'I did do.'

'About time.' Eileen's thin face stood out from the robust puffiness of the soldiers around. 'I don't blame you. Come and do a stint at the gun factory. You'll never look back. Too much going on up front!'

Margaret's laugh attracted someone she could not see during her talk about old times with Eileen. He told her afterwards how that vital and homely sound had gone right into his heart at a time when he met so much falsity night after night – whether he stayed in camp or not, which he usually did in order to write long letters to his parents back home.

And looking towards her laugh he'd seen someone who hadn't been there before, noting her long dark hair and the pink skin of her plump face. Every young girl was pretty, he admitted, especially if you'd parachuted in with the first wave of the invasion and had the total support of your friends scythed away in a few insane minutes, but *her* face was different, had a refined trust that, after her laugh, and while she was listening to her blonde friend, had a kind of profound and gentle helplessness. It was as if she'd come into the pub, he said, to wait for him as he had been waiting for her ever since getting to England.

He pushed his fresh yet strangely troubled face between Margaret and her cousin, buying a round for them just before closing time. She could not, even now, gainsay the fact that she was the reason for the drinks. Jimmy Chadburn seemed honest and fair of feature, except for the knife-scar caught in some tussle with a German during the Normandy landings which had closed the left side of his face up a bit.

But the right and best side was turned to her, and his inside soul seemed generous enough.

He treated her courteously, and always with a smile, dusted the chair before she sat down, opened the door and prevented her from being jostled as they went out. His teeth were so clean when he smiled that she might have known she couldn't trust him. And it was difficult to tell whether he was lonely or not – as one ought to be able to do with Americans who had so much money.

Large white single clouds passed swiftly through the sky, crossing the broad avenue of trees. She had sat down too long and the damp was pressing in. Tea-time would come and the kids would be home. There was no way or wish to stop the wheel turning day after day and week after week. But she dwelt a little longer on Jimmy Chadburn. He was her first love, yet she'd heard it said that whenever you start thinking of your first love you are about to meet somebody else. Well, she could wait, especially when it was a question of having to.

She kept no mementoes in life, except memory. All letters and photos were burned, and nothing of him remained. He had gone back to the wife he said he didn't have, and left her to nurse herself through the scorching deserts of betrayal and smashed love. How could anyone do such a thing to anyone else?

She supposed it was something all people had to put up with at one time or another. It was hard to think of anybody who hadn't. It was like a vaccination to stop smallpox eating you into a cancer.

The worst thing about being jilted was in the man you took up with afterwards. You acted joyfully because you thought it was all over, not knowing that this was the final bitter kick of it. She saw how true it was now, even though she kept herself free for two years, because it took that long to get over it, which seemed like no time at all when looking back.

It was good to get the ache out of her legs. She broke off a new and living bud, shredded its stickiness with a sharp fingernail, and could hardly remember where she'd met her husband, something that doesn't speak well for any man, almost proving you were never in love with him. Meeting Albert was probably the last flicker indeed of love for Jimmy Chadburn. Some people don't believe in love, which only means they'd never suffered from it. Yet if they hadn't she supposed they were lucky.

She reflected how Albert loved to make her cry, did everything to do so. It was never difficult, but he couldn't stand it when he succeeded, so jeered to make her stop. Walking down the street she slipped on a piece of rotten pavement, and he hit her, adding insult to injury in his usual way. He used to say all's fair in love and war, but she remembered that life itself was war to him, a war to get exactly what he wanted for himself. You had to be careful not to get in the way of what he wanted.

Asking herself what she'd done wrong to make him like this, it became obvious that she was only guilty of having married him – though by then it was too late. In any case he had an equal share of responsibility in having married her. No one could deny it. But to please him she'd have to go out one day and vanish, so that he wouldn't even have the bother of a funeral, though she didn't see why she should be the one to do it and make things easy for him.

After three years and three kids he left her, as she told Edie, 'without even a piece of bread between my lips'. That was the end of that, and as for mementoes, she'd burned even the memories inside herself, stamped on them whenever they threatened to come up, till they hardly ever did any more.

Roy John Callender was an exhibition diver and champion swimmer, whose name was occasionally seen in the more obscure columns of Nottingham newspapers. Though his exhibitions weren't so enthralling, nor his championships so spectacular, he was considered a man of fair showmanship and prowess in local terms, and all who had seen him dive agreed, over their sedentary drink of beer, that at thirty he was in his prime.

'When you cut into the water like a javelin,' he said to Margaret one night in the Maid of Trent, 'and go right down, you think you're dying because it don't seem possible you'll ever get up to fresh air and see daylight again. But you do. Dead right, you do. You don't want to move your arms, like they're tied up with ten balls of string, but they move by themselves and steer you level. Then they push you up, and when your head shoots out of the water you want to go up and up till you crack your noddle on the clouds.'

'Why do you do it, though?' she asked naïvely, even after this description which he had perfected over the years, and which half the people in the pub turned round to listen to.

He laughed fit to die, she thought, and told her when he could get his breath from it: 'I just like the water, I suppose!'

Several times in his career he had dived off Trent Bridge into a canvas area below. Dressed in a one-piece black costume he climbed on to the parapet and, after mock-gymnastics to loosen his limbs in the sharp summer breeze, he faced the chosen crowd with both hands clasped in the air. His stern expression, at the point of turning to begin his dive, changed to a grin of expected success.

Motorists leaned out of their car windows, and lorry drivers waved and wished him luck above the noise of their engines. The black and pink figure framed against the white sky of the distant war memorial turned a somersault above the bridge wall – then fell through the air towards the canvas area of bottle-green water.

He loved doing it, he told Margaret in the pub, because when he made that first great leap he thought he hadn't strength to do it properly, that he would smash himself against the dark stone of the bridge. But he managed it, and the feeling of dropping down so effortlessly and with such spot-on aim was the best in the world, except the sweet dreams that came after going to bed with a woman he loved – he winked.

She suspected him of piling it on a bit. But then, all men did that. He certainly looked a liar as he swaggered in and walked to the bar for his first drink of the evening. Tall and well built, he had a sharp pink face and dark hair receding in a vee back from his forehead.

He was no empty loud-mouth however, for he had done all he told her about, and spoke sincerely enough, though when Margaret questioned Edie as to whether or not she had ever heard of a champion swimmer called Johnny Callender Edie said she hadn't, but that that didn't mean much because she'd never heard of anything, anyway. So Margaret let the promise of him drop, her notion being reinforced that men were bigger bragging liars when they had something to brag about than when they hadn't. It was better to expect nothing so as not to be disappointed.

One afternoon a dark green van drew to the kerb outside the front gate and Callender himself came up the path with a television set in his arms. She met him at the door, flustered and laughing. 'Did you get that from under the water on one of your dives?'

He set it on the kitchen table, loosened his white scarf and unbuttoned his dark three-quarter overcoat. 'It's for you, missis. Or can I call you Margaret?'

'If you've brought that for me, you can. Shall I mash you a cup of tea?'

'It'll tek the sweat off me.'

'Sit down, then. What sort is it?' She dropped the kettle-lid, and bent to pick it up.

'A good one, don't worry. Brand new.'

'I'll bet it is.'

'No damaged goods where I come from,' he grinned, 'except me, perhaps.'

'You don't want to say that about yourself,' she said, with such seriousness and concern for the safety of his good name that he laughed out loud.

'What's bleddy funny about it, then?' she demanded, cut to the middle. She didn't like being made fun of just because she'd thought his phrase weightier than he could ever have done. 'If that's the way it is you can take your rammel and get out.'

'You don't think I mean it when I run myself down, do you?' he said, tears almost lighting up his deep brown eyes. 'Oh dear, love, when were you born?'

Having been out of circulation for the last nine years there was no telling when she was born, she told him. 'Though it might not have been all that long after you,' she added, 'so don't think yourself so smart.'

The tea-cosy was on the pot for five minutes till it mashed into a mellow brew, but then she poured it sharply as if to get rid of him as soon as possible. The bird warbled from its cage, and he promised next time to bring a budgie because it sounded as if it wanted a mate as well – helping himself to several spoons of sugar. He takes a lot of sweetening, she thought, and maybe he needs stirring up as well, or perhaps I do, though he's not the one to do it, swimmer or not.

'Boy or girl?' he asked, looking up, smile gone.

'Male,' she said, 'and it sings like a man as well. Men allus sing better than women, especially when they want summat. All a woman need do is bide her time. Then what she gets is twice as bad, I suppose.'

He sipped his tea as if she might have put a dash of ground glass in it. 'You sound proper old-fashioned.'

'That's nowt to what I *feel*.'

'Why don't you have a cup of tea as well, duck?' he said. 'I'm feeling a bit left out.'

'I was going to,' she said, beginning to like him again.

'Thought I'd get company after what I'd brought,' he reminded her.

It looked so much better than the cronky old set her brother had palmed her off with. 'Are you leaving it?'

'On approval. Depends whether you take to it.'

'Would you like some biscuits?'

'If there's cream in 'em.'

'I can tell you've been at tea with millionaires. It's plain biscuits at this house. If I got cream biscuits they'd go in a second.'

'Kids are like that,' he said, and she wondered if he'd got any of his own.

'Are you going to plug it in for me?'

He dipped a biscuit in his tea, and held it there too long so that most of it fell off. 'If I leave it, I'll have to.'

'It looks like it, don't it?'

The scalding tea went down his throat in one long gulp. 'Let's see to it, then.' He clattered the cup back to its saucer, and they went into the living room together.

He didn't move in, which she thought he might try in his brash fashion, but came to see her once or twice a week, and slept there. He was lavish in presents for the kids, though she saw as plain as day he didn't really like them, and that his generosity didn't come natural to him. He was uneasy under the weight of the kids when in their open good nature they clambered up as if to suck him dry. When Rachel wanted a bedtime story he almost snapped at the second asking. Margaret began to suspect he was married and had kids of his own, but when she tackled him about it he told her he was divorced.

'Why did you tell me you was single, then?'

They sat in a corner of the pub on Saturday night, and in spite of the noise that encapsulated them she almost hissed her question. He looked at her openly, as if proud of what he had done. 'I thought so much of you I didn't want you to think I was secondhand.'

She felt herself blushing. 'I'm the one who's secondhand, so I don't know what you've got to worry about.'

'That's different,' he said. 'I'm the one that's in love with you. If it was the other way round I wouldn't bother so much.'

'I don't know what to think.' She was bewildered at his calculated lies because she did not know how to let on she knew he was lying. His face deepened into seriousness, as if to disarm her even more, until she began to believe in him to such an extent that she wondered whether he wasn't about to ask her to marry him. He suddenly broke this intense silence by laughing out loud and calling the waiter to bring another pint for himself and a short for her.

Her disappointment at this breakage of their closeness increased even more because she did not know which of them was the cause of it. Another opportunity might not come around for weeks, and she didn't feel sure enough of herself to get it back on her own.

His face was such as held its own with the world, so you'd do well to look out for it putting one over on you, she thought, because like all men he treated you as part of the world as well. His face was a hard one, in spite of the gloss that came on it when he wanted something, yet she felt there was a soft centre somewhere – like in the tastiest chocolates.

She prayed for this to be true, because after they'd known each other a few months it was certain beyond all truth she was pregnant.

There was nobody she could spill it to but Edie. Her instinct told her that to let him know the news would drive him away clean and clear, which she didn't want to do, for though she'd started off being wary she now liked him enough to want him with her for good, if only he'd ever grow up and set his selfish mind to it.

The last thing she expected was to bring another kid into the world, but since one was indisputably on its way and might prove impossible to stop she ought to try and get used to the idea – not doubting for a moment that he'd help her all he could, and maybe actually marry her if nothing worked.

There was no point thinking yourself into a black sweat, so she went into the kitchen and put the kettle on for coffee. If she confided her trouble to Edie she might be able to tell her how and where to get rid of it. Certainly, she knew nobody else who would. She fancied there wasn't much Edie didn't know about a thing like that, though having an abortion had never been much in Margaret's mind when she got pregnant. But this time it was different, and nobody could tell her what to do with her own life and body. Three were enough kids in one woman's life, especially now they were getting on and the worst might soon be over.

When Edie pulled the chair from under the table to sit on, and sighed as if she had all the work in the world to do in the small space of her own house, and should never have left it for a moment, it was obvious she had something to tell Margaret, who therefore thought it friendly and polite to let her get it off her chest before coming out with her own worries. In any case, she welcomed a reason to defer it as long as possible.

'How many?' she said, reaching for the bag of sugar. 'What bleddy weather, in't it?'

'Four, Meg,' said Edie. 'Enough to turn you into a fish. Have you seen owt o' that chap o' yours lately?'

'He showed his face a week ago,' said Margaret, thinking it funny that Edie should mention him when he was on the tip of her own tongue.

'Is he married?'

Margaret thought it an outlandish question, and wondered what was coming.

'I hope you don't mind me asking,' said Edie.

'That's all right, duck. He ain't as far as I know.'

'I saw him in town yesterday, as large as life, with a woman and two kids trailing out of one o' them cheap clothes shops down Hockley. I'm not sure they was his kids, though it looked like it to me. I don't want to be nosy, but I thought you might like to know. The woman looked so miserable she must a bin his wife.'

She stirred Edie's coffee and pushed it towards her, thinking yes it was his sister because he'd mentioned her a few times, till another explanation came to her and she realized she was only making excuses for him. There could be no doubt he was married, because it fitted in with his actions ever since she'd known him. 'Thanks for telling me,' she said, drinking coffee to stop her lips trembling. 'I might have known.'

'They're all the same,' Edie said. 'It don't matter that much.'

'No,' Margaret said, 'it bleddy-well don't, I suppose. It ain't that I mind about him being married. But he might have told me. I hate sly and deceitful people. I expect he was frightened I wouldn't want him if he said he was married.'

'It's no use crying over it, duck,' said Edie, trying to comfort her, and cursing herself for a big-mouth when it suddenly came to her how things stood. 'We bloody women get all the bother, and the men go scot-free.'

Margaret's face was dry and stony: 'Nobody goes scot-free in the end.'

And she didn't ask Edie how to get rid of it, because she felt too much of a fool to let her know she was pregnant.

The hot and fine summer seemed to make it worse. She waited night after night, and even went to where he said he'd worked, but that was a lie too, for he wasn't there and never had been.

He didn't come for a month, so by the time she told him even her morning sickness was beginning to ease off. When he made an excuse to leave that same evening without going to bed with her, and saying he'd come back again when he'd thought what to do about it, she knew she wouldn't see him any more, but didn't want to make too much fuss in case it turned out not to be true and he came back after all. She laid the kids' things out for school and breakfast, her lips still wet from his one kiss. I shan't die, she thought, and I shan't starve, and neither will the kid I'll have.

What she would do, she thought one tea-time while seeing to the budgerigar, was wait till he next did a bit of exhibition diving at Trent Bridge, and then when he was about to jump she'd burst out of the crowd and run to him, shouting at the top of her voice that he was a rotten no-good get who'd got her pregnant and then run away and left her. Yes, she would. She'd hang on to him and go down into the water and never let go till they both drowned and were out of it for good. Let them put that in the Evening Post so that his wife could read about it while waiting for him to come home after boozing with his pals or from doing another woman. But maybe he'd led his wife a worse dance than he'd led me, and I'm well off without him in spite of having another one to feed and fend for.

The bird flew around the room while she cleaned out its cage. At the sound of seed spilling into its pot it darted back and rested a moment on her hand. 'Hello, my duck,' she said, knowing she'd do nothing of the sort, and not tackle Callender at Trent Bridge, 'you got over your little accident in the fire, didn't you?' – though not sure whether *she* would this time, as tears followed the too bright smile at her eyes.

She shut the door when it began to eat.

In the café, an old man sitting next to her began making funny noises.

He wore a hat and scarf and overcoat, so he wasn't even poor. But he was very old, in spite of a moustache and full head of white vigorous hair. She'd never seen him before, but it seemed nobody else had either, because they weren't disturbed by the noise he was making.

It wasn't loud, and didn't frighten her. She supposed that was why other people weren't bothered. But it was funny, somehow, though she knew it wasn't funny to him because who would feel happy with a noise like that for company — especially an old man who must be pushing eighty?

It wouldn't do to interfere, whatever happened. Maybe he was warming up for a little tiddly-song to himself. Old men were like that, and harmless as long as they weren't dirty as well. But on a bus once when she was twelve an old man put his hand on her knee. There's one thing to be said for an old woman: she wouldn't do a thing like that. So she knocked it away, without causing any fuss.

But if it came back she'd shout at the top of her voice: 'Get your hands off me, you dirty old swine.' Maybe he guessed what was on her mind, since he got up and shuffled out at the next stop. Perhaps he only wanted to tell her something, or was in need of company, or he was about to say she reminded him of his own daughter he hadn't seen for thirty years, not since she was a girl like her. Still, you had to look after yourself, even though she did feel a bit sorry for him.

Her tea was getting cold, but that wasn't the old man's fault, because he couldn't help the noise he was making. It sounded less and less that sort of noise the more it went on. She was the only one with ears. Or maybe the others hadn't washed theirs out that morning.

They sat with tea and buns, set in their newspapers, or staring into the air which must have been more interesting because they didn't even need print to hold them down. If you look into the air you look at yourself, and that must be better than any newspaper.

The old man was too busy with his tiddly-song to take much in. At the sound of such noise his eyes must have stopped looking at anything. Nobody else seemed to understand that his eyes had come to a dead end, for the few who glanced at him turned away as if they had seen nothing. Some talked together, and didn't even bother to look, though they knew what was going on right enough.

It made her uneasy, being by herself. He sat up straight as a soldier against the wall, a hand on the table beside his cup. By making such a noise he was trying to get in touch with someone, but he did not know who or where they were, which she supposed was why no one could bear to look at him in case it was them. It became more insistent until, to her, it appeared to fill the whole café.

She didn't find the noise meaningless or dispiriting, for it set her memory racing thirty years back to being a child and fading into sleep. Then, as now, she never went from the conscious world straight into sleep like maybe a healthy person would, but into another world between her and deep sleep itself, always a different place through which she had to pass before reaching real sleep, and she only knew she'd done that when she woke up.

She remembered feeling, once in this twilight zone, the horror of being about to die. A huge leaden sphere pressed against her brain as if to crush all five senses at once. As big as the earth, it rolled on to her, till her eyes saw only grey matter and her breath was starting not to pump. She called for her father, who came in and brought her back to full breath by some kind and trivial gesture of distraction.

Because of this outcome it was not a bad memory that the old man's noise had set off, yet now it began to annoy her, for she had come into the café for a cup of tea as a break from the grind of buying scarves for the children, and hadn't been in five minutes before bumping into this.

An older woman sitting on the other side had wire glasses and straw-blonde hair, and puffed a fag while looking out of the window as if to burn her way through the glass with the acetylene smoke of it. She was nearer, but Margaret couldn't imagine her being bothered by him in a hundred years – till she had the strange idea that maybe everybody else in the café had their heads filled with the same thoughts and words that she had.

Her laugh at this interrupted the noise coming from the man's mouth, her face turning red with shame because he must have heard her and imagined she was laughing at him. She was almost relieved when the rattle started again.

His tie-knot was slightly below the join of the collar. A hand was limp by his side, while the other jerked at the half-empty cup. She thought it a pity he'd let the tea inside get cold, then leaped up and opened his coat, trembling with embarrassment at her big belly getting in the way but acting as if it was the only thing left to do in her life: 'Are you all right? What is it then? Tell me, for God's sake?'

He wanted help, and she wanted help in order to help him, for her voice wavered at his eyes rolling, and the sound of finger nails scraping on tin coming from his clenched lips, pressed tight as if trying to stop something getting out for the last time. She was frightened at the sight of his convulsed body.

She pulled down the knot of his tie and flung it open, snapped his collar at the stud though it wasn't in any way tight at his withered neck: 'Where do you live, duck?'

Trouser-legs chafed at the supports of the table, as if they could stop him falling down to earth, because the bench he sat on was not enough. She looked from the double-white world of his pot-eyes and shouted in a panic: 'Can't somebody give me a hand, then?'

A waitress came over, more, Margaret reflected later, because she thought I might start to give birth if she didn't, than to be of much use to the old man. 'Is he badly?'

The noise stopped, and he was dead.

'You'd better call an ambulance,' Margaret said, 'and a copper. But he's still more alive though than you bleddy lot in here.'

The Second Chance

A swathe of Queen Anne's lace was crushed in the front wheelspokes as he pushed along the edge of a field, producing a summer smell pleasant to the nostrils. At the lane he climbed on to the machine and followed the lefthand rut, but when it became too deep and the pedals scraped its sides he balanced along the dry hump in the middle, hitting an occasional stone but staying on track. The thin blue-and-black band of a Royal Air Force pilot officer decorated each sleeve.

The sit-up-and-beg pushbike rattled incurably and had no three-speed. Chalk dust covered his shining toe-caps, but a few quick brushes with a cloth would bring the glisten back. It wouldn't do for the old folks to see him less than impeccable. Why a bike was thought to be more convincing in his approach he did not know. A bull-nosed Morris of the period would have been more in keeping, and in any case he wouldn't have cycled all the way from his airfield, as they liked to imagine.

At the stile he took the War Revision sheet from his tunic pocket. Major Baxter had folded it in the manner of a trench map from the First World War, so that a gentle pull at two corners brought the whole thing open. Sweat on his forehead cooled under the peaked cap. Dotted lines of the bridle path were clearly marked, but there were no signposts on the lanes. If, as was likely, the old man wielded his field service binoculars from the upstairs window he would already have seen him. He made an observable pause to look at the map before heaving his bike over. To do so was a clause in his instructions, and for the money he had made there was no point in skimping them.

It was an effort to lift the bike without spoiling his uniform but, putting his strength at the saddle and handlebars, he tilted the front wheel to the sky and sent it to the other side. The afternoon visit was preceded by a few hours of intense preparation, mostly the perusal of a refresher course which made him properly familiar with the person he was supposed to be.

435

He sat on the stile before climbing after his bicycle. White feathers of cirrus in the west were as yet only a wispy tenth or two, but a meteorological front was expected, and his study of such matters led him to predict rain by nightfall. He wasn't to know for sure. Perhaps the storm wouldn't come till tomorrow. There were no weather forecasts on the wireless in the days he was supposed to be living in.

Out of the next field came sharp stuttering cries from a score or so of sheep. The noise of ewes bewailing the loss of their lambs was continuous, and he felt better when the intensity of their distress was lessened by distance.

The old man brought Helen to the window so that they could witness him coming towards the house. At the next corner of the lane he would see them waving when he leaned his bike against a wooden gate and took off his cap to rake a hand through short fair hair. The telegram said he could only stay for tea, but they would be glad enough of that, living in a world where any sight of him could be their last.

'If you must go,' Baxter had said, 'and you must – we all know that, don't we, Helen, my dear? – then don't for God's sake join the army and have to march along those horrible *pavé* roads in France!'

He laughed, as he was meant to while they looked at the hump-haze of the Downs. He was genned up to the eyebrows: 'You don't go from a university air squadron into the infantry!'

Instead of marching at two-and-a-half miles an hour on cobblestones towards the Front as in the olden days Peter had flown at almost a hundred in a Tiger Moth, and later at over three times that in a Spitfire. They welcomed him at the gate as a perfect memorial to their twenty years of happiness – while he knew himself to be nothing of the sort.

Major Baxter found the features so similar, and mannerisms so close when he first noticed him at the bar of the pub-hotel in Saleham that he stood shaking his head as if not wanting to believe what he saw, while knowing it was likely that he would have no say in the matter. The uneasiness of sensing that he should draw back, mixed with a confused vision of what would happen if he did not, vanished like the sort of dream that couldn't be remembered on waking up.

The ordeal of seeing this spitten image of his dead son was so great that he forgot why he had come into the hotel. There was a smell of beer, dusty sunshine and olives (or were they pickled onions?) and a reek of tobacco smoke. He stood and patted the outside of each pocket to locate his cigarette case, which gave time, and saved him being noticed while in a state close to shock. To be caught staring would make him think he'd done something immoral, so he took out a cigarette and had, thank God, to search for a match.

He felt he might be going to faint, and the last time he had known such a sensation was when a shell splinter struck his thigh near Trones Wood in France, too long ago to bother. Having gone unhurt through so many dangers made him also proud of the fact that he'd never been stricken by an illness. Not even as a child had he broken bones or got put to bed.

He turned from his own image in the mirror, hair and moustache silver, tanned face gone pallid. A force that ached in his heels urged him to get set for the door and run, but he was unable to move for the moment, merely telling himself he must not speak to the young man sitting alone at the bar who, if he had worn an RAF officer's uniform with a pilot's white wings on his breast above the left pocket of his tunic, would have been none other than his actual son.

Baxter knew it was useless to say never because no sooner did the word manifest itself than the action began which drove him towards what he had decided not to say or do. To determine never to take a certain course deprived you of that flexibility of mind needed for solving a problem, and laid you open to doing exactly what you had resolved to steer clear of. He knew those 'nevers' all right! A soldier and a man of business had always to be aware and to beware of them. At the same time he realized that, as in every crisis, the necessary action would demand a combination of will, judgment and luck, a trio of factors he had rarely managed more than two of at any one time.

He had come into the hotel because his cigarette case was almost empty. His vigour made him more likely to admit that he had 'seen things'. But he hadn't. Yet having acted, even in so small a fashion, the shock was no longer disabling. To do anything at all would clear at least one part of the mind, and suddenly he found himself as far as the bar.

He was a large man, stout but erect, and a one-handed grip at the rail, vital to his pride, allowed him to appear nonchalant when the waiter came through an archway. The young man who looked like his son spoke before Major Baxter could give his order. 'A pint of your best bitter.'

'Yes, sir.'

437

'I have the most raging thirst.' When he drew out his wallet and opened it wide to pull a five pound note from an inner pocket Baxter's sharp eye took in the details of a formally lettered business card.

'It's the first hot day of the year,' the waiter said, robbing Baxter of saying the same.

'We waited a long time for a touch of the sun. Always have to in this country, I suppose.' The voice had a tone of lassitude and disappointment which Peter's never could at the age he had died. Yet it made him seem even more as if he might be Peter, who hadn't grown a day older in appearance but who, having seen everyone else put on the years, reflected the fact in his voice.

Baxter stood so that he could see the young man's face in the glass from both angles. Different images shifted and confirmed the exactness. But he questioned whether it was such a likeness, whether he hadn't in the space of twenty years forgotten what his son looked like, and whether the young man merely resembled one of the photographs in the snapshot album.

At sixty-six Baxter recalled how true it was that a few years after Peter's death he had, out of an inner and ever-burning grief, forgotten the precise shape of his son's features. Yet nowadays he was able to see people and events of twenty or even forty years ago with a sharpness that hadn't been possible when nearer to the circumstances themselves. Thus he remembered his son's face as if he had seen him only five minutes before, and knew it was the same in every part as that of the young man lifting the glass of beer to his mouth.

He asked for cigarettes, and a double whisky so as to make sure his impression was correct, and to convince himself that he wasn't going absolutely bonkers. He had little philosophy of life beyond the injunction to check everything once, twice, and three times – which was periodically necessary if you were to get anywhere, and defend yourself against the world.

'Passing through?'

He knew that the neutral and jovial tone was characteristic of himself. His left hand shook, but was controlled the moment he was aware. He hoped no one would have noticed the inner shaking of veins that led to his fingers. But by holding even his elbow still in its tracks he was afraid the whole limb might turn to stone. He saw his own features, and how the much whitened eyes bulged even more from their sockets, causing him to reflect that he always did look like a bloody fish, with too much eye and bristle.

The young man noted Baxter's smile, as well as his blue and white striped shirt, the grey tie and blue alpaca cardigan, and the heavy black horn-rims that looked like National Health specs but that no doubt cost a bomb-and-three-quarters at some posh optician's. He saw that he had grey hair, a moustache half hiding lips which he thought to be too thin, and deep blue eyes. Small town pubs were full of such lonely old souls, though Peter felt he had nothing to lose by answering:

'Driving to Brighton. I get so thirsty on the road, not to say bored.'

He wore a good jacket, and a shirt without a tie. Wouldn't allow it in the evening, Baxter told himself, even these days – conceding however that he looked smart enough. His hair had the close and even waves that had been his son's, and was similarly short. He clipped his words in the same way.

'Going there for pleasure?'

He turned, and by laughing at this harmless query fell into the trap Baxter had laid to gain several advantages at once, for while recording the full intensity of the grey-blue eyes, Baxter also got a sight of the teeth, and was able to gauge the tone of the laugh itself, as well as notice how he put slightly more weight on the left foot than the right. He used the word *uncanny* in his summing up because he couldn't think of one that fitted the coincidence more neatly. The shape of the fingers, the motion of the hands, the clean-shaven texture of the skin – were the same.

There was no reason to be unsociable. 'Heavens, no. Stay in Town for *that!*'

During one vacation Baxter's son had spread a navigation chart on the study table to do some plotting practice. He had looked over his shoulder and watched his hands manipulating a pair of dividers, opening and closing parallel rulers, wielding fine-pointed pencils, and dextrously twiddling the knobs of a Dalton computer. The fingers matched those now reaching for matches on the bar, and lighting the same brand of cigarette that his son had smoked.

Hating the nosey parker he had suddenly turned into, Baxter wondered what he could say next in order to delay the young man, who would otherwise finish his pint and motor off to whoever he was going to visit in Brighton, never to do this route again while he would be placed to meet him.

He was saved the trouble: 'It's work I'm bent on. Business, you know.'

'Are you now?'

The matter was left for a moment. Baxter thought he might offer him a drink, yet saw no point in keeping him. If he vanished for ever that would be fate, for both of them, as well as for Helen. He at least had been vouchsafed another sight of his son, and mulled on this till he remembered that Helen might wonder why he was late coming home. She wouldn't, and never had. When Baxter had come home that day and heard that Peter was reported missing presumed killed she was just turned forty, and had been concerned about nothing and nobody ever since.

After a long hot day in early autumn Major Baxter had returned from a field exercise with his Home Guard company. At forty-six years of age he was ready, with his good health and experience, to lead his men once more. Others like him had been in the trenches, and in defence would have the kind of staying power that the young couldn't know about. Nineteen-eighteen seemed like yesterday to those who had served in France, and they were excellent stiffening for the others, as well as being good shots.

Baxter was known as 'Old Scissors', and wore the faintest of smiles when he got them on parade, or had them semicircled about him for a lecture, because he knew they didn't realize that he was aware of his nickname. But they did. There was a point beyond which he wasn't much bothered, but it took him deep enough in the association for them to trust him, and be willing to follow him anywhere providing it wasn't too far towards the besetting sin of incompetence. He was a good leader, because he knew how to lead gently. Yet he was more aware of their limitations than he was of his own, and maybe that was the reason he was never given a battalion.

He came home exhausted and filthy, yet still excited from his time out of doors, throwing map case, field glasses and tin hat on to the stand in the cool hall. A seventeen-year-old had broken his ankle leaping a ditch, so he would have to call and see him tomorrow on his way to the office. The damned fool should have waded over, but he was a young bull who could hardly let experience take the place of brains because he hadn't yet got any. God help some of them if the Germans came, though they still had a few tricks tucked into their gaiters.

Helen stared into the food safe.

'Better shut it,' he told her, 'or the flies'll make an entry.'

She didn't turn: 'George, there's a telegram on the table.'

He saw it. 'Open it, then. Must be from your mother.'

'*You* do it.'

Unbuttoning his battledress tunic, he felt an unexplained rage eating at his backbone, as if the ache of two days were attacking him all at once. 'We'll see what it says, shall we?'

'No, don't.'

Her plea went into him like a thorn, but he kept his voice in its proper place, assuming that one of them would have to for the rest of their lives. 'Oh, come now, my love, close that thing, and let's have tea.'

It was as if she had turned to wood. He picked up the small brown envelope. The telegraph boy had known what was written there, and so had she, hands shaking as she scribbled in his receipt book for the telegram which they had dreaded since the war began.

She heard the faint rip as if the sky were being torn in two. 'Please!'

Impossible not to bring out the small piece of folded paper. She sounded as if she would never forgive him if he did, but what he read dimmed all feeling, such pain at least promising that nothing would ever hurt him again. Her eyes told him to say nothing, while he forced her as gently as was in him away from the food safe and into the living room. He obeyed her by not repeating the words of the telegram, and wondered ever afterwards why he had locked the message away with his insurance policies and never looked at it again.

Peter had cycled home a few days before his last sortie over France where he had been killed in his fighter above the towns and villages Baxter knew so well. While Helen slept he looked at his old maps and wondered where it was, but packed them away on hearing the shuffle of her feet as if they were love letters from some liaison which it would break her spirit to learn about.

She said nothing, but his nothing in response was of equal intensity. The perfect union between mother and son had been blighted by death. Baxter's own love, though it was all he had, seemed little by comparison, the sort of nothing that didn't even have anything beyond except nothing. But she didn't say a word, as he recalled, and neither could he, for any speech on the matter would have been so shallow as to have spoiled that ideal love.

The affection between father and son had also been perfect, in its fashion, but different in such a way that it would always remain impossible to define. There was no label for it, and he was not the man to give one, or to try and sort out whatever lay behind it if he did.

Not a tear had dropped from Helen's eyes in over twenty years. He would have liked to have seen some stain marking her cheeks, a sign of pain from which it might be feasible to recover. The thought sometimes occurred that maybe she wept in secret, but there was never any indication to reinforce – let alone confirm – such a suspicion. And if she did, which in spite of having known her so long he still couldn't be certain of, he had no right to venture into such an intensely personal area. Because she never wept, he learned to live without hope, and did so with no complaint.

He watched her hair turning grey, like a flower settling too soon into winter after an unexpectedly bitter frost in August. To anyone looking on, it appeared that she took Peter's death like others stricken in the same way, but the loss fixed her to the day on which the telegram came so that time had no effect on her soul.

Baxter had always imagined that the dead were the lucky ones. They had felt it in the trenches even if the saying had stayed unspoken, a common deception to make their peril more tolerable. But the death in this case had caused those who remained to die and Helen, who had taken the shock too profoundly for it ever to go away, wasn't lucky at all. He couldn't understand it, but had always thought that one day he might. Yet he understood perfectly. The fine balance kept him living, and drudged him along in a state which never failed to make people think that in spite of his occasional cynicisms concerning the uselessness of life, he too was 'putting a good face on it'.

Only half of her lived. Life was unjust to her in that he was able to absorb the shock with what appeared to be his more stoical nature – and perhaps, he sometimes thought, indifference. The heart can take only so much pain, yet it was also as if he had been used to such agony since birth. He was thankful that these deficiencies – if that's what they were – enabled him to provide the vital support. One of them had to, and the unspoken treaty allowed Helen to go on living yet never talk about her son.

Forever locked into each separate fire of deliberate forgetfulness was their only way of never putting Peter out of their minds for a single instant, and kept him more alive than if they had gone through endless seasons of grieving together. It was as if one word about him from either would consign him to a void into which all their memories would inevitably follow, and that was unthinkable.

But he continually pondered on ways of bringing Helen back to life without breaking their sacred pact. She stood in the garden and looked with vacant eyes as the engines of Lancasters or Dakotas or Spitfires sounded overhead. Peter's belongings of watch, spare uniform, trinkets and books came home, which Major Baxter signed for and locked away. A friend motored over with his bicycle, and thank God it was on a day when Helen slept from sheer weakness of body and spirit.

Doing the housework, or walking the garden, she would half faint for no reason. Nothing was diagnosed. For years a girl from the village had to be there if he was not. When the war ended he began to hope that she would one day come out of the near catatonic state into which she seemed locked for ever, but 'missing presumed killed' meant what it said, and there was no grave to set flowers on. She spoke, but used only the barest vocabulary to get through life, and nothing brought her clear of Peter's death, nor looked like doing so.

Music and voices blended from the dining room. The young man clacked his pint glass on the bar. 'Well, I must be going.'

Major Baxter drank his whisky. 'Not much of a meal you had.'

'I prefer to drive at lunch time. Less traffic on the road. I hate cars!'

'We all do. But we drive 'em.'

'Not to mention that twenty-mile red-bricked push out of London – through All-the-Croydons.' Peter looked vacantly at himself in the mirror, then turned away. 'I came via Leatherhead and Box Hill. Longer, but less dreary. I'll have tea later, in any case.'

He didn't care to ask a direct question, but there were occasions when all subtlety must be thrown aside: 'What sort of business are you in?'

Peter would no doubt have grown to show his lack of amusement in the same way: 'Books. The antiquarian kind. I'm going to Brighton on the off-chance of picking up a few. What do you do?'

'I'm Major Baxter – retired. Was in insurance.'

Peter's face lost all interest. 'Nice.'

'I have a lot of books.'

There was no plan, yet Baxter knew what would happen. The occurrence was packed within the limits of a scheme that was manoeuvring *him*, about which he could do nothing because the will to do, or not to do, had been taken away. It was a new experience, perhaps a necessary one, but he masked the fact that he didn't much like it by telling himself that at least it was happening late in life. Had he been younger, his pride would have spoiled it, while even now, an ever-present inanition might cause him to give in and do nothing.

Peter felt blood coming back into his face at the prospect of finding a well-tooled leather-bound hoard he only dreamed about. But there were probably no more than a few damp novels, a children's encyclopaedia, and a mountain of pulp magazines. He could smell them already. Hose 'em with petrol and apply a match. 'What sort of books?'

'Travel and topography mostly,' Baxter said. 'A few natural history. I sometimes forget what I *have* got. Fair bindings though, most of them. Came from my father, who collected all his life. Didn't have the heart to throw 'em out. But space *is* precious these days.'

It sounded exactly the stuff he was after, but it would be foolish to let the eyes gleam or muscles twitch over it. 'Do you ever think of selling any?'

Major Baxter ordered two whiskies. 'I might be, but look, Peter, why don't you come back and see them – if you're interested. Time is time, and nobody knows that better than I do.'

He recovered quickly from hearing himself called by his own name even before, as far as he knew, he had given it. At least, it was his middle name, the one his mother had used whenever his father wasn't close enough to hear.

He nodded at Baxter's idea, and agreed to follow his car, thinking he might make a fiver or so out of the weird old bloke before the day was finished.

Baxter shopped twice a week, and with all provisions stowed in the boot he purchased flowers from the funny little one-eyed woman who had a stall near the car park. After buying them on two occasions when Helen had been unable to leave her room, he felt he could no longer pass unless he took up a bunch of something. The one-eyed woman expected him to, or hoped he would, and you were obliged, really, to encourage a flower-stall, for they were rare enough these days. Unless there were carnations or mimosa it was often unnecessary to buy because Helen managed to grow some blooms each year in the garden. Mostly there wasn't much more he could take, because there was nothing she asked for, and little she appeared to need.

The major was a good leader because he drove with care, some would say slowly, deliberately taking bends and rounding corners he had negotiated for the past thirty years with a calculated sweep just short of stalling. Nevertheless he was amazed at how the little red underslung Morgan stayed in his rear mirror and never wavered.

One part of the winding lane was a green tunnel which opened out before turning a corner into a village. Beyond, he waited at a hump-backed bridge for a couple of cars and a tractor to come over, holding back whether or not he had right of way, because he was the sort of driver who tried to stop everyone else on the road from committing the mistakes he himself might have made if he did not hold his recklessness in firm control.

Peter felt confined for life as a part of a two-man bumper-to-bumper traffic queue set in rolling and wooded landscape on an empty road. No wonder we nearly lost the bloody war. There were two places at which it was possible to shoot out and overtake, but on such a narrow lane you could always rely on a souped-up bullet-like Mini to come round a bend at sixty and smash you for dead if you made that kind of move. It was no use anyway because he didn't know where the old man lived. Like all cunning slow coaches he didn't give his address so that, with it pencilled on the map, he might have scooted there by himself and waited at his leisure. Maybe he was a bit cracked, and would lead him a fifty-mile zig-zag before vanishing up the drive of some looney-bin or other. Yet if he had the books he said he had, perhaps it might be possible to pry a few dozen loose before other dealers got there.

'As far as I'm concerned,' his father had said, 'you only have two chances in life. You've had the first, and it landed you in prison.'

The days when he would have stood up for his father were over. Get on your feet for those who can help you, otherwise . . . He held his thumb *down* by the side of the armchair where it wouldn't be seen. 'I only got six months.'

Nearly drove into the old bastard. If he's so mean over his petrol, or careful of his skin, will he ever sell a book? A rabbit which ran along the lane suddenly stood perfectly still with fright, then vanished into the grassy bank as if part of the tarmac road had tipped up under its back legs.

'Only?'

'Well, I could have got more.'

445

'Yes, you'd have been sent down for two years,' his father shouted, 'if I hadn't paid for a solicitor and a barrister.' He had to calm himself or his heart would go splash. 'Cashing cheques with my forged name on them is all very well, but not other people's.'

'I served four months – with remission.' Peter could see the fact running through his father's mind that some people were very law-abiding in prison, and that if they were as well-behaved outside they would never get put into the place.

A second chance was like the second coming: when it appeared he barely recognized it. Flynn wanted him for his book business, and even his father thought it sound enough to spare a few hundred on. It seemed to offer a better living than that expensive school had prepared him for, which had only taught him (and the old bastard put on a higher moral tone to make his point) to be somebody he wasn't, so as to get things he had no right to, but in such a way that he wouldn't be able to keep them. And if he did bring something off he was bound to get caught sooner or later – as the silly ass found out when he tried his stunts on a woman who had more astuteness in her little finger than he'd ever have in the whole of his underworked backbone.

'If your mother had been alive I don't know what the hell she would have thought, though God knows, I don't think she would have cared one way or the other what you got up to, knowing what she was herself. When I met her she was pregnant, though a fat lot I knew. I fell in love with her. The war was on. And I didn't give a damn!'

He'd been drinking whisky at dinner, and was unaware of the malice in his voice, wouldn't in fact remember next morning, otherwise Peter would have given in to his rage and knocked him down. He rarely got drunk, and was in a good mood, and said he would put money into his 'trading venture' (so as to get me off his hands). He even remembered his promise the following day, by which time Peter felt it was rather too late to floor him for having been so vicious about his mother. Not that, at this turn of events, he still wanted to.

His mother had been dead a long time, and all he remembered were her nightly stories during the war when he was four or five which told of his father flying around the sky and coming to earth in a parachute of different colours. The tale often brought tears to her eyes, so after the first few tellings its mystery became tedious, and when he told her so, she didn't cry any more. But his father had been away in Scotland sorting out legal queries in the Pay Corps and hadn't flown in aeroplanes at all.

The greenery was rich yet still precise. Garden blossoms stood out delicately clear over the lane. Whenever the road took him to a crest the smokiness towards the horizon kept every detail distinct in the foreground, presaging the season about to break. He was unconcerned with what it might bring because he considered that, in spite of his stint in prison, life hadn't been too bad so far.

'It's five and three-quarter miles exactly,' the major explained before getting into his Austin A40 at the car park, but it already seemed like ten, in the unfamiliar area of sunken and twisting lanes whose short cuts the old bloke must have worked out some time before the Flood.

Major Baxter felt that the squat sports car had never been anything but set red in his rear mirror and waiting for him to move more quickly. But what was the use of it in this day and age? Still, no one had ever followed with such closeness and precision, though he was certain that Peter's pilot and navigator training would have allowed him to do the same. He had brought him up that way, as well as providing lengthy answers to every question, careful not to hide or mislead, and courteous in those innocent dealings between a father and son who had never spent much time together. He had sent him to schools which kept him out of trouble, so there hadn't been any of that and, as time went on, no gaps where it could have occurred, for he went from public school to university, and then via the air squadron to the volunteer reserve, leaving no periods either of idleness or neglect in which he could have contested the rules they had brought him up to respect. Baxter would have found such a dialogue hard to take, and had been glad of the way of life that helped to make it unthinkable. Whenever his son went back off leave it was as if he were returning to school after the holidays.

They'd had much to be grateful for but, like many such parents, had had to pay for it. In those days no one questioned their duty, probably because it had been so plain that they had neither wanted to – nor been able to.

Helen would be glad to see Peter before he went away as unob-trusively as he had come, for she would notice that he was well, and had grown no older while she had so unduly grieved. Perhaps it had been good that they had not mentioned him to each other these last twenty years, for the shock of seeing him might bring her from the prolonged malaise into which she had retreated. The major had not in that time seen one smile or heard any laughter. Her lips had thinned,

the mouth had straightened, the eyes had become dull and her movements slower. She spoke far from easily, yet with his help she kept the
house and worked in the garden, so that few would surmise she wasn't
living a kind of ordinary life – apart from the occasional breakdown.

They'd never had much to do with neighbours, while other members of the family had died over the years, or been killed in accidents,
or in war, or had emigrated, or had become so disaffected for some
reason that they didn't come within a hundred miles. Circumstances
separated the Baxters from everyone else, and they maintained a
dignity towards each other rather than to the rest of the world, thus
reinforcing a feeling that had already been there, but that grew
stronger the longer it went on after their son's death.

It was the best way they could find of living normally, though he
knew that compared to her former self she had altered so much as to
have died. He had married her, and Peter had come into the world,
and by this she had been killed. If he had relapsed into a similar death
such truths might not have occurred to him but, being the simple man
he was, and tending to be proud of it – suggesting that beneath the
simplicity lay a complexity of which he was even more proud – he
hadn't been able to die in that way. And being the kind of man who
wanted the richness of life to return to her, he thought that anything
was worth the attempt, and that this duplicate of their own son found
again and following in his car behind should bring her at least a few
moments of joy.

Tyres crunched gently to a stop on familiar gravel. Lifting two laden
straw baskets out of the boot he heard a few drops of rain clattering on
rose leaves and the roof of the brick garage.

'You're late, dear,' Helen called from the doorway.

He looked up, and noticed an edge of darkening cumulo-nimbus.
'We have a visitor.'

Peter stood by his car. These old well-kept country places could be
packed with all sorts of rare gew-gaws.

'Follow me in?' Major Baxter's plea would have been difficult to
ignore, though Peter considered doing so, because the tone suggested
that, after wasting time, energy and petrol there might not be any
books after all. Nevertheless, he asked to carry one of the baskets, not
knowing that Baxter had deliberately paused for him to do so after
recalling that his son Peter would have offered no less, for even at

twenty he had had enough imagination, as well as a shy sort of kindness, to think of others.

Peter put the basket nonchalantly over the left shoulder and held it in place with his right hand, showing freckles on the back of his wrist. Baxter's wife recognized him by this gesture before seeing his actual features, and her husband, with sharper sight, was close enough to notice that her lips were unusually tense.

From a distance she looked younger than her husband. She supported herself by the lintel, as if there was some weakness in her legs. Peter also noted the hesitation before she waved, and then called his name – with a smile that recapitulated for Baxter in one fell package the whole twenty years of her deprivation. The pain was intense, but he steadied himself while keeping back the vivid recollection of his own lost love.

His anguish did not alter the rate of his slow walk towards her. He didn't know whether to hope she'd see this young man as a stranger who reminded her of Peter, or that she would accept him completely as her one-time son. He didn't know which he wanted more, if indeed he now desired either of them. But her intonation of mother-chiding, suggesting she hadn't seen him for a week or so, hid a lack of awareness about what was happening, her smile at the same time putting her beyond the necessity for such perception.

Her face was unusually pale, and when she repeated his name it sounded like a call for help. 'Peter!'

Since leaving prison he had stiffened his spirit by priding himself that nothing could faze him, though he took it as strange that, like her husband, she had known his name before anyone could have given it to her. When it had happened at the hotel he hadn't liked it at all, but on hearing it from Baxter's wife at the door of their house, he felt pleased at such an agreeable welcome.

Baxter noted that she didn't weep at her son's return, or put her arms around him, or kiss him as if she were aware he'd been away twenty years and that every minute she had gone through enough to break any heart. Perhaps it was just as well. She led him into the house as if she had seen him only the day before.

A stick-and-umbrella stand was made out of an enormously enlarged shot-gun cartridge. 'Curious old thing, isn't it? Picked it up at an auction for a penny or two, years ago,' Baxter told him. 'Thought it would look rather good by the door.' He turned to his wife: 'He's come to see the books' – then followed them cautiously into the living room, as if she might suddenly be blessed with reality and blame him for this deception – though there seemed no chance when she turned to say:

'I do wish you would come home more often, Peter.'

The major smiled, and swung his shoulders back as if standing guard over some truth which he hoped neither of them would ever find. 'Maybe he will.'

The only books were a row of paperbacks on a window ledge. There was no television, either, though an old wartime one-band wireless set stood on a table by the door. He decided against lighting a cigarette out of an unexpected feeling of respect, as if he had been there before and told it wasn't the thing to do.

'I'm sorry,' he said, 'but I'm kept rather busy.' No apology had ever been easier to make. He hadn't known about their books, so there'd been no point in paying them a call. There was a stench in the place, confirmed when an enormous and obviously neutered tabby lifted itself from behind a copper plant pot, dropped softly to the floor like an over-sized floorcloth, and padded out of the room as if Peter were an intruder it didn't care to meet.

She peered lengthily at him from a few feet away, and even that didn't cause him the uneasiness it might had she been someone less strange. 'It's nice to be here, though.'

The major coughed. 'We're lucky to see him again – so soon.'

'I hear those planes flying over every night' – she waved towards the ceiling but looked at the floor – 'so I know you're so awfully occupied.'

It was difficult to tell what she saw. Her husband wondered, and stood as though ready to dash forward if she fell. She didn't. It was obvious that the visitor gave her strength. She didn't lean for support any more. Clear vision was on her side. She saw Peter, and if it was only a day since he had last called, it had been the longest she could remember. But some days were like that, and it was difficult to tell what made them so. Here he was, and she decided not to fuss too much. The furniture, curtains and walls looked clearer than for years, and reminded her that perhaps it was time to start cleaning the place, since it wasn't good for her only son to come home to a house that didn't glitter with tidiness.

It was easier to breathe when rain swept against the leaded windows, and now that Peter had come back she made up her mind not to give in to those inner powers that often beset her when he was absent. Occasionally, if the assault was too sudden, she went away to the coast, and George would say: 'You'll be as right as rain in a month.' She knew at such moments that because there was some anguish he could no longer take, she was to be put into an air-conditioned cork-lined box to be alone with her nightmares. When they receded she was allowed to come home, but she wouldn't go there again now that Peter was here. She didn't want to, and even George would not persuade her.

In his civilian clothes Peter looked almost the same as before going into the air force. She thought he must feel better to be out of uniform for a few hours, but wished he would smile, because he'd smiled a great deal as a child when he ran about on his own as if the flat and open garden was a maze to which only he had the key. Extending and complicating the invisible maze over the lawn kept him busy for hours. At each laugh he had worked out new twists and turns, or devised an exit that hadn't been there before, or discovered a quick way into the interior that nobody else had been able to find.

He was adventurous and self-absorbed but, after growing up, became serious and hardly ever smiled, and only laughed at moments when neither of them could see anything amusing, or when he thought he was on his own, as if his maze had been wiped out during the greatest disappointment of his life, which was strange, because nothing like that could have occurred, as far as she remembered. He'd turned into the sober young man they'd hoped for, and what could you expect except unexplainable melancholy with this war going on and on? It was a shame that children were brought up to face such troubles.

'I'll make you some tea,' she said.

A glance was sufficient for him to be able to describe someone afterwards, a method perfected in prison where to fix a person for any length of time might cause a fight. He took in enough of Mrs Baxter to remember her blue jersey and dark blue skirt, and that she had straight short grey hair, somewhat vacuous eyes, and dry pale skin which make-up might have camouflaged if she'd been by any chance expecting him. With such features she had once been a lively and goodlooking woman, but he saw that she was now at large in the territories of a fragmented mind, a state which, however, allowed her to maintain those appearances that she had always known were the height of decorous living.

'Mrs Bruce left us a pot of damson jam yesterday. We can have that for tea. You remember Mrs Bruce, don't you, Peter? She always asks about you.'

There was no need to use his powers of quick recognition in looking at Mrs Baxter, for it was plain that she wanted him to stare at her, though he didn't because it wasn't part of his nature to do what people expected. In any case a too studied gaze might disturb her husband, though he laughed on seeing him flush at the mention of Mrs Bruce, whoever she was, as if his embarrassment would have been the same whether he had slept with her or murdered her.

Baxter wondered how aware Helen was of the amount of time gone since Peter's last appearance. Certainly it wasn't necessary to tax his memory if Peter was supposed to have visited them in previous weeks. But there was no way of knowing, so it was better to let him talk, though what worried him at the moment was that Mrs Bruce had been dead fifteen years.

'Of course I remember her.'

The major's tone was one that he used to put people at their ease, though his laugh scared him in case it revealed anything. 'Perhaps he'd rather have a sherry. I got two bottles of Dry Sack last week.'

'I shall have to think about it,' she said, causing Peter to smile, which made her believe he was doing so out of affection. He had never found it difficult to endear himself to women, no matter how batty they were. One of his girl friends once took him to meet an old aunt, who had talked in the same outlandish way. In the encounter he had combined impeccable behaviour with an ability to carry on a conversation at cross purposes which won him the confidence of the half-crazed lady yet lost him his girl friend because she saw him, so she said at their parting, as being 'too bloody clever by half'.

'No, George. He'll have *tea*. I know my own son better than you do.'

Her vibrant tone concealed a weakness that neither could go against, and Peter had to tell himself that he had seen Baxter's glance in his direction before realizing that he had.

'All right then, dear.'

Helen detected their compliance, and smiled at Peter as if he would show her how happy she might finally be. He was on her side, and would defend her against the dark. He loved her, and his grey-blue eyes were opaque with a concern that would comfort her during any bout of desolation, though it seemed improbable that such could occur now that Peter had come home.

Her glances disturbed him, and he was glad to hear: 'You two go and look at the books, if you must. Afterwards we'll have tea in the dining room. It's such a lovely day!'

Baxter walked along the corridor with shoulders more bent than when they met in town, as if being at home made him older. The house smelled damp, and any books in it had probably gone rotten through being set in shelves against an outside wall. Peter clenched his fists at the idea that he had been tricked into wasting his time, and felt uneasy while following Baxter because he didn't yet know what if any profit he'd find by the end of the day.

'What's the idea, telling her I was your son?'

Baxter's heavily veined hand trembled at the knob as he closed the door. 'Keep your voice down.'

'Tell me what's going on, then.'

'I will, my boy, I will' – his sing-song suggesting he might never be able to. They were in a large study whose furniture, Peter saw, would notch up a fortune in the sale room. The Malcombe shotguns in their case must be worth a thousand. There were no guns finer. The major was delighted to show them, then returned both lovingly to their beds of green velvet. 'I'm afraid she does think you're our son.'

The admission demanded a calm response. 'So I gather.'

A lacquered desk shone with its tiers of many drawers. He'd never seen anything so fine. He walked to a butterfly collection on one of the tables, lifted the lid, and peered at their reminiscent colours. A faint smell of ethyl acetate came out.

Baxter looked over his shoulder, pleased at a common interest that might make them more friendly. It was easy to believe his son had come back, though he fought not to while watching him examine the butterflies as intently as if he really had leapt with swinging net between the bushes. 'He collected those.'

'I did the same, once,' Peter told him. 'Not on this scale, though.'

'We didn't stint him. There are moths as well. You don't see such things any more.' The major opened a cupboard that went from floor to ceiling, revealing exhibition drawers of shells, birds' eggs, geological specimens and beetles. 'They weren't all yours – his, rather. Collected some myself. That drawer was brought from India. Filled that one on the Nile.'

Peter walked to his books. People didn't usually know how to keep them. A man once took him to see hundreds that were heaped in the corner of a garden shed. The smell of mould was appalling. Some were good titles, but all had been ruined, and the only way to move them was with a shovel – straight into a furnace. These, however, were well-shelved and looked after, so it was only natural to expect difficulty in prising a few loose from the old man. He looked at their spines before Baxter unlocked the glass doors.

'Were these mine, as well?'

He opened a copy of Turton's *Travels on the Rhine* of 1828, fingers touching print and paper, then running across the fresh coloured plates. There was Fitzjohn's *Flora of India*, and a first edition of Goldsmith's *Wonders of Nature*. He reached for Sir Roderick Murchison's *Russia in Europe and the Ural Mountains*, with its coloured maps, plates and sections, published in two royal quarto volumes at eight guineas. God knows what it's worth now, Peter wondered.

Baxter pointed to a first edition of Ford's *Hand-book of Spain*, which led Peter to see, on the lower shelf, Penrose's magnificent *Principles of Athenian Architecture*, a folio volume with forty plates. He had a client for every book in sight. They would positively slaver at the feel, look and – he wouldn't be surprised – the smell of them.

Baxter's face became momentarily anguished. 'Most of them belonged to your grandfather.'

Peter unusually had some pity for people he knew well, and consequently had more than a little left over for himself, but he had none for Baxter, who would have to accept such dislike as part of their pact. What's more he was unwilling to waste too much time on something which kept him from the sort of idleness he called independence. He could have been in Brighton by now. 'What's in it for me?'

'Some are yours, of course,' Baxter agreed. 'You can browse through others when you come to spend a few hours' leave with your mother. The only time she smiles is when you're here.'

'So I gather.'

'It's a great blessing for her to see you after so long. She hasn't looked so well in years.' He spoke slowly in order to make sure there was no misunderstanding, though averting his eyes since to look up would give him the new experience of feeling slightly stupid before his son. He threaded his fingers so firmly together that the knuckles turned white. Then he closed the exhibition case of butterflies, all awareness of what had been decided gone from his face. 'Your mother hasn't had much of a life in the last twenty years, but perhaps things will improve now.'

The heavy books could not be carried safely under his arms. He had a vision of broken spines and scuffed pages – and of Baxter picking them up from the floor. The bargain was no confidence trick, poor old soul. He would defy even his own father to think so – not that it would matter if he did. Perhaps his quaint barrister prejudice about being in trade would lead him to see this little transaction as a more worthwhile manifestation of it. He placed all six books side by side on the table, then walked to the open window where he heard the insects living out their noisy lives under bushes and between grass stalks.

The major, erect and with springing steps, as if pleased that his mind was made up on a matter that had worried him for years, went to the desk and set his gaze at the lefthand column of small drawers. He didn't need to stare, but was putting on a show, Peter thought. He counted slowly from the top, took a small key from his coat pocket, and opened one:

'Have these.'

Peter had expected something else. 'Why?'

'He smoked them. They came back with his things.'

'So what?'

'You lit your last but one in the hotel.'

'You're very observant.'

'Yes. It's habit. And training.'

The name was the same, but the label a different design. The firm had kept up with the times. They were solid enough as cigarettes, and he rolled one between his lips in case the paper stuck to his skin. He didn't like being scrutinized, but wouldn't let it matter, as he scraped the match towards himself and looked hard at the flame to make sure it was alive. The tobacco was dry and tasteless.

When Peter let out the first puff of smoke Major Baxter saw that unless memory was trying to destroy his mind with pernicious inaccuracies his son's gestures were exactly repeated by this stray fellow who looked so much like him. He had never seen him light a cigarette without a flicker of distaste for the whole process curling his lower lip, before going on to enjoy it more than he should.

Peter pushed certain of his mean thoughts aside because he had the feeling that Baxter could read them as clearly as a title page in one of those mint first editions in the bookcase. He decided to be careful in handling this piece of luck, and be nice to the old girl when they went down for tea.

'Come on, Peter, I'll show you to your room.'

He wondered whether Baxter wasn't going barmy in an unspectacular way, in spite of his cunning expression. He seemed in thrall to something so monstrous that Peter wanted to get as far from the house as he could. But the rules of the game lay with Baxter. It would be cowardly to go, and deprive himself of knowing just what they were up to. At the same time he didn't like the fact that his curiosity was becoming even more important than the idea of getting something for nothing. Such a thing had rarely ended in anything except trouble.

Baxter's broad back led him along the corridor, through the dust zone and mothball layer to a converted attic. The studio-type window extending the length of the roof seemed out of character with the rest of the house. A brass telescope on a tripod was placed beside a star-globe, and Peter gripped his hands behind his back so as not to touch its brass framework of co-ordinates. He stood by a table that was covered with maps and drawing instruments.

'I taught him to use maps. Must have been better than me at it, at the end – and that's saying something.' Baxter saw reality in their grid lines and conventional signs, but recalled that his son had mastered their utility more to please him than satisfy any innate love for them. Something had gone wrong over the maps, and he couldn't be sure why, though it didn't seem important now that he had – as it were – come back.

The room had been kept tidy, and he imagined Baxter cleaning it every week. The iron grey-painted bed was made up. A fine-drawn line set out from a point on the plotting chart and ended where no towns were, as if whoever had been guiding his pencil along the ruler had heard a voice calling from downstairs and, Peter thought, having been brought up to instant obedience, had stopped work to answer. He had become a pilot, which was as far as he could get from the infantry of his father. When flying, he was on his own.

Baxter took a Royal Air Force uniform from the wardrobe and laid it along the bed. 'Want to get into that?'

His impulse was to say no, because he too had been brought up to say yes. He had worn a uniform for three years in the cadet force at school. There was also the other garb in prison, whose buttons were made of tin, not brass, and the material was horsecloth, unlike this smartly tailored well-creased blue with its pilot's white wings and officer's insignia. He took the flap of a front pocket between his fingers, thinking that if he had been twenty years older he would once have worn something similar, though it would probably have been khaki, and knowing his luck he'd have been brewed up in a tank, or dismembered around a mangled gun. 'It's good stuff.'

'Of course it is.' Baxter's sharp tone implied that he ought to realize that they had never given him anything except the best.

There was a school desk in one corner, with an inkwell which must have been regularly filled. The black liquid glittered like the tip of a snake's tail, and he drew back at the old man's voice: 'I'll leave you to spruce up a bit. I expect a good tea's being got ready. Don't forget to bring the cigarettes. And if you'd like to offer one to your mother, that's all right. It sometimes amuses her to refuse!'

He heard Baxter close the door. There was an old portable gramophone, and a pile of seventy-eight records on a separate table. When he tried to turn the handle he found it fully wound. He'd done nothing for himself, whoever he was. Peter fought off a wish to set it spinning and play a tune. There were foxtrots and tangos, and one or two classical piano pieces under the heap.

He again thought of running away, but what was the point? You always ended by going in circles. In the mirror, he wondered how much longer his lips would conceal the bitterness he felt. But he was happy, while knowing he was trapped. For the price of a few books he was doing a mad old woman a favour.

The uniform fitted, except for a slight pressure at the shoulders. He speculated on what books he would take, and on those he might help himself to on a further visit. Before going down to play his part, like someone who had once fancied himself as an actor, he tried to imagine what sort of person he had been whose uniform he was dressed in. The landscape helped, when he looked out of the enlarged window. The green hill in front was overpowering. Treetops of a copse on either side made a darker smudge, and to the right an unpaved lane led to a thatched farmhouse almost hidden by the thickening vegetation of late spring. Two horses walked across a field, and stopped under a tree to shelter from the rain.

Maybe the other bloke had died with this scenery in mind. He swore, out of pity. Bullets had shattered his plane, a handful of burning coals flung at his back with incredible speed. His parachute hadn't opened, and he had gone like a stone into water, stunned at the impact and dead before getting wet. He had come back to life. Peter smiled at the thought that the sky was his parachute, and would hold him for ever. He had never given into his father's bullying request that he get his feet on the ground. Perhaps he had taken his mother's story too much to heart.

The black shoes fitted. He pulled them off and walked around the room. He was hungry, a feeling which brought him closer to anger than at any time that day. Had he hated this view, and grown sick of looking at it, before leaving for the last time? He put the shoes on again, though they were stiff from lack of wear.

Baxter nodded towards the stairway. 'He'll be down in a moment or two.'

'Do you think he will?'

He watched her. She had thought of setting tea in the kitchen where Peter had liked to eat as a boy, but Baxter insisted on the dining room because it would be stupid taking Peter's mind back to those pampered days. He used the word 'stupid'. There was a war on, and one had to forget such times. He said 'one' instead of 'we' or 'you'. She had to admit there was no going back, and that she was – they were – lucky to have him here at all with so many boys – well, never coming home again. It wasn't easy to make out why he had reappeared when for some time she had thought him 'missing presumed killed', but here he was and it didn't do to question too much. You must enjoy happiness no matter where it came from, and whatever the explanation might be.

'No, don't call him.'

'Why ever not?'

'Just – don't, George.' She was determined to get her own way. It was so long since she had done so that she couldn't remember when it had last happened. But if she won her point now, it wouldn't matter, except that it wasn't really important. 'He must be tired.' Baxter noticed how embarrassed she was at saying so. 'You know he likes a quiet few minutes in his room, even when he can only spend an hour with us.'

She had made sandwiches, and smiled while altering the position of the cake on the table for the third time. He counted them. She wondered where Peter would sit.

He told her. 'Always by the fire. Even when it isn't lit.'

The photograph on the sideboard was tilted towards the window. There were resemblances in the straight but slightly thin nose, in the same lips and similar forehead. He looked like Helen. But the photograph was of an innocent young man who had loved and respected his parents. He had confided in them and you couldn't have asked for more than that. Pity he had to die. I didn't hang back for my country, Baxter thought, but if only it had been me rather than him. He sighed, having wished it every time his son had come to mind.

The photograph hadn't been in place for twenty years. They had never mentioned his name. There was no need to. She must have hidden it, and looked at it every day. He hadn't known. There was no reason why he should. Their grief occupied separate regions. He had been deceived. She had once gone to the clinic and forgotten to take one of the many paper bundles, and so had stayed twice as long. Now he knew that it must have contained photographs of Peter.

She was in the kitchen filling the teapot. He heard her trying to get the lid on, so went across the room to pick up the frame. The glass was about to crack in his grip. She would see the blood. He heard the tread of Peter coming along the hall and down the stairs, before the pressure could split his fingers.

She had changed her clothes, Peter saw, wore a white blouse and a pale grey, rather long skirt. Her nails weren't grimy any more. He took the heavy pewter teapot, wondering why her husband had let her fill and then carry it.

Her fingers shook. 'You always were kind.'

Baxter leaned against the chair, and Peter saw him looking at his wife as she walked around the table fussily re-laying it as if nothing would ever be right. Every time her fingers touched a plate her smile made her seem younger.

He felt that Baxter didn't like her smile. It made her look more normal, and therefore unusual. A visitor altered the atmosphere. He was afraid of what lay behind it. Lack of perception meant loss of control. An expression of hesitating tenderness was noticeable in Baxter, as if he saw an unpleasant aspect of her that he'd thought would never come back.

Peter held her chair, then sat down himself. Looking across the table he saw the major nod and smile. The drifting veils of rain had gone, and a shadow-line of sun crossed a pile of magazines in the window. He found it painful to watch her hand shaking when she tried to lift the pot. A trivial upset, such as the dropping of a spoon, would send her back into a state of fragile helplessness.

When he went to her she slapped him playfully away: 'If your mother can't pour you a cup of tea, then what use is she?'

Helen wondered why Baxter was so restless – though it didn't disturb her as much as when he was calm. He found it too peaceful, in fact, and had learned to tread carefully because in such tranquillity conflict was always imminent, and at such moments he thought about war with a touch of passion half concealed. Watching Peter and his wife, he knew there was something vital in life he'd never had, though he wasn't sure exactly what it might have been. Yet he knew that the love he had for his son was greater than Helen's. He smiled at the word 'eternal', and Helen reacted to it as if to mimic him when he turned for a moment from Peter. Whatever he hadn't got, it was obvious that Peter had, and had come back to stop him having to the end, though Baxter was willing to go without so as to give Helen the serenity she hadn't enjoyed for so long. There was nothing he would not do so that one day they would be able to talk about their dead son. But he was beginning to see that everything had its price.

He had learned in prison how to get secrets out of the walls, how to see through windows that did not exist, so it was easy to surmise, walking around the trap of his namesake's room, where the hide-outs of a tormented mind could be located. The diary rested on a ledge up the chimney, wrapped in layers of brown paper and pushed into the sort of canvas bag in which he took his gym shoes to school.

Careful not to pull down soot or pebbles, he carried it to the open window and shook the grit away. There had been no cause to start it before August, but after so many years he could smell his elemental panic through the faint pencilling when he did: 'Mummy and Daddy turned her away. I didn't write to them beforehand because I knew they would, though I had hoped they wouldn't. I can't believe it, but it's happened, so I have to. They didn't say why, but were quite firm about it as soon as they saw her. I didn't have the opportunity to tell them what she meant to me, but it wouldn't have made any difference if I had. I'm sure of it, but it doesn't make me feel any better.'

No fires had been lit in the grate. Such comfort might have spoiled him. Everything instead had been lavished on hobbies and education, which made the chimney a good place in which to keep his diary.

He read her full name scripted vertically down the page of half a week: Cynthia Weston, common enough with probably a few in every phone book in the country. Some days after her visit, and before Pilot Officer Baxter went 'missing presumed killed' there were more entries, but Peter was called down before he could read them. At the major's shout he anxiously placed the diary back in the soot, and stood up to make sure there was no sign of it on his uniform.

His mouth was half full of chicken-paste sandwich. Even the tea was good. No teabags here.

'Saw a couple of Heinkel One-elevens over France yesterday. Got one of them at twelve thousand feet. A cannon shell scraped my starboard aileron, but there was no trouble getting back.'

'It must be dreadful, for those poor French people,' she commented.

Baxter grunted. 'Didn't feel much for them in the last war.'

Her torment lasted till Peter came again, but on some visits she was uncertain who he was, and had to make up her mind whether or not to acknowledge that he was Peter whom she thought she had lost. The more hesitation, the greater her fuss when she did recognize him – Baxter had observed. At her distressed moments she knew him from his walk rather than his face. Sometimes he didn't even look like his photograph, poor boy, which was because he worried so much. The war seemed as if it would go on for ever.

'It looked beautiful from up there, those fields spinning under me. I saw the Heinkel hit the deck before any parachutes came out. Sorry about it, though.' He had practised reducing his smile to a look of ruefulness. 'I hate killing.'

'Didn't we all?' Baxter added that he knew those fields. 'We drove around there before the war. Don't you remember?'

'They were wonderful days,' Helen said. 'But so short.'

'On our way to the Loire.' Baxter usually smoked cigarettes, but occasionally lit a short well-worn meerschaum. He calmly released smoke away from the table: 'Stayed the night in Bapaume. Showed you my old sector on the Somme.'

Peter was tired of watching them adore each other, and suspected they only indulged in it when he was in the house. 'Of course I remember. I found a piece of shrapnel by the lane that led to the War Memorial.'

461

Baxter looked at him with suspicion, yet was grateful for such sharpness, with its hint of generosity towards his mother. Must have seen it in the drawer of *his* room. 'You've still got it, I suppose?'

'It's in my desk upstairs, wrapped in cotton wool, in a tobacco tin with an old ten franc piece.' There was no use denying anything. They could have whatever part of him they wanted – except that which would not even share its secrets with himself.

'You're too thin. I do wish you'd eat more.' Helen spoke as if all her troubles would be over if only his appetite improved.

He lit a cigarette with the crested silver lighter found on the bedside table. The flint had lost its roughage, but went at the second go. 'I'm really too full for anything else.'

Baxter disapproved of him having left nothing unturned in Peter's room. Peter smiled. Of course he had been through his things. What did he expect? Neither of them could dispute that they belonged to him.

'In the last war we couldn't get enough to eat,' Baxter said.

To get into a Spitfire and spill around the sky at over three hundred miles an hour was the perfect antidote to such a home life. Every take-off was a farewell. They hadn't even got his ashes back, not an ounce of salt or soil, only an ex-jailbird and con-man a score of years later to remind them of him. He touched her wrist, and picked up another sandwich. 'You're right. They're so good.'

'Your old school phoned the other day,' Baxter remarked, as if he too must play his part.

Helen poured more tea with a steady hand. 'They were really glad to hear about your adventures.'

'The headmaster read your letter to the boys.'

The notion of having grown up to become a credit to his school, not to mention a prime example of self-sacrifice, pleased him in a way he didn't like, though he put in: 'I only wrote what I felt. I just thought they'd like to hear from me.'

'You made them so happy,' she said. 'And us.'

However convincing he was, the little play had gone on long enough for today. The pendulum clock ticked sanely by the doorway. Didn't she know who he was? It was hard to imagine it could be otherwise. He felt sorry for her, but she wasn't the first person in the history of the world to have lost an only son. When he was fourteen a friend's cousin had run from the garden gate to be struck dead by a speeding car. He was an only child. His mother was a grey shadow, walking the streets but avoiding everyone when she could. She felt no offence when dodged in turn by those who saw her as too stricken for them to say anything that would make either them or her remember it without embarrassment. They were abashed at their helplessness, and she was too agonized to believe that any verbal contact would comfort her, or indeed that she would ever be sane again. Six months later she was working as a secretary in a solicitor's office – thinner, greyer, yet willing to talk about her disaster.

He fastened the top button of his tunic. 'I'll collect my books, and then I absolutely must be away.'

Her disappointment was easy to cover with a smile. A cake was packed in a box. I'll throw it out of the car. Every time he left there was a cake in a bloody box. The bow came undone as she put it on the table. But she retied it before the major could get up to do so – as she had known he would.

Baxter handed him his card by the door: 'Telephone when you can come again,' he whispered. 'Make it as soon as possible.' He had written his request on the back also, and there was a similarity to the sharp cramped handwriting in the diary. He put it in his flap pocket. Peter had no longer been a young man when he had scribbled those last entries.

He saw himself telling his tale in a Notting Hill pub. I've got this batty old pair who think I'm their pilot officer son killed in the war. He couldn't, though it was hard to give up what laughs he might get. Baxter admired his car:

'New one, isn't it?'

'I borrowed it' – he loosened his tie, and threw his cap on to the back seat – 'from the adjutant.'

A few more visits would complete his tour of operations. He'd often decided not to call on them again, not even for the cupboard of toys he had discovered under the stairs. He had taken away one or two that wouldn't look amiss in an antique shop window. But the Baxters had been different from his own parents in their treatment of the son they had once had, because they had kept all he'd ever possessed. *His* father had flung everything out when he'd gone to prison.

Baxter was whistling some idiot song from the thirties as he stood at the stove cooking breakfast. He stopped as soon as he was aware of

463

Peter's approach, and glanced at his undone tunic. When nothing came of it he went to work with the spatula to prevent bacon and sausages burning. 'Did you have a good sleep?'

Peter lit a cigarette, to cut the pungent smell of smoking fat. 'Marvellous, thanks.'

'The air's fresh down here, that's why. There are cornflakes over there. Sauce. Bread. Butter. Marmalade. All you need.' Every time he stayed overnight he was given the same instructions, as if he was never expected to learn. 'Grapefruit you'll find on the dresser.'

Whenever he had gone so deeply into sleep he wasn't hungry for breakfast, yet took one of the leathery, stained eggs on to his plate while Baxter sat to a meal of scorched streaky and broken sausages, surrounding it with blobs of sauce and dabs of mustard, as if laying out picquets against wily enemies waiting to launch a surprise assault from the wilds of Waziristan. When he suggested they go shooting that afternoon it was merely his way of giving Peter the morning to himself. 'We'll take the Malcombes.'

'All right.'

Baxter put both plates in the sink. 'Doesn't hurt to use them now and again. We might get a rabbit, or a pigeon if we're lucky. There's not much else around these parts.'

There was peace in the house, until an aggressive banging of church bells from the village began. The unholy assault on his senses as he wandered around the garden was so intense that he went up to his room and lay on the bed to look through the diary of his last year alive. A large greenish fly lifted into a zig-zag course before he brought a hand close to turn the page.

'I don't much care whether I live or die. In fact it would be easy for me to make sure of the latter.' The last entry came soon after, and he was disappointed that there was so little to read: 'Back to the squadron! I can't wait. Better there than here. More bang-on sport, the only sort I like.'

At lunch every button of his uniform was shining and fastened. He laid his cap carefully on the dresser, and as soon as Helen ladled the soup he said: 'I'm having trouble paying my mess bills these days.'

Baxter stopped eating, eyes flashing behind his glasses, as if the shock was greater precisely because he had expected it, and he was now uncertain how to respond. Peter couldn't decide whether he was the most devious bloke in the world, or the most dense. 'I'm afraid a few awkward questions are going to be asked.'

During the long pause Baxter's face assumed a blank expression, and became as sunburned as if he'd done another stretch in India. He was about to speak, but reached for his glass of lager, grunted, and drank off half of it.

Helen's hand lifted, and she looked at Peter. 'You must have been very careless.'

'I believe I was.'

'We shall have to help you' – though speaking as if she at least wouldn't mind.

'I'm sorry. It's an awful situation. But I need three hundred quid immediately. I'd hate the wing commander to find out.'

'You should damn well watch your mess bills,' Baxter grumbled. 'Take better care of things.'

He wanted to laugh at him squirming like a snail on a nail. 'I'll try – from now on.'

'It's easy to run 'em up, but hard to pay when the time comes.'

'I'm sure he *will* try,' said Helen.

The glare was steady with disapproval, but Baxter felt too unsure of himself to say much more than: 'Will he, though?'

Such well-contained rage could be ignored. 'I might.'

'You will, won't you, Peter?'

He hadn't stopped eating, so they couldn't complain of his lack of appetite. 'I'll have a go.'

It had been a gamble, though he'd enjoyed the risk, which seemed almost as good sport as going after the clumsy old Stukas. Top-hole, in fact.

'He's such a nice young man, isn't he, dear?' Helen said breaking the silence.

Baxter thought he might as well get something out of the situation, so looked as if unwilling to emerge from his sulk. 'Who?'

'Don't be silly, dear. You know who!'

She's never been deceived, Peter thought. She won't tell, either. It's Baxter who's deluded, though it'll make no difference in the end.

Baxter climbed a stile and moved across the meadow with the training and care of a lifetime. A couple of prime rabbits, ears at the sky, neither heard nor saw him. Peter stood fifty yards behind, aware that he would be hopeless in the matter. Two shots were so rapid that the noise rolled into one. Both rabbits spun on the grass, and Baxter ran from one to the other, stilling each with a chop at the neck.

'Damned good cat meat.' He wiped specks of vivid blood from his glasses, then put the empty cartridges into his game-bag with the rabbits.

In spite of his flying boots, he went forward more silently, but on squeezing the trigger found to his chagrin that he had forgotten to push off the safety catch. He felt better, however, when he fetched a couple of pigeons down: 'I'll get my batman to roast 'em on the spit!'

'You should. You seem to pay him enough.' Baxter was unwilling to call him a robber outright. 'I suppose you lost money at cards?'

Peter reloaded. 'It'll help pay my rent.'

'Or on women. That sort of thing.'

'Not at all.'

'Go on you can tell *me*.'

The wind had strengthened and changed direction. They couldn't get into the lee of it without wading the stream. 'I owe a packet on my car. Don't want them to fetch it back.'

'Mess bills are sacred. You should lay something by. Wouldn't hurt. Apart from showing the white feather, it's the worst thing out.'

He put the safety catch on. The temptation to become involved in the creation of a fatal accident was too great. 'I'll try to be more economical, but I'm afraid I'll have to come back for more if things keep getting out of hand.'

Peter watched him moving up the lane, game-bag slung too low behind, gun crooked in his arm, head looking to left and right as if dreading an ambush. By the dark copse he turned a corner, too angry to want his company on the way home.

He need never see them again, yet a new-found formality with regard to Mrs Baxter contained a certain amount of pity, and he decided to make a few more visits. He couldn't yet walk off with one of the Malcombe guns, though hoped to before the appropriate goodbye.

A voice grated into his ear like a file pulled across balsa wood. 'Peter?'

'It's the middle of the night, for God's sake.'

'It's me – Baxter. And it's nearly midday.'

The curtains were thin, and let in sufficient light for him to see his watch. God knows how he'd found the number. Maybe he'd followed him, or had him followed. Perhaps he'd searched his car while he'd been in Peter's room looking for more secrets, or gone through his things in Peter's room while he had been talking to Helen in the garden. But he'd never let them out of his sight or sound. 'What do you want?'

He saw Baxter in a phone booth near the market, just off the High Street, a pile of coins neatly stacked on the Bakelite shelf. Couldn't phone from home in case Helen heard. 'Your mother wonders when you're coming down for a day or two?'

Peter's lips were ready to shape obscenities at his pleading tone, but decided they were too good to waste at such a distance. 'Don't know when I can.'

'We'll be glad to see you. You know that. Don't you?'

His head ached, and he wanted breakfast to sop up the whisky he had been drinking till four o'clock. After days of intense work compiling a catalogue of their best books, many of which came from Baxter's choice collection, he felt the need of a long rest. 'Do I?'

'Can't you wangle a bit of leave? Even thirty-six hours?'

He hadn't been to see them for a fortnight, being tired of acting the part of their long lost son. When you found such easy plunder you were never far from being caught, so jump – before the axe fell. He put some encouragement into his voice: 'I'll see what I can do.'

His speech droned on through his hangover: 'Ask the CO. He'll let you have it. I remember him. He's a very good chap. I'm convinced he will.'

Still holding the telephone, he got out of bed and walked to the window, drawing back the curtains to let in daylight. 'I expect you're right,' he interrupted, trying not to laugh. 'He's such a ripping sport!'

Baxter chuckled. 'He won't refuse one of his best pilots.'

He lodged the receiver under his chin while lighting a cigarette. 'How did you find my number?'

'What number?'

How dense can the silly old bastard get? 'Telephone number,' he shouted.

'Oh, looked it up in the book. But don't forget. Come down and see your mother. She's not well.'

* * *

467

The pushbike idea was too much like hard work, but he'd agreed because Baxter did deserve some consideration after having parted with over a thousand pounds. He swore when his ankle caught on the pedals. Nor was the bike much good for carrying valuable old tomes in the saddlebag to his car parked at the station nearly six miles away.

He opened the War Revision map sheet with Baxter's name scrawled in pencil along the top margin. The folds were torn after much use. It was not necessary any more but Peter had cycled home on his last visit and used a similar map which, so Baxter insisted, he always carried even though he knew every lane and stile around.

When a piece of grit lodged in his left shoe he leaned the bicycle against a bush and scooped it clear with his thumb. There was a gap in the hedge. Damp soil, pocked by cow hoofprints, was scattered with bits of dead twig. He screwed up the map and slung it there.

At the lane a fat youth went by on a motorbike whose noise seemed to tear the heart out of the countryside. Peter glanced at the bulbous pale cheeks under a red helmet, and the hunched body dead-set towards the village. He mounted his pushbike and pedalled the last few hundred yards.

They stood at the gate like an advertisement for a life of happy savers and insurance payers. He thought Baxter's arm was around her, but couldn't be sure. When he was close he saw them wave.

'I shan't be seeing you for a long time.' They strolled back and forth on the lawn. 'The squadron will be packing up for the Middle East soon. I can't tell you exactly when because it's very hush-hush.'

The major's eyes suggested he'd already said too much. Didn't he know that rhododendrons had ears? He looked nervously towards the hedge, and then at Helen who said:

'We know you can't, dear.'

Brambles were growing outwards from the trees. The end of May had seen thunderous weather and a few hot days, and huge white Queen Anne's lace – as well as nettles – had become too tall to stand upright. The place looked more ragged than when he'd first seen it. 'There'll be promotion, though. Another step up.'

Baxter liked the idea. 'Be nice if you could reach squadron leader before it's over.'

If the war dragged on he might even get to wing commander, which would be one rank above major. Peter supposed it wouldn't do at all from Baxter's point of view.

'We'd be very proud if you did.' Her dress was too long, but she was smart and self-confident these days, and he was sorry for her that it was about to end.

The major walked with a stick. He wore a panama hat and a pale light jacket. 'We must mow the lawn sometime, Peter. Tidy things up a bit.'

His uniform was too hot, and he unbuttoned the tunic. A black-edged cloud which the met bods hadn't warned him about stood in the west. If Baxter grumbled at him for being improperly dressed he would tell him what to do with himself. Helen's ready smile made him think that she knew what was in his mind. Bad show. He had taken the diary home months ago, and there wasn't a word he didn't know by heart.

He sat on a straight-backed chair in the cool living room. Baxter made a jug of lemonade, and Peter hoped he'd splash in some gin. He didn't. The cat spread itself across a magazine on the window ledge like an old wine skin and closed its eyes. Helen's smile disconcerted him because it didn't quite fit what she was saying. She said with folded hands, 'I pray to God you'll be all right when you go overseas.'

'See a bit of the desert, mother. Have to brush up my navigation.'

Baxter put down his lemonade glass. His voice quavered. 'He'll do his duty, as we did in the last war.'

'I know he will.'

She wasn't absolutely sure, so he said: 'No worry on that score.'

He would have had no option except to have done it, yet knew that if he had to do it today he would be most unwilling, though to perform one's duty might at least help to pass the time. But the need for that sort of duty had not yet come, and probably never would till it overwhelmed him whether he wanted it to or not. He refused to let it concern him while there was an issue to be settled which did not conform to their ideas of duty at all.

'Mother, I wonder if you mind listening to me for a moment.' He heard his own voice with the same detachment as when he first spoke to Baxter in the pub. Since that meeting times had changed, though he wasn't sure by how much. The idea that under certain circumstances he would be like Baxter when he got to his age frightened him, and gave him the courage to go on: 'I have something to tell you.'

His sharp tone caused her to look up with an expression which asked who was this stranger in her house? Her son's face was grey. The features shifted from her, but when she smiled, as she must if the life she enjoyed with him was to remain, they came back, and his face turned

469

pale again. He always appeared as if exhausted, and she wondered what was wrong. Something surely was. The more she saw of him the more he looked like she felt. She wasn't his mother for nothing.

Peter hadn't heard such a laugh before, but Baxter had. Every time she looked at George, even when the three of them were happy together, he seemed afraid of something. But she didn't think it sufficient reason for Peter's face to turn into that of an ashen-visaged young man so close to death. She would try not to laugh again like that.

'Do you remember when I brought Cynthia home?'

'Who?'

George's hand lifted in a half secret motion meant for him alone.

'You remember. Both of you do.'

'Cynthia? Now, let me see . . .'

'You wouldn't let her stay.'

Peter was missing and presumed gone for ever. That trivial incident with Cynthia had only been known to the three of them. He had neither written nor telephoned for a month. The uncertainty had been appalling, but the agony of his death had erased the memory of those weeks. He had put a call through to his commanding officer, and when Peter did come back, nothing was said about Cynthia. Everyone had been sensibly forgiving.

He'd read the lines so often it was easy to speak them: 'Met Cynthia. This is the real beginning of my life. I know I'll never be happier.'

'What's that?'

'The secret thoughts of your one and only son. You brought me up to rely on you for everything, but when I came to see you with my girl you turned her away as if she were a . . .' His voice was about to break, and he thought tears already marked his cheeks, but pride stopped him lifting his hand to find out. 'I was open in those days, even honest, in spite of the war. There wasn't much else for me to do except get killed.'

Baxter filled his pipe, but laid it on the table unlit. He thought it only common sense to remind him that such a thing might have happened anyway, at which Helen hoped he wouldn't speak again for the rest of his life.

'It needn't. A lot came through it.' He smiled in the same resigned way as on the day they had made their feelings clear about *that* girl. It was the only time they had seen compliance with their wishes mixed with the bitterest despair. He was able to bring it back any time he liked.

'She wasn't our sort. We told you so at the time.'

'You did, but I was in love with her.'

Baxter stood up, and reminded him that he was pushing things just a little too far. There was no knowing to what lengths a jailbird and confidence trickster would go, however. On days when Helen had looked her normal self he often decided to tell him not to come back. It would be safe then to bring out that telegram (thirteenth drawer down from the right) and show her the news that Peter was missing and presumed to have been killed. He would say that if life was finished, then it was at an end for both of them. But it was clearly too late to do anything now.

'I wrote another letter to my school.' It was impossible to strike one without the other. When Cynthia appeared, she was turned away because they wanted him as much as possible to themselves in his last few months. By not seeing how vital his love affair was, they drove him more quickly to his death. They had let him down, one might say, but more fool he for thinking his parents would do anything else.

Baxter hoped he was mistaken at such malice. 'To your school?'

A photograph at home had shown him standing at attention in front of the cadet force armoury door, on which it said: 'England expects that every man will do his duty.' He was surprised not to have found something similar of Baxter's son upstairs. 'Yes, to my old corrupting school.'

With Baxter, self-preservation meant assuming an air of unthinking optimism. He recalled how, when Peter at other times had threatened to reveal something, he had made them even more proud of their perfect son by a last second divergence from it. 'They'll be delighted to hear from you.'

'Don't you want to know what I wrote?' He didn't altogether like this side of Peter's revenge. There seemed to be something of his namesake in him, after all. He much preferred to act the good son than indulge in the reality of his true self.

Baxter knew they had brought Peter up in such a way that he would surely have forgiven them if he had really come back to life. 'Don't listen to him.'

Helen saw her son, yet not her son. 'What's changed you, Peter?'

'I'm not your son.'

'You are. You always will be.'

He wanted to leave, but couldn't till he'd made them acknowledge what they had done. 'I told that pompous headmaster what a vicious little bastard I'd really been. I had great fun making a list of dirty books I'd read, and the money I stole, and equipment I wrecked and let others take the blame for. I explained how I hated the war, and all that crap about dying for one's country.'

Baxter's eyebrows lifted as if jerked by an invisible thread. Such a person shouldn't be allowed to live. 'Have you finished?'

'I listened to *you* often enough. It's my turn now. I died cursing, and throwing your stale lies back into your face. I'm not Peter. George talked me into it. Didn't you, George? He played a trick on you, Helen, though he doesn't know what stunts I worked on him when I came to see you while he was in town shopping. We had some good talks then, didn't we?'

She played into the game, and held his arm. 'We did, George.'

He wondered what other lies to tell. Baxter was too old to strike. A force of lightning would stab back at him. 'Don't go, major.'

Baxter was able to keep calm as long as any trouble stayed within the expectations of an uneventful life. He tried to remain immobile, to hold the pose for ever but saw, in enormous magnification, a shell going into the breech of a gun. It was big enough for a man to be encapsulated in the package. He shook his head at such a ridiculous picture.

'Peter's dead, but he could have got back to base after his last flight. His fuselage was riddled with bullets, but he was only injured. He rammed his plane into the Channel because his only thought was to end it all. I'll keep his uniform as a memento, and his diary, but I suppose you ought to have these.'

He worked his nails under a tip of his pilot's wings, and tore them off. They hit the table, and fell on to the floor.

Baxter knew that the end had come when, at the lowest point of unmistakable decline, he decided that something had to be done to prevent absolute disaster. Too late or not, you still had to act in order to maintain your self-respect, no matter what the consequences. He picked up the wings, looked at them for a moment, then put them in his pocket and walked away.

He had never left them alone together, and she stood up as if to make the most of it. 'You're not well.'

The truth he had spoken sounded so despicable that he wished everything unsaid. A window had been left open. Wind shook the curtains and the huge tabby cat jumped on to the ledge with a skinned rabbit leg in its mouth. He wanted to hear her say that Peter was finally dead, but she slumped back in the chair, her clarity dispersed as suddenly as it had come. The expression of despair startled him so much that he was unable to go over and comfort her. The right ascension denied itself absolutely. He couldn't walk away, either. Silence and stillness seemed the only safe possibility.

She made an effort, and spoke: 'We did the best we could – whatever went wrong. You'll do the same with your children.'

The cat was busy on the floor, and he pushed it from the raw meat. Helen flinched: 'Baxter never understood me. It wasn't his fault. He's not the sort of man to understand what's going on. I didn't know how to tell him, but if I had he might have changed so absolutely from the man I knew that it would have made things harder. I needed the person I already knew to help me through the terrors I hadn't known about up to then. Without being aware of it he passed *some* of his on to *me*.'

'I've nothing more to say.'

'Don't be sorry.'

'I'm not. I'm afraid.'

Baxter's footsteps sounded overhead, then the noise of his firm tread down the stairs. Every movement in the house could be heard from every other place in it. Peter didn't know from which way he would appear. The clarity he had forced Helen into brought more pain than he could bear, so the only thing left was to make his way back to the station on foot, crossing fields where normal air existed.

He said that he must go, and she agreed but hoped he'd come and see them again. He nodded to say he would, and she didn't believe him. He turned around, and hesitated when facing the hall door, a preliminary to his movement which was so slight as to seem almost a mannerism, and he was still in the living room when Baxter levelled his gun from the bottom of the stairs.

There was no need to aim. At such short range Baxter would scare him out of his wits so that he would never show his face in the district again – no mean feat with a foulmouthed plunderer who had taken their books and money. And neither would Helen expect him to come back after witnessing the comic antics of his departure. He had fouled her suffering, though he blamed himself for having lured him home that day. It was impossible to say what had happened during the making of a decision for which he could recall no clear feelings of responsibility. Such things happened in life – or they had with him. The same mechanism occurred again when, unconscious of any movement, and in no way making up his mind he pushed the safety catch forward and pressed the trigger.

The glimpse of George lifting his gun reminded her of one summer's dawn when she had seen him stalk a rabbit that had been ravaging the kitchen garden. He had got up specially, and in the first light he went inch by inch towards the spot where the rabbit quite plainly plundered the carrot tops and rows of peas, secure in its vandalizing gluttony. It must have taken him twenty minutes to get close – he in thrall to the rabbit and Helen fixed by him – before he risked a shot. She had never been able to observe him for so long without him talking to her or being aware that she was looking.

Peter stood, his hand at the cold door knob that had to be turned. He didn't want to go, but Helen suddenly urged him to *run*, her shriek striking the back of his neck:

'No, don't! George!'

The agony of her cry forced him to turn. Her eyes were closed, as if she didn't want to know who he was. He was given no time to consider the many reasons why this was so. She fastened her arms on him. Looking over her head he saw the levelled gun, and heard it become the end point of an exploding cone which knocked them against the door and covered his stung hands in blood.

The weight deadened his pain and enabled him to stay on his feet. She clung so hard that he couldn't hear what she was saying. The hand tore his uniform as he let her fall. The pain was like ice. Her burden smelled of death.

He wanted to say no, don't shoot, you have nothing to kill *me* for. His mouth wouldn't shape any words, as if he hadn't enough breath, and when he knew that he was helpless before the fact that there was nothing left to live for, he said: 'All right, then, kill me.'

Major Baxter turned his head slowly left and right, remembering something that had to be done, a minor item from long ago that it would be best to do now in case he forgot until the time came when it would be too late, as it was bound to if he didn't do it this minute, a piece of outstanding business that no one knew about except himself but which tormented him because the matter had been pending for so long.

An awkward reversing of the unfired barrel pulled the woollen tie loose from the folds of his jacket. The agony that would not let him talk produced only a simper. There was no atonement for what they had done. His lips were pursed: given time, he would break into a mindless whistling of some tune that would be familiar to all who heard it. He was taken by a sudden concentration of mind that nothing could break, and within it his placid expression said: yes, life is like this, and isn't the world a damned silly place to be in? An assertion he profoundly believed at the moment the explosion spread a volcanic crater backwards and changed his look to one which showed him trying to eat the moon.

A thunderclap rattled the windows. Peter curled on the floor. The sound pushed itself deeply in and then vanished as pellets of shot grazed his skin. The wind roared through a fever. His fever turned to icecold. Silence when the wind died made him feel he was resting on the ocean bed. Teeth bit into his finger ends. He heard Helen groan, and telephoned to get help.

He had been visiting them. He often did. They were like grandparents. There was a quarrel which he never did quite understand. Got some-what bitter, though. Hard to say why exactly. The old major tried to frighten him. Yes, that was it. To frighten *them*, if you like. He was fond of them both, and they normally got on very well. Can't think what came over him. Baxter's gun went off when he knocked against the stair rail. He must have slipped, dammit. Certainly didn't mean to shoot his wife, but when he did – by accident – he was so appalled that he killed himself. Who wouldn't be? Eh? The RAF uniform was a fad of theirs. He had been trying it on. They liked him to, occasionally, because it gave them a glimpse of their dead son, whom they said he resembled. Harmless enough, really.

The house and everything else would be his one day. The sooner the better, he told himself. Even the beautiful pair of Malcombe guns. No facts were altered. Can't trim facts. To backtrack by dead reckoning and try to find out how it had come about would not help, no matter how much he pondered. Nor could any inbuilt technological amanuensis have fixed it with any kind of precision. A square-search was out of the question. Interception problems were beyond his competence. Perhaps the triangle of velocities would help, or the probability of errors. But he didn't want to know. There was no purpose in knowing. Silence was freedom now that chaos had turned into order.

He was left with whatever ruins had been thrust upon him while he sat in the living room cleaning Baxter's guns – getting them ready over and over again in case that dreadful book-stealing con-man whose pictures were framed all over the house ever came back. He relaxed his stance only when Helen called from her wheelchair in the garden to remind him that they were going to a party in half an hour, and hadn't he better check the car and make sure that all was ready for him to get her into it?

'I will, my sweet,' he said, and whistled some mindless tune as he went outside.

No Name in the Street

'Do you know, you get on my bloody nerves, you do.'

Albert's black-and-white dog ran between his feet, making him scuffle out of the way in case he should tread on it and commit an injury. 'You've got on my bleddy nerves all day.'

It was almost dark when they set out for the golf course. A cool wind carried a whiff of hay from large square bales scattered about the field like tank-traps in the war when, as a youth in the Home Guard, he used to run from one to another with a rifle in his hand. It smelled good, the air did. He hadn't noticed in those distant days whether it had smelled good or not. Or perhaps he didn't remember. But you could tell it had been a hot day today because even though the wind had a bit of an edge to it the whiff of hay was warm. 'You do, you get on my bleddy nerves.'

The dog quickened its pace, as if a bit more liveliness would mend matters. And Albert lengthened his stride, not in response to the dog but because he always did when he made that turning in the lane and saw the wood's dark shape abutting the golf course. His dog anticipated this further increase of speed. Having been pulled in off the street a couple of years ago when it was starving, it couldn't afford not to. Even a dog knew that nothing was certain in life.

They'd come this way on most nights since, so there was no reason why it shouldn't know what to do. Why it got on his nerves so much he'd no idea, but what else could you expect from a dog?

'Get away from my feet, will yer?' His voice was little more than a sharp whisper because they were so near. The 'will yer?' – which he added with a certain amount of threat and venom – caused the dog to rub against his trousers and bounce off, then continue walking, almost in step despite both sets of legs still perilously close. 'You'll drive me up the pole, yer will. My nerves are all to bits.'

It wasn't a cold evening, following a hot day at the end of June, but he wore a long dark blue overcoat, a white nylon scarf, and a bowler hat, more because he was familiar with them than to keep warm. He felt protected and alive inside his best clothes, and in any case he usually put them on when he left the house in the evening, out of some half surfaced notion that if anything happened so that he couldn't get back home then at least he would be in clothes that would last a while, or fetch a bob or two at the ragshop if he had to sell 'em.

There was no reason why he should be this way, but that didn't make it less real. Apart from which, he couldn't go to the golf course wearing his shabby stuff. The adage that if you dressed smart you *did* well was about the only useful advice his father had ever tried to tell him, though it was so obvious a truth that it would have made no difference had he kept his trap shut, especially since neither he nor his father had ever done well at anything in their lives.

'Here we are, you aggravating bogger.' He stopped at the fence, then turned to the dog which, as always at this point, and for reasons best known to itself, hung back. 'Don't forget to follow me in – or I'll put me boot in your soup-box.'

No hole was visible, but Albert knew exactly where it was. He got down on his haunches, shuffled forwards, and lifted a strand of smooth wire. The dog saw him vanish. When he stood up in the total blackness of the wood, he heard the dog whine because it was still on the wrong side of the fence.

It showed no sign of coming through to join him, even though it was a job so much easier for a dog than a man. At least you might have thought so, but the bleddy thing was as deaf as a haddock when it came to telling it what to do. It hesitated so long that, after a suitable curse, Albert's pale bony hand at the end of his clothed arm at last appeared under the fence, grabbed it by the collar (you had to give the damned thing a collar, or somebody else might take it in) and yanked it through, briars and all.

It didn't yelp. Whatever happened was no more than it expected. 'You get on my bleddy nerves,' Albert said, holding its wet nose close, and staring into its opaque apologetic eyes.

When he walked along the invisible path he knew that the dog was obediently following. They went through the same haffle-and-caffle every time, and it got on his nerves no end, but it would have chafed them even more if the dog had done as it was supposed to do, because in that case Albert might not even know it was there. And then there would be no proof that he had any nerves at all worth getting on. He often told himself that there was at least some advantage in having such a mongrel.

He could do this zig-zag walk without cracking twigs, but the dog rustled and sniffled enough for both of them, biting leaves as if there was a rat or ferret under every twig. On first bringing the tike into his house it had shivered in a corner for three days. Then one morning it got up, jumped onto the table (treading its muddy paws all over the cloth) and ate his pot of geraniums almost down to the stubs. Afterwards it was sick on the lino. Then he gave it some bread and milk, followed by a bowl of soup (oxtail) – and from that point on there was no holding it. He even had to get a key to the food cupboard.

Albert hadn't felt right since his mother died three years ago, unable to work after losing her, finding that nobody would set him on at any job because they saw in his face that the guts had been knocked out of him. That's what he thought it was, and when he told them at the Welfare that he felt he was on the scrapheap, they gave him money to keep the house and himself going.

It wasn't a bleddy sight. The dog was eating him out of house and home. Every time he had a slice of bread-and-marmalade he had to cut some for the dog as well. Same when he poured a cup of tea, he had to put a saucerful on the floor. So you had to do summat to earn a few bob extra.

There was a bit of light in the wood now they'd got used to it, and when he reached the fence he saw that the moon was coming. It wasn't much of one, but it would be a help – without being too much of a hindrance. Sandpit holes in the golf course beyond glowed like craters. The dog ran into a bush, and came out more quickly than he'd expected, nudging his leg with something hard in its jaws. Albert bent down and felt cold saliva as he took it and put it into his pocket. 'That's one, any road. Let's hope there'll be plenty more.'

Occasionally when they found one so early it ended up a bad harvest. But you never knew. Life was full of surprises, and dreams. He had visions of coming across more lost golf balls than he could carry, pyramids that would need a wheelbarrow to take away. He saw a sandy depression of the golf course levelled off with them. He even had the odd picture of emerging from the wood and spotting a dozen or so, plain and white under the moon, and watching himself dart over the greenery, pocketing each one. In his dream though, the golf balls seemed soft and warm in his fingers as he slipped them into his topcoat pocket.

The dog brought another while he smoked a fag, but ten minutes went by without any more. 'All right,' he said, 'we'd better go and see what we can find. Best not get too close to the clubhouse: the boggers stay up boozing late enough in that cosy place they've got.'

His dog agreed, went through the fence this time even before Albert had finished muttering, glad to be in the open again. They said next door that his mother had to die sometime. Not much else they could say, being as she was nearly eighty. She used to talk to him about his father, who had gone to work one day twenty-five years ago complaining of pains in his stomach, and not come back alive. Something about a ruptured ulcer, or maybe it was cancer. There was no point in caring, once it had happened. The doctor had been kind, but told them nothing – a man who looked at you with the sort of glittering eyes that didn't expect you to ask questions.

Then *she* went as well. He bent down one morning to look, and saw that she'd never wake up. He sat with her a few minutes before going to get the doctor, not realizing till he got out of the door that he'd been with her ten hours in that long moment, and that dusk was beginning to glow up the cold street.

He was glad to be in the actual golf course because the wood was full of nettles, and brambles twisting all over the place. Stark moonlight shone on the grass so that it looked like frost. Even before he'd gone five yards the dog came leaping back, and pushed another ball into his hand, the sand still gritty on its nose. That was three already, so maybe a jackpot-night was coming up, though he didn't like to think so, in case it wasn't. Perhaps he should hope it would turn out rotten, then every find would be encouraging, though at the same time he'd feel a bit of a cheat if he ended up with loads. Yet he'd also be more glad than if he'd hoped it would finish well and it turned out lousy. He'd appear foolish sooner than lose his dream, though he'd rather lose his dream if it meant things seeming too uncomfortably real. The best thing was, like always, not to forecast anything, and see what happened.

Every golf ball meant fifteen pence in his pocket from the second-hand shop, and some weeks his finds added up to a couple of quid on top of his Social Security. He earned more by it than when he used to hang around caddying as a youth of fourteen before the war. Every little had helped in those far-off days, but there'd been too many others at it. Things had altered for the better when he'd got taken on at Gedling Pit, because as well as getting work he was exempted from the army.

After the funeral he sat in the house wearing his best suit, and wondering what would happen to him now. Going for a walk in the milk-and-water sunshine he wandered near the golf course one day and saw a ball lying at his feet when he stopped to light a cigarette. He picked it up, took it home, and put it in a cut-glass bowl on the dresser. Later he went back looking for more.

He ran his fingers over the hard indented pattern, brushing off sand grains and grass blades as they went along. It was an ordinary night, after all, because they found no more than four. 'Come on, then, you slack bogger,' he said to the dog. 'Let's be off, or you'll be getting on my nerves again!'

'It's a good dog,' he said, sitting at a table with his half pint of ale, 'but it gets on my nerves a bit too much at times.'

They wondered what nerves he had to get on, such an odd-looking well-wrapped up fifty-year-old whose little Jack Russell dog had followed him in. One of the railwaymen at the bar jokingly remarked that the dog was like a walking snowball with a stump of wood up its arse.

Albert sat brushing his bowler hat with his right-hand sleeve, making an anti-clockwise motion around the crown and brim. Those who'd known him for years could see how suffering had thinned his face, lined his forehead, and deepened the vulnerable look in his eyes. Yet they wouldn't have admitted that he had anything to suffer about. Hadn't he got house, grub, clothes, half pint, and even a dog? But whatever it was, the expression and the features (by now you couldn't tell where one ended and the other began) made him seem wiser and gentler than he was, certainly a different man to the knockabout young collier he'd been up to not too long ago.

He indicated the dog: 'He's got his uses, though.'

The railwayman held up a crisp from his packet, and the animal waited for it to drop. 'As long as it's obedient. That's all you want from a dog.'

'It'll have your hand off, if you don't drop that crisp,' Albert told him. The railwayman took the hint, and let it fall under the stool. The crunch was heard, because everyone was listening for it.

'As long as it's faithful, as well,' a woman at the next table put in.

You were never alone with a dog, he thought. Everybody was bound to remark on it before long.

'A dog's got to be faithful to its owner,' she said. 'It'll be obedient all right, if it's faithful.'

'It's a help to me,' Albert admitted, 'even though it does get on my nerves.'

'Nerves!' she called out. 'What nerves? You ain't got *nerves*, have you?'

She'd tricked him squarely, by hinting that some disease like worms was gnawing at his insides.

'I'm not mental, if that's what you mean.' Since he didn't know from her voice whether she was friendly or not, he looked at her more closely, smiling that she had to scoff at his nerves before his eyes became interested in her.

The dog came back from its crisp. 'Gerrunder!' he told it harshly, to prove that his nerves were as strong as the next person's.

Her homely laugh let him know that such a thing as strong nerves might certainly be possible with him, after all. She had a short drink of gin or vodka in front of her, and a large flat white handbag. There was also an ashtray on the table at which she flicked ash from her cigarette, even when there seemed to be none on its feeble glow, as if trying to throw the large ring on her finger into that place as well. Her opened brown fur coat showed a violet blouse underneath. He'd always found it hard to tell a woman's age, but in this case thought that, with such short greying hair fluffed up over her head, she must be about fifty.

'Let him know who's boss,' she said.

He felt the golf balls in his overcoat pocket. 'I expect he wants his supper. I'll be getting him home soon.'

Her hard jaw was less noticeable when she spoke. 'Don't let him run your life.'

'He don't do that. But he's fussy.'

He observed that she had mischief in her eyes as well as in her words. '*I'll* say it is. Are you a local man?'

'Have been all my life,' he told her.

She stood up. 'I'll have another gin before I go. Keeps me warm when I get to bed.'

He watched her stop at the one-armed bandit, stare at the fruit signs as if to read her fortune there, then put a couple of shillings through the mill. Losing, she jerked her head, and ordered the drinks, then said something to the men at the bar that made them laugh.

'You needn't a done that,' Albert said, when she set a pint of best bitter down for him. 'I never have more than half a jar.'

He needed it, by the look of him, this funny-seeming bloke whom she couldn't quite fathom – which was rare for her when it came to men. She was intrigued by the reason for him being set apart from the rest of them in the pub. It was obvious a mile off that he lived alone, but he tried to keep himself smart, all the same, and that was rare.

She pushed the jar an inch closer. 'It'll do you good. Didn't you ever get away in the army?'

'No.'

'Most men did.'

The dog nudged his leg, but he ignored it. Piss on the floor if you've got to. He'd go home when he was ready. 'I was a collier, and missed all that.'

She drank her gin in one quick flush. 'No use nursing it. I only have a couple, though. I kept a boarding house in Yarmouth for twenty years. Now I'm back in Nottingham. I sometimes wonder why I came back.'

'You must like it,' he suggested.

'I do. And I don't.' She saw the dog nudge him this time. 'Has it got worms, or something?'

'Not on the hasty-pudding he gets from me. He's a bit nervous, though. I expect that's why he gets on my nerves.'

He hadn't touched his pint.

'Are you going to have that?'

'I can't sup all of it.'

She thought he was only joking. 'I'll bet you did at one time.'

When his face came alive it took ten years off his age, she noticed.

He laughed. 'I did, an' all!'

'I'll drink it, if you don't.'

'You're welcome.' He smiled at the way she was bossing him, and picked up the jar of ale to drink.

Sometimes, when it was too wet and dreary to go to the golf course he'd sit for hours in the dark, the dog by his side to be conveniently cursed for grating his nerves whenever it scratched or shifted. At such times he might not know whether to go across the yard for a piss or get up and make a cup of tea. But occasionally he'd put the light on for a moment and take twenty pence from under the tea-caddy on the scullery shelf, and go to the pub for a drink before closing time.

If he'd cashed his Social Security cheque that day and he saw Alice there, he'd offer to get her a drink. Once, when she accepted, she said to him afterwards: 'Why don't we live together?'

He didn't answer, not knowing whether he was more surprised at being asked by her, or at the idea of it at all. But he walked her home that night. In the autumn when she went back to his place she said: 'You've got to live in my house. It's bigger than yours.' You couldn't expect her to sound much different after donkey's years landladying in Yarmouth.

'My mother died here.' He poured her another cup of tea. 'I've lived all my life at 28 Hinks Street!'

'All the more reason to get shut on it.'

That was as maybe. He loved the house, and the thought of having to leave it was real pain. He'd be even less of a man without the house. Yet he felt an urge to get out of it, all the same.

'So if you want to come,' she said, not taking sugar because it spoiled the taste of her cigarette, 'you can. I mean what I say. I'm not flighty Fanny Fernackerpan!'

He looked doubtful, and asked himself exactly who the hell she might be. 'I didn't say you was.'

She wondered when he was going to put the light on, whether or no he was saving on the electricity. He hadn't got a telly, and the old wireless on the sideboard had a hole in its face. A dead valve had dust on it. Dust on all of us. She'd picked a winner all right, but didn't she always? The place looked clean enough, except it stank of the dog a bit. 'Not me, I'm not.'

'There's not only me, though,' he said. 'There's two of us.'

She took another Craven 'A' from her handbag, and dropped the match in her saucer, since it seemed he didn't use ashtrays. 'You mean your dog?'

He nodded.

Smoke went towards the mantelshelf. 'There's two of *us*, as well.'

Here was a surprise. If she'd got a dog they'd have to call it off. He was almost glad to hear it. Or perhaps it was a cat. 'Who's that, then?'

'My son, Raymond. He's twenty-two, and not carat-gold, either. He's a rough diamond, you might say, but a good lad – at heart.'

She saw she'd frightened him, but it was better now than later. 'He's the apple of my eye,' she went on, 'but not so much that *you* can't come in and make a go of it with me. With your dog as well, if you like.'

If I like! What sort of language was that? He was glad he'd asked her to come to his house after the pub, otherwise he wouldn't know where to put his face, the way she was talking. 'The dog's only a bit o' summat I picked off the street, but I wouldn't part with him. He's been company, I suppose.'

'Bring him. There's room. But I've always wanted a man about the house, and I've never had one.' Not for long enough, anyway. She told him she might not be much to look at (though he hadn't properly considered that, yet) but that she *had* been at one time, when she'd worked as a typist at the stocking factory. It hadn't done her much good because the gaffer had got her pregnant. O yes, she'd known he was married, and that he was only playing about, and why not? It was good to get a bit of fun out of life, and was nice while it lasted.

He'd been generous, in the circumstances. A lot of men would have slived off, but not him. He'd paid for everything and bought her a house at Yarmouth (where he'd taken her the first weekend they'd slept together: she didn't hide what she meant) so that she could run it as a boarding house and support herself. The money for Raymond came separate, monthly till he was sixteen. She saved and scraped and invested for twenty years, and had a tidy bit put by, though she'd got a job again now, because she didn't have enough to be a lady of leisure, and in any case everybody should earn their keep, so worked as a receptionist at a motoring school. I like having a job, I mean, I wouldn't be very interesting without a job, would I? Raymond works at the Argus Factory on a centre lathe – not a capstan lathe, because anybody can work one of them after an hour – but a proper big centre lathe. She'd seen it when she went in one day to tell the foreman he'd be off for a while with bronchitis – and to collect his wages. He was a clever lad at mechanics and engineering, even if he had left school at sixteen. He made fag lighters and candle-sticks and doorknobs on the QT.

He could see that she liked to talk, to say what she wanted out of life, and to tell how she'd got where she was – wherever *that* was. But he liked her, so it must have been somewhere. When she talked she seemed to be in some other world, but he knew she wouldn't be feeling so free and enjoying it so much if he hadn't been sitting in front to take most of it in. She'd had a busy life, but wanted somebody to listen to her, and to look as if what she was saying meant something to them both. He could do that right enough, because hadn't he been listening to himself all his life? Be a change hearing somebody else, instead of his own old record.

'There's a garden for your dog, as well, at my place. He won't get run over there. And a bathroom in the house, so you won't have to cross the yard when you want to piddle, like you do here.'

He'd guessed as much, looking at it from the outside when he'd walked her home but hadn't gone in. It was a bay-windowed house at Hucknall with a gate and some palings along the front.

'It's all settled then, duck?'

'I'll say yes.' It felt like jumping down a well you couldn't see the bottom of. He couldn't understand why he felt so glad at doing it.

She reached across to him. He had such rough strong hands for a man who took all night to make up his mind. Still, as long as there was somebody else to make it up for him there'd be no harm done.

'Every old sock finds an old shoe!' she laughed.

'A damned fine way of putting it!'

'It's what a friend at work said when I told her about us.'

He grunted.

'Cheer up! She was only joking. As far as I'm concerned we're as young as the next lot, and we're as old as we feel. I always feel about twenty, if you want to know the truth. I often think I've not started to live yet.'

He smiled. 'I feel that, as well. Funny, in't it?'

She liked how easy it was to cheer him up, which was something else you couldn't say for every chap.

He polished his black boots by first spreading a dab of Kiwi with finger and rag: front, back, sides and laces; then by plying the stiff-bristled brush till his arms ached, which gave them a dullish black-lead look. He put them on for a final shine, lifting each foot in turn to the chair for a five-minute energetic duffing so that he could see his face in them. You couldn't change a phase of your life without giving your boots an all-round clean; and in any case, his face looked more interesting to him reflected in the leather rather than staring back from the mirror over the fireplace.

A large van arrived at half past eight from the best removal firm in town. She knew how to do things, he'd say that for her. Your breakfast's ready, she would call, but he might not want to get up, and then where would they be? Dig the garden, she'd say, and he'd have no energy. What about getting a job? she'd ask. Me and Raymond's got one, and you're no different to be without. I'm having a bit of a rest, he'd say. I worked thirty years at the pit face before I knocked off. Let others have a turn. I've done my share – till I'm good and ready to get set on again. She was the sort who could buy him a new tie and expect him to wear it whether he liked it or not. Still, he wouldn't be pleased if he took her a bunch of flowers and she complained about the colour. You didn't have to wear flowers, though.

He stood on the doorstep and watched the van come up the street. There was no doubt that it was for him. With thinning hair well parted, and bowler hat held on his forearm, he hoped it would go by, but realized that such a thing at this moment was impossible. He didn't want it to, either, for after a night of thick dreams that he couldn't remember he'd been up since six, packing a suitcase and cardboard boxes with things he didn't want the removal men to break or rip. He'd been as active as a bluebottle that spins crazily to try and stop itself dying after the summer's gone.

When you've moved in with me we'll have a honeymoon, she'd joked. Our room's ready for us, though we'll have to be a bit discreet as far as our Raymond's concerned. They would, as well. He'd only kissed her in fun the other night, but it had knocked Raymond all of a heap for the rest of his short stay there. He'd seen that she was a well-made woman, and that she'd be a treat to sleep with. He hadn't been with anyone since before his mother died, but he felt in need of a change now. I'll have to start living again, he told himself, and the thought made him feel good.

The dog's whole body and all paws touched the slab of the pavement as if for greater security on this weird and insecure morning. 'Now don't *you* start getting on my bleddy nerves,' he said as the van pulled up and the alerted animal ran into the house, then altered its mind and came out again. 'That's the last thing I want.'

He wondered if it would rain. Trust it to rain on a day like this. It didn't look like rain, though wasn't it supposed to be a good sign if it did? What was he doing, going off to live in a woman's house at his age? He didn't know her from Adam, though he'd known people get together in less than the three months they'd known each other. Yet he had never wanted to do anything so much in his life before as what he was doing now, and couldn't stop himself even if he wanted to. It was as if he had woken up from a dream of painful storms, into a day where, whatever the weather, the sun shone and he could breathe again. He smiled at the clouds, and put his hat on.

But if that was so, why had he got a scab on his lip? He'd been running the gamut of a cold a week ago, and had expected it to be all over by now. Maybe the cold had been operating at his innards even a week before that, and had twisted his senses so much that only it and not his real self was responsible for leading him into this predicament. He was disturbed by the possibility of thinking so. Yet because he wasn't put out by the impending split-up and change he'd rather think it than worry that he'd been taken over by something outside his control. You couldn't have everything, and so had to be grateful for the bit of good to be got out of any situation, whether you'd done it all on your own, or whether it was the work of God or the Devil.

'This is it, George,' the driver called to his mate's ear only a foot away in the cab. 'I'll pull onto the pavement a bit. Less distance then to carry his bits of rammel.'

He heard that remark, but supposed they'd say it about every house unless it was some posh place up Mapperley or West Bridgford. Maybe the dog caught it as well, for it stood stiffly as the cab door banged and they came towards the house.

'Get down, you bleddy ha'porth, or you'll get on my nerves!'

The dog, with the true aerials of its ears, detected the trouble and uncertainty of Albert's soul, something which Albert couldn't acknowledge because it was too much hidden from him at this moment, and would stay so till some days had passed and the peril it represented had gone. The dog's whine, as it stood up with all sensitivities bristling, seemed to be in full contact with what might well have troubled Albert if he'd had the same equipment. Albert knew it was there, though, and realized also that the dog had ferreted it out, as usual, which lent some truth to his forceful assertion that it was already beginning to get on his bleddy nerves.

The dog went one way, then spun the other. All nerves and no breeding, Albert thought, watching the two men stow his belongings in the van. It didn't take long. They didn't even pull their jackets off when they came in for the preliminary survey. It was a vast contraption they'd brought to shift him to Hucknall, and had clearly expected more than two chairs, a table, wardrobe and bed. There'd been more when his mother was alive, but he'd sold the surplus little by little to the junk shop for a bob or two at a time. It was as if he'd broken off bits of himself like brittle toffee and got rid of it till there was only the framework of a midget left. That was it. His dream had been about that last night. He remembered being in a market place, standing on a stage before a crowd of people. He had a metal hammer with which he hit at his fingers and hand till the bits flew, and people on the edge of the crowd leapt around to grab them stuffing them into their mouths and clamouring for more. This pleased him so much that he continued to hammer at his toes and arms and legs and – finally – his head.

Bloody fine thing to dream about. All his belongings were stowed aboard, but the terrified dog had slid to the back of the gas stove and wouldn't come out. 'You get on my *bleddy* nerves, you do,' he called. 'Come on, come away from there.'

It was dim, and in the glow of a match he saw the shivering flank of the dog pressed against the greasy skirting board. He looked for an old newspaper to lie on, and drag it out, not wanting to get his overcoat grimy. It was damned amazing, the grit that collected once you took your trappings away, not to mention nails coming through the lino that he hadn't noticed before.

'Come on, mate,' the van driver called, 'we've got to get cracking. Another job at eleven.'

There wasn't any newspaper, so he lay in his overcoat, and spoke to it gently, ignoring the hard bump of something in his pocket: 'Come on, my old duck, don't let me down. There's a garden to run in where you're going. Mutton bones as well, if I know owt. They'll be as soft as steak! Be a good lad, and don't get on my nerves at a time like this.'

The men in the van shouted again, but he took no notice, his eyes squinting at the dim shape of the dog at the back of the stove. It looked so settled, so finally fixed, so comfortable that he almost envied it. He wanted to diminish in size, and crawl in to join it, to stay there in that homely place for ever. We'd eat woodlice and blackclocks and the scrapings of stale grease till we got old together and pegged out, or till the knockdown gangs broke up the street and we got buried and killed. Make space for me and let me come in. I won't get on *your* nerves. I'll lay quiet as a mouse, and sleep most of the time.

His hand shot out to grab it, as he'd pulled it many a time through a

489

hedge by the golf course: 'Come out, you bleddy tike. You get on my nerves!'

A sudden searing rip at his knuckles threw them back against his chest.

'Leave it, mate,' the man in the doorway laughed. 'You can come back for it. We ain't got all day.'

Standing up in case the dog leapt at his throat, he banged his head on the gas stove. He belonged in daylight, on two feet, with blood dripping from his hand, and a bruise already blotching his forehead.

'Smoke the bogger out,' the driver advised. 'That'll settle its 'ash.'

He'd thought of it, and considered it, but it would smoke *him* out as well. Whatever he did to the dog he did to himself. It seemed to be a problem no one could solve, him least of all.

'It's obstinate, in't it?' the younger one observed.

'Go on, fume it out,' urged the driver. 'I'd bleddy kill it if it was mine. I'd bleddy drown it, I would.'

Albert leaned against the opposite wall. 'It ain't yourn, though. It's got a mind of its own.' It was an effort to speak. I'll wring its neck.

'Some bleddy mind,' remarked the driver, cupping his hand to light a cigarette, as if he were still in the open air.

'I can't leave it,' Albert told them.

'What we'll do, mate,' the driver went on, 'is get your stuff to Hucknall, and unload it. You can come on later when you've got your dog out. And if I was you, I'd call in at a chemist's and get summat put on that bite while you're about it. Or else you'll get scabies.'

'Rabies,' his mate said. 'Not fucking scabies.'

'Scabies or rabies or fucking babies, I don't care. But he'd better get summat purronit, I know that fucking much!'

Albert's predicament enraged them more than it did him, and certainly more than the dog. The only consolation came at being glad the dog wasn't doing to them what it was to him. He heard the tailgate slam during their argument, the lynchpins slot in, the cab door bang, and all he owned driven away down the street. There wasn't even a chair to sit on, not a stick, nothing on the walls, nothing, only himself and the dog, and that crumbling decrepit gas stove that she'd said could be left behind because it wasn't worth a light.

He sat on the floor against the opposite wall, feeling sleepy and waiting for the dog to emerge. 'Come on, you daft bogger, show yourself. You get on my nerves, behaving like this.' But there was no hurry. It could stay till it got dark for all he cared. He'd sat out worse things with similar patience. No, it wasn't true that he had, because the ten hours by the body of his mother had passed like half a minute. That was three years ago. He felt as if he had no memory any more. He didn't need one. If everything that had happened seemed as if it had happened only yesterday you didn't need to dwell too much on the past. It didn't do you any good, and in any case it was just as well not to because as you got older, things got worse.

It was daylight, but it felt as if he were sitting in the dark. The dog hadn't stirred. Maybe it was dead, and yet what had it got to die for? He'd fed it and housed it, and now it was playing this dirty trick on him. It didn't want to leave. Well, nobody did, did they? *He* didn't want to leave, and that was a fact, but a time came when you had to. You had to leave or you had to sink into the ground and die. And he didn't want to die. He wanted to live. He knew that, now. He wanted to live with this nice woman who had taken a fancy to him. He felt young again because he wanted to leave. If he'd known earlier that wanting to change your life made you feel young he'd have wanted to leave long before now. Anybody with any sense would, but he hadn't been able to. The time hadn't come, but now it had, the chance to get out of the tunnel he'd been lost in since birth.

But the dog was having none of it. After all he'd done for it – to turn on him like this! Would you credit it? Would you just! You had to be careful what you took in off the street.

'Come on out, you daft bogger!' When it did he'd be half-minded to kick its arse for biting him like that. He wrapped his clean hand-kerchief around the throbbing wound, spoiling the white linen with the blood. She'd asked if it was faithful when they'd first met in the pub: 'It'll be obedient all right, as long as it's faithful,' she had said. Like hell it was. If you don't come from under that stove I'll turn the gas on. Then we'll see who's boss.

No, I won't, so don't worry, my owd duck. He lay down again near the stove, and extended his leg underneath to try and push it sideways. He felt its ribs against the sole. What a damned fine thing! It whined, and then growled. He drew his boot away, not wanting the trousers of his suit ripped. He sat again by the opposite wall, as if to get a better view of his downfall. The world was coming to an end. It's *my* head I'll put in the gas oven, not the dog's. Be a way to get free of everything.

491

The idea of shutting all doors and windows, and slowly turning on each brass tap, and lying down never to wake up, enraged him with its meaningless finality. If he died who would regret that he had disappeared? Especially, if, as was likely, he and the dog went together. His heart bumped with anger, as if he'd just run half a mile. He wanted to stand up and take the house apart brick by brick and beam by rotten beam, to smash his fist at doors and floors and windows, and fireplaces in which the soot stank now that the furniture had gone.

'I'll kill you!' He leapt to his feet: 'I'll kill yer! I'll spiflicate yer!' – looking for some loose object to hurl at the obstinate dog because it was set on spoiling his plans, rending his desires to shreds. He saw himself here all day, and all night, and all next week, unable to lock the door and leave the dog to starve to death as it deserved.

His hat was placed carefully on the least gritty part of the floor, and he drew his hand back from it on realizing that if he put it on he would walk out and leave the dog to die. It's either him or me, he thought, baffled as to why life should be that way. But it was, and he had really pulled back the hand to wipe his wet face, his tears in tune with the insoluble problem.

He leapt to his feet, full of wild energy, not knowing whether he would smash his toffee head to pieces at the stationary hammer of the stove or flee into the daylight. He spun, almost dancing with rage. Feeling deep into his pocket, he took out something that he hadn't known was there because it had slipped through a hole into the lining. He dropped onto his haunches and hurled it at the dog under the stove with all his strength: 'I'll kill you, you bleeder!'

It missed, and must have hit the skirting board about the dog's head. It ricocheted, shooting back at an angle to the wall near the door. He couldn't believe it, but the dog leapt for it with tremendous force, propelled like a torpedo after the golf ball that he'd unthinkingly slung at it.

Albert, his senses shattered, stood aside for a good view, to find out what was really going on on this mad day. The dog's four paws skidded on the lino as the ball clattered away from the wall and made a line under its belly. Turning nimbly, it chased it across the room in another direction, trying to corner it as if it were a live thing. Its feet again sent the ball rattling out of range.

There'd be no more visits to the golf course tatting for stray balls. The dog didn't know it, but he did, that he'd as like as not be saying goodbye to his tears and getting a job somewhere. After his few dead years without one, he'd be all the better for the continual pull at his legs and muscles. Maybe the dog knew even more than he did, and if it did, there was nothing either of them could do about it.

The dog got the ball gently in its teeth, realizing from long experience that it must leave no marks there if the object was to make Albert appreciate its efforts. It came back to him, nudging his legs to show what it had got.

His boot itched to take a running kick at the lousy pest. 'That's the last time you get on my bleddy nerves, and that's straight.'

It was, he thought, the last time I get on my own. It wasn't a case any more of a man and his dog, but of a man and the woman he was going to. He bent down to take the gift of the ball from its mouth, but then stopped as if the shaft of cunning had at last gone into him. No, don't get it out, he told himself. You don't know what antics it'll spring on you if you do. Without the familiar golf ball in its trap the bleddy thing will scoot back to its hide-away. Maybe he'd learned a thing or two. He'd certainly need to be sharper in the situation he was going into than he'd been for the last few years.

He straightened up, and walked to the door. 'Let's get after that van. It's got all our stuff on board.' He raised his voice to its usual pitch: 'Come on, make your bleddy heels crack, or we'll never get anything done.'

With the golf ball still in its mouth there was no telling where it would follow him. To the ends of the earth, he didn't wonder, though the earth had suddenly got small enough for him not to be afraid of it any more, and to follow himself there as well.

The Meeting

She came through from the lounge, passing between two tables in the bar, and asked the waiter to get her a drink.

He noted everything about her: dark hair, pale face, red sweater, big bosom, black slacks and high heels. But there was too much shadow to see more than the barest details of her face.

On her way to sit down he asked her to join him which, to his delight, she did. He offered her a cigarette, and she took it.

'Are you lefthanded?'

'No,' she answered, 'but my father was. Are you?'

'No. My mother was, though. Are you married?'

'Was. We split up.'

'So did I.'

At least he wasn't secretive, which was a good thing, because she knew that secretive men were often rather simple in their relationships with women.

'The best women are divorced,' he said, 'it seems to me.' Every woman responded to flattery, in spite of female enlightenment, or whatever it was called, and he had long since told himself never to forget it.

She laughed. 'And the best men are married.'

'I can tell you don't believe that.'

She sipped her vodka. 'My husband was a spendthrift.'

'Vodka's best if you knock it back.'

'I know. He'd get through five hundred pounds like a snake on fire.'

He noticed the shifting unharnessed bosom under her sweater when she leaned forward to bring the ashtray close. 'Apart from that,' she added, 'he was a real old sour-socks! You remember that famous picture of "The Remittance Man Returning From Abroad" with his pathetic expression of wanting revenge yet also needing to be loved? I forget which museum it's in. He looked a bit like that. Very strong minded, in that he never knew what to do. Could only rest and feel wanted when he went into hospital to have his appendix out.'

'Tell me more about him,' he said, also leaning forward. 'You make me sweat.'

'Do I? There's not much to say, though. He was really a greedy little male chauvinist fascist under the skin. We had quite a time. He had that favourite male-swine's trick of pretending to be gentle and good humoured, while I was pushed into being outspoken and fierce. When we were on our own he was repressive, scornful, and plain bloody mean, just so that he could see my spleen burst when we were in company. The only way I could get my own back was to attack him in front of his friends – all of whom, I suspect, were having the same problems. Either that, or to give *them* a rough time. Then he'd have to soothe them, so that they all thought him a nice, diplomatic, and put-upon sort of person, while I was a shrew. He had a desert in himself, and tried to call it an empire.'

She looked very pleasant to him now. He wanted to asphyxiate himself on her two beautiful plump breasts, give her a kiss on the lips which would hopefully lead to a touch of the tongue, and end in an Epicurean lick of the epiglottis. 'I was happily married for ten years,' he told her, 'so I do have something to be pleased about.'

There was a tremor of curiosity in her deep blue eyes. 'What happened?'

'I came back early one day from my travels – I'm a commercial traveller.'

'So am I,' she put in quickly. 'Hosiery.'

'I'm in electronics. Well, I found her with my best friend. They were eating chocolate-covered wholemeal biscuits with slivers of Cheddar cheese. Both were in the bedroom, with nothing on. She'd been sleeping with him since just after we were married, but I'd had no idea. It had been the talk of the avenue for a long time and everyone thought that as a ménage-à-trois we were supremely happy. If he'd been a stranger I'd probably just told him to clear off, but because he was an acquaintance I half killed him. I threw my wife out as well, then put the 1812 Overture on as loud as possible till the neighbours had to break the door down and stop it. Then I was all right, and able to get back to work.'

'Do you always smoke a cigar as if it were a haystack?' she asked, when she'd stopped laughing. 'It reminds me of that delectable piece of haddock you usually get for breakfast at this hotel.'

'I like a good smoke.' He finished his whisky. 'A friend of mine drank a bottle of his wife's perfume after a three-day quarrel, and went blind. Nobody ever knew what they had been arguing about, because they led blameless lives, but he didn't get his sight back for a fortnight, and in that time she really went off the rails.'

She made sympathetic noises, unable to get upset about it. Evenings, after all, were the only times she had to relax. 'A friend of mine had been married to her second husband for two years,' she told him, after a long pause, 'and it suddenly occurred to her that she had never seen him shave. One day she woke up, and he was gone. His appetite, though, had been as regular as sin. She never saw him again.'

He called the waiter over for more drinks. 'Same?'

'All right. I prefer Dutch treat, though.'

'Don't worry, I can afford it. Trade's good. Everybody's got money to buy hi-fis and calculators.'

'They're fun, I know. But I'm making good money, too.'

'It used to be the tobacco that counts: now, it's pocket calculators!'

But she didn't laugh, asking instead: 'Do you think it's easier to recognize your own face or your own voice?'

'Know your enemy,' he replied, 'though not *too* well, or you may become like him – or her. Your face, I suppose.'

This seemed to upset her. 'I believe in the voice, really.' It had always been difficult to accept that she had delicate susceptibilities, and as for him – he'd usually preferred to learn the hard way. 'Get me a vodka then, for God's sake,' she said.

He thought she was going to cry, which seemed admissible in a big woman. They always cried sooner than small women.

'I read lately,' she said, making her usual good recovery, 'how common it is for a man and a wife to develop the same neuroses as they grow older together. What I think is that they fight each other's neuroses till a benevolent kind of stalemate takes over. This can go on until death. Quite often, though, one or the other can't stand such nullity and takes a lover so as to keep what individuality she's got left. But if it comes back completely it means a divorce. And then maybe they both begin the whole process again with their new partners – if they're idiotic enough. Maybe such things only happen to weak and ordinary people. But if they do, who does that exclude, I'd like to know?'

'It bloody well excludes me' – though he was sorry he said it so harshly and abruptly. That was the effect she had on him. 'Sex,' he countered, 'becomes too important in a marriage when not enough of it takes place. When the man and woman are so preoccupied with their work that they forget to make love as often as they need, they become antagonistic towards one another without knowing why. They only make love after a quarrel, so it seems that sex is more important than it should be. Or they get to think that the marriage is "based on sex" when it clearly is not.'

She hoped for something better every year, but it was always the same. 'I *did* try to save you.'

He put the expression on his lips that he could never control – simply, of course, because he didn't want to – a mixture of despair and disdain for her and all the world. It was unmistakable, and he always backed up the accompanying deadness of his eyes with some words or other: 'Those who save us destroy us, if we aren't careful to resist their blandishments after we no longer need them.'

With her usual bravado she drank her vodka straight off, which was no more than a cover while she took in his words slowly, so as to get the full cut of their blades. Then she picked up an olive and, carefully putting the stone on the rim of the ashtray, flicked it across the bar and into the lounge. She had picked it so clean with her teeth that it rolled along the well-worn carpet, and tapped against the reception desk – which a dark-haired intelligent-looking woman making enquiries about a room did not notice.

'You never miss,' he said. Her actions had always been the best part of her, in spite of her throaty voice.

'*I* work hard,' she said, 'so I have the right to relax in my own way.' He knew all that. By her travelling for a hosiery firm, their tracks crossed often, though each actual meeting had to be deferentially fixed. She was the *chief* traveller, and earned as much as he did.

Now it was his turn to feel like weeping, but he was able to say: 'People like us don't live long enough to see the results of their mistakes. And if they did I suppose they'd only look like glorious moments in an otherwise dull life. Even three hundred years wouldn't be enough.'

She touched his wrist, an indication that, in her view, he was improving.

This made him feel confident enough to add: 'It's a mistake to live in the future all one's life.' He tried to make a last bridge that might bring them together again. 'It's generally pretty miserable, because when you get old you have nothing to live for. Or so my instinct tells me, though I've always believed that instinct to be blind.'

Neither spoke for five minutes, and then she said firmly: 'I know you have. But the first thing you must realize about instinct is that it's not blind, then at least you might be able to get some advantage from it.'

Silence was still their enemy, so he put the usual question: 'What have you been doing with yourself this last year?'

She slurred her words. They were getting drunk. In the room they would, as usual, prove to be nowhere near it – but it was necessary for them to feel so in order to get there. 'I don't have much spare time. I know how to look after myself, though. What do you do?'

When their answers to the same questions coincided he knew they were getting to the end of the evening, though he added earnestly, 'Are you happy?'

She laughed. 'My lip feels dead.'

'Coffee?'

'Please. I read a lot.'

'So do I.' He called for a pot of coffee. It would be as weak as dishwater, merely causing him to get up every hour of the night. He thought it strange how some people never learn. Not to know how to learn showed a fundamental lack of intelligence, even though a person may be very bright and quick on the surface – he suggested.

She poured his coffee. 'Sugar?'

They had made each other suffer, so maybe that alone was love, especially since no marks showed. She used to think he didn't know how to suffer because he suffered too much in silence. If you were in love you'd have the generosity to let the other person see it.

'It seems ridiculous,' he said. 'Yes, I'll have some of that heart-attack white sugar.'

'Don't. I'd hate it if that happened. But what sounds ridiculous?'

'You know what I mean.'

'I don't know what you mean if you don't *tell* me. I don't live in the land of the unspoken any more.'

Everything had to be brought out. They were the ambassadors of two nations, and nothing could be left unsaid. 'Meeting once a year to see if we can't get back together again and make a go of it. That's what's bloody well ridiculous.'

In one way he was right, but at least they'd been able to talk in a civilized way whenever they'd met over the last five years. This hotel was beginning to feel like home. If he threatened to kill himself, or began knocking her about in his quiet far-off tigerish way as if to kill *her*, then at least she would be nearer help than in that detached suburban psycho-box they had lived in. People in that area who thought they'd heard screams would swear it could only have been cats – when it was too late. 'This is the way I like it,' she said firmly.

When they had lived together, their love, if such it was, had been one of incurable polarization. And however tempting it was to return to it she knew that, given her perverse temperament, she must never give in to what she craved. This was the closest she could get to happiness, and she must count herself lucky. She thought it the nearest he could get to it, as well.

His laughter sounded so genuine, and set apart from their insoluble dilemma, that she envied him, though she suspected it, because nothing he had ever done, no sound he had ever made when with her, was not part of some scheme to get at her. 'What are you laughing at?' she asked.

'I once knew someone who put back great quantities of gin, then suddenly stopped drinking on the advice of her doctor. Three months later she died of cancer. She'd been riddled with it. The booze had been holding it at bay.'

'I'll have to think of some good ones for next year,' she said, adding that she would certainly do without *that* kind of drink. He hadn't thought there was much point in it, but he always hoped. 'A score of beginnings,' he said, 'but never an ending in sight.'

If anything would win in the end, she reflected, it was his sense of humour. 'Let's go to bed.'

'I can't tell you how much I'm looking forward to it,' he said.

She was already standing. 'I have to set off for Bristol early in the morning.'

'And I have to go to Hull,' he said, seeing that it was to be the usual thing, after all, but happy at least for the night that was coming.

A Scream of Toys

Edie looked a long time at blue sky in a pool of water after rain before dipping her finger down for a taste.

It got wet. The edge of a cloud was bitter with soil and mouldy brick, telling her that the old backyard was in the sky as well. It was everywhere, even when she walked out and on to the street, and to the road at the end of the street, for wherever she was she knew she had to go back to Albion Yard because that was where she lived.

She liked the water best when it settled into a mirror and showed her face. It wasn't nice to taste the sky, but just to look at the big white cloud creeping back across her frock to cover both knees so that she couldn't see them. You got seven years' bad luck if you broke a mirror, so it was best only to look at it.

She stood up and waved the cloud goodbye, but still saw her mouth and hair saying hello to the sky. It couldn't talk to her, so what was the use? And if it did she'd cheek it back, her mother would say. She would jump in it except that she didn't want bad luck. If she got any of that her mam would smack her in the chops, and dad would thump her like he did mam when she broke the sugar basin last week.

A horse and cart went along the street loaded with bottles of lemonade that rattled against each other. If one fell she would catch it and run off to drink it dry in the lavatory – but it didn't. The big horse was black and white, and the man on the dray shouted and shot a whip at its neck. If a lemonade bottle did fall it would smash before she could reach out and hold it. It'd be empty, anyway.

She'd like to ride on the horse through the pools of water. It went by in no time, leaving big tods steaming on the cobbles. Mr Jones who worked on the railway opened his door and came out with a dustpan. He scooped 'em up and carried 'em back inside as if they was puddings straight out of the saucepan. She'd like lemonade better, but none fell off. He'd give the puddings to his pot plants for their tea. A woman came out with a broken shovel but she was too late. She would have to

501

wait till she heard another horse and cart, and until Mr Jones was at work, because he always got there first.

When she came back to the puddle it was still there. Nobody had dug it out and taken it away. They didn't like water because there was plenty in the tap, and besides, it was wet. It wasn't so big now though, because the sun had come out.

'You'll come to no good,' she said to herself, playing at her mother, staring at the fire and gazing at the sky. It was wrong to pull your knickers down and pee in water. There'd be no mirror left, but the pool would get bigger, though only for a minute. Johnny Towle put his finger there yesterday and she kicked him on the leg so hard that the buttons flew off her shoe. 'I'll tell yer mam I fucked yer,' he shouted right round the yard. She didn't know what it meant, but it wasn't good, so now she did know.

It was better to look down at the sky when she couldn't see her face.

Next day Johnny Towle came running into the yard, arms wide out, and a big round scream at his mouth, and his eyes shining like the black buttons she had kicked off her shoe.

'There's TOYS,' he shouted to everybody. 'A man's just left a big box of lovely toys at the end o't street. Quick, run, or they'll all be gone.'

'You're daft.' Edie didn't want to run, but her heart shook at his absolute certainty of this abandoned box of real yellow and red treasure-toys waiting for them to dip into and snatch, then take home and play with for ever. Not only his mouth had said it, but his whole body and legs as well, so it must be true, and she ran after the others to get her share.

All it was was a pile of cardboard boxes, and in their disappointment they kicked them to pieces. Johnny Towle booted them harder than anyone, as if he had been tricked as well, but they hated him ever after for his rotten scream of toys when there hadn't been anything but boxes.

When she mentioned it to her mother, her mother said she should have had more bleddy sense because nobody leaves a box of toys at the end of the street. Edie wanted to cry about this, but didn't because maybe one day they would.

When your bones ached you could see a long way off, the tool-setter had once said for a joke, fixing the belt on her machine so that it would go for another half hour at least. Some women were getting new lend-lease machines from America but her turn wouldn't come for at least six months, the gaffer said.

All dressed up and nowhere to go, she stood on Trent Bridge and looked into the water. It was a windy summer so her coat was fastened, causing half the month's toffee ration to bulge from her pocket. The water was like oilcloth. Her bones always ached by Friday night, but she had five bob in her purse, and no work tomorrow or Sunday, so the bit of a backache made her feel better.

When she turned round three army lorries went by and a swaddy whistled at her from the back of the last one. She waved back. Cheeky bleeder. But why not? Amy had asked her to go into a pub but she didn't because you had to be eighteen, though Amy didn't care, for she said: 'We have a sing-song, and it's a lot o' laughs. The Yanks'll always buy you a drink.'

The wind brought a whiff from the glue factory, and the water smelled cold. A barge made an arrow, and a man at the front who steered it wore only a shirt and smoked a pipe, and stared at the bridge he had to go under. She wondered if it would ever come out the other side. If it vanished in the middle and wasn't seen again it would be reported in the *Evening Post*. She wanted to run across the wide road and look over the parapet to make sure. You're not a kid any more, so don't, she told herself, watching smoke come up from its chimney.

She looked at aeroplanes flying over, small black shapes scattered across the sky. Maybe she would go to the Plaza picture-house and see Spencer Tracy or Leslie Howard or Robert Taylor. There might be ice cream on sale. Or she'd call at the beer-off for some lemonade and go home to drink it. If she went in the pub with Amy her mam and dad might be there. Or somebody would see her and tell them. After fifteen planes had gone over she lost count.

A man walked along, and stopped near her. They're going to bomb somebody, but they're brave blokes all the same. Oh dear. He leaned with his back to the bridge, looking at the wide road. He tilted his head at the noise of the aeroplanes, and spoke to himself. She laughed. He didn't like aeroplanes, she thought. His big moustache came over his lips like a bush. If it hadn't been for that he would have reminded her of Robert Donat, who had a thin tash.

She didn't want to look at him in case he thought she was looking at him, and then he would look at her, and she might have to look back, and if you looked at somebody they might not like it. They'd have to lump it, though, so she looked at him anyway. He had dark eyes, and laughed so that his teeth shone. He'll bite me if I don't go away, but it's my bridge as much as his.

The chill wind reminded her that there were ten Park Drives in her pocket. It was so cold she wanted to smoke. Her mam didn't like it so she could never have a puff at home. Her dad smoked, though. His pipe smoked all the time. You'll smoke yourself into a kipper, her mam told him every week when she got his tobacco from the Co-op. So she had to do her smoking at work, one a day in her dinner hour, a packet a week, which left three to spare. At Christmas a woman had given her some rum, and when they got back from the pub she was sick. Then she dropped asleep on a heap of uniforms. The gaffer came by, but didn't say anything. She didn't like boozing after that. The gaffer had had a few, as well.

He was like a soldier, but not quite a soldier, in his greeny sort of uniform. She wanted to walk away, and knew she should, but then he might follow her, so she stayed where she was. The water pushed and shoved itself under the bridge, but she couldn't look at it any more, in case it sucked her in. There was a bit of red and orange in the sky by the War Memorial and paddling pool. A woman walked along the embankment with a pram. The kid in it kicked a shoe off, and Edie heard a smack. Another army lorry came by, but the back was covered up.

The kid cried. She took her fags out, and the man stared so hard she put them back again. Then he smiled: 'You walk with me?'

Her grandad had lived with them, and she wondered why he got smaller and smaller. When he first came he was bigger than she was, but then he shrank till he was only a titch, and trembled when he got up from his chair at night to close the curtains. When he spilled his tea dad shouted at him. Fancy shouting like that at your own dad. He used to give her pennies but then he'd got no money left, so she gave him one of her fags when nobody was in, but it made him cough and he threw it on the fire, which was a waste. When he died he got buried, but mam and dad didn't wear black clothes at the funeral because they didn't have any, or couldn't be bothered, more like. They hadn't been to his grave since, but she'd gone twice and put wild flowers on, because you had to visit people's graves after they died. If you didn't they wouldn't remember you when you met them again.

It was a daft idea because where would you walk to when you met each other, but she took out her cigarette packet and held it towards him. You couldn't say what he was, because there were no badges on his battledress that told her anything. He was funny. He saluted her, then came and took a fag, looking carefully to choose one, though they were all the same.

'Thank you,' he said. 'Now, we walk?'

She felt a touch at her elbow, by a hand on its way to put the fag in his mouth. He puffed while it was still unlit, waved it about in his lips as she searched for a box of matches. Her dad bought a lighter at work which went nearly every time.

'I ain't got any.' She wanted a lighter for herself. Maybe she would buy one when the war was over, after she had got a bike and a handbag.

His face was misery, and she was tempted to laugh, till she thought he might not be acting. But he was. His eyes almost closed, and his eyebrows nearly went down to his nose. She had a photo of Robert Donat from *Picturegoer* under her mattress that she took out and looked at with her flashlight before going to sleep. He stretched his arms out wide, smacked his head – even louder than the woman who'd slapped her grizzling kid – undid his top pocket, searched half a minute as if expecting to find a leg of beef there, and fetched a single match out in his fingers. Then his smile was as big as the bridge.

She shivered when he looked at her, and at the lit match between his eyes. 'I'm Italian,' he said, 'prisoner of war – collaborator now.'

He's come a long way, she supposed – watching the lantern made with cupped hands, and then smoke as he put his head almost inside as if he was going to cook it. The dead match somersaulted over the parapet, and she thought she heard a sizzle as it hit the water and was carried away. It'll be in the sea by morning, she didn't wonder.

A man who'd lived next door chucked himself over into the water last year, and drowned. They found the body near Colwick Weir. He'd gone to the doctor's with a sore throat thinking it was cancer, and when the doctor said it was nothing to worry about he thought he was only trying to hide it from him, so he did himself in because he'd seen his mother die of it two years ago. There'd been nothing wrong with him at all, except that he'd gone off his head.

He held his cigarette close to hers. 'Now we walk?'

'You'll have to follow me.' She didn't mind at all when he bowed and took her arm. They said at work that foreigners were well brought up, though she supposed everybody was when they wanted something. But when you didn't think you had much to give it was nice to be bowed to like on the pictures, and smiled at, and walked with arm in arm. You didn't care whether it rained or not. And even without being told, he walked on the side the wind was coming from.

Two ATS girls looked at her gone-out. Seen enough, you nosey bleeders? she'd have said if they had stared a second longer. Officers' comforts was what they called them at work, where the two years spent there seemed as long as since she'd been born, a place where she thought she'd learned enough to last the rest of her life.

People couldn't see who you were with when it got dark, so she was glad when it did. Even when walking with Johnny Towle whom she had once gone out with she hadn't wanted to be seen because it hadn't got anything to do with anybody who she was with, and whether she was happy or not, or what they thought she was doing walking out at night.

He'd hardly said a word since leaving the bridge, and now squeezed her arm and walked in step and, as if realizing that such silence was no way to behave in face of his good luck at having found someone to talk to him, stopped abruptly and faced her. She was glad when he broke into her thoughts:

'My name is Mario. Your name, please?'

'Edie.'

'Edie,' he said, as if that settled something.

'That's right.'

Mario sounded like a woman's name to her.

'Twenty-eight years,' he said.

'What?'

'Age.'

She'd thought he was at least thirty.

'I'm sixteen,' she told him.

He said he was learning English and asked would she teach him. She said she couldn't teach anybody anything and that if he listened to her his English wouldn't be much good – though because she had sometimes come top of the class at school, she might try.

He said yes please when she stopped at the smell and mentioned buying fish and chips. At the shop you had to get in and shut the door before an air raid warden spotted the light, and Mario had never seen anyone vanish from his sight so quickly.

He leaned against a wall to wait. He almost went to sleep. How to wait was one of the fine arts of a soldier, and he still found it difficult not to regard himself as one. He also knew after eight years in the army that to receive and to have something done for you bound the person to you who gave or did it. There was no surer way. He had money in his wallet which he couldn't share with this pale dark-haired girl.

He had worked in South Africa, and saved it from his meagre pay, yet it was no use to him here. They had been fetched out of camp and put on a train to take ship for England at such short notice that he hadn't had time to change the two big notes for English money. It was true that the camp sergeants had offered to change them, but their rate was so low that he decided to wait and do it later. When they said you couldn't cash them in England he thought they were lying, but after he got here he found it was so.

The fact that he had been robbed never ceased to bite and hurt. It was only one of many such times that something had been taken from him. All through life you were robbed. At the beginning the greatest act of robbery was when you were taken from the safety of your mother's womb and fobbed off with air that barely allowed you to breathe. Nobody had any choice about that, but the various robberies of life multiplied thereafter, each occasion leaving you more at the world's mercy.

Everything contrived to separate you from that middle area of happiness and dignity. You could never escape the robbery that went on all the time. While you expected to lose watch, shirt, money or boots (having in any case done your share of robbery whenever you'd had the chance, for it was only the poorest of the poor who never got such opportunities) you didn't expect to be parted from your spirit.

He had been brought up to believe that his spirit was of little value, though he'd never accepted the fact. Even so your beliefs were continually waylaid and overwhelmed, but year by year they had become strong again, till such strength was the only thing of importance. As soon as this was realized your spirit got stronger until nothing could break it at last. It had survived the attacks of church and school, and then worst of all the God-almighty State in the shape of Mussolini standing on a shield and held aloft by his gang, the man and the Party you were expected to die for as you had once stood in church and been told to adore somebody who was supposed to have died for you — when nobody had a right to die for you except yourself, and what fool would want to do that? He had had enough for the rest of his life, and smiled at the truth that he would never be able to do anything about such assaults while he continued to blame nobody but himself. Being taken a prisoner of war was the final indignity, but it was also the point from which he had begun to hope.

The fat in the vat was smooth and smoky. The end of your finger would skate if it didn't get scorched. With three people in front she stared at the dark ice starting to split and bubble, and sending up shrouds of lovely mouth-smelling steam when the man poured a wire basket of raw chips in. His scrawny wife who wore glasses and a turban was pulling a handle on spuds that had been peeled white and then fell as neat chips into an enamel bowl.

'Two pennorth o' chips and a couple o' fish, please,' Edie said. She didn't know why she had left Mario outside in the dark, but it wasn't raining so she didn't worry. To be seen with a lad or a man would have made her feel daft, and being with an Italian was as bad as going out with a Yank, she felt, in that people said all sorts of rotten things, and if they didn't say so you could tell what they were thinking, though at work they might have had a bit of a laugh over it. One of the older women could pull a megrim if you as much as mentioned having a good time before peace was declared, in which case somebody was bound to call out: 'Well, Mrs Smith, it's a bleddy free country, ain't it?'

She hoped he'd be gone, but was glad he wasn't.

'Long time.' He hadn't expected to see her again.

She opened the bundle. 'I had to wait till they was done.'

'Done?'

'Cooked.' It was black but the stars were out, and the smell of vinegar and chips drew her face back to the batter-steam and fish clinging to her fingers. 'You'd better get some, or they'll be gone.'

He picked into the paper, and ate more as if to please her than feed any hunger. 'Good.' His approval seemed like a question. 'Thank you.'

Her smile could not be seen in the dark. 'Lovely, aren't they? They don't fry every night, so we was lucky.'

'You are a good girl.' He spoke solemnly, then laughed at her and at himself. The wall held him up. He leaned as if nobody lived inside the house.

He *is* funny, she told herself, though I don't suppose he'll murder me. 'Let's walk for a bit.'

He held her arm in such a way that it seemed to her as if he was blind or badly, and wanted to be led somewhere. 'I was in . . .' he began.

'In where?' she asked, after a while.

Their feet clattered the pavement. A soldier passed. Another man in the dark nearly bumped into them and stood for a moment as if to say something. He smelt drunk. If it was daylight he might have spoken but if so she'd tell him to get dive-bombed, or to mind his own effing business – whichever was more convenient to his style of life – as they said at work, with more laughs than she could muster at the moment. Mario snorted, as if thinking something similar. 'You're in Nottingham now,' she whispered.

'Nottingham, I know.' His normal voice made the name sound like the end of the world, and maybe it was, in the blackout, in the Meadows. 'I was in Addis Ababa. You know where that is?'

'I'm not daft. It's Abyssinia, ain't it?'

He laughed, and pressed her arm. She was glad at getting it right, saw a wild land full of black people and high mountains. Or was it jungle? As they turned into Arkwright Street the crumpled chip paper slipped from her other hand. There was always a smell of soot when it got dark, and a stink of paraffin from factories. A late trolley bus with lights hardly visible was like a tall thin house rumbling along the cobbles. The Methodist Hall was silent, all doors barred against tramps and ghosts.

'It in't a church,' she said. 'It's a British Restaurant. I sometimes eat my dinner there, because it only costs a shilling.'

He seemed to belong to her, even more so when he released her arm and held her hand. At the Midland Station he stopped. 'Not possible to go to centre of city. Not allowed for us.'

She was glad. In Slab Square people would look at them, and talk, and maybe call out. They turned back. She was also angry, because he no longer belonged to her when he couldn't go where he liked. There were different laws for him, so they weren't alone even while walking together in the dark. 'It's daft that we can't go downtown,' she said. 'It's not right.'

He held her hand again, as if to say that he was not blaming her, a warm mauler closing over her fingers. 'Not public houses, either, but cinema we can go.'

Nobody would take any notice if they went and sat on the back row, but it cost more than at the front. Youths would shout out, and there'd be a fight perhaps. 'We can go to the Plaza. That's a nice one.'

He pulled her close into a doorway. He smelt of hair and cloth, and stubbed-out fags – and scent. 'Tomorrow?'

'Don't kiss me, then.'

She couldn't fathom the scent. It wasn't even hair cream. His hair was dry. He didn't, and as they walked along wide Queen's Drive towards Wilford Bridge she shared a bar of chocolate and the bag of caramels from her toffee ration. You had to pay a ha'penny if you wanted to cross the Trent there, so they called it Ha'penny Bridge. To her it always seemed the only real way to get out of Nottingham, to leave home and vanish for ever into a land and life which could never be as bad as the one she'd felt trapped in since birth. But she had only been taken over to play as a child – or she'd gone across for a walk by herself and come back in half an hour because there didn't seem anywhere to go.

They passed the police station, and three years ago she had stood outside reading lists of dead after the air raid, long white sheets of paper covered in typewritten names. Spots of rain had fallen on them, and people queued to see if anybody was on that they didn't already know about.

Houses were heaps of slates, laths and bricks. If anybody was dead a Union Jack was sometimes put over. Johnny Towle's name was on the list. She'd only seen him the Sunday before, when they went to Lenton for a walk. He said he loved her, and sometimes she dreamed about him. A man stopped her when she walked by one smashed house and said: 'Would you believe it? My mother was killed in that house, and I put a flag over it. It ain't there any more. Somebody's stolen it.' He was wild. He was crying, and she told him before hurrying away: 'They'd nick owt, wouldn't they?'

She wanted Mario to talk because she didn't know what else to say after telling everything that had been in her mind, but he wouldn't. He didn't understand when she said: 'A penny for your thoughts!' Everybody must have something in their heads, but he only wanted to walk, and to listen to her, asking her now and again to explain a word he didn't know.

Before reaching the bridge she said: 'Let's turn round.' The thought of water frightened her, and she had no intention of crossing to the other side. Their footsteps echoed, and she was glad when she heard others.

'After Abyssinia' – his voice startled her – 'go to South Africa. A

510

long way. Then to England. Soon, Italy, when war is finished. I go to work. War is no good.'

'What will you do?'

'I do business.' He rubbed his fingers so hard that she heard chafing skin before actually looking towards it. '*Affari!*' he said, and she could tell it made him cheerful to say it, the first Italian word she had learned.

'*Affari!*' she echoed him. 'Business!' – so that she also laughed. 'I like that word – *affari*.' She would remember it because it sounded *real*. It was good to do business. Two years ago pennies were short for putting in gas and electric meters, so she and Amy did business by standing on street corners selling five pennies for a sixpenny bit. Some people told them to bogger off, but others were glad to buy. Then a copper sent them away, and she daren't do it again, though Amy did it with somebody else. She used to collect milk money at school so could always get the pennies. Mario laughed when she told him about it.

'*Affari?*' she said.

'Yes, *affari!*'

She knew nothing about him, but liked him because even English wasn't his language, and he had been all over the world. Unlike the lads at work, he was interesting. She took out another cigarette and, embarrassed for him at having to accept it said, hoping he wouldn't be offended: 'Ain't you got any?'

'No. We are paid sixpence a day. Italian collaborators' work. Pay tomorrow, so we go to the cinema, both, eh?'

They stood close so as to coax the cigarettes alight. 'You've got a one-track mind,' she said.

'You teach me English!'

On Arkwright Street they turned back towards Trent Bridge. She still wondered whether he was having her on. 'You know it already.'

'I learn. But speech makes practice. Good for *affari!*'

She laughed. He was funny. 'If you like. Pictures, then, tomorrow night?'

'Pictures? Museum?'

She knew it couldn't be hard for him to understand what was said because she'd never been able to talk as if she had swallowed the dictionary. 'No. Pictures means cinema. Same thing.'

She didn't want to lose him, but felt a bit sick after she had agreed. They said at work she never talked, not deep dark Edie Clipston at her sewing and seaming machine earning fifty bob a week. But she did

– when nothing else seemed possible. The lad who humped work to and from the machine tried to kiss her, and she threatened him with the scissors, but she let him last Christmas when somebody held mistletoe over them.

'It didn't mean anything, though,' she told Mario as they stood on the bridge. He had a watch, and said it was half past nine. He had to be in by ten, so pressed her hands hard, and kissed one quickly.

He walked away and she forgot all about him. She didn't know what he looked like, and wondered if she would recognize his face on meeting him again. But she felt as if the cobbles had fur on them as she walked back to Muskham Street.

Hearing no noise through the door she tried the knob and was able to go in, glad the house was empty. She filled the kettle and lit the gas. The cat rubbed against her ankle.

'Gerroff, you've had yer supper already.' It followed her around the room, mewing, so she gave it a saucer of bread and milk. Then she put coal on the fire. When they got back from the boozer they might wonder why she'd done so, but she didn't care what they thought.

Her father was tall and thin, and worked on a machine at the gun factory. He took his cap and jacket off and threw them across the sofa. 'Pour me some tea, duck.'

Her mother came in a few minutes afterwards, pale like Edie but her face thinner and more worn. She took off her brown coat with its fur collar and put it on a hanger behind the stairfoot door. 'What did you bank the fire up for?'

'It's cold.'

'It is when you stand in a queue to buy the coal.'

She sat by the glow to warm her hands. Her legs were mottled already from sitting too close too often. She had never queued for coal, anyway, because a delivery man emptied a hundredweight bag outside the back door every week.

'Kid's don't understand.' Her father nodded at the teapot. 'Let's have some, then.'

Joel Clipston had once spent four months in quod for 'causing grievous bodily harm' to a man who, wilting under opinionated hammerblows of logic during an argument on politics had called Joel's wife a foul name as the only way – so he thought – of stopping his gallop and getting back at him. Joel had kept silent in court, ashamed to say out loud what the man had called Ellen, and so he had no defence against having half killed somebody while waiting for opening time outside a pub one Sunday morning. He said nothing to the magistrate, and got sent down for 'such a vicious attack'. There are worse places than Lincoln, he said when he came out, though he was more or less cured of ever doing anything to get sent there again. For a while he roamed the streets looking for the man who had called Ellen a prostitute, but then heard he had gone into the army. If he don't get killed I'll wait for him when he comes out, soldier or not.

He lost his job over the court case, but now that the war had started it was easy to get another. He was set to digging trenches on open ground for people to run into from nearby houses when aeroplanes came over from Germany. If he worked twelve hours a day he made more money than he'd ever had in his pocket before. Then he got work as a mechanic, and found he was good at it. There was either no work at all, or there was too much, but never exactly as much as you needed. He preferred to read newspapers, play draughts, sit listening to the wireless with a mug of tea in his hand, or spend a few hours in the boozer, rather than work more time than he thought necessary — war or not.

They sometimes went over the river at Ha'penny Bridge and into the fields beyond Wilford. In spring, Ellen baked lemon curd tarts and made sandwiches, and Joel filled two quart bottles with tea for a picnic by Fairham Brook. The air seemed fresher beyond Wilford village, where the smell of water lingered from the river which rounded it on three sides.

Even though her brother Henry was younger he chased Edie with a stick, till the end of it flicked her, so she turned round and threw it into the river and both of them watched it float away like a boat. Joel was glad they got on so well. Henry was squat-faced and fair, while Edie was dark-haired and had olive skin like her mother.

Edie poured tea into his own big white mug, and put in a whole spoon of sugar. 'When the war's over,' he said, 'I'll get half a ton of sugar from the shop. Then I can put three spoons in. You can't even taste one.'

'Pour me a cup as well, duck,' her mother said. 'Where did you go tonight?'

Edie took the tea-cosy off. 'A walk.'

Her legs ached as well as her back. It seemed a long way that she had gone, though she remembered every place as close enough – but far off all the same when somebody talked to you who had seen so much of the world, and then kissed your hand. The pot was poised over the cup and saucer.

'Where to?' Ellen asked.

'I just went out.' She wondered what else there was to say, for it didn't concern anyone where she had been, and tonight she felt no connection to her mother or father, nor would she to Henry when he came in.

'Sly little bleeder!'

Joel tapped at the bars with a poker. 'You'll never get a straight answer from her.'

It had been the same ever since she was born, that if one of them started to get on at her, the other would always join in. She had the feeling that they knew where she had been, and wanted to drag her out of it and back to what she had always hated. She didn't know how they could tell, but was sure they'd twigged something.

'You ought to stay in at least one night of the week.' Her mother stood up to cut bread for Joel's lunch next day. 'And clean the house up a bit. I have enough to do as it is when I get home from work.'

She had noticed, as soon as they came in, that both of them smelled of beer. 'I go to work as well,' she reminded her mother, knowing when she spoke that they would have succeeded in pulling her out of her dreams. But she'd never say who she had been with. She brought more than two pounds into the house every week, which seemed enough for them to get out of her. 'I scrubbed the parlour floor last Sunday, didn't I?'

Hot tea sprayed over the saucer and the cloth, and the pot itself rolled itself on to the floor before she could stop it. The cup broke with the weight of the big brown teapot. She didn't know how. Dropped on to it. The noise shocked every bone, and she stood with fingers curled as if the pot were still gripped – or as if, should she keep them held like that, the teapot bits would reassemble and jump back into place.

In spite of her mother saying that she was always in a dream, that she was as daft as they come, that she had never known anybody to be so clumsy – and several other remarks that she wouldn't listen to but that would come back to her later when, she knew, she would have even less use for them – she felt that if there had been a hammer close enough she would have lifted it and smashed the remains of the teapot and cup to smithereens.

But she didn't care as she looked at the bits of pot mixed among the tea leaves and stains. She remembered Mario's face by the bridge, when he had taken the cigarette and put a hand over while lighting it, as close as if the whole meeting was happening bit by bit again. She saw both herself and him as real and plain as ever, the pair of them right by her side. The picture hypnotized her, and held her rigid with surprise and a feeling that gave some protection for what was sure to come now that she had smashed the teapot.

'She allus was clumsy,' her father put in, a mild response which told her to be on her guard. The jollier they were on coming home from the pub only meant that they would be even more nasty and hateful later. It was best to be out of their way at such times, but unless you went to bed there was nowhere to take refuge, and she didn't want to go to sleep so early after talking to Mario.

'I couldn't help it.' She heard the tone of fear, apology and shame, which made her more angry with herself than at dropping the teapot. The accident didn't seem important, anyway. She wasn't a bit clumsy at work. 'My fingers slipped.'

Her father put his half drunk mug of tea on the mantelshelf, as if it would be safe from her there. 'What am I going to do in the morning, then? There's nowt to make the tea in.'

If she looked up he would hit her, but in turning away she saw his grey eyes lifeless with anger, and his lips tight. Ellen picked up a few bits of the saucer from the cloth.

'Let *her* do it,' Joel said quietly. 'She dropped the bleddy thing.'

He sometimes chased her and Henry around the room in fun. All three laughed, but Ellen looked on as if thinking they should act their age and have more sense. But the last time Joel had been playful they suddenly felt too old for it. The time had passed when they could play together.

Edie sometimes said things without thinking, and when she did she was frightened. If she had known beforehand that she was going to be frightened she would still have spoken because she was never able to stop herself even when she thought about it. The words seemed to jump from outside of her: 'I'm not going to clear it up.'

He sat down with his tea, and she felt sorry she had cheeked him, so picked some brown sharp pieces of the teapot to put in a little heap on

515

the corner of the table. This methodical enjoyment of her task caused a flash of rage to blot out Joel's brain. Edie knew it was only right that she should try to clear the mess up, though her mother had already done most of it, and had come back from the coal place with a dustpan to start clattering bits on to it.

It couldn't have been worse if a ten-ton bomb had dropped on the place and killed them. All because of a teapot, Edie told herself, about to cry, as if she alone in her might and viciousness had broken the spirit of the house. There was such gloom that, after a few moments, the only thing possible was to laugh. She wanted to be walking again with Mario – while doubting that she ever would – crossing a bright green field with him, under a pale blue sky full of sunshine instead of bombers.

It was as if her father had picked up the wall and hit the side of her face with it. She wondered how he knew what she had been thinking. The blow threw her across the room, and coconut matting scraped her skin as she slid with eyes closed and banged her head at the skirting board. In darkness she saw nothing, but it was followed by a dazzle of blue lights as his boot came at her.

When her father lashed out like this her mother always got on at him to have more sense, and now she tried to pull him off, telling him not to be stupid or he'd get in trouble knocking her about like that, thinking of the times he'd pasted her, Edie supposed, but then wondering if she interfered out of spite, because he only answered by giving her another kick that was worse than the rest.

As she lay half stunned Edie knew she would go to the bridge again and meet him as often as she liked because he had been so gentle and interesting. They didn't know, but even if they did they couldn't stop her seeing somebody who made her feel she need never be anybody except herself.

After a parting half-hearted kick at her back which she hardly felt, her father sat down to light his pipe and finish his tea, ignoring her agonized and shouted-out wish that it would choke him.

The drawn curtains in her room made the blackout complete, but when she put off the light it was so dark she couldn't go to sleep. She ached from the last big kick but cried no more, not even when she hoped a German plane would drop a single bomb on them and make the blackout so final that they would never be able to switch a light on again.

She'd die of shame if daylight ever came, but if it did, she would never let anybody hit her again. If her father lost his temper and tried to, she would blind him with whatever she could grab. That sort of thing was finished from now on. She didn't know how, yet knew it was, because she had made up her mind, hoping that when it looked like happening she would be able to remember what she had made up her mind to do, and blind him no matter what.

She heard them arguing downstairs, though not what was said. Their speech sounded like the flood of a river hitting a bridge before going underneath. Now that she wasn't there they could start on each other. They could kill each other for all she cared. They had been cat-and-dogging it for as long as she could remember, but no wonder when she thought about what her mother used to get up to.

When dad was out of work – she would tell Mario (whether he could understand or not, because if you didn't tell your thoughts to somebody there was no point in living) – which went on for years and years, that mam kept going downtown at night saying she was off to Aunt Joan's, but one day after she'd bought some new shoes and a coat, and things for the house as well, and wouldn't say where she had got the money, dad followed and saw her on Long Row talking to somebody in a car.

He felt so rotten at the idea of her picking up men that he hadn't got the guts to put a stop to it. He didn't even let on he knew, though she must have known he did. But one night, after it had gone on for a long time, he decided he'd had enough, and caught her sitting in Yates's Wine Lodge as large as life with a man who'd had his nose blown off in the last war. Where the nose should have been there was wrinkled skin and two small holes that dripped if he didn't press a hanky to it.

When dad saw this he let his fists fall, but swore at them both and told mam never to come home again or he would murder her and the kids and then cut his own throat. Me and Henry liked what happened, because dad didn't even shout at us now she wasn't there. He pawned her clothes one day, and took us on a trackless into town and treated us to the pictures and an ice cream each with the money. The woman who lived next door often gave us toffees when we came home from school because she was sorry for us having no mother. It made us feel like orphans, and we liked that.

We were drinking tea and eating toast one night when somebody knocked at the door. The tap on wood was soft, as if a beggar was hoping we'd ask him in and give him some of our supper, and when dad opened it we were surprised to see old No-nose come in from the cold. Dad was mad at being disturbed from his newspaper and his peace, but No-nose asked: 'I want to know if you'll be kind and take your Ellen back.'

'Take bloody *who* back?'

'Your Ellen,' No-nose said.

Dad stood by the mantelpiece, as if ready to crank his arm up for a real good punch. No-nose stayed just in the door. He wore a nicky-hat and was wrapped up in a good topcoat and scarf – as well as gloves – because he had an office job and was better off than us. He would have been goodlooking if he'd still had a nose.

Me and Henry was too frightened to say anything, and when dad, after a bit of an argument in which nobody said much, said that mam could come back if she liked, No-nose looked as happy as if his nose had come back on to his face, which made us want to laugh – though we daren't in case dad turned on us.

He went out to get mam. She'd been standing at the end of the street waiting for him to come and tell her whether it was all right or not. No-nose gave us some chocolates and sixpence each, then went away after shaking dad's hand but saying not a word to mam. He only nodded at her, as if he'd had enough of the trouble she'd caused – though he was to blame as well.

When he'd gone mam sat on the other side of the fireplace to dad. They scowled at each other for half an hour. Then mam laughed, and dad said a string of foul words. He's going to get the chopper and kill her, I thought, but suddenly he was laughing and so was she. Me and Henry was even more frightened at that, and said nothing, because we weren't able to make things out at all.

Mam and dad kissed, and sent us to buy a parcel of fish and chips out of the few quid that No-nose had given her. Afterwards we had a good supper, and everybody was supposed to be happy, though I wondered how long it would last.

When Edie started to feel more sorry for them than for herself she fell asleep.

With her coat tight-wrapped around her, and holding Mario's two South African banknotes folded into her pocket, Edie went downtown into Gamston's Travel Agency to try and change them for him. She was glad that only one other person was being served as she opened the notes out and showed them over the counter, feeling daft because she had not been in the place before.

'Can't change 'em,' the bloke said, an old man with a moustache who first looked over his glasses at them and then at her.

'Why can't you?' Money was money, she'd always thought, and Mario had earned every penny of whatever it was called.

He held a pen, as if about to write all over her face. 'Because we can't. We're not allowed to, that's why.'

She stood, hoping he'd alter his mind, whether they were supposed to or not. 'Oh.'

'We can't anyway. It's regulations.'

He went to get a railway ticket for somebody but, not wanting to leave without doing what she had come for, she didn't move. Last night Mario had showed her some photographs of his mother and sister, and his two brothers, and they all looked as nice as Mario himself and she felt that if she couldn't get his cash changed she'd be letting them down as well as him. So she held up the large gaudy-coloured banknotes again.

The man came back. 'There's nothing I can do for you. It's foreign money, and there's a war on, and that's why we can't change it. Come in after the war, then it might be all right!'

'It'll be too late then. I need it now.'

A woman behind the counter put a cup of tea by his elbow, and maybe he didn't want to let it get cold because he said, as if ready to fetch the police to her: 'Where did you get 'em from?'

She saw by his face, and knew from his tone, that he thought she had nicked them or – she screwed the words painfully into her mind – earned them like *that*. Her mouth filled with swearing, but she couldn't spit it at him as he deserved, so walked out and then went quickly along Parliament Street towards a café where she could get a cup of tea.

The sun was in her eyes so she turned her back to it. When Mario walked on to the bridge she gave him the banknotes: 'Sorry.'

'No *affari*?'

'The bleeders wouldn't do it.'

He scowled. 'Bleeders?'

She explained.

'Never mind.'

Neither spoke for half an hour. They walked by rowing boats tied to wooden landing stages, and she wondered when and at what place they would reach the sea if she and Mario got into one of them. Maybe they'd land on a beach in Italy, and have no more trouble from anybody.

He held her hand tightly, so she knew he was brooding about something which it was no use asking him to explain. But he didn't seem angry. He was miles away, living in sounds and colours she had no hope of understanding, though she liked the warm and dreamy feeling when she tried to picture them. With an English bloke she wouldn't have had such dreams. They'd have joshed and teased like kids – whereas with Mario she saw mountains and yellow trees, and a sky so blue it would blind you if you looked straight at it. But she didn't want to because her dream was too far beyond her normal mind. You had to be grateful for small mercies, and this was bigger than most.

Grey water slopped at the concrete steps. There was a noise of children playing from the other side of the river. She felt easy with him because, though he had suffered and was far from home, he had a light heart and could make her laugh. But she took his larger hand in order to share his bitterness, and let whatever he felt was too much to bear pass into her. She had always known that there were some things you could only keep quiet about, though realized now that the one way of filling such silence was by touch.

The streak of green and blue turned into the last flush of the day. Children stopped playing suddenly. They were alone on the embankment with no one to see them. Not that she cared. She'd hold his hand whoever was looking on. They could take a running jump at themselves for all she'd bother. Once upon a time she had clutched her father's hand, but she hadn't spoken to that bully for days.

'Never mind,' she said to Mario. 'They're dirty robbers, that's what they are.'

Her whole body shook when he kissed her, and she could never remember feeling so protected.

'I love you,' he said.

She didn't know how to say anything. To speak like that seemed a funny way of putting it, though. They walked on, and she couldn't find words to answer, even when he said it again. It was time to say goodnight, and promise to meet another day, but she couldn't stop walking and say anything while still so close to that total change already made between leaving home and meeting him. To walk away from the comfort of holding hands seemed neither right nor possible.

She still felt stupid at not having got some English money for his foreign banknotes, but it was a failure that brought them closer, and made her want to stay longer with him, so that she was almost glad they'd been so rotten to her at the travel agent's.

A policeman stood talking to the woman tollkeeper who leaned by a tiny brick house to collect money from any carts or motors that went over Ha'penny Bridge.

'Not go there,' Mario said.

There was plenty of dusk to hide in, so she wondered what he meant. They were on the lowest step by the water which, had it come up another inch, would have flowed over her shoes. 'It don't matter, does it?'

'In camp at ten. No Italian out after ten o'clock.'

It was too late, anyway. The world was full of trouble when you did things that caused no harm. She wondered who started it, but didn't know. If Mario walked about after ten at night it wouldn't stop the day beginning tomorrow. 'Will you get shouted at?'

He smiled. 'I have given sergeant money. But the police don't know, and they ask for papers, maybe, then send me back, and tell Captain. Then Mario will not walk with Edie for three weeks.'

If they crossed Ha'penny Bridge to the fields they'd be safe from prying eyes – and from having to make up their minds to go anywhere. He pressed his face to her hair and said things she didn't understand but that she was happy to hear. She was also glad she had washed her hair last night.

He led her up the steps and back to the roadway. 'Police gone now,' he whispered.

She took two ha'pennies from her pocket. The old woman at the gate wore a thick coat and scarf to keep out the damp. The river pushed itself forcefully along, and the other side seemed far off from where they stood. The noise of a cow sounded from the fields.

The tollkeeper took her ha'pennies. 'You'd better be back before twelve.'

'Are you going to wind up the bridge, then?' Edie asked, thinking that coming back was too far in the future to worry about.

'Cheeky young devil!' the old woman called.

521

A sliver of sharp moon showed as if about to come down and cut the river to ribbons. But there were streaks of night mist towards Beeston, and white stars glittered above. Halfway over, Mario said: 'You give her money?'

'Only a penny. It's a *toll* bridge.'

'Toll?'

'Money to pay,' she said. 'Somebody private owns it.'

He walked more quickly. 'Not good.'

'It's always been like that.'

Her arm was folded with his so she had to keep pace. A plane flew over. 'One crashed last year. An American plane. The pilot knew a woman in a house at Wilford. He went over ever so low to wave at her. But he crashed, and everybody in the plane was killed.'

She didn't know whether he understood. It didn't seem to matter, but she went on: 'Five men died, and all for nothing. The pilot had wanted to say hello to his girl. And now she will wear black for evermore because he is dead. And she had a baby afterwards and they couldn't get married. She saw his plane blow up when it hit a tree with no leaves on in the middle of a field.'

'Bad story,' he said.

At the end of the bridge they walked down the lane, no lights showing from any house. They were used to the dark. She didn't know on which field the plane had crashed, but perhaps it was near Fairham Brook where she used to play with Henry when they went on picnics from Albion Yard. At work they'd said what a shame it was, and wondered whether the poor girl would ever get over it, and what would happen to her baby if she didn't, because she was packed off to live with her grandmother in Huntingdonshire. Others heard she'd killed herself, but all sorts of rumours flew about, and you couldn't believe anything, though she wouldn't be surprised.

When he stopped singing it was only to kiss her hand. She heard the grating cry of a crow from the river that looped on three sides of them. She liked his tune, and would have sung a bit herself if she had known it, though she was happy enough to listen as they went through the village that seemed dead to the world and into a field where they would stay till the bombers came home.

Confrontation

'When I last saw you – a year ago,' Mavis said resentfully, and with more disappointment than he cared to notice, 'you told me you had only three months left to live.'

He remembered it vividly, while reflecting that mendacity was an illness for which there was no proper cure. It was possible to recover from it, however, when you had no more need of such unsubtle ruses. In other words you might grow out of lying by the simple process of growing up. He hoped it was only a matter of time, that though old habits never die they might simply fade away.

It happened at June and Adrian's party, a disaster that was indeed difficult to forget. What's more, his ploy hadn't worked, so he might just as well have saved himself the trouble of lying. Yet it *was* undeniable that he had lied, and enjoyed it. He could only apologize to her – first, because he was still here on earth to make her remind him of it; and second, that he was still alive and might yet lie again.

His apology didn't seem to make much difference. Her disapproval was so profound that he saw some chance of them getting to know each other better. She watched him take a cigarette out of his packet, then put it back. He wasn't going to lie again, after all. Or perhaps it only meant he wasn't going to smoke much today. He was showing her that he was cutting down his smoke production, so that at least he couldn't convincingly repeat his lie of a year ago.

'I've only got three months to live,' he had said.

She laughed, loud. 'You're joking.'

The folds of her red-and-white African safari-wrap shifted under her laughter. She was big and fair and, talking to someone a few minutes ago, he'd heard that she had just left her husband. He thought he couldn't go wrong, until he told his silly lie.

'Well, no, I'm not lying, or joking, though it sounds stupid, I admit. I wish to God I was. It was only this afternoon that I was told.' He looked straight into her face, and watched the expression change. If you weren't merciless to people who made fools of themselves they would never believe in you again.

Her features showed an inner horror, as if she had touched previously unfathomed depths of callousness in herself – which frightened her far more than any predicament he might be in at having only three months left to live.

'I'm sorry,' he said, 'really I am. I shouldn't have told you. You're the first one. Why should I burden you with it? Even my wife doesn't know yet. I only heard today, in any case, and I haven't been home. I went to see a blue movie in Soho, then came straight on to June and Adrian's shindig.'

They stood in the small garden in which only a few others had sought refuge from the crushing noise because most people thought it was still too damp outside. 'Are you here because you know June – or are you a friend of Adrian's?' he asked, in what he hoped would be construed as a valiant attempt to change the subject.

It was his faint northern accent that brought back the feeling that he might still be lying. The only thing that stopped her disbelief was the fact that no one in the world would lie about such a matter. 'Both,' she told him.

'I don't even believe it myself,' he said, 'so if you think I'm lying I can easily understand.'

Maybe so few people came into the garden, he thought, because it was close to the main road, and a huge bar of orange sodium light glowing above the hedge had the ability to plunge its searching fire into any heart, and detect those untruths which everyone used at times like these. But against a *monstrous* lie it would have no power.

She felt herself unfairly singled out to receive this terrible information. It was as if someone had come up and married her without her permission. Her soul had been sold in some under-the-counter slave-market. At the same time she felt privileged to be the first one told – though a gnawing uncertainty remained.

'Forget it,' he said. 'I shouldn't have spoken. I feel slightly ridiculous.'

Her husband had never told her anything. If he'd heard from his doctor that he was going to die he'd have kept the information to himself and slipped out of the world without a murmur, so that she'd be left with the plague of having nagged him to death. Her frequent and fervent cry had been: 'Why don't you *say* something? Speak, for God's sake!' Once when they got into bed, after a day of few words passing between them, she said in a friendly tone: 'Tell me a story, Ben!' He didn't even say goodnight by way of reply. Thank heavens all *that* was finished.

She touched his wrist. 'It's all right. It's better to speak.' The glass she held was empty. In the glow of the sodium light it was difficult to tell whether he was pale or not. Everyone looked ghastly under it, and she understood why most of the others stayed inside. Adrian and June must have bought the house in summer, when the days were long.

'It's not,' he said, 'but I'm one of those people who can't really help myself. If I'm not talking I'm not alive. I often wonder if I talk in my sleep.'

Illness that is fatal, she had read, was nearly always brought on because the inner spirit of the afflicted person was being prevented from opening and flowering — or simply from a lack of the ability to talk about yourself and your problems. He didn't seem to be stricken in that way at all, though every rule had its exceptions — so they say.

'I've often thought of buying one of those ultra-sensitive modern Japanese tape-recorders which are switched on by the sound of your own voice,' he said, 'then playing it back in the morning to see if I've uttered any profundities, banalities, obscenities, or just plain baby-talk during the night.'

Her husband, who had been in advertising, had believed so much in the power of the spoken word that he would say very little, except perhaps at work, where it could be taken down and transcribed by his secretary, and used to make money. She dredged around at the back of her mind for something to say. Maybe her husband had been right when, in reply to one of her stinging accusations that he never said anything, rapped back: 'It takes two to make a silence.'

'But I never did,' he laughed. 'They're too expensive. Anyway, I might have said something that would have frightened me to death! You never know. And in any case, when I say something I like to make up my mind about what I'm going to say a second or two beforehand.'

'Is that what you're doing now?'

People were coming out through the open french windows with plates of food. Neither the sodium lights nor the damp would bother them if they had something to do, such as eat.

'Absolutely,' he told her, 'but because I'm talking to *you* I don't let it stop me.'

The northern accent, slight as it was, far from making him seem untrustworthy, now had something comforting about it. If he'd had the accent, and spoken very little, it would have been merely comic. But he had something to say, and that was different. He was also using it to good effect, she suspected.

'What work do you do?' It wasn't much to ask, but it was better than nothing.

He named one of the minor publishing houses, that was trying to become a big publishing house but was having a hard time of it. 'I work for them, but I'll be giving it up. *Force majeure.*'

'Perhaps things aren't as bad as you think.'

'The same thought crosses my mind – every alternate minute.' He suddenly got tired of it, and thought that if he didn't go and talk to somebody else he really would be dead in three months – or even in three seconds – from boredom. 'I must have a drink,' he said, glancing down. 'Be back soon.'

Later she saw him from a distance, talking intently to someone else. He came behind her in the queue for food, turned round because he had forgotten to pick up his napkin-roll of knife and fork, and looked at her as if she were a mirror. Thank God she'd stopped herself in time from smiling and saying something. After heaping up his plate with a choice of everything he walked over and talked to a woman with grey hair, an iron face, and a big bust.

She observed him for a while, convinced he wasn't spinning the same tragic tale he'd put out to her – though not doubting that it was something with an equal come-on bite. He wore a formal and finely cut navy blue suit, had black hair and dark eyes, which did make him look even more pallid under the light inside the house.

She asked someone who he was, and he said: 'Oh, that's Tom Barmen' – as if even talking to him was a peril no level-headed person got into, so she went upstairs to where June and Adrian kept the telephone directories, and found that he lived on Muswell Road, which wasn't far away. She dialled the number, and a woman's voice answered. 'Is that Mrs Barmen? I'm afraid I have rather sad news for you.' Someone had to tell her, after all.

* * *

'Would you rather be a man or a woman?' Joy Edwards asked, when Mavis got to the bottom of the stairs.

'Depends for how long,' she said.

'All day,' Harry Silk laughed, muscles bulging under his sweatshirt, a hand flattened on his bald head.

'Five minutes,' said his wife, heavily pregnant.

This was more like a party, Mavis thought, saying: 'Both at once? Or one at a time?' – and went to the bar for another glass of white wine, not caring now whether she got tight or not. She'd said all she had to say, for one evening at least.

When the doorbell rang, sounding faintly above the noise, she thought it was a taxi come to collect someone. Because it was after midnight one or two people had already left. A tall woman, still with her coat on, pushed through the crowd. By the kitchen door there was a crash of (unfilled) coffee cups, though the woman who had just arrived was not the cause.

'It's Phyllis Barmen,' she heard someone say.

She met him a year later at a publisher's cocktail party in the huge new Douglas Hotel. In the crowd she saw a hand throw down the end of a cigarette so that it went into a tray of peanuts instead of the ashtray. She looked up and saw who it was. He was dressed in the same suit, or one very similar.

'Did I?' he said, in response to her accusation. 'I'm sorry about that. Parties are so deadly boring.'

'The end of the last one, where we met, was quite exciting – I thought,' she reminded him.

'Thanks to you.' He looked as if he wished that *she* had only three months to live – or less.

'I suppose we should both apologize, really.'

She was totally miscast in her assumptions, he said to himself. Her mind was misshapen, the whole bloody lot warped.

She sensed she was misreading everything, judging from his mischievous look. It was devilish. She was glad there were other people around them.

'You were chosen,' he said. 'I knew I could rely on you, though you were so long going to the telephone that I was beginning to wonder whether I'd made a mistake. But when I saw you go up the stairs I knew I'd picked a winner.'

He had taken her seriously, at least.

She had taken *him* seriously, which wasn't bad going.

'I needed one more public set-to with my wife to end my deadly boring marriage,' he said. 'She wanted it too, so never feel guilty about it. It was quite mutual. We're well shut of each other now. I did feel sorry for June and Adrian, mind you.'

'So did I.'

'But they couldn't say they were bored for that last half hour. I haven't seen them since, though.'

'They miss you.'

'I'm sure they do.'

She couldn't resist gloating. 'All this is pure hindsight on your part.'

'There's no such thing as hindsight – in my way of looking at things.'

'You didn't plan it at all,' she persisted.

She felt so kicked in the stomach that when he asked her to go out to dinner after the party she said yes, and from that time on never had a moment to wonder whether she had done the right thing or not. It became more and more obvious, however, that she had been just as scheming when she'd gone upstairs to make the telephone call at June and Adrian's party, and over the years it was easy enough to make sure that he knew it.

The Devil's Almanack

Mr G. M. Stevens, postmaster of Biddenhurst, in the County of Kent, on Tuesday April 17th, 1866, at exactly nine o'clock a.m., was taking readings of the barometer, thermometer and hygrometer, and pencilling them into the blank pages of his specially printed almanack.

As he stopped to look at the rain-gauge he noticed, for the benefit of bird observers, that a muscular and energetic magpie flitted from the lawn and went into a willow tree which was just beginning to put on leaves. Tomorrow the solemn ash would come, and then the lime, followed by the maple, showing how true it was that the years went on and on, yet stayed the same.

He put a handkerchief to his nose to stem the flood – white spots on red one day, red on white another. He'd caught a cold (or the cold had caught him) when he'd got into a sweat digging his garden – or taking his readings twice a day: at nine in the morning and nine at night, winter or summer, spring or autumn, blue sky or blizzard, since the death of his wife ten years ago. The heavy soil-digging had put him into a sweat, and tired him. 'Come in, Gerald,' his wife would have called when the shower commenced, if she'd been alive. And he had wanted to go in, of course, to find the time by the chronometer, and record the shower in his almanack, but the last dozen links of soil had to be turned, otherwise when would the time come again?

You recorded the weather when nothing either good or bad occurred. You filled in columns of figures every day, read dials, fitted a neat extra leg to the month's gentle or jagged graph – when you didn't want anything to happen. But for how long had this labour-hobby held life back? A drop of sweat fell in the rain-gauge, and another hit the soil.

He was short and fat, and bald at fifty, but he stood up straight and pencilled rough calculations into his notebook. Cloud: cumulus. Amount: 7. From sun to cloud took little time when spring was a long while coming. Wind: west. You never trusted sunshine in the morning. It was beautiful, but menacing. You drank it in from the back step, the soft warm air vibrating with birds who suddenly knew why they were alive, hoping it would last but knowing it would not – the reality of birds who fed on ivy for their joy, the laudanum of sunlight for him, the sense of eternal wellbeing between waking up to take it, and going into the horrors, that fatal hiatus of any drug or drink or taste of pink-blue sky. Barometer: 29.937. Thermometer: 50. Hygrometer (Dry Bulb): 57½. (Wet Bulb): 48. Altitude: they say 400 feet, but no map shows it.

He smiled, glad the sun had gone so that he need no longer wish it would stay. Anxiety was both the spice and bane of his life. Lady Delmonden's black cat shimmered its midnight fur through the tall lawn-grass so that just its back was visible. He clapped hands but it didn't run, turned its head towards him, though he could see only its ears, and not the green-yellow eyes that managed to look so helpless and threatening at the same time. The ripple went to the hedge. Even cats are safe in Biddenhurst. It would soon be chill again.

He took the last reading and went indoors, glancing in at the parlour where his daughter Emily's body was neatly tucked on to the beige chaise-longue.

There had been no need for it, but there never is. He went into his study. God fulfils our needs, as we fulfil God's, and providing the compact is kept by all His creatures great and small – as well as by Him – we have no cause for fear in this life. But it troubled Stevens for a moment that he was worried by it – after promising himself that he wouldn't be. May the Good Lord strike me dead, he sighed.

He smiled at such a predicament, but became easy as he put in his last observation of the morning. Closing the specially bound fully-ruled logbook from the stationer's in Tunbridge Wells was a beautiful manoeuvre of finality, prelude to opening it again. In one compartment of his desk were half a dozen letters from Lady Delmonden to her son who started two weeks ago with his regiment for Gibraltar. Because he kept them neatly, their presence did not intimidate him. Their journey ended here, of necessity a short one, instead of where they were sent – those slim packets of tearful pleadings which he'd never thought would come from that tall, frigid, ugly woman.

Her soldier son was lean and fair, and ugly too. Disagreeable, until he chose to smile which – by its very rarity, like a primrose in bleak November – charmed the unwary or the stranger.

Emily had heard him kicking snow from his boots at the scraper outside, before he walked in with letters for the evening post. Counting stamps, she forgot whereabouts her finger had been on them when he demanded some for himself. That must have been how it started. From his study just behind, he'd heard the loud and throaty voice, but went on working out his average temperatures and comparing this year's monthly pressures with last year's. Had he been there to serve him would God have made it any different? If not that day, then another. Each day was the same, except for his recordings of the weather.

A sharp angle of shadow sliced the garden into light on one side and dimness on the other. White spots of daisies on either part, some blessed and the same amount not, and no one to say the why or wherefore of it. Perhaps the wind would change, bring back the sun to stay, feed the leaves and dry the grass, ruffle the cat's fur that once more walked across the lawn towards the kitchen garden, stalking all movement.

He came often after that, laughing as he bought more stamps, improperly confiding that he'd fallen in love and needed to send her letters every day, which put Emily off her guard while opening her eyes to him.

The heart would ache but never burst. The blood rose like burning paraffin. John would get no letters from his mother while ever he was postmaster here, unless by a fluke she dropped them in another town – though she was the sort of woman who these days would grieve only at home. Neither would she get any Royal Mail from him if he could stop it. In any case Delmonden, for all his show to Emily, was no writer of letters, cared only for his pleasures at other people's heartbreaks.

His one letter back which he had intercepted, and held open now to read again, was posted to his mother, and said that he, John Delmonden, after waiting a long time for a suitable ship at Weymouth, and then the appropriate weather, found that the army's dispositions had been changed, and that his regiment was ordered back to Dover – not far from Biddenhurst – so he would gallop over the Romney Marsh and come up through Appledore and Wittersham to see Emily Stevens.

'And mother, no matter what you say about her being below my station, I mean to marry her, and nothing will stop me, so set *your* mind to it as well. As you, and I suppose everybody by this time knows, we were married enough already – and now I aim to make it final. God willed I should not leave for Gibraltar, and I know His voice – by God! – when I hear it. Anyway, I shall go to her first when I get to Biddenhurst.'

No, he was such an engine as did not know what it was doing. At the same time he was as feeling as the barometer and the thermometer, the hygrometer and clock and calendar put together, only he was not responsible for moving the measurements of them. Everybody had their feelings, but thought little of their effect on others unless they knew God was reading and recording them hour by hour – and there were devils who did not care, even then.

How long could it go on? The columns of his readings made no sense. He closed the book, and gripped Lady Delmonden's letters to her son in his left hand, wanting to eat them, burn them, throw the bundle out through the rain at the stalking black cat with pink ribbon round its neck.

Ever since Emily was born he had been afraid of losing her, of her catching fever or consumption. After her mother died, his black dreams turned on taps of his own sweat at night. With blankets up and blinds drawn they harassed him in the darkest sleep, till he awoke happy it was all unreal – but weak, though able to go to her room where she slept, and look in at her untroubled face.

The earth wasn't generous in giving breath, because it wanted all people walking about to be under its soil and feeding it. It was the greed of the earth that made it beautiful. Life was a thin join of air in every body. What the Lord provides He takes away, but was it the earth, or was it God?

The soil gives abundantly to ivy tendrils and leaves, a parasitic growth whose coils lap as thick as pythons around tree-trunks and suck the tree's sap, till it dies and falls into a heap of dust to feed the earth. Likewise, ivy destroys a house. That picturesque green mat at the wall is a many-armed monster sent up by the rich vindictive earth to bring all things level with it.

Five drops of laudanum would not be enough – nor even fifty. He took the first letter of the bundle and tore it into confetti, and let it fall over the face of Emily. Her lips were thinner, the nose small and narrower at the bone than it had been, the forehead like paper. Be careful what you dread, in case you bring it to pass. But what you dread is only a warning of what the future has in store. Does God look over us from that far back?

Her face and form were littered with the paper bits of John Delmonden's letter. When he'd pushed the pillow against her mouth it was only to stop his own agony of what she had told him. He began pressing in order to hide her face, and went on with all his force when she was beyond consciousness because he couldn't bear the thought of her coming back and reproaching him for what he was doing.

Rain was tapping on the window. Perhaps the Romney Marsh would swallow Delmonden up for what he'd done. His hands were pale and puffy, and trembled as he tore the month of April out of his almanack, and made the scraps of that descend to join the other. The air was sweetening, the glass falling, the pressure a great weight on his eyes.

Each separate bone was bitterly tired. He steadied himself by the wall, the paper now the colour of laudanum, belladonna, gin, recalling how four years ago Lady Delmonden had quipped that such a widower as he get married again, that it was sinful to stay single on God's earth. Wasn't he lonely?

'I have a daughter to keep me company,' he answered – but she looked very strange at that.

A maid of hers would need a husband soon, she said, young, able, and bonny too. Perhaps he should have flowed with it – he tore March out as well, and the stitching came loose – but some stubborn notion gripped him, and he said no, and she was thwarted in her idea, so walked out cold-faced but polite, and never mentioned it again. But there'd been hidden pleading in her icy eyes. Six months later that same maid had a bastard drawn out of her, and who the lover was no one knew, except for certain hints about her roaming son.

Such a festering entered his vision when Emily told him the real truth of the tale he'd dreaded hearing when she came back five days after going with John Delmonden, and he joined it to the pictures in his own mind, and to Lady Delmonden's rigid face, and to her son's smile, and then to his new-found rage, and picked up the cushion because he couldn't bear the sight of tears on her cheeks. Was it only to wipe them gently away?

February and January, back to the hinges of the year. On January 1st there had been no cloud in the sky, a brilliant and empty blue all day, after the full moon of the night. What was the weather any more to him? Every subtle change of heat and sky he'd analysed, but what of the world inside his own flesh and blood, and that continent behind the pale blue eyes of Emily? It was all mystery, and his life had been an unchanging day that defied reading because he was locked blindly in his own brand of unknowing. The more you hide your soul from others the more it becomes hidden from yourself. But why hadn't he seen that until now?

He'd known she was dead, for ever and irrevocably, the moment he lifted the cushion, and so the calm of understanding took him under its protection. But as the hours went by he became less certain that she'd never talk to him again, and while taking his meteorological readings in the garden he forgot completely that she would not be walking about the house when he went back to it.

Bending down, he put his ear to her breast to see if any pulse was there. The feeling that someone would never come back again – all that his life meant to him – was replaced by the certainty that there were, after all, momentous things still to come.

One by one he pulled his almanacks to pieces and piled them into the parlour fireplace. He felt the excitement of a criminal as he knelt on the rug and shaped them down with his hand before lighting. Perhaps the flames would tell him something, the heat speak to the heat within. Emily moved – but it was a ball of paper to one side of the main heap, twisted by an unseen flame that had crept on an undercurrent towards it.

The enclosed space, the warm room he'd been used to with his wife and through his marriage, the semaphoring flame on the opposite wall, and Emily lying quietly on the chaise-longue, filled him with a joy of life such as he'd never felt. The music swirling and roaring fed his fibres, and blotted out memory so that his feelings were caged into this room and moment.

If there had been real music the ground would have opened more and he would have danced into it, a waltz for his feet, a gavotte for his arms, a minuet for his lips and eyes. But to feel the new rush of hope he sat on a straight walnut-backed chair midway between Emily and the fire, a final quietness in which he sampled the meaning of his past life. It held the agonies at bay, wolves beyond the windows and the wind.

The final black paper-ash crumbled. A draught came down the chimney and swirled it. When the birds stopped he heard its noise. It was a fair, fine day. The nothing-rain had passed over, only a threat. The curtains didn't meet, and a long sliver of sunlight hung from the ceiling.

A neighing horse outside displaced other noises, and he sat still, earmarked by the gap between its stopping and footsteps which ended with a knock against the side door. He reached to the shelf for his loaded pistol, and put it into his jacket pocket. Never let anyone know that you suspect them. Always keep secret those innermost perturbations that might otherwise ruffle the waters of their treacherous calm. Leave them in peace till the time comes to strike. The barometer's needle was set for a few days of good weather.

The knocking sounded again, and he sat down. It could be three times for all he cared – and would be. Let him hammer with his pampered fist. He didn't beat so loud when he came for Emily. He was an ill the world could well be purged of. Tears burst from his eyes when he looked at her. He'd heard them say that he was a wild man, but that meant he'd been afraid too long, set off for church too often perhaps, walking there with his back straight, but returning on his hands and feet. You can never get your revenge on someone who has given the first blow. Forget it, by destroying them.

He smiled, and stood as the third rapping began, walked through his study to the door and pulled it open. The hinges squeaked, alive. Everything had its own noise.

'What's wrong with you, Stevens? You must open the place. Are you ill?' Lady Delmonden pushed her way in. 'I *won't* stand outside.'

He felt the comforting hard weight of the pistol against his bone, his mind splintered at the shock of seeing her. She held an umbrella, as if to lean on it. 'Tell me' – she was taller, her finger lifted – 'has Emily had any word from my son?'

He knew he would have to speak, move his tongue with the same force as his arm when hard at digging. 'She tells me nothing.'

'I don't suppose she does, but I'll speak to her myself.'

'No' – he hadn't intended to say anything.

'Won't I? You must curb your temper, Stevens.'

If he didn't speak, he would shoot. 'No, I tell you.'

'Do you know what you're saying?'

He searched out his words, because he had never lied: 'She went on the coach to Tunbridge Wells. I'll send her to you as soon as she comes back.'

'Are you all right?' Her horse neighed again outside, a footman holding the reins.

'Yes.'

'Make sure you do, then. I can't be kept in the dark like this by the pair of them. Good day to you.' A final turn of rage brought her back:

'And next time I call on you, you will ask me into your parlour. Do you understand?'

'Yes, my lady.'

What did those blue eyes with the pale dead skin around them know? He looked as long as he dared into the waterfall of sky, as if he would collapse, hoping she would go, for his hand was on the cool handle of the gun. When she had come to him, and touted her pregnant maid, he had created in himself a complete scheme saying that really she wanted him to marry her, and this was her devious way of testing the ground for it. In her young years there had been stories of her runawayings and heart-stormings, but he knew that they were as nothing compared to his if he brewed up such ridiculous ideas as this. Who am I? he asked now, as he had then. I saw her first when she came with her mother, carrying a basket of cakes to the village school.

'Send her to me, then,' she told him.

He closed the door, and went back to his parlour.

Primroses, sorrel, violets and celandines were in Oldpark Wood, but he'd no energy to go and search out a few. As a child Emily had laid a bunch on his desk one spring. It's an inhuman machine that won't let you bring back such tender moments in all their reality. He smelled the soil as he pulled them up by the roots. He pondered on it in his fixity when even his eyeballs wouldn't move though he wanted them to. Hands on thighs, legs slightly apart, a scene set for his immobile head, waiting for Emily to breathe again.

Hours drew out. There was no time to act because time did not exist. On the sea the waves were molten metal, thin, without smoke. The motion and the endlessness made him sick.

Someone had come into the house. His eyes moved, sending a fissure of life back to his fingers. It was all plain now, and he called Emily in a normal voice, as if she would run to him. A chair went over in the study. He wished he had strewn her with flowers instead of those plague spots of paper bits.

'Emily!' Delmonden called.

He stood, and waited, awake again, calm even, but with a faint sweaty smile as if he'd turned back into a child. He wanted to be friendly and answer him, but was sly enough in his stunned and stunted childishness to know that if he did the frame of his new-found tenuous manhood would fall apart. For the first time he was aware of

536

the clock ticking on the wall, and thought it must have stopped yesterday, and for some unaccountable reason started again this second, it was so loud and disturbing as it hammered inside him.

The door was gently opened, and the floor creaked as Delmonden looked in. He tried not to stare at him, and turned aside.

'Why the devil didn't you tell me you were here? I don't want to see over your whole damned house.'

He was of the tall people who could walk in, and look for his daughter, sidestepping any man's freedom and dignity. There was no life without Emily. He wasn't afraid of him – as he had been when he watched the whole plot forming but told himself that his brain spun false pictures. What else is there to live for if you've stopped being afraid?

'What do you want?' – surprised at the clearness of his voice. He stood between the door and chaise-longue.

Delmonden must have ridden hard. His cloak was open – a dark suit under it, pale waistcoat, white shirt up to his throat, a florid ill-formed face just out of youth, a long clean-shaven chin. 'Why don't you let daylight in the place? Where is she?'

He stepped backwards to the shelf, a hand at ease in his pocket. 'She's not well.'

Delmonden came forward. He saw the road in front of him, pot-holes whose water reflected the variable sky. The rhythm of hooves still rang in his hearing. His eyes almost touched her forehead. 'I'll get the doctor. For God's sake, why didn't *you?*'

'She's dead.'

He felt his finger on the curve. It was like a hook, and the handle tilted, hidden. Forgive me, Lord: I know exactly what I do. The clock behind him seemed to explode, a noise blowing paper into the air as the bullet flew, a great stone at Delmonden's stomach.

He screamed, hand to the pain. He wanted to ask a question, but changed his mind: 'You devil! She hated you. I can see . . .'

The second ball hit him, this time the whole white of the sun before he fell.

Mr G. M. Stevens, late postmaster of Biddenhurst, was hanged at eight o'clock a.m. on June 6th at Maidstone Gaol, in the County of Kent.

When about to be executed the crowd threw soil and dung at him.

He saw these gestures merely as the earth extending a hand, welcoming him to become part of the good fellowship of the loam. The people were enraged by his indifference, because the trial revealed the abominations he had practised on the bodies of his victims. He had been able to keep them a further day before Lady Delmonden's tenants broke in and found them.

As the mob pelted him, he remained silent, looking at the sky, and feeling the air on his face. It was a south-west wind. The cloud: nimbus. Amount: 10. Temperature (as far as he could tell): 50. The parson had been good enough to inform him, before beginning his futile prayers, that the barometer read 29.620. A slight rain was falling.

His left hand reached for his almanack, and the crowd roared when it swung into the air.

The Fiddle

On the banks of the sinewy River Leen, where it flowed through Radford, stood a group of cottages called Harrison's Row. There must have been six to eight of them, all in a ruinous condition, but lived in nevertheless.

They had been put up for stockingers during the Industrial Revolution a hundred years before, so that by now the usual small red English housebricks had become weatherstained and, in some places, almost black.

Harrison's Row had a character all of its own, both because of its situation, and the people who lived there. Each house had a space of pebbly soil rising in front, and a strip of richer garden sloping away from the kitchen door down to the diminutive River Leen at the back. The front gardens had almost merged into one piece of common ground, while those behind had in most cases retained their separate plots.

As for the name of the isolated row of cottages, nobody knew who Harrison had been, and no one was ever curious about it. Neither did they know where the Leen came from, though some had a general idea as to where it finished up.

A rent man walked down cobblestoned Leen Place every week to collect what money he could. This wasn't much, even at the best of times which, in the thirties, were not too good – though no one in their conversation was able to hark back to times when they had been any better.

From the slight rise on which the houses stood, the back doors and windows looked across the stream into green fields, out towards the towers and pinnacles of Wollaton Hall in one direction, and the woods of Aspley Manor in the other.

After a warm summer without much rain the children were able to wade to the fields on the other side. Sometimes they could almost paddle. But after a three-day downpour when the air was still heavy

539

with undropped water, and coloured a menacing gun-metal blue, it was best not to go anywhere near the river, for one false slip and you would get sucked in, and be dragged by the powerful current along to the Trent some miles away. In that case there was no telling where you'd end up. The water seemed to flow into the River Amazon itself, indicated by the fact that Frankie Buller swore blind how one day he had seen a crocodile snapping left and right downstream with a newborn baby in its mouth. You had to be careful – and that was a fact. During the persistent rain of one autumn water came up over the gardens and almost in at the back doors.

Harrison's Row was a cut-off place in that not many people knew about it unless they were familiar with the district. You went to it along St Peter's Street, and down Leen Place. But it was delightful for the kids who lived there because out of the back gardens they could go straight into the stream of the Leen. In summer an old tin hip bath would come from one of the houses. Using it for a boat, and stripped to their white skins, the children were happy while sun and weather lasted.

The youths and older kids would eschew this fun and set out in a gang, going far beyond, to a bend of the canal near Wollaton Pit where the water was warm – almost hot – due to some outlet from the mine itself. This place was known as ''otties', and they'd stay all day with a bottle of lemonade and a piece of bread, coming back late in the evening looking pink and tired as if out of a prolonged dipping in the ritual bath. But a swim in 'otties was only for the older ones, because a boy of four had once been drowned there.

Harrison's Row was the last of Nottingham where it met the countryside. Its houses were at the very edge of the city, in the days before those numerous housing estates had been built beyond. The line of dwellings called Harrison's Row made a sort of outpost bastion before the country began.

Yet the houses in the city didn't immediately start behind, due to gardens and a piece of wasteground which gave to Harrison's Row a feeling of isolation. It stood somewhat on its own, as if the city intended one day to leapfrog over it and obliterate the country beyond.

On the other hand, any foreign army attacking from the west, over the green fields that glistened in front, would first have to flatten Harrison's Row before getting into the innumerable streets of houses behind.

Across the Leen, horses were sometimes to be seen in the fields and, in other fields beyond, the noise of combine harvesters could be heard at work in the summer. Children living there, and adults as well, had the advantage of both town and country. On a fine evening late in August one of the unemployed husbands might be seen looking across at the noise of some machinery working in a field, his cap on but wearing no shirt, as if wondering why he was here and not over there, and why in fact he had ever left those same fields in times gone by to be forced into this bit of a suburb where he now had neither work nor purpose in life. He was not bitter, and not much puzzled perhaps, yet he couldn't help being envious of those still out there in the sunshine.

In my visions of leaving Nottingham for good – and they were frequent in those days – I never reckoned on doing so by the high road or railway. Instead I saw myself wading or swimming the Leen from Harrison's Row, and setting off west once I was on the other side.

A tale remembered with a laugh at that time told about how young Ted Griffin, who had just started work, saw two policemen one day walking down Leen Place towards Harrison's Row. Convinced they had come to arrest him for meter-breaking, he ran through the house and garden, went over the fence, jumped into the Leen – happily not much swollen – waded across to the field, then four-legged it over the railway, and made his way to Robins Wood a mile or so beyond. A perfect escape route. He stayed two days in hiding, and then crept home at night, famished and soaked, only to find that the police had not come for him, but to question Blonk next door, who was suspected of poaching. When they did get Ted Griffin he was pulled out of bed one morning even before he'd had time to open his eyes and think about a spectacular escape across the Leen.

Jeff Bignal was a young unmarried man of twenty-four. His father had been killed in the Great War, and he lived with his mother at Number Six Harrison's Row, and worked down nearby Radford Pit. He was short in height, and plump, his white skin scarred back and front with livid blue patches where he had been knocked with coal at the mine face. When he went out on Saturday night he brilliantined his hair.

After tea in summer while it was still light and warm he would sit in his back garden playing the fiddle, and when he did everybody else came out to listen. Or they opened the doors and windows so that the sound of his music drifted in, while the woman stayed at the sink or wash-copper, or the man at his odd jobs. Anyone with a wireless would turn it down or off.

Even tall dark sallow-faced elderly Mrs Deaffy (a kid sneaked into her kitchen one day and thieved her last penny-packet of cocoa and she went crying to tell Mrs Atkin who, when her youngest came in, hit him so hard with her elbow that one of his teeth shot out and the blood washed away most of the cocoa-stains around his mouth) – old Mrs Deaffy stood by her back door as if she weren't stone deaf any more and could follow each note of Jeffrey Bignal's exquisite violin. She smiled at seeing everyone occupied, fixed or entranced, and therefore no torment to herself, which was music enough to her whether she could hear it or not.

And Blonk, in the secretive dimness of the kitchen, went on mending his poaching nets before setting out with Arthur Bede next door on that night's expedition to Gunthorpe by the banks of the Trent, where the green escarpment between there and Kneeton was riddled with warrens and where, so it was said, if you stood sufficiently still the rabbits ran over your feet, and it was only necessary to make a quick grab to get one.

Jeff sat on a chair, oblivious to everybody, fed up with his day's work at the pit and only wanting to lose himself in his own music. The kids stopped splashing and shouting in the water, because if they didn't they might get hauled in and clouted with just the right amount of vicious-ness to suit the crime and the occasion. It had happened before, though Jeff had always been too far off to notice.

His face was long, yet generally cheerful – contrary to what one would expect – a smile settling on it whenever he met and passed anybody on the street, or on his way to the group of shared lavatories at the end of the Row. But his face was almost down and lost to the world as he sat on his chair and brought forth his first sweet notes of a summer's evening.

It was said that a neighbour in the last place they had lived had taught him to play like that. Others maintained it was an uncle who had shown him how. But nobody knew for sure because when someone asked directly he said that if he had any gift at all it must have come from God above. It was known that on some Sundays of the year, if the sun was out, he went to the Methodist chapel on St Peter's Street.

He could play anything from 'Greensleeves' to 'Mademoiselle from Armentières'. He could do a beautiful heart-pulling version of Handel's *Largo*, and throw in bits from *Messiah* as well. He would go from one piece to another with no rhyme or reason, from ridiculousness to sublimity, with almost shocking abruptness, but as the hour or so went by it all appeared easy and natural, part of a long piece coming from Jeff Bignal's fiddle, while the ball of the sun went down behind his back.

To a child it seemed as if the songs lived in the hard collier's muscle at the top of his energetic arm, and that they queued one by one to get out. Once free, they rushed along his flesh from which the shirtsleeves had been rolled up and split into his fingertips, where they were played out with ease into the warm evening air.

The grass in the fields across the stream was livid and lush, almost blue, and a piebald horse stood with bent head, eating oats out of a large old pram whose wheels had long since gone. The breeze wafted across from places farther out, from Robins Wood and the Cherry Orchard, Wollaton Roughs and Bramcote Hills and even, on a day that was not too hot, from the tops of the Pennines in Derbyshire.

Jeff played for himself, for the breeze against his arm, for the soft hiss of the flowing Leen at the end of the garden, and maybe also for the horse in the field, which took no notice of anything and which, having grown tired of his oats in the pram, bent its head over the actual grass and began to roam in search of succulent pastures.

In the middle of the winter Jeff's fiddling was forgotten. He went into the coal mine before it was light, and came up only after it had got dark. Walking down Leen Place, he complained to Blonk that it was hard on a man not to see daylight for weeks at a time.

'That's why I wain't go anywhere near the bleddy pit,' Blonk said vehemently, though he had worked there from time to time, and would do so again when harried by his wife and children. 'You'd do better to come out on a bit o' poaching with me and Arthur,' he suggested.

It was virtually true that Jeff saw no daylight, because even on Sunday he stayed in bed most of the day, and if it happened to be dull there was little enough sky to be seen through his front bedroom window, which looked away from the Leen and up the hill.

The upshot of his complaint was that he would do anything to change such a situation. A man was less than an animal for putting up with it.

'I'd do anything,' he repeated to his mother over his tea in the single room downstairs.

'But what, though?' she asked. 'What can you do, Jeff?'

'Well, how do I know?' he almost snapped at her. 'But I'll do summat, you can be sure of that.'

He didn't do anything till the weather got better and life turned a bit sweeter. Maybe this improvement finally got him going, because it's hard to help yourself towards better things when you're too far down in the dumps.

On a fine blowy day with both sun and cloud in the sky Jeff went out in the morning, walking up Leen Place with his fiddle under his arm. The case had been wiped and polished.

In the afternoon he came back without it.

'Where's your fiddle?' Ma Jones asked.

He put an awkward smile on to his pale face, and told her: 'I sold it.'

'Well I never! How much for?'

He was too shocked at her brazen question not to tell the truth: 'Four quid.'

'That ain't much.'

'It'll be enough,' he said roughly.

'Enough for what, Jeff?'

He didn't say, but the fact that he had sold his fiddle for four quid rattled up and down the line of cottages till everybody knew of it. Others swore he'd got ten pounds for it, because something that made such music must be worth more than a paltry four, and in any case Jeff would never say how much he'd really got for it, for fear that someone would go in and rob him.

They wondered why he'd done it, but had to wait for the answer, as one usually does. But there was nothing secretive about Jeff Bignal, and if he'd sold his music for a mess of pottage he saw no point in not letting them know why. They'd find out sooner or later, anyway.

All he'd had to do was make up his mind, and he'd done that lying on his side at the pit face while ripping coal out with his pick and shovel. Decisions made like that can't be undone, he knew. He'd brooded on it all winter, till the fact of having settled it seemed to have altered the permanent expression of his face, and given it a new look which caused people to wonder whether he would ever be able to play the fiddle again anyway – at least with his old spirit and dash.

With the four quid he paid the first week's rent on a butcher's shop on Denman Street, and bought a knife, a chopper, and a bit of sharpening stone, as well as a wooden block. Maybe he had a quid or two more knocking around, though if he had it couldn't have been much, but with four quid and a slice of bluff he got enough credit from a wholesaler at the meat market downtown to stock his shop with mutton and beef, and in a couple of days he was in trade. The people of Harrison's Row were amazed at how easy it was, though nobody had ever thought of doing it themselves.

Like a serious young man of business Mr Bignal – as he was now known – parted his hair down the middle, so that he didn't look so young any more, but everyone agreed that it was better than being at Radford Pit. They'd seen how he had got fed-up with selling the sweat of his brow.

No one could say that he prospered, but they couldn't deny that he made a living. And he didn't have to suffer the fact of not seeing daylight for almost the whole of the winter.

Six months after opening the shop he got married. The reception was held at the chapel on St Peter's Street, which seemed to be a sort of halfway house between Harrison's Row on the banks of the Leen and the butcher's shop on Denman Street farther up.

Everybody from Harrison's Row was invited for a drink and something to eat; but he knew them too well to let any have either chops or chitterlings (or even black puddings) on tick when they came into his shop.

The people of Harrison's Row missed the sound of his fiddle on long summer evenings, though the children could splash and shout with their tin bathtub undisturbed, floundering through shallows and scrambling up to grass on the other bank, and wondering what place they'd reach if they walked without stopping till it got dark.

Two years later the Second World War began, and not long afterwards meat as well as nearly everything else was put on the ration. Apart from which, Jeff was only twenty-six, so got called up into the army. He never had much chance to make a proper start in life, though people said that he came out all right in the end.

The houses of Harrison's Row were condemned as unfit to live in, and a bus depot stands on the site.

The packed mass of houses on the hill behind – forty years after Jeff Bignal sold his violin – is also vanishing, and high rise hencoops (as the people call them) are put in their place. The demolition crew knock down ten houses a day – though the foreman told me there was still work for another two years.

Some of the houses would easily have lasted a few more decades, for the bricks were perfect, but as the foreman went on: 'You can't let them stand in the way of progress' – whatever that means.

The people have known each other for generations but, when they are moved to their new estates and blocks of flats, they will know each other for generations more, because as I listen to them talking, they speak a language which, in spite of everything and everyone, never alters.

The Gate of a Great Mansion

Fruit boxes were pounded against the shore by a snaking band of oil-logged water. The wood of the boxes was grey, hitting the rocks till it was splintered and stringy. Dead logs were covered in tar. Rotting offal, swirling from the town and jetties, was re-shaped and hardened into a kind of pumice by the battering ebb and flow of the wash. A stench hit the nostrils like ice when the wind veered full in the face. He lit a second pipe before the bowl was cold.

The whole flank of a three-funnelled steamer had gone to rust. Coolies going to work in the tin mines and rubber plantations of Malaya were so crowded on deck that it was hard to see where the mass of people ended and the superstructure began. One day the hulk will vanish in a typhoon, he thought, and the owners will retire on the insurance. A drum of paint costs treble what it does in Europe. Everyone says that business is bad, and they are right. You go inland for hemp, tea and timber, and get little or nothing when you bring them out. When it gets dark a clean wind pushes the stench aside.

The last chord of the sun's red disc was sucked behind the mountains. Take me with you, he said, when it wasn't so far down that it might not hear. He wanted sharp hooks that he could throw out to it for a free ride. He looked at the indigo sea chopping beyond his feet, and into the ink maw of the wider bottle. Nothing is free. Beyond the throat of rocks were stars. A lantern glowed at the prow of a sampan that went slowly towards the steamer. The peasants were dying from Revolution, Consumption and Cholera. They sleep-walk after imbibing the vile poppy dust of opium. Wireless telegraphy from Europe talks of war and prices.

He wanted only rain whenever he felt fever or influenza pushing his senses to their limits. The sun was on its way out, but one day it would come back to burn the world. The rain's cooling wash would flow down the veranda and along the gutters, would run through his veins and clear sludge from the mind, extinguish the unwholesome nightmare all around. He could only think when he was ill, yet his mind turned against him at such times. It must have been during similar feverish bouts that he had gone through the motions of coming to Amoy. He would not forget the smell of drying fish, even a hundred years after he had died.

Today he had been paid, and bought a sports jacket, so that there weren't enough dollars left for the instalment on his room. Both space and jackets were dear – for Europeans. Perhaps I can hold the landlord back till next month. Disturb him from his game of sticks and coins and a row of little books. Play it as long as you like, but I won't be here. If he throws me out, he'll get nothing, because you can't get taels (nor even *cash*) from a beggar. He's heard it often in the last year, but his look will say nothing yet all the same will say: a merchant's clerk isn't worth much. A Chinese can do the work better, and for less. Except that Poynter-Davis wouldn't trust one, though God knows why.

He walked. He was getting nowhere. The first sign of a fever was that the pipe tasted as if it were filled with a well-mixed compound of shit and soot. He was glad when it had burned away and he could knock out the dottle. His mother didn't know what her brother did for a living out here, only that he was 'doing well' – that magic phrase which was supposed to open every gate for the rest of the family. Nobody was 'doing well'. The Japanese were machine-gunning and bombing their sure way through Manchuria. The world was worn out. He stepped carefully in the dark. The noise of rats squeaking and scuffling away from his shoes made him feel that he was not entirely set apart from the world. He could no longer see the rusting flank of the decrepit steamer that would sink in a monsoon if it took him to England. It would be no easier trying for a job in Singapore or Penang.

He coughed from day to day, but illness was a fraud. Even if you were half dead you couldn't allow yourself to feel so at thirty-five. There were plenty of lights in the town. There was life. Amoy wasn't unhealthy any more. The old hands laughed, and spoke about heaps of corpses. The old always swore that things were better for everybody than they had been in their youth, but it only meant they had grown more tolerant of misery – or become richer on it.

Even the Chinese smiled. He hated himself when he shouted. Things were said to be difficult in England. There was no work. There was the dole for everybody. They used the word to terrify. If you came home, you'd go on the dole, they wrote. In any case, he didn't totally dislike it *here*. The stench of the town on one side and the odorous piss of sea on the other were homely enough, but his thoughts were caught in the unceasing and remorseless bang of the surf.

Letters were nearly two months getting home. He wrote every week, still the anxious boy who bothered them with mail. If they didn't look at the date they could imagine each letter took no more than seven days. *He* would have done, in their places. They'd be happier hearing only four times a year. His father at the bank and his mother at home were, in their old fashioned way, waiting for him to make a fortune in Amoy. Or Shanghai. Or Tientsin. Or Foochow. Anywhere, as long as he was out of the way. From the squalor of human souls you were supposed to get rich.

He could go back if his father died, and live with her. He never would. She loved him too much, she said, but would bore him to death because she hated him. He couldn't even go back into himself, not as he was before he came out. He would never find his own spirit as long as he stayed in Amoy. This country was too big. He had never known himself, even in a small place. It wouldn't be possible in the sort of life his father had always led, either. Six hundred pounds a year and a Morris car, and sending in the *People* crossword every week for sixpence.

He was jostled as he made his way towards the Bund. Coolies with stinking breath pushed against him. His tongue was rancid from fever. A hand went towards his pocket but he knocked it away. His Swan fountain pen was taken just after he arrived, but now he was forever on the lookout. A pair of eyes coming towards him showed the intentions of the mind that lived behind them. They understood each other, so he was safe. He, in his weakness, could ram with his shoulder, choking on the bad language that wouldn't leave his throat. Crowds always threatened when he wanted to be alone.

Sixteen years ago, walls of wet mud seeped through revetted fresh-smelling planks in Flanders. Walking the zig-zags of his sector, he had forced his way between the members of his platoon waiting to go over the top. That place too had been crowded, but he had felt good to be there. It was small enough in which to know himself. He could tell who he was, clambering the springy ladder and into the open as if into the unlit afternoon attic of a vast house visited as children. Would a ghost leap? A scimitar swing to chop off your legs? It hadn't. It was good.

He hoped his men would follow. They did. The scimitar got most of them, but it was better there than in school. A patriotic patrol cost fifty men. Life had become dimmer since. Nobody would follow him any more, which he understood because he couldn't even follow himself, since the only self he might have followed had vanished long ago. If it hadn't he would still not have known where to go.

At the height of his fever's influence (no one had diagnosed it, but only he knew a lassitude without pain or headache that had stricken him for no reason and vibrated as far as his brain) he had dreamed he was on a small flat-bottomed boat going between the high walls of the Yangtse Gorges beyond Ichang. He'd only heard the old hands talk of them, of the fact that the river was so boxed in by gorges that the sun could not be seen except at noon, and the moon only at its highest meridian.

But in his dream he was lying happily back, no oars rowing, no motor drumming, no diesel reek or anyone punting him through or pulling perilously from the shore, but going on and on towards the west as if travelling by a benign and co-operative current. In places the river banks sloped away and he could see the huts of a porters' village, or fisher-boats drawn up on the gravel. People waved, at first friendly and then warning him with more than menace if he didn't take notice.

The broad and often devastating flow of the Yangtse was east to the China Sea and the Pacific, but here he was on a current running him *west* through the heart of China. Fever played tricks with the soles of the feet, invented geographical flukes, altered the course of rivers and spun the cardinal points of the world. Fever made humanity feel that it might one day be possible to do the same.

He passed the kitchen, a jigsaw puzzle of culinary gewgaws. He got to his room, and lay down. Hunger was an act of spite on the part of the body. It reminded you to keep on living, and laughed like a demon when you did so.

The 'old hands' in their armchairs at the club, or in the lounge of the King George Hotel, mooned on about 'the China that we used to know, and how damned sad to see it change'. The more obvious it was that their days were numbered the more they thought the misery was picturesque. In reality it consisted of endless landscapes that dying coolies carried them through in their palanquins. They talked of bringing out turmeric and sugar from beyond Chungking, of transporting amber from the north, as well as getting bristles and silk from the wilds of Szechwan.

But in the dining room they also recalled the alluvial plains of great estuaries that kill as surely as famine. The moon rises and sets on destitution. Things he heard almost brought up the vomit. Some of the merchants were virtuosos in their sexual predilections.

Amoy was the gate of a great mansion, but it was a paper house, and the inside was rotten. From his bed he saw only the fire, the burning down, flames spreading and enveloping, that did not scorch when he put out his hands. He heard the crack of burning wood from the interior, and great sparks spitting fearfully out with the energy that only fire could give as huge beams collapsed, and cleaned everything, curing all hungers, even his own.

A Time to Keep

Martin drew the cloth from the kitchen table. An old tea-stain made a map of Greenland when held up to the light. He folded it into an oblong and laid it on the dresser.

After the anxiety of getting his brother and sister to bed he lifted his books from the cupboard and spread them over the bare wood, where they would stay till the heart-catching click of the gate latch signalled his parents' return.

He was staying in to see that the fire did not go out, and to keep the light on. He was staying up because he was older. When that unmistakable click of the gate latch sounded he would set a kettle on the gas to make coffee. Funny how thirsty they still were after being in the boozer all night. His two-hour dominion over the house would be finished, but as consolation he could give in to the relief of knowing that they had not after all been hit by a bus and killed.

Most of the books had been stolen. None had been read from end to end. When opened they reeked of damp from bookshop shelves. Or they stank from years of storage among plant pots and parlour soot.

He put a French grammar on to *Peveril of the Peak*, and a Bible in Polish on top of that. The clock could be heard now that they were out and he had extinguished the television. He sang a tune to its ticking under his breath, then went back to his books. He would start work next year, and didn't know whether he wanted to or not. Things could go on like this for ever as far as he was concerned. You got booted out of school, though, at fifteen, and that was that.

The certainty that one day he would be pushed into a job had hovered around him since he first realized as a child that his father went out every morning in order to earn money with which to feed them, pay the rent, get clothes, and keep a roof over their heads. His mother used these phrases, and they stabbed into him like fire. At that time work had nothing to do with him, but it soon would have. It was a place of pay and violence which his father detested, to judge by the look on his face when he came home every evening with his snapsack and teacan.

Under the dark space of the stairs he shovelled around for coal to bank up the dull fire – a pleasurable task, as long as the flames came back to life. A hole in the pan needed bigger lumps set over it so that cobbles and slack wouldn't spill on the mat between the coal-heap and grate. They'd rather have a few pints of beer than buy a dustpan.

He washed his hands in the scullery. He liked soap that was keen to the smell. Arranging his chair, he sat down again and lifted the cover of a beige leather-bound volume of French magazines. He read a sentence under the picture: a bridge over the River Seine near Rouen. In other books he was able to put Portuguese or Italian phrases into English. When a word appealed to his sight he manoeuvred through the alphabet of a dictionary to get at its meaning, though he never tried to learn a language properly. He handled books like a miser. In each one his name was written in capital letters, though there was no danger of them being stolen, because they were gold that could not be spent. The strange kind of hunger he felt in looking at them often fixed him into a hypnosis that stopped him using them properly.

If burglars came they would nick the television, not books. They were stacked according to size, then sorted in their various languages. Excitement led him to range them from high at both ends to small in the middle. He bracketed them between a tea-caddy and a box of his father's car tools so that none could escape. Then he spread them out again, like playing cards.

Summer was ending. It seemed as if it always was. He had a bike, but Friday night was too much of a treat to go out. He also thought it a squander of precious daylight on his parents' part that they should have been in the pub for an hour before it got dark. And yet, as soon as the outside walls and chimney pots were no longer clear, he swung the curtains decisively together, pushing away what little of the day was left. Once it was going, he wanted to be shut of it. He switched on glowing light that made the living room a secret cave no one could get into.

His parents were used to his daft adoration of books, but for anyone beyond the family to witness his vital playthings would make him blush with shame. Aunts, cousins and uncles would mock him, but what else could you expect? If it hadn't been that, they'd have teased him for something else. They had never actually seen his books, though they had been laughingly told about them by his parents. Books and the people he knew didn't belong together, and that was a fact, but he knew it was impossible to live without either.

He wondered what other eyes had slid across these pages. Their faces could be frightening, or happy. They had come in out of the rain after doing a murder. Or they closed a book and put it down so as to go out and do a good deed. How did you know? You never did. You had to make it all up and scare yourself daft.

In any case, how had they felt about what they were reading? What houses had they lived in, and what sort of schools had they gone to? Did they like their furniture? Did they hate their children? He would rather have been any one of those people than himself. Maybe nobody had read the books. They got them as presents, or bought them and forgot to read them. The thought made him feel desolate, though not for long. Books always took his mind off the world around. He lifted the picture-album of France, and pondered on every voyage the book had made. It had been to Chile and China, and all the other places he could think of, between leaving the printers' and reaching his table in Radford.

A clatter of footsteps at the yard-end and the boisterous notes of a voice he did not at first recognize dragged him clear. Print had hooks, but they were made of rubber. Before the warning click of the gate latch his dozen volumes were scooped off the table and stacked on the floor behind the far side of the dresser.

By the time the door opened the gas was lit and a full kettle set on it. He put sugar, milk and a bottle of coffee on the table, then sat looking through a car magazine as if he hadn't moved all evening. His cousin Raymond was first in the room. No stranger, after all. His mother and father breathed a strong smell of ale.

'He's the quickest lad I know at getting that kettle on the burning feathers!' his father said. 'A real marvel at it. I drove like a demon back from the Crown for my cup o' coffee.'

'And you nearly hit that van coming out of Triumph Road,' Raymond laughed.

Martin wondered whether he should take such praise as it was intended, or hate his father for imagining that he needed it, or despise him for thinking he could get round him in such a way. He was already taller than his father, and there were times when he couldn't believe it, and occasions when he didn't like it, though he knew he had to get used to it. So had his father, but he didn't seem bothered by such a thing. He decided to ignore the praise, though he *had* got the kettle on in record time.

'You brought him up right,' Raymond hung his jacket on the back of the door. 'He worn't drug up, like me.' He bumped into his aunt. 'Oops, duck, mind yer back, yer belly's in danger!'

Martin laughed, without knowing whether he wanted to or not. His father would put up with anything from Raymond, who had been to Approved School, Detention Centre and Borstal, though he was now an honest man of twenty-two, and able to charm anybody when he wanted. He did it so well that you were convinced he would never get caught stealing again. He could also use a bullying, jocular sort of self-confidence, having learned how to live rough, half-inch a thing or two, and die young if he must, without getting sent down every year for a Christmas box or birthday present. Another lesson well taken was that he must always look smart, talk clear and act quick, so that anyone who mattered would think he could be trusted. At Borstal he had done boxing, because it seemed that both God and the Governor were on the side of those who stored the deadliest punch. He had developed one as fast as he could, and wasn't afraid to use it whenever necessary. He was loyal to his family, helping them with money and goods to the best of his ability and hard work. He was often heard to say that he couldn't go back to his old ways, for his mother's sake.

Martin wanted to be like his cousin, though sensing that he might never be so made him look up to him even more. He was certainly glad he'd got the books out of sight before he came in.

Raymond, with his bread and cheese, and cup of coffee, was first to sit down. Martin moved across the room, leaving the fire to the grown-ups. The yellow flames blazed for them alone, and for their talk that came from the big world of boozers that he hadn't yet entered but was avid to. Raymond stretched out a leg, and expertly belched the words: 'Pardon me!' – at which they all laughed.

He held his cup for more coffee. 'I'll be off to Alfreton again in the morning. Help to build another mile o' that motorway. You know how it's done, don't you? I open my big gob wide. Somebody shovels tar and concrete in. Then I walk along shitting out motorway and coughing up signposts!'

'It'll soon be as far as Leeds, wain't it?' his father said quickly, trying to head off such remarks, which he found a bit too loud-mouthed.

Raymond detected the manoeuvre, and to save face, turned censorious: 'It would be, Joe, if everybody got cracking at their job. But they're too busy looting to get much done. The fields for miles on either side are laid waste by plundering navvies. Some of 'em sit around smoking and talking, and waiting for a turnip to show itself above the soil. As soon as it does, up it comes! They go straight into their snapsacks.'

He was a joker. They weren't sure whether it was true or not. No gaffer could afford to let you get away with not working full-tilt. But he *had* brought vegetables home. Ripping up a basketful was the work of a few minutes in the dusk: 'A bloke the other day came to wok in his minivan,' Raymond told them, 'and drove it a little way into the wood. He kept the engine running so's we wouldn't hear his chain-saw, but when I went in for a piss I saw the bleeder stacking logs in the back. A nice young pine tree had gone, and he covered the stump up wi' leaves. Nowt's safe. It's bleddy marvellous. He's going to get caught one day, doing it in the firm's time!'

Martin seemed born to listen. Maybe it went with collecting books. If he read them properly he'd perhaps start talking a bit more, and it might be easier then to know what other people were thinking.

'He don't say much,' Raymond observed, 'our Martin don't, does he?'

But he did at school. Among his pals he was as bright as an Amazon parrot. If he tackled a book properly, on the other hand, he might talk even less. It was hard to say until he did. Cut anybody's finger off who got too fresh. The teacher once stopped him bashing up another boy, and said if he caught him at it again he'd pull his arm off. He couldn't really be like Raymond, who'd once got chucked out of school for hitting a teacher right between the eyes.

'He'll be at work next year,' his mother nodded at Martin. 'It's looney to keep 'em till they're fifteen, big kids like him. Give him summat to do. *And* bring us some money in.'

'The bloody road tax is twenty-five quid now,' his father said bitterly, and Martin felt as if he were being blamed for it.

'I didn't have one for six months last year,' Raymond boasted. 'I stuck an old Guinness label on the windscreen. Nobody twigged it.'

Martin knew it wasn't true.

'You never did!' his father said, who believed it. 'I wish I'd had such an idea.'

'No, I tell a lie. It was only on for a fortnight. Then I got the wind up, and bought a real 'un.' He turned his grey eyes on to Martin, as if embarrassed by somebody who didn't continually give themselves away in speech. 'I'll get our Martin a job wi' me on the motorway, though,' he said. 'That'll settle his hash. He'll come home every night absolutely knackered.'

I expect I might, Martin thought. 'What would I do?'

'You'd have to get up early, for a start.'

That wouldn't bother him. Lots of people did. 'What time's that?' 'Six.'

'He's dead to the wide at six. It's all I can do to get him out of bed by eight o'clock.'

'I'm not, our mam.'

Raymond looked at the fire, as if he would have spat at the bars if it had been in his own home. 'I pass here in my car at half past. I'll pick you up tomorrow, if you like.'

'Will yer be fit for it?' his father wanted to know.

Martin, taking more coffee and another slice of bread, didn't think he'd heard right. He often looked at the opening of a book, and when he understood every word, couldn't believe he'd read it properly, and then went back to make sure. 'Tomorrow?'

'Well, I din't say owt about yesterday, did I?'

If Raymond said something, he meant it. He often said that you must regret nothing, and that you should always keep promises. It helped his reputation of being a man who showed up in a crowd. So he promised something in a loud voice now and again in order to keep himself up to scratch. 'I'll stop my owd banger outside the Co-op. If you're there I'll take you. If you ain't, I'll just push on.'

'I'll be waiting.' Martin felt like one of those sailors in the olden days who, about to set off west, wasn't sure he would ever get back again.

The sky was clear and cold. He saw it over the housetops, and above the façade of the bingo hall that he first went into as a cinema one Saturday afternoon nearly ten years ago.

The wet road looked as clean as if a light shone on it. He buttoned the jacket over his shirt. You never wore a top coat to work unless you were one of the older men. It was too early for traffic, making the road look different to when it was pounded by buses and lorries during the day. His mother had disturbed him from a hundred feet under the sand below the deepest part of the ocean when she had tried to wake him. She had to grab the clothes off him in the end.

Sandwiches bulged in his pocket. He enjoyed waiting, but his hands were cold. 'Never put your hands in your pockets when you're on the job,' Raymond had said. 'A lot of 'em do, but it don't look good.' He couldn't do it while waiting to go there, either. He wished he were setting off to work properly, and that he didn't have another year to do before he got real wages. There wasn't much point in starting work today, and then next year as well.

A postman went by on a bike. 'Morning, kid.'

'Morning.'

Raymond's car had rust along the bottom of the door as it swung open towards him. 'Get in.'

He sounded disappointed that Martin had been able to meet him. The car sailed up Wollaton Road like an aeroplane, spun around the traffic island by the Crown, and went along Western Boulevard. 'Tired?'

'It's a treat, being up early.'

'Bring owt t'eat?'

'Yeh. Mam forgot some tea, though.'

'I've got a mashing.' He played the car with hands and feet as if on a big picture-house organ. 'Sugar, tea, and tinned milk – solid like a cannon ball. Enough for a battalion. Trust our mam. She's old-fashioned, but she's a marvel all the same. You can stand a garden fork in *her* strong tea.'

Beyond the town there was a cloud like a big white dog. Martin yawned, and expected it to do the same.

'We like to start as soon as daylight hits,' Raymond went on. 'That's where the money is, in overtime. You don't mind getting out o' yer warm bed when you can mek a bit of money. I'd wok all hours God sends, for money. Watch the tax, though. Bastards will skin you dry, and fry you rotten. Dangerous work, as well. Nearly got scooped up by a mechanical digger the other day. But it's money that I like to be getting into my pocket, fartin' Martin! As soon as I know there's money to be earned I'd dig that soil up with my fingernails. They don't need to tell *me* when to start sweating!'

Martin had a question. 'What do you do with it?'

'Wi' what?'

'The money you get.'

'Ah! Booze a bit – that's me. Treat everybody – now and again. Save a lot, though. Gonna buy a house when I've got the deposit. Me and mam'll live in it. Not the other spongers, though. They wain't get a look in.'

His brothers and sisters had reputations as scroungers. Serve 'em right if Raymond dealt with them as they deserved.

The narrow lane was so rutted he thought they'd get stuck, the car swaying from side to side, sharp privet branches scraping the window. The wheels skidded on the mud in a couple of places, but it didn't bother Raymond. He steered as if in a rally car, then grumbled: 'Fuckers should have cut that hedge down' – seeing in his mirror another car grinding too closely behind.

As they topped the rise tears of muddy water lashed against the windscreen. When the wipers flushed over it Martin saw the vast clayey cutting between green banks. It was a man-made valley occupied by lorries, cranes, mechanical diggers. Those already moving seemed to be the ones that owned it. He was surprised at how few men there were, having expected to see them swarming all over the place.

Raymond drove parallel to the valley, and parked his car by a cluster of huts. He got out, and farted, then stretched his arms and legs. 'See that trailer?'

'Yes.'

'Well, I'm going to book myself in.'

The nearest wooden hut, full of tools, smelt as if it were made of still-growing trees. He expected to tread on leaves as he went in to have a look, but there was a crunch of gravel under his boots. His eyes were sore from little sleep. He yawned while trying to stretch his arms without being seen.

The sound of engines moaned and jerked from the canyon. They formed a chorus. There was never silence. Raw earth was being cleared. Soon it would be covered, and packed, and solidified, and paved to take traffic and huge lorries between London and Leeds. The men who did it knew what their work was for. They could see it as plain as a streak of paint across a piece of new wood. But it must go so slowly that a month was like a day.

Raymond came back wearing a helmet and a livid pink jacket. 'Don't stand idle,' he called sharply, so that Martin didn't know whether he was joking or not. 'Let's get on that motor.'

The dumper truck swayed as it went down the track hewn in the incline. The narrow ledge frightened him, for the dumper might tumble any minute and take both of them to the bottom. Raymond fought with the wheel and gears, laughed and swore as he swung it zig-zag along.

'This fucking thing – it's like a dog: I tamed it a long while ago, so you've no need to worry.' The machine went more quickly. 'If we don't get down in one piece, though, I'll get the push. That's the sort of world we're living in, Martin. Owt happens to this dumper, and I get my cards. Don't matter about us, if we get killed. We'll get compo, but what good does that do yer?'

He drove the petrol-smelling truck under the digger to take its load, then lumbered it back up the escarpment in such a way that Martin didn't think he'd tamed it at all. Tipping it from above helped to heighten the embankment: 'The bleeding gaffer wanted to know what *you* was doing here, so I told him you was the new mash-lad from Cresswell. He's got so much on his plate though, that gaffer, that he don't know whether he's coming or going. Looked a bit gone-out at me, burree din't say owt.'

After two trips Martin decided to stay on top. He could watch the beetling dumpers doing their work from a distance, which was better than being down among them. He remembered a word from school that would describe the long deep scar: geology, geological. The layers of gravel and grit and clay were being sliced like a cake so that the motorway could be pushed through into Yorkshire.

In a while he sat down. It was a struggle to keep the eyes open when you weren't thinking about anything. The wind died and the sun came out. He was dozing in its warm beams, then dreaming, but he never cut off from the distant punch and rumble of machinery, and the occasional shouting that broke through as if finding him at the end of a long search.

Diesel smoke wafted across. He opened his eyes so as not to lose contact with the sort of work he hoped to be getting paid for next year. Raymond nudged him awake: 'You poor bogger! A bit too early in the morning, was it?'

'No, it worn't,' he snapped.

'You know why, though, don't you?' He had a can of hot tea, and offered him the lid as a cup. 'Take this. I'll get some scoff.'

'Why?' The sweet strong tea went straight to the waking-up box behind his eyes.

'You stayed up too late. Can't go to work early if you don't get to your wanking pit on time. Not unless you're over eighteen, anyway. You'll 'ave to stop reading all them books. Send you blind.'

He'd heard that before – often. 'I'm not tired.'

Raymond rolled a neat cigarette. 'What about some snout, then?'

'No, thanks.'

He laughed. Smoke drifted from his open mouth. 'That's right. Keep off the fags. Don't booze, either, or go with women. Stick to your books as long as you can. And you know why? I'll tell yer: because fags pack your lungs in, booze softens your brain, and women give you the clap.'

With that, he went back to work.

Martin didn't know what to make of such advice, so it didn't seem important. He wished he had one of the books he'd stacked and shifted about on the table last night, even if it was only the Bible in Polish, or the Italian dictionary. When dumper trucks again moved into the canyon, and the first one came back loaded, they didn't interest him any more, though he thought they might if he sat at the wheel of one like Raymond.

An hour later he was so bored that he felt hungry, so finished off his last cheese sandwich. Sitting high up and set apart gave him a picture-view. Nothing happened, and he was bored, yet everything moved so slowly that he wouldn't forget it as long as he lived.

Raymond's truck was easy to recognize. He saw clearly across the whole distance, and watched him go with his load up the far slope of the motorway. A wind blew from the streets of a town on the skyline, as if someone on the church top in the middle were wafting it over. With his vivid sight he saw Raymond's truck go behind a long low spoil bank, the helmet moving slowly. Then his body reappeared, and finally the truck again.

It was manoeuvred into a clearing for about the twentieth time, and guided close to the escarpment by another man. It waited a few seconds, as if to get breath, then it tipped its load. There was no pause before setting off quickly towards the excavation for another.

He stared more closely, imagining he was Raymond sitting on the truck and working the levers, confidently steering after four years' experience, smelling old oil and new soil and wondering how much he would coin that day. He wouldn't mind working here, even if he did have to start by seeing to the men's tea and running errands from one hut to another. A mash-lad was better than a school-kid.

The truck reversed towards the precipice at a normal and careful speed. At dusk they'd drive back to Nottingham. Maybe Raymond would call at home for a bite to eat before going to where he lived in the Meadows – though it wasn't likely because he never went visiting in his working clothes.

He could almost hear the engines speeding up. 'I'll get this one over with,' Raymond might be saying, 'then I'll pack it in and piss off out of it. Done enough graft for one day.' He sensed the words going through his brain. He said them aloud, as if to save his cousin the thought or energy.

He couldn't say who was tired most: him, Raymond, or the man whom Raymond's dumper truck knocked flying over the almost sheer slope. The man had sauntered out of the way as usual but then, for a reason which was hard to make out (though he was sure there must have been one, since there always was a reason – for everything), he leapt back against the truck as if to dive underneath.

It wasn't easy to decide the exact point of impact. The man's spade turned in the air, and Martin swore he heard the clatter as its metal head caught the side of the truck.

The body rolled down the steep bank and smashed into a mechanical digger. He watched Raymond jump from his seat. Other men lined the top of the spoil heap. Two or three, Raymond clearly among them, started to scramble down.

The whole heart-side of Martin's body was dulled with pain. It lasted a few seconds, then left him feeling cold, wind-blown and gritty at the eyes, which now seemed to lose their vision. The sound of an ambulance came from far away as he walked towards the huts. His legs and arms shivered as if from cold. He gripped himself till it stopped. The flashing blue lights of a police car bobbed along the hedge-top.

He noticed how pale Raymond was when he got into the car an hour after his usual knocking-off time. He smoked a cigarette, something he said he never did when driving. 'That pig-copper told me I'd killed 'im on purpose,' he shouted above the engine as it roared and sent the car skidding along the muddy lane. 'They said I must have been larking about.'

'I didn't see yer, and I was watching.'

'A few others was as well, so I'm all right for witnesses. But can you believe it? Killed 'im on purpose! One of the blokes I'd known for weeks! Can you imagine him asking a thing like that? Must be rotten to the bloody core. He just jumped in front of my truck.'

Martin felt as if he was asking the only question in his life that needed a proper answer:

'Why did he do it?'

After half a minute's silence, which seemed so long that Martin thought his cousin would never speak again, unless to tell him to mind his own business, Raymond said: 'You won't guess. Nobody on this earth would. I'll tell yer, though. He dropped his packet o' fags in front of my truck, and because he thought the wheels would crush 'em, he jumped to pick 'em up. The daft bastard didn't want to lose his fags.

Would you believe it? Didn't *think*! Blokes who don't think deserve all they get. I'd have given him half of my own fags though, if only he'd left 'em alone.' He smiled bleakly at his untested generosity. 'Can't understand him doing a thing like that. I thought I knew him, but bogger me if I did. You don't know anybody, *ever* Martin. So never think you do.'

'He's dead now, though.'

'The daft bleeder.'

Martin said he was sorry it happened. He hated feeling the tears at his eyes as sharp as glass. 'Who was he?'

'An old chap, about forty-odd. Happy old chokker. He was allus singing, he was. You could tell from his mouth, but nobody ever *heard* him because of the engines kicking up such a noise. He didn't sing when he thought we could hear him. Funny bloke altogether. All my life I've been careful, though, that's the best on it. I never wanted that to happen. I'm not a murderer, it don't matter what that copper tried to say. "I'm not a murderer, your honour! Honest, I'm not!" That's what I'll shout out in court when the case comes up.'

Back in the lighted streets, Martin said nothing. He had nothing to say, because everything had been *done*. His cousin drove with one hand, and held his wrist tight when he reached across with the other. 'I'm glad you came to work with me today, any road up, our Martin. I wouldn't have liked to drive home on my own after that little lot. I'll tek you right to your door. Don't say owt to your mam and dad, though, will yer?'

'Why?'

'Let me tell 'em, tomorrer.' He was on the edge of crying. Martin never thought he'd feel sorry for Raymond, but he did now. He felt more equal than he'd ever done – and even more than that. There wasn't much to look up to. The big mauler was crushing his wrist. 'Aren't you going to the boozer with 'em tonight?'

He drew his hand off, to change gear before stopping at the White Horse traffic lights. 'I think I'll get off home. Mam might go out and get me a bottle of ale from the beer-off.' He winked. 'If I ask her nice.'

Nothing could keep him down for long.

Martin wasn't as tired as he had been by the motorway. When his parents drove to the boozer he got his books out of the dresser, instead of going to the last house at the pictures as was usual on Saturday night.

The clear clean print was a marvel to his eyes. He started to read the first page, then became so drawn into the book that he didn't even hear the click of the gate latch when it sounded three hours later.

The Sniper

Just before closing time in The Radford Arms an old man leapt up on a table and started to dance. The other drinkers were so preoccupied that his clearing of pint jars with such speed went unnoticed, though some of them saw how his polished shoes in which their faces shone tapped with a clever sort of energy on the wooden top.

The landlord was trying to decide when to put the towels on (for in Nottingham the clocks seem notoriously unsynchronized in this respect), and for a few minutes his fingers ferried a hand along his watch chain as if he wouldn't get out his timepiece till everyone saw him and ran in panic to the bar for their final pint – which some of those who considered themselves more deprived than the rest had already stood up to do.

The old man sat as much by himself as was possible on a Saturday night, by the door from where he had a good view of the saloon and could judge when to act. He waited till near closing because at turned-eighty his energy was limited. Everyone later agreed on his cunning, for he caught the landlord at a time when he was unable to imagine such an occurrence, which allowed the old man to get in some minutes of tap-dance and sing-song before the night was brought to an end.

As he waited by the dregs of a second pint, his free hand began to shake, and his slate-grey eyes took on such a glitter that it seemed unlikely they provided him with much visibility. He drew his sleeve across his mouth to wipe the beer away, but also to erase any tremble which might betray his intention, suggesting a strength of character from former days that had not yet totally vanished. He blinked nervously and, when his arm came down, his tongue darted twice across his lips. He wore a knotted tie over a white collar that turned up at the ends, and it could be seen that his dark grey jacket and trousers didn't quite match.

In the general astonishment at the clattering dance everyone looked at his shoes rather than his face, sensing that if a collapse were to come it would begin with them, and they would see the full drama from the start. Yet the face was more interesting if only because it was difficult to fix on, and hard to accept what it was saying to those who thought only to observe the feet. Anyone who did look at his lips might realize he was trying to tell them something.

His hands were held flat in front as if to push off his audience should they try and drag him down – as he expected and dared them to. They hardly heard the tapping of his feet, and few made out the tune he was singing, for the pub was far from quiet. His mouth moved to a definite song but the words were hard to catch. He relived the murder, but no one listened to his gospel-truth. His sneer was like spit in their eyes though they did no more than grin, or call to get his knees up, or ask him to remember his age and not to be such a loon. Or they ignored him while supping their final jars.

He would dance while he could, and tell again what he'd whispered in that shell-hole near Gommecourt fifty years ago. He shouted names and phrases, and sometimes made them rhyme, till a few listened, though heard little that made sense. He tapped the rhythm and told it clear, and wondered when they'd pull him down and ask why he'd never been taken to the cop-shop and relieved of his money, belt, braces, shoes and false teeth, and got thrown into a stone cell, and brought into court (where he'd have said nothing from start to finish), and finally taken into the hangman's yard as a proper end to a wickedness he hadn't repeated to a soul till an age when the edge of his younger days came back and time had no meaning because there wasn't much of it left.

Every stone had beetles underneath. They lay still and quiet, because of all creatures on earth they were good at knowing how, but in the last few months they'd been growing bigger, till he felt the boulder ready to surge into the air and crush him to even less than a beetle when it came down. The crime had kept him loving and industrious ever after, and even now God hadn't paid him out.

Nevill passed the house of a blacksmith's noisy family. The up-and-down stretch of common known as the Cherry Orchard was blocked from the west by Robins Wood. The sun glowed on a bed of clouds, and the surrounding grass appeared so green from his place of hiding that it seemed as if a secret kingdom shone from under the ground.

Too far off to be noticeable, Nevill saw the man walking towards the wood – having been daft enough to think that secrets could be kept. Silence increased the quality of the glow. The stark side of the trees stood out as if they would melt, part of the most perfect summer since the fourteen-year-old century had turned.

Nevill watched Amy follow her fancyman from the lane, by which time he was already waiting in the wood. He plucked a juicy grass stem and, now that they were out of sight, moved along a depression – in case they should be looking from the bushes – towards a spot a hundred yards above where they had entered.

A breeze which carried the smell of grass made him hungry. He had come out before his tea, tracking to where he thought she had gone. There had to be a day when he came home early. The farmer he worked for lent him a gun so that he could stalk hares and be sure of hitting them. He moved like a tree that seemed always in the same place to the delicate senses of a rabbit. Then he took five minutes to lift his gun so that they didn't stand a chance. Even so, one sometimes escaped in a last-minute zig-zag too quick to be sighted on. Because the farmer gave only one cartridge at a time he could afford no waste. A big rabbit lasted two meals, and made a smell for any man to come home to.

The last of the sun flushed white and pink against his eyes. A raven circling over the wood told him they were still there, and hadn't gone out the other side towards the west. Its black gloss turned purple in the evening light.

Kneeling, he wondered whether or not to go back to the house and leave them alone. Now that he knew for certain, there seemed no point in pursuing them, for he could call the tune any time he liked. But his legs wouldn't stop his slow encroachment on that part of the wood they had gone into. A cloud of gnats pestered him. If he had been walking at a normal pace he could have reached home and forgotten all about it, but the deliberate putting forward on to the grass of one foot after another was as if he advanced on a magnetized track impossible to sidestep.

Shadows aggrandized each tree and solitary bush. Two rabbits ran from the wood. One stared at him, then sat up and rubbed its paws, while the other turned away with its white tail shivering in the breeze. He heard a hooter from Wollaton colliery, and the blink of his left eyelid wasn't sufficient to warn the rabbits, one of which was big enough for the pot.

Fingers itched for the safety catch, the shotgun lifting inch by inch. One would be dead for sure, but he fought his instinct, staying the gun while in the grip of something firmer. Rabbits swarmed so much this summer that a week ago he caught two with one bullet.

The long dusk began. A platoon of starlings scoured back and forth on a patch of grass to leave no worm's hiding place unturned. He wanted to light his pipe and smoke off the gnats, but any movement might reveal his place, so he became a flesh statue with head bowed, green jacket blending into green.

The crack of twigs sounded and she walked, without turning left or right, straight across the Cherry Orchard and back towards the lane. It wasn't the nearest way home but, when close to the house, she'd expect him to see her coming from the Woodhouse direction in which her mother lived. He smiled at such barefaced cunning, in which they'd talked up their little plot together, he deciding to stay another ten minutes in the wood after she had got clear of it.

Nevill needed only a few paces to reach the trees. Dodging the brambles, he walked from the thigh, toes and balls of the feet descending so as to avoid the heel on unseen twigs. He heard the stream that ran down the middle of the narrow wood. Blackberries were big and ripe. A pigeon rattled up, and he made towards its noise, advancing at the crouch, knowing every patch because his cottage was on the northern tip. When a match scraped along a box he stiffened.

The odour of fungus and running water on clean pebbles was sharpened by the cool of the evening. It wasn't quite dusk, but Nevill had to peer so as not to mistake him for the shadow of a bush. Looking for the first star, he lowered his head before finding one. The sky was still pale blue.

He saw him by the stream smoking a cigarette. A loosened tie hung around his neck, and he irritatedly brushed leaves from the legs of his dark suit. He whistled the bars of a tune, but suddenly stopped, as if not wanting to hear anything that would take him so far from what had just passed between him and Amy.

Nevill lifted the gun, butt-first. When a frog plopped into a side arm of the stream he saw the rings, and the man turned sharply at the noise as he decided it was time to get out of the wood. After two paces a shadow came at his head which had the force of the world concealed in it. An electric light went on for a second and revealed the trees roundabout. Often when a rabbit wouldn't die he battered the neck, and his rage was so great that it was no more difficult to smash the man's temple while he lay on the ground. There was a smell of hard drink when he knelt to make sure he was dead.

At the edge of the wood dusk was coming across the Cherry Orchard like a scarf. When Nevill fired, a rabbit spun on the ground. Then he fastened its two back legs together and walked towards the darker part of the common.

Standing at the door to look for him Amy heard the shot softened like a thunderclap in the distance, and shivered at the evening chill. Nevill passed by the blacksmith's house and went down the lane, under the long railway bridge to Lottie Weightman's beer-off in the village. He sold his rabbit for sixpence, then drank a pint. They were talking about the war, of how everybody was going, some saying what damned fools they were, while others thought it the only thing to do. He sat observing them with his slate-grey eyes, smiling at their expressions that did not seem to know what life was about.

Next day he went back into the wood and, hanging his jacket from the spike of a dead branch, hauled the body from its hiding place. He scraped off the turf and hacked at the roots. The soil was dry, but moistened lower down. With Amy last night he had lain back to back, thinking he'd never touch her again. Each press of the spade, pull at the handle and lift, reinforced his feelings about her. From the clear land of the Cherry Orchard he heard children, so put his jacket on and went swiftly to the edge of the wood.

'You can't come in 'ere.'

They were three ragged-arsed kids from Radford. 'We only want blackberries.'

'It's private.'

They grumbled.

'Gerroff – or you'll get a good hiding.'

He looked as if he'd do it, so they went, though one of them called from a distance and before fleeing 'Fuckin' owd bastard!'

He worked more quickly and, when the neat oblong hole was deep enough, heard the body thump to the bottom. The smashed head vanished under a first curtain of soil. Dead twigs and leaf-mould disguised the grave. He leaned against a tree to smoke his pipe, till sweat subsided and his breath came back, then he walked through the deepest grass to get the soil off his boots, for it wouldn't do to be untidy if you were going into town.

Walking up the hill towards Canning Circus he met others on the same errand. He spat on both hands for luck and rubbed his palms on hearing the clash of a band outside the drill hall, thinking that the army would be as good a place to hide as any.

The smell from his skin went as quickly as the spit dried. After passing the medical and getting his shilling he drank a pint in the canteen. Two hours later and still in their own clothes they were marched back down Derby Road to tents on Wollaton Park – only a mile from the wood where the fresh body lay buried.

Farmer Taylor could keep his job at fifteen bob a week. With two hours off the next day, he called to say he had packed it in, and expected to be turned out of his cottage, but the farmer smiled: 'I knew you would. I told you he'd be the first to go. Didn't I tell you, Martha? You wait, I said, he'll go, Nevill will! I'll lose a good man, but I know he'll go. Wish I could be in the old regiment myself. I know of no finer thing than going to fight for your country.'

There wasn't much need to talk. He was invited into the parlour and given a mug of ale.

'You'll mek a fine sowjer,' Taylor went on. 'I expected no less. Come and see us when you've got your khaki on.' He gave him a florin above his wages: 'Your wife can stay in the cottage. I'll see nowt happens to her.'

'I expect she'll be able to look after herself,' Nevill said cheerfully.

The farmer gave him a hard look: 'Ay, you'll mek a fine sowjer. Your sort allus do.'

He went home: 'I've gone and enlisted. You can carry on all you like now, because I won't be coming back.'

She gave him some bread and cheese. 'God will pay you out, leaving me like this.'

He wanted to laugh. When she went on the prowl for her man it wouldn't do her much good. He went upstairs to change into his best suit. The small room with its chest of drawers and flowered paper was part of them, as was the bed with its pillows and counterpane. She kept the house like a new pin, he had to admit, but it made no difference. He tied his working clothes and spare boots into a parcel and pushed it under the bed with his toe-cap. He wouldn't be back for any of them. Most other men in camp wore their oldest clothes, some nearly in rags, but he wanted to look smart even before the khaki came. If they took him away to be hanged he didn't want to take the drop looking like a scarecrow.

He stood in the doorway for a last look at the kitchen. 'Everybody's rushing to the colours.'

'More fool them. It doesn't mean you've got to join up as well. You're nearly thirty: let the young mad-'eads go.'

He didn't know what she had to cry for. She should be glad to get shut of him. He put two sovereigns between the pot cats on the shelf: 'Don't lose 'em.'

When she took off her pinafore and began to fold it he was frightened at having taken the King's shilling. One thing led to another when you killed somebody. Birds were whistling outside the open window. She'd hung the mats on the line. In his weakness he wanted to sit down, but knew he mustn't.

She rushed across to him. He lost his stiffness after a few minutes, and held her. They had been married in Wollaton church five years ago, but when they went upstairs he felt that he hadn't known her till now.

He forgot her grey eyes and her auburn hair when walking back by the dark side of the wood. If God paid him out it would be because God was a German bullet. As for the bloke whose brains he had knocked in, it served him right. He was tempted to dig by the bush and look at the body, to make sure everything wasn't happening in the middle of a dream, but he didn't have a spade.

The day was rotting. He breathed dusk through his nostrils, a smell that was enough to turn you as balmy as a hayfork, especially in such silence before rain. Happiness made him walk upright across the Cherry Orchard without looking back.

'You'll dig yourselves ten feet under,' the sergeant shouted, 'when the first shell bursts.'

On parade he was ordered to tie a white tape on his arm, the mark of a lance-corporal, till uniforms came and he could sew on the proper stripe. He was a more promising soldier than the rest, for he did not live from day to day like most of the platoon, not even from hour to hour as some of them cared to. He existed by the minute because every one contained the possibility of him being taken off and hanged. The grave was a deep one, and the man not known in the district – he reasoned hopefully while lying in the bell tent with eleven others and listening to raindrops hitting the canvas. It was also a time when scores of thousands were going to other towns to get into their favourite regiments, so maybe no one would even look for him.

During every package of sixty seconds he gave absolute attention to the least detail of military routine, and became the keenest man in the platoon. When rifles were issued he was careful that each round reached a bull's eye. The sling was firm around his arm and shoulder, body relaxed, feet splayed, and eye clear at the sights.

Every battalion had its snipers. 'On a dark night a lighted match can be seen nine hundred yards away,' they were told, 'and that's as far as from the Guildhall to the bloody Castle!'

It was also the distance from here to where *he* was buried, Nevill thought.

'Pay attention, or I'll knock your damned 'ead off!'

The sergeant savvied any mind that wandered, and Nevill knew he mustn't be caught out again.

He slid into the loop-holed sniper's post built by the sappers in darkness. Sacking was around his head, and mud-coloured tape swathed his rifle. He looked slowly from left to right, towards wire and sandbags across ground he had been over in darkness and seen in daylight through a periscope. He knew each grass-clump and crater. A faint haze hovered. Smells of cooking and tobacco drifted on the wind. He savoured the difference between a Woodbine and a Berlin cigar, till a whine and a windrush eruption of chalk and soil caused his elbow to tremble at a shell dropping somewhere to the left. The camouflage net shivered. He heard talking in the trenches behind. An aeroplane flew high.

Amy worked on filling shells at Chilwell factory, earning three times the amount he got as a corporal marksman, but he sent half his pay for her to put in a bank, though he didn't expect ever to get home and claim it because either a bullet or a rope (or a shell) was sure to pay him out. I always loved *you*, and always shall, she wrote. Aye, I know, same here, he answered – but not telling what he knew, and cutting her from his mind in case he got careless and was shot. He smiled at the justice of it.

In the space between one minute and the next he expected to see a party of men coming to get him for the hangman's yard whose walls would smell like cold pumice and rotting planks. He was ready for it to happen from any direction he could name, so that even in the débris of the trenches there was no one smarter at spotting misdemeanours in his own men, or fatal miscalculations on the enemy parapet.

A machine gun half a mile away stitched thoughts back into his brain, eyes turning, head in a motion that scanned the faint humps of the broken line. He didn't want to give up his perfected system of counting the minutes which kept him going in a job that held little prospect of a long life. All snipers went west sooner or later. He was glad that whole days passed without thinking of Amy, because she took his mind off things.

A smudge of grey by a sandbag, and then a face, and he lined up the sights instantly and pressed the trigger. The crack travelled left and right as he reloaded almost without movement, the bolt sliding comfortably in. The bullet took half a second to reach the face that had sprung back. He heard the word for stretcher bearer – *krankenträger* – and he wanted to laugh because, as in a game of darts or cribbage, he had *scored*. The more he killed, the less chance there'd be of getting called to account. He didn't want to know more than that. It was dangerous to think. You're not here to think but to do as you're effing-well told – and never you forget it or by God I'll have your guts for garters and strangle you to death with 'em. But they didn't need to roar such rules at him.

A retaliating machine gun opened from three hundred yards left. He saw the gunner. Chalk that jumped along was nowhere close enough. An itching started on his cheek, and an impulse to scratch was fought down. When it came back he turned his body cold. It was an almost pleasurable irritation that couldn't be ignored, but he resisted it, minute by minute. You had only to be at the Front for an hour and you were as lousy as if you'd been there ten years.

Last week he'd had a fever, and hadn't been able to do his work. No sniper was allowed out with a fever or a cold. With a fever you shook, and with a cold you dozed – though a true sniper would forget such things in his moment of action. Yet an experienced sniper was too valuable to waste. He sensed as much when he moved along the communication trenches at dawn or dusk, and observed how the officers looked at him – after their first curiosity at seeing such an unusual specimen – as if he were a man singled out for a life even worse than death, cooped up like a rat that only waited its turn to kill without fair fight. He knew quite plainly that many didn't like him because sniping was a dirty weapon like poison gas or liquid fire.

The trench was disturbed. Every eye fixed his stretch of land. They looked but did not see. He let his body into complete respose so as to make no move. The range card was etched on to his brain, and his eyes caught all activity, had even sharper vision because of the body's helplessness. The whole view was exposed to his basic cunning. His itching leg was forgotten when he pressed the trigger and killed the machine gunner.

Out of the opposite trench, a few fingers to the right, came a man who stood on the sandbags and beckoned. He wore a dark suit. A tie was unfastened around his neck. He bent down to brush chalk-grit from his trousers. When he straightened himself, he smiled.

Nevill lay in the water of his sweat, his teeth grinding as if to take a bite out of his own mouth. His body wasn't dead, after all. The man was afraid to come closer. Grey clouds formed behind his head, till he became part of them, when Nevill took a long shot almost in enfilade, and brought down a man who looked up from the second line of trenches.

If the man had still been alive Nevill would have shouted at him for his foolishness. Mistakes were as common as Woodbines. Even the old hands made them occasionally, as if tired of a caution which wouldn't let them be themselves. Something inside decided, against their will, that they'd had enough. In an unguarded moment their previous carefree nature took over – and they died. He smiled at the thought that no such fecklessness could kill him, no matter how deep down it lay.

He couldn't get out of his place till darkness. Danger time was near. If he chanced one more round they'd get a bearing and smother his place with shot shell and shit. Papier mâché heads painted to look real were put up so that when the sniper's bullet went clean through back and front, a pinpoint bearing could be made between the two holes which would lead with fatal accuracy to him. So when he saw a head tilted slightly forward and wearing no helmet he didn't shoot. If he kept as still as dead they would never see him, and he'd known all his life how to do that. When he played dead he was most alive. He felt like laughing but, knowing how not to, was hard to kill. As if in agreement the earth rumbled for half a minute under another nearby burst of shell. It grew in intensity till it sounded like a train going through Lenton station. He wanted to piss, but would have to keep it in.

Tomorrow he would be in a different position and, corked face invisible, could start all over again. He lay by the minute, sun burning through clouds as if intent on illuminating only him. A shot at dusk might succeed, when the setting sun behind sharpened their line of trenches, but only one, because they would be waiting, and he was too old a hand to get killed just before knocking off time.

Raindrops pestered a tin can, and caused an itch at his wrist. There was better visibility after a shower, though gas from his rifle in the dampened atmosphere might give him away if he fired. Their eyes were as good as his when they decided to look. He felt like a rabbit watching from its burrow, and counted the minutes more carefully. If they found him, he'd die. He craved to smoke his pipe. No sniper was taken prisoner. Nor their machine gunners. He felt cramp in his right foot, but tightened himself till it went.

The minute he woke in the morning, either at rest or on the march, or in the line, his first thought was not to decipher where he was but to realize that he hadn't yet been taken up for the man he had killed. He kissed his own wrist for luck. Other soldiers round about wondered why he smiled, while they only scowled or cursed.

Lying in his cramped hole sometimes brought on a faintness from which the only way out was to spread arms and legs as far as they would go, then get into the open and run. He would certainly be killed, so when blood packed at the extremities of hands and feet, thereby thinning at the heart, he called the minutes through and counted them. Sixty minutes made a platoon called an hour. Twenty-four hours formed as near as dammit two battalions of a day. He deployed his platoons and battalions of time and sent them into the soil. A shell once burst too near and he pissed into his rags – but kept his place and his life. When a machine gun peppered around no-man's-land in the hope of catching him, a man from his own trenches stopped the racket with a burst from a Lewis gun.

The minutes he hewed out of life, from the air or his own backbone, or plucked even from the din of the guns, saved him time and time again. In pushing aside the image of the hangman coming to get him across no-man's-land (or waiting in the form of a Provost Marshal's red cap when he went back through the communication trench and up towards the broad light of the day that was to be his last) he had only to punctuate his counting of the minutes by a careful shot at some flicker on the opposite sandbags. Away from the trenches, he could not wait to get back, even if on frontline duty as one of a back-breaking carrying party, or as an enfilading sharp-shooter during a trench raid. But mostly he belonged in a sniper's position that needed only eyes, brain and a steady finger at the trigger while he lay there all day and counted the minutes.

A week in the trenches was as long as a month or a year. He counted the minutes while others marked off the days. But all of them were finally without time and covered in mud, one in ten lost through shellfire, raids, frostbite and bullets.

They drudged to the rear and one night, wet from head to foot, Nevill joined his company in a rush across the churned turf of a field towards the bath-house. Everyone stripped to let the sanitary men get at their underclothes. Lice were everywhere. Scabies was common, and spread like chalkdust on a windy day. Some scratched themselves till bloody all over, and were treated with lavish doses of sulphur – which might give them dermatitis if they got too much of it. Nevill endured the terrible itching, even in his sniper's post, but on normal duty he woke himself after a few hours' sleep by a wild clawing at his clothes.

Water gushed from the taps only one point off freezing. They had expected it to be hot, so sounded as if a pack of ravening lions had got loose. The captain, transfixed by their mutinous swearing, hoped the sergeant-major would be along to get them moving into the water no matter how cold it was. Hard to understand their rage when they endured so much agony of life and limb on duty in the trenches. One man slipped on the slatted planks, and cursed the army.

'This is the last straw!' he shouted.

No one laughed, even when he was advised: 'Well, eat it then.'

Nevill, the icy chute spraying at him, let out a cry that stopped everyone's riotous catcalls: 'Fucking hell, it's too hot! It's scalding me to death. Turn it off! I'm broiled alive. Put some cold in, for Christ's sake!'

They began laughing at the tall thin chap fooling around with knees and knackers jumping up and down, a look of mock terror in the fiery stillness of his eyes and the falling line of his lips.

Once fastened into the separate world of his own outlandish shouts, Nevill went on calling loud and clear: 'My back's on fire! I'm broiling in *hell*! Turn that effing water off, or put some cold in, *please*! This steam's blinding my eyes. Turn it off!'

Others joined in and shouted the magic phrases like a chorus line at the music hall. They no longer hung back, but took to the water without further complaint.

Nevill stopped, and gripped the soap to wash. The muddy grime swilled off, and his face turned red as if steam had really worked the colour-change, not shame. Then he laughed again with the others while they blundered around fighting for the soap.

They collected warm and fumigated underwear. After breakfast came pay parade and later, with francs in their pockets and a few hours' kip behind their eyes, they were away to the estaminet for omelette, chips and wine, where they went on singing Nevill's catch-line: 'Turn that effing water off, or put some cold in please!'

What made him shout those words he didn't know, but the captain marked him for his sergeant's stripe, seeing a priceless NCO who could control his men by firmness – and displays of wit, however crude. Apart from which, there was no better off-hand shot in the battalion, though as a sergeant his sniping days were over.

After a hard week's training for 'the battalion in attack' they went back to the line with buckles, boots and buttons shining. The noise of guns took up every square inch of air around the face, kept a trembling under the feet for days. They said the gunfire brought rain. Cordite gathered full-bellied clouds that emptied on trenches to make all lives a misery. At the best of times a trench was muddy. The common enemy was rain, and the guns that shook soil down.

The few shells from the other side blew the earth walls in, no matter how well-revetted. When Nevill was buried he thought the hangman had come and gone already. He smelled quick-lime. In his tomb, yet knowing where he was, made him wonder if the man had been alive when he had buried him in Robins Wood. But he hadn't gone back till next day and he'd been dead by then right enough.

Nevill was earthed-in with bullet pouches, water bottle and rifle. In other words – as Private Clifford said, who found him more alive than two others whose names he couldn't remember as soon as they were dead – he was buried with full military honours, and you couldn't want more than that, now could you, sarge?

The pattacake soil-smell was everywhere, and the only thing that saved Nevill was his tin hat which, being strapped firmly on, had enough all-round rim to trap sufficient air for him to breathe till he was pulled free.

Every fibre of skin bone and gristle vibrated to the pounding. Could anything live under it? He drew himself into his private world and remembered how Amy had answered that she had nothing to forgive him for. She was never to realize he'd known about her love affair, though no doubt she wondered still where the chap had hopped it to. Maybe to the Western Front, like the rest of us. And if he hadn't sent a letter, what was funny in that? Nevill felt almost sorry she'd been ditched by two instead of one, though perhaps it wasn't all that rare when so many men had gone away at once.

Yet he needn't have worried about her wellbeing, for she sent him a parcel of tinned jam and biscuits and salmon, and a note saying she was working at Chilwell Depot till as close as she could get to her confinement which, he surmised, couldn't by any stretch of counted minutes be his kid. By earning her own money she could do as she liked, and in any case he had bigger things on his plate than to care what she got up to. 'I expect my missis is having a little bit on the side while I'm away,' he heard Private Jackson say. 'Suppose I would if I was her, damn her eyes!'

Being in a webbing harness of cross-straps and belt, with all appurtenances hanging therefrom, made him feel he no longer belonged to himself, since a devil's hook in any part of his garb would swing him from here to eternity without a by-your-leave. He had a date with some kind of hangman and that was a fact. The unavoidable settled his gloom, and was only lifted when his duties as platoon sergeant made him forget.

Under the hangings of equipment he was almost skeletal. The other sergeants – when he shared Amy's food parcel – chaffed that a bullet wouldn't find him. But he ate like a wolf, and no flesh grew. He worried, they said. He worked too hard. He was never still. You needn't let a third stripe kill you. The men didn't like him, yet under his eternal fussing felt that he would never let them down.

Drumfire crumbled the walls between compartments of the minutes. A shake entered his limbs that he had seen in others, and which he thought would never afflict him. As a sniper he had gone over after the first rush of infantry, but now there would be no distinction. He'd be in the open without his hideaway. It wasn't the first time, but they'd been trench raids, and not the big attack. He held his hand down, and counted till the trembling stopped.

578

The guns were finishing off every living thing, and all they had to do was walk across on the day and take over what was left. 'Only, don't scratch your lily-white ankles on the rusty barbed wire, lads. And don't fall into an 'orrible shell-hole. And if you see a hot shell sizzling towards you, just push it to one side with your little finger and tell it to piss off' – he'd heard Robinson diverting his mates the other day. Nobody else thought it would be a walkover, though he supposed a few of the brass hats hoped against hope.

He walked along the trench, lifting his boots through the foot-depth of mud.

'Had yer rum?'

They read his lips in the noise. 'Yes, sergeant.'

'Had yer rum, then?'

'I'm tiddly already, sarge!'

'Answer properly when yer're spoken to.'

There was no doubt about the next one: 'Had yer rum?'

'Yes, sergeant.'

'Wake up then, or you'll be on a charge.'

'Bollocks.'

He swung back. 'If yo' don't have less chelp, Clifford, I'll put yer bollocks where yer fucking 'ead should be.'

The man laughed. 'Sorry, sergeant.'

Live and let live. He moved on. 'Had yer rum?'

'It makes me sleepy, sergeant.'

'You'll wake up in a bit, never bloody fear. Had yer rum?' – and on till he had made sure of everyone.

He stood by a ladder and drank his own, except for a drop in the bottom which he threw into the mud for luck. They called it the velvet claw because it warmed yet ripped your guts. Some couldn't take it, but those who could always drank any that went buckshee.

He saw that the stars had turned pale. The guns made a noise that two years ago would have torn him apart had it been sprung on him. He pressed his feet together so that his knees wouldn't dance. There'd never been such a week of it. Every minute was hard to drag out. Darkness was full of soil and flashes. The counting melted on his tongue. For a moment he closed his eyes against the roaring light, then snapped them open.

One dread stamped on another. Explosions from guns and Stokes mortars dulled the feel of a greased rope at the neck. His cheeks shook from the blast of a near-miss. With bayonet fixed and day fully light the only way out was over the bags and at the Gerries. The shuddering of his insides threatened to send him into a standing sleep, so he moved up and down the trench to cut himself free of it – and to check every man's equipment. Nothing bore thinking about any more. Under the feet and through the mud a tremor which rocked his temples was connected to a roar in the sky travelling from the south. Another explosion came, and more until the final whistles began. They were letting off the mines before Zero.

Faces to either side were dull and shocked. One or two smiled stupidly. A youth muttered his prayers (or maybe they were curses) and Nevill knew that if he stopped he wouldn't be able to stand up. They were trapped, no matter what they had done. The straight and cobblestoned gas-lit streets of Radford replaced everything with carbide-light clarity. It was a last comforting feel of home, and when it vanished the trap was so final that it seemed impossible ever to get out, though he never lost hope.

Some leaned, or tried to fold themselves, wanting soil for safety. One man was eating it, but blood and flesh and scraps of khaki were up the side of the trench, and his arm was gone. Nevill shouted at them to stand up. He was thrown to one side as pebbles and slabs of chalk spattered his helmet, but he still called hoarsely at them to stand up to it. Screams came from the next bay, and another call for stretcher bearers. Lieutenant Ball examined his luminous watch, and Nevill wondered how much longer they'd be.

Over the parapet he saw flashes in the smoke and mist, an uneven row of bursts where trenches should have been. His watch said seven twenty-five. Amy's letters showed more tenderness than either had felt when they were together. There was more than there would ever be for him should he get back, because it wasn't his baby she was carrying. He won his struggle against her memory by counting each blank minute, knowing there weren't many left before they ascended the swaying ladders.

It was a hard pat on the shoulder that made him turn:

'Yes, sir?'

A company runner stood by. The pale-faced lieutenant of nineteen looked forlorn under his helmet, but regained sufficient competence to tell him: 'You're to go back to Battalion Headquarters, Sergeant Nevill.'

'Now, sir?'

Lieutenant Ball smiled, as if to indicate that such a lunatic signal had nothing to do with him. 'Seems so. You're to go out of the line.'

Nevill gripped his rifle, a vision of himself raising it to the 'on guard' position and bayoneting his officer. The horror of it broke his habit of obedience.

'What for, sir?'

The barrage would lift any second. Lieutenant Ball looked at his watch again, and didn't turn from it till the guns stopped. 'How do I know?'

The hangman would be there, for sure. 'Let me go over, sir. I've waited a long while to have a proper go at them. I can see what they want at Brigade as soon as I come back this afternoon.'

Nevill had fathered the platoon, so it would be vile not to let him take part in the big attack. Silence was filled by the noise of the birds. They were always busy, even when the guns were at it. He stuffed the message into his pocket and said:

'See that you do.'

'Thank you, sir.'

Whistles cut along the crowded slit in the earth, and Nevill shouted them into the open.

Full daylight met them as soon as they were up the ladders. Many clawed their way by planks or soil to gain freedom from the stink, shadows and uncertainty of the trench. Men on either side were falling under loads they could hardly support. Highstepping through their own wire, they went on under the mist as if that too weighed more than they could carry.

Shells of shrapnel balls exploded above their heads. They stopped silently, or rolled against the soil as if thrown by an invisible hand. Or they were hidden in a wreath of smoke and never seen again. The wire was like a wall. The guns had cut only one gap so they were like a football crowd trying to get off the field through a narrow gate on which machine guns were trained.

He sang to himself, wanting to get on. The men walked slowly because they couldn't go back. The biggest paper bags in the world were bursting above their heads. Minutes were unimportant. Every second was a king. He had to see his men through the wire. Lieutenant Ball disappeared as if he'd never existed. When they lagged, Nevill cursed from behind. He wanted to run but didn't know whether front or back would be any good so got ahead to coax them through bullets and shrapnel:

'Come on, move. Keep your dressing there. Keep your dressing. Keep moving, lads.'

They couldn't hear, but read his lips if they saw them, and came on, as if they too had been counting the minutes, and were terrified of some hangman or other. He wanted them to know that safety lay in doing as they were told and in getting forward. A few of his platoon were in advance of the company. He didn't know where the others had gone. While still in the German wire more shellbursts caught them. He was anxiously looking for a way through. You couldn't hear the birds any more. Machine guns never stop.

He knelt and fired towards the parapet, loading and reloading till he felt a bang at his helmet, and was pulled as if he were a piece of rope in a tug-o'-war. If it went on he would snap. In the darkness someone screamed in one ear when he was drawn icily apart, and he wondered why there was no light, thinking maybe they were going to bury him in Robins Wood, except that he was in France near a stink-hole called Fonky-bleeding-Villas.

He didn't know who was trying to yank him clear, but there was a smell of steel that burned so fiercely it turned blue. He rolled over and over. He opened his eyes, and took off his waterbottle to drink. The shrapnel had stunned him but he was unhurt except for a graze on the scalp.

The man by his side said: 'Not too much, sergeant. We'll need it for later.'

The stream in Robins Wood ran through his mouth. He counted the minutes to stop himself drinking to the bottom. 'Who are yer, anyway?'

'I'm Jack Clifford, sergeant. You know *me!*'

'I was bleddy stunned.' He looked around. 'Where's your rifle?'

'I lost it, sergeant. I don't know.'

'Oh, did yer? You'll be bleddy for-it, then.'

He began to cry.

'Where are yer from?'

'Salisbury Street, sergeant.'

'Got any Mills bombs?'

They were too far off to be any use, but he had.

Pulling off his burden of equipment, and without his helmet, Nevill edged to the rim of the crater. A leg with a boot on it hung over the other lip. He beckoned Clifford to follow, but indicated not too quickly. After a full minute, raising his head, and positioning himself, he fired a whole clip at men on the German parapet. Clifford got higher and threw a grenade, shouting: 'Split this between yer!'

Machine gun bullets swept across. Clifford screamed and rolled back.

Something had struck Nevill's shoulder, and his arm felt as if gripped by an agonizing cramp, but with shaking hand he bound both field dressings across Clifford's white and splintered ribs: 'That'll see yer right till we get back. The fuckers are picking us off like rabbits. We don't stand a chance, so we'd better stay where we are.'

'The red caps'll 'ave me. I've lost me rifle,' Clifford said.

Nevill wanted to tell him that it didn't look as if anybody would have him any more, though you couldn't say as much to a young lad. 'Them boggers wain't come for you,' he comforted him. 'It's me they're after. They sent a signal for me.'

'They don't come over the top,' Clifford said, 'do they?' He tried to spit, then seemed to think that if he did he'd die. 'Not them, they don't. If the Gerries didn't shoot 'em, *we* would, wouldn't we, sergeant?'

'Happen we might. Just keep still, and don't worry.'

Blood was pumping like a spring in autumn, but he knew no tourniquet would hold it. 'Let me tell you summat,' Nevill said, thinking to take his mind off it.

Clifford tried to laugh. 'What, me owd cock?'

'In September, I murdered somebody. Lay still, I said, and don't talk.'

His white face grimaced in agony. 'You're having me on?'

'Before I enlisted, I mean.'

'Got to save our strength. The Gerries'll get us.'

Nevill fought to stop himself fainting. 'No time. I'll tell you about it if you'll listen.' He looked around as if someone else might hear, then pulled Clifford towards him with a desperate grip, shouting into his ear when shells exploded close, and telling his story so that Clifford, behind eyes that stared wildly one minute and were closed the next, couldn't doubt his confession.

A greater truth was choking him, but he forgot to be afraid of machine guns and searching shrapnel while Nevill spoke his deadly tale in which he embroidered the homely Nottingham names to divert Clifford from the agony that would not let him live. He brought in the sound of Woodhouse and Radford, Robins Wood and Wollaton, Lenton and the Cherry Orchard and all the streets he could think of, as many times as possible to divert him and make his account so real that even a dying man would see its truth – though hoping by a miracle the talismanic words would save his life.

'It's on'y one you killed, sarge,' he whispered. 'Don't much matter.'

After dark Nevill dragged him a few feet at a time. 'Find somebody else,' Clifford said. 'I'm finished. I'll never be old.'

Nevill had to get someone back to safety. 'Don't talk so bleddy daft.'

He carried him a yard or two, thinking that as long as he hung on to him he need never consider the hangman again. He sweated grit and spat blood and pissed sulphur – as the saying went – and knew he was always close to conking out.

'Why are we in a tunnel, sergeant?' Clifford's eyes filled with soil and tears. 'Yer off yer sodding nut. Yer pulling your guts out for nowt.'

Occasional rifle shots sounded, but the machine guns and artillery had ceased. 'They'll hang me,' he said. 'Shut up.'

Clifford pulled both legs into his chest, choking on his blood. 'They'll shoot me, without me rifle. I don't like this tunnel, though. We went over the top, didn't we, not in a tunnel. Must a bin a mistake.'

He knelt close and saw his face in the light of a flare. 'Yes, we did go over the top, and you're wounded, you fool, so shut your mouth.' He whispered into his ear as he lay down beside him: 'A real Blighty one yer've got. You'll be out of it for *good* soon.'

English voices called low in the darkness, and stretcher-bearers found them. When they pulled at Nevill's arm to part him from Jack Clifford he screamed in agony.

The adjutant went through the rolls at Battalion Headquarters and said: 'Sergeant Nevill? Wasn't he the one we sent the signal for? Don't suppose he got it in time. All they wanted was for him to come back and explain why he had indented for too many ration replacements last week. We'd have put him down for a medal, bringing in a wounded man like that while he was wounded himself, if only the chap hadn't died.'

When Nevill was demobbed in the spring of 1919 he went back to Nottingham and found Amy. She had her own small house, and took him in as if he'd just come back from shooting rabbits in Robins

Wood. Three months later she was pregnant again, and he was already at work on a mechanic's job that was to last thirty years. He looked after Amy and her first son, and then she had two by him, but he was never brave enough to tell her what he told Jack Clifford near Gommecourt. He was on the point of it often, but sensed that if he let it out they wouldn't stay together any more.

Those good souls who helped old Nevill from the table in The Radford Arms averred he was no more than a bag of skin and bone. He trembled as they sat him down, and the landlord nodded at one of his bar-keepers to bring a dash of whisky and water. It had already passed closing time, and two more men who were also good enough to order him something were forced to drink it themselves.

'Funny bloody story he was trying to spin us,' one of them said, 'about killing somebody in Robins Wood.'

'Couldn't make head nor tail of it. I've known him years, and he wouldn't hurt a fly. A bit senile, I suppose. Come on, get that turps down your throat, then we'll drive him back to his missis in Beaconsfield Terrace.'

Nevill thought he would have a word or two if ever he met Jack Clifford again about the secret he'd foisted on him but which nobody else had taken notice of when he let it out in the boozer. Not that he had much of a wait before discovering whether or not he'd see old Jack. Nobody was surprised when old Amy found him dead one morning, sitting fully dressed by the fireplace. Having heard about his dancing on the table in the pub, the neighbours had supposed – as they said at the funeral – that it couldn't be long after that.

Brothers

In the ten minutes or so while Ken dealt with his large white mug of tea he didn't take his hand from the handle once, not even when the mug was resting before him on the table as if, Tony thought, he was frightened of somebody coming in and snatching it away.

'I don't know what I'll do. I can't even think.' Ken's voice sounded vacant and forlorn. Though not aware of pitying himself it was beginning to get through that you only lived once. He'd always known – and who didn't? – but regarded the fact as not worth bothering about. The green progress of summer made it more insistent however, as also did the discouraging fact that he had lost his job at the factory.

Thin rain fell noiselessly into the backyard beyond the window. In work you could choose your friends, but out of it you couldn't, so he had come to see his brother, and he didn't know why, because they had never felt much sympathy for each other. He didn't expect any help. His problem was too big for that, and problems were always your own, but he had just wanted to say hello. The only time he looked away from his tea was to glance at his own polished boots, which unaccountably made him put his hand to his throat and realise he wore no tie.

'I don't know what you can do.' Tony stood. It was his dinner time, and soon he would have to get back to work rewiring the canteen of a local small factory. Ken wanted something, and Tony didn't like to think so because he wasn't sure what. He'd never seemed much in contact with the world, our Ken hadn't, and Tony recalled their father saying about him that he was just bright enough to realise he wasn't all there.

Ken had never understood how they could be brothers, being so physically different. He was tall and lean, with a moustache, and almost bald (or so it had seemed in the mirror that morning) but Tony was short and stout and round faced. Eyes almost closed and a wide smile showed he was thinking of something funny, but he was too tight-arsed to share the joke with anybody else, certainly not with his brother. Only

587

when they looked each other square in the eye did they know they came from the same family.

Ken took a final swig at his tea. 'Well, I didn't come here to ask for anything. I suppose we ought to meet now and again, though. We're brothers, after all.'

Tony had to agree. 'That's true enough,' but as if he'd also been wondering what they had in common. Behind him was a big colour television, and half a dozen shelves of video films arranged in the recess like books in a library.

Ken lit a cigarette, and leaned back in his chair. If Tony wanted him to go, let him say so. 'The gaffer gave me five hundred quid when he laid me off, so I don't suppose I can grumble.'

'That's the trouble, working for a boss,' Tony said, puffing his thin little cigar. 'Sooner or later you get the push.' He told the familiar tale of how, on coming out of the army, he put a card in his front window saying: ANYTHING REPAIRED. 'I couldn't lose. If it was a wireless, you knew nine times out of ten it was summat to do with a plug or a loose connection, or a dud valve. Wirelesses was easy, in them days. If it was a watch or clock it was either a bit of dust in the works, or it wanted winding up. Or one hand was so close to another it stopped both from moving. You'd be surprised how many people don't know a watch wants winding up. Or they didn't then anyway. The same with most things.

'I'd sometimes get called out only to mend a fuse. And if it was owt more complicated I'd tek it to a place in town, and charge the customer a commission. You can always mek a bob or two in this world. After a while there wasn't much I couldn't fix in the electrical line: vacuum cleaners, fridges, televisions. Then I moved out of the front room, and rented my own workshop. Took on another bloke to help. Got my own firm going in no time.'

The most successful cowboy in the business, Ken thought, but now he knew so much he wasn't a cowboy any longer. Last year he went to Benidorm, and this year he was taking Molly to Greece. 'I like to go abroad now and again,' Tony went on. 'Got a taste for it in the army, after my year in Germany. Anyway,' he winked, 'I like to see all them topless girls dodging about with a volley ball!'

Ken didn't begrudge him any of that. Nor did he really mind being out of work. He was nearly fifty, anyway, and would get the dole. He didn't suppose he could be thrown out of his flat, though sometimes he wouldn't mind, seeing as how far above the ground it was. Then there was the noise from neighbours, and it got damp when rain blew horizontal from Derbyshire.

All his life he had gone from one job to another because there were plenty to be had and none had seemed good enough. He'd got on well with most gaffers, though, working hard because he liked doing the best he could, and because time went quicker that way. When he realised that even doing the best bored him he opted for another job. Nor did the gaffers want him to leave, but what changes they offered to make him stay had never seemed interesting enough.

When they sat in the armchairs Molly came in with the after dinner cup of tea, and Ken was surprised to see one for him. He remembered her being as ripe as a plum and very good looking, but now she was a dowdy little woman with a few teeth missing. She apologised and said she'd broken her plate that morning, and Ken was surprised that Tony hadn't been able to fix it. He didn't say so, but there was a slight glint in Molly's eyes as if she'd known what he was thinking, and she smiled on handing him a cup of tea he didn't expect because he'd already had a mug. On the other hand he supposed it was a signal that after he'd drunk it Tony would say he had to drive back to work. His little red van was parked outside the terraced house for which he paid only fifteen pounds a week to the council. Then Ken knew he would be sent on his way.

At election times Tony put a Conservative poster in his window, not a big one, only a label really, and Ken wondered what his brother had to conserve. He was the opposite, but didn't put anything in his window. If he did only the birds would see it as they swooped by, because it was ten floors up, one of the high-rise hencoops nobody liked living in.

'I expect you'll have to sell your car,' Tony said, putting three spoons of sugar in his tea. 'Won't you?'

He sounded as if he would enjoy seeing him do it, so Ken laughed. 'I'll be lucky if I get enough to buy a pushbike, and even then it'd be secondhand. I only gen fifty quid for my old banger, and it's bin more trouble than it's worth. You're right, though. I shan't be able to afford the tax and insurance.'

'Cut your coat according to your cloth,' Tony said.

'That's my motto – allus has been.'

Ken had done that all his life anyway, because he'd had to. That was the sort of family they came from, with six kids altogether, and their father earning just enough as a shop assistant at the Coop to keep them alive. But the more cloth Tony got, as it were, the more he put into the bank, though he was no miser when it came to holidays and a bit of enjoyment. Apart from the van he had a new Cavalier, which he kept locked in a garage off Alfreton Road for fear somebody would set fire to it in a riot, or drive it away and push it in the Trent for a bit of fun when they'd finished, which could always happen these days. Black or white, the boggers stopped at nothing. Ken stood at his window once and saw some lads down below looking at his car. One of them shook his head, and they went away laughing, to look for a better one.

Too much time was going by, and the ash from Ken's fag fell onto the carpet. Tony noticed: 'I don't think it'd suit me, being without a job.'

'I'm out every day looking for one,' Ken said, 'don't worry about that.' Not that he would worry. But he'd been turned down at half a dozen places already because of his age, he supposed, so he might not bother anymore, though if he did he wouldn't go to the job centre and apply through them.

Tony with a wider grin suggested that if his brother didn't stick his nose into their office every day and get that bit of paper, and go out to try for a designated job, he wouldn't go on being eligible for the dole. Maybe that's how far he would fall, then he wouldn't care anymore, knowing – as their mother always used to say – that you couldn't fall off the dogshelf. Then he might plonk himself on to me, Tony thought, either to borrow something, or to cadge a bed for a few nights when he was slung out onto the street.

The street had altered during the stay at his brother's house. Tarmac and pavements turned into silk and every car was washed clean, even his own as he stooped inside and twisted the key. More often than not it started first time now that his job had gone west.

He had to go home and change the budgerigar's water, and smiled at the thought that that was all he had to do. In one way he fancied being out of work, or would if he had enough money to keep him halfway happy.

He raised his foot from the accelerator and flashed a bus out of its stopping place. A gentleman of leisure, that's what I'll be. Shooting along the boulevard by the supermarket and hosiery factory, he turned left at the traffic lights. I've done my stint since I was fifteen, so somebody else can have a go on the treadmill. He was a bit slow at getting away, and a souped-up white van to his right set a horn screaming that almost blew him out of his seat, followed by a bawled curse as it leapt forward.

What was the hurry? They'll get to the coffin soon enough. It parked only a couple of hundred yards ahead, and the driver, a shaven-headed bully with an earring, ran into a shop with a parcel under his arm.

Maybe he had a girlfriend there, though it seemed as if everybody in the world had an irritable form of St Vitus flu, people either half doped, or in a rage to set on each other and do murder at the slightest provocation.

He used to amuse himself imagining how an unstoppable civil war might begin: late on Saturday night a man, well satisfied with his evening's boozing, and all set for home, stood on a pub step for a moment to clear his throat. Someone in the dark nearby thought his sound was the beginning of some sneering remark aimed at him, so clocked him one. At the noise of the fight people came out of the pub, and joined in for the fun of it. It turned into such a set-to that the police were called, and the riot spread over the whole area. When TV cameras were set going the people started throwing petrol bombs, just to give the crews better footage, and those seeing it on their screens in other towns sent their streets up in flames as well. Finally they had to bring in the army to mow the boggers down.

In a way he liked the picture, but while parking hoped that one day everybody would be cured of their madness and be able to live and let live with each other. That'd be the day, he thought, sorting out the four keys to get into his flat as if it was Fort Knox. He didn't see why not, and hope never did anybody any harm.

A ladder leaned across the pavement and Ken wondered about the old-fashioned saying which told you never to walk under one because it brought bad luck. Surely such notions are now forgotten or no longer believed in. But no, during his time standing there to take out a fag, strike the match and light it, three people avoided the ladder by walking out on to the road, all of them a lot younger than him. He did the same, and went on his way up to the Castle.

He'd struck lucky, and got two hundred quid for the car, from somebody who was into vintage makes. It wasn't that old, but would be in a year or two. He'd be vintage as well soon enough, though doubted whether anybody would pay as much for him. Even he would think twice about giving more than a bob or two.

On the other hand he knew himself to be priceless, getting up to the Castle top without too much heavy breathing, and walking along the parapet which used to be known, and probably still was, as Suicide's Leap. At least the air's good up here. Used to be all smoke, and now it's clear as far as the hills – and the power station. One time you heard the noise of mayhem from the scruffy houses of the Meadows, and the grunt of trucks, but today it was muted except for motor traffic on the road at the bottom of the sandstone escarpment.

The way to the bottom was long, and the body would bounce forever before hitting the railings. A few bushes growing out from the stones might stop your fall, as if to brush the dust off your coat so that you would be tidy before strolling into heaven – though it might be Hell for doing something like that.

The body would spin a bit, it was bound to, and you wouldn't end up tidy at all. If you chucked yourself off on the q.t. – and funnily enough there wasn't anybody about at the moment on the long wide terrace – the only witnesses would be the birds, who wouldn't be surprised because they'd seen a lot of people doing it over the years. 'Another bloody fool,' they'd say. 'Christ! Just look at him' – then go on whistling.

After the final wicked thump, which he could hardly bear to think about, he knew there would be no bloody Heaven or Hell for him, just blackness. Having imagined the smash so vividly, almost with real pain, he felt as if he had done it, and thought that would have to satisfy him till death came for real from he didn't know where.

A loop of approving wind spun from behind a corner of the stark Castle, and he buttoned his coat against it. Loving his life, whether joyless or not, he lit a fag and walked smiling down into the town for his morning cup of coffee. Then he would buy a paper and go home to read, and feed the bird, which had always seemed happy enough in its cage.

And maybe somewhere at the back end of the newspaper there would be a few lines about a silly old sod who had stood on the wall of Nottingham Castle and got a medal for not slinging himself off.

But they don't print things like that, do they, then, my pretty little budgie? Tut-tut-tut – come on, and get this lovely birdseed in my hand. There, I knew you would. Tastes like the best steak to you, don't it? What nice smooth feathers you've got. I wish I had a coat like yourn. That's right, eat your fill.

After I've fried myself an egg I'll close all the windows and let you out of your cage for half an hour. You'll like that, won't you? Brothers, did I hear you say? Don't talk to me about brothers.

The Caller

The usual yew tree stood umbrageously in the churchyard, in an area of green and among the gravestones. 'There's always a yew tree,' Stephen said knowingly, leaning against the wall where they had parked the car. 'Always has been. The archers cut their longbows and arrows from them. For the price of tuppence they did for the French chivalry at Crécy and Agincourt. That very tree, I wouldn't be surprised.'

His reservoir of general knowledge was remarkable, Sarah thought, for a man under forty who had just retired from the frantic life of a whiz-kid on Throgneedle Street. She wasn't sure they were doing the right thing, but anyway he was dead set on getting out of London and taking up the life of a country gentleman. For some reason he had pinpointed this village, saying he would live here and nowhere else, only there wasn't a house for sale, and all the neighbouring agents said so. He had badgered them for weeks but, look as he could, there was no place to be had.

It had been hard to park because of a funeral. Mourners came out of the church and followed a trolley, which looked as if it could hardly support the weight, to a graveside beyond the yew tree, where lips of earth indicated the hole. 'I expect it's a local who lived to be ninety,' he said, 'but let's go and see what we can find out.'

'I'll get the umbrella from the car,' she said. 'I think it's going to rain.'

'It usually does at a funeral.' He unlatched the gate and, walking up the steps, slipped forward on the asphalt, but managed to right himself before a nasty crash. They stood behind the line of half a dozen people, in time to hear the vicar, or whatever he was, in a white surplice, intoning his ashes to ashes and dust to dust piece. When they saw the widow Sarah nudged him in the ribs: 'Surprisingly young for the wife of a ninety-year-old, don't you think?' The black draped woman took a lump of soil from a proffered spade and let it fall, with copious tears, onto the box.

Sarah always admired the way Stephen was able to begin a friendly conversation, often in the most unlikely conditions, and supposed that to be why women found him so compelling. She had seen him go up to someone at a party he hadn't seen before, and in minutes the head would be bending forward to hear more, whoever it belonged to laughing at whatever line he was putting over. To her, only his wife for ten years, he spoke little, and in the morning was never in a mood less than dangerous if you happened to speak yourself, more especially if he'd had something to drink the night before, or come in so late from the office that he had been seeing a girlfriend and couldn't tolerate waking back into the deadly reality of marriage.

If they did live out here he would be free of the fleshpots and temptations of London. Her few friends spoke up against leaving the flat in Maida Vale, so it was doubtful they'd ever call to see her in this remote place. As for having to give up the gym, she supposed country living would throw up enough activity to take its place.

He talked to the man next to them: 'I'm awfully sorry. Was he your brother?'

The man's laugh caused other people to look in his direction, but it was more as if amused by the increase of rain than at the demise of someone else. 'Good Lord, no. My brother-in-law. My sister's husband is a term I like better' – from which they deduced that he hadn't been much liked, and she knew Stephen very much wanted to find out why. The rest of the mourners dispersed, cars already starting to move. Stephen introduced himself formally, and the man said his name was Larry. 'Did he live in the village?'

'They did, but my sister won't be staying here much longer. She has no good memories of the place. Can't stand it, in fact.'

'Yes, I can imagine.'

The man laughed again. 'Oh no you can't. She had one hell of a life with him, and wants to put as much of it behind her as soon as she can.'

'What did he die from, then?'

He took out a tin of Gold Block and filled his pipe, as if needing to calm himself at such talk. 'Car crash. What else? That 303 gets like a battlefield at times. They reckon it was about two in the morning. Nobody saw it. The police thought he must have nodded off at the wheel, but my view is that some husband he had cuckolded drove him off the road. He was that sort of chap. My sister doesn't know how lucky she is. He didn't take two years to die, nor get sent home in a plastic

594

bag. But she thinks he'll probably come back to haunt her if she stays in this village. He was always in and out of women's beds, so you could say he had it coming to him. Anyway. I must look to my sister. She's had a blow, all the same. Nice meeting you.'

'Where is her house?'

'Oh, just down the road from the pub, on the right. Stands on its own. You can't miss it. A long house, hamstone, plenty of ivy.'

They left the car, rather than move it a few hundred yards, and could just see the house from the pub window while eating their lunch. 'It's exactly the thing.' He chomped at the beef on his large plate – with all the trimmings. 'I'll be there as soon as it comes on the market. It's a beauty.'

She ate her cheese and baked potato, pleased at his smile.

'It's almost too good to be true.'

'Things sometimes are. But I'll be down again in a week, to knock on the door, and ask to see the place.'

Three months later they moved in, pantechnicons – they needed two – leaving just room for cars to get by on the village street. Stephen in his joy couldn't resist helping the men to shift furniture onto the pavement, while Sarah in the house busied herself telling them where to put things, and making pots of tea whenever Stephen gave the hint. The men were quick in their work, too much so, for they dropped a container of her best china, laughing that they would get it back on the insurance – not a good omen, she thought.

She had never known him so happy, yet felt that something wasn't quite right with the place. Certainly it was perfect for him, she could see that, with its neat beams and inglenooks, ivy at the door, a large and splendid living room, and a top floor studio to hide himself away in and call it work, and apple trees in the garden. Nothing more that either could want, they would even have a bedroom each, yet an aura lurked about the place which disturbed her, though not apparent to him as he whistled and sang and then, when the removal men indicated that they could do the work themselves, wandered around the house and garden, almost gloating at what he had come into. It was the first house they'd had, and not a thing needed doing to it on moving in.

His joy continued after the men had gone, when he went upstairs to unpack the boxes containing his books and computers. She stood at the Aga cooking their first meal there as if someone were looking over her shoulder. She wondered why the dead man's wife had put herself through such an uprooting to get away from the place when her husband hadn't even died there. The village had shop, pub, post office and a filling station on the outskirts, and from what she'd heard, the women had gone to live in a hamlet only ten miles away, which had none of these.

'I like the meat rare.'

'What?'

Raindrops spattered the window, and she shivered. She went to the foot of the stairs, spatula in hand. 'Darling!'

He sounded annoyed at being disturbed. 'Yes?'

'Did you speak?'

'Only to myself, I expect.'

The day had been long, almost like three days, coming from the London flat after handing keys and best wishes to the new tenants, then the three-hour drive, and all the bother of seeing things put in their right place. She felt utterly wrung out, so exhausted as to be hearing things. But she could have sworn somebody had spoken, so distinctly he must have been right behind her. She'd even felt breath on her neck.

'I'm not sure I like this house,' she said when they were eating, a bottle of Bordeaux open before then.

'That's a right bloody helpful thing to come out with when we've just moved in.' His elevated moods were easily punctured. Normally she would think before speaking, but maybe the first glass of wine, with immediate effect because she was so tired, had betrayed her. He broke the sullen silence: 'And why aren't you sure?'

'There's something – well – spooky about it.'

He finished his second glass. 'Oh my God! You – to say a thing like that.'

'I thought someone talked to me while you were upstairs.'

'Well, I didn't hear anything. Nobody spoke to me. It must have been someone passing the house. The window's open, so you'd easily hear conversation from outside.'

She laughed at such an obvious explanation. 'I suppose you're right. Glad to know I'm not going out of my mind just yet.'

'That'll be the day.' It was the beginning of September, darkness already coming earlier than she liked. 'I'll pick up those drops from the lawn tomorrow. Some of them are Bramleys, and I'll make a pie.'

They usually slept in separate rooms, but he wanted her in his bed on the first night. She was put off by noises in the attic, as if a squirrel was loose, or a pigeon had found a way in or, at times, someone was drumming impatiently with their fingers. Waiting for us to finish, she thought.

'I'll go up there in the morning, and if I see any sign I'll put traps down. A dab of Somerset brie on each one should tempt the little devils to their doom.' She didn't know whether he had heard it as well, or was only trying to calm her. Either way, she didn't like it, and had to fake her pleasure.

There was so much to do in the next few weeks, arranging the furniture, stacking shelves in the kitchen, dusting and sweeping, filling the wardrobes with clothes, and cupboards with bedding, that they took little note of life in the village, only too glad to fall into a dead sleep in their separate bedrooms at night.

But Sarah's sleep was far from dead. First there were the dreams – nightmares, more like – which she couldn't tell Stephen about. He might be upset, though he was looking less happy the longer they were in the house, a further reason not to tell him. Her dreams were like a full theatre, with lights, noise and human movement. A face which she thought she had seen before kept appearing in the glare. Much of her day was taken up trying to place it, Stephen often accusing her of not paying attention to what he was saying. The face was that of a man in early middle age, in full vigour, eternally persuading her to come with him, his expression one of promise and charm, as if to lead her to a state of endless pleasure. But he always spoiled it by waving her away when she had made up her mind to follow, implying that he would come to her, and when he did she turned to see streaks of blood on his distorted face.

One morning Stephen said: 'I seem to be going through a spate of the most peculiar dreams.'

'Oh, do you?' she said brightly, pressing the coffee grinder which made such a noise that she wouldn't have to hear what he had to say for twenty seconds.

'I dream I go outside to the car,' he said, 'and all four tyres are flat, and there's this dread that I have to get in and drive away to save my life or yours. Another time the whole windscreen's gone, and the car's covered in dust and cobwebs, as if they hadn't been used for years. Then again I was driving along the dual carriageway and the car went out of control. I expect it'll pass. Sounds as if I'm afraid of going impotent.' He kissed her. 'No sign of it, though.'

She poured water into the pot. 'I should say not,' but she didn't tell him about the laughter she heard when they were making love. Maybe it wasn't fair not to tell him her own dreams, but it would be too ludicrous to do so, like someone saying: 'I've got cancer,' and the person replying: 'How strange! I have it as well.' Not the thing to get into at all.

The fact was that they were here, and you had to press on with your life. Nothing could go on forever, either good or bad. If things got better you were lucky, and if they became worse that was only a sign for them to improve, in any case. She would like to think so, and could when the dreams hadn't bothered her for a week, in which case where had he gone, and why? The possibility that she might be missing his attentions now seemed worse than the dream itself.

Stephen said to her one morning, after coming in from mowing the lawn and cutting the jungle back: 'There are times when I think of getting out of here.' She wanted to say: 'You're right. We must. It's not good for either of us,' but a vision from her wayward dream, of the man so charming and persuasive, showed with a finger to his lips for silence, and she obeyed. Even worse, feeling a joyful lightheadedness, she said: 'But why? We're just about settled in. And we've done so much work to make the place comfortable.'

He sat down and peeled an apple, giving half to her. 'I'm so glad you feel that way. We'll stay, then. It was only an aberration.'

She hoped so, yet didn't think it could be. He'd heard something she hadn't, or maybe even seen something, therefore she ought to know about it, but had stupidly put him off from explaining, and couldn't now reopen a wound he'd been too glad to close.

With a sink in her bedroom she didn't need to use the bathroom to do her teeth. A light above the glass showed her drawn features: she had certainly lost some pounds in the last few months, which she was pleased about, though not at the scheming yet frightened expression in the eyes that looked back, which also showed the man standing behind her, and she decided to carry on as if he wasn't there, though knowing that it was the request on his face that forced her to keep looking at him and not shout for Stephen, as if her life depended on it even more than did his.

Her cold body thawed and became warm, as a grey wraith hardly visible came around and touched her breast, the sensation as if done by a real but gentle hand which knew exactly the pressure to exert, then withdrew at the same moment as the face disappeared like a light out of her life. A last glance at herself before getting into bed showed flushed cheeks, and an avid glint in the eyes which denied her exhaustion.

A few nights later, when it began, she put a dot with a circle round it in her handbag diary, in pencil and not easy to see. Reading in bed, her habit before going to sleep, she found the pages increasingly difficult to turn, and looked to see if anything was sticking them together, though nothing was apparent. She smiled at taking it for a sign of lights out, no disagreeing about that, put the book down, settled the pillows, and drew the sheet up to her neck, feeling for the switch.

The blackness was complete, also the silence. In London, no matter where you were, there was always the distant roar of traffic, but here, except for a late car going through the village, it was bliss. Blackness and nothingness should have been perfect for being pulled into oblivion, yet it rarely was. Those nights she got to sleep easily provided the weirdest and thickest of dreams.

She was on the way, when someone tugged at her sheet, no mistake, wanting to get into bed, and it could only be Stephen, though she must have been nearer to sleep than she thought because there had been no noise of an opening door. 'Oh, leave me alone tonight,' she said. 'I'm too tired.' No one was there, but she was caressed as in a dream come to life, unable to resist until drawn into a sleep without visions.

The awakening was better than for weeks, even months. All day the sensation lasted, and in the evening she suggested as a treat, mainly for Stephen, that they drive five miles to the local town and eat at the Red Lion.

'I don't know why it is,' he said, 'But I'm nervous about getting in the car these days. It's as if I've had an accident recently, and scared of being at the wheel again. I can't explain it more than that.'

Well, she thought, you'll damned well have to get used to it, because we're living in the country, and if you don't you're stuck. 'Then I'll drive,' she said. 'No problem,' a response which surprised him, because she hadn't really asked what the problem might be. She didn't say it, but he probably intercepted her words. Any such thing was likely in this house.

'No, it's nonsense,' he said. 'I'll drive, of course, but I want to go in on my own, and get a very elaborate takeaway from the Indian restaurant. The old Tandoori's supposed to be excellent. You can set out the candles in the dining room while I'm gone. I'll get everything going that looks good.'

'And all the trimmings?' she said archly.

'You bet.' The gleam in his eyes showed his distrust of everyone, but especially her, she thought, though he tried to show that she wasn't included in it. She kissed him. 'I can't wait, so don't be long.'

He was longer than she thought, though half expecting he would be. Whoever or whatever had got into her bed last night had left her so excited it would never do to mention the phenomenon to Stephen. She knew she ought, but if she did maybe the visitations would stop, and not only that but perhaps it would disturb Stephen enough for him to have his dream of country living blasted sufficiently to give the whole experiment up and move back to Town, and she didn't want to do that to him.

Even now, alone in the house, Ralph, as she called him, was with her. She felt the familiar draught as he came to look over her shoulder while she was reading her book, as if taking in the lines slightly quicker and wanting her to turn the pages before she was ready. But she held back, unwilling to let him have it all his own way, thought he was so tangibly present that it became hard to concentrate. Then he left her, so abruptly that it was impossible to know why. For a while she felt bereft, as if betrayed, irritated at the emptiness of the house, for he had gone right away from it she was sure, as if called out on an urgent errand.

She felt sweat on her forehead, and reached for a paper towel, but the skin was dry, and she wondered if she weren't going a shade crazy in wanting him back, the sudden absence of someone she was used to now painful to her. She stood to light a cigarette, which she hadn't done since coming to the place, but luckily Stephen always kept a few packets scattered around, having started again recently.

To the town and back shouldn't take more than an hour, even if he had to wait, which you invariably did at a takeaway. She put plates in the oven on low, then heard the car stop quickly, and a violent bang of the door as he got out. She'd put the porch light on to guide him in, and went to help with his boxes, but he almost knocked her down as he came to the door, took her by the waist, and pulled her back into the kitchen. She had never seen such a look of fright on anybody's face: 'What is it?'

'I wish I knew. But I'm sure somebody tried to kill me, and I can't think why. On the way back something dark and grey seemed to sit on the windscreen. I couldn't see a thing, whatever it was, so put on the brakes. I skidded and grazed a bank, then nearly hit another car that came around the bend with lights blazing. Then whatever it was cleared off. At first I thought it was a person, then I wasn't sure.'

'It could have been a freak mist. You get them sometimes.'

'I'd like to think so.' He paused, and stared across the room as if seeing it again while – and she couldn't help such a banal thought coming to mind – the boxed food in the car was getting cold. 'But I don't. I can't,' he added. 'It came only for me, like a panther, dark grey, jumping across.'

'It was one of those things,' she said, 'Accidental. Best not to imagine it was anything else. How could it have been? We live in the real world, after all.'

He looked at her, unbelieving, while she opened the cupboard and took out a bottle of Jameson's, and poured a good measure for him and a smaller one for herself. 'Let's have a drink. Then we'll get the food and pop it in the oven for a few minutes. I'm starving, so you must be as well.'

'All right. Nothing else to do.' He gulped the fiery liquid.

'But I got a fright, let me tell you,' wondering at her divine calmness about the matter, appreciating it all the same, because it wouldn't do for two people to get locked into whatever it was.

Stephen fitted well into the life of the village, and bully for them they made it easy, for he went twice a week to the pub and always came home saying what a good and interesting couple of hours he'd had. They talked gardening, he told her, and sport, agricultural matters, and dispensed local happenings of the past, and any present peculiarities. Someone talked him into exhibiting vegetables at the annual village show, and he got second prize for a huge cabbage, which pleased him in a way she never thought such an accomplishment would. There was even talk about coopting him onto the village council, though since the incident in the car the glamour had gone out of the possibility, in that he had stopped talking about it.

She saw this so clearly that she was sorry for him not being able to fight what was troubling him, or not having the greater courage by somehow giving into it, as she had done, fighting it if he had to, enduring it at least. 'I want to stay,' she said, when he spoke of leaving.

601

'I'm just about getting used to country life. I never thought I would. But it suits me now. I've slowed down. I've forgotten London.'

He went out in the car as rarely as he could get away with, letting her drive when something was needed from the little supermarket in the town. Hitherto not liking to be much at the wheel, she now enjoyed it, exploring the lacework pattern of narrow lanes till getting to know all the short cuts of the area, discovering wayside shops and farms which were good for organic supplies, where to pull in for the best honey, or free-range chickens, the best village for its butcher, or what town had the most elaborate deli. And she was always conscious of her shadowy lover hovering either beside her or on the back seat, giving indications on sharp bends or dangerous corners, and on straight stretches muttering phrases of love and adoration into her ears, and promising to display further expertise during the coming night.

'You've forgotten London,' Stephen said angrily. 'But I haven't. All I know is that we were happy there, even though I did agitate to move down here. I only remember how idyllic it was between you and me, looking back on it.'

'It's amazing how things change,' she said.

'Or how you do. Or they seem to have. That's what foxes me. I thought you'd jump at the chance of living in London again. It was hard enough getting you out here, God knows.'

'I'm used to it now.'

'Yes, but used to what?'

'I just can't chop and change.'

'Nor can I. But I have to get away. There's something weird going on in this house.'

The laugh surprised even her, a shock at its tone which seemed to search out every corner of the large living room for refuse, ringing from beam to beam, from inglenook to window seat. The flames in the fireplace danced at the prolonged sound.

He was deep in the armchair, then she was on the floor, the laughter following her from the blow at her head. He was standing over her. 'Never laugh like that again.' His hands shook, as if he hadn't finished, so close to killing her.

'Never, you understand?'

He had some justification, but she gloated at his loss of self-control, until the pain began burning in her cheek. He'd never hit her before, and she felt the glowering disapproval of her lover. More than that, a desire for vengeance. 'That's the last time you hit me,' she called in her rage.

'You asked for it.' He slumped back into a despair she had no pity for. 'I'm sorry, though. I don't know what got at me. I couldn't help it. It wasn't me.'

'It god-damned well was,' she cried. 'The last time. You understand?'

Close to tears, he went from the room, leaving her to straighten up the small table knocked over in her fall, and set the lamp straight.

During lunch, having again worn himself out in the garden, he told her he was going to London in the morning. He'd seen an advertisement for a large flat that would do for them, in Ealing. 'I just want to see what it's like. It's in our price range, and we'll have no trouble selling this place, even though it is haunted.'

'Haunted?' She crushed a laugh. 'Who told you that?'

'A bloke in the pub some days ago. He said he was joking afterwards, but it struck a chord in me. So what do you think about a move back to London?'

She didn't, not at all. 'Well, if you have to, then I suppose that's all right.' The answer was too ready for her to think she would ever go. She liked it here, but let him think not, if he cared to.

He set off at nine, midday-midweek for the best traffic conditions, so she had the day to herself, to enjoy the house, to do what she would, to eat when she liked, to take a bath in the afternoon, sit in the summerhouse and hope for sun, stroll to the end of the village and back – her best day in the house so far, because no one else was there – until she lay in the bath and the water rippled for no good reason that she could see. The indistinct cloud rolled over her, and liked what it saw, then left her to the pleasures of herself. She didn't feel its presence for the rest of the day, as if it too wanted rest, or had something to do elsewhere.

As evening came on she tidied the house, stowed yesterday's newspaper into its place under the staircase, noticing the details of two flats circled with purple felt pen, the large one he said he was going to see, but also a studio flat at Notting Hill Gate, which she supposed he would call at as well, though why? She considered all the possibilities, nothing too outlandish or outrageous to go through her mind. Either he intended someday living alone, or he intended fixing up a place to put a girlfriend in. There was no other explanation.

When he got back she would rail him about it, and though at the

603

moment her thoughts lacked animosity, she would certainly get herself up to it when the time came. Maybe he hadn't even gone to London at all, knowing she would check the newspaper, and accept that reason as an alibi. He said he would be back by dark, but it was dark already. She supposed he had gone carousing with some of his old friends from the finance place, all hugger-mugger at a pub in the city, or he was cavorting with one of his old flames – hard to say what put such thoughts into her mind.

She sat before the living room fire with a plate of biscuits and cheese, and a cup of tea, happy not to have cooked a meal. Stephen always laid a fire on the morning after they had used one, so it was only necessary to hold a long match to the paper and sticks, and bring in a couple more logs to replace those she'd put on. She began to want her love, and wondered where he was, too much to be deprived of both.

Unable to sit still, she walked out to the conservatory and watered the plants. If ever she lived here alone she would get a cat. She liked cats, so beautiful and unobtrusive. Hardly possible to have one in a flat, not fair to them, but here it would be perfect, and she didn't know why she hadn't thought of it before – though not a nice moment with Stephen on the road from London.

Or was he? If he was staying overnight there was no point waiting up. It was gone ten and he should have phoned – if he wasn't coming back. Maybe she would never hear from him again, a notion that intrigued more than alarmed. People vanish, she'd seen notices of missing persons in *The Big Issue*. Even these days it was possible. Perhaps I'll bump into him on Waterloo Bridge in ten years time, burdened down with plastic bags full of rags and old newspapers. She laughed at the way her thoughts were going, the tone of her amusement recalling the evening he had hit her, and surely would again if he had heard this one. But he wasn't here, and she could laugh as loud as she liked.

She thought about what kind of cold supper would be tasteful enough to have ready when he came in, but after looking at television for an hour she saw it was after midnight, and wondered why he didn't phone. In the armchair she must have fallen asleep, for it was almost one. Then she remembered he had a mobile in the car, so could have stopped in any layby and called, unless he was trying to punish her for something she didn't know she'd done. Yet she had never found any malice in him, not to that extent at least, and while searching her memory for any she might have missed it occurred to her that she could phone him. The number was so long she had to look in her address book, never able to remember so many digits, but there it was, and she dialled. It was ringing.

'It's me,' she said. 'Who else did you expect?'

His voice was stiff, and unreasonable. 'No one. I'm on my way to my lovely little haunted house.'

'What nonsense. Where are you?'

'On the 303, where else? About halfway. I got caught up with a couple of old friends.'

'Thought so. Oh, and did you like the big flat best, or the little one? Or both?'

'I couldn't face looking at either. Wobbled a bit there. I'll get in the inner lane and slow down. Hard to drive while I'm talking. Anyway, I'm coming home to you. I still don't like London.'

'That's all right, then,' she said.

He sounded little-boy bereft. 'You don't sound as if you'll be glad to see me.'

'Of course I will. What makes you think that?'

'Oh, I don't know. But thanks a lot.'

'Love you, you know that.' She tried to sound as if she did, and he seemed taken in. 'Love you, too,' he said, soft and low. Then a cry: 'Oh, oh my God —' Atmospherics were so loud they tickled her eardrums, and then silence.

Something had happened, and she knew who had done it. She went to the cabinet to bolster herself with a double whisky for when the inevitable visit took place, as she knew it surely would, when a shade crossed her eyes as if to say that from now on all would be well.

A jet fighter came low over the house, as they did three times a week, a carpet of sound laid across the fields and then pulled up as the plane sped on its way. 'I only wish you could do something about them as well', which persuaded her that nothing in the world ought to be regarded as serious if you wanted to survive in it. 'Well, shall we go to bed now? You've earned it, and so, I suppose, have I. But you've taken a bloody liberty, thinking that's what I wanted.'

Maybe he was too tired from the work. What work? After she'd drunk her coffee he came back, as if to be with her when the police arrived, unobtrusive, half apologetic, sheepish, yet also self-satisfied, proud you might say, cocksure for certain. He was with her, but being with herself she still hoped to hear BMW tyres on the gravel outside the door. Near misses on the motorway happened all the time, though he ought to stop and say that he was all right.

Two cars came, one with a blue light flashing. A male officer and a policewoman stood in the kitchen. 'It must have been about one o'clock. No other vehicle was involved. For some reason or other he went out of control. Well, that's our assumption. Another vehicle reported seeing him on his mobile, but didn't give us his name. We got there soon enough, and pulled him out. Funny how he didn't look much knocked about. But it was too late to do anything about it. It's still a bit of a mystery, though, why he went off the road like that.

She enjoyed the homely Somerset accent of the woman, while willing herself to go white in the face with shock at what was heard. In bed she was aware of being comforted in her grief, tears being quickly dried when the pillow should have been wet. She drifted down into paradisal dreams, into light from darkness, sleeping as if to wear off the exhaustion of years.

On waking it was impossible to tell who, where or what she was, for a moment or two. For the next two weeks she became two people, one in the vaults of a painful anguish and then, at night on getting into bed, the mistress or victim – she was never to know which – of the shade who lay by her. Her sister at the funeral said she must sell the house, and get a flat in town, become her old self again, but Sarah turned the idea down: 'Stephen wouldn't want it. He loved the place.'

'He didn't the last time I spoke to him. He was getting to hate it,' she said. 'Some psychobabble about it being haunted. He sounded really disturbed, as if the whole thing was getting on his nerves. I don't think I'll ever get over him being killed like that. I was very fond of Stephen.'

'It's beginning to rain,' Sarah said. 'We'd better get everyone back to the house.' And then out of it, she added to herself as they went down the sloping paved path, wanting to be alone with her love, who would stay with her for life.

Spitfire

The silver Supermarine Spitfire was of the finest quality steel, Donald knew, having worked at engineering firms most of his life. A jaunty and effective apparition in the damp November air, the plane seemed about to lift into the murk, its pilot to seek adventures unto death.

Dates on the gravestone tallied with a brave man's life. He hadn't died in his cockpit but lived to be seventy-eight, so what better memorial to defy time and weather? A lot must have been paid to get the model lovingly chromed, an outline anybody should be able to recognise, being shown so often on television. He'd also read books about the Battle of Britain and, smoking a cigarette before setting the roses in front of Edith's headstone, mused on the aircraft as if willing it to rev up and take off in a benefit performance for him alone.

He'd heard you should be done with grieving after a year, but he couldn't eliminate the good times they'd had in their married life, nor the awful months of Edith's dying either. He stayed longer on his visits rather than less, sometimes for an hour or more, little enough on recollecting how tall and bonny she had been before getting cancer. He always came on Saturday, because saying hello again, and asking how she was, inspired him to carry on through the weekend.

After twenty years of marriage she was surely still there in the flesh, often wanting to know why they were talking in a graveyard instead of being at home waiting for the kettle to boil, or why he wasn't in the garden he had made so beautiful for when they first went into the house. His visits always seemed too short to get the best out of such memories, living alone so painful to the spirit, and no good for the body, and the fact that she was dead was hard to let go of, which was why his time by the grave did not diminish.

No reason in any case why it should but, as if to take his mind from her, and shake off the painful turmoil – which she would not begrudge him – he wondered about the man who had flown the Spitfire in his youth, no comparison with his bit of National Service after the war. Such blokes as the pilot did five years or more, and many never came back. If they had the country might now have been a better place to live in.

Whoever called at the Spitfire grave laid more exotic flowers than his could afford to be. He once purloined the head of an orchid to put between his daffodils, and give Edith a laugh. The person who brought such a resplendent bunch would hardly miss it.

He liked to speculate on what emblem would adorn his grave when he died, should there be anyone to put it there. A micrometer, perhaps, or a spanner, which made him smile, because who would wonder about his life on seeing such common tools. Maybe the pilot, back from the war, had become a solicitor, or an engineer building bridges, or the managing director of a factory, though he must have known that nothing would be as exciting as doing aerobatics and having eight machine guns clattering away in the wings. You had to admire and envy him for having handled a plane like that.

The laying of flowers done, he felt the damp, and buttoned his overcoat. The red flare of the poinsettias under the Spitfire headstone lit the sombre air, and he wanted to know who had placed them there, saying aloud to Edith, without worrying that a man four graves along the row would think him soft in the head: 'I'll come on Sunday next week, so don't be surprised at me leaving it till then.'

'I'll wait,' giving the same old mischievous laugh, which had often been an indication that it was time for them to go to bed. 'I know your game,' she went on. 'Getting nosy in your old age, are you?'

He could go to the cemetery in the car, but didn't want to lose the use of his legs, like so many who drove to the shops even though they were only a hundred yards from their door. He enjoyed the twenty-minute stroll back to his council house, crossing the main road and junking though the estate. The only other outing made with any purpose was to the small town library in midweek to change his books.

On Saturday morning he was up and dressed before realising his decision to call at the grave on Sunday. But he couldn't wait, the usual day too firm to be resisted. A change of routine might disturb Edith, so he would do it when more reconciled that she was only dust and mud and too long dead to speak to him anymore, if that time ever came, for he never stopped asking himself why her and not me, and knew he'd be done with mourning only when the question ceased to nag.

She indicated, before dying, that he should get married again, but apart from the fact that he couldn't see any woman wanting him, he thought the notion very cold indeed. 'I never will,' he told her.

Unable to alter the mechanism of his action, he went on the same day through winter into summer, his puzzlement as to who put flowers on the Spitfire grave not a luxury to be thrown away. If there was any chance of meeting the person, he didn't want to be seen tending Edith's grave with flowers so much inferior. In summer he could cut a large bunch of white chrysanthemums, a swathe of marguerites, and a few orange and yellow dahlias from his garden.

No need of an overcoat on the hot day coming up, though the dry summer did little good to the garden. He walked through the quiet Sunday streets with yesterday's newspaper enveloping the long stalks of his flowers. A Jack Russell terrier ran from a gate and nearly got hit by what must have been the only car out at that time of morning. Curses gridlocked in the throat of its owner, Donald a few yards ahead amused at his language. A kick at the dog's ribs and a wild yelp: 'Gerrin, yer daft bleddy ha'porth! That's the second time yer've done that.'

He wandered across the main road without waiting for the lights to change, another reason for going on Sunday, which he should have done from the beginning. Being so early meant a few extra words with Edith, till several families came into the cemetery, changing flowers, talking loudly, even laughing on their day out with the dead, so many he waited at the tap to fill his vases, wanting to get his prime duty done then give his mind to whoever would come to the Spitfire grave.

Luckily the weather was pleasant, and there were sandwiches in his pocket in case the wait was long. He was hungry but didn't want to be caught with a mouth full of bread and cheese. On the other hand he had to eat sooner or later. A flask of tea recalled that whenever he and Edith went any distance in the car they always packed sandwiches and took the big thermos, not caring to stop at a service station and get stomach cramps. Your own food and tea tasted better than whatever you could get on the road, as well as saving money. 'Well, I always said that, didn't I?' She reminded him, though her voice seemed less clear these days.

The sandwich went in a few appetising bites, washed down a treat by hot sugarless tea. The Spitfire grave couldn't have been much attended to for a fortnight, so maybe whoever it was had gone on holiday. Somebody like that might have a house in France and spend the summer there. Lucky for them. He couldn't go away, even if he had the money, having to be at Edith's grave every week. Not grieving so much was one thing, but he would have to bring flowers now and again.

Birds entertained you with their song, so much green in a graveyard to attract them, but by late afternoon he was the only person left, and knew it was time to go.

A pulsing at his temples told him that, late as it was, the woman who came though the gate was on her way to the Spitfire grave, not only because of the flowers but from the way she looked in its direction, and walked in a straight line rather than use the paths.

He knelt, hoping that Edith had told him in no uncertain terms to arrange the flowers again, sly looks at the woman a few feet away. She was about sixty, with the palest of faces, and a band of grey hair across her forehead, the pallid sort of skin that went with dark eyes and a slender figure. He didn't doubt that she was the wife, though a good few years younger than the pilot.

She laid down the flowers, taking her time, then stood upright to touch the Spitfire, curling her fingers around the neck, and running them along the body to the tail. A steely rim on high white clouds glistened like the metal of the plane. There was something of a puzzle about her smile as she lifted a hand in the air as if to let the plane go free, or to hear what he inside had been saving to tell her.

You always looked for tears in a cemetery, but she had none, attended to the business of dividing the flowers into two heaps. She took a pair of shears from a basket to cut grass that grew wild when left too long in summer, a waterproof sheet under her knees, the clip-clip above other people's noise.

'The grass grows too fast,' he called.

She smiled, her accent not quite local. 'I've never known it not to. I was on holiday last week.'

'Did you go abroad?'

'No,' she said, as if it was beyond her too.

'Do you have a long way to come every Sunday?'

'From Carlton.' She saw this tall man, who stood erect to talk, with his thatch of short half-grey hair, looking about fifty, though he could, she thought, be a bit older.

'That's a good few miles.'

'Five or six,' she said. 'We did live around here, but I left after he died. I wanted to change my environment. It's no use grieving too long.'

He offered a cigarette, surprised that she took it, leaning forward to a light so that he caught a whiff of her perfume. 'You come here often enough,' he said. 'I always see your flowers.'

Her laugh was throaty and genuine. 'No too often. My daughter comes sometimes. She thought the world of him. But it looks like rain, so I'd better be getting on.'

He turned to sort out his flowers again, and on looking up she was halfway to the gate, her coat flapping open. She couldn't have thought much of the pilot, otherwise why had she gone to live somewhere else? It only occurred to him when he was halfway home that he hadn't asked about the model aeroplane.

Sitting in the kitchen with the light on after dark, a moth came through the open window, did a dance around his large fist by the cup of coffee. When it settled he watched its whiskers, and brown sweptback wings, a sinister little bomber quite unlike the silver grace of the Spitfire, but he felt consoled by its company for a while until, not wanting to damage it, he cupped it in his hand, a fluttering against the flesh of his palm, and watched it fly away as he closed the window.

Next time he asked straightaway about the Spitfire. 'He must have had quite a time, flying one of those.'

'You might think so.' She took the old flowers, which he considered still fresh enough to decorate Edith's grave, and dumped them on a heap by the tap. He followed with her jars as well his own.

'Do you want these filled up?'

'You've saved me a journey. Yes, both of them.'

Plenty of time, he took them back, Edith no doubt smiling to herself under the soil. Well, there was no harm in helping somebody.

The lilies were so long she took scissors from her bag and clipped a few inches from each. 'I shan't be doing this too much from now on. A year's enough, don't you think?'

'You mean you won't come anymore?'

'I expect I shall, but not so often.'

He looked at the plane, securely bolted into the concrete of the headstone, nose at a slight angle as if to give safe lift on take off. 'You'll miss the old Spitfire.'

She stood, the job done. 'It makes your back ache, all this bending.'

'Not mine. I worked in a factory, and got used to it. What did your husband do?'

He was fascinated by her look of anger. 'He flew no Spitfire, I'll tell you that.'

He thought she might be about to cry, but realised she was too angry. All he could do was wait. 'It's a good model, thought.'

'I hope he's flying it in Hell.'

'He wasn't a pilot, then?'

'Pilot?' She put the clippers and knee pad into her bag, and he wondered if she would say anything more – to the nosy old bogger he must seem. 'Pilot? Not him. But he pretended to make them, in a shed at the bottom of the garden. Some he must have made, because he used it for an alibi. He would get over the wall and drive off to see his fancy woman. He spent a lot of time with her, but as long as he held up a Spitfire now and again when he came back into the house I believed he'd been where he said he had.'

To hear all this was more than he had expected, but she went on: 'I sometimes think he only ever made one, and there it is, stuck on his grave. He told me he made lots, and gave them to his best customers at his video and telly shop in town. When I found out what he was up to I told him he had to see no more of his girlfriend, or I would leave him. Then he started to ail. His heart went. He said I'd willed it on him. Well, I did. It had to be me, didn't it?'

Now she was crying. 'And I felt so awful at having done it. When he asked me just before he had the second heart attack to put the Spitfire over his grave I promised I would. I never stopped loving the devil, though. But what can you do?'

The idea seemed unthinkable, so he had to ask: 'And you won't be coming again?'

She wiped her eyes with several sheets from a box of Kleenex. 'I didn't say that, though that's what he deserves. I haven't told anybody about all this before.'

'It's because nobody's asked you, I suppose. My name's Donald.'

'Mine's Teresa. And who's in that grave of yours?'

'My wife. She died eighteen months ago.'

'And what took her?'

'Cancer.'

She fastened her coat, though he couldn't think what against. 'It's all over the place. But it's been nice talking to you. I have to come here now and again, though, to remind myself why it is I live alone.'

He liked her smile, and the sense of humour that had carried her through the troubles. 'We'd better go, or they'll be closing the gates. If we're locked in we might get pulled under by the dead, and I don't want to go there just yet.'

She laughed now. 'Well, we wouldn't would we?'

'I wouldn't anyway.'

'No, nor me.'

'I might see you next time, then.'

'I shouldn't wonder.'

He hesitated. 'Unless you want to come across the road now and have a drink before you go home.'

'I'd like to, but I've got somewhere to go this evening.' She touched his hand. 'Still, I expect I'll be here next week.'

He noticed it well before reaching the grave. A shape had been taken out of the air. Somebody had come with tools and done a very neat job of detaching it with screwdriver and metal saw, maybe thinking to make a nice Christmas present for his lad.

The cemetery seemed empty without the plane, as if there was no reason left for him to be there. Even the arrow in Robin Hood's bow had been nicked from the statue by the Castle wall, and if that wasn't sacred to the people of the town then neither was God Almighty. They must have come over the gate like thieves in the dark. It's no use supposing the world's full of such villains, either, though it only needs one to make you think so.

'Would you believe it?' she said. 'I can still see it, yet it's gone right enough. It must be flying in a strange place by now.'

'I hope the pilot's taking my wife for a ride.'

'That wouldn't surprise me at all.' A laugh suggested she wasn't too upset at the missing plane, not as uneasy as he had been for some moments. 'Let's hope it brings the bloke who stole it some luck,' he said. 'Not that I think he deserves it.'

She laid down her flowers, and took his arm. 'It's given me quite a jolt, all the same. I suppose it was only to be expected.'

'Isn't there another in his hut?'

'Not as good as that one was.'

He wanted to make sure. 'If you found one I could fix it on for you, stronger than before. They'd have to take the gravestone as well, and how they'd get that over the wall I wouldn't like to think.'

'I won't bother. It's no use trying to mend the past.'

He saw some sense in that. 'How about going for that drink now?'

The completed their obsequies sooner than usual, and walked out of the cemetery together.

ACKNOWLEDGEMENTS

The stories in *The Ragman's Daughter*, *Men, Women and Children* and *The Second Chance* were first published or broadcast as follows:

Guardian; Pick of Today's Short Stories; Argosy; New Statesman; Transatlantic Review; The Daily Worker; London Magazine; New Yorker.

Encounter; Nova; Morning Star; Penthouse; Winter's Tales.

Bananas; BBC Radio; Granta; Guardian; Literary Review; Nottingham Press; New Review; Prairie Schooner; New Yorker; Nottingham Quarterly; Punch.